Korval's Game

Baen Books
by
Sharon Lee &
Steve Miller

The Liaden Universe®
Fledgling
Saltation
Mouse and Dragon
Ghost Ship (forthcoming)
The Dragon Variation (omnibus)
The Agent Gambit (omnibus)
Koval's Game (omnibus)
The Crystal Variation (omnibus forthcoming)

The Fey Duology
Duainfey
Longeye

by Sharon Lee
Carousel Tides

Korval's Game

Sharon Lee
& Steve Miller

KORVAL'S GAME

Plan B copyright © 1998 by Sharon Lee & Steve Miller.
I Dare copyright © 2002 by Sharon Lee & Steve Miller.
Introduction © 2011 by Sharon Lee & Steve Miller.

Liaden Universe® is a registered trademark.

A Baen Book

Baen Publishing Enterprises
P.O. Box 1403
Riverdale, NY 10471
www.baen.com

ISBN: 978-1-4391-3439-9

Cover art by Alan Pollack

First Baen printing, May 2011

Distributed by Simon & Schuster
1230 Avenue of the Americas
New York, NY 10020

Library of Congress Cataloging-in-Publication Data

Lee, Sharon, 1952-
  Korval's game / by Sharon Lee & Steve Miller.
    p. cm.
  ISBN 978-1-4391-3439-9 (trade pbk.)
  I. Miller, Steve, 1950 July 31- II. Title.
  PS3562.E3629K67 2011
  813'.54--dc22

                                    2011002042

Printed in the United States of America

10 9 8 7 6 5 4 3 2

CONTENTS

INTRODUCTION

❉❉❉❉❉❉❉❉❉❉❉❉❉❉❉❉❉❉❉❉❉❉❉❉❉❉❉

SO WHAT'S YOUR GAME, NOW?

WE'LL HOPE THAT YOU'VE READ most of this space opera series before you get to this book, *Korval's Game,* because, honestly, a lot has gone before. Not only will some of the words sound odd if you're just starting, but so will some of the ideas. The two novels here are the culmination of a seven book run, so be understanding if you've somehow stumbled here first. Baen has already published *The Dragon Variation* and *The Agent Gambit* encompassing the first books of the series—that's the best way to get your "What has gone before" fix for this book.

Right from the start of the Liaden Universe® series, we, the authors, knew that Clan Korval was up to something. And the reason we knew it was because Korval's Liaden and galactic contemporaries all knew it, from the heads of clans and secret organizations down to the meanest corner stall market trader waiting for the final consolidated pod to be unloaded from a Korval tradeship's once a decade visit.

Now, if this happens to be your first visit to our universe, you've come in at an exciting time, because Korval—well, Plan B is in effect, and that's the title of the first book you'll read here. And right, since *Plan B is in Effect* means that the Clan had already been doing *something* now they're doing something else, or maybe something *more*.

Korval was a player wherever they showed up, and often where they didn't, and if no one was quite sure what their game was, exactly, there was no doubt that they knew what they were about. So thought their enemies and their friends, and so of course did society at large.

At the start of *Plan B* there's much doubt about the future of Clan Korval, though, from within the Clan. Plan B was always a last ditch thing, and this implementation is far more free form than any of the people in charge like—including the fact that not everyone is sure *who* is in charge. The grace of allies is good, but when two different enemies send their best at the same time, things can get interesting, indeed.

Sometimes, winning and survival are not the same thing, and winning is paramount. Miri and Val Con, stalwart friends and lovers though they be, have different talents and abilities—and the adventures in this book require them both to permit the other to walk into war alone.

I Dare is a novel where both kinship and the Liaden culture's understanding of itself are tested, with the internal conflicts of the seven original novels coming into strong focus. Readers find most of their favorite characters at work in this one, sometimes in roles that are unexpected. On top of that, the game is still afoot; with the Council of Clans, the Liaden Scouts, and Terran mercenaries all game pieces in the confrontation with the Korval's most ardent and secret enemy. And then there's the problem of what do you do with a Clan that is seen as a threat to a planet, anyway?

In addition to pulling together all the threads form the earlier books *I Dare* also ends with the promise of more to come, with the introduction of Theo Waitley, a promise already fulfilled with the publication of Theo's story in *Fledgling*, *Saltation*, and the forthcoming *Ghost Ship*. The Liaden novel *Mouse and Dragon* is also available from Baen, and it fits into a strategic spot, feeding into and drawing from the mini arc encompassing *Local Custom*, *Scout's Progress* and *Mouse and Dragon*; some will suggest that *Ghost Ship* only be read after *Mouse and Dragon*.

Baen will shortly be releasing one more Liaden Universe® reprint omnibus: *The Crystal Variation* (including *Crystal Soldier*, *Crystal Dragon*, and *Balance of Trade*). The novels run the gamut from Space Regencies to Space Opera. All are character-driven; all were fun to write and, we hope, fun to read.

If this is your first encounter with a Liaden Universe® book—welcome. We hope you'll find this a start to a lot of good reading. If you're an old friend, stopping by for a revisit—we're very glad to see you.

Thank you.

Sharon Lee and Steve Miller
Waterville Maine
September 2010

PLAN B

A Liaden Universe® Novel

For the Friends of Liad: lisamia keshoc.
We are in your debt.

LIAD:
Department of Interior Command Headquarters

❀ ❀

> *Here we stand: An old woman, a halfling boy, two*
> *babes; a contract, a ship, and a Tree. Clan Korval.*
> *How Jela would laugh.*
> —Excerpted from Cantra yos'Phelium's Log Book

THERE WAS TIME, but neither night nor day.

Time. Current time on twenty planets was counted along the digital displays in the long left wall. The light was impartial, unchanging. Shadowless.

In addition to the silent, steady chronometers, the room contained a desk upon which sat two screens—one large, one small—a keypad, some few files of hard copy, a stylus. Behind the desk was a chair; in the chair was a man.

Those who owed allegiance to the Department, to the Plan, addressed him as "Commander" or, formally, "Commander of Agents." That was enough.

Commander of Agents touched his keypad, advancing the file displayed upon the larger screen.

Blindfolded and questioned—if any would dare it—he could easily have recited the entire contents of the file. He perused it without reading it, as another might shuffle and deal hand after hand of Patience, mind wrestling a problem light years beyond his busy fingers.

The immediate problem was threefold, the sections named thus: Clan Korval, Val Con yos'Phelium, Tyl Von sig'Alda.

Clan Korval. The Department of Interior had long been aware of the danger presented by Clan Korval, that maverick and most oddly successful of clans. The Department of Interior had taken measures—bold measures—in the past, with an eye toward nullifying Korval's menace. The culmination of these measures was the recruitment of Korval's young nadelm into the Department and the subsequent redesign of that same Val Con yos'Phelium into an Agent of Change.

That stroke, brilliant and necessary, had produced uncalculated results. Korval became aware of the Department. And, being Korval, measures—bold measures—had been taken. The Department found its name spoken in public places; long-stable funding sources came under scrutiny, several dummy accounts were unmasked and summarily closed by the Masters of the Accountants Guild, the funds returned to the Council of Clans.

Not satisfied with such unseemly commotion, Korval moved again—and more boldly yet. The clan vanished—ships, children, servants, and pets—all, all gone from Liad.

Not quite all.

Commander of Agents touched his keypad. One of the line direct remained upon Liad: Anthora, youngest of the adult yos'Galans, who had prudently moved to the ancient and formidable Jelaza Kazone, Korval's first base of planetary operation, and was living there retired. For now.

Commander of Agents advanced the file, eyes looking beyond screen and data. Korval was out *there* somewhere. Who knew what they might do? Or when?

The Commander considered the probability that they had gone entirely, leaving behind one too odd to understand her peril. Were Korval to abandon Liad and accept sanctuary from Terra, the balance long in favor of Liaden trade missions and Liaden expansion would be at risk. The children of yos'Galan were half-Terran. Mongrels. They might well go to kin.

The Commander was not one to feel qualms. The various actions against Korval, including fomenting revolution on the world of Korval's oldest trade partner, were necessary to reduce Korval's influence and bring about the true ascendancy of Liad.

The recent revolt had not been an entire success, for Korval's old ally and sometime bedmate had prevailed. Still, it would be a generation before the economy of the planet healed, and the political conflicts would take a dozen dozen relumma to settle.

More, there was rumor that one string not yet strung to the bow of the alliance was now gone. The Commander allowed himself a faint smile: fight them over and over, covertly, and even Korval must fall. They had almost been eliminated twice now.

The Commander blinked. This time, perhaps. On *his* watch.

This nearly open flight was unfortunate, and unexpected. That Korval searched for their missing delm-to-be was certain. To allow them to locate and reclaim Val Con yos'Phelium would be an error. A very serious error.

A most successful Agent, Val Con yos'Phelium. There was that in the madcap Korval genes that inspired its members to excellence, whatever course they might chart. Before the adjustment of his loyalties, Val Con yos'Phelium had ridden the mandate of his genes to a certain pinnacle of achievement: Scout Commander, First-In. A man of infinite resource, a pilot from a clan that bred for pilots; intelligent, flexible and—after suitable training—exquisitely deadly, he had among his armament the greatest of all an Agent's weapons, the Probability Loop.

The Loop allowed an Agent to calculate odds of mission success and personal survival. To some extent, it served as a predictor of coming action, and as a strategy program. There were, of course, certain other mandates implanted, as well as a self-destruct subroutine. These mandates and subroutines were provided to ensure that an Agent remained loyal to his mission, to the Department, and to the Plan. It should not be possible for an Agent of Change to break training.

And, yet, there was evidence—disturbingly strong evidence—
that Val Con yos'Phelium, delm genetic of a clan that seemingly
valued random action just slightly less than piloting skill, had
broken training.

So. Agent of Change Tyl Von sig'Alda had been dispatched on
the trail of a rumor, to seek Val Con yos'Phelium along the ways of
an interdicted world, to offer transport to the home world, to
debriefing and recalibration. Had the Agent merely come against
mischance, these things would be accepted. Had he suffered severe
mischance, Agent sig'Alda was to bring his Commander a body, a
skull, sections of vertebrae—*proof.* An Agent was no such thing to
be carelessly left lying about the galaxy, after all. Especially no such
Agent as Val Con yos'Phelium.

Commander of Agents came to the end of the file and closed
it with a flick at the keypad. He leaned back in the chair which
conformed to his body's shape, and briefly closed his eyes.

Agent sig'Alda had been gone some time. It was understood
that ransacking a low-tech world for one man—or one corpse—
might consume time. The Commander was prepared to wait some
small time longer, before loosing another Agent to the search.

Commander of Agents opened his eyes, seeking the smaller
second screen.

This screen showed a sector map. Marked plainly on the map was
Interdicted World I-2796-893-44, where Tyl Von sig'Alda sought Val
Con yos'Phelium. An amber light near the world marked the location
of sig'Alda's ship, as reported by the concealed pin-beam locator
beacon. Some time ago, the beacon had reported that it was on world
and Commander of Agents had allowed himself hope.

Alas, the ship lifted very soon, thence to dawdle in orbit now
several more days, so the scent that had enticed Agent sig'Alda to
the planet's surface must have proved false.

Commander of Agents moved his eyes to the chronometered
wall. He was due in conference very shortly, where another portion
of the Department's Plan would be reviewed.

Korval's links with outside interests were being attended to,
carefully. It was the Commander's thought that Korval had dwindled

to the point of being too few to attend to their own security. Thus a test case. It would do Korval no good, should *Dutiful Passage* fall.

Hands on the armrests, the Commander pushed his chair back, glancing to the beacon screen—and freezing.

For the beacon's light was no longer the placid amber indicative of a stable position. It blazed green on the star map, its glow eclipsing the world called "Vandar" by its natives, the pre-Jump coil-charge smearing the telltale into a blur. Coordinates appeared at the bottom of the screen, the beacon phased from green to turquoise, then flared into nothing as it and the ship around it entered Jump.

Commander of Agents reached forth a hand and tapped a command into his keypad. The home system of the interdicted world melted from the screen, replaced by another map, this with a ship route limned in red.

Commander of Agents leaned back in his chair, and allowed himself to believe that all was well.

Tyl Von sig'Alda was Jumping for Waymart.

And from Waymart it was but two Jumps to Headquarters.

STANDARD YEAR 1396:
Vandar Orbit and Jump

❀ ❀

SHE WAS QUICK, canny, and careful, a former mercenary master sergeant with the battle wisdom of a hundred combat encounters behind her.

He was not without resources, trained first as a scout and then as an Agent, but the knife nearly penetrated his guard, so smoothly did she manage the thing. He snatched her wrist as it snaked past, shifted balance for the throw—and ended the move in an ignominious twisting breakaway as she broke his grip and rode the attack forward.

She danced back to the metal wall, gray eyes intent, muscles coherent; poised, not stressed; the sweat bathing her face the residue of physical exertion, rather than strain.

She let him regain stance, she allowed him time for orientation, time to conceive and launch an attack; uncommon courtesy from so deadly a battle-mate. He feinted with a move out of L'apeleka, saw the grin flit across her face even as she shifted balance in proper response to the phrase.

He danced another half-phrase of the Clutch discipline, choosing a subtle variant beyond her current level of attainment. He was not really surprised when she moved smoothly in response, timing perfect as a heartbeat. His mental Loop, residue of his days as a full Agent of Change, indicated her chance of besting him in this encounter was nearly seventeen percent—four times higher than it had been half a year ago.

She charged.

Training took over and his hands flashed out, faster than thought. The knife spun away as he caught both her wrists this time and took her with him into the somersault, both aware of the constraining walls.

She twisted and broke half free. He countered, snaking around and pinning her flat against the metal floor, one hand tight under her chin.

"Yield!" he demanded, trying not to see how easily his fingers encircled the fragile column of her throat.

She sighed slightly, considering him out of calm gray eyes. "Sure," she said. "What the hell."

He laughed, taking his hand from her throat and rolling away to prop hip and elbow against the cold deck. "Not quite the attitude I might expect from a seasoned mercenary."

"No sense gettin' killed," Miri said reasonably, grabbing his free hand and laying it over her breast. She squirmed a little, as if to settle more comfortably against the deck plates. "That's better."

"Fraternizing with the enemy?" inquired Val Con.

"Taking a little rest with my partner," she corrected him sternly. "Liadens and Terrans ain't enemies—they just don't get along too good."

He opened his green eyes very wide. "Don't we get along, Miri?"

"Yeah, but see," she said earnestly, reaching to touch his right cheek and the scar that marred the smooth golden skin, "we're crazy. And that's besides you being a scout and having this funny idea about how Liadens and Terrans and for-space-sake Yxtrang are all from the same stock."

"It is true," Val Con allowed, feeling her heartbeat through the breast nestled in his palm, "that scout training may have identified those characteristics that are classified as 'crazy' and honed them to a fine degree. However, the hypothesis of the common root of the three human races is from my father's studies." He smiled. "So you see that insanity is hereditary."

"Yeah, all you do is believe it." She stretched suddenly and sat up, face abruptly serious. "Tell you what, boss: I think I'm cured."

He rolled over onto his back, crossed his arms behind his head and considered the other thing inside his head—a precious gift, balancing the Loop's distasteful, inevitable presence.

Legend said that lifemates had often been linked this way, soul to soul, not quite sharing thought, but rather sharing intent; joying in a knowledge of each other that went deeper than any kin-tie. That he and Miri should be so linked, now, when Liad's wizards were on the wane and lifemates were merely in love, was wonderful past belief.

"Boss?"

"Eh?" He started and smiled at the ripples in the song that was Miri in his head; smiled at the frown of concern on her face. "Forgive me, cha'trez. I was thinking." He stretched and sat up next to her. "I believe your estimation is correct, however: you certainly fight as if you are cured."

"Huh." She shook her head. "You need somebody around can really give you a workout."

"So? You very nearly had me. Twice," he added thoughtfully. "Miri."

"Yo."

"Where did you learn the response to that Clutch move?"

"The second one?" She shrugged. "Seemed the only logical way to go, given how you shifted . . ." Her shoulders dipped, upper body sketching the essence of the move. "Yeah . . ."

"Ah."

She glanced at him suspiciously. "Ah, is it? What's that supposed to mean?"

"Nothing, Miri," he said meekly; and grinned in shared joy when she laughed.

"So, partner, seeing as we both agree I'm cured, how 'bout you bust this tub outta orbit and we get a move on."

"It must certainly be my first wish to please my lady and my lifemate," Val Con said, coming to his feet and offering her a hand in graceful Liaden courtesy. "But I wonder if you can suggest where it is we should get a move on *to*?"

"Had to ask, didn't you?" She rose lightly, gripping his fingers for the pleasure of contact rather than because she required assistance. "Let's go up front and get some tea." She led the way, hand stretched behind her to his as they moved through the narrow corridor to the control cabin.

"Family of yours is on the lam, right? When's this Plan B thing go outta force?"

He hesitated. Miri considered herself Terran, though she carried a Liaden house-badge among her dearest treasures, and had agreed, perhaps too hastily, to share life with a Liaden. She had not been raised to the tradition of clan-and-kin, and the first eight months of their mating had been spent on an Interdicted World, learning to survive and prosper in a culture alien to them both.

"Plan B," he began slowly, feeling his way along thoughts that seemed to shift nuance and urgency as he tried to convey them in Terran. "Plan B may be called into effect by delm or first speaker in the instance of—imminent catastrophic damage to the clan. It is thus not established lightly, nor do I think it—goes out of force—until the dangerous situation has been resolved. I believe this may be its first use."

"Imminent catastrophic damage to the clan," Miri repeated, gray eyes sharp on his face. "What's that mean? Who's the enemy? And how do we get past them and connect with your family?" She frowned, chewing her lower lip. "I take it you *want* to connect up?"

"I—yes." Such clear knowledge of his own will was still unsettling to him, who had only shaken off the mind-twisting Agent training with the help of Miri and the luck. "It is possible that the danger is the Department of Interior," he said. "After all—" He waved a slender hand at the neat little ship enclosing them, "the Department managed to locate us and send an agent after, and we were most wonderfully lost."

"Much good it did them," Miri commented, meaning the Agent, dead at the Winterfair on the far-below surface.

"Much good it very nearly did us," Val Con retorted warmly, meaning the wound she'd taken and the Agent's too-near success in completing his mission.

"Yeah, well . . ." she shifted, reached to take his hand again. "You talked to your brother Shan, you said . . ." and that made her uncomfortable, he could tell from the subtleties of her mind-heard song.

"I am not," he said gently, "an expert at speaking mind-to-mind. In fact, the whole exchange must have been on Shan's skill, without anything at all from me. I can't even bespeak you, Miri, as closely as we are linked."

"Tried it, have you?" She grinned briefly. "But didn't your brother tell you what kind of danger?"

"Just that Plan B was in effect . . ."

"Moontopple," Miri muttered and Val Con laughed even as he shook his head.

"Things were rather confused at the time, recall. The Agent was hunting me, you and I were separated, Shan was talking inside my head—and very annoyed he was, too! We hardly had time to set up a rendezvous before contact was cut."

"So you did set up a meeting!" Approval lightened her face. "Where?"

He took a deep breath and looked her steadily in the eyes. "At the home of your family, Miri."

"My fam—" She stared at him, dropped his hand and backed up, shock rattling the constancy of her song. The back of her knees hit the edge of the co-pilot's chair and she sat with a slight bump, eyes still wide on his face.

"Look, boss," she said finally, "I ain't got a family. My mother's dead—died my second year in the merc. And if Robertson *ain't* dead he oughta be, an' I don't wanna be the one does the deed."

"Ah." Sorrow touched him: Clan-and-kin, indeed. He perched on the arm of her chair. "The family I meant was Clan Erob."

Her hand dropped to the pouch built into her wide belt. "Clan Erob," she said huskily, "don't know me from Old Dan Tucker. I *told* you that."

"Indeed you did. And I told you that Erob would not shun you. You have—what? Twenty-eight Standards?"

She nodded, wariness very apparent.

"So," said Val Con briskly. "It is high time for you to be made known to your clan and to make your bow to your delm. Now that you are informed of your connection, you would be woefully rude to ignore these duties."

"And besides, you told your brother to meet you there, so that ends that. Might just as well go there, *first*," Miri glared at him. "I just hope you know where it is, 'cause I sure don't."

"I know exactly where it is," Val Con said, taking her hand and smiling at her.

Miri sighed, though she did return the pressure of his fingers. "Why don't that surprise me?" she asked.

"NO," Miri said flatly, teacup clenched tight in a hand gone suddenly cold.

"Cha'trez . . ."

"I said no!" She glared at him over the cup-rim. "This is your idea, Liaden, not mine. You wanna visit a buncha strangers and claim favors, *you* take sleep-learning to find out how!"

"I already know how," Val Con snapped. "And the case is, my lady, that you will be claiming not favor, but rightful place, based on kinship. Proof will be properly offered, in the form of—"

Miri slammed the cup down. "A piece of enamel—work my grandma most likely swiped from some poor sot in an alleyway somewhere, along with everything else in his pockets!"

". . . a gene test." Val Con finished, as if she hadn't spoken.

She took a hard breath against the upset in her stomach.

"Don't need to talk to get a gene test done. Comes to that, I can talk, some. You taught me Low Liaden. No reason why you can't teach me enough High so I don't embarrass you."

"Miri—" He sighed, raising a hand to stroke the errant lock of hair out of his eyes. Miri bit her lip, knowing as plain as if he'd spoken that he'd noticed her upset inside his head, just like she could see his frustration inside hers. And he'd figured out she was far more upset than she should be, given the request, given the partnership, given the love.

"It is not a question," he said now, "of shaming me. We are lifemates, Miri: I am honored to stand at your side. But there is this other thing, when one is lifemated—would you send me into battle without insuring that I knew the field as well as you?"

"Huh?" She shook her head. "Likely get you killed, holding back information. And I'd have to give you everything I had, 'cause you never know beforehand what's gonna be important."

"Exactly." He leaned forward, holding her eyes with his. "We speak of the same situation, cha'trez. Liadens . . . Liadens are very formal. Very—structured. There are six ways to ask forgiveness—six different postures, six distinct phrases, and six separate bows—and none of the six is what a Terran would call an *apology*. Apologies are—very rare." He pushed at his hair again, leaning back.

"You speak Low Liaden—adequately. You have some High Liaden from book-study—enough to get by, I think, if we merely work together on your accent. But language is such a small part of communication, Miri! It is as if I gave you pellets, but failed of giving you the gun."

She closed her eyes; opened them. "You studied this Code-thing, right?"

"Right." He was watching her, very wary. "I grew up in the culture; studied the Code through sleep-learning to correct my understanding of nuance; took what I had learned and shaped it in keeping with my own melant'i. Your melant'i is not mine, Miri. I cannot teach you how to present it. But your lifemate may counsel you on how best to guard it."

"Is there a book?" She was conscious of her breath—shortened and half-desperate—of blood pounding in her ears and sweat on her palms. "Can I study it out of a book, and then you and me can work on the accent?" *Does it have to, HAVE to be sleep-learning, gods?*

"The—book—is actually several volumes," Val Con said softly;

"several large volumes. I used to stand on them to reach the top shelf in my uncle's study, when I was a child."

"Must've been an easier way up than that," Miri said, half-grinning.

"There was," he said repressively; "but I was forbidden to climb the bookshelves. My uncle was quite clear on the point."

She laughed. "That uncle of yours had his share of trouble."

"It is true that Shan and I tended to embrace—inappropriate—necessities," he murmured; "but Nova was quite well-behaved as a child." A ripple of the shoulders. "Mostly."

Miri choked back another laugh. "What about the baby? Anthora? She as bad as the rest of you, or did your uncle get some sleep?"

"Ah, well, Anthora has always been Anthora, you see. Her necessities are often on another plane altogether." He tipped his head, green eyes very bright. "What distresses you, Miri?"

"I—" *Hell, hell, HELL and damnation!* Memory triggered and for an instant she was in the stifling cubicle in Surebleak Port, fourteen, brain-burned and reeling; and the tech was telling Liz, "I'm sorry, Commander. Doesn't look like she can take sleep-learning."

"Miri?" The fingers brushing her cheek were warm; out of the present, not the past. "Cha'trez, please."

"I can't." She swallowed; focused on his face. "*Can't*, boss, get it? Liz took me to a Learning Shop in Surebleak Port to tack on Trade before we left planet. Damn near killed me. Tech said—said I couldn't take it. Sleep-learning. Found out later that—defectives—can't take the—strain on their brains." She managed a wobbling grin. "I know I'm not supposed to tell you I'm stupid . . ."

"Nor are you defective." He stroked her cheek, her forehead; lay his fingers lightly along her lips and then let them drop, eyes troubled. "Tell me, were you given a physical before you took the program?"

She shook her head. "Just plugged in and left alone. It started to hurt—I remember screaming, trying to rip the wires out—"

He frowned. "Why not use the dead-man switch?"

"What dead-man switch?"

Anger, jolting as an electric shock—*his*, not hers; then his voice, very calmly. "A dead-man switch is required in all sleep-learning modules. Lack of the switch would cost a Learning Shop its license to operate."

Miri closed her eyes, suddenly very tired. "So, who checks licenses on Surebleak?"

Silence; then a sigh and the warmth of his fingers closing around hers. "Let us go to the 'doc, cha'trez."

SHE STOOD QUIETLY at his shoulder while he made the inquiry, in Trade, so she could read it: MIRI ROBERTSON: PROGNOSIS FOR SLEEP LEARNING.

The autodoc took its time answering, lights flickering while it consulted its data banks. MIRI ROBERTSON WILL INSERT HER HAND INTO THE UNIT, it directed, a small slot opening to the right of the keypad.

Miri stuck her left hand in as far as it would go, felt the tingle; heard the chime and saw the words. MIRI ROBERTSON WILL WITHDRAW HER HAND.

The slot closed and the screen cleared. More lights flickered. Then: RECUPERATION NEARING COMPLETION. SLEEP-LEARNING ALLOWED FOR MAXIMUM THREE-HOUR SHIFTS, NOT EXCEEDING THREE SHIFTS PER DAY; MINIMUM BREAK SHIFTS TWO HOURS. SUPPLEMENTS SUGGESTED AFTER EACH LEARNING SHIFT TO INSURE RECUPERATION AT CURRENT SATISFACTORY RATE. DISPENSED BELOW.

"I suggest," said Val Con softly, "that you are better nourished than you were at fourteen. I also suggest that this module is properly tuned and equipped." He slipped the supplement pack out of the dispensary and handed it to her. "An Agent is too valuable to lose to brain-burn; a failed mission far too high a price to pay for faulty machinery."

She stared at him; turned to look at the module, complete with dead-man switch, open and ready to receive her.

"Three hours?" It seemed like three centuries.

"It is the most efficient block of time," Val Con said gravely, and stroked her hair. "Miri, I swear that you are in no danger."

She looked at him, remembering the pain and the burning and the terror. "It's really that important?" But of course it was that important. He was her partner. It was his responsibility to see she had what she needed to survive; what she needed for them both to survive.

"OK," she said, and suddenly, desperately, reached up to kiss him. He hugged her tight.

"I will be watching," he murmured. "Malfunction triggers an alarm on the pilot's board. Use the switch, if you feel any discomfort."

"Right." She stepped back, stuck the vitamin pack in her pouch and went over to the module. She lay down and took a grip on the switch. Val Con lowered the lid.

The connectors slid out of the mattress and out of the canopy, stinging a little as they pierced her. Miri closed her eyes against the starless black overhead, and let the program take her.

A TWO-TONED CHIME was going off insistently in her left ear, gradually gaining volume. Miri opened her eyes and sat up, blinking in bleared confusion at the nest-like unit, its black dome lid raised.

Right. Learning module.

She struggled out of the nest and took a couple of deep breaths, head clearing rapidly. Behind her the chiming changed from a two-note chiding to a one-note demand. Frowning, she turned, saw the slip of paper sticking out of the slot near the timer and yanked it free.

The chiming stopped.

Miri frowned at the paper. The words blurred out of focus; steadied: *Absorption rate 98% overall. Feedback accurate 99.8%. Self test consistent 98.4%.*

Miri shook her head, remembered the packet of vitamins in her pouch and went to get something to wash them down with.

Val Con was coming toward her as she entered the bridge and she froze, mind presenting a good dozen ways to address him; combinations of bows and salutations branching off into a veritable jungle of possibilities, none seeming more right than another. The combination for greeting a senior officer presented itself and she grabbed it, executing the bow in barely proper time.

"Sir," she said, remembering to straighten before speaking, and to speak with the inflection of respectful attention, "I have completed my session with the Instructor."

Both brows shot up before he returned her bow, briefly, and with subtle irony. Miri was dismayed; recalled that one might accept idiosyncrasies of style, so long as they did not cross the line of what one's own melant'i would tolerate.

"Ma'am," Val Con said, senior to junior, though with an undefinable under-inflection, which seemed to echo the irony of his bow, "I am delighted to find your time with the Instructor so fruitfully spent. However, I believe that the length and—intimacy— of our relationship might allow you use of my name."

"Yes, certainly . . ." But *that* combination did not arise and the more she scrambled to find a mode that would allow it, the more confusion rose. She lost the timing of the conversation, shattered cadence and art, was adrift in an echoing sea of inflection.

"Miri."

She looked up at him, helpless to choose from the endless and proliferating possibilities; unable to define herself, since she could find no way to define him.

His hand closed over hers. "Miri. Stop worrying at it, cha'trez. Let it find its level and settle."

The Terran words wrenched her out of confusion; she sagged against him, suddenly aware that she had been holding herself at full attention.

"I don't guess I learned how to just use somebody's name," she muttered.

He hugged her. "That's Low Liaden. 'Val Con-husband,' remember? Eh? And 'Val Con-love.' Much nicer to hear from you than 'sir.' I thought I was in black disgrace."

She snorted a laugh. "Worried you, too."

"Certainly."

She laughed again and pulled away, shoving the piece of paper under his nose.

"Came out of the machine. Any idea what it means?"

"Ah." He slipped it from her fingers; read it with a nod. "On many worlds it would mean that you are a genius, Miri. The module is set up to test gain and chart the student's recall. A defective person, for instance, would have been expelled from the program after the first test demonstrated that no learning had taken place. Those scores," he handed the paper back, "will have triggered an accelerated program."

"Genius?" She frowned at him, then at the paper.

"Genius." Val Con sighed gently; reached to tap the paper. "On Liad, these scores would gain you admittance to Scout Academy. Since you have also demonstrated ability to operate—and prosper— in a low-tech culture, you would likely be admitted to the middle class."

"I ain't a pilot," Miri protested, thinking that scouts were the best there was. Thinking that Val Con was a scout. Thinking that it had to be a glitch in the machine somewhere. Thinking . . .

"It can be arranged," Val Con was saying, "to have groundwork laid for piloting lessons while you are sleep-learning—a matter of appending the program to your study of the Code. It is only a preparatory program, of course, but I can teach you the math and the board-drills."

"Sure," Miri said, absently.

"Good. Would you like some tea?"

"Huh?" She shook out of her reverie, looked at the paper again—written in Liaden, she noticed, then, but was beyond being surprised. "Tea'd be fine, thanks. Gotta take my vitamins anyway."

"Yes." He went to the menu board and she followed. "I suggest you use the Rainbow tonight, cha'trez, to anchor today's learning. Tomorrow you should be able to do all three sessions."

"All three—!" She glared at his back and then sighed, recalling another bit of learning. "Guess if I'm gonna have this melant'i stuff to take care of, I'd better get the rules right." She took the cup out of his hand.

"Genius, huh?" She shook her head. "Tell you what, though, boss—I don't feel the least bit smart."

DELGADO:
Bjornson—
Bellevale College of Art
and Sciences

※ ※

". . . **COFFEE**, flapjacks and YOO-oo-OO!" The voice wavered unmelodically, though with evident sincerity, from edge-orbit across the general beam and into the tiny professorial office. The man at the desk glanced over his shoulder at the beam-set, frown flickering into a smile as he recognized Number Three-Fifty-Eight singing his way into port, if not into the heart of *Vail Runner's* satiric mistress, as he did precisely at the professor's midnight, every night.

"Speak to me, beautiful Captain!" the singer urged against the background chatter of half-a-hundred ships, from port to the fringe of the third world out; and in blithe disregard of the possibility that there might be any number of beautiful captains within hearing.

"Sorry, Three-Five-Eight. Thought you were in the middle of breakfast." The woman's voice was cool, with an undercurrent of amusement, precisely as always. The professor smiled again and turned back to the screen and the thesis he was grading.

A singularly disappointing document, truth told; even though the author had not been one from whom he had hoped great things. However, one liked to know that a *little* learning had taken place, even in the least promising of scholars. Ah, well, they were but at the mid-term. Perhaps guidance might yet produce thought.

So thinking, he brought his wandering attention more firmly back to the thesis, seeking the most profitable means of providing guidance. Behind him, Three-Fifty-Eight pled his case with the cool-voiced lady, one tile in a familiar, comforting mosaic of voices. The professor listened with half-an-ear, then with even less, as the key to guidance presented itself and he gave it his full attention.

❊ *ATTENTION! ATTENTION!* ❊

It snarled across the familiar mosaic like an angry boot heel. The professor had already spun in his chair, dark eyes intense on the squat receiver as if he would see through it to the ship that carried so urgent a message.

ATTENTION! ALL JUNTAVAS EMPLOYEES, SUPPORTERS, DEPENDENTS, ALLIES SHALL FROM RECEIPT OF THIS MESSAGE FORWARD RENDER ASSISTANCE, AID AND COMFORT TO SERGEANT MIRI ROBERTSON, CITIZEN OF TERRA; AND SCOUT COMMANDER VAL CON YOS'PHELIUM, CITIZEN OF LIAD; TOGETHER OR SINGLY; REDIRECTING, WHERE NECESSARY, YOUR OWN ACTIVITIES. REPEAT: AID AND COMFORT TO MIRI ROBERTSON AND/OR VAL CON YOS'PHELIUM IMPERATIVE, PRIORITY HIGHEST.
MESSAGE REPEATS. . .

That quickly it was done, gone; leaving nothing but dead beam for a heartbeat—for two. . .

"What the hell was that!" The irrepressible Three-Fifty-Eight.

"Courier ship," snapped someone else and, "You should've seen that brother go! Third planet kick-off, skimmed in, dropped it and gone!"

Five days out. The professor eased out of his chair, went with wary, silent grace across the room to the little receiver, staring at it as if it had suddenly become something quite else.

"Scout Commander Val Con yos'Phelium," he whispered, extending a hand to touch the power-off. "Scout Commander Val Con yos'Phelium . . ."

He turned, paced the length of the tiny office—five of his strides—and the width—five more—until he came again to the desk and the work awaiting him. A hand slipped into one pocket; emerged—and he stood staring down at the flat gleam of a ship's key, incongruous in his soft, scholar's palm.

Professors of cultural genetics did not as a rule own spaceships. He sighed and slipped the key away.

So deep a cover, constructed over so many years. . .

He shook his head, banishing the thought with the key and sat once again to his work, trying to recapture his previous mood of gentle instruction. Screen-light gleamed off his single ring—three stands of silver, twisted into a flat knot, worn on the smallest finger of his left hand. After a moment, he sighed again, leaned back in the chair and closed his eyes.

Scout Commander Val Con yos'Phelium. . .

LYTAXIN:
Approaching Erob

❀ ❀

HOUSE. She was sure that was the word. House.

Sleep-learning had reinforced her vocabulary, made her comfortable with sounds and meanings, and the recent social encounter at the landing field had almost convinced her she had all things Liaden by the scruff of the neck.

House.

It was huge.

Miri stopped on the crest of the gentle rise, staring up at the long expanse of velvet-lawned hill, and the u-shaped sweep of gray-and-black stone, several stories high. The house, that was. She looked at Val Con.

"Are you *sure*?"

He glanced away from his own study of the landscape, one brow quirking. "It does *seem* to be a clanhouse," he murmured; "but recall that I have never called upon Erob, either."

She took a deep breath. "It's as big as a hyatt," she told him, stating the obvious in as calm a voice as she could muster. "A *big* hyatt. Maybe we got the wrong directions. Maybe it is a hyatt, which ain't all that bad. We could maybe get a room if we got enough money, and call ahead."

Val Con grinned and stroked her cheek. "This is a frontier world, cha'trez—the entire clan would live in one house, plus necessary staff, plus guesting rooms, contract-suites, administration, supplies.

"Recall that this is the capital-in-fact of the planet until they recover from the revolt—actually the center of the world in some ways even before." He lifted a shoulder. "I would say that they have no more space than they likely need, depending upon the size of the clan and the amount of administration they feel it necessary to perform."

"Gods." She looked at him, suddenly struck with a thought. "Is *your* house this big? The one you grew up in?"

"I grew up in Trealla Fantrol," he said softly; "yos'Galan's line house. It is very grand, of course, but not nearly so large as this. Korval has never ruled the world." He offered his hand, smiling.

After a moment, Miri dredged up a smile of her own, wove her fingers around his and went with him, toward the house.

THE GOOD THING about being on world was the smells. The breeze. The colors. The hand in hers. The quiet.

That was an odd one, Miri realized as they walked paths that had only recently been guard marches and troop routes. Quiet.

As many worlds as she'd been on, none of the planetfalls had been like this. Leisurely, and—aside from her own certainty of ruin at the end—calm. The weapons checks were habit, the vitamin dosages learning aids rather than war-prep, the entry to atmosphere a tourist's wonder of ocean, continents, and icecaps.

They'd come in as the cordon around the planet was being dismantled. Troop and guard ships alike had failed to notice them— as Val Con had prophesied—and there'd been no alerts, no threats, and no danger.

For three orbits Lytaxin had spun below them. The radio had told the tale pretty clearly: A stupid and bungled coup attempt followed by a dirty little war mostly confined to a single continent. The mercs had come quickly.

What they hadn't gotten from the radio they had soon enough from Riaska ter'Meulen. Now *there* was a person who could talk. She'd limped out of the office of the little general aviation field, to Miri's eye unflapped by the sudden and unannounced appearance of their—of the Department of Interior's—vessel.

"Scouts," she'd said, nodding a rather unconventional kind of a bow at both of them. "How may I be of service? And how shall I register your visit?"

Val Con returned the nod with a formal bow. "Of your kindness, register the ship as *Fosterling*, out of Liad, piloted by Val Con yos'Phelium, Clan Korval. Business of the clan."

The woman made her own bow at that point and Miri's new-poured training kicked into gear. Val Con's bow, acknowledging what?—personal debt, personal respect?—to the clan of an ally or friend of his clan? And ter'Meulen's bow acknowledging . . . acceptance of respect and recognition of the—honor, was it, of being so acknowledged?

She walked with them across the airfield, discussing the war, her limp growing more evident with each step. She stopped them in front of an open hanger housing a vintage ground attack aircraft.

"Pilot of Korval, I expect you are well-placed to assist us. This is the official airfield defense craft. It and its kin were gifts of Korval, and before the war we had perhaps a double dozen of them. There were five here, but all save this one went off in The Long Raid. I understand that the contingent on the islands were destroyed by our side, and Erob's allies in the highlands used theirs until they were relieved by the mercenaries. The Long Raid was their idea, I gather—stuff enough fuel and strip enough weight to get them 'cross the ocean . . ."

Val Con listened, quiet, while Miri nodded at the good sense of the tactic. Sounded like the kind of thing Kindle would pull together.

"Many planes were shot down—where Clan Kenso got weapons like that I'd give the rest of my leg to know!—and so I have this . . ." She bowed toward the plane—fond respect, Miri thought.

"Parts are hard to come by, and while this one flies, and will continue in its duty, it would be good to have spare parts. If there might be a way—the patterns and the equipment that built them are on Liad, in your own shops."

Val Con bowed. "As time permits I shall speak to the first speaker."

Riaska ter'Meulen bowed. "I am grateful."

"Cars are yet in short supply," she said then. "May I call the House and have them send, or may I offer you service of my flitter?" A wave of a hand indicated a tiny craft—barely more than a cabin over a lift-fan.

Miri stirred, in no hurry to raise the house and seeing no need to deprive a wounded woman of transport.

"It's a fine day," she said to Riaska ter'Meulen, in the mode of equals, "and we've been long aboard. A walk will be welcome."

The woman bowed again, willing equality. "As you say. Allow me to point you on your way."

THEY STOPPED just short of the three low stairs leading to a sort of black stone dais and a front door that was all pieces of high-glaze tile forming a field of indigo, across which a crimson bird stooped toward a gold-limned mountain, far below. Miri felt the hairs lift at the back of her neck and her free hand touched her pouch, where a miniature of that very design rode, perfect in every detail.

She shook her head sharply and frowned, slanting a glance at her partner's face; saw him gazing with sharp interest to the left.

"You gonna ring the bell or not?" she demanded.

"In a moment." He set off across that soft, resilient lawn purposefully; fingers still firm and warm around hers.

And stopped in front of a tree.

It was a largish tree, Miri thought, with a pleasingly tree-like trunk and nice, broad, four-fingered leaves a shade greener and a shade less blue than the grass. Nuts or seedpods hung in clusters here and there and the whole thing smelled good, in a kind of olfactory tree-ness.

Val Con loosed her hand, took another step toward the tree and bowed. Deeply. With the stylized hand-sign that offered instant, willing, and unquestioning service.

"I bring thee greeting, child of Jela's hope," he said in the High Tongue, but in a dialect beyond any of those Miri had studied in her crash-course sleep-learning. She thought it might be related to the mode used by the most junior servant to the ultimate authority—and then thought that was crazy.

"When last this one visited the homeworld," Val Con was telling the tree, "thy elder kin yet flourished, grew, and nurtured. The charge is kept and the guard continues. When next this one is upon the homeworld, thy name shall be whispered to the elder's leaves."

He stood for a moment or two then, head bowed, maybe listening to the little rustling sounds the breeze made against the leaves. Then he bowed again, like he was going to ask a favor.

"This one has not had grace of Jela's children in some years, and this one's lady has yet to know the elder. In need, this one asks the boon of two fruit, and one leaf."

He stepped forward then, reaching high; and pulled two nuts free from the lowest cluster. He plucked a leaf from the same branch and stepped back, bowing thanks.

Grinning, then, he cracked a nut and handed it to her; cracked open the second and pulled the shell apart, revealing a plump pink kernel.

"These are good," he said, back in Terran. "I ate quite a number of them when I was a child, to the gardener's dismay."

Miri pulled her own nut apart, blinking in surprise at the aroma. She paused in the act of fishing the meat out and looked at her partner.

"It's a nice tree, boss. Does it talk back?"

"Eh?" He blinked, then laughed. "Ah, I had forgotten . . . There is a very old Tree on Liad that my clan is—involved with. A long story. The name of that Tree is Jelaza Kazone. This tree here is a seedling of that, so it behooves me to pay courtesy, wouldn't you say?"

"Um." Miri nibbled the kernel, finding it delicious. "How do you know this one's related to yours?"

"There is only one Jelaza Kazone," Val Con murmured. "And Korval does occasionally seal—certain—contracts with the gift of a seedling."

"Right." The nut was gone. Miri sighed in real regret and looked up as Val Con handed her the leaf.

"Wear this in your belt, cha'trez. Are you done? Good. Let us ring the bell."

THE DOORKEEPER WAS YOUNG, narrow-shouldered and too thin; the fragile bones almost showing through the translucent golden skin. His hair was pale red, shading toward blond, and tumbling over a high forehead, not quite hiding the bruises at both temples, where the combat helmet had been too tight. The blue eyes were wary, with a darker shadow, lurking far back.

"Delm Erob?" he repeated, looking from Val Con to her and back again. And seeing, Miri knew from the slight change of expression, two soldiers, coming where they shouldn't be, asking for somebody they had no business to see.

"The delm is quite busy," he said now, speaking the High Tongue in the mid-mode reserved for strangers whose melant'i was yet unclear. "If you will acquaint me with your difficulty, sir— ma'am—perhaps I may direct you to the proper person."

"It is essential," Val Con said, his own mode shifting subtly, so that he spoke from senior to junior, "that we speak to Delm Erob with all speed, young sir."

The boy's cheeks flushed darker gold, but he let no hint of that spurt of temper enter his voice. "I must insist you acquaint me more particularly with your mission, sir. If you are separated from your unit—if you have not received proper pay—if you have missed your transport—none of these difficulties will be addressed by Delm Erob, though Clan Erob is able to solve any or all for you. I merely require adequate information."

Not too bad, Miri thought, for a kid who was obviously out on his feet and at the tail end of seeing and doing a bunch of stuff he'd probably rather never have known about. The blue eyes shifted to her and she gave him a grin of encouragement before the sleep-learning kicked in and let her know that was a mistake. The kid frowned, eyes suddenly hard.

"Have you been in our garden?" he demanded, mode shifting

fast toward belligerence, courtesy forgotten in outrage. "Have you defaced our tree?"

Miri came to full attention, eyes tight on his. "We have certainly not defaced your tree!" she snapped, in a mode very close to the voice she used to chew out a soldier who'd been particularly stupid. "We asked grace for the leaf and it was freely given."

The boy's face altered amazingly, shifting from outrage to shock to a sudden dawning dread. He touched his tongue to his lips and brought his eyes back to Val Con.

"We do," Val Con said, gently, and still only in the mode of senior to junior, though he could have done much worse to the kid than that, "very much desire to speak with Delm Erob. Now, if possible. You may say that the Second Speaker of Clan Korval is calling, regarding a daughter of your House."

THE KID HAD GONE to get his boss, leaving the two of them to kick their heels in what sleep-learning suggested was a formal reception parlor.

Miri pictured him running down the long hallway the minute the door was shut and grinned as she glanced around, wondering what this room had over the one at the front of the house they'd almost stopped in. The kid had actually crossed the threshold of that room, and Miri got a glimpse of white paneled walls and uncomfortable looking furniture before he apparently thought better of it and stepped back with a slight bow and a murmured, "Follow me, please."

So now, the Yellow Salon, and another kid, a little younger than the first, bringing wine and glasses and a porcelain tray of cakes. She kept her eyes averted, after one disconcertingly bright blue glance that seemed more interested in Val Con than in her, and bowed real pretty, asking if anything else was required in a voice that said she hoped not.

"Thank you," Val Con said gravely. "The solicitude of the House gives gladness."

"Sir." The kid bowed again and escaped, forgetting to wait for the door to fully close before she ran.

Miri grinned again, slid her hands in her belt and wandered over to look out the window, squinting a little against the sun.

"There's your tree, boss."

"So?" He came over, shoulder companionably touching hers as he took in the view. "But that is not my Tree, Miri. That is Erob's tree. Mine is much older—and taller."

"Sounds like a quibble to me," she said. "If this one's a seedling off yours and yours is the only one there is, besides its own seedlings . . ." She stopped, cheeks heating in an unaccustomed blush.

Val Con laughed.

"Ah. Clan becomes discovered."

"Real funny . . ." she began, and then cut off as the door clicked.

Val Con went silently toward the center of the room, Miri half-a-pace behind his right shoulder.

The woman who entered the salon had not run full-tilt down the hallway, but she hadn't dallied, either. She was gray-haired, gray-eyed and golden skinned, wire-thin and charged with energy. Two heavy lines were grooved horizontally across her high forehead; more lines ran starkly from nose to mouth. Still more lines radiated from the corners of her eyes, puckered now as she stared against the sun. She was dressed simply, in what sleep-learning told Miri was house-tunic, and tight trousers tucked neatly into a pair of buff-colored short-boots.

All business, she marched across the buttery carpet, stopped a precise four paces before Val Con and bowed crisply, hand over heart.

"Emrith Tiazan," she said in a low, clear voice, "Delm Erob."

Val Con made his own bow, more fluid than hers, though as deep. "Val Con yos'Phelium, Clan Korval."

Miri tensed—but the old eyes stayed on Val Con.

"Yes," she said. "You have your father's look."

Val Con bowed again, slightly—and with irony, Miri thought.

Emrith Tiazan might have thought so, too; she lifted a sharp-bladed shoulder, and let it fall. Miri again tensed to make her own bow, but the old woman seemed intent on ignoring her.

"I'll tell you plain, Korval, before we sit to tea and cake and behaving as though we're civilized—it's no joy to see you at this time, tree-kin though we be. We're just through with a matter that will heal in a generation or two—if all goes well and no one breeds another hothead like Kel Bar Rentava. I am aware that Erob owes a contract-wife this term, but while plain speaking's in force I'll tell you that the one we'd settled on went the soulroad in the war." The old face shifted then, all the lines tightening, but her voice stayed smooth.

"They shot her down—Clan Kenso. She was the very best we had, and they shot her down. Her ship crashed in the rock plain, east of here. I expect we have all the pieces, by now."

She closed her eyes briefly; lifted her shoulder again. "I'll have nothing of such excellence to offer Korval until Alys comes to her growth—nine years, perhaps. Alys should do very well—but she'll be no Kea Tiazan."

There was a silence.

Miri's mind raced, but nothing from her own experience or from the sleep-learned stuff helped her make sense of this one. The old lady was clearly at the end of her rope, worn to skin, bone, and character. Her mind might even be wandering, though Miri doubted that. It might have been that Val Con's clan and Clan Erob had sealed an alliance with a marriage, when this lady had been a young delm . . .

"Forgive me," Emrith Tiazan was saying to Val Con, "if my frankness offends. I've no time for wasteful courtesies and it is certainly not necessary for Erob to stand upon ceremony with our old ally, Korval. We have always understood each other very well."

"In this instance, however," Val Con said neutrally, "understanding may have fallen short. I assign no blame, nor does frankness offend." He reached out to capture Miri around the wrist and drew her lightly forward to stand at his side. "I present my lifemate, Miri Robertson Tiazan, Lady yos'Phelium."

The gray eyes in their golden net of wrinkles went wide, then narrowed as they swept Miri from face to feet. The glance scathed, lingering longest on the leaf before whipping back to Val Con.

"So! You discover a houseless favorite and you *dare* bring her to *me*? I shall acknowledge her, shall I, and give her place among the clans? Korval presumes—and presumes too far. I will remind you that you *guest* with Erob. Your whim is not law here!"

That was enough. Miri moved, deliberately turning her flank on the old lady and her rage.

"I tell you what, boss," she said, in her flattest, ugliest Terran accent—one-hundred-percent Surebleak. "I ain't about to join this outfit, genes or no genes."

"Ah," said Val Con.

"*What* did you say?" demanded Emrith Tiazan, in Terran, though Terran slurred and softened and pronounced like Liaden.

"I *said*," Miri snapped, in the stiffest mode she could call to mind from the High Tongue, "that it is not the place of a high commander to reprimand another commander who is come to parlay."

For the space of two heartbeats, Emrith Tiazan stood frozen, and then she bowed, very gently.

"Forgive me—madam," she said, the High Tongue carefully conveying equality of rank. "You spoke of genes. I desire further information upon the subject as you believe it to concern yourself and—this outfit." She paused. "If you please."

Miri hesitated, more than half determined to walk out the door and down that long hallway and out into the sunshine. *Ought to be able to find the merc camp without too much trouble*, she thought; *get a hot meal and a place to bunk. . .*

"Miri," Val Con said softly. "Will you show Delm Erob your heirloom?"

Damn him, she thought; and then sighed and worked the catch on her belt-pouch. She fingered the disk free and held it out to the old lady, belatedly remembering to bow.

Emrith Tiazan glanced briefly at the shield, then turned to the obverse, frowning at the engraved genealogy. She looked back at Miri.

"How came you by this?"

"I have it from my mother," Miri said, matching the other's mild tone; "who had it from hers."

"So." The old lady looked at Val Con. "This appears genuine."

He lifted a brow. "Many clans possess—protocols—for deter-mining authenticity."

She stared at him. "Indeed. You will excuse me for a moment." She turned and marched out of the room without waiting for their permission.

The door had barely closed when Miri swung around. "What is this? How come she thinks you came here for a contract-wife? If you're pulling one—*one*—of your damned Liaden tricks, that old lady ain't gonna have to bother taking you apart, 'cause I'll do it for her, you understand me?"

"Yes, Miri," he said meekly, but for once meekness failed to gain her smile. She stood glaring, poised on the balls of her feet, a trained fighter, more than half-ready to fight.

Val Con took her hand, led her to the couch by the refreshment table and sat down. "Miri." He tugged gently at her, patting the cushion beside him.

For a moment he thought she'd refuse, yank her hand free and stomp away, as he had been certain she would earlier, and he with no choice but to follow his lifemate. . .

"Hell." She flumped down next to him and dropped her head on his shoulder. "You're more trouble than you're worth, you know?"

"Shan has often expressed that view," he said, sighing in mock remorse. "The two who know me best cannot both be in error."

She snorted a half-laugh; stirred and sat up. "That kid who died—Kea? She was a pilot."

"So are you."

"Like hell—" The door clicked and she swallowed the rest of that argument.

Emrith Tiazan stopped before the couch and held the disk out to Miri, bowing with careful equality. "This has tested genuine." She straightened and looked at Val Con. "Genes, you believe?"

"I have no doubt," he said calmly. "You will, of course, wish to attain your own surety."

"Of course." She went across the room to the desk comm and touched a button. In a very short while, the door opened to admit the young doorkeeper. He flicked a nervous glance at the couch, then bowed deeply to Emrith Tiazan.

"My delm desires?"

"You will go to the older storehouse and find in Room East 14 a large package stasis-locked and wrapped in blue silk. Bring it here. You will bid Win Den tel'Vosti attend me here. You will likewise bid the senior medical technician, adding that she shall bring her sampling kit."

The boy touched his tongue to his lips, bowed, turned—

"An Der."

He glanced back over his shoulder. "Yes, Aunt?"

"You will speak to no one, excepting tel'Vosti and the senior med. You will go to the storeroom alone and bring what I require away with your own hands."

The boy bowed again. "I hear," he said—and ran.

"WELL, EMRITH?"

The old man leaned on his stick in the center of the room. "To what do I owe this interruption of my studies?"

"Studies!" The delm stared at him for a moment, then moved a hand, directing his attention to the couch. "I make you known to Val Con yos'Phelium, Second Speaker for Clan Korval. Korval, my kinsman, Win Den tel'Vosti, thodelm."

"So." The brown eyes watched with seeming amusement as Val Con stood and made his bow.

"My Lord tel'Vosti."

"My Lord yos'Phelium." The return bow was more complete than Miri would have expected, given the cane. "Your father was a rare one for Counterchance."

"So my uncle has told me, sir."

"Er Thom yos'Galan? Now *there* was a demon for the game! Very good he was—a thoughtful, subtle player, no shame. We came even, the times we played. But Daav . . . I believe I may yet owe him a cantra. Perhaps two. I'll consult my account books. Do you play?"

"A bit, sir, but not to match my uncle."

"Pity." The brown eyes sharpened. "You'll want to have that wound looked after, of course, before you meet the House."

Wound? What wo—Sleep learning surfaced and Miri gulped against the sudden *understanding* of what it meant, to be a Liaden with your face scarred . . . .

"Thank you, sir," Val Con was saying calmly. "It's healed cleanly."

"Win Den." Emrith Tiazan began, but tel'Vosti had come to attention, as if he were a corps captain facing another, and half-sketched a salute.

"It is your campaign, sir."

"*Win Den.*" This time his delm's voice could not be ignored. She moved her hand. "I am told that this lady is Miri Robertson Tiazan."

Miri came to her feet and bowed into those amused brown eyes.

"Well, and why not?" said the old gentleman, returning the bow with a certain flair.

"Lady yos'Phelium," Val Con murmured in the room's sudden stillness and tel'Vosti straightened with a laugh.

"Aha! A man who wishes to be absolute of his assets! My felicitations, sir! Perhaps you are not so poor a player of the game as you would have me believe." He glanced back at Miri.

"You are a soldier?" he asked, in the almost-friendly mode of Comrade.

"I was," Miri said, allowing him the mode, though not without a few mental reservations. "I retired a year or two ago."

"Indeed? At what rank?"

She eyed him warily, wondering where this line of questioning was going; wondering, with a sudden spurt of panic, if he was trying to figure her melant'i and if it was going to come up to par. "Master sergeant."

"Master sergeant." He said it like a caress. "And your age is?"

"Twenty-eight Standards." She considered him, the lurking amusement, the straight shoulders, the cane, the mane of pinkish hair. "More or less."

He laughed and glanced at Emrith Tiazan, who stood, grim-faced and silent, near the desk.

"So you tell me you retired two years ago, with the rank of master sergeant. A private troop, perhaps? Industrial?"

"No," Miri had to tell him, against a building wave of dread. "Mercenary unit." She mustered enough nerve to glare into his perpetual amusement. "I was with the Gyrfalks before I retired. I began in Lizardi's Lunatics, which is how I came to be a sergeant in the first place. We got into a spot of trouble, command-chain broke down . . ."

"So you were made field sergeant." tel'Vosti tipped his head. "But your rank was upheld, once the—trouble—was past. And the Gyrfalks raised the stake by a star."

Suddenly, amazingly, he bowed. "A Master of mercenary sergeants by the time you attained twenty-five Standards! A significant feat, Lady yos'Phelium, for I have seen the Gyrfalks in action. Their conduct is always professional and they are most resourceful. Their services do not come cheap—am I correct, Emrith?—but they are worth their weight in cantra, each of them. Korval does well to guard his assets."

The door clicked, and opened to admit the wide-eyed doorman, barely seen behind the flat crate he carried against his chest. After him came a stern dark-haired woman in a crisp coverall: the senior med tech.

"Great," Miri whispered to Val Con, as tel'Vosti and the delm turned away to deal with the new arrivals. "Now maybe we can get this over and get outta here."

THE CRATE HAD BEEN PLACED against the desk, and the blue silk drawn away. Emrith Tiazan knelt before it and with her own hands loosened the seals. An Der helped her rise, a solicitous hand at her elbow, a ready arm by her waist.

She shook him off and stepped back. "Open it," she said harshly, and the boy bent to comply.

Val Con drifted forward, Miri at his side. They stopped to the right of Win Den tel'Vosti, who stood with both hands covering the knob of his cane, no amusement at all in his face. The med tech had shrugged and gone over to the couch, perching on the wide arm and watching the proceedings with a sort of distant interest.

An Der wrestled the cover loose and stepped away.

The med tech drew a noisy breath in through her teeth.

Nobody else moved at all, and Miri frowned, wondering why an old mirror should be the focus of such tension, such expect—

"Oh, shit," she breathed, and moved away from Val Con's side, staring at the reflection that didn't move—didn't move because it was a painting—a portrait, not a mirror. A portrait of a woman in flying leathers and loose-laced white shirt, arms crossed under slight breasts, legs braced wide, gray eyes direct in a willful, intelligent face, and the copper-colored hair done in a single long braid, wrapped three times around her head.

"Miri Tiazan," Emrith Tiazan said, voice still strained. "Who left the clan in disgrace."

"Who put the clan in disgrace by leaving," tel'Vosti corrected. "Be precise, Emrith."

"It is disgrace to ignore the delm's order!"

"But she never did ignore it—as you well know. She merely asked leave to postpone contract wedding until love's seed should bear fruit. Tamishon was in no great hurry, being content to know the contract was valid and eventually would be fulfilled. Four month's delay was no cause to abort the babe." He turned to Miri and bowed slightly, indicating fuller information forthcoming.

"The lad was dead, you see—she'd get no other child from him. And Baan Tiazan was a tyrant who ruled both his daughters hard, eh, Emrith?" He moved his shoulders when she gave no answer, amusement back in his eyes.

"She was not always dutiful, understand—that would be unlike her name. But she acquiesced in the large things, and made shift to come the sophisticate, in company."

Miri shook herself. "She ran away to have her kid," she finished, in Terran, too shaken to sort through sleep-learned modes. "She crashed on Surebleak and couldn't get home . . ."

"Is that what came of her?" tel'Vosti asked softly. His Terran was better than the delm's. "We had wondered."

She shook herself again, ran the Rainbow, fast, to get distance from the shock of the picture and the tension focused now on her. "I'm guessing," she told tel'Vosti. "She's dressed like a pilot—and there ain't any reason to choose Surebleak, when you got the whole galaxy ahead."

"So," he said, and looked ready to say more.

"There will be a gene test," Emrith Tiazan snapped. "Med Tech, attend your duty!"

The tech came to her feet, looking open-mouthed from the picture to Miri. She looked finally at the old lady and bowed, rearranging her face into an expression of cool interest.

"As you say," she murmured, and drew a flat kit from her utility pocket. "If the young lady will attend me here . . ."

THE BLUE DRESS felt nice.

It looked nice, too, Miri decided. In fact, she looked amazingly respectable for a woman who had lately been a mercenary master sergeant, a bodyguard, a fugitive from justice, a woman of all work, and a singer.

Whether she looked respectable enough to please the circus gathering in the reception room below was something she'd find out far too soon.

She took one last turn before the mirror, admiring the way the bluestone necklace lay just right against her throat. She was wearing her hair loose, held back with a set of deceptively simple silver combs. Central stores, located in the cavernous belowstairs had provided dress and combs. The necklace and matching ring were hers, gifts from Val Con, from a time when gifts from Val Con were potentially deadly.

"Very elegant," she told her reflection, and bowed pleasure at making acquaintance, remembering to include the hand-gesture one used toward newly-met kin.

"Gods," she said, and came slowly erect, as if the woman in the mirror might jump her. "Oh, gods, Robertson, what the hell have you gotten yourself into?"

Val Con's dressing room—the 'apartment' set aside for their use was bigger than Zhena Trelu's whole house, back on Vandar—was on the opposite side of the bedroom. There were three other rooms—a parlor, an office and a bookroom, plus a bathroom the size of Lytaxin spaceport and a balcony that looked out over the East Garden.

A huge bed commanded the bedroom. Flowering vines grew up two of the posts and all over the canopy, dripping long tendrils like flowering curtains around the sides. Miri shook her head. Liadens . . . A whole room just to dress in, a garden growing in the bedroom, and a bunch of other stuff, here and there, apparently just done for pretty. She bit her lip, recalling the apartments she'd lived in as a kid, an endless succession of rats, peeling synth-lam walls and near-paneless windows leaking Surebleak's frigid winter winds.

"Forget it, Robertson," she whispered; "you ain't going back there. Never going back there."

The bed-flowers were pale blue with soft white stripes, lightly and agreeably perfumed. On impulse, she pulled one free and tucked it behind an ear as she continued across the cream-and-blue carpet to Val Con's dressing room.

He caught her eyes in the mirror as the door opened, and smiled.

"Cha'trez."

She tried to smile back—saw her reflection's mouth wobble and then straighten in distress as the big gray eyes got bigger, taking in the ruffled white shirt, the rich dark trousers, the green ear-drop and finger-ring—all the accouterments of a Liaden gentlemen about to attend a formal dinner.

Val Con spun, eyes and face serious.

"Miri? What is wrong?"

"I—" she shook her head and managed to dredge up a half-convincing grin. "You look like a Liaden, boss."

"Ah." His face relaxed and he came across to her, lifting a hand to touch her hair. "But, you see, I am a Liaden, which no doubt accounts for it."

"That's probably it," she agreed and sighed. "You ready to go face the lions?"

One brow rose. "Clan Erob? Hardly lions."

"Yeah, and suppose that gene test comes out negative? *You're* OK, but I ain't the kind Erob usually has to supper."

"And the portrait of Miri-eklykt'i?" He touched the flower behind her ear with a gentle forefinger.

Miri sighed, recalling with a certain queasy vividness the face of the woman in the old painting. The resemblance was spooky enough if she *was* that one's granddaughter. . .

"I don't guess coincidence'll cover it, huh?"

"It seems unlikely in the extreme." He touched the flower again, then drew it from its resting-place.

"Not," he murmured, "for this sort of dinner."

"Huh?" Miri followed him into the bedroom. "It's against the law to wear flowers to dinner?"

"This particular flower," said Val Con, placing it gently in a cut crystal water glass, "is an aphrodisiac."

She blinked at him; blinked at the canopy. "And they've got 'em growing all over the bed?"

"What better place?"

"Right." She closed her eyes, willing tense muscles to relax.

"Miri?"

She looked at the pattern of him inside her head—bright and clear and beloved—then opened her eyes and grinned wryly at the proper Liaden gentleman before her.

"Tell you what, boss: This whole masquerade's gonna come crashing down over something as stupid as that flower. If you hadn't been here to tell me before I went on down, I could've blown everything." *Everything*, she thought: His melant'i; the melant'i of Line yos'Phelium; her own insignificant amount—all gone. Because of a flower.

"I ain't up for this," she said suddenly, feeling the panic boiling in her stomach. "Look, boss, I'm a soldier, not an actor—and nobody down there's gonna believe for one minute that I'm Lady yos'Phelium. Let's see if we can't catch the old lady and tell her we made a mistake, OK? All the mercs in the city right now, there's bound to be somebody around who owes me dinner—"

"Miri—" That quick he was across the room, arms around her tight, cheek against hers. "It is not a masquerade, cha'trez. It is truth. We are lifemates. And a portion of our shared melant'i involves standing as lady and lord to Line yos'Phelium." He laughed softly. "For our sins."

She choked a half-laugh and pushed her face into his shoulder. "I'm gonna wreck your melant'i."

"No." He kissed her ear. "My lifemate is a lady of intelligence, wit, and courage. How else could it be, but that her melant'i supports and enhances my own? And together—" He slipped his hand under her chin and tipped her face so she could see the bright green eyes, awash in mischief. "*Together*, cha'trez, we are—" he bent his head, put his mouth next to her ear and breathed "—*hell on wheels.*"

"You—" She laughed and hugged him hard before stepping away and taking his hand. "All right, let's go meet the family."

She stopped him at the hall door, though, struck by one more detail.

"We gonna let on I don't know your family from sliced bread? I don't think even tel'Vosti'd like a lifemating where I ain't met your First Speaker, much less you got her permission."

"A valid point," Val Con murmured and tipped his head, staring hard at nothing, with his brows pulled slightly together.

"Line yos'Phelium," he said after a bit, "presently includes Kareen, my father's sister; her son Pat Rin, and his heir, Quin. My father is Daav yos'Phelium, who is eklykt'i. His lifemate, my mother, was Aelliana Caylon. She is dead. I was fostered into the household of my father's cha'leket, Er Thom yos'Galan, and his lifemate, Anne Davis. They, also, have died. Shan is Lord yos'Galan, Nova is First Speaker, Anthora is—Anthora." He paused.

"yos'Galan children are Padi, who is Shan's heir, and Syl Vor, who is Nova's. Korval's seat is Jelaza Kazone; yos'Galan's Line House is Trealla Fantrol. We are located to the north of Solcintra City. The ship of which Shan is captain and master trader is *Dutiful Passage.*"

Miri considered him. "That's it?"

"Yes."

"Nothing else?" she persisted. "I don't wanna trip up."

"This should be sufficient to see us through dinner," Val Con said softly. "It is scarcely to be expected that a new bride will have complete intimacy of her lifemate's clan."

"Great." She shook her head as he opened the door and bowed her through ahead of him. "All right, Liaden. Just remember—it's your neck we're gambling with."

SHE'D NEVER seen so many redheads in one place.

The reception room was jammed with them, male and female; old, young and in-between, with hair shading from the lightest strawberry blonde through orange, mere-red, auburn and a particularly striking mahogany.

Hand resting on Val Con's arm, Miri considered the crowd, noting the eyes that slid toward them and slid away—and also something else.

"You're *tall*!" she blurted, remembering at least to whisper, though there was no one directly beside them.

One eyebrow slid upward. "A little above middle height," Val Con acknowledged, lips twitching. "For a Liaden."

He glanced across the room to where Emrith Tiazan stood talking to tel'Vosti and a youngish woman with carroty hair piled high on her head. "We to the delm, now, cha'trez, to make our bows."

And to hear the results of the gene test. She sternly put down the rebellion in her stomach and walked head up at his side, fingers curled lightly around his wrist, trying to act like she didn't notice the way conversation ebbed at their approach and picked up again, once they were past.

"Is this a good idea?" she muttered out of the side of her mouth.

"No, of course not," Val Con muttered back and she almost laughed.

Emrith Tiazan's face saved her—half-relieved and half-approving, as if she'd expected them to show up for dinner in leathers. Miri felt a spurt of sympathy as she bowed respect for the host, Val Con bowing at the same instant.

"Ma'am," he said, soft voice pitched so that it carried across the still sea of redheads, "we offer thanks for the grace and care the House has shown us."

"It is the House's honor," the old woman said into the silence, "to guest its ancient ally and friend." She looked up across the room then, and raised her voice, though it wasn't necessary.

"Hear me, my children, for I tell you of wonder and joy. Come to us only today is Miri Robertson, who is of Erob by Tiazan, this without doubt." She looked hard at Miri out of stern gray eyes.

"Turn," she ordered, still loud enough for the whole room to hear, "Miri Robertson Tiazan, that your cousins may see your face and rejoice."

Sure. She squared her shoulders and turned, looking out over the mob and seeing precious little rejoicing—unless you counted an orange-haired somebody around eight or ten—she wasn't too good at guessing ages that young—who was grinning fit to split her face.

"See also Val Con yos'Phelium," Emrith Tiazan continued behind her, "Thodelm and Second Speaker of Clan Korval, our oldest and most honored ally. It is through Korval that we rediscover our kinswoman." There was something of a stir at that and a bigger one when Val Con turned around to face them.

"It is further told the clan that Miri Robertson Tiazan and Val Con yos'Phelium have each seen the face of the other's heart and, having seen, joined hands and hearts and lives together."

Sleep-learning kept Miri from a gulp; years of dicing and playing cards for kynak and money kept her face straight. *Damn,* she thought, *put that way it sounds all mystic and misty and stuff, when it's just him and me holding together and doing what needs doing . . .*

The carrot-top who'd been talking to Emrith Tiazan and tel'Vosti came forward and bowed, thin face earnest.

"Line Tiazan acknowledges Miri Robertson Tiazan and welcomes her with joy."

Miri returned the bow, hand automatically signing recognition of kinship. "Lady Tiazan, I am honored."

tel'Vosti stepped up next, bowing all courtly over his cane.

"Line tel'Vosti sees Miri Robertson Tiazan with delight, welcomes her with honesty and acknowledges her with anticipation."

She almost grinned at him, but sleep-learning kicked in, and pattern recognition with it, adding up all the things the Code didn't say, like that Liaden society was controlled, yeah, and formal, sure, and all those pretty words and modes and gestures were the weapons you used to survive in an unending, cut-throat competition. Melant'i and Balance. Face or no face. And here was tel'Vosti, who had lived a long lifetime immersed in well-bred in-fighting, giving her a non-standard greeting, there in front of delm and everybody. Tweaking her, he was. Trying her, to see what she'd do.

She bowed, timing it to centimeter and millisecond. "My Lord tel'Vosti." High Tongue Equal, that was the mode; it leaned on Val Con's melant'i, but that was fine, since he was thodelm just like tel'Vosti, and the whole room had just heard the delm say she was a thodelm's lifemate. "I see you with appreciation, hear you with understanding, and acknowledge you with trepidation."

The brown eyes gleamed; the rest of his face remained merely polite. No way to tell if she'd scored points. She didn't think she had. But she didn't think she'd lost any either. Even was OK; tel'Vosti'd said it himself, when he'd been talking about Val Con's uncle. Inside her head Val Con's pattern held steady, inscrutable as a mandala.

The delm stepped forward, indicating Thodelm Tiazan with a backhanded wave. "Your cousin Bendara, daughter of your late cousin Cel Met Tiazan."

The carrot-top gave a little bow, barely more than a heavy nod of the head. "Cousin Miri."

Miri gave the bow back, "Cousin Bendara," straightened and felt Val Con shift, oh-so-slightly, at her side. She directed Bendara's attention his way with a copy of the delm's backhanded gesture. "One's lifemate, Val Con yos'Phelium."

Bendara bowed again, a shade deeper than equality of rank demanded, as if maybe Val Con had more time in grade. "My Lord yos'Phelium."

"My Lady Tiazan." His voice was soft as always. She couldn't see his bow.

The delm waved for her attention again, this time for a man of late middle years, hair aggressively red, hazel eyes hooded.

"Your cousin Dil Nem, son of your late uncle Kern Tiazan."

Again the heavy nod, the exchange of names; the pass on to Val Con.

"Your cousin Ilvin, daughter of your cousin Jen Sar Tiazan, who is from clan at present."

"Your cousin Kol Vus . . ."

"Your cousin . . ."

Miri lost count, very likely lost names, after the first dozen or so. Her head was beginning to ache with all the cool, polite faces and she started to want a slug of kynak. She gritted her teeth and bowed kinship to tel'Vosti, damn him: "Your uncle, Win Den tel'Vosti, son of Randa Tiazan and Pel Jim tel'Vosti."

There was another blur of names and faces after him; the next she took clear note of was the last.

"Your cousin Alys, daughter of your cousin Makina Tiazan, who is from clan at this moment."

Alys, who would be "very well," but never a Kea Tiazan. Alys, who they were going to offer as a contract-wife to Val Con, when she came of age.

She made her bow, very serious, and stood tall, all three and a half feet of her, curly, orange-y hair held down by the brute strength of three formidable-looking combs. The brown eyes shone with something past curiosity or even friendliness and Miri caught her breath. She'd seen that look on recruits, sometimes, the ones who fancied themselves "in love" with the commander.

"Cousin Miri," she piped up, "I'm happy to see you."

Oh, hell. Like she didn't have enough trouble without an elf hooking onto her. Miri returned the bow with matching dignity.

"Cousin Alys, I am happy to see you." She made the backhand wave toward Val Con and repeated the weary formula for the last time, moving the kid along. She wanted that drink bad, she thought, and looked up to find Emrith Tiazan watching her, something like approval in the lines of her face.

"Appropriately done," the old lady said. "We now go in to dinner. Win Den, attend me, by your grace."

tel'Vosti stepped forward and offered his arm, which she took, allowing him to lead her down the room toward the door at the opposite end. The mob of redheads made room for them to pass, but nobody followed.

"Us now, cha'trez." Val Con's voice was soft in her ear as he took her arm. "You did admirably."

"Easy for you to say," she muttered. "I'd rather sing for my supper, though. Any day."

"I NEED A DRINK."

Miri leaned against the wall just inside their private parlor, eyes closed against the scented darkness. Dinner had been horrible. Her place had been set with an arsenal of forks and tongs and spoons and knives, all of which, sleep-learning told her implacably, had a specific use. She'd fair busted her head while she'd waited for the first course, trying to remember the long list of foods that could and should be addressed with each implement.

Then the first course was served and she'd broken out in an ice-cold sweat as dish after unidentifiable dish went by. She'd snuck a look to see what Val Con was having; took a little of that and nibbled while she tried to do her conversational duty to the woman on her left. She'd left the wine strictly alone, terrified at getting even a little fuddled with all those new cousins watching and keeping score.

"A drink," she said firmly. "A *big* drink."

"Certainly," Val Con murmured in her ear. He slipped a hand beneath her elbow. "Come sit on the couch, cha'trez . . . There. Red wine? White? Jade? Canary? I believe—yes, there is misravot, if you would prefer . . ."

Miri sighed, leaned back in the cushions and finally opened her eyes. Val Con had lit the low-lights—the ceiling sparkled with starring pinpoints; the carpet glittered like new snow.

"What do I know about wine? You pick."

"All right," he said, and poured pale green wine into two crystal cups. He brought them to the couch and handed her one, raising his own in salute.

"To Lady yos'Phelium, my love."

She laughed and shook her head. "Why not to Lord yos'Phelium?"

"Lord yos'Phelium was not courageous, nor did he comport himself with anything but mediocrity." He touched her cheek. "Miri, you are a treasure."

"If you say so," she said dubiously and sipped her wine. "I think it's pretty brave, myself, to trust everything to somebody who don't even know what fork to use—" She shook her head. "Who knows what fork to use," she corrected herself, "if there'd been a clue to what the food was!"

"Ah, I had wondered why you ate so little . . ." He tipped his head. "You must not let it burden you," he said softly. "You imagine my melant'i is so fragile it will shatter at your slightest error. Instead, it has—resilience—and certainly strength enough to withstand my lifemate's mistaking a fork—or even using a fork instead of tongs!" He tasted his wine, suddenly serious.

"In all matters of importance—in your conduct toward your delm and the head of your line; in your answer to tel'Vosti—you were above reproach. If in less vital matters you err, or simply choose to disregard the Code, then it is—a nothing. People will say, if they say at all: 'Ah, she is an original.' Which is no bad thing."

"An original?" She frowned and shook her head.

Val Con sighed. "It is one of the reasons I insisted you learn the Code from the source, rather than from my tutoring," he said slowly. "Each individual takes the Code and—shapes it—according to his own character and necessity. Now, I have, perhaps, taken too much from my uncle's tutelage—or learned too young, as Shan would have it—so my manner tends toward coolness and extreme precision." He sipped wine, brows drawn.

"Shan is an original," he murmured: "his manners are appalling, but his *manner* pleases. Anthora follows his style. Pat Rin is very correct, but easy, so the correctness seems joined to and flowing from his melant'i. Nova—" he shook his head, smiling with a touch of wistfulness. "I once overhead someone say he would rather meet an angry lyr-cat unarmed, than Nova and I in a reception line."

Miri laughed.

Val Con leaned over and kissed her.

"Mmmm," she said and shivered delightedly as warm, knowing fingers stroked down the line of her throat.

"You find me too Liaden, Miri?" Val Con's voice was husky in her ear, his cheek soft against hers.

She breathed in the scent of him and let the breath go in a half-gasping laugh as desire broke over her. "The clothes threw me," she murmured. "Why don't you take 'em off?"

He laughed gently, took her wineglass and bent to put it aside, his weight pushing her into the cushions. Then his lips were back, demanding full attention, while his hands stroked and teased and finally found the fastenings of the dress and loosed them.

She tried to return the favor, reaching to open the fine white shirt, but he eluded her hands, keeping her pinned and all but helpless while he slipped the dress down over her shoulders and a bit further, nuzzling her throat, kissing her breasts, her belly . . .

The dress was gone. She reached again to help him out of the shirt, aching to feel his skin against hers—and was fended off with a breathless laugh: "Ah, not so greedy, cha'trez . . ."

Mouth and hands engaged her full attention once more, the soft fabrics of trousers and shirt stroking against her nakedness alternately frustrating and exhilarating.

At some point, he picked her up and lay her down again on that high, wide bed, and was gone for a moment, returning with his hand full of bed-flowers.

He covered her in them, laughing; crushed one in long fingers and stroked the fragrance across her breasts. She shivered and laughed and twisted, pulling him down and mock wrestling, desperate to have him, with an urgency the flower-scent fed.

He laughed, fingers and lips teasing; but allowed the shirt—and at once allowed everything, abandoning the role of command as she bit and kissed and stroked and the flowers were crushed beneath them and gave up their seductive odor.

She lay across his chest, teasing, nearly lazy against the flower's urgency. Val Con's eyes were half-closed, his face blurred with desire, hands stroking, beginning to insist. But he wasn't in control now, she was. She rubbed against him, felt his hips move and laughed as she kissed his ear.

"So greedy, Val Con . . ."

A laugh—or a soft groan. "Miri . . ."

She closed her eyes, concentrating on the feel of him, on the warmth, on how well their bodies fit, on the desire barely restrained, soon to be loosed.

She looked at the pattern of him inside her head.

And—*reached out*, very softly, to stroke it and breathe on it and—kiss it—and love it and desire it and—

Beneath her, Val Con went utterly still. Miri opened her eyes.

"Cha'trez . . ." He touched her face, his eyes wide and shocked-looking, as if he'd been suddenly wakened. "Miri, what are you doing?"

She looked at him through slitted eyes, still more than half cuddling the pattern of him—the *him* of him—against her, feeling the love flow from her; feeling it return, enriched and expanded.

"Loving you," she managed. Then, as the distress in his eyes began to resonate in his pattern. "Should I stop?"

"No." His hands closed hard around her waist and he rolled, spilling her over into the crushed flowers and him hard and urgent atop her. "Never stop."

It was bodies, then, and lust and the flowers and finally two voices crying out as one in joy and wonder.

They were still tangled around each other when the timer shut the room lights down. Both were fast asleep.

DUTIFUL PASSAGE:
In Orbit

❀ ❀

"ONCE MORE," First Mate Priscilla Mendoza called, "sequence twelve . . . *now*!"

Inside the lifeboat the pilot hit the sequence. Outside, the laser turrets swiveled, left, right, up, down, extended and finally withdrew into their shielding.

"Great!" she said. "Shut her down, Seth; we're meshed."

The little ship obediently powered down and the pilot slipped out of the slot, slamming the hatch.

"Last one," he said. "Time to take on the Yxtrang."

Priscilla blinked up at him—long, rat-faced, laconic Seth, matter-of-factly installing laser cannons on lifeboats. "Is that what you think we're going to do?" she asked. "Go to war with the Yxtrang?"

Seth shrugged, bending over to gather up his toolkit. "Can't think of anybody else'll fire on escape pods," he said calmly. "Terrans won't. Liadens won't—pay all that weirgild?" He grinned, a surprise of white teeth in his narrow face. "Never met a Liaden crazy enough to bankrupt himself on a sure thing."

Priscilla smiled back and slung her tool bag over her shoulder. "So it's the Yxtrang, by process of elimination?"

"Seems reasonable," Seth said, ambling at her side down the service hall to Bay Four. "Either that, or Shan wants an ace up his sleeve." He shrugged. "Never known Shan to make a bad play, where the ship was concerned. I'll follow him on this one."

Priscilla stopped and looked directly into his eyes—mud brown and smallish—Healer sense tuned to read every nuance of his emotive pattern.

"Seth, it's not Yxtrang. But it could still be very dangerous. People who well *might* fire on an escape pod, and Balance be damned. We don't know that they will, but we aren't at all convinced that they won't." She paused and packed the next words heavily, timing them to his inner resonance. "Be certain, Seth. There's still time for you to ship down—no blame."

He stared back into her eyes, more than half-tranced.

"Shan found me in a backworld dive," he said, so softly she strained to hear. "I was scraping out a living running in-system ore boats and garbage scows. Drinking too much, doing too much smoke. Lost my family in an Yxtrang raid—wife, kids, parents. Went off my head, I guess. Came to, eventually—no money, no job, and no friends. Shan needed pilots—'Always need a good pilot,' he said—gods, I can still see him coming into that dive—skinny, shoulders not filled yet, cutting deals like a pro—sixteen, maybe seventeen Standards—with that white hair and a kid's face and those eyes. Never seen eyes like that . . ." He blinked; shook his head and Priscilla let him break the trance.

He sighed. "Shan got me out of there—out of *all* of there. Gave me a chance. 'My man,' is what he told the port guard. 'That's my man, sir; and he's wanted at his post.'" He nodded sharply and turned away, heading doggedly down the hall.

"If it's Yxtrang or if it's something worse," he said as Priscilla fell in beside him, "I reckon I can man my post."

SHAN LOOKED UP as she entered his office, smiled wanly and returned to the screen. Priscilla crossed to the bar and poured two glasses of wine—red, for him; white, for her—and carried them back to the desk. She slid into the chair opposite and waited, holding the glass and running through a low-level exercise to restore tranquility.

"Thank you, Priscilla." He picked up his own glass, waved it in ironic salute and took a healthy drink.

"You're welcome," she murmured, reading the worry and the exhaustion and the sparking nervous energy overlaying his emotive grid. "The First Mate reports all lifeships armed. Field tests remain to be done, but everything reads fine on the circuits." She sipped wine. "Seth Johnson chooses to remain with his Captain."

Shan sighed. "Seth Johnson is a sentimental fool," he said, and nodded at the screen. "We have a match."

"So soon?"

"Amazing, isn't it? With so many gene-maps in the galaxy?" He grinned tiredly. "I played a hunch—that notation on Sergeant Robertson's birth certificate—*mutated within acceptable limits*—you recall?"

She nodded. "You thought that might mean 'partly Liaden.'"

"And my thought has proved correct—I tell you, Priscilla, I'm not a master of trade for nothing! Though you would consider that a scout might more fully communicate—but I digress. How unusual." He took another swallow of wine and waved at the screen. "Miri Robertson's gene-map matches that of Line Tiazan." He eyed her expectantly.

She sipped her wine, knowing that her temple training had taught her more than enough patience to wait out one of Shan's rare silences.

"You disappoint me. Don't you have the least wish to know who the devil Tiazan is and where we'll be meeting my wretched brother?"

"But I was certain you were about to tell me."

"Unkind, Priscilla. I can't think why I lifemated you."

"Because I let you talk as much as you want."

"Do you? How odd. Especially as I have the distinct impression that I'm talking less than I ever have. But, I perceive you a-quiver with curiosity and hasten to explain."

He set his glass aside with a flourish and sat up straighter in the chair, humor vanishing from face and emotive grid.

"Tiazan is First Line of Clan Erob," he said; "which has its seat upon Lytaxin. So to go to 'Miri's people' as directed by my brother and delm-to-be, we need merely go to Lytaxin. Very simple, once one has the proper information. What astonishes me particularly is that for once in his life Val Con seems to have done exactly as he ought."

Priscilla blinked. "He has?"

"As I said, astonishing. Though, to be just, Val Con *often* does as he ought. Of course, he just as often does precisely as he pleases. I expect there's a deliberate pattern involved, calculated to a hair's breadth to appear random. One afternoon when I'm bored I'll feed the parameters to the tactical computers and see what they make of it. But to continue! Erob is Korval's most ancient ally. The family diaries speak of Rool Tiazan and his lifemate, leaders of the dramliz, who chose to evacuate the Old World on the ship piloted by Cantra yos'Phelium."

Priscilla allowed a wisp of inquiry to escape her and Shan nodded.

"Rool Tiazan had read the luck, you see—and the luck sent him to Cantra yos'Phelium."

"Rool Tiazan was a full wizard, then," Priscilla murmured. "He had the Sight."

"Apparently so, since *Quick Passage* and her passengers eventually came safe to Liad."

"And all that time since the ship came to Liad, Korval and Erob have been allies?"

"Actually a bit longer than that," Shan said. "Cantra's log indicates that she and Jela—her partner before she took on the revered yos'Galan ancestor—had known Rool Tiazan and his lady some time prior to the evacuation. If it comes to that—recall that I promised to amaze, Priscilla!—we're a bit more than allies. More accurate to say cousins—or half-clan, there's a word! Ever since the ship landed on Liad, Tiazan and Korval have been sticking to an arrangement—actually a protocol, all properly signed and sealed—a schedule of a contract-marriage every three generations, with the child going, in unfailing sequence: Erob, Korval, Erob, Korval . . ."

Priscilla frowned. "You said Tiazan and Korval—"

"So I did, and so it was. Korval seems to have sent equally from yos'Phelium and yos'Galan, but Erob seems only to have sent from Tiazan, never from the subordinate Line. In any wise, the schedule demanded a contract wedding this generation. yos'Galan was sent last time, and the child came to Korval."

"And Val Con knew all this?" Priscilla demanded.

Shan shrugged and reached for his glass. "Now that's a different question. Unless he's knocked his head rather sharply, he certainly recalls our long association with Erob. That a mating was mandated and that yos'Phelium must send—I doubt he did know that. I only know it because when I was First Speaker in Trust, I received a note from Great-great-great Aunt Wayr yos'Phelium, dated one hundred ten Standard years ago." He sighed. "I sent it forward a little time more, to Val Con's thirty-fifth Name Day: a puzzle for him to solve on the day he becomes delm."

"But Miri Robertson is Line Tiazan, and she and Val Con are *lifemates* . . ."

Shan nodded. "The child of a contract-marriage would have gone to Erob. But the children of a lifemating will come to the clan sheltering both partners."

"And Val Con will not leave Korval for another clan." She made it a half-question, and Shan answered with unwarranted soberness.

"Val Con is Korval Himself—the one who will be delm. He *can't* leave. There's no clan in the Book who would have him." He sighed. "Korval has this certain—reputation. Even among our allies." He stared into the dregs of his glass, then all at once seemed to shake himself and looked over to her with a wry smile.

"It's been a long day, Priscilla. Will you join me for a nap?"

"Certainly." She came gracefully to her feet, despite the weariness that grated behind her eyes and pulled at her back. "Ken Rik has shift-authority and will call if there's a problem."

"Wonderful," Shan muttered, stepping aside to let her procede him into their private quarters. "I always wanted to be captain of a military vessel, Priscilla. Remind me to give my brother a very sound shaking, when we finally catch up with him."

"Yes, dear," she said placidly and turned to give him a hug.

LYTAXIN:
Erob's Clanhouse

🐢 🐢

VAL CON struck the last note, held it and looked over to Alys Tiazan, standing alert by the audio unit. He nodded and she pressed a key, ending the recording. Val Con lifted his hands from the keyboard and smiled.

"I thank you, Miss Alys. Your assistance was invaluable."

"You are kind to say it," she responded, very properly indeed, for one rising ten Standards, and then dimpled. "But you had much better have had me than Kol Vus, you know. He fidgets awfully!"

"Then I was doubly fortunate to encounter you," Val Con said gravely, touching the omnichora's power-plate. "Shall we play the tape back, do you think? It would not do to give Kol Vus a muddy recording, when he has been so gracious in accommodating me."

"But he must do that, mustn't he?" Alys said, with the cool matter-of-factness of childhood. "After all, you are Korval."

"So I am, but I am also a guest in your house. Allow me to possess some address, I beg."

That bought a bright glissade of laughter, after which she considered him for a moment more soberly, face intent and looking, so he fancied, very much as Miri had, at ten.

"I don't think you're the least frightening," she stated at last and Val Con inclined his head.

"You relieve me."

"Now you sound like Uncle Win Den," Alys told him severely, and bent to the audio unit, pressing three keys in sequence.

Music swelled out of the tiny unit, filling the room to the walls.

The name of the piece was *Toccata and Fugue in D Minor* and it had been written many years before Terrans achieved the stars by a man named Johann Sebastian Bach. It had been Anne Davis' favorite piece of music, and for this present purpose Val Con had striven to play it in precisely her style.

The role of Clan Radio Tech Kol Vus Tiazan in the project was to seal the brief recording to Lytaxin's perimeter beacons. Ninety seconds, Val Con thought, would surely be long enough for Shan to descry their mother's favorite and read into it verification that Val Con awaited him on world.

The music-fragment ended, snapped off clean at 90 seconds, and Val Con again inclined his head.

"I believe that will serve the purpose quite well. May I discommode you further, Miss Alys?"

"You would like me to take this down to Kol Vus?" she asked, rising and sliding the unit's carry strap over her shoulder. "That's no trouble. I need to pass the comm room on the way to my tutor." She hesitated. "You play very nicely. I would be happy to hear more, if time allows it during your guesting."

His touch on the omnichora was god-gift, honed by years of study. He could easily have been a master musician—a *maestro*, according to Anne, who had taught him his scales. But he was Korval: Stranger passions claimed precedence.

He smiled at the child before him, her hair a riot of orange curls, her eyes an intelligent, sparkling brown.

"I would be honored to play for you, Miss Alys. Only name a time."

She tipped her head, apparently consulting some inner schedule. "Tomorrow?" she said eventually. "In the hour before Prime?"

"Done," he said gravely, and bowed as one accepting a treasure.

She did not, as he expected, erupt into giggles at this, but returned the bow most creditably, murmuring an exquisitely proper "The pleasure is mine."

She straightened, then adjusted the strap across her shoulder and smiled. "I have to go before my tutor tells Aunt Emrith I've been late again."

"Please do not allow me to be the cause of such distress to the House," Val Con said, and that *did* draw a giggle, cut off as she slipped out the door and pulled it closed behind her.

He stood alone in the music room, considering his options. Miri was closeted with Erob's Historian, filling details in the lives of Miri-eklykt'i and Katalina Tayzin—an interview that promised to be both lengthy and productive of an uneasy temper in one's lifemate.

His duty plainly lay in the direction of Erob. Some explanations must, in courtesy, be made to the delm of Korval's oldest ally, and yet . . .

Music tingled in his fingertips, awakened by his brief playing for the beacon. Surely, he might steal ten minutes to set the rest of the music free?

Slowly, knowing that duty called him elsewhere, yet unable to resist the lure of a concert-quality instrument perfectly set in a room tuned for its unique voice, he went to the omnichora, sat on the bench and pressed the power plate.

THE WALL HE FACED over the omnichora was mirrored.

Val Con sighed, recalling the revulsion on several faces last night, despite the courtesy due a guest; wondering if he should have followed tel'Vosti's hint and had the scar canceled.

The scar was there for a reason, after all; he might have had the autodoc erase the wretched thing anytime during their voyage from Vandar. He had chosen to allow it to remain, a constant and sometimes painful reminder of the wages of foolishness.

"No more than you traded for, young sir." He heard Uncle Er Thom's dry reproval in his mind's ear, and half-smiled in agreement.

It would be another matter entirely, he told himself, fingers adjusting stops and frequencies, had the cut failed to heal—or if one's lifemate objected to the mar. But the wound was clean, as he had told tel'Vosti, and Miri made no objection.

"No call," Uncle Er Thom's voice instructed him from memory, "to concern yourself with the comfort of non-kin. Korval acts upon its own necessities. Let others mind their melant'i."

"Yes, uncle," he murmured, and touched the keyboard, softly playing the cool and logical line of his uncle's musical signature, that the boy Val Con had composed many years ago. His ear caught a possibility in the old theme and he played on half-aware, letting his fingers find what they might.

Let others mind their own melant'i. An old lesson, that; among the first. One kept one's own care close, for clan, for servants, for kin . . . Val Con's fingers faltered on the keys.

Shan would be here—soon.

Shan was his cha'leket, the brother of his heart. Shan might well mind the scar. Might well mind other things, truth told; things that would distress one who had helped a green-eyed fosterling grow. That would surely distress one who was a Healer and able to see what was now that fosterling's soul.

The Department of Interior . . . the Department of Interior had done much damage, severed memories, stolen home, love, music, mother—". . . our mother," Shan's voice said from years gone. "Your mother's gone, but you can share mine, all right?"

Our mother . . . Anne Davis: chestnut hair, merry dark eyes, clever hands, scented with bound books and flowers; wide-hipped and full-breasted, as many Terran women; full with laughter and passion and more than enough love for the children of the house— her own three and the child of her lifemate's cha'leket. She had taught him to play the 'chora, taught him his letters—Terran and Trade—wiped tears, comforted child-woes and halfling griefs, shared out justice and kisses, rejoiced with him when he was accepted to Scout Academy—

And the Department of Interior had stolen her.

"My kinswoman . . ." He recalled his own voice, telling Miri—a Miri nearly lost, gods; wary-faced and distrusting, as she had very good cause to be. "My *kinswoman*—" without feeling, without even such a memory as flashed now, of big, warm hands holding his, shaping tiny fingers above the keyboard.

His right hand dandled True Scale as his left rose to adjust stops. Both hands centered above the keyboard, and at once came down, with sure authority, sweeping headlong into the *Toccata.*

It allowed much, as great music does, endless opportunity for variation and lessons from one's own fingers being among the chiefest of its joys. But their mother had loved it for its own sake, as well, and he played it that way now, as he had for Shan, while memories, suppressed and twisted and made strange—repulsive— by intent of his enemies, loosened and flowed and touched him true, until he closed his eyes and gave himself to the music and the remembering and didn't even know if he wept.

The music reached a natural end, as music will, and his fingers went still upon the keys. After a moment, it occurred to him that he was no longer alone in Erob's music room and he opened his eyes.

"Hi," she said from her perch on the polished curve of a listening-stool. Her hair was braided today; he saw the copper length of it gleaming down her back in the mirror. She was dressed in a rich yellow shirt and soft trousers the color of Shan's favorite wine—proper attire for an extended session with the clan historian. She leaned forward, eyes intent. "You OK?"

"I believe so." He took a breath and smiled. "Yes."

"Good." She shifted on the stool. "Came to tell you that I got a break from the question-and-answer bit. Historian says he'll see me for more after lunch. Not bloody likely, 'cause I already got a headache with remembering stuff that happened when I was three years old and would've sworn yesterday that I didn't know anything about." She stood abruptly.

"I'm going down to the merc camp and see if I can't find the 'falks—maybe Jase." She bit her lip, and he listened to the song of her that played inside his head, hearing the thin notes of exhaustion, and a certain wistful sadness.

"I know you don't think much of Jase," Miri was saying; "and you got no call to love the Gyrfalks. Folks here seem to appreciate them a bit though—" she chewed her lip again, and the chords of her song strengthened and clarified—"But you're welcome to walk that way with me, if you want to."

"I want to," said Val Con, touching the 'chora's power-down and standing. He smiled at her, relieved to see her return smile burn away the wariness in her eyes. "Thank you for inviting me."

"WHEN DO YOU THINK your brother'll get here?"

Val Con laughed softly. "Weary of being clan-bound so soon, Miri?"

She'd been squinting up into the bright sky, as if she might see the *Passage*; now she transferred the squint to him.

"Means you don't know," she surmised. "This mind reading stuff don't seem very efficient."

"Alas. I was offered use of the House's pin-beam so that an answer to *when?* might be achieved quickly. Unfortunately, one must know the position of the beam's target, and Shan has all the galaxy at his beck—and hyperspace, as well."

"Pin-beams're expensive," Miri commented.

"Erob may not consider it so, weighed in balance."

"That eager to get rid of us, huh?" She shook her head at him, mock stern. "You got some reputation among the home-folks, Liaden. And to think I was worried about wrecking your melant'i."

He laughed and swept a sudden bow—from lesser to greater, as she read it. "Had I not said that it was your own melant'i would carry us?"

She grinned and took his hand, and they walked across the fragrant, sun-warmed grass.

"Talked to tel'Vosti a bit while I was waiting for the historian to show," she said, slanting an idle glance at his face. "Said he knew your father real well."

The pattern of him inside her head flashed and tightened. "So, it seems that all of Erob knew my father," he snapped.

"Huh?" She stopped, yanking him to a halt, and frowned up into his face. "There something wrong with that?"

His pattern snarled and an acid wash of frustrated pain

cramped her belly, so that she dropped his hand and half-cried out in astonishment.

"Miri!" His hands were around her waist, easing her down to sit on the grass. "Cha'trez?"

Worry was added to the emotional hash, mixing badly with the pain and the anger.

"You're hurting me," she gasped, eyes closed as she groped for him inside her head. "Stop it, boss—the pattern . . ."

Shock turned her icy, and the next instant she was the eye of a color-storm—*redyelloworangegreenblueviolet*—as the Rainbow whipped 'round her, and some unknown inner sense registered the near sound of a door opening—and closing.

Stillness, within and without.

"Gods." She let out a shuddering breath, tipping forward in controlled collapse until her forehead touched her knee. "Gods, gods, gods." She sat up and opened her eyes.

Val Con sat cross-legged before her, hands loosely cupping his knees. "Is the pain gone, Miri?" His voice was as calm as his pattern.

"Gone," she agreed and licked her lips. "What *was* that?"

Puzzlement shadowed his eyes. "I am without information. If you could describe the phenomenon, we might achieve understanding."

"Right." She frowned. "Told you that tel'Vosti had known your father, and you got pissed—saw your pattern—cramp up, kinda. And when I asked you what was wrong with that I was all of a sudden furious—frustrated—like I'd been banging my head against the same brick wall for years and wasn't any closer to busting through . . ." She sighed and reached over to take his hand, looking into his eyes worriedly.

"Seems like I must've gotten it straight from you, somehow," she said slowly. "Wasn't really that the *pattern* was hurting me."

"Ah." His fingers tightened around hers. "And you have never experienced this before?"

"No . . ." She shifted a little, thinking. "But I never did anything like I did last night before, either—just reaching out and *touching* the pattern. Never occurred to me. Maybe I got—sensitized—or something."

There was a small silence before he said, "Or perhaps Priscilla, who is after all dramliza, might have done—something—to me by way of insuring that I might hear Shan."

Miri blinked thoughtfully. "Something to that, ain't there? You can't tell—naw, I guess not."

"I—felt—despair and distress coming from you at the Winterfair," Val Con said softly. "But it was clearly emanating from *you*. I did not experience your emotions as my own." A faint wisp of something like hunger escaped him and Miri chuckled, squeezing his hand.

"Just as well—but you're talking emergency situation. Maybe that's the tip-off. Some kind of emergency hooked up with your father?"

Val Con sighed and lifted a hand to stroke the hair out of his eyes. "Only that he lost his lifemate—my mother—to assassins and, after taking Delm's Counsel, left his clan and his heir in the hands of his brother Er Thom, and went off into the wide galaxy, seeking Balance."

"And never sent word back," Miri finished, and shook her head. "Bad business, tel'Vosti said."

"tel'Vosti is more correct than he knows," Val Con murmured. "The options revealed by Delm's Counsel were a war with the Terran Party, who had employed the assassin . . ."

"Which would mean a war with Terra." Miri frowned. "Bad choice."

"My father thought so, as well. So he took the second option, which was slower, and less sure, but, if it worked, more fruitful." He sighed. "Or so it says in Korval's Diaries. The plan itself is not detailed." He glanced away; caught her eyes again.

"Tradition is, should an individual be estranged for twelve years, he is considered dead to the clan and the date of his desertion recorded as a date of death. Traditionally, the head of line announces the death and makes the notation."

Miri touched his cheek. "You didn't do that."

"Daav yos'Phelium is eklykt'i," Val Con said, coming smoothly to his feet and offering her his hand. "Momentarily beyond the clan. Korval's records show nothing else."

✳ ✳ ✳

JASON CARMODY walked down East Axis, an island of blonde quiet among the noisy, purposeful bustle going on all around.

Every so often, Jase turned aside to talk to this one or that; on two occasions he ducked inside half-dismantled tech-sheds to supervise some particularly tricksy bit of equipment balancing. Merc Center would be stripped down to dirt by this time tomorrow. Dawn the day after would find only torn meadowlands and a network of synthphalt service roads, already crumbling back to sand.

Jase ducked out into the sunlight and stood, techs and troops flowing around him like a dusty leather river, staring at nothing in particular and gently stroking his beard.

Eight days to Fendor, if the transport was on time. It had been known to happen. More often it wasn't, but the Gyrfalks had another contract pending, so they'd paid a premium for a guaranteed pick-up. Sometimes that worked. In the meantime, Suzuki and the spec-team were on their way to negotiations, leaving Jason, the tyros, and the low-ranks to break camp and tidy up.

Jase sighed and shook his massive frame into motion, going with the flow down East Axis until it intersected with Command Way, where he turned off, heading for his quarters.

"Jase!" The voice from behind was familiar, but not urgently so. Jason checked his stride unwillingly, half-minded to go on.

"Jase!" the voice persisted. "Jason Carmody!"

He sighed and turned, hoping the problem wasn't going to be too time-consuming and scanning the scurrying crowd, looking for a face to match the voice.

"Jason."

She was a mere four of his paces before him, a red-haired Liaden woman in a yellow shirt and burgundy trousers, comfortable boots, belt, pouch, no apparent gun. Her hair was single-braided and fell below the holsterless belt. A man stood at her right shoulder. Jase flicked him a look, established that he was Liaden, too—scar across the right cheek, dark hair, no gun—before bowing to the woman.

"Yes, ma'am," he said in respectful Trade, cudgeling his brain to recall which of Clan Erob she precisely was. "What can I do for you?"

The woman blinked, flashed a quick glance at her companion and drifted a step closer. Something in the way she moved sparked a flicker of deeper recognition, gone even as he fumbled for it.

"What the hell's the matter with you, Jason?" she demanded in Terran. "Tell me I can come back anytime I want, then forget what I look like inside of a year?"

"*Redhead*?" Jason very nearly goggled, at last seeing past the disguise of rich clothes to the lithe, familiar body, the sharp face and dark gray eyes. He fell to his knees, which put him only a head or so taller than she, and flung his arms wide.

"Gods love us all, my darlin'!" he cried. "Come and give Jason a kiss!"

"YES, BUT DARLIN'," Jason was saying, handing kynak all around in the privacy of his quarters, "if you and Tough Guy was comin' to Lytaxin anyway, why not just come with us in the first case? We'd have saved you a good bit of time."

Miri lifted a shoulder and flashed a grin at her partner, who was perched on the arm of her chair. "Had a spot of trouble to clear up first."

"Spot o'trouble, indeed!" Jase sprawled on the thick rug, taking up most of the available floor space, and braced his wide shoulders against the side of a wooden chest, the delicate hand carvings just visible through the mars of rough travel. He waved a massive hand in Val Con's direction. "You didn't have that facial decoration last time I saw you, did you, my lad?"

Val Con considered him out of bland green eyes. "No."

"Wouldn't've thought there was much out there fast enough to touch you," Jason persisted. "Polesta still ain't recovered from that little love tap you gave her. Actually heard her say 'please' to the muster-clerk this morning. Enough to give a man religion."

Miri laughed. "Make a soldier outta her yet. How'd the campaign go? When you shipping out?"

"The angels won," Jase said comfortably; "and the employer was prompt with regard to the fee. Paid in full, yes, indeed, and due to ship out tomorrow."

"Tomorrow?" Miri's shoulders sagged; and Val Con shifted slightly to press against her.

"Now, now, my small, take heart. You know what transport pilots are: why book three runs when six're offered? They're bound to make at least two on time."

She laughed and sipped a little of her drink, laugh turning to a gasp and half-choke.

"A little out of the way of it, darlin'?"

She managed a grin and shook her head. "Been drinking wine lately. 'When on Maris. . .'"

"'Drink what they offer'," Jase finished and knocked back a quarter of his glass. "Only too true. About this other thing, though; you know we're not throwing you to the beasties. Sign back up where you belong and there's a place on the transport with your name on it. Suzuki and me're still wanting to give you that lieutenant's badge . . ."

"Yeah, well . . ." She sighed, not daring to look at Val Con. "Thing is, we just got here yesterday and there's some stuff I still gotta do, being as they're my clan and all . . ."

Jason stopped with his glass halfway to his mouth. "Who's your clan, Redhead?"

"Umm—people up at the house."

"What!" Jase sat up straight, hitting his head a solid *whack* on the overhanging chest-top. "What house—the big house? *Erob's* house?"

She looked at him doubtfully. "Yeah."

Jase slapped his thigh. "I *knew* they were right 'uns! The old lady with the ring—damn me if I didn't think she was familiar the first time I saw her!" He suddenly seemed to do a double take. "That is *your* clan, Redhead? Eh? Not your partner's?"

"My clan," Val Con told him softly, "has its seat upon Liad."

"Mine," Miri said, half-grinning. "Late-breaking news, appalling everybody from the delm down, except maybe Alys and tel'Vosti."

"The General? You could easily do worse by way of relatives. The General's worth all four of my uncles—with a grand-dame thrown in! And young Alys shoots like a trooper. I wish I had a tyro as sharp with a yessir as she is!" He slid back down against the chest and had another slug of kynak.

"But you haven't said what you've been about, my small, besides the clearing up of business."

"Well, let's see . . . Got into it a bit with the Juntavas—their mistake, really—but I guess that's all straightened out by now. Spent some time, ummm," here she glanced at Val Con for a moment, "out of touch, sort of. Little bit of action there. Worked some odd jobs, did some singing and celebrating . . ."

"Directed the defense that turned an enemy invasion into a rout," Val Con's quiet voice picked up; "without loss to home guard. Learned High and Low Liaden, mastered the salient points of The Liaden Code of Proper Conduct, began the study of the opening equations and board-drills, sufficient to attain the level of provisional pilot, third class."

There was a small silence, during which Miri tried to decide whether to break Val Con's arm or only his jaw, then Jason cleared his throat.

"That right?" He shook his massive head. "Busy, my small—and here I was afraid you'd fall into trouble, what with having idle time on your hands." He looked at Val Con.

"You're a pilot, are you?"

"Master level, yes."

"And you been teaching Redhead piloting." He stared off into the far corner of the ceiling for a moment, then looked back at Val Con. "Your opinion, as a Master level pilot, is that Redhead is capable of attaining what class?"

There was a small pause. "Second class, easily," Val Con said. "If she chooses to apply herself, first class is certainly within her reach. Master—" He moved his shoulders. "It is too soon to know."

"Well," said Jase and finished off his drink. His eyes came back to Miri with something like wonder. "Your partner telling it square, darlin'?"

"Yeah," she said, throwing a glower at Val Con, who lifted an eyebrow. "Yeah, he's got it right."

"Well," Jase said again. "Might have to make that a captain's badge." He held up a hand. "Suzuki has to OK it, too—you know the drill. Learning how to pilot, tacking on both brands of Liaden . . ." He sat up straight, carefully avoiding the chest lid.

"I know Tough Guy's your partner. If you want to talk further on it, I can commit the 'falks to a pilot's slot at a rank comparable to his grade in—?"

Miri grinned wickedly. "He's a scout," she said, feeling Val Con shift sharply beside her. "Scout Commander, First-In."

"Ooof!" said Jason—and laughed. "You don't brag on yourself, do you, my son?"

"One does," Val Con told him, "what one does."

"Right you are." He laughed again. "Scout Commander . . . but you look to be at liberty, if I might say so. If you want work as a pilot, or if there's something else, the unit could only profit."

"I—" Val Con hesitated, alive to the sudden note of longing in the sense of Miri within him. He glanced down into her eyes. "There are discussions to be made," he said, and she nodded, wistfully.

"It sounds good," she told Jase truthfully. "And I want it—but him and me still got some stuff to clear up. You're going back to Headquarters, right?"

"For a time—there's a new contract on the burner, though, so it looks to be a jump-in/jump-out. Suzuki's gone to start the talk—which I assume you knew, since you didn't ask for her."

"Heard it on the chatter when we were coming in." Miri nodded. "I'll leave a message, after this other stuff gets settled." Val Con stirred slightly. "Or, at least, after we got a better idea of what's happening." She sighed and looked up at him. He lifted a light hand to her cheek.

"Know you can't hold an offer like that forever—" she said to Jase's suddenly speculative eyes.

"Never mind it, my small. If you decide you want us, believe that we want you! Anytime, anywhere, any terms. Why, I'll even give you my slot—"

Miri laughed and came to her feet. "Gods, look at the time!" she said, flicking a slender hand toward the window and the reaching orange rays of sundown. "We're gonna be late for dinner, boss."

"Alas," Val Con said, standing. He bowed slightly to the towering Aus. "Honor attended the asking," he said stiffly. "My thanks to you and your troop."

"That's all right, son. I know quality when I see quality—not quite as thick as that!" Jase laughed and loomed to his feet. "Walk you to the access road. Pretty planet. Pretty sunsets."

THE THREE OF THEM stopped at the place where East Gate had been earlier that afternoon, and Jase bent nearly double to hug Miri and plant a kiss firmly on her mouth.

"Take care of yourself, my small."

"You too, Jase. Best to Suzuki. Tell her. . ."

The message was swallowed in the sudden appalling uproar—a banshee wail from the lone communication pole still upright beside the comm shack—and startled beeps from a half-a-hundred personal communits.

"Air attack—popped up over the mountains—reentry speed—" Miri could barely hear the words pouring from Jason's communit against the siren's wail and the new sound, a sound like a thousand thunderstorms, all letting loose at once.

"Bastards tricked us! Pull everyone . . ." Jason cut off in the middle of issuing orders to stare.

In the sky: A formation of deadly shapes, black against sunset orange. As they watched, one peeled off—another—a third, toward the distant city and the closer town.

"Oh, shit," breathed Jason. "Redhead—"

Redhead was already gone, moving flat out down the synthphalt toward Erob's house, her partner a fleet dark shadow at her side.

Warning to the civilians in hand, Jason whirled, bellowing to his troops.

"Yxtrang coming in! Blood war!"

14th CONQUEST CORPS: Lytaxin

ALONE AND WEAPONLESS, he held the planet.

It was an accident and one that would cost *someone* a stripe or two, though not himself, who had neither stripe nor rank to lose. The moment was laden with irony, had one taste for it—that Nelirikk No-Troop should be first Yxtrang upon this world, before even the General.

Having devoted most of ten Cycles to acquiring a taste for irony, Nelirikk embraced the moment and looked about him.

The world was beautiful and lush—exactly the sort of place Liadens usually chose to colonize. The wind—warm, yet edged now with evening-chill—brushed against his clean-shaven face, treating him to natural odors for the first time in—ah? those same ten Cycles! The noises behind him were those of war, but not yet the smells.

"Try now! Try again!" came the order from the ship.

Nelirikk rotated, put his foot back onto the landing chute, and with a swing of the solid metal mallet struck the recalcitrant holding lug. The mallet's head bounced uselessly on the first strike, and the

70

second—but the third strike was true, and the offending lug shot free and rolled away into the crushed field grass.

Automatics took over then, and Nelirikk bounded away in time to avoid being run over by the command cars coming hastily to life in the chute.

He ran farther, perhaps, than was required—and then a few steps more.

Behind him: sounds of motors, of shouting, of feet, hitting the metal plank in troop rhythm. Before him: free growing plants, high-flying birds, and flowers. Nelirikk filled his lungs with fragrant air; sighed it out grudgingly.

A small gray animal poked its head out of the high grass just beyond Nelirikk's grasp, ears perked, eyes bright. It jerked abruptly upright; showing front paws very hand-like, and in a nose-twitch was gone. Two soldiers hit the grass from the landing tube, took aim instantly—and held fire pending orders. Nelirikk breathed a second sigh—and was instantly aware of this new irony, that a no-troop attached to an invasion force pledged to slay thousands of sentients should feel relief at the escape of a squirrel.

Someone shouted then and Nelirikk jumped aside, saluting the General's car, as even a no-troop must, then melted away, alone of the crowd without duty or orders, to watch as the troops and vehicles of the 14th Conquest Corps turned the pretty land into Field Headquarters.

THE GENERAL'S WORD brought him to the war room, a grim-faced Captain Kagan as his guard. Nelirikk's greedy eyes sought this screen, that, taking information in rapidly and indiscriminately.

So—there was no capital ship arrayed against them in space, though there was strong resistance on the coasts of this continent and heavier fighting on the other continent, where they had inadvertently landed in the midst of mercenaries preparing to leave. Locally—

"This is the man, General."

The General looked at Nelirikk, perhaps recognized him. Nelirikk stood at silent attention, face expressionless, hungry eyes hooded.

There were three men under guard behind the General. Two were corporals Nelirikk had dealt with recently; the other was an officer he didn't recognize.

"No-Troop." The General demanded his attention. "Describe to me the situation you encountered at landfall."

"Sir." He brought his fist up in salute. "I was strapped in at the advance station. The ship touched down and the landing chute began its extension, however the lead vehicle—your command car—did not move. The chute completed its extension, but the column remained still.

"Under orders, I investigated the situation and discovered that the explosive lugs had failed to fire and that the metal retaining lugs prevented your car from moving. I reported and was ordered to remove the impediment. I pointed out that disarming the explosive devices would prevent potential injury to the craft and your car. They were disarmed, I knocked out the metal lugs with a mallet, and the invasion proceeded."

The General stabbed a finger at the first corporal.

"You—what was your role?"

"Sir. I set and checked the retaining lugs in orbit. All was well. Sir."

"And you?"

The second corporal was visibly sweating, her youth perhaps preventing soldierly performance.

"Sir. I—my duty was to set the power cords to the explosive lugs, as ordered by Over-Technician Akrant. They checked out correctly on Test Circuit B." She choked. "Sir."

"Akrant, your report?"

The Over-Technician answered easily enough—too easily, Nelirikk thought.

"All tested according to spec, General, and was rechecked. It wasn't until we set down that I discovered that Corporal Dikl had utilized reserve circuits which required pilot intervention to operate in atmosphere."

Corporal Dikl broke into a fresh sweat, her eyes showing a bit of white around the edges.

Nelirikk, hearing as the General no doubt heard, could have advised her not to worry, but a no-troop speaks when a no-troop is spoken to, and at no other time. Nelirikk turned his attention to the proliferation of information about him.

The air power charts showed the largest aircraft concentrations on the coast. The nearest to Field Headquarters was a small base, doubtless related to the—yes; a town and a large holding were equidistant from the field. Which meant it most likely held civilian craft—easy pickings. Another screen showed the numbers of the dropjets sent to secure it, and the transport bringing in a hundred of the deadly Spraghentz—the infantry—support aircraft—that would occupy it.

Other screens—uplinks and downlinks—were coming on line now: locations of ships in orbit, radar and other scans, visual searches, live transmissions from the front.

"No, sir," said Corporal Dikl, with unsoldierly fervor, "I was working from training manuals. I'd never done the procedure before."

Nelirikk squinted his eyes slightly, focusing on a screen across the room showing the view from the combat camera of an interceptor. He found the cue number, checked the screens.

Bomb and strafing run. That same small airfield, on automatic target. The plane lifted and—Nelirikk's heart climbed into his throat. He blinked, checked the vision screen against the radar scans, but it had moved to the next scan—looked back at the radar screen.

It wasn't there.

He sighed. His once-exemplary eyesight was failing and had played him a shabby trick. As if such a ship would be found among a small field of backward civilian craft.

"On Akrant's orders?" the General demanded of the corporal. Nelirikk sniffed. Now, *there* was a dead career. Called without rank twice by the General during Inquiry? Might as well begin tearing off the stripes and swallowing the badges.

Again the camera-screen showed the tiny airfield, this time from the vantage of a low-level run. And there, among the tall trees and with a slight hill behind it, was a thing of awful beauty.

The beauty lay in the deadly, competent lines.

The awfulness—was it that such a ship should die—if die it must—fighting, rather than destroyed ignominiously upon the ground? Or was it that he was reminded all at once of his own ship— the *Command's* ship. Always the Command's ship, for a troop owns nothing but his rank and his booty.

Duty turned him toward the Captain.

Thought stopped him.

He was Nelirikk No-Troop, permitted to speak when spoken to. He had been given leave by his assigned commander to speak to the Inquiry. Speaking without permission would cost—

The missiles were launched: they struck and crumbled a building. The view in the screen slipped as the plane turned and set up for the next run. The radar cross-scans showed no sign, the computer listeners heard no slightest whisper, the metallics—

And what *would* it cost him? He'd had ten Cycles of shame.

Decisively, he sought the Captain's eyes; signed for permission to speak.

The Captain's face clouded. He deliberately looked away. Nelirikk glanced back at the screen. Someone—an air controller— had finally sighted the beautiful ship. It sat in a visual freeze-frame as the computer made analysis, the null-image of the comparative radar etched over it.

The view from the field showed an aircraft rising in opposition. An antique by its look and in the air only by the grace of the Gods of Irony. Impossibly, it wavered into the horizontal—*fired*, by Jela! on the rushing dropjet—and was lost to view.

And there, in the corner screen, the spire of that—other-ship!

The screen froze again, as if someone lacking proper information was trying to figure out—

Nelirikk broke position, took three hasty strides toward the Controller.

"Hit that ship! Do it now!" he demanded.

There was instant silence in the room. The General turned to stare. Captain Kagan's weapon was in hand.

The screen showed the ship again, and the silly, greathearted antique, as well, rushing headlong against the cream of Yxtrang fighters. The camera showed it circling slightly as if to protect that ship—and the closing fighters lost one of their number as the antique apparently unleashed all of its weapons at once before it was shredded into smoke. But its mission had been accomplished: the attack was diverted away from the beautiful ship.

"Hit that ship now!"

"No-Troop. Explain yourself!" Kagan's voice was grim.

On the screen, the first pair of Yxtrang fighters leveled out before the camera plane, began a sweeping turn—

Glare! Glare!

TRANSMISSION LOST

Freeze-screen came back up, picture telescoping in on the deadly ship sitting there beneath the trees, the shielding hill behind it.

Nelirikk looked at the gun, looked back at the screen.

"Scout ship," he said, calmly. "That's a Liaden Scout ship, Captain. If it's not destroyed immediately it could take out a battle-ship!"

"Control! ID that ship!" The General at least had ears.

"Sir. No ID on record. We've never captured or seen one—"

"*I've* seen one," Nelirikk spoke before the General, against best health. "Take it now, before it's fully activated!"

"Control!" ordered the General. "Get another flight in there. Take it out."

"You'll need something bigger. Call the transports back before they get in range—" Nelirikk heard his traitor voice correcting, apparently determined to have him shot. "It's space-based—coil-fields, power magnetics—"

"Silence!"

Nelirikk fell silent; heard the mistaken order relayed.

"No-Troop will remain silent!" snarled the General. "You, Controller, will keep me informed."

Nelirikk watched the camera screen, heard as if from another galaxy the demotions behind him: the corporals busted a level each, retaining rank but losing pay and time in grade. The over-tech was now a life private in grocery supply, proper punishment for a stupid error. To trust to training-manual performance for a thing of such importance!

The camera screen came up, showing four planes ahead of the camera plane. Munitions tumbled away, heading for the pretty ship—

Glare! Glare! GLARE! And a wildly swinging picture, smoke on the fringes—TRANSMISSION LOST

"**GENERAL,** Flight 15 is not transmitting and does not show on scans." The controller's voice was level, soldierly, merely imparting the facts.

The General's voice bordered on frenzied. "I want the *Barakhan*. Now. No one will mention No-Troop's insolence or this occurrence outside of this room."

For several moments there was nothing to see, and then a new camera—from quite a distance—hazarded a looksee and then was gone: the flash of an energy weapon was unmistakable.

"Sir, *Barakhan* is in position and has acquired the target."

The camera screen came up once more and Nelirikk watched as the horrific fires of proud *Barakhan*, dimmed only slightly by atmosphere, punched through to the scout ship, leaving bright, dancing shadows behind his eyelids. He saw, incredibly, the small ship fire back, the first wave of the battleship's energy deflected up and away by some tremendous effort of shielding.

Now the small ship could be seen from a more distant camera, firing in several directions as the General raised his voice.

"Bring all available batteries to bear, transports . . ."

And that quickly it was both too late and all over, for the Liaden ship had launched missiles and beam hard on target in the moments before it exploded, leaving a smoking crater in its stead.

He had no doubt of it even before the stunned com tech relayed the word. "General—the Spraghentz—the transport is gone!"

Nelirikk blinked—once, twice. "Honored foe," he thought treasonously, for Liadens were never such, "we salute you."

The General turned from the screen and folded his hands upon the table. "No-Troop will report to Security with Captain Kagan," he stated. "Now."

STARS LIKE FISTS OF ICE above the rocks and trees.

Nelirikk sat with his back against a boulder, rifle and pack to hand, and stared at the stars until his eyes teared, ringing each bright dot with rainbows.

Ah, Jela, to be once more upon a world!

This, *this* was what they'd trained him for, from the time they'd plucked him from among his fellows in boot camp. They'd trained him for exploration, made him something other than a mere troop, that the Troop and the Command might be served more fully. Training . . .

He closed his eyes, abandoning himself, here, under the free stars, to memories he had not dared recall in ten full Cycles.

Training, yes: piloting, scouting, weapons—not only the soldier's carbine and grace blade, but also other, more subtle things. They'd trained him to operate—to make judgment and form appropriate response—without recourse to superiors, regulations, subordinates, or comrades. Trained him to make decisions. Trained him to impart information. Trained him, even, to command.

They'd made him a misfit, that they had. A troop with a voice of command. A commander with imagination. They'd made him a misfit and sent him alone to the stars, to find out—to report back. And when he returned from his most important mission with urgent information? Why, then they'd made him a no-troop, and buried his report so thoroughly that not even a description of the ship had survived.

Nelirikk sighed.

His mess orders had last—and quite recently—changed hands in an all-night betting game of the officers. Rumor was that Captain Kagan had lost one of the bouts of small-skills, and thus won the housing of the no-troop. Nelirikk had not been assigned to Captain Kagan's command, nor had he been given duties within the Troop. He had merely been relieved of the chit entitling him to eat from

Captain Bestu's supplies and given another with Kagan's account number on it. To have that same no-troop call a General's attention upon himself had done Captain Kagan's credit no good at all.

Nelirikk opened his eyes and stared wearily up at the stars. In a moment, he straightened, ran through a mind-clearing exercise he'd learned with the rest of his age-mates in the creche.

The General, now. . .

Security had taken him to a room that held no sign of the devices most usually employed to punish the recalcitrant. Neck-hairs prickling, Nelirikk glanced around him, locating at least three grills and two lights that most likely held microphones and cameras. Three chairs, two computer terminals, a table upon which sat a carafe of water and three glasses—unthinkable courtesies for a rogue no-troop. Nelirikk was suddenly very tired.

Without orders he should not sit.

He sat.

No voice from a hidden loudspeaker ordered him up.

Security would have his records and files, Nelirikk considered, and would know his training and abilities—

Would know that he was not to be trusted, though some chance cruelty of the High Command dictated that he should be made to continue living, rather than receive the simple back-of-the-head execution Security itself had recommended. Security would have the file that said Nelirikk Explorer was hereinafter and forever Nelirikk No-Troop, shamed and shunned—the only living Yxtrang to have been captured by a Liaden.

Caught in a trap—tricked, as Liaden scouts had been tricking Yxtrang for untold years—and then *let go*, to return to his commander and report, half-dazzled by the possibilities he glimpsed within the information the scout had—knowingly?—given. He'd described the ship . . .

So they'd taken his report, ignored it, isolated him from the small cadre of Yxtrang explorers, made him a no-troop and forgot him.

And now he was here, a rogue no-troop, apparently so weary of his dutiless life that he interfered with command level action in the

General's own war room! An explorer might possibly have done so, without punishment.

If there were any explorers left. He'd searched for traces of the unit, using stolen computer time and unauthorized glimpses of ship movements through distant portholes—to no purpose. His terror was that they had disbanded the explorers, and made him no-troop in a far different way.

"*Hup!*"

He came to his feet, at attention. The General stood before him, comrade close, eyes full of calculation, the tattoos of rank and achievement not quite disguising the unnatural ruddiness of his face.

"You retain your alertness, No-Troop."

"A soldier survives through alertness, sir."

The eyes narrowed.

"I have reviewed your records," the General said, "and I understand how you might have been able to identify a ship unknown to our scanning program. I understand how you might react without permission and assume compliance. I understand, also, that you have disturbed the organization of my war room."

A statement of facts required no reply. Nelirikk continued to look eye-to-eye with the planetary commander.

"What do you say of your insolence, Nelirikk No-Troop?" the General demanded. Nelirikk avoided the sigh.

"Sir. I sought to serve the Troop, and gave warning of clear danger. Pilots are not to be wasted—"

"Silence!" roared the General. "Do not consider yourself a pilot, No-Troop. That honor was long-ago forbidden you."

He turned abruptly, jabbing a finger toward the table and the computers. "Sit."

The General took the second chair, tapped in a request and leaned back as the battle-site filled the screen.

"Now, No-Troop, why do you think such a ship would be on this planet? Why did it remain grounded rather than rising to the fight? Mere Liaden cowardice?"

The urge to look wonderingly at the General was strong;

Nelirikk instead stared at the screen, restructuring the logic chain he had formed in the war room.

"I have given this matter thought, sir. However, I have little information about the current military situation—"

"You need none. Speak to this case!"

Nelirikk did sigh, very quietly.

"Yes, sir. In this case several possibilities exist." Unconsciously, he moved into the lecture technique he'd learned for briefing fellow explorers.

"One possibility is that the ship was under repair and unable to lift. Supporting information is sparse—no repair machinery was observed about the craft. Another possibility is that a junior officer during the commander's absence manned the ship. We then have a reason for the delay in firing, and also for the failure to lift and engage."

The General gave a mildly approving click.

"Another possibility," Nelirikk continued, "is that the ship was unmanned and computerized self-defense functions were in force. Or that the crew was aboard and deliberately sought to escape notice so that a later strike at a capital ship might be launched. My assumption is that *Barakhan* took damage from that last bolt—"

"An invalid assumption, No-Troop. So small a ship, and firing through atmosphere, to touch *Barakhan*?" The General waved a hand in negation.

"I saw the ship fire when the particle-beams began the attack. A charged beam could well use the same path to—"

"I am not interested in traitorous assumptions!" the General snarled. "I asked you for whys."

Nelirikk stared at the screen—at the crater where the pretty ship had been—until the view changed to a map of the surrounding area.

"Sir. It is possible that the ship was ordered to remain grounded in order to defend an important center or person." He pointed.

"I propose that the town, the nearby command base, or the remaining mercenary troops are of special importance. That small plane, trying so bravely to hinder our jets—it may be that by luck we were attacking the escape ship of an important person."

Nelirikk paused, staring at the screen.

"Recall that by drawing fire the ship has taken out a number of our drop fighters and has forced a demonstration of our overhead strength. A scout might trade his ship for such information. For this possibility, I assume standard invasion policy has been followed and the planetary satellite net has been destroyed."

The General was eyeing him, displeasure apparent. "You insist on this scout, do you?"

"If all Liaden ships of that size were as powerful, sir, I believe Liadens would even now be pursuing us across the galaxy."

"Fool!" The General's fist rose, but, remarkably, no blow landed. He twisted in his chair, frowning heavily at the screen. "Hear yourself—naming Liadens—*Liadens!*—brave, assigning soldierly virtue to a race long known to be weak and honorless—*animals*, No-Troop. You entertain the possibility that the 14th Conquest Corps might be routed by *animals*."

Nelirikk said nothing.

The General shut down the display. "We have discovered maps and a short-range radio transceiver in a captured enemy vehicle. I understand from your records that you are fluent in the language of Liaden animals and can read their scratchings as well."

The General rose, walked to the brown-gray wall and back.

"You will be outfitted for a special mission. You are to infiltrate the area bounded by a triangle of this airfield, this town, and this command center. You will be given the transceiver and the maps I spoke of, as well as a recall signaler. I will issue a weapon from my office. Security will issue a kit and a blade."

He came to Nelirikk's chair.

"We make use of your training and inclinations, No-Troop," he commented; "and allow you to avoid fighting."

Nelirikk sat quietly, refusing to show any reaction to an insult that would have demanded blood to balance—ten Cycles ago.

The General's lips pursed, as if he would spit; then:

"Let me be clear: You are to gather information—which you will note on the map. You are to return to the pick-up point no later than the tenth planetary dawn after you are released. This is a combat order."

Nelirikk straightened, unable to control the quickening of his heartbeat. A combat order! Was he reinstated, then—once more a part of the Troop?

"Be sure you understand your orders entirely, No-Troop," the General advised him. "Deviate from them and you will be shot. Not even a Heroic Explorer's Starburst certificate in your file can protect you from proper punishment if you fail a combat command!"

Ten Cycles of keeping his face quiet served him well. But the blow was severe. Odd, that so sudden a burst of hope should leave such agony in its wake.

On the hillside, under the hard, beautiful stars, Nelirikk stirred and came out of his thoughts. The shattered hope of reinstatement had faded in the resolution of a mystery ten Cycles old. Almost, he was content. For he knew at last why they had not executed him.

The General had thought he'd known—had thought Nelirikk used the protection of a Hero's status to wreak havoc in the war room and flaunt command. The General had not taken into account the slowness with which such news trickles down through the levels, from the High Command to the soldier. Even the announcement of so signal an honor might take a Cycle or two, depending on battles and tours of duty. Nelirikk smiled at the sky: Heroic Explorer's Starburst!

It would have been awarded for the odd moon, of course. Strangely dense, with an atmosphere capable of supporting Yxtrang or Liadens, green-blue bushes and a storm-driven climate that brought daily rain to every spot on the surface.

He was a Hero, though his face bore no trace of the honor; and, like all Heroes, his name must now be listed on the Great Board at Temp Headquarters.

The Command preferred Heroes to die in battle—preferably in great victories.

As Lytaxin was likely to become.

Nelirikk picked up the pack and the long-arm, though he had no illusions regarding either. He rose easily to his lean height, smiled again at the stars and looked around at the velvet night.

A pretty planet. To die in open air would be a boon.

LIAD:
Department of Interior :
Command Headquarters

COMMANDER OF AGENTS stared at the beacon screen, which informed him that Tyl Von sig'Alda's ship tarried yet about the planet of Waymart.

Days, about a minor Terran world offering nothing that an Agent in fulfillment of his mission might require?

He thought not.

Alas, other thoughts proliferated, chiefest among them that Val Con yos'Phelium had overpowered his brother Agent during Jump—and yet why simply *hang* there, when Waymart's sole charm was that it offered so much possibility in the matter of Jump points?

Commander of Agents frowned. Were he Val Con yos'Phelium—and not inclined toward a debriefing—he would make all haste to fling his vessel into Jump, thence to plan and make such arrangements as he might for re-entry into normal space.

Perhaps yos'Phelium had escaped to the planet's surface? But there was no record of the ship having done other than held this middling, dawdling orbit for several days. A painstaking reading of back files discovered no harm the vessel might have taken.

The thing made no sense.

Commander of Agents disliked nonsense—intensely.

Eyes on the beacon screen, he considered whether it was more prudent to dispatch a second Agent to Waymart, or a team of lesser operatives, such as he'd already dispatched to Lufkit, where Agent yos'Phelium's break from discipline had first manifested.

He had settled upon sending the team and indeed moved his hand somewhat toward the toggle that would summon his second to him when the beacon screen flashed. The amber light that denoted sig'Alda's ship and its conditions flared bright, began blinking, and brought up windows full of warnings: system overload, weapons released, coils overcharged, Jump coil engaged, ERROR, ERROR ERROR—

Commander of Agents flung out a hand as if to make adjustments, to resolve the problem, to disengage the coils—too late.

Commander of Agents blinked, then leaned closer to read the message at the bottom of the black screen.

NO SIGNAL. TRANSMITTER DESTROYED.

SHALTREN:
Juntavas Headquarters

❀ ❀

SAMBRA REALLEN, Chairman Pro Tem of the Juntavas, folded her hands upon the desk and looked up at her two large visitors.

"I regret that our actions on your behalf have as yet produced neither Scout Commander yos'Phelium nor Sergeant Robertson, Aged Ones. I would remind you—with respect—that the universe is wide."

"Indeed it is," rumbled the largest, who called himself Edger. "Yet I had anticipated speedy reaction from our kin. News of our search should most surely have reached them by now. Yet we have no word. No whisper of possibility. It distresses me, Sambra Reallen. I begin to believe our kin are perhaps lost more deeply."

She drew a breath, careful not to let a start of alarm betray her. Had she not been present when these two beings destroyed both her predecessor and his weapon, and that with a mere three notes of alien song? What might they not be moved to, did they come to believe these claimkin of theirs dead?

"I think there no reason to consider them so profoundly beyond us," she said, keeping her voice level with an effort of will that started sweat beading in her armpits. "Merely, they may have gone to ground on one of the lower tech worlds, where word of our search would not travel so quickly. Eventually, they must leave their safe place. And when they do, they will make themselves known to us."

"And yet," said the second turtle, with a diffidence that sat oddly upon one so large, "why should they so?"

Both Edger and the Juntava stared at him, at which he ducked his head, moving his three-fingered hand in a gesture of—apology, thought Sambra Reallen. Or possibly of obeisance to Edger, who was larger-shelled and therefore in a position of command.

Edger moved his own hand. "You have asked. Can you answer?"

The smaller—Sheather, his name was—raised his head. "T'carais, I can."

"Do so."

"Yes, T'carais. Consider that our sister and our brother are masters of survival, though pursuit of art renders them no strangers to violence." He stopped and Sambra Reallen leaned forward, impatient for once of the mannerisms of long-lived Clutch-turtles, who might take as much as twenty human minutes for a pause of courtesy.

"Go on," she urged and there was an edge along her voice, so that Sheather looked at her out of his great eyes, then inclined his head.

"You are correct. I ask forgiveness, that I am careless of your time."

She waved a hand. "Granted. But say on—why shall your kin hide from us?"

"Why," said Sheather, blinking his eyes solemnly, "only because when last our kin had treat with yours, the Juntavas did their most to slay them. Neither our brother nor our sister is such a fool that they would willingly place themselves into the hands of a known enemy."

"Hah!" She sat back, staring at him and feeling dread like ice in the pit of her belly. For he was correct. Val Con yos'Phelium—a Commander of Scouts, no less!—and Mercenary Sergeant Miri

Robertson had no cause to love the Juntavas, and many reasons to avoid them. The message the courier ships carried was, perforce, brief, and offered no reasons for the abrupt change of Juntavas policy with regard to the Turtles' kin. Who would of mortal necessity be compelled to consider the message a sham—or bait—and thus exert themselves doubly to avoid anything even remotely attached to the Juntavas.

Edger was looking at her. "Do you agree with my brother's summation, Sambra Reallen?"

She took a breath and met his eyes with what calm she could, who faced a being that could destroy her with a note. "Aged One, I do."

"So." He appeared to consider for a moment, then inclined his great head. "We shall go now, Sambra Reallen, to consider between us what might now be done to retrieve our brother and sister. Do you the same, of your kindness, and let us come to you again in three days' time to compare thoughts and perhaps build a more worthy plan of action."

They were not going to kill her out of hand? Relief left her giddy, yet she summoned the strength to stand, to bow. "Aged One, I shall be most happy to speak with you, three days hence."

"So it shall be," said Edger, turning ponderously toward the door. "I thank you for the gift of your time."

"It is freely given," she managed, though her legs shook with the strain of standing. It took them a few minutes to navigate the door. When they finally passed beyond the entry-eye, the door slid shut on its track and she collapsed onto her chair, uncertain whether to laugh, scream, or cry.

"IT COMES TO ME," Edger murmured into the soft silence of their evening habitation, "that you have thought more widely yet upon our sister Miri Robertson. Is it so, young brother?"

Sheather lay his hand flat, feeling the tiny rug fibers prick his palm. So many small bits of fluff, united in will to become a carpet!

"It is so," he answered softly, and raised his eyes from the study of the rug. "In truth, elder brother, there is little else with which I may occupy myself, here in this time and place. We have set motion upon certain projects with regard to our brother and sister. And now we wait. At home, waiting is put to use, for the benefit of the clan. But here, there are no knives awaiting sheathes. There are no young to instruct or any elder requiring my aid. So, indeed, I have thought much upon our sister, and studied what I might of her history."

This was rather a lengthy speech for Sheather, who was the most retiring of Edger's many brothers. However, Edger merely inclined his head.

"Ah," he said. "I would hear the tale of your study, if you would honor me, brother."

There followed a pause, of middling length for Clutch, then Sheather spoke again.

"Miri Robertson, Mercenary Soldier Retired, Personal Bodyguard Retired, Have Weapon Will Travel."

Edger moved his hand in acknowledgment. It was not so ill a name, for one yet young. A Clutch person who had seen his first Standard century might easily and without dishonor tend a lesser. Spoken fully, Edger's own name consumed several hours. Edger had seen seven Standard centuries, start to finish, and his name was not yet complete. It was the tragedy of humans, that so many died before attaining even a tenth part of their name.

"I placed my attention," said Sheather, "upon that portion of our sister's name 'Mercenary Soldier Retired.' I discover that there is a database, elder brother, containing the active rolls of every unit of mercenary soldier registered with Command upon the planet Fendor. It is accessible from yon device." He nodded across the room to the terminal built into the far wall.

"From this database I find that our sister holds the esteem of Suzuki Rialto, Senior Commander, Gyrfalk Unit and Jason Randolph Carmody, Junior Commander, Gyrfalk Unit, though she no longer holds herself at their word." Sheather hesitated.

"I comprehend that the bond between our sister and these commanders of gyrfalks is that of kin, T'carais."

"Ah." Edger felt a flutter of what might have been called excitement. "And your studies led you to believe that Miri Robertson may have called upon her kin to shelter herself and our brother."

"So they did," Sheather acknowledged. "However, I felt my understanding to be yet imperfect and set myself the task of tracing our sister through the ranks of mercenary soldiers, in an effort to identify others of her kindred."

"And has our sister other kin among the mercenary soldiers, younger brother?"

"One other," Sheather said, and closed his eyes for a minute or six. Upon opening them, he resumed.

"This other is an elder, brother. She has known our sister since our sister was an eggling and stood as sibling to our sister's mother. I believe, if our sister were indeed to seek shelter from her soldier-kin, she would seek it first from this elder."

Edger considered this for a time, eyes slitted in the dimness. Across from him on the floor, Sheather sat respectfully silent, studying the weave of the carpet.

"It is well-reasoned," Edger announced in the fullness of time. "Surely even so masterful an artist as our sister must seek an elder's wisdom in the face of such difficulties as the Juntavas offered. An elder of quiet renown, based perhaps upon a backworld . . . such might offer greater immediate safety than the kin of our brother, who live busy and open upon Liad."

"These were my thoughts as well," said Sheather. "Most especially might they seek this elder, should one or both be in need of healing." He held up a hand. "I heard the Juntavas say that neither was harmed, my brother. I heard the recording of our kin, stating the same. Yet my heart whispers that the Juntavas have lied to us many times. And how easy to compel our kin to lie, as well! Merely threaten either with further harm, did they not speak what was required. I think we may not assume our kin were unharmed, merely upon the word of the Juntavas."

"You speak wisely," Edger said. "Have you the name of this elder? Her location?"

"Her name is Angela Lizardi, Senior Commander Retired, Lunatic Unit Inactive. She makes her home upon the world called Lufkit."

LUFKIT:
358 Epling Street

✺ ✺

THE DOORCHIME SOUNDED loud in the cluttered room. Frowning, Liz lowered her book and raised her head, listening to the tinny echoes fade and die. She listened a moment longer, then bent again to her book.

The doorchime sounded.

Taking her time about it, she slipped a marker into the book, laid it atop several other bound volumes on the table beside her and levered out of the chair.

The echoes of the third chime were still fresh when she pulled open the front door to look out. And down.

Large violet eyes thickly fringed with dark gold lashes looked up at her. "Angela Lizardi?" The voice was as lovely as the eyes, low and seductively accented.

Liz nodded.

"I hope you will forgive this imposition," said her caller, apparently oblivious to Liz's lack of cordiality. "I am come on behalf of Miri Robertson. You are her friend. I thought you might consent to—help."

Liz frowned and took a moment to consider the rest of the face: high cheeks, pointed chin, biggish mouth, complexion carrying the faintest blush of Liaden gold. The shoulder-length hair was a richer gold, but not as dark as the long lashes.

She pulled the door wider and stepped back. "Come in," she said, and it sounded like a command in her own ears.

Her caller seemed to find nothing amiss in her manner; she stepped inside and waited patiently while Liz locked the door, then followed her back to the main room.

Liz sat in her chair and the little woman stood before her, putting her forcefully in mind of the last person to stand there. "Redhead's Liaden," she called him in her head, since he hadn't told her any name. Liz very nearly snorted. Liadens.

"Well," she snapped at this one, "you got my name. Let's have yours."

"I am Nova yos'Galan," the woman said readily, and it seemed she was on the verge of something else, but stopped herself. Liz saw her right hand move, thumb rubbing over the ring on her second finger.

"And you're here on behalf of Redhead," she prompted.

"On behalf of Redhead," the other repeated slowly, and moved her head, sharply. "Miri Robertson. And also on behalf of her lifemate."

Liz blinked. "Redhead ain't married," she said flatly. "Not her style."

"Her partner, then," the golden woman persisted. "A dark man—green eyes . . ." She reached into a sleeve-pocket, offered a rectangle of doubled plastic.

Liz took it; sighed at the hologram it enclosed. Well, at least she'd find out his name.

"Or her friend," the Liaden was saying, softly, almost pleadingly. "They were together . . ."

"He was here," Liz admitted at last, looking from the picture to her visitor and back again. Even given the difference in coloring, the resemblance was striking. She handed the 'gram back.

"Relative of yours, is it?"

"My brother," Nova said softly. "He was here some time ago, I think. Perhaps as much as a Standard?"

"No more'n six, eight months." She shrugged. "Redhead sent him by to collect something. Her partner, is what she told me."

"So." The word was a hiss of satisfaction. "They were pursued at that time, though I am not certain of the nature of the trouble. It is known that they left planet, traveling together; that they disappeared together . . ."

"Then you know more than I do," Liz said. "Last I heard, he thought they'd be able to outrun whatever mess they were in. Said when Redhead left he was going with her. Glad to hear they got off Lufkit. He seemed sound enough, and Redhead's no slack." She frowned. "But you're saying they didn't get wide of it."

"No. I am saying that they are presently—missing. They are not in places one would expect; they have not contacted appropriate persons. My brother has sent no word to his clan, or to—others."

Liz straightened in her chair. "That means they're dead." It was suddenly hard to breathe, thinking of Miri dead.

"No," said Nova yos'Galan again; "only that they are missing. There are indications that they may be missing for good cause. That they dare not send messages." She took a breath. "I must ask a question of you, Angela Lizardi. Forgive the necessity."

"OK," said Liz, still trying to figure what kind of trouble was *that* much trouble, and where the girl would go to ground.

"It is in my mind," Nova murmured, "that Miri Robertson is Liaden. My eldest brother tells me that it sometimes does happen that a half-blooded—even a full-blooded—Liaden will be born on— an outworld. Will have papers stamped 'Mutated within acceptable limits.'"

Liz sat very still, staring at the lovely face before her, while her mind's eye conjured up another face: Katy's face; worn to fine, supple gold, stretched over a fragile bone frame.

"Redhead's part Liaden," she said slowly. "Robertson was Terran, no question. Katy could've been half-Liaden, could've been full—she never said and I never asked. Don't even know for sure if she told the kid. Not the kind of thing you tell your kid, if you figured her to be stuck on Surebleak for the rest of her life."

"But Miri Robertson *left* Surebleak!" Nova snapped. "Do you know the name of the clan? Katalina Tayzin? There is no such name within the clans, though a few might be possible, given accent, vowel shifts . . ."

Liz hesitated; thought again of Redhead dead. "Something," she said, grudgingly. "Katy had a thing . . ." She closed her eyes, reaching for the memory. "Gaudy thing," she muttered. "Flat disk. Enamel work. Fine stuff—that's what I know now. Probably Liaden. Liadens do that kind of work—so fine you can hardly see the wires holding in the colors. Lots of colors . . ." She shook her head. "Never did make any sense of it."

"It looked like this?" Nova held her ring out, room lights skidding off bronze scales and green leaves. Liz narrowed her eyes.

"Like that," she allowed. "Different design, but that's the idea."

"Ah." The Liaden woman nodded as if to herself. "Then Miri Robertson is descended from one in the line direct. The search becomes simpler."

"That a fact."

Nova glanced up sharply. "Do you recall the design of this disk your friend had, Angela Lizardi? If—"

"I'd know it if I saw it again," Liz said lazily, watching through half-slitted eyes. "What're you gonna do now?"

"Run a search across all clans, specifying disappearances of those in the line direct within the last—sixty—Standards. That done, I shall try to match 'Tayzin' and, if the luck is willing, my brother shall be found."

"Not exactly encouraging." Liz stood. "OK, let's go."

Nova stared. "Angela Lizardi, I regret—"

"Don't have to. Redhead's my kin, near as I have any kin, and she's in trouble. Seems to me you're just a little more concerned with recovering this brother of yours than you are about what happened to her. Come here snatching at vapor-trails, thinking the thing's solved because you got a wisp of something to start a computer scan with—" She shook her head. "Seems like I got a responsibility to go along and assist the campaign, if you know what I mean. Make sure Redhead gets a fair shake, if and when we turn the pair of 'em up."

"It may be dangerous," Nova said flatly.

Liz shrugged. "I ain't out of practice with a gun, and I figure I still know a trick or two, hand-to-hand." She looked down into her visitor's lovely, cold face. "*Eldema*, your brother called me. That's 'first speaker,' right?"

Nova nodded.

"So, if one of my clan's missing and likely in some kind of jam, then I got a clear-cut obligation, don't I? As First Speaker?"

A pause, followed by a sigh.

"That is exactly correct, Angela Lizardi. The obligations of First Speaker are quite clear." Another sigh, and a glance at the watch she wore strapped to her wrist. "When can you be ready to leave?"

"Just let me get my kit," said Liz.

LUFKIT:
Lufkit Spaceport

❀ ❀

THEIR FOOTSTEPS echoed off the floor and reverberated in the corrugated metal walls of the service tunnel. Liz walked one step behind Nova yos'Galan, duffel slung over her right shoulder and service pistol on her belt, scanning over the little blonde's head into the metallic dimness ahead.

The corridor bent and straightened in a abrupt dogleg, showing Liz the end of the tunnel and the vapor glow of port lighting against the blue-black drop of night.

Nova yos'Galan continued her rapid, steady pace; stepped over the edge of the tunnel into the yard and turned to the left, Liz just behind.

There wasn't much doubt where they were headed; only one ship sat on a pad in this part of the yard—a sleek little scooter, the unfamiliar lines of which were lit by the honed brightness of a labor-spot, which also picked out several crimson coveralls.

"Thought you said you were ready to lift," Liz hissed. "Looks like the maintenance crew ain't done yet."

The Liaden woman flung one sharp glance over her shoulder. "Maintenance crew! That's a hotpad!"

And she was gone, running toward the spot and the three red-covered figures.

Liz blinked and swore and jumped after her. She'd figured the Liaden woman was in a hurry, but to go to the expense of a hotpad—a guaranteed short-order lift-off, anytime 'round the clock; and an assurance that no port maintenance crew would do anything but steer wide of the area—!

Ahead, Nova yos'Galan had checked; Liz came even with her. "Could be just a mistake," she muttered, but her gut didn't believe it, and her head was working the moves, given the three in sight; wondering how many were out of sight, around the other side; wondering if they were the fighting kind or the running kind. The Liaden woman didn't even spare her a glance.

One of the coveralls turned, started, yelled, hand snatching at belt. The shot sang past Liz's ear as the three of them bolted, fanning wide.

"I've got left," Nova snapped and Liz was spinning, target marked; gun out and up; spitting—once—and she kept moving, swinging back toward center, crouching, gun ready. A shot chewed gravel at her feet and her answer jerked the man's head up and back before he slammed flat and stopped moving at all.

The third coverall was down, Liz saw, straightening slowly: a huddle of blurred red in the leakage from the spot. Nova was running toward the ship.

The fourth one broke from behind the ship just as she came level with the spot.

Small, slim—Liaden, most likely; Liz thought, holding her fire—sprinting for the tunnel, no weapon out, no backward look.

Liz straightened. Scared stupid, she judged; might as well let her go.

By the spotlight, Nova yos'Galan spun, knees flexed, gun up and steady in a two-hand grip, picture-book perfect.

The slim runner was halfway to the tunnel, arms pumping.

A pellet pistol spat, once, and the runner stumbled, staggered another step forward.

The pistol spoke again—and the runner fell, arms flailing. Liz swallowed her yell; took a breath against the bile rising in her throat and walked, slowly, toward the spot.

STRAPPED INTO THE CO-PILOT'S SEAT, she stared at the perfect, golden profile; at the shapely hands, steady and certain over the unfamiliar board. Murder. Nothing but a senseless killing, no matter that Liadens rarely took prisoners. *Wouldn't done any harm to let that kid go*, Liz started to say, and forced the words back down her own gullet. Not her business.

Nova flipped a toggle. "Tower, this is KV5625, Solcintra. Lift initiates in five seconds. Out."

"Tower here, KV5625. I—umm—"

Liz kept the grin from reaching her face with an effort, trying to remember if she'd ever heard a pilot give the Tower clearance before.

"Is that a clear?" snapped Nova.

"I—yes," Tower managed, with belated decisiveness. "You're clear to lift, KV5625. Tower out."

"Recorded. KV5625 out." The toggle flicked off and quick golden fingers danced over the board, green go-lights glowing to life under the magic touch. Liz heard the teeth-aching screech as the magnetics kicked in; felt the pressure start—and was suddenly slammed back into her seat, shockstraps jerking tight.

"Ooof!"

Violet eyes flicked over her and the acceleration eased slightly. Liz took a hard breath against the pounding of her heart.

"You make that brother of yours look like a ray of sunshine," she snarled, and saw again the runner falling, shot in the back, and the woman next to her calmly holstering her gun and turning to inspect the hull for damage.

Nova yos'Galan barely smiled. "Only wait until you meet my elder brother," she said, hands flashing over the board. There was the barest shudder as the ship switched from magnetics to full power. "He takes an hour to say yes—and two to say no."

"Terrific," muttered Liz and tried to find a comfortable way to sit in the too-small chair. She gave it up about the time they achieved orbit and the power scaled down to maintenance; glanced over at the pilot's station and took a deep, careful breath.

Nova yos'Galan sat rigid in her chair, fists clenched on the armrests, eyes screwed shut, lips pinched to a thin, pale gash. She was shaking. Hard.

Liz cleared her throat. "You get hit?" she asked, knowing, *knowing* that there was no way—

Nova started, eyes opening and closing immediately, as if the sight of the pilot's board was too much for her to bear. She took a long, ragged breath and leaned woodenly back in the chair.

"I have never—killed—anyone before," she said, and tried another breath.

"Aah, hell . . ." Liz thought about that one, suddenly seeing the runner's death in a very different light. She unhooked the shock-webbing and pulled the flask out of her pouch; telescoped the lid to full extension and poured a healthy slug.

"Here you go."

Violet eyes slitted. Liz pushed the cup toward her, encouragingly. Nova closed her eyes.

Liz sighed. "When Redhead—Miri—had her first action," she said, keeping her voice conversational; "she had a slug outta here."

The eyes opened again; locked on the cup. "Did it help?"

"The shakes," said Liz, easily. "It helps with the shakes, girl. Ain't nothing except experience helps with the other."

One slim hand left the armrest, unclenched and took the cup. Liz nodded.

"You want to knock it back quick," she advised. "Don't go sipping at it like it's some fancy, hundred-year-old brandy. All it is is kynak. Go."

Obediently, Nova lifted the cup and threw it down her throat like medicine.

"Ah!" Tears started to her eyes, ran down her cheeks; she choked and Liz pounded her on the back, retrieving her cup in the process.

"Drunk like a merc!" she said cheerily and shook her head, abruptly more serious.

"Thing to remember is you don't have to kill everybody on the field," she said, keeping her voice easy, without judgement or condemnation. "Wasn't any real reason to kill that last one. She was just running to get away."

Nova shook her head, unlatched the webbing and sighed. "You do not understand."

"So explain it," Liz invited, still easy in the voice.

Nova sighed. "There is danger," she said. "I told you that there was danger. My brother—there are—persons—hunting him. These—they fired on the First Speaker. It is the First Speaker's duty to survive, to serve the clan."

Liz stared. "First Speaker? Girl, I'm no First Speaker—that was just what Redhead's Liaden—"

"*I* am First Speaker," Nova said, flatly; "of Clan Korval. I could not take the risk."

Liz thought about that one, too, as she unscrewed the flask and had herself a shot, and finally shook her head.

"I can see where you might think that. But you're saying this brother of yours has got trouble of his own—in addition to the trouble him and Redhead were trying to lose?"

Nova sighed again, and leaned forward to stare at the piloting readout. "Circumstances are not quite clear, Angela Lizardi." She glanced over, violet eyes bland and beautiful. "I have several matters to discuss with my brother, when I see him again."

"Yeah," said Liz, thoughtfully; "I can see that, too."

DUTIFUL PASSAGE:
Jump

❀ ❀

A CERTAIN AWKWARD PRIDE suffused the ship. Shan felt it as an electric undercurrent as he approached the tower.

The ship's mood disturbed him. Barely three hours ago they'd been escorted to their Jump point by Portmaster Vinikov's hastily cobbled armada, and the crew—his crew of mannerly merchanters!—was inebriated with the glory of it.

He'd called battle stations; and it had become immediately and painfully apparent that there wasn't a ship in-system that outgunned *Dutiful Passage*. Indeed, the ten military ships comprising their escort were badly outclassed: the *Passage* had three battle pods in reserve, with the others triple-targeted. They could have broken the system defenses, held the planet hostage.

Portmaster Vinikov and her fleet had held position until the *Passage* Jumped.

If he decided to turn rogue . . .

Shan shivered.

The problem was power.

Suddenly the crew was aware of the ship's power. Suddenly, they had an inkling of Korval's strength.

As would Korval's enemies, of course, for such an escort could hardly go unremarked. Within days the galaxy would know that *Dutiful Passage* had pulled away from Krisko, the Tree-and-Dragon at every name-point, and transmitting not the neutral ID of a freighter, but the strident warn-away of a battleship.

I dare: Korval's motto.

Octavia Vinikov knew the motto; knew a thread or two of Korval history.

Octavia Vinikov had seen her old drinking friend and chess partner leave dock commanding a warship, and acted as a portmaster must, to ensure the safety of the port; though she must have known, canny tactician that she was, that her armada could never withstand an attack from the *Passage*.

Shan sighed. "Gods defend the innocent," he murmured, and pushed his palm against the comm-room door.

"Innocent? Who's innocent?" demanded the familiar voice of Senior Radio Technician Rusty Morgenstern.

Shan managed a wan smile. "We're all innocent, my friend," he said and nodded at the console Rusty sat before. "How fares the new set-up?"

"Almost done. Would've been done, if we hadn't got a lot of last minute stuff in code because of the farewell parade." Rusty grinned, soft, round face glowing with martial importance before he bethought himself of something else and rummaged briefly on the console's ledge.

"Got a couple here for you—"

He held out a sealed envelope with a holostripe across the seal.

Shan lifted his eyebrows.

"It came out in code after I decoded it," Rusty explained, suddenly diffident; "so I thought I ought to . . ."

"Of course." Shan took the package and weighed it idly in his hand. "From now on anything like that should be routed directly to me on the—"

Rusty nodded seriously.

"I tried that, but Priscilla said you were almost at the door."

"I see. And did Priscilla tell you anything else?"

"Just that I should double check all outgoing channels and be sure we've got Tree-and-Dragon on primary and back-up, and to do the same for the lifeboat comms when I get the chance."

Shan shook his head ruefully. "I see I could have saved the steps."

"Naw, one of us had to see the other. Need your signature on this."

Shan looked dumbly at the official-looking orange card: Korval's sigil was printed at the top; at the bottom were the words "Code Confirmation."

He looked at Rusty and caught the thrill of the other man's fear.

"It's in the book, Captain," he said carefully. "I'm sorry . . ."

"Yes, it is, isn't it, Radio Tech?" Shan bent and scrawled his name. He handed the card back with a straight look into worried brown eyes. "I'm sorry, too."

Rusty nodded, countersigned the card, carefully peeled back from front, and held out the second copy.

Shan tucked the card away, hoping he'd remember to file it at some point, then stuffed the envelope in the same pocket.

"Thank you, old friend. Carry on."

He left then, weaving a brief tapestry of good will to chase away Rusty's fear.

THE FIRST DISK held the information he'd been expecting from their agent in-system: an up-to-the minute listing of the locations and schedules of those Korval and Korval-allied ships still on regular trade runs, plus the first and second choice fall-back points of each.

To obtain more than that would require Nova's First Speaker's key.

Just as well, Shan thought with uncharacteristic grimness. *Better that I don't know it all*. He extended a long arm and activated his link with the first mate's station on the bridge.

"Priscilla, I'm sending up some information to go under Captain's Seal. Do take a moment to glance at it and memorize three or four coords from the bottom half of the list."

"Yes, Captain. I'll take it at number four."

He copied the information to her terminal and memorized two new coords himself. He already knew the others.

That done, he moved to the second disk.

He laughed aloud when the code formed on the screen: "Poor Rusty!"

Of course the key wasn't filed in the ship's codebook—how could it be? It was built on the constantly changing situations of four different correspondence chess games.

Shan tapped in the algebraic codes of the last move in each game.

Na5xBb2. 0-0-0+. d5xe4. g6.

He paused with his finger on *go*, considering the last notation. That pawn chain was an awfully tempting target and would take—

"Fool!" he snarled under his breath and smacked *go* with such force that the terminal beeped in protest. Flutter-witted Shan—trust him to worry about the outcome of a chess game with Plan B in effect!

He ran the codebook command and glared at the reformed screen. The decoded message was blunt. Adrenaline surged and he hit the direct line to the cargo master's office.

"Man the reserve bridge," he snapped as soon as the line came open. "I'll be with you momentarily."

There was one heartbeat of startled silence. "Yes, Captain," said Ken Rik, and the line went dead.

The next call was to the first mate's station.

"This is the Captain. Do me the kindness of calling battle stations—yellow alert. When you have 80 percent compliance, go to red."

"Shan, we're in Jump."

"Indeed we are. Call battle stations. And put Gordy in charge of . . ." He glanced at the ship's master plan posted above his desk. "Put Gordy in charge of courier boat thirteen. Now."

The sounding of battle stations nearly drowned out his next words, which were, "Always remember that I love you, Priscilla."

✳   ✳   ✳

THE HEADSET of the light duty pressure suit Shan wore brought him the harsh sound of breathing. Deeper inside weapon pod six, Cargo Master Ken Rik yo'Lanna wore a heavy duty suit against the possibility of booby traps or contamination.

"Fingernails," Ken Rik muttered, fury and terror making an interesting counterpoint to the bloodlust in his voice. "One an hour, and then the toenails—with my own set of grab calipers, I swear it. Just promise me the opportunity—gods! Three more, Shan! I'll peel his face with a diamond-dust plane . . ."

"Do you have that, Priscilla?" Shan murmured into his link with the bridge. "Three more. These in sub-bay six. What's our count now?"

"Fourteen." Her voice was cool in his ear, soothing Healer nerves rubbed raw with Ken Rik's emotions. "The computer builds a pattern suggestion. It—"

"Another!" Ken Rik snapped. "This one's bad. Active. Rigged into the Jump scans."

"Location?"

"Access panel between sub-bay six and the emergency power module. There's a thin wire running off it through the panel edge. I can—"

"*Don't touch!*" Priscilla cried, Command Mode freezing even Shan for a moment.

"As you say, Lady. As you say." The old cargo master's voice held a note of near hysteria.

"Ken Rik, that is not to be touched," Priscilla said, very carefully—very gently. "I have a feeling . . ."

Shan shivered, though this was not the first time Priscilla's wizardly powers had saved a life.

"A feeling?" he ventured.

He heard the buzz of an open line, but it was nearly a minute before she spoke.

"Intent," she said finally. "That one has malicious intent behind it. I—"

"They all have malicious intent!" Ken Rik broke in, but Shan had already gotten his lifemate's meaning. The other devices had

been set as—devices, hardware necessary to accomplish a goal. What Priscilla sensed around this latest trap was the lingering taste of anticipation and desire.

Whoever had set that booby trap had *wanted* them to die.

"Yes, friend," Priscilla was telling Ken Rik; "but you cannot see the pattern I have here on the screen. There's a density and—"

"Spare me the obvious, girl," Ken Rik snapped. "It's a spiral, any fool can see that! And as it spirals in toward the power storage and capacitor banks it gets more and more dangerous. We dare not make one mistake in disarming them. We dare not believe we might even find them all! I haven't begun to look in the firing heads . . ."

Out of view of everyone, Shan nodded. Someone had carefully planned the death of the *Passage*. Planned it to be mysterious and untraceable—an explosion in Jump, confined to the Jump locus—matrix—not much chance of survivors from that!

"Ken Rik, mark your place, leave the access panels open and come to me here." He hadn't intended his tone to be so sharp, or the order so abrupt.

"At once, Captain." Relief washed some of Ken Rik's terror away, but Shan scarcely noticed.

"Priscilla, cut pod six to minimum power. Shift as many of the crew as possible to the opposite side of the ship. Discounting Ken Rik and myself, you have eight full pilots. Keep three with you, send one to the inner bridge, and station two outside my quarters, to be given access to the captain's controls, should necessity arise. You will have Gordy go to Storage Unit 117-A and remove what he finds there to the courier boat. Once back at the boat he is to go to internal power and be at battle stations with the other pilot.

"And, Priscilla—please be good enough to pull and cross link every file we have on the theoretical and practical aspects of the mathematics of Jump."

"THE SITUATION," Shan said carefully, "is quite awkward."

He glanced up into the split-screen where nine serious faces watched him, even as he watched them: Gordy, his foster-son—and Priscilla's—tight-lipped and gray-faced beside the large eyes and dark face of Thrina Makami; Vilobar, mustache shiny with sweat; Seth, laconic as always; Priscilla. . .

It was hard not to watch Priscilla. He would have rather been on the bridge, where he could take comfort from her presence, but the melant'i of the situation was plain. Resources needed to be spread out as much as possible. Both ship and crew had a better chance if at least one pilot survived—

"Weapons pod six has been—mined. Booby-trapped. Sabotaged while in storage."

There was a brief outburst of anger and fear; Shan raised his hand and quieted the noise.

"Who? It doesn't matter for the moment. How? Apparently under the guise of maintenance the proper fittings were from time to time replaced with fittings containing built-in bombs. How did we know? I received a coded pinbeam from—an impeccable source. Claiming the pod seems to have set a number of rumors into motion, not the least of which is that the galaxy should soon hear of the destruction of a major Liaden trade vessel under mysterious circumstances.

"As far as we are able to determine, there are more than fifteen explosive devices on board, all designed to do some damage, several designed to do maximum damage. The difficulty is that the devices have a variety of timers and triggers associated with them—at least one appears to be Jump-activated—and we very probably have not seen all the devices. Master Ken Rik believes the chance of finding and disabling all these traps before Jump-end is vanishingly low."

He looked at each of the nine serious faces in turn. No one seemed unduly distressed. He glanced down at his hands, big, brown, clever hands, folded quietly, the Master Trader's amethyst shining like a small purple sun in the light of the instrument panel. He looked back at the screen.

"In normal space I would merely reset shields and take the calculated risk that we would be far enough away from the thing when it exploded—or use it for target practice if it didn't.

"Here, we have a different situation. We are, as you all know, in Jump, and cannot maneuver. On the other hand, the physical laws regulating Jump suggest that an explosion in the connected pod will release the energy therein which will then duly fill up the Jump locus-matrix with itself, the total energy/mass equivalency of the system not being altered. Does anyone disagree?"

Nine dismayed faces reflected agreement.

Shan sighed.

"The captain sees no immediate clear answer either. I suggest each command location consider alternatives for the next twelve minutes, on my mark. We shall then reconvene. Pilots, I give you my mark . . . three—two—one—now!"

"POGO STICK!" Vilobar protested, smoothing his mustache nervously. "I can't see how—"

"No arguments," Shan directed. "We're taking ideas now."

"No, but the springs—if rocket thrust won't work maybe springs will!" Gordy pelted on, overriding both the older pilot and the captain. "Put them in the connecting passage, compressed, attached to the support arm. Cut the connections—the springs will uncompress and push the pod away. Then we retract the support arm . . ."

". . . use the pod's own screens, if we can trust them. Once we achieve separation it depends on philosophy. Will energy flow through the whole system, or does loss of physical congruency stop energy flow?"

Seth looked up from his scrawled notes, and gave a wry grin. "If it works we'll give the philosophers and physicists plenty to argue about."

". . . cut the entire pod mount away, if we must," Ren Zel said rapidly. "The power expenditure is within tolerances, as is the weakening of overall ship structure. We'd likely lose the cutting team . . ." He glanced up, eyes bleak in a politely expressionless Liaden face. "Necessity, Captain."

This, too, Shan limited to twelve minutes; there really was not enough time to decide how much time there was.

SHAN STARED AT A SCREEN filled with a growing forest of landing struts, braces, jacked platforms, and the occasional shadow that was one of the volunteers, making fine adjustments, doing the best they could to get even pressure.

Ken Rik had charge of the volunteer team. There had to be a pilot in it, and an old first classer, Ken Rik had said with a sobering lack of his usual vitriol, would be less missed by ship and crew—if something went awry—than a master pilot. Even a master pilot who was a thorough young idiot.

Shan watched and waited. On his second screen he saw Priscilla, likewise waiting, and was surprised by a surge of longing so intense his eyes teared. He was going to have to do something soon about adjusting priorities; this keeping the ship's first and second officer apart for security considerations didn't have the feel of a long-term working solution.

"That's the last," Ken Rik announced from within the pod, still in that disturbingly calm tone. "We're coming out now, Captain."

"Fine," Shan said. "Each of you count off as you come into the hall. We don't want to leave anyone in there with that thing."

He touched a key, bringing up an image of the pod's basewall, and increased magnification until the painted markers loomed—one mark every half-meter, to allow measurement of a movement the instruments could not detect in Jump. Movement that could not happen in Jump.

According to one theory.

Shan sighed. He'd calculated that they would achieve a separation rate of just under one half meter per second, under normal conditions. Who knew how fast the rate would be in Jump, where there was neither speed, nor distance, nor direction—assuming Gordy's "pogo stick" worked at all?

"Five." Rusty's voice in the count-off reflected nothing but exhaustion and Shan felt a burst of affectionate sympathy for the pudgy radio tech. Then it was Ken Rik, signaling into the camera, speaking over the com.

"Everyone clear, Captain. Give us twelve seconds to clear the hall . . ."

"You have forty-eight, starting with my mark. Three—two—one . . . mark. Priscilla?"

"On it, Captain. At minus twelve seconds we start powerdown. The pod sequencer will cut the meteor shield for twenty-four seconds, after which collision shields come up."

"Effectively sealing the ship off at pod six access hall while pod six tumbles down to hell. We hope." He shook his head, noted Ken Rik's all clear—twenty-two seconds—and glanced back to screen two.

"Please allow the ship's log to show that Gordon Arbuthnot is confirmed this day as pilot third class and entered as a candidate for provisional second class."

The crew, on battle stations, got a twenty-four second warning, for what it was worth.

The *Passage* gave a slight—even a familiar—shrug as the external pod clamps were withdrawn. Nothing changed on the screens.

Twelve seconds. Nine. Six. Three. Two. One. *Shrug* . . . the internal pod clamps withdrew—

His prime screen showed dozens of landing struts flexing, jack stands kicking sideways, platforms shaking—and there was the tiniest of lurches, as the third screen showed the markings on the basewall: one half meter . . . one meter . . . more . . .

The monitor showed a half-second blur as the pod twisted under the uneven push.

And then there was gray. Jump gray. No pod. No basewall. No hastily painted measurements. Gray.

Priscilla was looking at him from screen two.

"Instruments have lost the pod, Captain. No reading from docking radar, Jump-matrix screen shows no change. Meteor shield goes up in six seconds . . . we've got a report from inertial guidance comp: point-two-five meter per second adjustment."

So. For good or for ill. Whatever they had done was done, and the outcome was upon the knees of the gods. Shan reached for the controls and shut down the grayed screens.

"Thank you, Priscilla. I suggest we meet in our cabin for lunch. We have six hours to Jump-break and I will spend at least one with you."

LYTAXIN:
Erob's Combat
Practice Grounds

🌀 🌀 🌀 🌀 🌀 🌀 🌀 🌀 🌀 🌀 🌀 🌀 🌀 🌀 🌀 🌀 🌀 🌀 🌀

IN THE DISTANCE was the tree, gift of Korval. Beyond that, the house, and well beyond that, the foothills and small mountain range named Dragon's Back. Somewhere there, on the lower of the mountain humps, was another gift of Korval.

This was a tower. Called Dragon's Tooth for reasons none could give, it currently housed three spotters, a circumstance that had charged Win Den tel'Vosti with glee.

"A fine use we make of Korval's contract-suite, eh! Well enough, niece Miri, that you come to us lifemated, else you and your term-husband would have taken residence in Dragon's Tooth, and nothing either might do to prevent it!"

"Pretty far to walk for breakfast," Miri commented, which observation tel'Vosti was pleased to greet with laughter.

On the other side of the Dragon's Back was rough country indeed, and beyond that occasional farms and forestry plantations. The Yxtrang had not penetrated there as yet and the spotters in the Dragon's Tooth were looking down at and beyond the tree, and Erob's House. Using a good telescope they kept watch on movements close to the coast, ignoring the fields below the house itself, where only those expected yet trod. The mists of morning made the observer's job difficult, the Yxtrang destruction of most of the satellites in orbit made it vitally necessary.

"HEH UP!" Miri's voice echoed over the grounds and the members of Unit 1, Lytaxin Combined Forces, fell back from defending and attacking positions and turned to face their captain.

"Rotation!" Miri commanded, and those who had been defenders last round moved left to pair off with a new partner.

"Ain't proper training if they just work with one partner," Miri had said at the beginning. "We'll keep shifting 'em around, make 'em learn as much as they can; force 'em to be flexible. Maybe . . ."

Maybe, Val Con thought now, drifting along the line with seeming randomness in his role as the captain's second, *just maybe some of them would survive.*

Survival, of course, was problematical for all, though a measure of luck had attended the deployment of the Yxtrang invasion force. The majority of invaders had landed nearer the coast, with a mere battalion or so landing within striking distance of Erob's lands, though the Loop assured Val Con that a battalion of battle-hardened Yxtrang was likely sufficient to the task of overcoming the remnants of the mercenary units and Unit 1, Lytaxin Combined Forces.

Miri had nicknamed her command the "Lytaxin Irregulars," which was a comment after all on the state of most of the defending forces facing Lytaxin's tidy little difficulty. Aside from one of Jason's crack units, even the named and recognized forces were amalgams and hastily restaffed shadows of standing merc units. Val Con sighed, hid the Loop's predictions away in a corner of his mind, and came to attention with the rest of the troop on Miri's command.

"Partners A, C, E," Miri shouted. "Defend!"

His assignment this drill was the overseeing and correction of the attackers, speaking with the captain's authority and his own expertise in hand-to-hand technique. It was an assignment like most of the others he carried within the troop where he held no rank other than that of scout—and of Miri's partner.

The field was silent, awaiting the captain's next order. Val Con closed his eyes, recalling the Yxtrang landing.

He and Miri had been running to warn the Erob when the flight of attack craft circling overhead drove them to cover. The attackers dove toward the airfield, which sustained several passes before ter'Meulen's plane had risen in challenge. By then, the biggest roar in the sky had been the approach of the troop and transport ship.

Stupidly, the Yxtrang had attempted to take *Fosterling* out with a strafing run. The awesome fall of wreckage from the sky had been the result of that error—and the local keep's salvation.

Then came thunder from the sky and thunder from the ground as *Fosterling* replied to an attack from a space-based enemy. Valiant vessel—and all, eventually for naught. His ship was gone. Clonak ter'Meulen's heir was gone. The remnant of Erob's air fleet was gone. And he, a pilot of Korval, was grounded, charged with training children in the arts of death.

"Heh, go!" Miri commanded and the field went from absolute stillness to frenzied motion. Several pairs did absolutely the wrong thing. Miri headed for Trianna and Ilvin, as Val Con cut off An Der's charge with a sharp "Hold!"

"An overhead approach is acceptable for machete or broadsword," he told the boy's bruised blue eyes. "It is an inefficient technique for survival blade, in that it leaves the attacker vulnerable to a fighter with longer reach. Given the likelihood that the opponent you may eventually face with this blade will be considerably larger than you, the proper thrust is low, to surprise and injure, while making of yourself the smallest possible target. Then, an upthrust to chest or throat—thus." He demonstrated the sequence against an imaginary giant, reversed the blade and stepped aside. "The drill, if you please. Use your brain; terror wins no battles."

The boy took the weapon, bowed as student to honored instructor, and again faced his partner. Val Con watched them execute a far more reasoned drill and then moved down-line, pausing as necessary to correct, demonstrate, encourage.

"Heh, up!" The command rang out and all movement stopped.

"Drill done!" Miri called. "Return knives to Kol Vus. All at liberty until mess-call."

Val Con felt his shoulders sag in relief. It was amazingly tiring, this training of children and the Housebound. He began to walk toward Miri, and saw Emrith Tiazan and Win Den tel'Vosti bearing down on her from the opposite edge of the field.

"Scout!" The big voice bellowed from behind, booming with excitement. Val Con ground his teeth and kept walking; he had no wish to deal with Jason Carmody at this instant.

"Hey, Scout!" Jason insisted. "Over here, double-time! Got something to show you! Number one priority!"

That was final, then. Val Con sighed. A commander's priority outweighed any desire a man might have to protect his lady from the stresses of dealing with her kin.

He turned, and very nearly stared.

Jase grinned and dragged a sleeve across his forehead, leaving a streak of grime. His well-kept ponytail was in disarray, fine golden hairs pulled loose from the ribbon and standing out from his big head like an aura. His leathers were muddy and scuffed; there was a purpling bruise on one tan cheek, just above the beard-line; and his wide azure eyes were full of demonic glee.

"Look a sight, I'll wager," he said cheerfully. "Wasn't time to find my ball dress, though. This is hot, my son—got somebody you need to talk to!"

Val Con's heart stuttered. *Shan*? he thought, then nearly laughed.

Yes, he told himself, *very likely. As if Shan is so lacking in wits he'd endanger his ship and the a'nadelm's life by running an Yxtrang blockade.*

"You there, Scout?" Jason's eyes were sharp on him.

Val Con raised an eyebrow. "I am here, Commander. The question is: Where is this someone I must talk to?"

"Icehouse." The grin cracked free again, wild with pride. "Man, wait'll you—Hey, Captain Redhead!"

"Jase," Miri's voice was quiet, and a little husky from shouting practice commands. She smiled at Val Con and slid a comfortable arm around his waist.

"They're lookin' good out there, darlin'. When you figure on turning 'em loose to whip ass?"

Miri tipped her head and Val Con felt a sharpening in his own psyche, as if he was engaged in weighing values he recognized on some level past mere thought.

"Can take some heat, if you got it to share," Miri was telling Jason, calmly. "Ain't up to a pressure-cooker, but I figure to hold our own in a spat."

"Might have something to share, at that. Depends on what the Scout can get out of—"

"And what," demanded Emrith Tiazan arriving on Win Den tel'Vosti's arm, "is of such importance that Captain Robertson must need turn her back on me and walk away?"

There was an instant's silence.

"You're top brass, Jase," Miri muttered, and the big man started slightly before he bowed to the delm.

"Sorry, ma'am," he said, schooling his big voice to a polite boom. "I need the Scout and Captain Robertson to step along with me, Priority One."

tel'Vosti grinned, but Emrith Tiazan only glared, letting the silence stretch until it became a danger even Jason felt. Val Con shifted slightly, drawing the big man's eyes.

"It is possible," he murmured, "that Delm Erob will wish to survey this top priority, as well."

Jason looked doubtful, but produced another bow on the delm's behalf. "I'd be happy to have your assistance, ma'am—and General tel'Vosti's, too."

Erob inclined her head, her arm still twined with tel'Vosti's.

"Lead on, Commander," she ordered. "We are delighted to lend our—assistance."

DESIGNED TO WITHSTAND THE RIGORS of quick-freeze, the vacuum of freeze-drying and, coincidentally, the detonation of a small bomb, Erob's back-up freeze-plant made an admirable prison.

The corporal on guard at the door offered the information that Doc Tien was still inside, guard-crew with her, all according to the commander's order.

Jason nodded and pointed to the monitor. "Take a look," he said. "It's the best I can tell you."

It was difficult to see anything but the size of the prisoner, with the medic and the guards all around. Still, Val Con felt his pulse quicken even as Miri turned to stare up at Jason.

"What'd you do?" she demanded. "Crack an Yxtrang across the head?"

He grinned. "Damned near broke my carbine. That brother's head is *hard*."

"Yxtrang?" tel'Vosti squinted at the monitor. "You captured an Yxtrang? Alive? My dear Commander! You bring us hope."

Erob turned her head stiffly.

"Hope?" she snapped. She glared at Jason, for all the worlds like a strike-falcon baiting a bear. "What good is it, Commander? Shall we start a zoo?"

Jason laughed, short and sharp.

"Guess you could at that," he said, stroking his beard. "Put me and him in the same cage. He's just about my size, give or take a headache." He shook his head. "But his worth is what he knows and where he was. Found him up the hunting park. Alone."

tel'Vosti and Erob got very quiet. "So close?" Val Con murmured and Jason looked down at him, suddenly serious.

"Up on the east ridge," he said; "buncha hundred meters down from the top. Couple klicks out from where Kritoulkas is holding line—show you on the map." He grinned again and pointed at the monitor. "But what d'ya think, Scout? Ain't he a beauty?"

"He does seem to be indicative of his type." Val Con turned back to the screen, trying to see through a burly guardsman to the prisoner himself. "You say you hit him across the head?"

"From behind," Jason admitted, somewhat sheepishly. "He'd just got through sending a fongbear on its way and I fell on him like the mountain coming down. Seemed like a good idea, but, damn, then I had to carry him out!"

Miri laughed, eyes on the monitor. "How bad's he hurt?"

"Doc's checking. Once I found out I was in one piece I real quick sprayed him with a double-dose of Sleep-it from my medkit. Put his gear in the other room, there. 'Spect the scout'll want to see it."

"Will you?" Miri muttered.

Val Con sighed. "I anticipate the need. Jason seems to have surmised that a scout will speak Yxtrang."

"Oh." Miri blinked. "Have to rig up a talkie, I guess."

"Perhaps." Inside the freezer-bay, the medic had straightened, shut down her monitor and moved toward the door, shooing the guards out of her way like so many chickens. Val Con felt himself go cold as her patient was finally and fully revealed.

Something of his shock must have reached Miri through their lifemate link. She leaned close. "Boss? You OK?"

"OK—yes." He spun as the door opened, claiming the doctor's attention with a hand-wave.

"That man—is he whole?"

She shrugged, Terran-wise. "He'll do. Sleeping pretty sound." She glanced down at the med-comp. "If he's got reactions anywhere approximating a Terran of like mass, he ought to be out of it in forty minutes—an hour at the outside."

"Hour to look at his stuff," Jason said. "And to figure out how best to ask him." He paused and looked straight at Val Con. "You can talk to this guy OK, can't you, son?"

"Talk to it!" Emrith Tiazan repeated, somewhere between horror and fury. "Korval—are you able to speak to that thing?"

But Val Con was at the monitor now, studying the image of the man in the room beyond, thinner than his length predicted, stretched across a bed made of six hastily arranged packing crates, and covered with a standard merc pack-blanket. His short-cropped hair was light brown in color, the features of his face indistinct behind an intricate mask of tattoo.

"Korval." Erob again. He was mightily weary of Erob all at once, as he was weary of Jason and the war they had not yet engaged. This man here. This man. . .

"Korval!" Emrith Tiazan snapped, no doubt relying on the Command Mode to turn him. "I require response. Are you able to persuade that thing to speak to the point?"

It was a wrenching effort of will to turn away from the monitor and the image of the sleeping giant. He came about slowly, feeling his face stiffen into unaccustomed lines, as it would, of course, following the tutelage of the old tapes. He felt the proper phrase rise to consciousness, and then to his lips.

Erob's face showed fear; tel'Vosti's disquiet. Jason actively goggled. Miri alone moved—to stand between himself and her delm, and to lay her hand upon his sleeve.

"Easy, boss."

The old learning let him loose, so that he smiled at her through the hunger of his need, and lay his other hand over hers.

"Forgive me," he said to Erob's startlement. "The Yxtrang language is difficult and in some ways uncouth. In certain matters, however, it is perfection itself."

He glanced over his shoulder for a last lingering sight of the screen.

"I am able to speak to this man," he told Erob softly. "Indeed, we spoke at some length when last we met."

She stiffened. "Do not trifle with me, Korval."

Val Con regarded her blandly. "I do not."

It was tel'Vosti who moved this time, to take the old lady's arm and very nearly shake it. "Let the boy be, Emrith! This is not the time to stare a dragon in the face."

Val Con turned to Jason. "I will inspect his equipment," he said, his eyes straying back to the monitor. "Do give me a whetstone, and a length of good rope. I shall speak with him alone, when he wakes."

"Right!" said Jason. "Whatever you say."

Val Con nodded. "Exactly as I say." He glanced at Miri and smiled, suddenly and joyfully, into her worried eyes. "With my captain's permission, of course."

NIMBLEDRAKE:
Between Planets

"THAT ONE," Liz snapped, certainty hitting her system like a jolt of Stim.

Beside her, Nova yos'Galan blinked, then fingered the controls, bringing the image into close-up.

"Look carefully, Angela Lizardi. You are certain?"

"Told you I'd know it if I saw it again," Liz said, shaking off the dregs of her drowse. "That's the one."

It wasn't much to look at, compared with some of the other Liaden clan sigils they'd scanned over the last couple hours, but made its point with a purity of line that Liz at least found—refreshing.

Nova yos'Galan had turned from her study of the screen and was looking at her out of wide violet eyes. "You are certain?"

Liz frowned. "How many times you want me to say so, Goldie?"

She had discovered rather early in their association that Nova yos'Galan did not care to be called "Goldie." She thus reserved the name for times of special aggravation, of which, unfortunately, there were many. The Liaden woman had a gift for setting a body all into angles.

This time, however, the nickname earned neither darkling glance nor frown of disapproval. Instead, Nova turned back to the computer display and fiddled the buttons on her armrest until the sigil was replaced with a screen full of Liaden characters. She fiddled some more and the words dissolved. When the clan badge was back on-screen once more, Nova spoke, calmly and without inflection.

"That is the badge of Clan Erob."

Liz frowned again, trying to read something from the side of her companion's face or the set of her shoulders, which was about as useful as trying to read a meteor shield.

"If your friend held such a thing, she was of Erob, through Line Tiazan. *Tee-AY-sahn*," Nova breathed and grimaced. "Katalina *TAY-zin*. Pah!" She turned and looked at Liz once more, eyes shielded now, hard as amethyst.

"Be—very—certain, Angela Lizardi."

"Think I'm playing with your affection? That's the design. I'd know it if I was blind."

"Clan Erob," Nova said again, flat-voiced.

"If you say so. Got a problem, Goldie? What're they, the Capulets?"

Puzzlement flickered in the depths of the violet eyes, and was gone in the next instant. "Indeed, no. Clan Erob is none other than our eldest ally. We were to have shared genes again this generation, as I recall it."

"That so." Liz chewed on it a couple seconds. "Damned if I can see why you're cooked, then. If Redhead and that brother of yours are married—and I ain't believing *that* 'til I got it from Redhead herself—but *if* they are, seems to me you oughta be booking the band for the reception and pulling together a guest list."

"Hah." The stiff golden face relaxed into what passed for her smile. "But you see, I, too, entertain some . . . astonishment . . . at this lifemating. My brother Val Con, you understand, is not— biddable. It would require but a word in his ear that he must marry to Erob and we should find him looking in all directions, save that one."

Liz laughed. "Him and Redhead are well-matched, then. And you and the rest of the family better stand back!"

"Well," Nova's smile deepened, actually touching the depths of her eyes before she turned her attention back to the screen. "Our search is made easy," she murmured, plying the buttons and shutting the search program down. "We to Lytaxin, Angela Lizardi, there to put our various questions to my brother and to Miri Robertson." She rose, shaking her golden head at the blank screen before glancing down to Liz, pale lips still curved in her slight smile.

"And to Delm Erob, most naturally."

"Sounds like a plan," Liz said and climbed to her feet, stretching tall. "You know how to get us to Lytaxin, I take it."

Nova bowed slightly. "Simplicity itself."

EROB'S HOLD:
Freeze-Dry Prison

❋❋❋❋❋❋❋❋❋❋❋❋❋❋❋❋❋❋❋❋❋❋❋❋

"THIS GUY IS A SOLDIER?" Miri's voice held palpable unbelief.

Val Con looked up from his frowning inspection of the captive's pack.

"All Yxtrang are soldiers," he said, only half-attending what he said. "This one had been something more, once." He gestured with a mouse-nibbled ration bar. "He seems to have fallen on evil times."

Abruptly, he pitched the bar back into the pack and stood frowning into its depths. "Something's amiss."

Miri laughed. "Screwier than a hive of hurricanes," she agreed. "Take a look at this rifle."

He laid the pack down and went to where she had the bulky long-arm arranged across two packing crates. He knelt opposite and looked at her quizzically, but she only grinned and waved a hand. "All yours."

The rifle was clean and well oiled; to first and second glances a proper, soldierly weapon, though something about that nagged Val Con as he bent closer to inspect the firing mechanism and auto-circuitry. He checked, glanced up at Miri.

She nodded. "Looks like maybe him and the weapons-master wasn't on terms."

"So it does." He rocked back on his heels, brows pulled sharply together. "And no need for him to be carrying such a thing at all."

"Why not? Makes sense to take a rifle with you, if you're going for a stroll in enemy territory."

"It does indeed, for a soldier," Val Con said softly. "But not for a scout."

Miri blinked. "Scout?"

"Explorer, it would be rendered from Yxtrang. But—scout, yes."

She shifted carefully, drawing his eyes. "You said you know this guy?"

"Ah, no." His smile flickered, banishing all but a shadow of the frown. "Merely, we had spoken once, many years ago. I held captain's rank then—very young and very certain of immortality." He grinned. "Shan all but ordered me out of the scouts, when I told him the tale. I've rarely seen him so angry."

Miri looked at him carefully. "Which tale was that?"

"The one in which I caught an Yxtrang scout studying the same world I was conducting studies upon, snared him, spoke with him, and then let him go."

"Thought you should've cut his throat for him, is that it?"

"Thought I should have rather cut and run at the first indication that there were Yxtrang of any sort on-world." He smiled again. "Shan has a great desire for those of us under his care to behave with what he considers to be proper caution. But he sets so bad an example, cha'trez . . ."

She laughed and shook her head, pointing at the rifle, the pack with its load of defective gear. "Hell of a way to outfit a scout."

"I agree." The frown was back. "Even if he were sent as a decoy—an explorer might conceive of such a plan . . ."

"Let himself be captured?" Miri stared. "Yxtrang don't let themselves get captured, boss. You know that."

"Yes, but this one has had experience of being captured," Val Con said, "and is a scout besides. Though it would be rational to equip a decoy well, to bolster the fiction that here was a soldier upon some other mission."

"Think he's an escapee—a deserter?"

Val Con shook his head. "In that case, one would be certain to appropriate working weapons, good food—the edge on that survival knife is so dull he could only use it as a crowbar or an ice-chop!"

Miri sighed and came to her feet. "Puzzle, ain't it?" She glanced at her watch. "We're at twenty-five minutes."

"So." Val Con rose. "I'd best have these things with me."

"I don't like you going in there by yourself to talk to him," Miri said, suddenly not his partner, but his lover and his lifemate. "Take a guard."

He smiled and came close, touching her cheek with gentle fingers. "It will be well, Miri." He bent and kissed her forehead. "Besides, he's tied up."

DREAM AND MEMORY danced for the pleasure of the Gods of Irony.

In the dream, he was caught, trussed like a rabbit and swinging from a tree, blade and pistol riding, remote as the Home Troop, in his belt.

In the dream, he roared abuse at his captor, who sat cross-legged on the moss below, absorbed in sharpening his knife. Memory provided an odor beside alien air, which was the scent of the oil the other applied now and then to the surface of the whetstone. The slide of blade along stone was comforting, a commonplace in a situation for which there was no analog.

The smell and the sound persisted, though the dream began to fray. The smell and the sound and the ropes, crossing snug over his chest, pinning his arms to his side, binding his ankles tight.

He opened his eyes.

Light stabbed, igniting a rocketing pain in his head, throwing reality momentarily awry, so that he snarled out of memory:

"Isn't that knife sharp yet?"

"The knife," answered the soft voice that had haunted his sleep these long, weary Cycles, "is sharp again, Ckrakec Yxtrang."

The sharpener lifted his head then, wild brown hair tumbling half into eyes like sharp green stones, and his face—the face—the face of his ruin, smooth and unchanged through the Cycles— though not quite. The right cheek now carried a mark very like a *nchaka*, or maturity scar.

"*You!*" He had meant to roar; instead a harsh whisper emerged as he tensed against the ropes.

The Liaden scout bowed from his cross-legged perch atop what seemed to be a packing crate. "I am honored that you recall me."

"Recall you!" The trade language failed him in that instant. Almost, breath failed him. Abruptly, he relaxed against the bonds and lay his head back, exposing his throat.

"If the knife is sharp," he growled in the Troop's own tongue, "use it."

The scout selected a strand of rope and tested the quality of the edge. Shaking his head, he took up the whetstone once more and resumed his sharpening.

"It would be more pleasant," he said, so softly it was a strain to hear him above the burr of stone stroking steel, "were we to talk."

"Talk." He twisted his head to stare, mouth curling into a sneer. "Still no taste for a soldier's work, Liaden?"

The unkempt head rose, bright eyes gleaming. "I see I have not made myself plain." He lay the whetstone by, and held the knife carelessly in one hand.

"The last time we spoke I was graceless," he said eventually in High Liaden. "I neglected to give you my name and rank. Nor did I request yours." He slid from the crate to the floor, blade still negligent in a frail hand.

"Shall we play the game out?" the Yxtrang demanded in Trade. "Though if you imagine that puny knife is enough to—" He hesitated because the little Liaden had moved silently out of his line of sight.

"Play the game out?" That soft, womanish voice, so compelling, unforgettable, once heard . . . The scout came back into sight. He brought the knife up, as if considering its ultimate merit, and brought it flashing down, suddenly held very business-like, indeed.

The Yxtrang stiffened, anticipating the pain as the blade sliced between his left arm and side, neatly parting the ropes.

"I am currently attached to the local defense force," the scout said in conversational Trade, as he moved south relative to the position of the Yxtrang's head. "A military necessity, as I am sure you understand. My name is Val Con yos'Phelium, Clan Korval, and I hold the rank of Scout Commander."

The knife flashed again, parting the ankle ropes. The scout nodded and jumped back to the top of his crate, folding his legs neatly under him.

"You are?" he asked in quiet Terran.

The Yxtrang lay unmoving, considering the knife, the scout's smallness, his own reach and the distance that lay between them.

"Your name and rank, sir?" The Liaden persisted, this time in Trade.

Cautiously he moved his legs, flexed arm and chest muscles against the loose bindings.

The scout sighed. "Conversation consists of dialog," he remarked in High Liaden and tipped his head to the left. "The request in your own language seems unnecessarily abrupt, though perhaps I judge it wrongly." He straightened.

"Name, rank, and troop!"

The Yxtrang snorted and sat up, putting his eyes on a level with the Liaden's. "Your accent stinks like a charnel-house."

"As well it might," the scout said calmly. "I meet very few people native to the tongue who are willing to converse with me. Your name and rank? No?" He reached behind and hauled a battered pack onto his lap.

"I find here that you are attached to the 14th Conquest Corps."

He said nothing and after a moment the scout worked the pack's fastening and rooted about inside, head and shoulders all but vanishing. He emerged eventually, held out the bulky Security-issue blade, and cocked an eyebrow.

"The 14th Conquest Corps equips troops shabbily, don't you think?" He waved it away, thinking of his own knife, that rode in his boot-top, that they had never taken from him, that had an edge to cut hullplate and—

"A knife is a knife, after all," the scout insisted. "I admit this one has seen ill days, but a few minutes' work will put it right. And it is surely of a size more fitting to yourself, Explorer, than to me." A moment passed . . . two.

"Take the damn thing!" the Liaden shouted in Troop tongue and thrust the knife forward.

Hounded, he took it, stared at it, and lay it down beside him. He should unsheathe it, he knew, and use the dull blade to skewer or to bludgeon the scout. It was his duty to report back to the Troop, to—

The scout was offering the whetstone.

"Your blade," he said, "needs care, Explorer."

"I am not an explorer!" That came out a proper roar, lancing his head with pain.

The little scout didn't flinch. "No? And yet I first found you behaving in a very scout-like manner, piloting a single-ship and making very curious studies. Surely you were an explorer then, at least?"

"No longer." The snarl startled stars across his back-eyes, and he winced, unsoldierly.

"You have been given medical attention," the scout murmured, "though it was predicted that your head would ache for a time after you woke."

"Medical attention? Why?" He leaned forward, shouting into the small, bland face. "Scout, are you mad? I am Yxtrang! You are Liaden! We are enemies, do you recall it? We are made to hunt and kill you!" He sat back, away from the face that neither flinched nor crumbled in terror.

"Occasionally," he continued, more quietly, "you kill us. But it is not done that you hit your enemy over the head with a rock and then call the medic to repair his wound."

"I did not hit you over the head with a rock, Explorer—"

"I am not an explorer! *Look* at me! Captured! *Captured like a cow for slaughter*! Twice to fall alive into Liaden hands! I am a failure, a weakness, and a shame! Rightly I am Nelirikk No-Troop!"

"Catch!" The command was Troop tongue. His hand flashed out—and he discovered he held the whetstone.

"What shall I do, Scout Commander?" he inquired with heavy sarcasm, "sharpen this blade so you may cut my throat? Or should I cut my own? That—"

"Would be a waste of talent," interrupted the scout. "I have contempt for the 14th Conquest Corps, who put their insignia on such equipment as they give you—explorer, no-troop or common soldier!" He hurled the pack off his lap. Nelirikk caught it as it struck his chest.

"A canteen with worn filters, a knife so dull it's more bludgeon than blade—yes, you still have the one in your boot, and I see you cared for it—out-of-date ration packs, half-nibbled by mice; a fire-starter in danger of burning out on next use—"

"Surely, Commander," Nelirikk said with sudden weariness, "you know how it is to equip the expendables?"

There was a small silence. "Are explorers expendable, then?" the scout asked softly. "Are they so little valued that they might be sent out all but weaponless to chase bears in our park, with never a thought to the waste, should the bear prove superior today?"

"Explorers are not. No-Troops are."

"Ah." The scout sat quiet for a moment, as did Nelirikk, who wished he might lay back down and go to sleep against the pounding misery in his head.

"Here," the scout said abruptly; "this is also yours."

He opened his eyes and stared at the rifle in dawning horror.

"You're not going to let me go!"

"Take the rifle," the scout commanded. "It's heavy!"

He grabbed and sat holding the thing in one hand while he stared at the Liaden.

"I would not advise attempting to fire it," the little man said conversationally. "I am not certain if the firing mechanism or the chamber will go first. If the pin goes, of course, you are simply disappointed when you pull the trigger. But if the chamber blows, Explorer, I suspect you will be either blind or dead."

"Scout," he said, very carefully, "you are aware that I can smash you to jelly with this rifle, whether it is in condition to fire or not?"

"Certainly. But, before you do, there is another defect I would like to point out." The scout came to his feet upon the packing crate, and there was a sudden crystal gleam in his left hand, a flash and a pressure on the rifle—which had abruptly lost four inches of barrel.

Nelirikk looked at the severed segment, and then at the crystal knife in the scout's hand.

"I note this further defect," he said. "It is one I might not have discovered until it could not be remedied."

The scout nodded, crystal blade vanishing as he resumed his seat. "Precisely. Like the canteen, if you had come across bad water."

He snorted. "I am not going to drink bad water, Scout."

"No. You'll not die of bad water."

"What will I die of?" Nelirikk looked directly at his tiny enemy. "Answer me, Scout Commander—will you give me the honor of a firing squad? It is more than a no-troop deserves."

"Yes," said the scout softly. "I know."

There was another silence, then the scout spoke again. "But what befell you? Explorer to no-troop . . ."

"What befell me? *You* befell me! What else should happen to a soldier who survived the dishonor of capture?" Nelirikk rubbed the back of his neck, trying to finger away the worst of the headache.

"Security recommended execution. But the Command supposed I might yet have knowledge useful to the Troop, coward though I am." He looked back at the scout, sitting so attentive atop his crate.

"Ten dutiless Cycles, of eating after the *soldiers* had their fill, of speaking when spoken to, of being the loser's prize in games of skill between the captains! Ten cycles of scut-work and kicks and being banned from the piloting chambers—because you befell me! You should have cut my throat ten Cycles ago, Liaden. Be a soldier and do it now."

The scout was staring at him, wonder on his smooth-skinned face. "You *reported*," he breathed, so softly he might have been speaking to himself, except the words were Yxtrang, as was the shout that followed: "Gods damn you for a fool, man! Whatever prompted you to *report* it?"

Nelirikk stiffened. "What else should a soldier do?"

"Who am I to know what a soldier will do? But an explorer will use his brain and look first to his duty."

"You," Nelirikk suggested, with wide irony, "did not report."

"And be planet-bound for years, while my head was drained of every nuance of our encounter, and my abilities languished? I was trained as an explorer and discoverer of worlds—to do less than that work was to fail in my duty to my teachers."

The anger hit all at once—he saw it reflected in a sudden widening of the scout's bright eyes. The waste of it! The years of shame might never have been! He might have advanced the Troop to a dozen new worlds. He might have—

He took a breath and brought the scout back into focus, noting with something akin to approval the soldierly way in which the Liaden sat his post, eyes wary and hands ready—much good it might do him against Nelirikk's bulk and strength.

"You have endangered your teachers and your people," he said, "by failing to report. How if they settle that world we found together, while some of the Troop do the same?"

"My report indicated that I had identified at least one example of a potentially sapient race," the scout said; "and recommended the planet be studied again in a generation."

"You know that planet, Scout! There were no more sapient . . ." Nelirikk choked suddenly as the phrasing overtook him; gasped, "Me?"

"You," said the scout calmly. "I never considered but that you would do the same."

"Then that is the difference between us," Nelirikk said heavily. "For I only thought to do my duty, and report everything to the Troop." He looked up. "Kill me, Scout Commander."

The scout shook his head and the wild brown hair fell into his eyes. "As to that," he said. "I must speak with my captain and receive further orders." He unfolded his legs and dropped to the floor, soundless and graceful as a squirrel, passing just beyond Nelirikk's reach on his way to the door.

"Care for your blade, do," he said as he touched the button set into the door. "I will speak with my captain and return."

The door opened and the scout slipped through, leaving Nelirikk alone with his weapons.

THE DOOR ROLLED CLOSED behind him, amber overhead glowing bright.

"Sealed," said the guard, and voices broke all around him, sudden and bewildering as a hailstorm.

In Liaden: Erob and tel'Vosti.

In Terran: Jason.

Variously:

"Well, what'd he say?"

"Is the information useful?"

"Are they going to attack through the park?"

"Well done, well done, excellent!"

"Shall we dispose of it now?"

Val Con gulped air, got his mental feet under him with wrenching effort and ran the Rainbow. He sorted the crowd and found Miri, silent and serious by the monitor, touched the song of her within his head and smiled into her eyes before glaring at the noisy rest and waving a hand for silence.

It came instantly, and he breathed a sigh of relief.

"The project requires time," he said in Trade, to avoid having to say it again. "Circumstances exist." He glanced over Erob's head to the towering Aus.

"Commander Carmody, have you plans regarding the upkeep of your prisoner?"

Jason laughed. "Upkeep? That's two steps ahead of me, son—I just thought you might get something useful out of him!"

"So I may," Val Con said. "However, he has not been well-cared-for by his troop of late. If I might—"

"Hell, bet he's hungry as a freeze-toad at ice-out! Boy that size's gotta eat as much as I do. Here . . ." He slapped a leg pocket; pulled out four ration-packs and tossed them over. After a moment, he unsnapped his canteen and held it out. "Best believe *these* filters are good."

Val Con bowed and heard Erob catch her breath, no doubt scandalized that one of Korval should acknowledge so deep a debt to a mere Terran. "My thanks, Commander. Shall I need to obtain your permission regarding any steps I might find it necessary—"

Jase waved a hand. "Do what needs done. You're a scout, ain't you?"

"Indeed," said Val Con softly; "I am a scout." He turned to Erob, amused to find tel'Vosti's arm firmly through his delm's, fingers curled unobtrusively around her wrist.

"Erob." He gave her full measure in the bow, made the sign of an equal requesting favor with his unladen hand.

"I see you, Korval."

"This prisoner was taken upon your lands. He is housed within your prison and lives at your pleasure. In recognition of these things, I request that I be allowed to deal with him—with this person Nelirikk—as my melant'i and the necessities of Korval dictate." He straightened and looked her full in the face. "On Jelaza Kazone."

Breath hissed out of her and tel'Vosti's fingers tightened about her wrist. "I require a fuller accounting of Korval's necessities," she said, as was her right in this.

Val Con bowed again. "I have former acquaintance with this Nelirikk. We met many years ago, when he was explorer and I scout captain. At that time, I dealt—inadequately—with him, and now wish to honorably correct an error in judgment."

"Honor? With that?" She flicked a glance at the monitor, which showed Nelirikk seated upon his makeshift cot, stoically sharpening the larger knife. "It is an animal, Korval."

Val Con sighed. "Erob, he is a man."

"And you would attempt Balance with it." She stared at him, at Jason, back at the Yxtrang. "So you feed it and allow it to sharpen its weapon. You think yourself able to take it, I assume. Mad your line and house may be, but I never heard that you were suicides."

He bowed ironically. "I am to take this as your agreement to uphold my necessities regarding this man?"

She was quiet a time longer, staring at the monitor until tel'Vosti shifted at her side. Her permission, when it came, was resigned. "Deal as you must, Korval. You will, in any case."

"My thanks, Erob. Korval is in your debt."

He turned back toward the door, rations and canteen in hand; saw Miri lounging by the monitor. "Hey, Cory," she said in Benish, which only they two among those assembled spoke. "You have a minute to talk?"

"Certainly." He grinned at her. "As many as you like."

"Good." She nodded, keeping to Benish. "Your intentions with this soldier are? I see no worry, here." She touched a finger to her temple. "Tell me the plan."

"Yes. This man is a treasure, cha'trez. It is imperative that we do not waste him."

"Hmm. But he talks like he thinks he's got no worth—talks like maybe he'll cut his own throat."

Val Con stiffened. "Miri. How do you know what he said?"

She jabbed a finger at the monitor. "Heard him."

"Yes," he said carefully. "But when he said those things, he was speaking Yxtrang."

"Yx—" Her eyes widened, finger rising once more to touch her temple. "You speak Yxtrang," she said, very carefully. "I don't speak Yxtrang."

"Not," he agreed with matching care, "so far as I know."

"Shit." She lapsed back into Terran. "Tell you what, boss: we gotta figure this thing out before somebody gets killed."

He flicked a glance at the monitor.

"Yeah, yeah. Necessity and all that. What's the backup? You want me in there, too?"

He heard the flat note of fear in her voice and in the internal song and reached to touch her cheek, scandalized old women be damned. "I may need to call upon you, cha'trez, my Captain. But at this moment, if you permit, Nelirikk and I have certain philosophies to discuss." He smiled and lay his finger lightly on her lips. "It will be well, Miri."

"You keep *saying* that," she complained, around the concern he felt almost as his own. "Just don't get yourself killed, OK?"

"OK," he said. The door cycled open and he stepped back into prison.

PUTTING THE KNIFE right soothed—and gave him time to think, to measure his weaknesses and his strengths.

The rifle . . . Nelirikk nearly spat.

Given a decent kit it could be restored; but he lacked the kit. He might also construct a small bomb from the components that still functioned, if he had time. He doubted the scout would be gone for more time than was required for the knife, and there was certainly someone monitoring the small scanner in the ceiling-corner.

A bomb, therefore, would be useless both as a surprise and as a vehicle for escape, given the solid masonry all about.

The knife-edge was superb now, for the stone was of excellent quality. These were the sorts of things one looted for on a Liaden world: the little things that worked better or were more elegant.

It was odd that beings which the Command taught were merely vermin should have the way of making such fine things, Nelirikk thought suddenly. Similar objects, made by Yxtrang hands, tended to be serviceable, but uninspired.

And an enemy had freely given this stone, that he might bring his blade to an honorable edge!

An edge that could now easily pass entirely through something as thin and fragile as the scout.

Alas, throwing such a bulky blade would be inexact at best, and it was folly to suppose the scout could thus be taken by surprise. Worse, the scout carried a personal weapon that sliced gun-steel like cheese. What it might do to flesh and bone—

He thought about that.

It might be possible to goad the Scout Commander into using the crystal blade. It might be possible, after all, to die a hero's death, with no Yxtrang ever knowing that Nelirikk No-Troop had failed yet again, that—

There was anger.

Nelirikk explored it, for anger sullies thinking.

When he thought of the scout, there was anger, distant and indistinct, as if a cloudy remnant of those years of intensely focused pain hung between them, obscuring what might be truth.

When he thought of the rifle—

His heartbeat spiked, and he very nearly brought the blade to his own throat as the shame of being given a useless weapon broke across him.

Stupid. As always. With an effort, he calmed his thoughts and considered the blade and the scout anew.

What did he know of Liadens, in truth? That they were people—sentient and self-aware—must be clear to the dullest of the Troop, no matter the Command's teachings. As *people*, then, following custom and system of their own devising . . . Was it conceivable that Liadens practiced some alien honor? Was it possible that this one left his enemy specifically alone, granting him honorable opportunity? The knife was very sharp: three rapid motions would solve many problems.

Nelirikk hefted the blade; sheathed it with a sigh. After a moment, he drew his grace blade from its snug boot top and used the whetstone on it.

Tending the blade was soothing. Perhaps the scout found it so, as well.

"I SEE YOU, EXPLORER."

Nelirikk looked up from his task, eyes narrow on the bag the little man carried.

"I see you, Scout."

Val Con nodded and resumed his former perch, settling the bag firmly in his lap. The Loop was disturbingly before his mind's eye, elucidating a 27 percent likelihood of an immediate attack, and an even more disturbing refusal to project an ultimate Chance of Mission Success or Chance of Personal Survival.

Light glinted from the blade Nelirikk was sharpening—a fine thing, as like the larger blade as a screwdriver was to the Clutch knife he wore in his sleeve.

He rummaged in the bag and tossed a food pack lightly toward the Yxtrang, who snatched it and the next comfortably out of the air, and sat holding them in his hand.

"Food?"

"Food," Val Con agreed. "Commander Carmody believes a soldier should be permitted to eat."

Cautiously, Nelirikk bent and returned his knife to its boot-sheath, expression unreadable behind the tattoos.

"Do eat," urged Val Con. "I suspect they may be better than the rations you were issued."

Nelirikk frowned at the Terran-lettered labels.

"You would eat this?"

Val Con laughed.

"It is not nearly as delicious as the rabbit one snares oneself, I admit. But the mercenaries buy their own food—surely they would not poison themselves. Most certainly not Commander Carmody, who gives this from his own day-kit."

He used his duty blade to open a ration pack while the Yxtrang sat watching.

"Shall we trade?" Val Con murmured, triggering the tiny heating element. "Are you concerned for the quality?"

Almost, it seemed that Nelirikk might laugh. He pointed toward Val Con's food.

"The explorer," he said, hesitantly, "is unfamiliar with local custom."

"Local custom is that hungry persons may eat. If you dislike what you have, you may have some of mine. There is water here, too, if you'll share the canteen. Or use your own, if you trust the filters."

"Eat," the Yxtrang repeated quietly. He opened the silver packet, discovered the tray and tray mechanism quickly, triggered it, stared again at the label.

"What food is this?"

Val Con glanced at the bright lettering. "Prime salmon. Excellent—though I hope you will not find it necessary for me to share it."

Nelirikk looked up sharply, wariness clearly visible through the facial decorations.

"No?"

Val Con laughed. "The food is good. But on my last mission the God of Quartermasters saw fit to supply my captain and myself with a year's rations of salmon and crackers—and nothing else!"

The Yxtrang sampled the fish carefully. In a moment he was eating with gusto.

"TELL ME MY DEATH, Scout Commander."

They had finished eating and the small man had passed over the canteen. Together, they had gathered the remains of the food and put them in a recycle box, and now they looked at each other.

"How shall I die?" Nelirikk repeated, the Yxtrang words bittersweet in his mouth.

"I do not know," said the scout quietly, also in Yxtrang. "The orders I have are simply to do what must, of necessity and honor, be done."

"Honor?" The word seemed to hang overlong between them— he had not meant it as a challenge, in truth, but what could a captive-holding troop know of honor?

The Liaden shook his head; shifted on his seat.

"My curiosity and arrogance seem to have caused you much pain. I had never meant for a fellow seeker-of-worlds to suffer— certainly never as you have suffered. So, I seek to balance the evil I brought upon you."

Nelirikk stared, trying to grapple this concept into sense. The scout spoke of *personal* responsibility—*personal* retribution, personal action. The oddness of it made his abused head throb.

"Balance." He tasted the word for connotation—for implication.

He looked at the Liaden, sitting so solemn atop his crate, seeing no trace of humor, or malice, or deceit, or any attitude of attack. No attitude of defense.

Yet—questions of honor with *Liadens*? Those worthless enemies who had no respect, who—treated a man like a soldier, when the Troop had thrown him away.

"Balance," he said once more, and contrived a stiff, seated bow.

"Your ship, Scout Commander."

The green eyes were cutting sharp upon him. "Yes."

"The reason I am here," said Nelirikk, slowly, "is that during the strike on the landing field I showed your ship to the forward controller. A no-troop may not speak unless spoken to—" Nelirikk thought a moment of anger and glanced at the blade, which sat idle as he spoke equitably to an enemy.

"Despite the regulation, I gave warning that your ship was dangerous—that I had seen its like before. I told them to take it out—"

The Liaden had stiffened, face intent.

Nelirikk leaned an elbow on a knee, meeting those sharp eyes with puzzlement and some sadness.

"There is your balance, Scout. Freedom for freedom. For over-stepping—for causing a general to seem a fool—I was sent to explore boundaries and map the importance of your ship's defense."

"It seems a balance for generals and units," the scout commented.

"Yes," agreed the Yxtrang. Then, thoughtfully: "Was there a junior officer onboard? Did you lose troops from this?"

"No, thank you. The ship—I could not return in the ferocity of the attack. The ship defended by—reaction."

"I saw it return fire to orbit," Nelirikk said, "but was told that it did not."

The Liaden nodded.

"Fired upon from orbit, it would return fire to orbit. The beam would be weaker, but enough to singe, I warrant."

"So." The Yxtrang's grin was savage. "Seven drop-jets and a strike on the battleship, at least. Your ship did you well, Scout Commander." He paused. "It was a ship to behold."

The Liaden acknowledged this with a sketched salute, smiling wanly.

"Did proper duty," agreed Val Con. "As you did. As I've done." He looked up sharply, waving a thin hand for emphasis.

"Does it strike you as a wasteful—even artificial—equation, Nelirikk Explorer, that doing proper duty tends to result in destruction?"

The question jolted—the more so because he had asked it of himself, as a thinking person must, while he had been explorer, and while he had been no-troop. His answer came a heartbeat later than it should have.

"The Troop survives! The Command survives!"

The Liaden moved his shoulders, expressive of some emotion Nelirikk could not name.

"Very true. Faceless and interchangeable, Command survives. I tell you that I, Val Con yos'Phelium, know about duty. Duty says you and I must fight, eh?" He brushed hair out of his face. "Duty demands that I attempt to kill the closest peer I've met in several Standards. Duty demands blood all too often—in this time, what does it demand of you, Nelirikk?"

It was hard, that answer, but it was in him, blood and bone. Any soldier would have answered the same.

"Duty demands that I call fire on your brave ship, Scout. It demands that I kill you, given the opportunity."

"And then?" the Liaden insisted, *pushing* with mere words! "What demands, after I die?"

"That I escape, back to my unit to—"

"To report and be shot!" shouted the scout.

Nelirikk bent his head in the Liaden way. "I might instead be used as a target for knife practice."

The Liaden looked a bit wild-eyed.

"Do you wish to fight?" he demanded.

"Scout, I must!" Nelirikk looked to the blade.

"Is it true," asked the scout, very calmly, "that two men of equal rank might fight for the higher position?"

"Yes," Nelirikk agreed, wondering at this change in topic.

"And that then, the winner commands the loser?"

"With the concurrence of the next above in the troopline, yes."

"Ah." The Liaden slid abruptly down from his perch, head tipped up to stare into Nelirikk's face.

"I propose," he said, "a contest." He turned his back, walked to one end of the room and back, eyes brilliant. "I propose that we fight—for duty's sake. We will fight as equals—scout to explorer. If you should win, I will take your orders. If I win, I will sponsor you to my captain for admittance to the troop—pledged to me and my line."

Nelirikk sat speechless, staring at the manic little man, who grinned at his stupefaction. Fight a Liaden for troop position? Treat scout equal to explorer? Who would enforce a win? The difficulties. . .

"*Are* you mad?" he asked slowly. "How could you hope to win such a contest? I'm strong, fast, and weapon-wise—"

"Mad?" The scout's grin grew wider. "It is madness to waste resources. It is madness to give in to the faceless. I will represent you—Nelirikk Explorer—to my captain—should I win. I swear it by Tree and Dragon! If you win—"

"If I win, Scout, you will likely be dead!"

The little man came forward, stopping just within Nelirikk's reach, face and eyes gone child-solemn. "Would you really waste so valuable a resource?"

Nelirikk stared, put his hand on the troop blade—and took it away again.

"I hope I do not waste resources," he said. "But where will you find a neutral here to serve as referee? How could we break?"

The scout waved a hand airily. "Technicality," he said. "Mere technicality. Do you agree in principle? If so, we will be able to devise details."

Nelirikk sighed, then slowly stood.

"It is better to do something than nothing. I know that you won't feed an enemy forever." He bowed, stiffly, but with good intent. "For duty and for balance. May you be strong for the Troop."

The Liaden returned the bow with fluid grace, then brought his fist to his shoulder in a proper salute.

"As you say," he agreed, and climbed back atop his crate. "Let us now consider technicalities."

❊ ❊ ❊

TOGETHER, they pushed the storage crates in front of the door. On them went: a rifle, a pack, a long-knife, boots, another pair of boots, several more knives—including one sheathed in fine black suede, the handle of which gleamed like polished obsidian.

They stood, toe-to-toe and barefoot, scout and explorer.

The Yxtrang looked down on his toy-like opponent, a line from a camp-song echoing briefly in his head:

A soldier's opponent is more than might—
Little Jela was a demon to fight. . .

For clarity they went over the agreement, first the Liaden and then the Yxtrang, each speaking in the other's language to be sure there was no difficulty in translation.

"Thus shall it be," came the Liaden words from the Yxtrang: "should I prevail in this contest, I shall pursue my duty as I see it, you subordinate. Should the win be yours, I shall pledge myself and my services to you and your line until released."

"The win," said the Liaden in Troop tongue, "goes to the first able to count three on a vulnerable opponent; the loser yielding at once."

They backed away, then, each looking the room over, perhaps measuring the luck of this or that corner, or seeking an advantage of light, or filling their mind with a last living vision, each already distant from the world.

THE TIMER ON Val Con's watch beeped.

He moved forward slowly, accepting both the necessity for motion—from the L'apeleka stance, *Desiring Difficult Desires*—and the need for caution.

From the other side of the large room came the Yxtrang. The face behind the tattoos had gone distant: intention hidden deep within the eyes while the huge body came forward gently, gracefully, inevitably. Val Con noticed that the Yxtrang's feet, like his hands, seemed disproportionately delicate.

L'apeleka demanded the right elbow forward now; the Yxtrang answered by crouching a shade lower. Val Con pulled the arm in, saw his opponent's shoulder rise in proper reaction.

They were beginning the dance with caution: both testing responses or lack of, until at once they were in and close, arms in motion, knives the honest threat. Could-be threats were of this, that, or the other throw or kick, a punch hidden behind the placement of elbow or flick of wrist.

Nelirikk feinted, saw the feint ignored, the threat parried before execution.

Val Con's Loop evaluated the situation: a clear 43 percent Chance of Mission Success.

The Loop flicked away, lost in the sudden hugeness of the explorer, looming above, knife held so—

Val Con ducked, twisted—heard the hum of blade passing over—close to his ear, saw the big man recover a trifle slowly, used the heartbeat to barely touch an ankle with the blade—

And was past and behind, where he needed to be, but the foot placement warned him and he whirled away just ahead of the kick, Nelirikk grimacing with the effort it cost him to keep balanced.

The wall was barely an arm's length from Val Con, forcing him to dart in close again. He found the move in L'apeleka: *The Blizzard Swirls.*

Hands, arms, legs, knees, feet blurred with the sequence—he got a kick in on a solid thigh, a knifeless punch high on a shoulder— and tried to dance away—too late!

The answering blow caught his shoulder, he spun with it, tumbled, whipped around to find the Yxtrang in full charge, leapt, kicked solidly at the face—and caught the ear as the other's knife slashed his tough combat leather leggings.

Disengage.

The room was silent but for their breathing, and they backed away, each searching for signs of damage. The Yxtrang's ankle had a small spot of blood; his ear was dark red. Val Con felt a slight sting; shrugged it out of consciousness—damage to his right leg was minor—no more than a scratch.

Nelirikk adjusted his belt with a quick hand.

Val Con tried to move in; was held off by the other's long reach.

He moved left; found himself faced. Right—and again the move was there, checking him, boxing him, trying—

Nelirikk was trying to get him into a corner, arms low and spread.

Val Con feinted right, feinted left, went straight in for half-a-step, then dove for the right arm, blade nipping out as he tucked—rolled—and felt the force of the blow on the floor behind him, gained his feet and whirled in time to see the Yxtrang's blade bounce, once.

He was too slow: the knife was recovered.

Both were sweating now; the floor was slick with it and with dripped blood, making a slip or misstep all too likely.

As if by common consent they moved downroom to a drier patch of floor. It seemed neither wished to be on the right side of uncertain footing.

CMS flashed behind Val Con's eyes: 41 percent.

He grimaced, and the Yxtrang started moving in, perhaps taking it as a sign of despair.

Val Con drew back as if to throw the blade; Nelirikk glided casually away, adjusting his belt as he came back again, hands protecting face but leaving shoulders and thighs vulnerable. Val Con glanced at the unbladed hand—empty.

Three seconds! How many times had they already threatened each other with—

Val Con tried again to close; was fended away. Nelirikk lunged, Val Con twisted, avoided, skidded on dampness—snatched a moment to recover his balance.

A moment was too long—a heavy arm swung out, slamming him off his feet and into the wall. He bounced, rolled and came up, knife in hand, shoulder aching, but unbroken. There was blood on the floor from his leg.

This time he feinted a slip as the Yxtrang closed; wrapped himself around that massive knife arm and punched his blade into the upper shoulder.

Nelirikk grunted, shook—and Val Con was airborne again, flung loose like a hound from a bear. He came up and around as his opponent tossed his knife to the undamaged left hand and charged.

Val Con gave ground, saw the trap—

Nelirikk slipped on a smear of blood—and Val Con raced by, elbow lifting to fend off the descending blade—which was sharp, gods; a proper soldier's knife, fit for slashing leather, flesh, bone . . . The blood was quick. Hot.

CMS flashed; he ignored it. What did the Loop know about necessity?

He slipped.

The Yxtrang nearly fell on top of him: he scrambled away in time to avoid the lunge, jumped to his feet, wiped the blood off his arm, saw the depth of the cut, shuddered—and moved in.

Move in. Move in. Move in. He needed to be inside that long reach if he had to kill the Yxtrang, if neither would yield—

He ducked back, avoiding a fist. Saw the curiously graceful hand move toward belt and check as he feinted in.

So he charged. Straight at the huge man, blade ready to slice or cut and—

He skidded, lost his knife, slid behind the Yxtrang, who snatched—and Val Con's good hand flashed out, snagged the ring of metal on his opponent's belt, and yanked.

Nelirikk saw the scout's knife on the floor, bent, grabbed—

But Val Con had it now: a thin strand of cutting wire as long as his arm. He hugged the giant's leg, pulled the wire loop hard— twisted, half-avoiding the hammer-blow of a huge fist—and hung on, *hung on* to the wire cord while oceans roared inside his ears and his vision went gray, ebbing toward black and Miri was there, terror sheeting her face, her hands overlaying his own on the wire . . .

The explorer went down. Val Con hung on grimly; clawed back to sense, pulled his knife to him with his bloody leg.

"One, two, three . . ." he gasped—let go the wire and came to his feet, as he must, knife in hand.

The Yxtrang lay half-sprawled on his side, knife held at throat-level, eyes distant. He sat up slowly, knife still high, eyes on Val Con's face. With his free hand he fingered the bloody loop around his legs, mouth tight.

Val Con stood back warily, wondering if he could dodge a thrown knife, or avoid a sudden desperate lunge.

Nelirikk explored the place where the wire lodged in his right leg. A spasm of pain crossed his face, eloquent despite the tattoos. Carefully, he turned the knife in his hand, holding it by the blade as if to throw, weighing its balance—

Then held it farther out, toward Val Con.

"I neglected to ask," he said in neutral Trade, "what language I should use when speaking to your captain."

Val Con sighed, slid his knife away, and accepted the offering. He cleaned it carefully against the sleeve of his fighting leathers, inspected it, and found its edge undamaged. He extended a hand to the Yxtrang, who hesitated before using the assistance to stand.

"You have accepted a brave challenge, Explorer," Val Con said in Yxtrang. "I must have the rest of the pledge before I may present you to my captain."

The big man half-lifted a fist to salute, caught the gesture, and made a ragged bow. "As you say." He paused a moment, either to recruit his resources or to puzzle out the most proper phrasing.

"I, Nelirikk . . . *I*, Nelirikk Explorer, pledge myself on Jela's honor to the person and line of Val Con yos'Phelium. My blood is yours, now and until my death. May your orders bring glory to us all."

Val Con bowed and held the heavy knife out across both palms.

"Your blade, Nelirikk Explorer. Wear it and use it as required, by my consent. The Tree and Dragon is now your shield also: I trust you will bring honor to us all."

Nelirikk took the blade in wonder.

"Can you walk?" Val Con asked him.

"If required, my leader."

Val Con shook his head. "Scout is sufficient for now, I believe. Do you rest while I go to bring my captain."

MIRI WHIRLED from the monitor as he came through the hatch, slamming her gun home with one hand and unclipping her belt-kit with the other. Behind her was Jason—and behind him were tel'Vosti and Erob.

"It is done." Val Con said. "Miri, you will need to—"

"Hold him, Jase."

Val Con stiffened; heard as if it had only now begun the song that was Miri within him—heard the terror and the beginning of the metamorphosis into anger. He sighed and leaned back into Jason's bulk, muscles shivering with reaction.

Miri slashed the ruined sleeve to expose the knife wound, sprayed it with antiseptic; reached for a pain bulb—

"No! Miri, you must talk to—"

She looked at him straight, gray eyes wild, and wiped the sweat from his face with an antiseptic cloth.

"You're mostly OK." Half question, half accusation.

"Yes. Some pain, some wounds that will heal, but—"

"What in hell were you trying to pull?" she yelled, terror abruptly sublimated into rage. "Next time you want yourself dead, try a step off a hundred meter cliff! Whatever gave you—"

She bent over the arm, still yelling, slipped for a moment into an argot that made even Jason cringe and slammed back into Terran for, "Jase—gimme a double staple patch outta your kit."

"Miri," Val Con said.

She swabbed his face again—hard; leaving the bitter taste of antiseptic in his mouth.

"Miri?"

"You ain't answered me, soldier! I wanna know where you got permission to pull such a damn fool stunt!"

"Necessity. Miri, please. It is done."

"Done is it?" she snorted, and knelt to get at his leg. "You look it."

"Attend me!" Val Con insisted, voice rising. He heard a faint pop as a sweat bubble broke in his ear.

She came up fast, eyes blazing. "Don't you lose your temper at me, you scruffy midget!"

For one searing moment, Val Con thought she might actually strike him, so exalted was her fury. Apparently Jason thought so, too, for he dropped his grip and stepped back.

Miri took a deep breath, hurled her free hand into the air and leaned close.

"So tell me, *partner*," she said, so sarcastically Jason retreated another step; "what's the plan? Huh? What'm I supposed to do now? What's the new gag? Yours all the way—so tell me about it."

The sarcasm hurt; his arm hurt and every other bit of him, too. Ridiculously, he regretted the warm solidity of Jason to lean against, and took a breath, pitching his voice for neutrality.

"Miri, my Captain, I request that you also give aid to the man inside this room, who is waiting to see if you will accept him as a recruit."

Her fear flared and his own anger melted. He reached to touch her cheek, which caress she allowed, shoulders losing some of the tension fury had lent.

"I said that I would sponsor him to you," he murmured. "Do me the honor of at least speaking with him before he bleeds to death."

She stared at him, anger and terror evaporating into wonder. "You want me to accept an *Yxtrang* as a recruit in a Terran-Liaden unit?"

"If the captain judges it wise," he said carefully.

She considered him out of wary gray eyes. "And if the captain thinks it's the worst idea she's heard since she left Surebleak?"

"That is the captain's right," he acknowledged. "But you will still wish to speak to this Nelirikk and show him some care, cha'trez."

"Why should I care a plugged bit what happens to him?"

"He is pledged to serve us, Line yos'Phelium," he explained. "There are—obligations. Such as seeing that one's servant has proper medical attention and does not needlessly suffer."

She flung hand out toward the sealed hatch. "We *own* that?"

"Certainly not," said Val Con. "One cannot own a sentient being."

"Right." She closed her eyes. "Other people," she said, apparently to the room at large, "give their wives flowers."

She spun on her heel, eyes snapping open. "Open the door," she told the door-corporal and glanced back at Val Con and Jason. "The two of you got me into this; the two of you can tag along."

※   ※   ※

NELIRIKK STOOD, awaiting the return of the scout. He dared not sit on one of the crates, for fear his wounded legs would fail when it came time to rise to the captain's honor. He had made scant effort to clean himself, for it was no disgrace, that a captain might see a soldier fresh from soldier's duty.

There had been a voice raised in the outerways; a murmured answer that must be the scout—and the raised voice once more, swearing, as he'd monitored from time to time from Terran ships.

If the raised voice were the captain, it would seem to register displeasure with the performance. It suddenly occurred to Nelirikk to wonder just how persuasive was the scout, and he worried somewhat, and shifted on his aching legs—

The door cycled open, admitting a procession.

The scout led, limping, with field dressings on arm and leg. Immediately behind was a Terran male who filled the doorway with his bulk—a full-sized soldier, dressed for war, yet looking like some scraggly farm-peasant, long-haired and bearded, without tattoos of rank or maturity-mark. Still, he moved with assurance; with command: A proper captain!

Behind came a tiny red-haired figment—an apprentice soldier, doubtless brought early from the creche in the emergency of the invasion—carrying what appeared to be a medical kit.

The scout paused, swept a bow and nearly slipped on the slick floor. The larger man turned his head to snap a command at the soldier in the doorway: "Get a mop and cleaners!"

"My Captain," the scout began, and Nelirikk turned his face more fully to the bearded man, thinking that it would not be so bad, to serve a captain at least of proper size . . .

"My Captain," the scout repeated, and bowed profoundly, head near touching his knees, as the figment continued forward, thumping the equipment she carried onto a nearby crate, striding past the big man and the small one, to stand wide legged directly before Nelirikk, matchstick arms folded across scant chest.

"Well?" she snapped, and Nelirikk's mouth opened in response to the command-voice before his mind recalled that it was not yet his place to speak. The scout it was that answered, properly—and most gently.

"Captain, this is the man I propose to add to the unit. Nelirikk Explorer, he is called; a thoughtful fighter and—"

The captain shifted; frowned. "Introduce me."

"Yes, Captain." The scout bowed obedience; Nelirikk brought himself to stiff attention, striving to ignore his injuries and the persistent buzzing in his ears, the while his mind raced to encompass a captain who was smaller even than the scout and—

"Explorer, attend! Here is Captain Miri Robertson, commanding Action Unit 1, Lytaxin Combined Forces! Captain, I bring you Recruit Candidate Nelirikk Explorer."

Nelirikk stared straight ahead, as proper, while the tiny creature unfolded her arms and walked almost casually around him, inspecting. From the corner of an eye, Nelirikk saw the large man grin, then go soldier-faced as the captain completed her circuit.

"Is this the man who was carrying that stupid rifle?" she demanded of the scout.

Nelirikk kept his countenance. The question was reasonable, after all; and the part of his sponsor to explain.

"Yes, Captain."

"Hmmmph." She walked behind him once more. "What in the hell is this?"

"I took it from his—"

"Can he talk?" snapped the captain.

"Yes, Captain." The scout effaced himself and the large man grinned into his beard.

"Explorer," the captain demanded his attention. "This thing you're tangled in. What is it?"

Nelirikk stared straight ahead, concentrating on the proper formation of the Terran words. "Captain. A Shibjela. If the captain pleases."

The scout stirred within Nelirikk's vision, eyes gone intent.

"Translate that," ordered the command-voice and the scout bit his lip.

"I . . . In Trade: Jela's Neck-jewel. Jela's Necklace, in High

Liaden . . ." He paused, thumb rubbing over fingertips, as if he felt the texture of nuance and sense. "In Terran . . . perhaps Jela's Noose. Or—"

"Got it," the captain interrupted. She resumed her cross-armed stance directly in Nelirikk's line of sight. "Explorer. Do all Yxtrang carry one of these?"

Excellent! The captain thought quickly and to the point!

"No, Captain. My—the unit where I take my training pays homage to one of the original members. All who train there carry Shibjela. Other units have—"

"Other toys," she finished for him and barely turned her head.

"Jase."

"Captain Redhead?" The bearded man did not bow, though his expression showed clear respect.

"Got one of your toys?"

The big man grinned, stepped forward and produced an oddly shaped piece of wood. It was perhaps a club, though it looked frail for such work; slightly edged, highly polished. Nelirikk's hand itched for it, to test balance and theory.

"Ever seen one of these?" the captain asked, walking to his left.

"No, Captain," he said, noting that the captain appeared to possess several names.

"Good. So we have some secret weapons, too." She was behind him again.

"This hurt?" she asked, and he felt a sear of pain where she touched him above the bleeding leg wound.

"Yes, Captain," he said, neutrally.

"Ought to. Looks pretty ugly. Can you fight?"

"Yes, Captain." He hesitated. "Now?"

"No!" She was before him again, head tipped back so he could see a grim face no larger than the palm of his hand, dominated by a pair of fierce gray eyes. "I mean—can you fight well? Ain't no slackers in my unit, you understand? My soldiers fight!"

"I can fight, Captain. I have many years of training. I use the autorifle, the—"

"Skip the sales pitch. How many languages you speak?"

"Yes, Captain," said Nelirikk, wondering—and then recalling that this was the captain who attached a scout to her command. "Languages: Yxtrang, Liaden, Trade, Terran, and Rishkak."

"Fine. You know how to take orders?"

"Yes, Captain."

"If I tell you to charge head on against armor and all you got is a rifle, will you?"

"Yes. Captain."

The gray eyes considered him blandly. "You really think you can take orders from somebody like me?"

He hesitated fractionally, began the proper answer—was cut off by a sharp wave of a child-like hand.

"You tell me what you think, Explorer. The truth, accazi?"

"Yes, Captain. It—occurs to the explorer that the captain is—very small."

Incredibly, she laughed. "Yeah? Well, it occurs to the captain that you're out of reason tall. If you can't take orders from me, I'll just hand you over to Commander Carmody and let him sort you out. I didn't go asking for another scout in this unit. Seems to me one's all the trouble I need." She blinked thoughtfully. "Might be easiest just to let you loose."

Nelirikk gulped. "Captain—"

"Dammit, Redhead!" Commander Carmody yelled, drowning every other sound in the room. "You can't do that! The stuff he knows? Why, darlin', the man's *beautiful*! We can't just be throwing him back in with some bunch o'rowdies who don't even keep the mice from the larder!"

"Great," she said expressionlessly. "You want him?"

"Now, now, my small, you know he's best off with you. Seems him and the scout there understand each other fine."

"That's what scares me," said the captain, with a noticeable lack of fear in either posture or face. She sighed and turned back to Nelirikk.

"All right, Beautiful, you had time to think it over. Which is it, me or Commander Carmody?"

He looked at the scout, who returned his gaze blandly; at Commander Carmody, who shrugged and put his hands behind his back; at the captain herself.

"The scout sponsors me to his captain, who has the wisdom to value the—resource of an explorer. I pledge to obey the captain's orders, if she will accept me into her troop."

"Hmmph. You know anything about first aid?"

"Yes, Captain."

"Good. Help Commander Carmody patch you up."

"Yes, Captain."

The bearded man came forward, med-box tucked under one arm. The captain went to the crate that had been the scout's seat and hoisted herself up.

"Explorer, you're gonna cause me lots of problems, you know that?"

"I had not considered, Captain. I—"

"Consider it! You got 'til this first aid stuff is done and then I want you to tell me what problems I might have with you and because of you—and how to fix them. Think hard, accazi?"

"Yes, Captain." Commander Carmody had set the box aside and was on one knee behind him. Nelirikk felt him touch the Shibjela and pick up the ring-end.

"All right, now, boyo. I expect this'll sting a mite." His understanding of Terran was perhaps flawed, for the quick jerk that pulled the cord from its nesting-place excited an agony as exquisite as it was, mercifully, brief. He bit his lip, soundless, and concentrated on remaining upright.

There was a slight hiss, a coldness, and then a numbness on the wound, followed by the sound of his uniform leg parting. Resolutely, Nelirikk turned his thoughts to the problem his captain had assigned.

"CAPTAIN. Study indicates that each small problem generated by recruiting an explorer to your troop comes from a single, large problem."

The captain turned her attention from the Scout, with whom

she had been conversing in a language Nelirikk didn't know, and frowned.

"That so?" she asked, but the question was apparently rhetorical, as she commanded immediately: "Elucidate this larger problem—and its solution."

"Captain." He brought fist to newly bandaged shoulder in salute before he recollected such a gesture might well give insult.

"The large problem is that the explorer is Yxtrang and the troop you command is not. The solution . . ." Embarrassing it was to have to give such an answer. Embarrassing and hardly indicative of any value he might bring to her troop. Nelirikk kept his face soldierly. "Captain, I conclude that there is no solution. Biology is fact."

"Biology," she corrected, "is *a* fact." She came to her feet, there on the packing crate, and crooked a finger. "Come here."

He moved forward two steps and stopped as he sensed the scout's increased tension.

"I said," the captain snapped, "come *here*."

"Yes, Captain." One eye wary on the scout, he came forward until his toes touched the crate she stood on. Even with that added height, he looked down on her and had a moment to consider the thick coil of hair wrapped tight 'round her head before she tipped her face up to him.

"What's all this stuff?" she demanded, tracing lines across her cheeks with a forefinger.

"Captain. *Vingtai*—marks of rank and . . . accomplishment. Done with a needle, to be permanent."

"Right. What's yours say?"

Nelirikk blinked, dared to flick a look at the scout and was answered by the quirk of a mobile eyebrow.

"Captain," he said respectfully, returning his gaze to her. "On the right—insignia of born-to Troop. The name is perhaps Jela's Guard Corps. In Terran I do not—"

She waved a hand. "Close enough. What about the left?"

"Captain. The left cheek marks me explorer. The double lines there show me—show me no-troop. These others . . . creche mark, apprentice troop, honors of marksmanship and piloting. This . . ."

His hand rose and he ran his fingers lightly down the right cheek, feeling the old scar, nearly hidden by the layers of tattoo.

"This is *nchaka*," he said slowly. "When a soldier is done training and has his own weapons given, Sergeant of Arsenal bloods the grace-blade, to show the edge is sharp." He hesitated; glanced at the scout. "Point of information. If the captain pleases."

She waved a hand. "Go."

The word seemed to connote permission, rather than an order to leave, though literal translation—Nelirikk sighed. "Yes, Captain. History tells that *vingtai* were used by the first soldiers because it gave fear to Liadens."

"Gave fear?" The frown cleared. "Right. If it stops 'em for a second and lets you get the first strike in, it's worth the effort. I guess."

She glanced over to Commander Carmody.

"Need us a medtech, on the bounce."

"All yours, darlin'," the big man said cheerfully and strode over to the door, shouting orders into the room beyond for someone or something called "Chen."

"Tech'll be able to hack an erase program for the tattoos," the captain was telling the scout; "probably do a skin-tone, too. What about the hair? And—" She turned. "Can you grow a beard, Beautiful?"

Nelirikk stiffened. A beard? Did she think him a farmer? A merchant? A—Terran commander? Very nearly he let go another sigh. "Captain, it is that a soldier does not have a beard. It is part of discipline."

"Hmph. So, if you just ignored discipline for a couple days, would you start to grow a beard? Or are you like this one here?" She pointed at the scout, who lifted a brow, but remained silent.

"If discipline were ignored," Nelirikk said stiffly, "the explorer would begin to sprout hair on his face. With the captain's permission, it would then be very hard to read the *vingtai*."

"Not a worry," she assured him; "we're gonna get rid of all that facial decoration first off." She turned back to the scout, leaving Nelirikk gasping mentally. "How 'bout hair and beard? Anything we can do there?"

"Perhaps hormones and a shot of accelerant," the scout said

softly. "He should spend the night in the 'doc in any case." He made a slight bow, slanting his eyes upward. "If the captain pleases."

"Big joke, huh? Just wait 'til—"

"Captain." Nelirikk had found his voice at last. She turned toward him.

"Yes."

"Captain, will you remove—" his hand went to his cheek, traced the familiar swirl of his Home Troop, touched the *nchaka*.

She frowned. "You said you wanted to soldier in my unit, didn't you?"

Nelirikk gulped. "Yes, Captain."

"And you said you wear those things to give fear to Liadens, right?"

"Yes, Captain."

"Well, my troop ain't giving fear to Liadens. My troop is aiming to give fear to Yxtrang, you got that?"

He stared, wrenched his mind toward thinking about Yxtrang as the enemy—and touched his maturity-mark once more.

"I understand, Captain."

She shifted on the crate and caught his eyes in a glance so fey he found he could not break it.

"You gonna be able to run this gag, Beautiful?" Her voice was comradely, though the Terran words confused.

As if she sensed his confusion, she asked again, in High Liaden: "Are you able to nurture the children of your actions, Nelirikk Explorer?"

He bowed. "I am held by my word to an—honorable opponent. It is understood that the troop failed in honor and sent me to find my death. I strive to do better for the children of my actions."

"Right." She was back in Terran. "When were you supposed to be picked up?"

"In six days, local midnight."

"OK, give the scout your ID, we'll take care of that detail. In the meantime, your orders are to cooperate with Chen, heal up, eat and rest. Have to spend a day or two in here, I think—" she glanced at the scout, who nodded thoughtfully.

"We'll get you a computer and a tech to show you the basics. The scout'll work up an outline for you to follow. *Information*, OK? And in your spare time, you can brush up on your Terran. Can't have you mistaking an order in the heat of things." She jumped down from the crate and stared up at him, a long way. "Questions?"

His head spun; he was suddenly as weary as if he had been fighting for days and sleep seemed very sweet. "No, Cap—" he began, then: "Yes, Captain. What will be my position in the troop?" Did they mean to keep him here in this cage, inputting data until he ran dry? Something in him refused to believe it of the scout, while all his life's accumulated experience clamored that it was the only rational use they might put him to.

"Position in the troop, is it?" She frowned. "You will be the captain's personal aide. You will report directly to the captain." Her eyes gleamed. "That OK by you?"

The captain's personal aide? Nelirikk blinked and looked to the scout, but was unable to read anything in that smooth face but a weariness as profound as his own.

"That is OK by me," he said, and tried not to see Commander Carmody's grin. "Thank you, Captain."

"Don't thank me yet," she said grimly and Commander Carmody laughed.

She turned away, the scout attentive at her elbow, then checked and turned back.

"'Nother thing." She pointed at the Liaden. "You gave him an oath, swearing to protect him and his line, right?"

Nelirikk grabbed after his wavering attention. "Yes, Captain."

"Yes, Captain," she repeated and sighed. "You ask him what that *means*? You ask him if he's got triplets, or an aged father?"

Liaden clan structure was a complex social architecture. Nelirikk had studied it, as one studies everything available regarding an enemy, but had no confidence that his understanding approached actuality. He tried to keep the dismay he felt from reaching his face.

"No, Captain."

She sighed again. "Gonna learn the hard way, ain't you?

Anything short of a direct order, if a Liaden asks you to do something, *get details*, accazi?"

"Yes, Captain."

"Fine. Now, the details you didn't get in this case include the fact that the scout and me are lifemates." She came a step forward, peering up into his face. "You savvy lifemates, Beautiful?"

"I—am not certain, Captain."

"Get certain. The broad outline is that him and me are one person. If I go down, the scout speaks with my voice. If the scout goes down—"

Something of his dawning distress must have shown after all, because she grinned and nodded her head.

"Tricky, right? Gotta watch him every minute." She glanced at the doorway, which was cycling open to admit a team of two, pulling a gurney, which supported a whole-body med-box, or autodoc, according to Terran. Nelirikk looked at the captain doubtfully: such things were reserved for generals. . .

"That's Chen," the captain said. "Gonna get cracking on those cuts and erase the tattoos, all according to orders." She paused, tapped her cheek where his carried the *nchaka*.

"You don't worry about this one—man's scars are his own—but the tattoos make you look like an Yxtrang, when what you are is an Irregular. Can't have you gettin' shot by our side when Commander Carmody thinks you're so valuable, right, Jase?"

"Right you are, Captain Redhead! I think he'll look charming in a mustache, Chen."

"Do our best," the tech said easily as he approached Nelirikk with a hand-reader. "All right, son, roll up the sleeve, and let's see what you're made of."

Sighing, Nelirikk obeyed, and when he looked around again, he was alone with the techs.

LUFKIT:
Epling Street

❖ ❖

THE DAY WAS FINE, the sun high, the air bright and bracing. Sheather filled his lungs appreciatively as he moved down the soft strip of *concrete* toward the living-place of Angela Lizardi, Senior Commander Retired, Lunatic Unit Inactive.

The T'carais, his brother Edger, did not accompany him on this mission. They had reasoned that two of the Clutch, walking together in an area where non-humans were not often found, would excite comment among the local population. Worse, the novelty of the sighting would doubtless sharpen memories. Dull remembrance was in the best interest of Clutch and human-kin, should one such as Herbert Alan Costello, the Juntavas buyer of secrets, find this place and begin his askings.

So did Sheather come alone to Angela Lizardi's home-place, bearing a message from T'carais to Elder and another, which was to be said to Miri Robertson and Val Con yos'Phelium, should the Elder deem it fitting that Sheather see and speak with those valued persons.

The numbers on the door-fronts counted this way: 352, 354,

356. The door that adorned the number named 358 was heavier than those other doors adorning other digits. This door was hewn of wood, not formed of plastic. This door was scarred and gnarled, beaten by weather. It stood before him with the aloof impartiality of an Elder, minding such duty as was its own, and which was far beyond the ken of a mere Seventh Shell.

Halted by the door, Sheather stood, great eyes dreaming on the scarred wood, accepting the awful dignity of the barrier. After a time, when it seemed right to do so, he lifted his hand and pressed a finger very gently against the glowing white button set in the portal's frame.

Beyond the scarred elder wood, music chimed, high and brief. Sheather waited.

After a while, it seemed right to press the button once more. Again, the music sounded.

The day was noticeably less bright when Sheather assayed the button for the third time. Music sounded, distant behind the door. Closer to hand, another music spoke.

"The lady gone away."

Carefully, for he was well aware of the fragility of even full-grown humans, Sheather turned. Carefully, he looked down.

A human eggling stood by his knee, face uptilted like a flower, brown eyes opened wide.

Humans thought Clutch big-voiced. Sheather made what effort he could, to shape his voice smaller.

"I am looking for Angela Lizardi, pretty eggling. Do you say she has left her home-place?"

The petal-pink skin rumpled as feathery brown eyebrows contracted.

"Lizzie-lady gone," she stated emphatically. "Momma say. I like Lizzie-lady."

"Your regard does you honor," Sheather said solemnly. "Do you know when Lizzie-lady left this place?"

The face puckered again, eyes misting in thought. Sheather stood respectfully, awaiting the outcome of thought.

"Dilly!" That voice was older, sharper. Sheather took his

attention from the eggling and discovered a woman bearing down upon him, the child, and the door.

Straight to the eggling rushed the woman, bending to snatch her hand, then snapping upright with such force the child was jerked an inch or two off the soft concrete.

"How many times do I have to tell you not to talk to strangers?" the woman asked the child, her irritation and anger plain to Sheather's ears.

"The eggling did me a service," he said. The woman's eyes flicked to him and she went back a step, taking the child with her. "I am in possession of a message for Angela Lizardi and the eggling tells me she is away from home. Might you know the day upon which she is expected to return?"

The woman blinked, jerking the child close to her side. "Liz left sudden a couple days ago. Sent me a note to keep an eye on the place. We used to watch each other's places, back when I first come onto this street. Liz traveled more back then. Where she went this time or when she's coming back . . ." The woman shook her head, backing away another step. "She didn't say. None of my business. All she asked was to keep an eye on the place."

"I understand," Sheather stated, remembering to moderate his voice. "It is not my intention to call you from your duty. I am . . . sorry . . . not to have met Angela Lizardi at home. Perhaps I shall find her at home another day."

The woman frowned, thrusting the eggling as far behind her as possible while still maintaining a firm grip on her hand. "If I was you and I wanted to get a message to Liz, I'd go to Soldier's Hall and leave word there. Chances are she'll have given them someplace to find her."

"Thank you," said Sheather, inclining his head. "Your suggestion has merit."

"Glad I could help," the woman said and abruptly spun, snatched the eggling into her arms and dashed hastily down the walk.

Sheather paused to review his actions, but could identify nothing in his conversation or stance that might have suggested danger to the woman. Still, he conceded, where the safety of an eggling was the stake, it behooved an adult to be seven-times prudent.

Soldier's Hall, now. He felt he understood the location of that building, on the other side of the city. He would first go to his brother Edger and report these happenings outside the home-place of Angela Lizardi. Most especially would he report the Elder Door and the wise eggling. And then the two of them might walk out into the coolth of Lufkit's evening and seek Soldier's Hall together.

EROB'S HOLD:
Practice Grounds

❀ ❀

NELIRIKK EMERGED from the luxury of the autodoc healed, well-feeling and clean-faced, but for the *nchaka* and a startling bristle of silky brown hair sprouting between nose and mouth. The hair of his head had likewise sprouted from the soldier's crop he had worked so hard to maintain to a softly curling mop fully four fingers long.

As he scraped the stubble from his chin with the razor General Stores had provided, along with leather clothing such as he had seen others wearing, he studied this new face in the mirror.

The eyes—dark blue, surrounded by short, thick lashes—were as always, startling in the naked expanse of his face. The *nchaka*—that was comfort, though it was barely more than a beige thread in the unrelieved brown of exposed flesh. The beard, the self-same beard that had plagued his face for all of twenty-five Cycles, was a comfort. By the time he finished shaving, he thought he might recognize himself, were he to come upon a reflection unaware.

One Winston—a soldier old in war, as Nelirikk read him—arrived as he was finishing the breakfast that had been brought to

161

him and for an hour it was drill—signals, emblems, insignia and call signs—until the old soldier announced himself satisfied.

"That's fine. You keep that hard to mind, now, hear me? Hate to have to shoot you 'cause you missed a call."

Mindful of his status as recruit, Nelirikk saluted as he had been shown. "Sir. I will not shame your teaching."

Winston laughed and waved a hand, already moving toward the door. "Hell, I ain't no 'sir,' boy. Just stay alive and keep Cap'n Redhead the same, and you done me all the honor I could want."

The door opened and Winston was gone; it stayed open to admit a technician and the scout. The technician pushed a gurney bearing a computer. The scout had a loop of cable over one shoulder.

"Explorer, I find you well?"

Nelirikk bowed, hand over heart, as he had seen the scout give to their captain, and answered in Terran, as he had been addressed.

"Scout, I am more well than I have been in many Cycles."

The little man nodded as the tech pushed the gurney against the wall, locked the wheels down and pulled out the keyboard.

"The med tech tells us that you were sadly undernourished. He took the liberty of injecting vitamins and supplemental nutrients." He smiled. "We are charged with 'feeding you up,' which directive I hope you see fit to take as an order."

He moved to the gurney. The tech took the cable, deftly made her connections and left with a nod to them both, uncoiling the cable as she went.

The door stayed open after she exited.

Nelirikk looked to the scout, but the scout was at the computer, touching the on-switch, nodding as the screen came live.

"I have constructed a program," he murmured, "as the captain directed. Attend me, if you please."

Nelirikk came forward and stood at the scout's right hand, marveling again at the other's seeming frailty. Yet he had fought like a soldier, winning through to his goal despite the logic that said he was too small to prevail.

One thin hand moved on the keypad. The screen flashed and Terran words formed.

"You will be given a question. Two consecutive returns signals an end to your answer. Should a point require clarification, you will be prompted. When all is made clear, you will be given another question." He looked up, green eyes bright.

"Questions and prompts are in Terran, to aid you in perfecting your grasp of that tongue. Should it be required, a touch of the query key, here, will bring up a rendering of the same question in Trade."

"I understand," Nelirikk said, around the chill in his belly. The man beside him tipped his head.

"Shall you honor your oath, Nelirikk Explorer?" he asked, of a sudden in the Liaden High Tongue. "Or is it that you believe I shall not honor mine?"

Nelirikk took a breath. "Scout, it will take many days to empty me entirely, no matter how clever your program."

"So it would," the scout said in brisk Terran. "However, the captain cannot spare you from your duty for many days. You are required to report to her at evening arms practice. In the meantime, this is your duty and I will leave you to it. After you have given me your recall code."

Nelirikk stood for a moment, then forced himself to move over to the place where his pack lay beside the shameful rifle. He had sworn, he reminded himself, as he reached inside and removed the recall beacon. He had sworn, and the Troop had sent him to die, which was the least of the Troop's sins against him.

Yet, it was as hard as anything he had done in his life, to pull the beacon out and lay it in the fragile hand of a man of the race of the enemy.

The scout received the beacon with a bow, green eyes solemn.

"Battle-duty, Explorer. I do not ask you to forgive it. I only say that I would not require it of you, for less than the lives which must be preserved."

The understanding of an arms-mate, from one who was no soldier? Nelirikk felt something in him ease, and he nodded in the Terran manner.

"I hear you. It is no shame, that a soldier fight as a soldier must."

He drew a breath. "You will wish to know the place," he said, and rummaged in the pack once more for the captured map.

"Here," he said, unfolding it on the floor between them. The scout knelt down to see where his finger pointed, studied the area and nodded—nodded again as Nelirikk recited the procedure for sounding the recall.

"I shall contrive," he said, rising lightly to his meager height. "And now I shall leave you to your duty, and attend mine. I advise you—as a comrade—be on time to the captain."

A bow without flourish and he vanished through the open doorway. Nelirikk cinched the pack, picked up the useless rifle and walked over to that tempting portal. The small stone room beyond was empty, though there was doubtless a sentry outside the door in the right-hand wall. Still, a blow from the rifle would settle a sentry and gain him a working firearm.

The rifle was heavy in his hand. He had sworn, by Jela. And the Troop had sent him uselessly to die.

Nelirikk walked back inside the larger room, lay the rifle next to the pack and carried a packing crate over to the computer. He sat down, adjusted the height of keyboard and screen, read the first question, and began to type.

"OK," Miri told her troops. "Dismissed. Arms drill in an hour."

The vets she'd inherited—a couple 'falks, like Winston, who'd asked for the patrol, and a handful of others who had been separated from their units by the invasion—swung on out toward the mess tent like they'd just had a nap instead of a twenty mile hike. The greenies mooched out considerably slower, a couple walking like their feet hurt. Which, Miri conceded, they probably did.

In point of fact, her own back hurt from the unaccustomed weight of a full equipment pack, rifle and comm. But she stood tall until the last of the Irregulars was out of sight before sighing and reaching for the straps.

"Tired, cha'trez?" His voice was in her ear, his hands taking the weight of the pack as she eased it down.

"Tell you what it is," she said, as his hands settled on her shoulders, "I got soft."

"Ah," Val Con replied, comprehensively. His fingers were kneading gently, finding and smoothing the knots in her muscles, apparently by instinct. Miri sighed and bent her head forward. He rubbed the back of her neck.

"Gods, that's good. Don't get carried away, though. I wanna be alert when I introduce your pet Yxtrang to his unit."

"*Our* pet Yxtrang," he corrected, softly. She felt him shift balance, and then shivered with pleasure as he ran his tongue around the edge of her ear.

"Watch that stuff. I'm an officer."

"So am I." He nipped her earlobe lightly, hands pressing her waist.

Miri sighed, savoring the sensation a second longer, then slowly straightened. Val Con released her immediately, though she seemed to feel a moment of wistful lust, echoing and enforcing her own feelings, just before she turned to face him.

"Got more ways than a kitten, don'cha?" She smiled, reached out to touch his cheek, tracing the line of the scar.

"If the captain pleases."

"Big joke," she said mournfully, shaking her head. "Now, I think the new addition to the family is just as respectful as he oughta be. Do you good to watch how he carries on."

"I assure you, I intend to watch how he carries on very carefully, indeed."

She cocked her head. "Hey, you were the guy took his oath and sponsored him into the Irregulars. *Now* you got second thoughts?"

"Say rather that I do not dice with my lady's life. Nelirikk undertakes no easy thing here. To completely cut himself off from his people, his culture, his language? Worse, to give an oath of service and go to live among the enemy, the most of whom see him as an object to be vilified, hated, and feared?" He shook his head.

"Wishing only to honor his oath, yet he may fail of it."

Miri stared at him. "So you figure he'll crack quick?"

"I figure," Val Con said, taking her hand and beginning to walk slowly in the direction of the mess tent, "that the luck has favored us, in that Nelirikk has been so badly used by his people. I take him for a man who possesses a strong and innate sense of Balance, else he would never have allowed himself to be persuaded to that oath. If we are clever, and give him what he starves for—work, discipline, and respect—we may yet preserve him."

Miri chewed on that awhile as they continued their meander across the grass. "How come you're so interested in this guy? I know you said you owe him, but there's something more than that, ain't there?"

There was a small silence. "This *Jela* whom Nelirikk swears by—he of the neck-jewel?"

She nodded.

"One of the founders of Clan Korval was Cantra yos'Phelium's partner, a man named Jela, who had been a soldier. It is Jela's Tree that our clan watches over, in fulfillment of an oath he had from Cantra to keep it safe, should he fall. My study of Korval's Diaries inclines me to believe that Nelirikk's Jela is that identical soldier."

"Oh."

Diaries from a time before Terra had space. A soldier in the family who happened to have the same name as some Yxtrang war-leader. A tree which was paid the courtesy of a bow and a promise to recall it to its parent. Miri sighed to herself.

He believes every word of it, Robertson. Look at the man's pattern. He might be crazy, but he ain't lying.

"So what's that make you?" she asked, as they approached the mess tent. "Cousins?"

He smiled and squeezed her hand lightly. "More like students of the same master."

She let him see her sigh this time. "OK," she said. "We'll give the man his shot."

"Thank you, cha'trez," Val Con murmured, dropping her hand and allowing her to preceed him into the tent. "And remember, I will be watching."

THE VETS ARRIVED on the field first, took their places and composed themselves to wait for the newbies to straggle in and sort themselves into lines.

A tall figure strode smartly across the field, straight up to where Miri stood near the situation board, Val Con at her back.

"Reporting for duty, Captain." Nelirikk snapped a sharp salute, now he had the merc way of it. Not only that, he was on time—not late, not early. *On time.*

Bland-faced, she took his salute, then walked around him as she had the first time, with him nothing but blood, sweat, and nerves and looking as much like a street brawler as a soldier.

Today, leathers gleaming and boots glowing, he was clearly a soldier. His utility belt held its pouch and the knife he had used in the fight with Val Con, enclosed in a battered but well-oiled sheath. He stood at attention like he meant it, eyes front while she completed her leisurely circuit.

He was big, but totally lacking the exuberant massiveness that characterized Jase Carmody. Nelirikk, Miri thought, lived private. His eyes might give him away. Maybe.

Without the tattoos, his face was ordinary: two eyes, a nose, a mouth, and a decidedly square jaw. The rapid-grown hair was sandy brown and wavy. The mustache was a sandy brown brush over the thin unsmiling mouth.

Circuit done, she crossed her arms and looked up at him.

"Explorer. Is your kit complete?"

"If the captain pleases. I have not a sidearm."

"I see that. Anything else missing?"

"No, Captain."

"Enough ration-bars for your needs?"

"If the captain pleases. I am not informed of a mission. The kit and rations are more than adequate for general use."

Miri nodded. "Can you march in those boots today?"

"Yes, Captain."

"Could you march in them again tomorrow?"

"Yes, Captain."

What she did then was probably as stupid as anything Val Con'd done on behalf of this man, but she didn't question the right of it. A soldier who didn't have a sidearm was no soldier at all. Nelirikk, a pro, would know that, right down in his gut.

"Think you can work with the quartermaster?"

The tiniest flicker of surprise at the back of those careful blue eyes. "Yes, Captain."

"Good. After arms practice, you'll draw a sidearm and ammo."

"*Yes*, Captain."

"All right," Miri said, flicking a look over the field. The lines were formed now, soldiers at field rest. Time for class.

"Consider yourself on duty. And remember to draw extra protein and a second dessert at mess. Orders from the head med tech."

"Yes, Captain."

She marched forward, Nelirikk at her shoulder. Val Con took his usual place, a little off to the side of the main action, and stood there, bland-faced and perfectly calm. His pattern, when she looked at it, displayed some interesting tensions, but no real alarm. He was watching, like he'd said. Aware of the possibility of danger.

"All right, Irregulars," she called out over a field that was suddenly very quiet, indeed. "This is Beautiful. He's my aide and he'll be assisting in today's hand-to-hand drill. Squads count off by threes and—"

"That is an Yxtrang!"

Oh, hell, Miri thought, locating the miscreant. jin'Bardi. Of course it *would* be jin'Bardi. Man hadn't given her a minute's peace since he'd showed up at Erob's in the first wave of refugees from the city. Worst part was, when he put his mind to it, he could soldier.

"No chatter!" Reynolds, that was, a vet from Higdon's Howlers, and, like the rest of the vets, strawboss to a double-dozen newbies. jin'Bardi, predictably, ignored him.

"I say that thing is an Yxtrang, Captain! Do you deny it?"

Miri glared him down the field, which didn't do much good, jin'Bardi being a mean-tempered somebody, and answered, voice level and pitched to carry to the last soldiers on the field.

"I say this man is an Irregular, mister. Report for kitchen duty after arms practice." She looked out over the quiet field. "Count off."

"And I say no!" jin'Bardi left his place and ran toward her. She felt Val Con shift—stopped him with a shoulder-twitch.

"At ease, Beautiful."

"That is not a man!" jin'Bardi yelled, voice echoing over the field. "And if you think that it is, you are not fit to lead this unit!"

You damn fool, Miri thought at jin'Bardi. The vets exchanged glances among themselves, and Winston took the lead.

"Now, see, among us real mercs, there's a tradition, kinda, where if somebody don't like the way the captain's leading, they can go hand-to-hand and whoever wins, their opinion wins, too. I ain't especially advising you to try that against Cap'n Redhead. What I'm advising for you is to take the fifty years kitchen patrol you just earned, and get back in line so's we can drill."

He paused and looked around the field, his gaze crossing Miri's for an instant. One eyelid flicked in a wink.

"I ain't got no problem with Beautiful joining up. Fact, I'm glad to have him. Can always tell a real soldier by the way he keeps himself, and shows proper respect to command."

The tension was easing out of the field—or it would have if jin'Bardi hadn't chosen that particular moment to sing out, loud and clear: "Fine, then! I challenge the captain here and now to hand-to-hand combat."

Miri sighed wearily, sensing rather than seeing Val Con drifting in from the sidelines. Beautiful stood at her back, at ease like she'd told him. She hoped.

"jin'Bardi, you got a deathwish?"

"Afraid to fight me, Captain?"

"In your dreams." Damn the man. Nothing for it, now. "Troops!" she shouted across the field. "Form a circle."

She unbuckled her belt and handed it to Beautiful, who slung it over his right shoulder, which, by a fascinating coincidence placed her sidearm in position for a reasonably quick draw. He folded her battle-jacket carefully and placed it between his feet.

jin'Bardi stripped off his belt and jacket and looked around, but nobody was offering to hold them. He dumped the jacket onto the ground, belt on top.

The circle had formed to include Beautiful. Winston was on one side of him, Miri noticed. Reynolds was on the other. Val Con was on the far side of the circle, not quite directly opposite Beautiful. She hoped he had sense enough not to interfere with this one. There really wasn't any need for him to be concerned. She could take jin'Bardi hand-to-hand. The problem was going to be remembering not to kill him.

In the center of the circle, she turned to face jin'Bardi.

"Beautiful!" she called out. "Give the mark."

"Mark in three, Captain. One Captain. Two Captain. Three."

jin'Bardi came in fast, like she'd known he would, trying to startle her into a stumble. She sidestepped, got a foot around his ankle and a hand under his elbow and let him do most of the work of flipping himself onto his back.

He hit hard, but came up in a quick snarl of motion, and was heading back, low this time, and it wasn't until he was right on her that she saw the telltale gleam.

She twisted and at least he knew better than to lead with the knife. She countered with a move Val Con had taught her, dancing away, feinting in with a kick, tempting the knife.

And jin'Bardi, the idiot, took the bait.

It was quick, then. She slapped the knife away and gave him a ride over her shoulder, slamming him flat. The air went out of him with an audible *whoosh* and while he was seeing stars, she spun, grabbed the knife, and spun back, pinning his arms with her knees, and put the edge under his ear until she saw the first drop of blood and real fear in jin'Bardi's eyes.

"Give me one reason why I shouldn't cut your stupid throat!"

He stared up at her, and it was terror, now, and she kept the knife snug, wanting to be sure he was going to remember today's lesson for the rest of his life. No matter how short it was.

"If the captain pleases." The recruit's voice was near and respectful.

Now what? "Permission to speak."

"Thank you, Captain. This fighter shows potential of becoming a skilled soldier, with training."

Mithras, give me strength.

"You offering to take him on, Beautiful? Whip him into shape?"

"If the captain pleases. For the good of the troop."

jin'Bardi's eyes were showing a lot of white. His face was an interesting sort of greenish-gold color and wet with sweat. Miri leaned close, talking real quiet.

"I'm going to move the knife, jin'Bardi, and then I'm going to stand up and back away three paces. Then you're going to stand up and present yourself to Beautiful. Vary, and you're meat. Are we clear?"

"Clear, Captain," he managed, sounding pretty hoarse. He swallowed. "I yield," he added. High Liaden.

"You bet," she returned in Terran, and took the knife away.

She rose, backed away and stood holding the knife while he climbed painfully to his feet and walked over to where the big man stood between Winston and Reynolds, his face impassive.

jin'Bardi was shaking and he must've been hurting, but give him credit, he walked right up to Nelirikk and saluted.

Nelirikk didn't move. "It is proper discipline to thank the captain for a valuable lesson."

There was a moment of utter stillness from jin'Bardi. The circle waited. In her head, Val Con's pattern was cold, watchful, and stringently calm.

Slowly, jin'Bardi turned and bowed. "Thank you, Captain, for a valuable lesson."

"No problem," she said and looked up at Beautiful. "Take this guy to the medics and have them check him out, then report back here. Give my stuff to Winston."

"Yes, Captain." A salute. Her belt and jacket changed hands and Beautiful moved back from the circle. jin'Bardi, shoulders slumping, began to follow, was stopped by a raised palm.

"It is proper discipline," Beautiful stated, remorselessly unemotional, "to take leave of the captain."

Once again, jin'Bardi turned, made the effort and straightened his shoulders, snapped a salute. "Captain."

She nodded. The two of them moved away and the circle began to come apart. Miri walked forward.

As he came even with the situation board, jin'Bardi abruptly spun. "I want my knife back!"

Nelirikk stopped. "If the captain pleases," he coached, "may I have my weapon."

Miri stopped, feeling the weight of the thing in her hand, and something tickling at the edge of her mind. The balance was good . . .

"You want this?" she snapped.

"Yes," jin'Bardi snapped back and that quick the knife reversed itself and she threw.

The knife tumbled in the air, traveling fast, much too fast for jin'Bardi to have time to move. The blade passed so close to his cheek it seemed to glide over the skin, then buried itself deep in the situation board, a lock of his hair pinned tight.

"Say 'thank you, Captain,'" Nelirikk directed into the absolute stillness that followed the knife's *thunk*, "'for returning my weapon.'"

jin'Bardi licked his lips. "Thank you, Captain," he said faintly, "for returning my weapon."

After a moment, Nelirikk reached over and pulled the knife from the board. He offered it, hilt first, to the shaking Liaden.

"Soldier, your weapon. Inspect it for damage as we walk to the medical center."

Around her, she started to hear buzzes as the Irregulars shook themselves back into normal mode. Miri turned, caught Val Con's eye and decided she'd worry about where she'd learned how to throw a knife like that later.

"All right!" she shouted, over the growing noise. "Squads count off by three for hand-to-hand drill! Double-time!"

LIAD:
Department of Interior
Command Headquarters

🏵 🏵

THE OPERATIVE commissioned to discover what nature of mishap had destroyed Tyl Von sig'Alda's ship, innocently in orbit about the busy world of Waymart, had filed her report.

Despite that this document directly contravened several apparently known facts, Commander of Agents readily accepted the operative's assertion that no such ship had been in orbit about Waymart during the span of days designated in the search grid, nor had such a ship exploded upon the day, hour, and nanosecond also named. The operative expressed herself quite certain of these things.

Commander of Agents ordered the operative to her immediate superior for deep questioning under the drug, but it was a formality. He believed her report, utterly. Oh, certainly, he had the raw data received from the hidden transmitter upon sig'Alda's ship, as well as his own excellent memory of event. Mere facts.

And facts, as any Agent knows well, are open to manipulation.

Seated behind his desk in the room of chronometers, Commander of Agents indulged in fantasy.

Tyl Von sig'Alda, the fairy tale went, had not departed the world of Vandar. Indeed, let it be that he had died there, during that brief period in which his ship had rested on world.

Val Con yos'Phelium, rogue Agent, having overpowered the man sent to return himself or his severed head to Headquarters, used the ship's key and lifted to orbit. There, he had not after all dawdled, but engaged himself in a fever of busyness, first seeking and then subverting the hidden beacon, the existence of which he would have easily deduced. That done, he had Jumped, but never, so Commander of Agents was willing to wager, for Waymart.

Or perhaps he had, as he was both subtle and intelligent.

In short, Commander of Agents concluded his fantasy, Val Con yos'Phelium could be anywhere in the galaxy, not excluding the hallway outside his Commander's door.

A peculiarly unnerving conceit, that.

It would all, of course, need to be checked.

With a feeling not unlike dread, Commander of Agents leaned forward and touched the switch that would summon his second to him.

A team of Agents, so he considered, in the few moments before that efficient person appeared. Certainly, a team of Agents to Vandar, to discover the whereabouts of Tyl Von sig'Alda, or the manner of his death. What else? How might they now discover a hint to Val Con yos'Phelium's thought, a clue that might point to his ultimate destination?

"You summoned me, Commander?" His second bowed and then stood silent.

Commander of Agents stirred, issued his orders regarding the team and the maximum priority mission they were to undertake. His second bowed. "There is something else?"

Where? Where might he go, whose clan, save one, was scattered to the Prime Points? What cause might move him more strongly? Balance? Or the safety of his kin? What reason might be read into random action? Which actions were deliberately random? Which only mimed chaos, with cold reason as the lodestone?

Where would he go, with all the galaxy to choose from?

"Dispatch a team to Jelaza Kazone," Commander of Agents said to his second. "I do not wish Anthora yos'Galan to depart her clanhouse just now. Contain her, first. If necessary, detain her."

His second bowed. It would be done.

"Also," Commander of Agents said, hearing himself with something akin to astonishment. "The raw data regarding the Terran female. Robertson. Have that sent to me here, Commander's Priority."

Again, his second bowed. "At once, Commander."

LIAD:
Jelaza Kazone

⊛ ⊛

IT WAS LATE when she closed the old book and returned it to its place among its fellows. That done, she stretched, hands high over her head, feet above the floor, chair tipped nearly horizontal. For the count of ten, she held the position, taut, every muscle straining. On eleven, she went abruptly limp, breath exploding outward in a "hah!" that echoed along the metal walls.

The chair snapped back to vertical and she laughed, using one hand to push the wild tumble of dark hair up out of her face. The other hand she held negligently downward, palm out, fingers curled in silent summons at the comb that had deserted its duty and now lay on the floor three feet beyond her languid grasp.

Thus summoned, the comb flew to her hand. She used it to anchor the hastily twisted knot of her hair, fingers lingering along the satiny wood. This was a precious object—carved by Daav yos'Phelium, Val Con's true-father, to adorn the hair of his own dear lady. It had come to Anthora on her halfling nameday, given by Val Con. Thus, the gift was thrice precious and it was the ornament she wore most often.

176

She stretched again, somewhat less heroically and accompanied by a yawn, then gently came erect. Youngest of the yos'Galans, she had inherited the full body of their Terran mother without the height necessary to satisfactorily complete the effect. Still, she was of Korval, and a pilot of the line, light on her feet and elegant in her bearing.

She turned now, spinning a graceful circle, and called aloud, "Lord Merlin? Come, sir. We walk and then we sleep."

Her voice came back from the metal walls, deep and nappy as velvet, with a ring that glittered off the edge of the ear and might, after all, have been the walls.

From somewhere down within the books came a "Mmerwef!" and the thump of something solid striking carpet. A moment later, a rather large gray cat sauntered 'round the edge of a shelf and looked up at her out of round golden eyes.

Anthora smiled and moved toward the door, the cat flowing along at her ankle. He waited patiently while she worked the pressure-latch and followed her into the paneled hallway, then waited again while she canceled the lighting and sealed the library tight.

Duty done, the cat and the woman walked down the hallway and out into the inner garden.

THE GARDEN was lit by star-shine—well enough for one who knew the way. Anthora walked slowly, savoring the night air, cool with the scent of growing things. Down and 'round the path she walked, til she came to the center, the heartplace, of the garden, and here she left the path, and moved across the moss to lay her hand against Jelaza Kazone, Jela's Fulfillment, known to the World as Korval's Tree.

"Good evening, Elder," she murmured, and felt her palm grow warm, where it lay against the bark. She breathed deeply of the cool, minty scent and leaned back, settling her shoulders comfortably. At her feet, in a vee made by two shallow roots, Merlin tucked himself, front feet under his chest, golden eyes slits of satisfaction.

In the minty dark, Anthora closed her eyes. Purposefully, she filled her lungs with the scented air, Jelaza Kazone warming her back through the house tunic she wore. Slowly, as if of their own volition, her hands rose, palms vulnerable to the stars.

Anthora opened her Inner Eyes across the dazzle of the galaxy and in nightly ritual, began to count.

There, the cool flame that was Nova, blurred by the veiling of hyperspace. And, there—Shan, warm as a hug. Through him, less Seen than extrapolated, Anthora found Priscilla. And there—there was Cousin Pat Rin, aloof, as ever.

It was a foolish ritual in its way, there being no aid she might send to those so distant, should she find them in distress. She lived in no little dread, who was considered the heedless one, of the night she might count one frail candle missing and nothing she could do to recover the flame.

Still, she persisted, taking comfort where it was offered—and so far tonight she had counted four—Nova, Shan, Priscilla, Pat Rin— safe, for now, and treasured.

So, onward. She took another deliberately deep breath and cast her mind out once more. Val Con . . . She found him, his flame brilliant as before the Wrongness, which Anthora now knew was named the Department of Interior, and at his shoulder a bonfire, which was Miri—his lifemate, whom Anthora had yet to embrace in a sister's welcome.

Well enough, six, and herself made seven. She brought her thought toward an easier goal, touched the children—Quin, Padi, Syl Vor, Mik and Shindi—and Great-aunt Kareen yos'Phelium, and Cousin Luken bel'Tarda, bright, all bright, in their safeplaces, then took deeper breath and flung her mind wider still.

She had first noted this one during her pregnancy with the twins. In that heightened state of power, it had been as plain to her as a comet on the horizon. Now, it was the glitter of a jeweled pinhead, sometimes sensed, sometimes seen, and sometimes lost entirely in the clamor of the worlds intervening. Tonight, she thought she would miss it, then caught a flash of its unique glitter, at the extreme edge of her ability to read.

There was no name to put to this tiny gem of flame, yet she

welcomed it as she welcomed the flames of her named and known kin and dreaded its loss as nearly.

So then, of adults, counted and known, nine. Of children, the full complement of five. Clan Korval, numbering precisely fourteen, from the eldest to the youngest. The warmth at her back grew briefly warmer and Anthora smiled as she lowered her hands.

Fifteen, of course. One did not discount the Tree.

But even with the Tree, it did seem few—very few, indeed. No skill that lay to her hand would reveal the number of those who hunted them—but she guessed them to be far in excess of—fifteen.

She opened her eyes and stepped away from the Tree, but without the spring of joy the counting of her kin most usually gave her. Instead, she bade the Tree good evening in a tone that was nearly somber, and went softly across the mossy carpet to the paved path, where she paused and glanced back.

"Lord Merlin?"

The cat opened his eyes, stood, stretched and sauntered to her, stropping once against her leg before preceding her down the path, to the house and bed.

EROB'S HOLD:
Practice Grounds

꙾꙾꙾꙾꙾꙾꙾꙾꙾꙾꙾꙾꙾꙾꙾꙾꙾꙾꙾꙾꙾꙾꙾꙾꙾

QUICKLY, he discovered the joy of having too much to do.

It was made quite clear that he was to be the captain's shadow and bodyguard, and to perhaps carry extra communication equipment if required. He was then a specialist attached to the captain by her order, outside the ordinary line of command.

There were times during the day when he was ordered to this place or that to return with a map or disk or perhaps a bottle of something, and there were times when he stood watch duty as was his right.

He knew, too, that he never stood watch alone—and that was understood as well.

At first, the scout was always within range, the Captain's Blade, as Nelirikk came to consider him, ready to slay any who might harm her. Gradually, the scout became less evident—was then missing entirely, sent here and there by the captain's word—or by the word of those others, of higher command.

He met with those others—Commander Carmody, who proved himself an astute and cunning officer, and an elderly Liaden who was made known to him as "General," a patriarch of the captain's clan—as well as seniors of mercenaries and house guard.

By Yxtrang standards they were woefully understaffed in the mid and low-level officers, but truth known, they were fighters and not functionaries.

They asked him fact and opinion, numbers and names, battle plans and supply schemes. He told straightforward, and after a short time he understood they were not threatening when they asked "What makes you think that?" or "Why would that be the case?"

In short, they treated him as he had not been treated since his days of exploration: as if he had a mind as well as eyes. He spent more time with the AI computer: its questions were wonderfully complex, and his respect for the scout grew wider.

When he was not with the captain or in mess, he found it difficult not to be doing things. He studied as well as he could, spending hours in serious contemplation of colors and their meanings. And, on the midnight that the scout and half-a-dozen veteran soldiers awaited what transport the Yxtrang should send to retrieve one they would rather had died, he began his dedication gift to the troop.

The command of the combined Terran and Liaden forces headquartered here now knew much of what he knew, Nelirikk thought, as he carefully plied needle and thread. They knew and in the process of laying all before them, he had discovered truth. And in truth, after so many Cycles of bitterness, he found a certain peace.

The 14th Conquest Corps had quite liberally interpreted the orders it had received. He'd heard the rumor—and since none feared a no-troop, whose word was nothing but sound—he'd heard it in numerous places.

The 14th Conquest Corps had determined to treat the target of a long-planned multi-Corps invasion as a Target of Opportunity. It was a bold move, born of the intelligence that the target world was in upheaval. It was a move that—if successful—would advance the 14th to leadership over the 15th and 16th after too dismal a turn as back-up and support auxiliaries.

So, the 14th was reaching hard, straining for glory. Rather than take one continent fully and await the 15th, it had gone for both of the large ones. The need, after all, was to own the planet when the other units arrived.

If the 14th merely fell short of its boldness—took one continent, but not both—the 15th would likely land troops and claim the victory for its own, relegating the 14th once again to back-up.

However, if the 14th were defeated. . .

Could such soldiers as he had seen here defeat the 14th Conquest Corps?

Nelirikk considered that, snipping and sewing in the nighttime camp.

The Irregulars—his home troop—held a number of strengths: Its captain was war-wise and intelligent, neither over-bold nor underconfident. The scout was a strength, as the captain's near advisor, as trainer in hand-to-hand, and as fabricator of weird devices of surprising effectiveness. The unit contained perhaps twenty such as Winston, old in soldiering and canny in the field.

That many of the Irregulars were raw—was weakness. Their overall numbers were, also, a weakness, but balancing that was the accumulated experience of the senior officers and the fact that the Yxtrang general had not yet had time to secure more than a foothold on either continent as a base.

The 14th, Nelirikk considered, at last laying down his needle and stretching out on his cot, might well find itself with a war on its hands.

HE WOKE ABRUPTLY, aware of some change too subtle to name, opened his eyes and saw the scout—a thin shadow against the dimness in his quarters—cross-legged and at ease on the locker at the foot of the cot.

The thrill of the discovery lay in its message. The scout was indeed *that* skilled. It was an honor to be aligned with such a man.

"I regret," Nelirikk said to the silent shadow, in Trade, for that was the language of the troop, "that my current position makes a salute awkward, Scout Commander."

"A salute is out of order in the present moment. I come

as—comrade, let us say—for your former comrades have proven themselves unworthy of the honor." The scout spoke his piece in Yxtrang.

Nelirikk felt a strange stir. Was this good news or bad? If the ambush had been successful then—

"I was within view of the site designated some time prior to the appointed hour. I remained twelve twelves of ticks beyond. There was no sound, Explorer. No sighting."

Shame was a rush of adrenaline that brought him upright on the cot. "By Jela, for a knife to cut their throats! They—"

"They used your drop-off as a recon run. I suspect they even now listen for radio reports to determine how far you might have come before being beset." This was in Terran. The captain had warned him of this—that he would need to "think lively" if he were to follow conversation between herself and the scout.

There was a moment of silence, then in Liaden came a sentence spoken as if it were Yxtrang, hard-edged and short.

"We speak now of Jela, whom you claim as near-clan."

Nelirikk went still, looking carefully at the shadowed scout.

"If I have offended, I would know why. Jela's Troop was always honorable."

"Indeed," the little man said quietly. "I am pleased to know that. For you should know that my clan is respected, my house among the oldest on Liad. We are generally accounted honorable, if misguided. The name of my house—and of the tree which stands over it—is Jelaza Kazone."

The Liaden words swept by and it took him a moment to register the under sounds. Running them past his inner ear once more, Nelirikk shook his head, Terran-wise.

"I cannot make whole what you tell me, Scout," he said, "other than your house name is similar to Jela's."

"No. Not an accident. Not merely similar. The house *is* Jelaza Kazone." There was a pause then, and a shift in language:

"In Terran it becomes 'Jela's fulfillment' or, perhaps, 'Jela's promise.'"

The language shifted again, without strain: "Trade might have it as 'Jela's contract' or 'Jela's dream,' depending on the speaker and how they think of Korval."

The scout went back to Liaden, the sentence spoken with inexorable exactness: "As I say, Explorer-bound-to-Korval, my family, Clan Korval, is accounted honorable by many, and we of the blood still live in the house first-built by Jela's arms-partner and bed-mate, Cantra yos'Phelium. Our motto is *I Dare.*"

The words echoed, found their match in the language of the Troop, and Nelirikk heard his own voice, chanting the campfire tale from his youth:

"*And when Jela had faced this challenge, and made his dozen upon the day, a soldier called out from the ranks, 'How do you dare this, small soldier, when one rush could take you down?'*

"*Jela shrugged, and smiled, and with knife in sheath and empty hands shown all around, said, 'I dare because I must. Who will dare for me, if I dare not dare for myself?'*"

Nelirikk sat quietly, recalling the fierceness of the struggle between himself and the scout—and the irony of it. That two of Jela's own should contend so! And who but the smallest should win? He laughed, softly, in the dark.

He sobered then, recalling things that the Troop did not know—or did not tell.

"Did Jela die on Liad, then?"

"Alas," said the scout, as sober as if the death had been yesterday. "Jela took one too many rear-guard, permitting his partner and her ship to escape. That, after all, was the essence of their agreement: he to guard the ship so the Tree might win through, she to guard the Tree, should he fall.

"She came away with his son-to-be-born and the very Tree that stands above my house. The tree here—Erob's large tree—is a seedling sent to seal the alliance between our two houses. And I must thank you for the Jela story, for it is not one we have in the Diaries."

"Diaries?" Nelirikk felt hunger lick through him. To read Jela's own words? "Jela's diaries?"

"Not precisely, though some of the log entries are surely in his hand. Jela's last years were spent with the space captain, my ancient grandmother. In her logs and diary she wrote down much wisdom, some her own and some his. The delms of Korval have kept the Diaries up, and study of them is part of each clanmember's education, so we do not forget that which must be recalled."

It was then that the scout offered treasure.

"Should we find ourselves able to leave here and return to Jelaza Kazone I will undertake to show what I may of Jela, if you like. The first diary entry of him, and the tree he carried out of a desert far, far away."

Seated as he was, Nelirikk contrived to bow. "A boon I would count it."

The scout inclined his head. "As it is in my power, Explorer."

There was not much to say then. Eventually, the scout stood, bowed formally and with meaning entirely too fine to be read properly in the available light, and slipped silently into the night.

DUTIFUL PASSAGE:
In Jump

Primary operations had been moved to the reserve bridge. Priscilla, in charge of Second Team, was at station on the main—no, Shan corrected himself—on the trade bridge. He gritted his teeth and ran the board checks with a thoroughness they scarcely required, since it was the third check he'd initiated within the last half-hour.

The mood on the reserve bridge was of tension harnessed into purpose. The mood of the captain was of frantic worry degenerating into terror.

Shan closed his eyes, deliberately removing himself from board-drill and bridge, and ran the Healer's mental exercise for distance under duress and calmness under calamity.

He sighed once, centered in an unruffled crystalline pool, then opened his eyes again to the reserve bridge.

Or the "war bridge" as Uncle Daav had used to call it—most likely to tease Shan's father. Shan's recollection of Daav yos'Phelium was sparse, and memory's eyes had lately tried to translate the barely remembered features into Val Con's well-known and beloved face.

Val Con, who they were to meet at Lytaxin. Val Con, who

would be delm—and quickly, it was to be hoped, so he might sort
this mess they found themselves in and show the clan its enemy.

Val Con, who had supposedly killed a man to gain his spaceship, who had warned Shan away from "appalling danger" while the
Passage was being rigged for death—

"We break Jump within the twelve, Captain," Ren Zel said
quietly from second board, and Shan pushed all such thoughts away,
even the growing fear that Val Con had not managed his murder,
and was himself dead on some backworld—aye, and his lifemate
buried with him.

"I have the mark," he told Ren Zel. "Prime to me, second string
through four toggled in sequence. Courier boat thirteen is cleared to
depart the instant we break—your call, pilot."

Ren Zel flashed a look over-full with dark surprise, then
inclined his head. "Captain."

"Trade bridge standing by, Captain," Priscilla's voice was calm
as always, but the corner of the screen that should have contained
her image was gray, gray, Jump gray.

"Acknowledge," he murmured. "Reserve bridge is sequenced
backup boards two through four. Trade bridge should stand ready
to take fifth string—captain's bridge?"

"Monitoring, Captain." Seth was as matter-of-fact as if they'd
been discussing routine shuttle maintenance. Or as if he didn't
know that matters would be very bad indeed by the time control of
the ship shunted to the captain's bridge.

Ten seconds to break-out, by the countdown at the bottom
right of the screen . . . nine . . . eight . . . seven . . .

There was no room now for silly worries; no room for anything
but the weary, familiar, bone-known drill while the ship gave one
last gasp around them and the gray screens shattered into stars and
an alarm went bong and . . .

"Courier, hold!" Ren Zel commanded and the collision warning
howled as the main screen filled with the image of the tumbling
abandoned weapons pod. . .

"All shields!" Shan called out even as his hands slapped the
toggles.

The screen flashed, blurred—and the ship shook as the tremendous energy of the explosion bathed the *Passage* in radiation so fierce the shields flared.

"Air loss, Captain," Priscilla reported from the trade bridge. "Pod dock holed—emergency seals on."

"Get it!" Shan commanded, scanning the gauges, shifting a finger to touch another control. "Tower. Rusty, what do we have?"

"Ears," came the laconic reply; "but not many. You're carrying lots of stuff in the shield fields, Captain, and it's blocking most incoming . . ."

The main screen showed a throbbing blue-green shimmer with an occasional lightning-like flash. Shan flicked a glance at the filtering gauge and nearly gasped at the energy required to dim the scintillations to this near-blinding brightness.

"Mother attend us!" Priscilla cried. "Shan—"

"I see it." He flicked toggles, shunting computer time to the analysis board, which gobbled every nanosecond greedily—and offered up a schematic of the problem: The pod's energy and remaining ionized mass was caught between the shield layers, trapping the ship within a hollow sphere of deadly energy. If that searing plasma touched the *Passage*—

"Ren Zel, cycle the outer shield down to 200 kilogauss if you please. I'll take the inner up as high as I dare—and then you'll cut entire. On my mark."

"Yes, Captain."

"Mark."

"Two, Captain. One, Captain. Half. Quarter. Tenth—down!"

Shan nodded, though Ren Zel was too busy to see, and phased the inner shield up. The maneuver was chancy, placing the lighter coils of the meteor shields at risk—but that was minor for the moment—

He felt it then, as would the rest of the crew: the grate of a piercing headache as the magnetic and other fields phased in, coursed through the controlled shield and leaked into the ship.

Shan grimaced and cut back, watching the main screen as he did, seeing the filtering levels falling, falling . . .

"Engineering, magnetics check. All nonessential crew, magnetics check!" Priscilla's voice cracked over general in-ship as Shan brought the shields to a more reasonable level and the remains of the weapons pod blew into space like the gaseous nebular remnant of a supernova.

"Air report!"

"Under control, Captain. The pod bay took a direct strike from debris—a twelve centimeter hole and twenty centimeters of fracture."

Shan shuddered. Debris coming through an armored pod door with that much force—he could have lost a dozen people!

"We've got a temporary patch up," Priscilla continued. "We can replace that whole wall with a modular fix once we're—"

"Position report, Captain. Tactical report, Captain." Ren Zel's voice betrayed nothing, pitched exactly loud enough to override Priscilla's report.

"Tactical?" Shan asked.

"Tactical," Ren Zel affirmed. "There are warships all over this system . . ."

"Tower here! Shan, this feed—" snapped Rusty, quickly followed by Liaden-accented Trade: ". . . system is under attack by Yxtrang. Repeat, this system is under attack by Yxtrang. All shipping be warned. Flee and bring aid. This message by order of Erob."

"That's from a booster transmitter somewhere about six hours out," Rusty said. "I—"

"Bastards! Got you now! Ah-*hah*! We got you now!"

"No chatter!" Shan called out against Seth's bloodthirsty glee, and looked to Ren Zel, who was coolly accessing the military files available to his key.

"Hold a moment, pilot," he said quietly. "I have additional information here."

IDs blossomed across the long-screen as he shunted the auxiliary files available to the captain and first mate.

What Shan noticed first was the battleship, flanked by two cruisers.

The second thing he noticed were the swarm of smaller vessels, in-system strike-ships, clustered around the dreadnought like bees around a teel blossom.

The portion of his mind not engaged on the level of sight nudged him into awareness that the feed from the system beacon was still coming through, and that he was hearing—music. Heartbreakingly familiar music.

Val Con had made it to Erob.

It was Priscilla who noticed the other thing, and who said it quietly, on private line from her station to his.

"They've landed on Lytaxin, Shan."

Shan nodded and leaned back in the pilot's chair.

"So they have, Priscilla," he said, staring at the tactical screen, where the blockade was outlined, ship by deadly ship, cutting the *Dutiful Passage* off from Val Con—and from Korval's future.

He sighed.

"So they have."

THE ANNUNCIATOR sounded as Shan began the calculations necessary for the final definition of the secondary equation. He called "Come!" without taking notice of the fact and dove deeper into the beguiling intricacies of vector-graphs, real-time movement, gravitational fluctuations, relative mass ratios, velocity transfer rate, and the potentiality of random speed shift.

A spiraling approach such as the *Passage* was currently committed to was impossibly complicated even without an Yxtrang armada between them and the target planet, he thought hazily, manipulating factors of seven. The math comp suggested applying a factor of 267 to shift potential and he OKed that with a finger-tap.

Not that the Yxtrang had taken any particular note of the battleship in their midst, after an initial flutter of radio exclamation. It was to be expected, however, that they were reserving their most serious displeasure for the *Passage*'s closest approach, and if one extrapolated a grav-flux rate directly proportional to the movement of the primary natural satellite...

Equation framed, the computer announced some little time later. Shan blinked at the screen.

"So you say." He sighed and leaned back, calling up a Healer's relaxation drill to chase away the ache in shoulders and back.

"Well," he said to the computer, tapping the *go* key. "If you think you've got it framed, let's see it, don't be shy."

"Captain?"

"Eh?" He glanced up, blinked the larger room into focus, and blinked again as he discovered the figure of his foster son, perched uneasily on the edge of one of the two visitor's chairs across the desk.

"Hello, Gordy. I didn't hear you come in, but I expect I must have let you in, mustn't I? Math does such very odd things to one's perceptions, don't you find?"

"Sometimes." Gordy's face was paler than usual and showing heretofore unsuspected lines. He pointed at Shan's computer. "I've been doing some math myself, if you've got a minute to check me."

Such seriousness. One should not have lines of grimness sharpening one's features at nineteen. Shan sighed and extended a long arm, saving the frame with a rapid series of keystrokes. He glanced up again.

"The name of your file is?"

"Murder."

Shan stared, ran a quick scan of that utterly serious emotive pattern and lifted both brows. "Auspicious."

The corners of Gordy's mouth tightened, in no way a smile, and he folded his hands tightly together on his knee. "Yessir."

Murder was a series of three interlocking equations, as deceptively simple as haiku. Shan's hands went cold on the keypad as he scanned them. He looked at Gordy, sitting so still he fairly quivered with strain.

"These are quite attractive. Would you mind awfully if I frame my own set?"

Some of the stress eased from the boy's eyes. "I was hoping you would."

"Fine. A few moments' grace, please. Get yourself something to drink, child—and bring me a glass of the red, if you will."

"Yes, Father." Melant'i shift—and of a sort one rarely had from

Gordy, who was after all a halfling, and full of a great many useless notions regarding dignity. Shan returned his attention to the screen.

Fifteen minutes later, he sat back and picked up his glass, tasting the wine before he looked across at the waiting boy.

"I regret to say that your projections seem accurate in the extreme. My own calculations indicate explosive conditions reached eight nanoseconds before your model, but I suspect this is merely a reflection of the difference in our ages. Youth is ever optimistic."

Again, the tightening of the mouth, while the brown eyes shone with abrupt tears.

"I ran a sim," he said, voice grating huskily and then cracking. "Worst case, we lose *everybody*, Shan."

"Precisely why it's called worst case." He tipped back in his chair and had another sip of wine. "Don't look so ill, child. You've served warning. The patch on that thrice-damned pod is an unacceptable stress point. If we have to maneuver suddenly—if we have to maneuver and *fire* at the same time—poof! As you say, we lose everybody." He shrugged.

"Nothing for it but to go out and do a proper fix."

Gordy stared. "With all those Yxtrang out there?"

"Well," said Shan, with a casualness Priscilla would have known was all sham, "I don't expect they're going to be leaving soon, do you?"

"YOU ARE NOT GOING out there to repair that pod mount!"

Shan paused with the wine glass halfway to his lips, face etched in disbelief. "Your pardon, Priscilla? I cannot believe that I heard you correctly."

Black eyes flashed and her mouth tightened ominously. "You heard me."

"Well, if you will have it, I did." He moved to the bar and set the untasted glass next to the decanter of red before turning to her again, a frown on his face. "Need I remind you that I am captain of this vessel?"

"All the more reason for you to stay away and let someone else do it!" she cried, body taut as a harpstring, projecting passion with such force Shan's teeth ached.

He took a deep breath. "I suppose you have someone else in mind?" He inquired, keeping any hint of irony out of his voice.

Priscilla glared. "Yes, I do. Me."

"Oh, much better!" he approved, and the irony this time was impossible to leash.

He was warned by the flare of heat against his cheek, had time to think a thought and *reach* before the wine erupted from the goblet and, given direction by Priscilla's fury, smashed into a storm of blood-red droplets a whisker's breadth from his face.

"Oh dear," Shan said softly, looking down at the carpet. "We seem to have made a mess, Priscilla."

"A mess . . ." She was looking a trifle dazed, as well she might. The amount of finely tuned energy required to move a coherent volume of wine the specified distance with such rapidity and without breaking the goblet was certainly considerable. She closed her eyes and whispered something Shan thought sounded suspiciously like, "Mother grant me patience," before opening them again.

"Shan," she said carefully; "what is that?"

"That?" He caught the glimmer of what his construct must look like to her Inner Eyes and smiled.

"Oh, *that*! Well, I don't know how it should happen, Priscilla, but I became concerned that you might be going to dash a glass of wine into my face. Given the conviction, I thought it expedient to arrange for a shield of sorts. Pretty clever I thought it, too, especially on such short notice. But now I perceive that I should have arranged for something a bit more—encompassing—for here's the carpet, all spotted up and—"

"Damn the carpet! Shan—" Passion of a different sort broke and he found his eyes full even as hers spilled over and she was that quickly across the room, cupping his face in her hands.

"Shan, for sweet love's sake, don't go out there! Something—something *horrible*—will happen. I—"

Gently, he put his own hands up, running his fingers into her black curls and looking closely into her eyes. "A foretelling, Priscilla? Something that you *know* is true?"

His palms were wet with her tears. He saw the uncertainty in the

back of her eyes before she shook her head. "I—I'm not sure."
Passion flared once more. "Let me do it. The tests—"

"The tests show that you rate either excellent in manipulation
and very good on speed or very good in manipulation and excellent
in speed. The same tests show that the captain rates consistently
excellent in both manipulation and speed. We have two Master
pilots on this ship—the captain and the first mate. It's sensible to
have one with the ship at all times. Since I out-test you on the repair
module—just barely, I admit it!—and since speed and manipulative
excellence are both very likely to be factors in making the needed
repairs, I am the best choice." He sighed and dropped all shields,
letting her see the truth in him.

"This is no act of heroism, I swear it to you. If Ren Zel, Seth, or
Thrina were more able, the task would be theirs."

Priscilla's face was troubled. "But not mine," she murmured.

Truth was truth, and only truth was owed, between lifemates.
"Only," he admitted, "under severest compulsion."

She stepped away from him, shaking her head. "You'd rather
make me watch you die."

"But I have no intention of dying, Priscilla!" he cried, with
counterfeit gaiety.

And felt her pain in his own heart, twisting like a sudden knife.

OUTSIDE REPAIR was tedious, nerve-wracking work, in this case
made more nerve-wracking by the interested presence of several
Yxtrang warships. That the residents of the warships were more
than a little vocal in their interest had early on moved Shan to cut
his open beams to three: direct to the *Passage*, direct to Seth, and
conference.

Seth was assigned as pointguard between Shan and the interested
enemy, a task he undertook with a worrisome degree of enthusiasm.
However, though two flights of insystem fighters had passed
foolishly close to the edge of the *Passage's* range during the last few
hours of welding, sweating and swearing, Seth, the *Passage* and the
Yxtrang had all managed to keep fingers from firing studs. Shan
indiscriminately thanked every god and goddess he could think of

for this rare display of moderation on all sides, and sweated even more in the heavy-duty suit, in an agony to finish before someone mislaid their common sense.

"I believe that's sealed," he murmured at too long last. "Ren Zel, check me, if you please. I don't really feel up to coming back outside tomorrow to patch the keyhole."

"Equations set and sim running, Captain." Ren Zel's smooth-toned and proper Liaden voice was as bracing as a cool breeze. "We have compliance to the one hundredth and fifth percentile, Captain."

Relief so exquisite it was almost pain. "Wonderful. Seth, my sharpshooter, we're going back inside. Allow me, in the fullness of time, to buy you a glass of that reprehensible rotgut you drink."

"You're on—ah, hell, here we go again. Yxtrang flight-squad just inside eyes-screen eight. Must be flying school today."

"Let's hope it's not target practice, shall we?"

"They've been real polite so far," Seth commented. "I'll swing out and give you some room, Captain. The sooner I get a glass of rotgut in my hand, the happier I'm going to be."

"Spoken like a sane man, Mr. Johnson. Back off to vector sigma-eight-three, and I'll slide around to Bay Six."

"Gotcha. Changing vector—now."

"*Passage* note following vectors and track. Intend to intersect with Bay Six in—Seth! Screen four!"

Two of the Yxtrang craft had peeled out of formation, local velocity increasing to an insane level. Seth threw his own vessel into an evasive tumble that should have skated him toward the *Passage's* well-protected belly and safety. Of a sort.

But Seth did not choose the life-saving maneuver. Instead, his tumble spun him *away* from the *Passage*, vectoring with the Yxtrang fighters.

One came after him, gun turrets tracking as they held the target despite the craft's maneuvering. The second fighter kept on—a straight, one would have said suicidal, run in toward the heart of the *Passage*. Toward Shan.

Multiple voices filled the void's radio frequencies. Shan's "Seth, return to ship!" was nearly overwhelmed by Priscilla's calm, "Safety interlocks off, full battle condition. On my mark, gunners."

Seth's voice broke into the end of Priscilla's instructions, on the dedicated beam between the lifeboats. "One family's enough. I'm on your man. They're after the lock."

It was all true in the tumbling way things happen in space; Seth's course had altered enough that his gun was tracking the lead enemy, the ship tracking him began to maneuver its way closer, and the lead Yxtrang was closing rapidly on both Shan and the lock he'd need to enter.

"Your screen six," came Priscilla's calm voice, this time tinged with an ice that made even Shan's blood run cold. "This is the attack. Gunners, your mark. Three and Five spot Seth. Teams Four and Six spot the captain. Everyone else—standard defense."

Screen six showed a flight of five fighters whose meandering courses had suddenly become one.

The fighter tracking Shan veered away from the collision course, and Shan's reflexes brought him back toward the lock, and then away, away. . .

"Shan, we . . ."

"Can't risk an open lock. I'll loop around and see . . ."

"They're pairing up on you, Shan," came Seth's warning.

Shan felt a momentary touch of love so sweet and full it nearly overwhelmed him. Then he felt a wrenching he understood all too well; Priscilla had gone behind her strongest shields, as she must. As he must.

"Shan, close in on pod four!" Seth urged.

Shan cursed the little lifeboat: fighter it was not, despite the add-on guns. More massive than the fighters by dint of its planetary capability, it was never meant to fight a space battle.

His stabbed at the release button, flinging the valuable remote repair unit into space to gain a measure of response.

"Shan!"

Seth's scream came at the instant the first Yxtrang fired; then there was static and a missile to be dodged and another. Shan felt the g-forces pushing him sideways as the little craft answered helm and then the first Yxtrang ship was pieces in the void as Seth's elation echoed across the radio and the second Yxtrang was turning ever so quickly for another run at Shan.

Shan's screens glared bright as *Dutiful Passage* went to war.

THE VERY FIRST CONCERN was the larger fighter flight; the two that were behind that, closing at high speed with some larger ships intermingled, would wait.

Priscilla ignored the screen that showed Shan's ship: he'd done as Seth suggested and closed in on the *Passage* as best he could. Her concern now was weapon-mix and security; it wouldn't do to show their full capability quite yet.

"Team Two," she said quietly into her mike. "Fire at will."

The ship's automatics cut in. She felt the minute tremble as the guns began their rapid fire and the ship compensated. It would be seconds before the Yxtrang crossed their path, and a good radar system might give them warning. Priscilla spoke to the mike again.

"Team Three, wide area coverage around Team Two's center. If you get a veer, target it in."

"Cluster incoming; looks serious." This from Ken Rik on the inner bridge.

Priscilla's attention snapped to screen three—several of the larger ships further out had launched their weapons and were already dropping away from their escort of fighters. Too far for a missile shot. Still.

"Team One, your target is the hindmost of the midrange ships in Sector Three; your next target is next closest to us. You are cleared for two bursts each. At will."

Her eyes had already found the sight she wanted to see: Shan's boat close in to the *Passage*, firing an occasional burst toward something out of her sight.

The next screen showed it: Seth was still hanging away from the *Passage*, staying between Shan and the remaining fighter from the original attack group. He seemed to have earned some respect from the Yxtrang pilot.

A shudder went through the ship, followed by another.

"Team One. Bursts away, Priscilla," Vilobar's voice in her ear was calm. Perhaps he was calm. Inner senses stringently locked away, she chose to believe so.

The beams were a battleship's weapon. The beams—pulses actually—technically moved at just under the speed of light and carried with them a baleful mixture of particles, magnetic flux, and high speed atomic nuclei. She looked to her screens.

Unanticipated, Team One's bursts tore through the incoming cluster of missiles, and a few of the intervening fighters as well, leaving behind an awful shadow of explosions. A moment more, and the hindmost ship was incandescent fog.

Radio noise, already full of sputters and crackles from the first beam's passage through the Yxtrang, became a roar and hiss, and a second roaring followed as the second of the midrange ships followed its sister to vacuum.

"Fleas! Fleas!" Seth's voice was insistent in her ear. "Fleas!"

She slapped the switch, grabbed the screen and saw Seth's boat madly whirling and firing.

Watching, she thanked the Goddess for Seth, for his loyalty, and behind her Wall, among that which was locked away for this while, she feared—terribly—for his life.

For, in fighting to stay between Shan and the enemy, Seth had encountered a horde of the stealthy fleas—one-man ships barely more than a powered and hyper-armed space suit.

On visual she saw what she feared: his boat was dodging a dozen or more of the things, and though he had speed, they were a cloud around him, each firing and trying to attach weapons meant to mine a warship's hull.

"Seth!"

That was Shan, and now his boat was closing, firing, whirling, ramming.

"Twenty-three, Shan." Seth said. He might have been counting cargo pallets. Then, sharper—"I see their mother!"

The little boat whirled purposefully, the guns firing at a small dark spot in space as it picked up speed. Out, out, into the cloud of fleas and beyond. Away from the *Passage.*

"No!" Shan's voice was strong with Command. It made no difference.

The side of Seth's boat erupted. It spun, then—incredibly—straightened course, moving yet toward a nearly invisible spot against the stars.

"Damn," Seth said, and he was gasping. "Drinks are on me! Thirty-three." A pause. "Don't do anything stupid, Shan."

Then Seth's boat crumpled and exploded against the dark plastic mother ship of the Yxtrang fleas.

"Priscilla!" Shan's voice, high and hoarse.

"Teams Five and Three. Take it out." The ship shuddered and the bursts were away. The fleas' mother died in a flare of vapor.

"Priscilla, accelerate," Shan—no, *the captain* said into her ear. "There's a cloud of fleas closing on you."

His boat was spinning, moving, dodging, guns flaring—and each move taking him further and further from the *Passage*. From safety.

"Shan—"

"That is an order," he said, cold in command. "Accelerate!"

"Yes, Captain." Behind the Wall, she screamed and railed and rent her garments in anguish.

On the war bridge, she spoke quietly into her microphone, relaying the order to accelerate.

SHE HAD MEMORIZED this computer code seven Standards ago, offering at the same time a prayer to the Goddess, that she would never need to use it. Her fingers shook as she entered it now, but there was no shame in that. Neither the Goddess nor melant'i demanded fearlessness in the performance of duty, merely that duty was done.

The screen blanked as she entered the last digit, taking even the window at the bottom right corner, which elucidated the progress of lifeboat number four toward the planet surface. There was silence in the captain's office, as if the *Passage* were mulling over her request, and more than half-inclined to refuse it. Priscilla folded her cold hands together on the wooden desk, waiting.

The *Passage* made up its mind with a beep and a flash of letters on her screen.

❊   ❊   ❊

DUTIFUL PASSAGE OFFICER ALTERATION ROUTINE.
BEGIN RUN:
RANK: CAPTAIN
HISTORY: SHAN YOS'GALAN, CLAN KORVAL
ER THOM YOS'GALAN, CLAN KORVAL
SAE ZAR YOS'GALAN, CLAN KORVAL
CANDIDATE: PRISCILLA DELACROIX Y MENDOZA,
CLAN KORVAL
HISTORY: PET LIBRARIAN
PILOT THIRD CLASS,
TRAINING SECOND CLASS
SECOND MATE
PILOT SECOND CLASS,
TRAINING FIRST CLASS
FIRST MATE
PILOT FIRST CLASS, TRAINING MASTER
ACCEPT: COMMUNICATIONS MODULE
EMERGENCY MODULE
LIBRARY MODULE
OVERRIDE MODULE
NAVIGATION MODULE
WEAPONS MODULE
MAIN COMP
ACCEPT: PRISCILLA DELACROIX Y MENDOZA,
CLAN KORVAL
RANK: CAPTAIN
ADJUSTMENT: CAPTAIN'S KEY FILE
ACCEPT
AUXILIARY INFORMATION: RANKS FIRST MATE,
SECOND MATE, THIRD MATE UNMANNED. HIGH RISK
CONDITION NOTED. OPTIMUM SOLUTION: APPOINT
OFFICERS: FIRST MATE, SECOND MATE, THIRD MATE.

MINIMUM SOLUTION TO UNACCEPTABLE RISK
CONDITION: APPOINT FIRST MATE.
END RUN

※　※　※

The screen blanked once more. Priscilla extended a hand that still showed a tendency to quiver and tapped in a retrieval request. A heartbeat later, Plan B lit her screen.

※　※　※

A changing array of safeplaces shall be maintained at all times, in the event of immediate, catastrophic threat to the Clan. There is no shame in strategic retreat. Even Jela sometimes ran from his enemies, the better to defeat them, tomorrow.

Keep the children safe. Honor without love is stupidity.

This by the hand of Cantra yos'Phelium, Captain and Delm, in the Third Year after Planetfall.

※　※　※

The screen beeped, indicating the existence of an auxiliary file. Priscilla accessed it with the touch of a key.

This message was not nearly so ancient. In fact, it was mere weeks old, dispatched by Nova yos'Galan, Korval's first speaker in trust, to Shan yos'Galan, captain and thodelm.

※　※　※

Plan B is in effect. Assume our enemy omnipresent and dedicated to Korval's utter ruin. Contact no one, for we cannot know which alliances stand firm and which are rotted out from the core by the work of our enemy. Arm the Passage. *Secure yourself. Repeat: Plan B is in effect.*

Keep safe, brother.

※　※　※

Priscilla sat back in Shan's chair, staring at the screen. They had armed the *Passage*. They were, as far as conditions allowed, secure. The ban on radio contact was subject to captain's interpretation, given those same conditions. She touched another key, sealing the files once more. The diagram of Shan's descent to Lytaxin reappeared in the bottom right corner of the screen.

Eyes closed, she considered priorities.

The ship's priority, that there be at least one other in the command chain, should the captain fail, was best acted on at once. The radio . . . She reached out and flipped a toggle.

"Tower."

"Rusty, this is the captain," she said quietly.

There was a short, electric pause, then a respectful, almost somber, "Yes, ma'am."

"Please do me the favor," she continued, hearing her own voice take on Shan's speech pattern, "of constructing an anonymous message to the appropriate authorities regarding Lytaxin's situation."

"Yes, ma'am," he said again, then: "I'm assuming we don't want to give away our name or our location."

"That's exactly what we don't want, Rusty. Can you do it?"

"Take a little fiddling, but—yeah. I can do it. You want to review before implementation?"

"Please."

"Will do," he said, and his voice was brighter, as if the promise of a problem he was able to master had cheered him up. "Tower out."

"Thank you, Rusty. Captain out."

THE SCREEN on the side of the desk was live, displaying the current crew roster, but the decision had been made before ever she keyed in the request to see that document.

Priscilla sighed. Ten Standards she and Shan had captained the *Passage* between them. To name another to take the place she had made for herself, as duty demanded that she take Shan's rightful role was—not easy. Yet it must be done, for the safety of ship, crew, and kin. The temple had schooled her well in duty, before she had ever dreamed of Liad.

Priscilla closed her eyes and called up an old exercise—one of the first taught to novices in temple, honing her anxiety into purpose. She had barely opened her eyes again when the door chime sounded.

"Come," she said, and the door, obedient to the captain's voice, slid open.

"Acting Captain." He bowed respect from the center of the room and straightened, awaiting her notice.

She took a moment to consider him: A medium tall man, as Liadens measured height, skin an unblemished medium gold, hair and eyes a matching medium brown, neither beautiful nor ugly, not fat nor yet thin. He wore no rings of rank nor any more simple adornment. His shirt was plain and pale, his trousers dark, his boots comfortable and well tended.

He was a pilot of some note—first class verging on Master—and she knew him for a quick and incisive thinker. The information that he possessed humor would have startled many of his crewmates, but none of those would have said his judgment was unsound, or that his temperament was other than steady.

He was also inclined toward austerity, which was worrisome, Priscilla allowed, even when it was austerity applied to the best good of ship and crew.

From her seat behind the desk, she inclined her head and moved a hand toward the pair of visitor's chairs.

"I have a proposal to put before you, my friend," she said in mild, modeless Terran. "Will you sit and listen to me for a moment?"

"Gladly," he responded. His Terran was heavily accented, though his comprehension was excellent. He took the chair nearest the corner of the desk and folded his hands neatly upon his knee.

Priscilla closed her eyes briefly, opened them and considered Ren Zel's quiet face. She remained, perforce, behind her Wall, reduced to reading the emotions of others from the shifting clues of expression and bodyline. Like most Liadens, Ren Zel was a master at keeping his emotions well away from his face.

"An announcement will be made to the entire crew within the hour," she said, and took a breath, enough air, certainly, to force the few words out. "The ship has accepted me as captain."

Face smooth, Ren Zel inclined his head. "Has there been— word—of Captain yos'Galan?"

Priscilla shook her head, gesturing at her screen and the diagram describing the descent of lifeboat number four. "He will make planetfall within the next few hours. After the lifeboat is stable, we'll rig a punchbeam. For the moment, we—assume—that Captain yos'Galan is alive, but unavailable to us. Circumstances dictate that the ship be served by a full captain." "Assume," Ren Zel said, voice expressing interest without judgment, which was only prudent from a man reared in a culture where a judgment expressed outside of one's proper area of concern might well result in honor-feud. Priscilla was free to ignore him, but she would have to stretch—and endanger her own melant'i—to read insult into his question.

"Assume," she repeated, and smiled with good intent, if limited success. "Understand that I am—shielded away. Without Healer skill. There are exercises I must soon undertake so that I may serve the ship as it must be served, but for the moment, I have no more knowledge of Captain yos'Galan's safety than what I can read from the tracking computer and from my own desires."

Something moved in the brown eyes. She thought it might have been pity. "I understand. Forgive me. I had not intended to cause you pain."

"You have a right to ask—to know. Shan is your captain, after all."

"Indeed, I owe him my life," Ren Zel murmured. "And yourself, as well."

In lieu of being able to pay Shan directly, Priscilla thought wryly and deliberately suppressed the shudder of anxiety. She lay her hands flat on the desktop and looked at him.

"Then perhaps you will find this proposal even more interesting," she said and tipped her head, seeing wariness at the back of his eyes.

"You know that we are short-handed, that we have been short-handed since the *Passage* became a full-scale battlewagon."

Ren Zel inclined his head. "And with the loss of Pilot Johnson and Captain yos'Galan we become less rich in resource."

"Exactly. In a ship—rich in resource—the second mate would move to first, third to second, and a third mate would be chosen by the captain."

"We do not have this luxury of personnel," he agreed. "We are at war."

She nodded. "The ship requires a first mate and the captain must decide who will serve the ship best. I propose yourself for first mate, unless you can think of a compelling reason why you shouldn't be."

Shock stripped his face naked. He sat—just sat—and stared at her for the space of three heartbeats. He closed his eyes then, and sat through two heartbeats more. He opened his eyes and they were distant, his face without expression. When he spoke, it was in High Liaden, in the mode called Outsider.

"The captain is reminded that one is clanless, with neither name nor kin nor melant'i to support one. The ship is best served by one who is alive."

"The captain recalls most vividly that you have been reft of your birthright," Priscilla said carefully, following him into Liaden, but only so far as Comrade mode. "The captain points out that your piloting license bears a name—Ren Zel dea'Judan. The captain fails of recalling a single instance of that name being dishonored in the several years of our association. The melant'i which you embody is pure. The ship can be no better served."

There were tears in the medium brown eyes and she dared not unshield, even to offer comfort. Instead, she sat and waited while he mastered himself, while he thought it through, and when he rose to bow acceptance.

"Captain, I am honored. I will serve willingly, with all my heart."

She stood from behind the desk and returned his bow, reaching into High Liaden for the ritual phrase spoken by a delm when accepting a new member into the clan.

"I see you, Ren Zel dea'Judan, First Mate. The ship rejoices."

Tears again, hidden by a hasty bow. "Captain."

She smiled slightly and shook her head. "First lesson," she said in Terran.

Quickly, he looked up, brown eyes bright. "Yes?"

"My name is Priscilla," she said, and held her hand out to him.

THE CREW, at battle stations, accepted her ascendancy to captain and Ren Zel's appointment as first mate with somber approval. She had detailed their mission: to take up defensive orbit about the planet and await the aid that surely must come in response to Rusty's carefully anonymous pinbeams.

"In the meantime," she said, "Captain yos'Galan's lifeboat has entered atmosphere. We will attempt to establish a dialog via laser packet when he comes to ground and we are sure his position is stable."

"Why not just use the radio?" That was Gordy, face tight, voice harsh with pain.

"The Yxtrang may ride our radio wave down to the planet surface and discover the location of an object we value," Ren Zel murmured, before she could frame a reply. "They have surely marked that one pod escaped the battle, and they must wonder after its worth. A laser burst is not so easy to follow, so we may shield Captain yos'Galan while informing him of our vigilance."

In the screen, Gordy nodded, jerkily. "I see. Thank you."

"Other questions?" Priscilla asked, and there were none, so she released them to their duties or their rest, then turned to Ren Zel.

"First Mate, the shift is yours."

He bowed, accepting the duty. Priscilla hesitated.

"Ren Zel."

He looked up.

"I—there are preparations that I must make," she said, slowly. "Preparations which are . . . of the dramliz. I will be in my cabin for the next few hours, but I will not be available to you." She bit her lip, and added that most dangerous of Terran phrases, "I'm sorry."

He moved his hand lightly, as if clearing the air of a faint wisp of smoke. "Necessity. I, to my duty. You, to yours."

She smiled, then. Almost she laughed. Practical Ren Zel.

"Of course. How could I have forgotten? Good shift, my friend."

"Good shift, Priscilla."

SELF-HEALED, and whole once more, Priscilla drew a breath in trance slightly deeper than the one before. Her lips moved. The voice of her body whispered a word.

Weapons Hall leapt up around her, mile-thick walls breathing chill and fell purpose.

One did not seek this place lightly. Many—most—of those trained as Sintian Witches never had need to come here, though all were taught the way. It was the peculiar misfortune of those who had been born Moonhawk to know the way to Weapons Hall all too well.

Priscilla moved silently over the stone floor, her cloak pulled tight against the chill. At the end of the hall, she paused, frowning down at a blood-bright spot against the worn rock bench. Bending, she picked up a round wooden counter like those used in gaming houses, bright red in the center, but losing its paint along the rim. She smiled slightly and curled her fingers over the token, feeling it warm against her skin, and moved forward once more, to the long, weapon-hung wall.

The tale is that, for every art of healing, for every spell of joy a Witch masters, there is a weapon hung in the Hall, which is its dire opposite.

The tale is true.

Priscilla walked the long, weapon-thick wall. Three times, she put out her hand and when she lowered it, a portion of the wall stood bare. At the end of the Hall, weapons chosen, she closed her eyes and raised her arms and was gone from that place that was nowhere and nowhen.

IN THE BED she shared with Shan, Priscilla's body stirred. Breath and heartbeat quickened. Black eyes opened. Blinked.

She stretched, then, fully back in the body, and noticed that her right hand was clenched tight. Raising it, she carefully opened her fingers and looked in wonder at the round wooden counter, brave crimson enamel worn away around the rim.

To her newly wakened, battle-honed senses, the little token vibrated with power, with . . . presence. Carefully, she opened her thought to the artifact—and nearly cried aloud with wonder.

The wood was alive with Shan's presence.

She held it in her hand while she dressed, loath to surrender even so tenuous and strange a link with him. When she had wriggled, one-handed, into her shirt, she slid the token into her sleeve-pocket, taking care with the seal.

It wasn't until she had stamped into her boots and gone into the 'fresher to splash water on her face that it occurred to her to wonder what Shan might have found awaiting his hand, in the Witches' Hall of Weapons.

NIMBLEDRAKE:
Ending Jump

LIZ PUNCHED the third button from the top in the fourth column from the right, which probably said "tea" as plain as the nose on your face, if your nose happened to be Liaden. Since hers wasn't, she'd memorized which buttons Nova pressed to draw what kind of rations.

She fished the cup out of the dispenser and punched the button again, then walked both cups carefully down the narrow hallway to the piloting chamber. They were due to fall out of Jump pretty soon—a way stop, not Lytaxin itself.

Nova was at the board, which was where Nova mostly was, except for an odd hour of sleep, or a short stroll down to the canteen to draw tea or food—that she ate and drank while sitting watch over her board.

"Here you go, Goldie." Liz slid one cup into the holder of the arm of the pilot's chair, and, juggling the other cup, got herself into the cramped co-pilot's seat.

"My thanks," Nova said absently, busy with some figuring on a tiny work screen set off to the side of the main board.

"No problem," Liz said, anchoring her cup and pulling the webbing across. Not that Nova was likely to give them a thrill breaking Jump—she'd shown herself far too able a pilot for that. But, in Liz's experience, accidents did happen, and the ones who were prepared were the ones least likely to get hurt.

"Planning on making a long stop?" she asked. "Or just using the revolving door?"

Nova looked up, golden brows pulled tight. "Revolving?" The frown cleared in the next instant. "Ah. I see. We shall pause long enough to hear the news, then move on. If the luck smiles, we will be dining with Erob twenty hours hence."

"Terrific," Liz said, without emphasis. She had a careful sip of her tea. "You got a pretty good handle on Terran," she said. "Haven't managed to really stump you yet."

"Were you trying?" Astonishingly, Nova looked amused. "But you might consider my handle to be not quite what it should be, when you learn that my mother was Terran."

Liz managed not to choke on her tea. "She was?"

"Indeed, and a scholar of linguistics besides." There was a muted chime in the cabin and Nova turned back to the screens.

"You will excuse me. We approach Jump end."

Liz settled her cup in the slot and eased back as well as she could in the chair, so of course they phased into normal space with no more happenstance than the usual snap of transition.

Nova was busy with the board. Liz picked up the plug she'd been given, as she thought, to keep her quiet during just such periods of pilot concentration, she slipped it in her ear, doodling with the one dial of the dozens decorating the board that she was allowed, even encouraged, to touch.

For a while there was nothing much. The usual traffic talk and between-ship chatter you'd get any time you broke system. Then there was something else. Liz froze, holding the setting steady, and pulled the plug out of her ear.

"Nova."

A flash of violet eyes none too pleased. Liz held out the earplug.

"Gotta hear this. Priority One. I picked it up on the shipping channel."

One slim hand moved, sideways to what it had been doing, slapped a toggle and the speaker came live.

"Repeat. All vessels shipping to or through Lytaxin space are warned that Clan Danut is invoking the war-impaired shipping clause of all contracts and will not carry, deliver, or receive goods bound for Lytaxin, based on reliable information. This by order of Delm Danut."

In the pilot's chair, Nova took a deep quiet breath. Liz looked at her.

"You know them?"

"Clan Danut," Nova said, still staring at the board. "They are a small clan; their principal warehouse is on planet here. If they were not certain, they would not speak." She moved then, hands dancing along the controls.

"WE SHALL CHECK another source, Commander Lizardi, for if one trader announces such news, another has information a little fresher!"

Liz watched as Nova's hands touched this comm-panel and that, heard what might have been a Liaden cuss word as a loud monotone note sounded, then saw hands busy again.

"It would be good of you to fetch more tea for me, and some of the board-biscuits—sixth key on the right side of the warmer."

Liz noted the half-cup of tea still locked to Nova's chair, but figured she could tell when she should be elsewhere for a moment.

As fast as Liz rushed for the vittles, whatever secrets the Liaden woman wanted hidden were still her own when she got back.

"Strap in this time, Commander," said Nova, hands busy on the board yet again. "We Jump as soon as our orientation and speed are correct."

"Whoa!" Liz started to reach out and get hold of a wrist, then thought better of it. "Where you putting out for?"

No answer.

"Answer me, Goldie, I got a right to know."

"Indeed you do," Nova said, her voice a calm and shocking counterpoint to her busy fingers. "We are going to Fendor, Angela Lizardi."

"Merc Headquarters?" She blinked. "What're you gonna do? Hire yourself an army?"

"If necessary. Jump phase in 20 seconds. Erob is Korval's ally. We owe assistance in peril. And I have evidence from a pinbeam bounce that my brother and his lifemate are on Lytaxin as we speak."

Nova turned her violet eyes to Liz. "The mercenaries will have ways of determining if this rumor is true. Am I correct?"

Girl was too damn bright, Liz thought, and sighed.

"Yeah," she said, "they probably do."

"I thought so," said Nova, and the ship snapped into Jump.

LUFKIT:
Merc Hall

❀❀❀❀❀❀❀❀❀❀❀❀❀❀❀❀❀❀❀❀❀❀❀❀❀❀

THERE WAS a wonderful bustle of busyness, a splendid to and fro, not unlike to art. Not unlike at all, Edger considered, watching the hasty humans dart up and down the wide hallway. The art of which his youngest of brothers, Val Con yos'Phelium Scout, was a master.

He tarried by the door some noticeable time, by human counting, his brother Sheather at his side, absorbed in the spectacle.

Not all was hastiness within the hall. Here and there, at appropriate and artful intervals, were arranged islands of stillness: a counter, a computer, and a human sitting behind a table. It was these still islands which, in a soaring of art, inspired the most of the hastiness, Edger saw, noting with a connoisseur's eye the flow of tensions, light and human plain song between and among the stillnesses.

He could have tarried in contemplation yet some while, save that the introduction of himself and his brother into the fringes of the work did subtly alter the flow, and exerted compulsion upon one of the centers of stillness, requiring the human seated behind the table to rise and throw himself into the hasty human river. In a very short time, indeed, by Clutch standards, he emerged and engaged in that activity known as "salute."

"Sirs. I'm Sergeant Ystro Ban. Is there some assistance I can offer you?"

"I thank you, Sergeant Ystro Ban, and honor your inquiry. We come seeking a soldier and were told she might have left word of her whereabouts with kin at this hall."

The Sergeant's face knotted up most wonderfully and his eyebrows went up and down rapidly.

"Well, sir, we don't normally just give out the whereabouts of one soldier. If you like, you can leave a message for her here and I will personally make sure she gets it, when she reports in."

"I regret that our need is more pressing than that, Sergeant Ystro Ban," Edger said, and with no real astonishment then heard his brother Sheather's voice, questioning most mildly.

"I wonder, Sergeant Ystro Ban, is it always so bustling in your hall?"

"Huh?" He looked over his shoulder as if he had forgotten the bright, busy clatter in the course of their discourse together, then shook his head.

"Naw, this is something special. Got a blood war on our hands and everybody who can carry a gun is signing into the rescue team."

"Forgive me," Sheather said. "A blood war? What has gone forth?"

Sergeant Ystro Ban shrugged. "What it looks like is a Yxtrang invasion force came into Lytaxin system and set up housekeeping. Trouble is, there's mercs trapped on the planet, and we don't aim to let 'em fight this one without backup."

Edger exchanged a glance with his brother Sheather, who blinked solemnly and asked yet again.

"Which mercs are these, Ystro Ban, who are trapped upon Lytaxin?"

"'Bout half of the Gyrfalks, is what we heard here." He moved his head from side to side. "Word is Suzuki's on Fendor, which is fine by me. Wouldn't want to be on the same planet with Suzuki right now."

"It is these Gyrfalcons who are kin to our sister, Younger Brother?" Edger asked slowly.

"Brother, I believe they are."

"Ah." Edger turned his saucer eyes to Sergeant Ystro Ban. "Can you tell me if this hastiness we observe here will be replicated upon Fendor Mercenary Headquarters? And perhaps in other like halls?"

"Damn straight," said Ystro Ban.

"I understand you," said Edger and again sought the eyes of his brother, which were bright with the same thought, he would swear, that illuminated his own mind.

"I detect the hand of a great artist, Oh, my Brother," Edger said.

"I also," Sheather returned.

"And what more like our sister, that she should aid her kin in peril?"

"Nothing more," said Sheather.

"So." Edger turned back to the still and patient human and lifted a large three-fingered hand.

"I thank you for the gift of your time, and the jubilation of your news, Sergeant Ystro Ban. Do you go yourself to Lytaxin?"

"Couldn't keep me away with a battalion."

"I am gratified to hear it. Perhaps we may see you there. Come, Younger Brother, and reflect upon the depth of our brother's art, who inspires us to ever hastier action!"

LYTAXIN WAR ZONE:
Altitude: 12 kilometers

❀❀❀❀❀❀❀❀❀❀❀❀❀❀❀❀❀❀❀❀❀❀❀❀

HABIT almost killed him.

Shan flicked on the lifeboat's homer and directed its attention to Lytaxin Spaceport, his own attention more than half-occupied with keeping the clumsy little craft airborne and relatively upright while nursing the sadly-depleted fuel supply.

So far, he'd managed to avoid meeting anyone with a general grudge against Liadens and his goal was to come to ground before he did. The lifeboat's pitiful guns were all but exhausted and the thought of trying anything resembling evasive action against atmospheric fighter craft was enough to make his stomach knot.

Anxiously, he ran his eyes over the displays. Skies showed clear on screens one, two, three, and four. Good.

Screens five and six were something else again.

He had been at Lytaxin Spaceport no more than four Standards past. Then, it had been a bustling, mid-sized port, with half-a-dozen public yards and a sprinkling of private. There had been traffic, lights, and people—ships. Ships on hot-pads. Ships on cold-pads. Ships under repair and ships being hauled from one pad to another.

What remained was wreckage. Glass-edged pits marked the places where ships had been caught unaware, murdered while they slept. The Port Tower was a cowed, half-melted framework of naked girders. The blastcrete streets had been bombed into gravel pathways, separated now and then by segments of fencing. Twisted metal was strewn haphazard and the blasted pathways gleamed where glass had run in rivers, and frozen again where it lay.

Destruction burned his eyes and his hands were moving across the board, ripping the lifecraft into another course entirely before his thinking mind fully realized his error.

The lifeboat bucked, responsive as a rock. Shan swore, briefly and with sincerity, flicked a glance at the falling fuel gauge and thence to the screens, which showed plain, placid sky all about.

More than a touch of the luck in that, he owned, and no more than he had traded for, should the screens suddenly show him the very Yxtrang fighter craft he wished so ardently to avoid.

But, if not the Port, where might he go on a planet riddled in war?

"To Erob, of course," he muttered, fighting the lifeboat's tendency to go upside down relative to planetary surface. "Do try not to be a slowtop, Shan."

If Erob were overrun by Yxtrang, scattered, murdered and no more? Shan sighed and glanced again at the fuel gauge.

"Why to Val Con, naturally enough. And pray the gods he's close by."

It was not wise, what he did next, and he was certain his teachers in Healer Hall would have counseled strongly against it. But there really was no choice, given the fuel gauge—riding in the red zone, now—the planetary maps the lifeboat did not carry and his own rather strong disinclination to die.

The little ship was steady for the moment. Shan gripped the edge of the console, closed his eyes and dropped his inner shield.

There was no time for finesse, no time to prepare himself properly. He brought Val Con's emotive template before his Inner Eyes and flung himself open, spinning out in a search that was far too wide, concentration centered on that unique pattern.

He found instead a vast and welcoming greenness, familiar from childhood, comforting as the touch of kin.

Shan took a breath and abandoned Val Con's template, listening for what the Tree might tell him.

It was not, of course, his own Elder Tree, but Erob did keep a seedling. Nor did Jelaza Kazone necessarily speak to those who served it, but it had ways of making itself and its desires known.

The Tree was not read as a Healer might read a fellow human. Rather, the Tree borrowed referents from one's own pattern, displaying them in sequence at once familiar and vegetative.

Thus, the message arranged itself within Shan's senses: Joy— Welcome. Joy—Welcome. Joy—Welcome. Spice—whiff and stem— snap, from a memory of breaking off a leaf. The taste of Tree-nut along his tongue. A second impression of leaf, and a sense of pushing, gently, away.

He was aware that his hands moved across the board and was helpless to stop them. After a short struggle, he did open his eyes and found the dials a blur, the fuel gauge half-gone in red. Within, the Tree touched one last memory—warm lips laid soft against his cheek—and withdrew. Shan slammed his Inner Wall into place, shook himself and looked to the screens.

Number three showed an Yxtrang fighter, growing rapidly larger.

THE TREE'S INFLUENCE upon his body had produced a set of coordinates, residing now in the console's readout. Shan flicked a toggle and locked them, sparing a moment to hope the Tree possessed an adequate understanding of the limits of fuel and the action of gravity on an unpowered object.

The fighter loomed larger. Shan turned his attention to the guns.

Pop guns they were, though Seth had put his to good account, and badly drained besides. Shan's hands flashed over the board, shutting down auxiliary and non-essential systems, shunting the extra power to the guns. The energy level crawled upward, stabilized well below the ready line.

Shan chewed his lip, checked the board, checked the fighter—gods, *close*—checked the screens—and stopped breathing.

The Tree's coordinates were bringing him in on an encampment. He could discern tents, machinery, *soldiers* mistily in screen six. There was a standard, snapping bold in the wind below: an enormous white falcon stooping to its kill down a field of starless black.

Terrans. And no doubt close enough to the place the Tree had intended him to go. But not with an Yxtrang on his tail.

His hands moved again, dancing over the board, shutting down everything but air and the computers, sending every erg of energy to the guns and *still* they held below the line.

Shan flicked a glance at his pursuer, another at the camp and the surrounding terrain. He reached up and pulled the worksuit helmet over his head, hit the toggle with his chin and tasted canned air. His hands moved across the board, shutting down ship's life support, feeding the energy to the guns.

The gauge topped the line. And stopped.

Inside the helmet, Shan nodded and made one more adjustment on the board, draining what was now the topmost cannon, feeding everything he had into the belly gun.

Power surged in the single live cannon. He could have wished for more. He could have wished for both guns full primed and on-line. For that matter, he could have wished for a ship to equal the one that came against him, but time was short. He had what was needful.

Just.

He flicked a toggle, relieving the boat of its mindless adherence to the coords, and slowed, dropping a few artfully wobbled meters toward what appeared to be a canyon, or possibly a quarry, at the extreme edge of the encampment.

Behind him, the fighter took the bait.

The other pilot jammed on speed, guns swiveling. Shan waited, wobbling slightly lower—though not too low—toward that tempting rocky edifice. Waited until the fighter was committed, until there was no possibility of a fly-by—and no possibility of a miss.

Jaw locked, he whipped the thrusters, spending the dregs of his fuel. Agonizingly slow, the lifeboat tumbled. The fighter snarled by, the other pilot seeing the trap too late. Shan hit the firing stud, and the single canon blared, hot and bright and brief.

The fighter exploded, raining burning bits down into the encampment's perimeter.

And lifeboat number four, guns and fuel utterly expended, fell the few remaining meters to the planet's surface.

HE OPENED THE HATCH into the wary faces of two soldiers— one Terran, one Liaden—both holding rifles.

Quietly, he stood on the edge of the ramp, gauntleted hands folded before him. He'd taken the helmet off, exposing his face and sweat-stiffened hair; the land breeze was cool against his cheeks. The sounds were bird sounds, and the slight wind abrading leaf and grass.

It was the Terran who spoke first, sounding friendly despite the carbine she kept pointed at his chest.

"You OK, flyboy? Nasty fall you took there."

"Thank you, I'm perfectly fine," Shan assured her. And smiled.

The flip maneuver had worked precisely as he had hoped. The lifeboat had fallen about 12 meters, to land, right side up relative to the ground and unharmed, on the rock apron at the entrance to the quarry. The pilot had received a stern shaking and would have bruises to show, but the space suit and crash webbing had cushioned the worst. "Perfectly fine," stretched the truth, given other conditions, but not nearly into fantasy.

The Terran nodded and turned to her mate.

"Call and let 'em know we're bringing him in."

He slung his rifle, pulled a remote from his belt and spoke. "Quarry patrol. We have the pilot, safe. Will transport." He brought the unit to his ear, listened with a frown, then thumbed it off and hung it back on his belt.

"The sub-commander wishes to speak with him," he told his partner.

"Right," she said and jerked her head at Shan. "OK, friend. Let's take a walk."

Eye on the rifle, Shan hesitated. The woman shifted, her demeanor abruptly less friendly. He held up his hands, gauntleted palms empty and unthreatening.

"I do beg your pardon! I have no wish to keep the sub-commander waiting, but the case is that I am separated from my ship and I have every reason to believe that an attempt at contact will be made, once it is recognized that my position is stable. I should be here to receive that message when it comes."

The woman shook her head. "Sorry, pal. Sub-Commander Kritoulkas wants you and we're under orders to bring you. Wouldn't care to have to shoot you in the knee and carry you myself, but we can do it that way, if you insist."

Shan lowered his hands, taking a deep breath to push the sudden rush of distress down and away from the present moment.

"I would hardly wish to put you to so much trouble. By all means, take me to Sub-Commander Kritoulkas."

SUB-COMMANDER KRITOULKAS was a sour-faced woman with iron-gray hair and a prosthetic right hand. She glared at Shan where he stood bracketed by his two guards, sweaty and out-of-breath from his hike. Heavy-duty work suits are not made with strolls through the woods in mind.

"What else?" she asked, transferring her glare to the Terran soldier.

The woman saluted. "He did say he was separated from his ship, ma'am, and expecting a call."

Kritoulkas nodded. "Tell Comm to keep an ear out." She glanced at Shan.

"Anything we should say for you?"

He considered her blandly. "That I am safe and among friends."

"Think so, do you?" She looked back to the soldier. "Pass it, if the call comes. Dismissed."

The soldiers saluted and were gone, leaving him alone with the sub-commander's glare.

She sighed and braced a hip against her desk, folding her arms over her chest.

"OK, we'll take it from the top. Name and rank. If any."

"Shan yos'Galan, Clan Korval," he said. "Captain of the battle-ship *Dutiful Passage*."

"Battleship," she repeated and shook her head. "You don't look much like a soldier to me. Course, you don't look much like a Liaden to me, either." She shrugged. "Whatever. What're you doing here, Captain?"

"My ship took damage and I was separated during an Yxtrang attack that was launched during outside repair."

She nodded. "That's one. Take a step further back and tell me the other one. Why is your battleship in this system?"

Shan sighed, shifting his shoulders inside the hot, heavy suit. He emphatically did not want any more questions from this abrupt, sour-faced woman. He wanted a shower. He wanted his lifemate, his ship, and the familiar routine of the trade route. None of which he was likely to receive in the near future, if ever again, though the shower might just be possible, if he were polite and answered the sub-commander's questions.

So.

"Family business. My clan is allied to Erob, and I have reason to believe that my brother is here."

"Yah? Name?"

"Val Con yos'Phelium." Shan watched her face closely, but saw no recognition there.

"Not somebody I come across. You sure he's here?"

"I am positive that he is here," Shan told her, the recollection of that painfully familiar music flowing from Erob's warning beacon vivid enough to raise tears. He blinked.

"Perhaps another name," he said to Kritoulkas' glare. "Miri Robertson?"

That meant something to her. She straightened, glare melting into astonishment. "Redhead? She's here, all right. Think she'll own you?"

"Yes," he said, by no means sure of it.

Sub-Commander Kritoulkas nodded.

"OK, Captain, here's what. Gonna have to pass you up-line

anyhow, that being where we got folks who are real interested to hear about what things look like upstairs. We'll keep an ear on your 'boat down there and let your ship know you're among friends." Her mouth twisted a little at that. It might have been a smile.

"Meantime, we got a shift-change coming up in about four hours, which is about enough time for you to clean up, get something to eat and a catnap. Under guard, you understand, because I'm damned if I believe you're regular military and I ain't having you endanger my people."

A commander's natural concern was the welfare of her people. Shan's opinion of the sour-faced sub-commander rose slightly and he nodded.

"I understand entirely, ma'am. Thank you."

She snorted, and raised her voice, bawling for "Dustin!" A shortish Terran strode in from his post outside the tent and saluted. "Yes, ma'am."

She jerked her thumb at Shan. "Take this guy to draw clothes and a couple sandwiches. Shower and time-out at the medic's station. Stick close and get him to the departure squad on time."

Dustin saluted again. "Yes, ma'am." He turned and nodded at Shan, face and eyes neutral. "OK, sir, let's go."

He turned toward the door, heard Kritoulkas clear her throat behind him.

"One more thing, Captain."

He looked at her over his shoulder and, incredibly, saw her grin.

"Damn good shooting, coming in."

SHAN LAY ON THE HARD COT, head on a crinkling, antiseptic-scented pillow, and closed his eyes. He had showered, and put on the fighting leathers provided by the quartermaster. He had forced himself to eat one of the half-dozen sandwiches Dustin had pried out of the mess tent, and had drunk several cups of water. Now, more or less alone, if one discounted the guard at the cubicle's entrance, he prepared himself to enter trance.

He took a breath, and another, building the correct rhythm.

The noises of the camp faded, his heartbeat slowed. When the time was proper, he slipped over into trance.

Healspace is formless, a void of warm frothing fog. There is nothing but fog within Healspace—until something more is required.

Warm within the formlessness, Shan spoke his own name. He smiled at the man who stepped out of the fog to join him, and extended a hand adorned with a purple ring to take a hand on which an identical stone flashed its facets against the fog. With the deft surety of a Master Healer, he opened a line of comfort between them.

The turmoil he confronted was acute: Grief, joy, guilt, fury, bereavement, horror, love, confusion, repugnance. My, my, what a muddle, to be sure, but after all, demanding nothing more taxing than a Sort and a touch of reweaving. His scan found no irredeemable catastrophe, no resonance which so imbalanced the personality matrix that forgetfulness must be imposed. The matter was not at all complicated, and work could go forward at once.

In Healspace, there is no time. There was the work, and the results of the work, Seen by Healer's Eyes. The work consumed the time that the work required. When it was done, Shan smiled at Shan, opened their arms and embraced into oneness.

Healed and at peace, he turned in the foggy nothingness of Healspace—and checked.

This place was not Healspace. Nor was it the medic's tent cubicle. This place was stone, strange and brooding: A vast stone cavern, or so he thought at first. Then he saw the weapons, hung orderly along the wall.

The weapons . . . shimmered, in their places, as if each held its present form by whim and might as easily be something, quite, else. He focused his attention on a particular sword, and felt it slip from edge to shield, from shield to explosive, from explosive to . . .

"Good moon to you."

The man's voice was beautiful. The man, seated on a stone bench to Shan's right, was lean and hawk-faced, the black braid of his hair vanishing into the tattered shadow of his cloak. A red counter moved in his long fingers, appearing, disappearing. Appearing. Gone.

"Good moon," Shan returned calmly, while with Healer's senses he tried to Sort this place that was no more physical than Healspace, though it certainly was not Healspace. Nor had he ever met another in Healspace, save one he had called, or who had called him.

"Ah, but you haven't met another," the man in the cloak said, his fine black eyes glinting amusement. "I am you. Or you are me. Oh, my . . ." In his fingers the counter flashed and vanished. He smiled. "I can see language is not going to be useful in this conversation."

"I'm familiar with the concept, as it happens," Shan said, reaching out with Healer's senses to touch the other. He encountered a cool smoothness very like a Healer's protective Wall. "But we can hardly become all of myself if you are shielded away."

"Clever child. But as you say, this is not the sweet floating dream of a spellmist. This," he gestured, grandly, with one long, sun-darkened hand. A silver dagger appeared in that same hand. He considered it, shrugged and thrust it through his belt.

"This," he repeated, drawing the word out, "is Weapons Hall. You are here because you have found it necessary to be armed. Do tell me why."

Shan frowned, allowed himself to wonder if this after all was madness. Perhaps he was even now dying in the wreckage of the repair pod, his mind spinning a last, rich fantasy to disarm itself.

"Nothing so precipitate," the man in the cloak said softly. "As you well know. You are strong, hale and sane. That being so, I must again ask—why come here?"

"I don't know that I meant to come here," Shan told him. "It was necessary that I Heal myself, before I did damage. There is a war, you see, and the sub-commander is correct, damn her. I'm not a soldier. But the world is under attack. I must be able to fight. I must be able to—use all of my resources."

"And you trained as Soulweaver, the Mother be praised." The man tipped his head. "*When* are you? Captain of a ship that sails between the stars, and more than a touch of the Dragon in you. And your lady is a Moonhawk. I begin, I think, to see."

He stood, flinging the cloak behind his shoulders, revealing a shabby black tunic and patched black leggings.

"I—we—have been here no more than six times since Moonhawk showed me the way. We've never loved the place, nor sought it out of power-lust. Time, you understand, is not very orderly, but I do believe this is the only occasion upon which I met myself here." He beckoned and Shan went forward to take the strong, callused hand.

"Shan is my name in your when?"

"Yes," he said, as they walked toward the shimmering wall of weaponry.

"In this when," the man lay his hand upon his breast, "your name is Lute. Let us arm me well."

THE WORLD looked different, even with his eyes closed.

The information that came through shuttered eyes somehow told him it was afternoon; it also told him that one wall of the tent where he'd been allowed rest-space was in shade.

His left arm was slightly warmer than his right—the sun was on that side of the tent.

There were sounds, each fraught with meaning: he could hear the quiet, regular step of someone walking a guard path; he could hear an occasional low mumble of voices, which meant that he was in an area where security was a concern.

Even the sounds he wasn't hearing meant something. He was alone in the tent, the med-tech having gone elsewhere for the moment.

He savored the information coming in, sorted it and milked it dry of meaning, while some back corner of his mind not engaged in this vital task was explaining very calmly that these things meant nothing to him. He was a master of trade, a Healer—a peaceable fellow, really, despite his place in the line direct of a clan descended of a smuggler, a soldier, and a schoolboy.

yos'Galan—the schoolboy's line—had always been respectable, though, in all fairness, the genes had been mixed across lines so often that it was difficult now to know where respectable yos'Galan began and pirate yos'Phelium ended.

Outside the tent, from the sunny left, came two sets of quiet footsteps, accompanied by the low murmur of a woman's voice. He caught the word 'backup' on the edge of hearing that seemed much sharper than usual, then the steps went beyond the tent and Shan realized he was ravenous.

He opened his eyes and sat up in one smooth motion. The cubicle was as he recalled it; the remaining sandwiches still wrapped under their cool-gel.

He made short work of them, feeding a hunger so great it was almost nausea, at the same time aware that he could always eat one of the ration bars tucked into his combat belt, if the sandwiches proved insufficient to his need.

As he ate, he considered. He was often hungry after a visit to Healspace—perhaps a two-sandwich hunger, he thought wryly, unwrapping the last of the food Dustin had wrangled from the mess tent. When he and Priscilla had traveled so far in spirit to talk to Val Con—both of them woke starving, having lost a tenth or more of their bodies' mass. *Magic*, Priscilla had said then. *Strong magic uses an immense amount of energy.*

So, Shan considered, polishing off the fifth sandwich with a sigh, Lute's Hall of Weapons must be very strong magic, indeed. He sat back on the cot and shook his head.

"Shan," he murmured, mindful of ears close by, "what in the blessed name of sanity have you gotten yourself into?"

He hadn't taken much from the Hall: a knife and a shield. Things that would serve any soldier well, Lute had said, then held out a thick manuscript. *Soldier Lore* was written across the face of its leather binding in the ornate characters of a language Shan was positive he didn't read.

"Behold, the most useful of all the weapons in the hall," Lute said with a flourish. "Take it."

Shan did, looking at his mentor—at himself—doubtfully. "It's rather heavy, if one is to be marching about. Which seems to be my next assignment."

"Nonsense," said Lute, "it's not heavy at all." When Shan looked again at his hand, the manuscript was gone.

It appeared that the lore of a good soldier was still with him; his bones felt steeped in it.

Shan shook his head and, in an instinct that was in no way his own, began to take inventory.

He had no gun, no sword, no distance weapons whatever in his belt or pouch. The blade he did have was neither a combat blade nor a bayonet, but part of a folding utility kit.

In an emergency, however, *Soldier Lore* informed him, a blade is a blade, so he inspected it carefully, oddly pleased with its quality and balance. He'd held worse and used it to good purpose—he shook his head, banishing the memory that was not his—It was *Val Con* who had the passion for sharp edges of all types; peaceable Shan was accurate enough with his pellet-gun, but he tended to rely on Healer skill as protection from harm.

Weapons check complete, Shan turned his mind to other details that required attention. He stood and walked out of the tent.

"Dustin?"

The startled guard's about-face nearly took Shan's mind off his purpose. The gun had come around—but not dangerously so.

"Sir. I thought you were gonna sleep till the cows came home."

"Are we expecting cows, Corporal? I didn't think . . ."

"Naw," the man waved the expression away with his free hand. "Just meant I was sure I'd have to rouse you when the time came. You've got another hour or so, if you wanna catch another snooze. Sir."

"I have slept, thank you. Is there a way I can check on the boat I came in on? It would be good to know if any messages have come through—or gone out."

"I don't think the sub-commander wants you just wandering around. Sir. It might be better if you'd just go on back inside and—"

SHAN SIGHED INWARDLY. *Soldier Lore* noted that the corporal could be taken, if need be. He was measuring Shan's distance by soldier-speed, not by pilot speed.

Abruptly, a memory flashed of Cousin Luken bel'Tarda, as un-war-like a man as one could wish.

"All I ask," the gentle mannered merchant would say, as the child Shan tagged after him through acres of warehoused carpets, "is an honest advantage. When I have that, the other party is nearly always positive that my position is weak."

Shan tipped his head, deliberately meek, and reached out, oh, so gently, with Healer sense, inspiring Dustin with goodwill.

"Corporal," he said, voice and face all calm reasonableness. "I've spent the better part of a day inside my work suit inside a lifeboat. At least grant me a chance to walk around."

Corporal Dustin blinked and Shan moved closer, looking gravely into eyes the color of nutmeg. "I suggest you take me to the departure point," he murmured. "I should get a feel for my boots, if I'm going to have to march in them."

Dustin blinked again, glanced down at the boots the quartermaster had supplied. After a moment, he nodded.

"Yessir. We can move in that direction. Might happen we can at least take a glance toward that spitfire of yours when we go by."

Shan smiled and withdrew the tendril of goodwill. "Thank you, Dustin."

THEY HAD PASSED several sentries, but it became quickly apparent that Sub-Commander Kritoulkas did not believe in concentrating her people in one spot. Dustin directed him this way, that way, up a series of trails, all of which showed use, but none that were obviously more important than another.

Shan nodded to himself, pleased with the sub-commander's arrangements—and then, on the very edge of his sharpened hearing, caught a sound.

He listened, ignoring the sound of Dustin's boots scraping against stone: a familiar sound, common in ports and cities. . .

"Dustin," he said softly, "do we have heavy-lift rotor-craft on our side? Perhaps two or three of them?"

The corporal flicked him a startled look, stopped heavily and took his hard hat into his hand. He cocked his head to one side, listening—then snatched for his belt comm.

"Traffic," he said distinctly. "Possible copter noise, any ID?"

"Traffic," came the quick reply. "Ear's going on. Reports to Traffic Two, thank you."

Shan listened. The sound was distinct, now, though it was difficult to be sure of direction through the canopy of trees.

He thought of his late spiral worldward, the rotor noise growing in his ears. From what he recalled, the sounds were coming—

"From the coast," he said, abruptly. "At least two!"

Dustin looked at him seriously, nodded, and thumbed his Communit again. "Traffic Two, we have estimate of two plus rotors coming from the coast."

"Traffic Two acknowledges. The Ear says three, real low. Thanks, son." There was a slight burp then and the whisper of a new message from a dozen spots in the nearby woods.

"This is the Dealer, this is the Dealer. Shuffle the deck, please, and cut it three ways. Player names the game."

"Good ear, sir," Dustin nodded respectfully at him. "Best move with me. If we get separated—anyplace where there's a definite Y in the trail you'll find a dugout about ten meters in toward the empty side, long as you're inside the camp. Might need to hunt a bit. If there's crossing trails you should see a faint fifth trail—look on the opposite side of that."

Shan nodded, pleased again with the sub-commander.

By now the sound was a definite heavy chop. Coming in low. Fast and low.

At the first Y they came to Dustin took him straight ahead into the woods. The corporal ducked low beneath a branch, and disappeared. A moment later Shan found the dugout and dropped in beside him.

Shan felt the dugout slope deeper into the earth, could see where portions of the wall had been reinforced with local wood and branches. One of the cut branches, as tall as he and with a few gray-green leaves still clinging to it attracted his attention. He leaned against the branch. It flexed slightly, but felt sternly durable. His hand went around it comfortably. . .

"This is the Dealer, this is the Dealer. We've got a three-handed game of Stone Poker. Cards are on the table. Jacks are wild. Spectators will refrain from spitting."

Dustin nodded. "C'mon, Sir. Jacks are wild means every available hand. Stone Poker means they're up toward the quarry somewhere—"

"My boat!"

"Yessir. Or maybe the Yxtrang wreck."

There was a roar overhead. Dustin ducked back into the dugout. Shan, peering upward through a gap in the trees, saw three black forms lifting into the sky—heading back toward the coast in a hurry.

"That refrain from spittin' stuff," Dustin said, easing out of the dugout. "That means no shooting til we get orders, sir."

Shan looked at him and held out his empty hand and his stick.

"Yessir, I know. Please follow me."

He began to do that, then realized that the sound of the retreating rotors had changed somehow. He fell to his knees, found the gap in the sheltering branches—

The last of the copters was moving very slowly, almost hovering. Perhaps they had spotted someone or—

A figure appeared from the belly of the copter, sliding down a cable made visible by his motion. A second figure followed, and a third. Four. . .

There were eight of them on the ground, the last having dropped a good distance as the rotor began to move away.

"Sir?" Dustin had missed him and returned, sounding both relieved and annoyed. "Sir? You'll need to come this way—"

Shan stood, automatically brushing the dirt from leather-covered knees.

"Corporal, that last copter dropped eight soldiers over this way."

"I didn't see it," Dustin said doubtfully.

"I did. They must be on that rise over there. Slid down a rope in a hurry."

The comm burped and gave out a muffled chant.

"This is the Dealer. Side-bets are in order when you see cash. Repeat, side-bets are in order when you see cash."

Shan glanced at Dustin's worried face, eyebrows lifted in question.

"Sir, that means we can engage if we have to, local unit leader to decide." He grimaced. "Guess that's me."

He reached for the comm and thumbed the switch.

"Traffic Two, chance that eight slid down a straw near—" He waved a beseeching hand. Shan nodded, pointed as best he could through the trees.

"Traffic Two, that's maybe eight down the straw near hill four."

There was a pause then, and Shan could feel the tension building in the man's emotive grid.

Finally, "This is Traffic. We have the straw report. Confirm visually, says The Dealer. Tell me go."

"Gone," said Dustin and tucked the communit in its holster, switch off.

SHAN WISHED he'd had a chance to break the boots in. As it was, he'd have sore feet tonight. If the luck smiled, of course.

He also wished he had something more than a branch and a utility knife for weapons. He'd considered making a spear out of the stick—it was nearly his height and reasonably straight—but he didn't have the necessary time. So he carried it, hoping balefully that he now knew how to use a cudgel if he needed to.

The going was slow. They'd climbed down a hill and now were inching up a rocky slope sparsely studded with trees. Portions of the slope were nearly cliff, and it was Dustin's knowledge of the trails that kept Shan from taking several bad turns.

Halfway up the hill they heard muffled voices, speaking a language that Shan's sharpened hearing found unfamiliar. Dustin glanced back, signaling by tapping his ear and then waving an empty hand around the land.

Shan nodded, concentrated. After a moment, he pointed carefully to his left, but still uphill.

Ever more slowly they climbed, with Shan from time to time cringing at the amount of noise Corporal Dustin threw into the wind.

The alien voices wavered, lowered. Dustin looked back to him and Shan concentrated, heard not with ears this time, but with

Healer sense: eight intent patterns, one lanced with red sparkings of pain. Shan swallowed and pointed for Dustin—to the left yet, but not nearly so far uphill.

At a crawl, they went on.

A few moments later Shan saw his first Yxtrang. And then his second, third, fourth, fifth, sixth and seventh. They stood alertly on the edge of a shaded pocket of bush and branches just above a near vertical rock drop.

Each carried weapons, some several. Shan recognized a sniper gun, four carbine equivalents, a heavy automatic weapon, and what looked like an anti-armor tube.

When his eyes got used to the light, Shan saw his eighth Yxtrang. That one was sitting down, in the dim pocket of bush, employed in fashioning a rough splint for his left leg. He stood, almost fell, and eased himself carefully back to the ground.

Voices again, as two of the standees leaned in toward the pocket, followed by a snarling phrase that might have been an order given.

One of the standees saluted, fist thumping to shoulder, then the seven whole Yxtrang dropped into trail crouch and moved off, melting quietly into the landscape.

Shan considered the remaining Yxtrang, who had readjusted the splint and was prying himself to his feet by using his rifle for a cane. It came to him, calmly, that a rifle was a far better weapon than a stick. He looked over to Dustin.

It took several moments to make the Corporal certain of what he wished to do, and more than a little exercise of his own will over the other man's to still the argument he saw leaping in the nutmeg eyes.

He moved slowly, silent over the rocks and twigs, and came up on the pocket of brush. He had a moment's vertigo, as he stared down the steep incline and he wished in that moment with all his heart to be back on the *Passage*, and never again be the man who had formulated—who would carry out—this plan.

He shook himself and crept forward a few more inches, making sure of his grip on stick and knife.

The Yxtrang looked up, surprised by the sudden, sure intrusion into his safe place, the trigger of his rifle-cane well away from any useful finger.

Shan moved, the cudgel swung in a knowing arc, slamming the hand that fumbled at the gun, taking the other man off balance, onto his injured leg. Shan closed, the cudgel rising quickly to catch the thrust of the Yxtrang's knife. The eyes that locked on his in the moment before the cudgel crushed the man's windpipe knew no pity, sought no quarter.

The Yxtrang's body went over the lip of the pocket, the knife still uselessly clutched in one hand.

Shan sighed once, short and sharp, and bent down to claim his rifle.

EROB'S HOLD:
Practice Grounds

THERE HAD BEEN two meetings—one, the scout and captain alone in the privacy of the tent they shared, Nelirikk standing guard at the entrance, as was his right and jealously held duty.

That meeting, the first, had been a quiet thing, for all that it danced through four separate languages, and at the end of an hour they two had emerged and walked shoulder-and-shoulder across the practice field, Nelirikk in his place as rear-guard, until they came to the command tent.

The meeting there had not been so quiet.

Commander Carmody and aged General tel'Vosti—they heard the captain out with the respect due her rank and battle years. The elder female civilian—the delm of the House to which the captain and the general belonged, and to whom each owed differing degrees of allegiances in a pattern which Nelirikk had not quite puzzled out—that was something else.

"You will send your lifemate alone into a nest of Yxtrang?" she demanded, the Liaden High Tongue sounding like splinters of glass.

"High melant'i, indeed, Lady yos'Phelium. But, tell me, do,

what you expect one man might accomplish against a horde of
ravening animals."

There was silence in the command tent for a moment and the
old general looked no less grim than the Terran commander.
Captain Miri Robertson sighed and shook her head.

"Couple points you're missing," she said, using Terran to
counter the blade of the old lady's outrage. "First off, the man's a
scout. He don't wanna be seen—you don't see him. Second, he's got
a touch with an explosive that's really something special. Third
thing is?" She looked at the old delm until that one stiffly inclined
her head.

"Third thing is," the captain said then, "is it's his idea. I don't
like it any better'n you do. Spent the last hour trying to talk him out
of it. Won't give an inch. Stubborn, too, while we're airing his faults.
But the fact of the matter is he's got a point. He's got a chance of
getting in, creating serious damage, and getting back out alive.
He's the only one we got that I know of has that chance, with the
possible exception of Beautiful, here. If we don't stir Yxtrang
around, keep 'em off balance and blow us up an ammo dump or
two, we're all gonna be real sorry, real soon."

"Good soldier sense, from scout and captain," the General said.
"Make your bow to the truth, Emrith."

She glared. "I have seen enough war to last me this lifetime and
the next, Win Den. And I say to you that, dragon or scout, the only
likely outcome of this lackwitted scheme is that he will die."

"Not necessarily," the scout murmured, and smiled when the
delm's eyes crossed his. "I do hold—certain—skills, besides having
the advantage of knowing my targets in advance. I may die, but I
assure you that it is much more likely that I will come away whole,
and return to stand at my lady's side."

Erob sniffed and used her chin to point at Nelirikk, where he
stood guard inside the entrance.

"If that has an equal chance of creating mayhem and escaping,
why not send it?"

The scout shook his head in the Terran manner and bowed
lightly in the Liaden.

"Why so," he said, and to Nelirikk's ear the tone was almost teasing, "should the luck frown and I fall, I will have left my captain with a like weapon with which to continue the war."

"I'll OK it," Commander Carmody spoke then and nodded at the scout. "Draw what you need from stores, and mind! If you take that flitter, you bring it back, boyo. Am I clear?"

The scout bowed once more, eyes serious, though his mouth smiled. "You are clear, Jason. Thank you."

IT WAS ON THE SECOND DAY after the scout quit camp that Nelirikk was called to the command tent once more.

He went hurriedly, with a nod for the comm tech who had been testing his memory of call code and band protocol, and arrived to find commander, general, his own captain and the full complement of minor staff awaiting him.

"Sit down, Beautiful," the commander said, giving him the grace of his field-name, and with a wave that might have been an acknowledgment of Nelirikk's salute, or part of the order to be seated.

"Them big hummers of rotor craft," the captain said, without preamble. "What do they carry? Troops, equipment, special weapons? You got the floor."

It took him a moment to realize that he was not being offered a floor as his own, but the opportunity to speak.

"Captain. When well supplied, each can carry eight dozens of troops, or field artillery and four dozens. I have not the range of them since they may carry auxiliary fuel tanks instead of troops.

"They can be used well for forward supply, but are light on top and side armor. They are not attack aircraft and their gunners are but four. It is not unusual for them to drag—drop troops.

"Rumor is that the landing structure was designed for lighter work and is always under repair. Their crews think themselves far above the troops they ferry."

"Well, there's a bit of good news," Commander Carmody commented. "Too good to work as hard as they could for the ground guys."

"How many?" the captain demanded, intent. Nelirikk shook his head, Terran-wise.

"Each regiment has different numbers. I saw four pods of three at the base I was sent from."

"Fifteen hundred troops might thus be moved in a short-range rush, were everyone crammed to overload," said the general, looking up from the paper which was not filled with idle doodling, as Nelirikk had suspected, but a dense line of manual calculation.

"Gotcha." The commander nodded at tel'Vosti.

"Explorer," asked the general, "are they well supplied?"

"Sir. I do not know the mission. I cannot hazard to say."

"Good boy," the old soldier said unexpectedly. "Don't let us wish ourselves into troubles." He glanced speculatively around the table before he spoke again.

"Tell me, Explorer. If you were on the spot, and you knew there to be what might prove to be a courier boat for an opponent's battleship landed within range, what would you do?"

"Courier for a battleship?" The concept amazed. Yet the question was obviously serious. Nelirikk applied himself to the answer.

"If the general pleases. I would send one pod—three—well equipped soonest. A second pod would be fueled and ready for loading depending on need. I would also increase pressure everywhere that I could to disrupt . . ."

"Thank you," the general said, holding up a hand and nodding. "So would I."

Nelirikk sat a moment in uncomfortable silence as something was decided in several glances round the table.

"Yessir," Commander Carmody said, perhaps to himself. "When this little dust up is over, I'm gonna go up the park and find me that fongbear up there and pin a medal on his chest." He came to his feet and Nelirikk jumped up, snapping a salute, only to find that the other was bending over a kit belt.

The commander extracted something small from the belt and handed it to the captain, then turned to Nelirikk, a pistol in his hand.

"Beautiful, we're sending Redhead's Irregulars out in harm's way, and she refuses to budge without you."

The big man extended the pistol, butt first. Nelirikk understood that he was to take it, and did so, stunned by the purity of its balance, its perfect, deadly elegance. The grips were carved of wood, the metal a wondrous satiny. . .

"Took me the same way, first time I saw it," Captain Redhead said from his left. "But listen up, Beautiful—Commander Carmody ain't done yet."

Nelirikk snatched after his wandering wits, raised a hand to snap a salute and was waved into stillness. The commander pointed.

"That pretty belongs to Senior Commander Rialto and if anything happens to it—or to Captain Redhead—she'll give me hell. Bring them both back. That's an order."

His salute was waved away again and the commander held out another large hand.

"You'll want the ammo, too, boyo."

SOME THINGS, you didn't question.

Like when the man you'd married, thinking it was bad enough he was Liaden and thodelm in a House she'd figured out by now was one of the fifty called High—when the man you'd slit your own throat before you saw him hurt came to you the night he left for something that might not let him back alive and murmured, "Cha'trez, you must know this. I am Nadelm Korval, by lineage. You are nadelmae, by right of our mating. Should I fall, you must claim the Ring and as delm keep Korval safe."

You heard that, you just nodded, and pulled him close in the dark, and you didn't ask, *So, who do I claim this Ring from and why should they believe me?* and you didn't say, *What makes you so sure I'm gonna outlive you?* You just nodded, and held him and listened to his heart beat, strong and steady next to your ear, and then you kissed him and you let him go, the night swallowing him up, like he'd never been at all.

Likewise, Miri thought, looking down at the golden gyrfalcon in her palm, you didn't ask why Jase Carmody picked you for the hot seat, if he happened to find Nirvana, this war. You just took the token and didn't make a fuss, kept it close and hoped to every possible god of war and peace that you never had to show it.

Miri pinned the token to the lining of her sleeve, then sealed the battle jacket and looked up at her tall shadow.

He looked down at her, dark blue eyes alert, brown face expressionless. She'd gotten used to him, mostly, but there were times, like now, when she felt ice sweep down her backbone, remembering what this man was.

Going into battle with an Yxtrang at your back. Robertson, if I'd've known you were going to turn out a nut case I'd've left you on Klamath.

Miri sighed and straightened, giving her aide a grim smile.

"OK, Beautiful. Let's round 'em up and move 'em out."

THEY SAT IN WHAT ORDER they could in the back of a large farm truck bouncing its way along unpaved track. The captain had appointed of her troop three lieutenants, naming them properly First, Second, and Third, and she also appointed the sergeants. The under-officers then appointed the squads.

It was what one might expect of a unit put together of remnants and volunteers, moving in all haste toward its first blooding. Still.

The captain sat to his left, her eyes closed, though her grip against the catch-rope was not that of a sleeper. Nelirikk cleared his throat.

"Captain?"

The fierce gray eyes snapped open. "Yo."

"I have not had time to finish properly, but I have been working on something for the troop, if you allow."

She sat up straighter, looked into his face with a curious expression.

He reached among the hastily stowed supplies, and pulled a plain cloth sack from between several sealed containers of explosives.

"I had hoped to make it more complete, but glory comes upon us quickly . . ." he said, deftly fitting together the lengths of tubing.

Holding the staff in the crook of his elbow, he then took the square of labored-over cloth from the bag, unfolding it as gently as he could in the crowded, lurching truck.

The captain stared, and for a moment he thought that he had offended, that she would reject his gift to the troop—

"That's some piece of work," she said, taking a portion of the flag in her hands. She looked up at him, feral eyes bright. "Your idea?"

"Captain. Yes. A gift for the unit for being permitted as a recruit. If it pleases."

The nickname of the unit, 1st Irregulars, was rendered in the trade language, as befit a troop made from as many different sources as theirs: bronze letters on a black stripe fully a third of the flag deep. The symbol—ah, that had been a hard night's thought!—a knife in silver with two sets of wings, one black, one white, set on a green field. One set of wings were dragon's wings, to honor Jela's arms-mate, who had founded the House of the scout. The blade was Jela's own symbol, of course; and the other set of wings was from the bird of the Gyrfalks.

"It pleases," the captain said amid the growing buzz of interest as others of the troop began to take notice.

"Hang it up," she said, then, and he did so, fastening it to the top of the distaff, where it hung, brave in its solitude, without yet the proper complement of captured enemy flags to adorn it.

"That's good," the captain said, softly. "That's real good, Beautiful. Turn it around now, so everybody can see." She came to her feet and jumped lightly onto the seat, one small hand on the catch-rope.

"All right, listen up! We still got us a bit of riding before we start our march, and we got one more important decision to make. First off, I want squads together."

In a remarkably short time and with only a little too much jostling, the squads formed themselves.

"OK!" called the captain. "Some of you close by saw what I have here. The rest of you take a good look at the unit's flag! Now you got a choice. You can go out there and fight and hope no one notices you. Or you can go out there and fight and let 'em know you're there. Which squads ain't interested in carrying the unit flag into our first fight? Hold your hands up and sing out!"

The close-packed squads were abruptly silent, sitting as still as they could.

The captain let the silence stretch, then flashed a grin at the assembled soldiers.

"Darn," she called out, "that's gonna make my job harder. Be sure you understand that this is serious stuff. Which ever squad carries this flag is gonna get a lot of heat. It'll be noisy and it'll be for keeps. You'll have to run with it and protect it, and, most important, you'll have to bring it back safe."

Nelirikk, holding the standard high, felt his heart lift. For here, indeed, was a captain. On the spot, she created a competition, offering the flag. It was the preparedness check-and-drill, with officers standing by to see what needed remedy, what weapons were underprepared, which squad's knives were out of place.

The truck cranked, lurched, and ground to a halt that shuddered every bone in the back. Nelirikk glimpsed forest through the open hatch, with hills sloping away, and an overgrown path too narrow to permit passage of the vehicle.

"All out!" the newly appointed sergeants bawled. "Fall in!"

"Troop Beautiful." The Captain spoke quietly under the noise of evacuating the truck. "Please do the honor of marching the unit's flag down to squad three and turning it over to their bearer."

He stared. After a moment, he remembered to breathe. "Captain," he said, though it was not his place to remind a captain, "I am not in the line of command."

She grinned at him. "Orders, Beautiful. And always remember— volunteering is its own reward."

FENDOR:
Mercenary Headquarters

THE DOOR GUARD looked first at Nova, taking in the leathers, the face, and the frown. The second look caught Liz, who nodded easy-like and lifted two fingers in casual salute. The guard nodded back.

"ID?"

"Lizardi," Liz said and obediently stared down the bore of the retina-reader. It beeped positive and the guard slung it back over her shoulder.

"Her?" A jerk of the head at Nova, standing silent and astonishingly patient at her side.

"She's with me."

"Recruit?" Palpable disbelief, there.

"Lookin' to hire."

The guard's face cleared. She nodded to Nova and touched a stud on her belt. The door behind her slid back along its track and she stepped aside to let them pass. "Cleared to Dispatch. Need a guide, Commander?"

"I remember the way, thanks," Liz said and stepped forward, Nova yos'Galan following a respectful two steps behind.

�֍ ✖ ✖

FENDOR 'quarters doubled as Home and it was always hopping. This evening, the place was wall-to-wall with mercs, many with kits on their backs. Liz frowned. Something was up. Something *big* was up. She lagged half-a-second and let a crew of six pack-bearing techies get in front of her.

"Might be hard for you to hire," she muttered as Nova came abreast. "Looks like some big doings."

"Only lead me to Dispatch, Angela Lizardi. I anticipate no difficulty in hiring."

Liz snorted and lengthened her stride as much as conditions allowed. A couple minutes later, she took the right into Dispatch, which was crazier and more crowded than the main hall, and forged ahead toward the counter without bothering to make sure the Liaden woman was still with her.

She broke into the clear space before the counter and grinned in sudden delight.

"Hey, Roscoe!"

The square built little guy hogging the main screen looked up, bald head gleaming under the lights. Raisin-colored eyes scanned the crowd, pinned her. The enormous mustache—black like he was twenty instead of rising sixty—lifted in a grin.

"Lizzie! I known this one bring you out from hidin'! Come over an' tell me who you got."

She shook her head and walked over to him, reaching across the counter to grab both shoulders.

"What happened to your pigtail?" she asked, remembering the shiny, foot-long braid that had been his pride, even above the mustache. Roscoe pulled a long face.

"Ah, I sell it to buy a watch for m'wife, but you know what? Bitch leave me anyway." He laughed—a roar that belonged to a man twice his height—grabbed her forearms and squeezed—gently, because Roscoe was stronger than he looked. "Lizzie, you lookin' damnfine. I get relief in two hour. You stick aroun' an' we do a mattress test, eh? I book you in second wave." He dropped her arms and bent to the computer. "Tell me who you got."

"I don't have anyone," Liz said quietly.

"We wish to hire," Nova yos'Galan added from her side. Roscoe looked up, blinking his hard little eyes.

"You want to hire? You got to wait. Suzuki's hiring everything got a gun." He made a shooing motion with his hands. "Come back two, three day, we maybe got a couple 'prentices lef' for you to hire."

Nova shook her head. "My business is urgent and I *will* hire soldiers," she said, firm, but not with the blaze of temper Liz had expected. "Please let it be known that I will double the payout on Suzuki's contracts."

Roscoe stared at her for a beat of three before he looked over to Liz.

"Who the hell this?"

"I will pay," Nova stated, cutting Liz off before she could answer, "in cantra."

Roscoe pursed his lips. "She crazy?" he asked Liz.

"You could say."

"Fine." Roscoe looked back to Nova. "You crazy. You gotta hire. You pay in cantra. Nothin' I can do. You talk to Suzuki, cut you own deal. Then I make it OK wit' the 'puter. *Ichi?*"

"*Su bei*," Nova said surprisingly. "Where may I find Suzuki?"

"You stay put. I bring her here. No way I miss this one." He grinned and flipped a toggle on the board. "Suzuki, you come front Dispatch," he said into the mike. "Somebody you gotta meet."

She had expected another such as Angela Lizardi—rangy, tough, and tall. But the woman for whom the crowd parted minutes later was no taller than herself, sturdy and efficient. Her hair was very short and very black. Her eyes were chips of blue ice, set at a slant in a composed, determined face.

Nova straightened, for if Val Con himself had named Angela Lizardi first speaker, then the woman who came now was surely a delm.

The woman stopped at the edge of the crowd with a nod.

"Liz," she said and her voice was quiet and clear. "We can use you."

"So Roscoe said," Angela Lizardi replied in her laconic way. "But I'm here with her." She jerked her head and Nova found herself caught by those slanting blue eyes.

The owner of the eyes bowed, not a generic, Terran, surrogate handshake bow, but something that recognizably approached the proper mode between strangers of unknown rank.

"Suzuki Rialto, Senior Commander, Gyrfalks Unit."

Nova bowed as between equals and saw interest move in the blue eyes. "Nova yos'Galan, Clan Korval," she returned. It was perhaps not best wise to give her true name within this crowd of unknowns, but one wished to deal honorably with honorable persons. She straightened.

"You may know us as Tree-and-Dragon Family."

The other woman's interest intensified. "Indeed, the unit has done business with Tree-and-Dragon in the past. What may I be honored to do for you, ma'am?"

Good. A person of integrity and quick wit. Nova inclined her head. "I have need of soldiers, Commander. Many soldiers, and at once. I am informed by this person here," she used her chin to point at Roscoe, "that you are hiring everything that has a gun. I submit that my need is at least as great as your own and ask that we work equally toward equal ground."

She heard Angela Lizardi snort, but did not deign to look at her. Suzuki Rialto's face betrayed slight interest, and a tinge of regret.

"It must of course pain me to deny Tree-and-Dragon Family this consideration," she said, most properly. "However, my need overrides every other conceivable need in this galaxy or the next. I am blunt with you, ma'am. You will forgive me when I say that I have people trapped upon a world under Yxtrang attack." She swept a small, square hand out, indicating the now-silent crowd.

"What you see here is a rescue force. You may outbid me—in fact, I don't doubt that you can. But I do not believe you will hire one soldier until we have rescued our own."

But Nova was staring at her, feeling a certain sense of wonder unfolding within her and tasting, *tasting* the tang of the luck, Korval's curse and Korval's blessing.

"Under Yxtrang attack?" she repeated, to gain the time she required to assimilate it and then shook her head as her mother had often done, not to express negation so much as baffled amaze.

"Commander Rialto, it may be we have a common goal."

Suzuki Rialto tipped her head. "Please explain."

"My brother is on that planet—local name Lytaxin. And the lifemate of my brother, as well."

"That's Redhead she's talking about there," Angela Lizardi put in and the other woman looked at her sharply.

"She says," Liz added. "I don't put much stock in that side, myself. Last I knew, she was calling him her partner." She pointed her finger and Nova raised an eyebrow. "Show Suzuki your picture there, Goldie."

She reached into her sleeve pocket for the folder, opened it and offered it to Suzuki Rialto, who took one quick look and laughed.

"Him? Last *I* saw them, she was as likely to kill him as kiss him."

Nova felt her lips twitch, all at once in sympathy with her new and unknown sister. "It is a common dilemma, when one deals closely with my brother," she said solemnly, closing the folder and slipping it away.

Suzuki grinned, then let the expression fade to one of calculation. "It seems our goal is the same, ma'am, as you have pointed out. I suggest that I am skilled in the hiring and outfitting of soldiers, as is Commander Lizardi. You are yourself perhaps skilled in an area where my expertise has currently fallen short."

Nova inclined her head politely, acknowledging the truth of the other woman's words and her own willingness to hear more.

"In what manner might I assist you toward attaining our common goal, Commander?"

The blue eyes met her straightly—the look of a delm, in truth.

"We need ships," said Suzuki Rialto.

Nova truly smiled, then, and bowed.

"As it happens, I can locate ships."

"I thought you could," Suzuki said gravely and offered her arm. "Let us retire and discuss particulars." She looked over to Miri Robertson's first speaker. "Liz? Are you in?"

"Couldn't keep me out with a battalion."

EROB'S BOUNDARY:
Quarry War Zone

※ ※

THERE HAD BEEN opportunity to kill more Yxtrang, on the way from the pocket of brush to the quarry entrance. Dustin had accounted for two and Shan three—one of those a lucky shot into the impenetrable treetops, prompted by the very faintest of out-of-place leaf rustle.

But the quarry. The quarry was where the heavy action centered.

"Looks like they're after your boat, sir." Dustin whispered, as they crouched behind a conveniently placed boulder. The lifeboat was precisely where he had left it, upright in the entrance to the quarry, closer to the mercenaries' line than the Yxtrang.

"Indeed it does, Corporal, but why? It has no fuel. It has no weapons. It has a radio, but surely the Yxtrang have their own radios?"

Dustin looked at him oddly. "Hard to tell why 'trang'll do anything. Maybe they want it for a war prize. Important thing is, if they think it's worth arguing over, we gotta be sure they don't win the argument."

At the moment, it appeared that Sub-Commander Kritoulkas' regulars were holding their own in the argument. The Yxtrang

248

liberally sprinkled throughout the trees opposite were actively involved in the dispute, but had made no push to advance their position. Shan sank a little lower behind the shielding boulder, thinking about that.

"Are we seeing a diversion, Corporal?" he asked finally. "Or are they waiting for friends?"

"Hard to say, sir." Dustin was moving, inching his rifle into position. Shan looked, saw the target, looked again and chose his own mark.

The argument continued, and all at once the Yxtrang began to move, pushing their line grimly forward. Behind them, deeper into the opposite wood, Shan's sharpened hearing registered the sound of heavy equipment, distinct even in the fury of the firefight. He flicked a look at Dustin.

"There's something big moving in the woods."

The corporal nodded, face pale except for the thread of blood down one cheek, where a chip off the boulder had cut him.

"I feel it," he said, mouth tightening. "Get ready to fall back, sir. They were waiting for the armor to catch up with them."

Around him, then, he felt a—withdrawing—as, one squad at a time, the mercenaries melted back from their positions. Across, the Yxtrang pushed forward, and the sound of the armor moving was thunder in the ground, rattling through his chest and into his head.

"Now," Dustin said. "Fall back." Shan nodded and heard the other man leave, even as he tried to recall if he had seen anything like anti-armor, in his brief and all-too-incomplete tour of the mercenary encampment.

Where, he wondered, *are they withdrawing to that will stand safe against a tank?*

A pellet struck his boulder, spraying his face with gravel. Shan ducked, found the range and fired. An Yxtrang soldier crumpled out from behind a bush that was too meager to shelter him and didn't move again.

He was alone on what had been the mercenary line, Shan realized, and about to be overrun by Yxtrang. Yet, why should he fall back, when the means to kill the oncoming tank was right here?

The lifeboat's coils still functioned, after all. It was but the work of a moment to set them to overload.

Decision taken, Shan began at last to move from cover to carefully chosen cover, angling toward the lifeboat.

BEAUTIFUL was two steps behind her, armed like an officer, and almost totally silent, which was more than she could say for the rest of the unit.

There'd been a kind of constant crunch as the Irregulars moved through the woods—nothing to be done about it at this point—and then a single distant boom, as if something really big had blown up.

That one was a puzzle. It wasn't the sound a shell made being fired, or the sound it made hitting something, usually. And it sure couldn't have been an ammo-dump because Miri knew Kritoulkas had been running mostly with carry-it-yourselves.

Her people did pretty good at not stopping when the guns started chattering.

There was a lot of gun noise she didn't recognize right off and that made her nervous, because if she didn't know the sound it was likely to be Yxtrang caliber stuff.

The battle-flag was about twenty steps ahead of her, wrapped tight around its staff. The squad that had it was moving out. Likely they thought they'd show up, unroll the flag, and scare Yxtrang back into space without a ship.

Not bloody likely.

The key here was going to be showing up at all. The Yxtrang, even if there were a lot of them, probably had their hands pretty full because Kritoulkas was bossing a near-pure Gyrfalks crew.

The communit in her pocket hadn't buzzed, which was good news—it meant Jase and the house guard were still holding a quiet fort. Be bad if the Irregulars didn't have a place to go home to, once the party was over.

She signaled a stop, waved her three lieutenants in. One of them hunted out this way, regular.

Beautiful was there, back to her. He was carrying his field pack and two extra ammo boxes for the automatic weapon carried by the flag-bearing unit, no complaint, no slowdown. At halt he'd dropped the boxes and instantly gone on alert.

Miri saw how he watched: lower level of trees, mid-level on rock-piles and such, eyes long enough on each spot to catch color or movement. The greenies either stared hard at one spot and waited for it to grow wings or swiveled their heads around so fast they'd get themselves whiplash.

She took her time deciding on the next phase of the march. The sounds were heavier to the west, which the local looie thought meant they were centered on an old quarry on the south side of the merc camp. That could be good if it meant Kritoulkas had the Yxtrang pinned down. The firing was getting pretty heavy . . .

She nodded, reluctantly broke the squads into two groups. The smaller group, four squads under the local, would take the uphill side. As they closed into the quarry they'd follow some path he knew.

Her main group of six squads would waltz right on down the main trail, trusting that the sub-commander was still holding up her end of the bargain with the mercs.

She felt eyes on her, turned to see Beautiful looking at her.

"What's up?"

"Nothing is up, Captain. No air cover. No sign of ambush in the trees. No listening devices."

Inwardly, Miri sighed. "I meant, what's bugging you? What should I know?"

"Captain, only the single large explosion. By now if there was artillery it would be in use. We have here one hundred. Probably the unit we will face has more."

"Great. Even odds."

She wasn't sure if he got the sarcasm; he simply nodded and asked permission for a drink from his canteen, since action might come upon them anytime.

The distant shooting went almost quiet for a moment or two and then became insistent and rushed.

She knew the sound of that—one side had managed to mass a bit of a charge. The heavy, nearly steady beat of a Paradis 88 made her suppose the Yxtrang were on the move against a well defended spot.

She waited while the lieutenants carried her news to the sergeants, and then they moved on, the crunch of boots not nearly as loud as the growing noise of battle.

THE FOUR SQUADS under the local lieutenant melted away as best they could. The main body continued ahead, with the sound of firing heavy and the acrid smell of battle permeating the air. Forward motion halted abruptly. Soldiers dropped, taking cover. Ahead, the woods were noisy, like whoever was there didn't care if they were heard.

Miri dropped, felt the presence that was Nelirikk, positioned like a bodyguard, protecting her back, while his height still allowed him to see beyond her.

The noise stopped as suddenly as it started, and then there was a more distant sound, as of confident marching. Miri began moving toward one of her lieutenants when the woods near her lead troops exploded with the sound of a Paradis 88.

The targets were up on the hill, and Miri could suddenly see the movement and hear the return fire of dozens of alien weapons. There was a whoosh, an explosion and scream—but by now it was clear which side was which and her lead troops opened live fire on an enemy for the first time.

It was obvious they'd stumbled into a flanking movement by the Yxtrang, one that the Paradis had been supposed to foil.

Now it was their turn, and she signaled her squads into a battle line, tried to straighten out a kink that could be dangerous. The folks on the hill hadn't been expecting quite so many people, apparently, but they were still willing to fight.

It was hard to tell, but it looked like there were more and more of the Yxtrang up on the hill, as if the whole damned bunch of them had tried an end around.

The Irregulars were returning fire, but the lead squad was in big trouble and likely to get cut off. The Yxtrang were concentrating fire there, and there were more of them on the hill, so many that it looked like a charge forming.

Miri pulled the whistle from her pocket, sounded the attention blast and the double-pulse of short pullback. The Irregular's firing dropped decidedly then as they all tried to worm backward five meters like they'd been taught.

"Beautiful, up there. A charge forming?" Miri yelled.

"Yes, Captain. I believe it likely."

"Tell that crew there to open up with their toy. Now!"

Nelirikk crawled to the crew with flag still wrapped tight, carrying the boxes of extra ammo to them, taking time to point out the most likely route down the hill . . .

There was something quite satisfying in the chatter of the Sternbach. True, it wasn't a Paradis 88, but it should do. She glanced back at the smoke-wreathed gun crew.

Shit. Now they were for it.

The gun crew sat behind their almost-shield of a downed log, the Irregular's battle-standard waving insults at the enemy.

Unexpectedly, up on the hillside, a spot of color showed, flapped—snapped to blood red.

Nelirikk was suddenly beside her, low to the ground, a very real grin on his face.

"Captain, we face Tactical Assault Twenty-Two. They are very famous for their attacks!"

She cussed but he didn't hear, for at that moment the woods screamed with Yxtrang rage and the charge began.

THERE WASN'T TIME for finesse. Miri blew the command that released squads to sergeants. And when she turned to repeat the call in the other direction, she saw the Yxtrang behind them.

This charge was really aimed at the Sternbach—in fact both of them were. The unit was falling back on its own accord toward the flag; the Yxtrang were heading there, too.

A young trooper—one of the refugee volunteers—fell half a yard away, the side of his face gone. Miri dove, snatched up his rifle and fired into the oncoming mass while the Sternbach kept up its end of the conversation, and the Paradis—

An Yxtrang fell at her feet, dead, and the short sharp sound of a pistol going off behind her warned her to turn.

The pistol spoke again and there was a wounded Yxtrang flung by her. He started to rise, and she took him out, spinning into a forest of blades as the Yxtrang wave and the 1st Irregulars crashed together and merged.

Miri fired, dropped her man, found another target, and heard Nelirikk scream, "Yadak!"

She saw the blade flashing downward, killing-bright in a huge hand, swung the rifle up to catch it—

From behind and above, Nelirikk's arm swept out, into the blade, smashing it out of the Yxtrang's hand and Nelirikk's hands were around a throat, crushing, and he roared out, "Irregulars! Irregulars!"

The Sternbach chattered on and other voices took up the yell, "Irregulars!" and the flag stood over it all.

NELIRIKK'S ARM was bandaged, but his care was for the flagstaff, whereon he hung—upside down—the flag of Tactical Assault Twenty-two.

Miri waited for yet more casualty reports, watching as the crew of the Sternbach fieldstripped it lovingly.

"Beautiful," she said finally. "What's yadak?"

"Captain." He was carefully looking more at the flag-project than at her. "Yadak was the field name of a dead man. It means nothing."

Miri nodded. She'd been afraid of that. "So you knew that guy. I'm sorry—"

He shrugged, discomforted by more than the wound, Miri thought.

"Yadak made many errors, Captain. He joined the 14th Conquest Corps. He came with them to this planet. He volunteered for Tactical Assault Twenty-two. And he attacked my captain with a machete while she stood command over a unit with Jela's insignia on its flag."

"You mean he shoulda known better?"

He took his time answering.

"Captain, Yadak and I both learned at Jela's feet. He left the home unit before I did, seeking action." He looked at her, blue eyes bleak.

"Yadak did not believe much in tradition. But, yes, Captain. He should have known better."

THE POSITION of lifeboat number four had been stable for some time. Ren Zel touched a switch on the main board.

"Tower." Rusty Morgenstern's voice was scratchy with fatigue.

"This is the command helm, Radio Tech," Ren Zel said, as gently as one might in the sometimes bewildering modelessness of Terran. "Please do the grace of directing a laser-packet beam to these coordinates—" The transfer was made from his screen to Rusty's with a keystroke. "Alert this station when a dialog has been established."

"Will do."

"Thank you," Ren Zel murmured, and hesitated a moment over the proper phrasing. "Do honor your rest-shift, Radio Tech. The ship depends upon your acuity."

There was a slight pause, followed by a sound that might have been a grudging chuckle. "Caught me, did you? I'll hit the sack as soon as we get Shan on the line. Tower out."

"Command helm out."

He returned to his duty. The watch-points reported nothing untoward. Apparently they had won a measure of respect from the Yxtrang in their first encounter.

Or the Yxtrang were biding their time.

Regardless, the *Passage* continued its spiral orbit toward Lytaxin. Ren Zel pulled up an auxiliary screen and began to calculate approach vectors, measuring this orbit against that, in terms of best defense of the world below. . .

At some point he became aware of a presence beside him and looked up to find Priscilla Mendoza standing quietly at his shoulder, her eyes on the watch screens.

"A quiet shift, First Mate?"

"A quiet shift, Captain. Lifeboat four has come to rest. The Tower is attempting to establish contact. The Yxtrang have been— circumspect."

"Well for the Yxtrang," she said, moving her eyes at last from the screens and smiling at him.

Ren Zel went cold, and in that instant she reached out to lay a hand on his shoulder—a sister's touch, warming, yet inexpressibly painful to one who was dead to three sisters of his blood.

"It's Weapons Hall," the woman before him was saying, her deep voice resonant; her black eyes brilliant and fierce. "I told you I had preparations to make. For the good of the ship."

"So you had." He cleared his throat. "One had not anticipated . . ."

She laughed, rich and full, drawing the eyes of the duty pilot in a quick flick over a shoulder before he returned to his board.

"No, how could you? I barely anticipated it myself, and I've been to Weapons Hall more times than I can count." Her eyes strayed again to the watch-screens, touched the corner that elucidated the position of lifeboat four, and moved on to the work screen.

"You're calculating defensive orbits. Good. We'll also want to bracket that battleship. Have you found anything like a defense system?"

"Debris," Ren Zel said, reaching to the board and bringing up the charts. "Ship's records indicate satellite defenses in orbits correlating to the orbits of clustered wreckage." He looked up into those brilliant black eyes. "The Yxtrang were thorough."

She nodded.

On the main board, the channel light glowed to life.

"Tower here."

Captain Mendoza leaned over his shoulder, extending a long arm for the switch.

"Hi, Rusty."

"Captain," the Radio Tech said seriously. "Wanted to let you know—there's no answer on that punchbeam."

Ren Zel held still, watching the side of her face, refusing to allow himself despair. For after all, there were many reasons why the laser-packet to lifeboat four might have gone unanswered, and not . . . all . . . of them were dire.

"I see," the captain said quietly. "Keep trying, in quarter-shift rotation. When the reply comes through, notify me immediately."

"Yes'm. Will do."

"Good," she said. "And, Rusty . . ."

"Ren Zel already read me the riot act," he interrupted. "I'm turning the Tower over to Tonee and Lina and getting me some shut-eye."

"Lina?" the captain repeated, blankly.

"Yes, Lina." The voice of the ship's librarian came briskly out of the speaker. "I speak Yxtrang, Priscilla."

"You do?"

"Certainly," Lina said, as if it were the most commonplace of talents. "Why not? The scouts gave the tapes. It would have been a poor use of the gift, to allow them to languish."

"Of course," the captain said seriously, but Ren Zel thought he saw the corner of her mouth twitch. "Carry on. Captain out."

"Tower out," Lina said. The line-light dimmed and the captain turned her brilliant eyes back to himself.

"Speaking of off-shifts—First Mate, I believe the shift passes."

He made to rise from the command chair, his eyes touching the screens once more. "Captain—" he began, and froze.

In watch-screen three—a blot of nothing where moments before the instruments had reported clean space.

"Fleas," he said, hand sweeping out for the all-ship. "All crew, attend! Fleas at three o'clock! Battle stations. Level red."

Beside him, he heard—no, he *felt*—a gasp, and his eyes leapt in some fey instinct to the corner where the coordinates for lifeboat four should be displayed—

And read instead the stark message from the tracking computer:

CONTACT LOST. LIFE POD UNIT FOUR OFF-GRID.

THE EXPLOSION WAS—beyond his expectation.

When the ground stopped bucking, and after prudently giving it another few minutes to re-acquaint itself with a less volatile state of being, Shan sat up, sticks and gravel raining off his shoulders.

He had expected a . . . significant . . . result from overloading the lifeboat's coil circuits, and had taken care to put what he believed to be a sensible distance between himself and ground zero, dashing like a long-legged hare through the forest, stasis box under one arm, bulky Yxtrang rifle in the opposite hand, to drop at last behind a solid-looking boulder and bury his face in the mold.

He had not expected a force that would uproot trees around him, shattering boulders less stalwart than his chosen cover, and throwing cargo-holds of dirt and gravel high into the air.

In the aftermath of the shock came a silence so profound Shan wondered if he had been deafened. He stood, shaky, but keeping a good grip on the rifle, and wiped his face on the leather sleeve of his combat jacket. The silence was terrifying. The wreckage of downed limbs and exposed roots, bewildering. If the lifeboat's last duty had caused such damage here, what must the site of the blast be like?

"Really, Shan," he said, and it was a relief to hear his own voice, blurry and cracked as it was. "You might have killed someone."

Abruptly, he sat on the ground behind the boulder, jaw clamped against a sound that might with equal possibility be laughter or a scream. Automatically, he began an inventory.

The rifle was unharmed, the magazine full. The Yxtrang soldier's ammunition belt, too large for his waist, was slung from shoulder to hip, like a bandoleer. The Yxtrang's grace-blade, which Dustin had retrieved along with the belt, hung within easy snatch of his right hand.

Weapons counted and made certain of, he turned his attention to the stasis box. It was dented, the Tree-and-Dragon scratched, but the seal had held. He smiled when he saw that and lay his palm over the scratched insignia.

. . . more than a touch of the Dragon in you . . .

He shook his head sharply.

Priscilla, he thought, painfully, *is not going to take the news that the lifepod is off-grid with equanimity.* No more than he would, had their places been exchanged. Though it was to be hoped that his lifemate would have had more wit than to detonate a coil-driven vessel on a world-surface.

Sounds were beginning to nibble at the edge of the silence. Shan raised his head, listening, sorted out gunfire, some distance to the east.

Nodding, he came to his feet, picked up the precious box and the rifle and looked around him.

The fallen trees gave almost too much cover, the grounded branches were more hazard than assistance. So, he took a few moments to plot his course, from this rock, to that log, to that tree, to *that* one, and then to that large red rock, where he would plot the next stage of his travel.

HE WAS IN THE MIDST of his third stage of travel toward the battle-sounds when his open Healer sense caught a familiar glimmer of pattern. He altered course and in a very short time was face to dirt-smeared face with Corporal Dustin.

"Sir." There was honest relief and not a little wariness in the nutmeg-colored eyes. "Thought we'd lost you."

"Only temporarily misplaced, for your sins," Shan said, slipping behind the corporal's sheltering log and settling the stasis box close.

"You near the big blast?" Dustin asked.

"I'm afraid I'm the one responsible for the big blast. If the coil circuits in a spacefaring vessel are simultaneously closed and set to charge at full, they will overload and catastrophically give up their energy in something just under five Standard minutes. I can do the math for you more precisely later, if you find you're interested."

"I'll just take your word for it," Dustin said. "Sir." He chewed his lip. "Shouldn't there be a safety trip, so you don't overload by accident?"

Shan looked at him. "There is."

"Right." Dustin sighed. "Yxtrang armor?"

"I'd wager a cantra, if I had one, that the Yxtrang armor is not going to be a problem, Corporal. They were stopping to inspect my boat as I fled . . . What's the situation here?"

"We're pretty scattered. Got seven, eight, within sight. 'Nother half-dozen down along the stream. Gin's got fifteen to the rear and hugging the hill."

Twenty-eight soldiers. *Seasoned* soldiers, Shan corrected

himself. Soldiers who knew their business and operated like professionals. He looked at Dustin.

"We should consolidate, sweep in toward the quarry and secure the ground."

"Yessir." Dustin reached to his belt, pulled out the comm and flicked it on.

"Traffic Two, captain's gonna swing us back the way we come."

There was a moment of startled silence, then Sub-Commander Kritoulkas' voice came from the comm, very distinctly.

"Put the captain on."

Dustin handed the unit over. Shan found the talk button on the side and depressed it.

"Good evening, ma'am."

"You." Her tone was not cordial. "You happen to know anything about that lifeboat?"

"It seemed expedient to dispose of the object of the quarrel," Shan told her earnestly. "Especially as there was Yxtrang armor approaching."

"Great. Tell you what. Have Dustin move the crew—they know the drill. We're getting some help down from the house that'll make up the second hand. You stay pegged right where you are and wait for them. Keep the comm and tell me what you see. Can you do that, Captain?"

"Yes, ma'am."

"Then do it," she said, and the line went dead.

THEY FLUSHED TWO POCKETS of Yxtrang on their way down toward the quarry. They took an anti-air tube from the first bunch and a couple more casualties from the second before Winston got close enough to lob in one of Val Con's homemade Grenade Surprises.

From the second bunch, then, they got two Irregulars dead, five of what Beautiful identified as Troopers Regular Field Long Arms, and the ammo belts that went with them. Miri sighed. The dead now numbered twenty, all greenies. The injured numbered slightly more, with five or six needing a 'doc pronto two hours ago.

The sweep went on, with the Irregulars and the bits of Kritoulkas' crew they picked up along the way hopefully pushing what Yxtrang were left down toward the quarry and into the second sweep line of seasoned mercs.

Some would get away, of course, running ahead of the closing jaws to regroup and—maybe—await pickup. The object wasn't to kill every Yxtrang in the park. The object was to secure the area to the old quarry and hold the line.

Miri scanned the terrain ahead. They ought to be coming up on the Eyes Kritoulkas had posted at the hinge-point pretty soon. When they hit that point, they'd swing south a little to close the loop, then squeeze back in toward the quarry.

"Captain," Beautiful said from behind her, but she'd already seen him—a lean figure in battle-leathers, ammo belt slung bad-ass style across his chest, a rifle—correction, an Officers Personal Duty Long Arm—held ready, but not threatening anybody.

It wasn't until she'd left the line and gone closer that she saw the white hair under the helmet, the winging eyebrows and the silver eyes she'd seen once before, in a dream that was true.

She stopped, pushing her own helmet up with a fingertip, saw him look first for the insignia, then back, for her face. He recognized her with a lift of white brows.

"Captain—Robertson?"

She sighed. "It'd have to be, wouldn't it? With the kind of luck I've got?" She ran her eyes over him again: dinged up helmet, filthy face, scuffed leathers and that damned bandoleer. And the rifle. Where the hell had he gotten that rifle?

"I haven't been having the best day myself," Val Con's brother told her in a voice that had probably been real pretty, fifteen bad frights ago. "I do think I ought to mention, however, that there is an Yxtrang standing behind you."

She turned her head enough to glimpse Beautiful out of the edge of her eye.

"Get used to him," she said. "His name's Nelirikk Explorer and he's sworn to Line yos'Phelium." She pointed.

"Beautiful, this is the scout's brother, Shan yos'Galan."

"I give you good greeting, Shan yos'Galan," Nelirikk offered in High Liaden.

The silver eyes closed, as if maybe Val Con's brother had just gotten a bad headache. Not that Miri blamed him. His eyes opened and he inclined his head.

"I give you good greeting, Nelirikk Explorer, oath-bound to Korval." The eyes moved to her. "Where is Val Con," he asked, back in Terran. "By the way?"

She shook her head, briefly flicking her attention to the pattern of him inside her head: busy, concentrated, *intent*. Aware of danger, but not in trouble.

"'Nother part of the woods. He's doing just fine, and he'll be real glad to see you, when we're all back in camp."

He held still a second, like maybe he was considering how much profit would come to her from lying to him. She didn't blame him for that, either, but waited until she had his nod before pointing at the comm on his belt.

"Kritoulkas says to pick you up for the sweep and leave Scotty here on comm-call," she told him, jerking her head to the Gyrfalk leaning heavily on the rough crutch.

He nodded again and pulled the unit free. Miri took it and handed it to Beautiful, who carried it over to Scotty and bent to help him settle into cover. The silver eyes followed him, face displaying a sort of wry resignation.

"You do get used to him, after a while," Miri said, and Val Con's brother looked back to her.

"I'm certain that one does," he said politely.

THE WORN RED COUNTER was in her hand, hot with Shan's presence. Shan's living presence. She was aware of it, and then not, as the demands of defense claimed her attention.

"Gun Teams Three and Five, fire at will."

The *Passage* shuddered. Her screen showed a brief blaze of clean space in the wake of the charge, filling as she watched with the mushy nothingness that was the fleas' signature.

Mother, how many can there be?

The red counter flashed in her fingers and there was a wrench and—*she stood high on her toes, craning over the cornstalks, staring down the blue sky to the ragged black horizon, and the wind of their coming was a furnace blast and where they passed, nothing was left alive. . .*

Her hand swept across the control board, struck one toggle: "Engineering, half-power to main engines, on my mark. Mark." Another: "Piloting, on my mark accelerate ship's rotation to plus fifty percent." And a third: "All crew, strap down! Repeat. All crew, strap down!" She took a breath and touched the last toggle.

"Piloting, you have my mark."

The ship paused, gathered itself and began, slowly, to spin.

"Engineering, when we achieve plus fifty percent on spin, increase power to main engines to three-quarter."

"Engineering. Aye to three-quarter on plus fifty."

"Priscilla," the voice was very soft. "What do you?"

She turned toward Ren Zel, strapped in as ordered at the auxiliary board, caught the edge of his fear with that sense that wasn't Healer sense at all, but a far more frightening Sight, which was the burden of those who had been to the Hall.

She took a breath, banishing her knowledge of his secret terrors.

"The fleas," she said to his worried eyes. "Long-range weapons are useless. We could empty everything we have and still not stop them all. And we don't know how many have managed already to get inside the watch-points. If we increase ship's spin—"

He inclined his head. "Those which have not yet anchored themselves shall be thrown off and those who approach will have difficulty matching vector. As well as gravitational problems." He paused, frowning past her shoulder as the *Passage* tumbled around them.

"If the captain will allow me, there is another item of close-in defense which may be utilized."

She waved a hand for him to continue, saw the flash of the red counter along her fingers.

"The meteor shield. Should we adjust spin to opposite— matched as close as we are to a planetary gravity field, a charge will be built . . ."

. . .and the space between ship and shield would be filled with an effect not unlike an intense aurora. Which would fry everything in its field.

Priscilla looked at her first mate, past the properly expressionless Liaden face to the horror and the resolve within him.

"Necessity, Captain," he said, softly.

She nodded. "Necessity, First Mate." And touched the toggle for Piloting.

A HALT WAS CALLED when they reached the southernmost point of the sweep. Shan bent carefully, set the box between his feet, straightened, and closed his eyes. His bruises had stopped bothering him some time back, swallowed up in a weariness so vast that he considered it perfectly possible that he would fall asleep where he stood.

There were others on the march in worse shape than he— walking wounded. He could see the blood-red glimmerings of physical pain amid the larger matrix of the unit, as well as every conceivable shading of terror, stress, and anguish. Eyes closed, he shifted, thinking muzzily that he should do something about that. He was a Healer. People needed him.

He took a breath, ran a rapid exercise to energize himself—and saw the brilliant pattern of Val Con's lifemate very near at hand, attended by a massive calmness of mauve and mint.

Shan opened his eyes.

Val Con's lady was less than an arm's length away, the tattoo- less Yxtrang at her back. She was holding out a canteen.

"Thought you might could use a drink," she said. "Since you lost your own jug."

Water. The thought woke a torment of thirst. He took the canteen and put it to his lips. The water was warm, tasting faintly of plastic, and he savored it more than the most precious wine in yos'Galan's renowned cellar.

He allowed himself two exquisite swallows.

"Thank you," he said, offering the "jug" back to her.

She waved it away. "Keep it," she told him, the wave turned

into a point at the scratched and dented stasis box. "What's in the keep-safe?"

He looked at her. "Seedlings."

"Seedlings," she repeated, expressionless, then nodded. "Beautiful here can carry that for you."

Shan froze. "I beg your pardon," he said carefully. "I may not have made myself clear. This box holds half-a-dozen stasis-bound seedlings from Jelaza Kazone. It's my duty, as a pilot of Korval, to carry them to safety."

Val Con's lady held up a small hand. "I *said*," she repeated firmly, "Beautiful can carry the box for you."

It was, in any light, an order. She was Val Con's lifemate, and Nadelmae Korval could certainly order mere Thodelm yos'Galan as she chose in matters of Tree and clan. And in all good soldier-sense, the box was weighing him down, slowing him down, making him a less effective soldier. As commander of this particular military action she could just as easily order him to leave the box, as hand it over to . . . He looked up into Nelirikk Explorer's face, gathered himself for a deeper looking—and saw the big man bow his head.

"Be at ease, Shan yos'Galan," the Yxtrang said in High Liaden. "I am of Jela's own Troop. The seedlings of his Tree are safe with me."

"*Jela's* Troop?" Shan repeated.

Not possible, he thought first. *After all these years?*

If that isn't like Val Con's damnable luck, he thought second, with a touch of what he suspected was hysteria, *to pick up this particular Yxtrang, of all possible*—He snapped off that thought as a third occurred to him.

"Do forgive me if I raise a painful subject," he said to the Yxtrang, in Terran. "But I wonder if you had previous acquaintance of my brother. Perhaps eleven or twelve Standards ago?"

"Yes," Nelirikk said.

"And you've sworn yourself to his line?" Shan demanded. "I'd have rather thought you'd try to murder him."

"He tried," Miri Robertson broke in. "But the deal was that whoever came out winner in armed combat between the two of them would be boss, and Val Con won." She jerked her head. "Time to move out. Give Beautiful the safe."

He did as he was told, but it was with a definite pang that he saw the big hands close over the Dragon seal and lift the box away.

HE WAS BEYOND WEARINESS, into a state of hyperaware numbness, where every leaf-twitch abraded and the taste of emotions around him seared.

It was Healer sense that saved him.

The emotive grid was alien, dark with blood lust, dank with deep-held horrors. Shan felt it in the instant before the twig snapped under the force of the Yxtrang's charge.

There was no room to bring the rifle up, no time to go for the knife. The axe blade descending toward his head was black, light absorbing and wickedly sharp. Shan shouted—what, he had no idea—and *reached*, grabbing for the shield he had used to save him from Priscilla's wine-shower, a far-away lifetime ago.

The axe sang downward. Bounced. Broke.

The Yxtrang screamed rage and Shan *reached* again, into the dank undergrowth of horror, snatched up a squirming, squealing nightmare and threw it with every erg of his will into the Yxtrang's waking mind.

The scream this time was not rage. The Yxtrang threw away the axe haft. Hands clawing at his eyes, he whirled, crashing back the way he had come as gunfire exploded on all sides.

Shan sprang to the left, fell heavily behind a log, brought his rifle up and fired into the Yxtrang charge.

It was a quick, dirty fight, the Yxtrang being armed with nothing more than the standard long-arm and apparently without an officer to command them. The charge into the sweep line was ill conceived—or the last valiant act of desperate men. In either case, there were twenty of the enemy counted dead among the trees when the noise was finally over.

Shan sagged behind his cover, cheek on his arm, wondering, in a sort of foggy apathy, if he would be able to stand when the order came, much less walk.

Behind him, a leaf scraped leather and he rolled, rifle swinging up to target—

"Peace, Shan yos'Galan." Nelirikk Explorer dropped beside him, astonishingly quiet for so large a man. Feeling somewhat sheepish, Shan lowered the rifle.

"The captain sends to find if you are wounded."

Wounded? He tried to focus attention on his body, but gave the effort up after a moment with a frustrated shake of his head.

"Merely exhausted. I think. This is not the sort of outing I'm accustomed to."

Surprise showed on the big man's face. "No? But surely you have been a soldier?"

Shan sighed and dropped his head back on the ground, watching the other through half-closed eyes. "I have never been a soldier," he said, as clearly as his abused vocal chords would allow.

There was a short silence. "And yet you bring glory to the troop, for to capture that rifle was not easy. Unless you made your kill from afar?"

"From all too near," Shan assured him. "It must be noted, however, that the previous owner of the rifle was wounded. And I had a very stout stick."

"Stick." A grin cracked the impassive brown face. "Truly you are of Jela's get, and the scout's brother."

A whistle sounded: three short blasts, pause, one long.

Nelirikk stirred. "That is the call to move on. Stay vigilant a short time more, Shan yos'Galan. We are on the last leg of sweep. When we reach the quarry, there is rest."

The whistle sounded again: one short. Nelirikk grinned.

"My captain calls," he said, and vanished into the trees.

After a moment, Shan pushed to his feet, settled his helmet and stepped back into line.

BORDERING EROB'S HOLD:
Behind Enemy Lines

❊ ❊

THUS FAR, Nelirikk's information had been accurate in the extreme.

Val Con crouched in the slender concealment of an armored landcar's rear wheel-well and peered cautiously out. His time in the generator shed and in the ammunition cache had been well spent, and he flattered himself that his most recent efforts in the motor pool would not be found despicable.

As he worked his mischief, he counted—air transport, land transport, foodstuffs and stocked ammo. The count had confirmed Nelirikk's theory that the 14th Conquest Corps, in its stretch for glory, had perhaps over-reached itself.

And would soon be overextended more seriously still. Footsteps sounded, loud in the night. Val Con ducked further back into his hiding place. Two sentries tramped by half-a-foot from his nose, eyes straight ahead, long-rifles resting on broad Yxtrang shoulders.

Val Con held his breath, exhaling very softly when finally they were past. His internal clock gave him two hours until the generator shed opened the evening's festivities. Time enough to create conditions productive of even more consternation before he removed to the flitter.

Carefully, using all of his senses, he checked the immediate area for watchers. Finding none, he eased out of the motor pool and melted into the shadows at the edge of the troop-way.

Some minutes later he entered a barracks, ghosting down the cot-lined aisles. He paused here, there and briefly by the soldierly caches of battle gear at the base of each cot—silent, quick and unhesitant.

The luck was in it, that he encountered no wakeful trooper, though he was forced to freeze in place for a time his heightened senses demanded for hours when a long form shifted in its nest, muttering an irritable order to one Granch to have done and fire the damned thing.

The trooper subsided without coming to a sense of his true surroundings, and Val Con ghosted on, out of the barracks and into the night.

THE COMMUNICATION center was his last call of the evening. Deliberately so, for anything he might contrive there would need to go forth quickly, and at an increased risk of his capture.

Val Con sank into the thin dark place between a water tank and a metal shed bearing the Yxtrang symbols for "Danger: High Voltage" and assessed the situation.

Communications Central was well lit and very busy, indeed. There were two sentries at the entrance and a constant hubbub of coming and going. Val Con frowned, noting the abundance of officer's markings on the scarified faces of those frequent arrivals and departures.

Something had happened. Something big had happened. He *knew* it.

He sank back in the shadow of the two buildings, watching the crowd come and go. He checked his internal clock. Fifty Standard minutes before the first explosion took the camp by surprise. Not enough time, good sense argued, to listen at Yxtrang doors in the hope of hearing something worthwhile.

And, yet—If the 15th had arrived?

He slid to the very edge of the shadows, held his breath, chose his path across the brightly lit roadway, and waited. His patience was shortly rewarded by the simultaneous arrival of three agitated officers, whose jostling at the door distracted the sentries' attention just long enough for him to dart through the dangerous light and into the shadow behind the flimsy temp structure, where he followed the wires to his goal.

LIAD:
Jelaza Kazone

❈❈❈❈❈❈❈❈❈❈❈❈❈❈❈❈❈❈❈❈❈❈

ON THE SUNNY EASTERN PATIO, Anthora yos'Galan looked up suddenly from her breakfast, and frowned as she scanned the empty lawns.

"Jeeves . . ." she murmured and the hulking robot standing near her chair replied, its voice proclaiming it a male of Terra's educated class:

"Working, Miss Anthora."

"I . . . believe . . . we may have company. Four individuals?"

"One to each compass point," yos'Galan's butler said smoothly. "Shall I deal with it?"

She was silent a moment, biting her lip and considering the patterns of the intruders. Coldness, imbalance, disharmony and ugliness—each so like the other that one nearly became persuaded they thought with one brain. But, no. She had seen the like of these before. The work of the Department of Interior was impossible to mistake, once seen.

"How did they get in?" she asked the robot.

"Accessing perimeter files. I have an anomaly, sixty-three seconds in duration, one-half hour ago. My apologies, Miss Anthora. They came through a particularly resistant section of perimeter. I see that stronger measures are called for, though one dislikes employing coercion."

She turned her head and blinked up at the featureless ball of its "head," momentarily diverted from the threat of potential assassins.

"Coercion? Jeeves, my brothers told me you were a war robot before they reclaimed you to be our butler. Surely you've practiced coercion in the past."

"One may be practiced in an art of survival without necessarily enjoying it," Jeeves commented, moving a pincher arm toward the teapot. "May I warm your cup?"

"Thank you," she said and held it out, silent until the tea was poured and the pot replaced.

"Tell me the truth, Jeeves. *Were* you a war robot?"

"I was many things, Miss Anthora. As befits the motivating force of an Independent Armed Military Module. Shall I deal with the interlopers on our lawn? It won't take but a moment."

Anthora sipped her tea, and extended her thought to the eastern pattern. Idly, experimentally, almost playfully, she exerted her will against the chill ugliness. And felt something move, deep within the construct imposed by the Department of Interior.

Anthora sipped again, shook her head, Terran style, and lazily set the teacup aside.

"No," she told the robot, "leave them. They won't be staying long."

EROB'S BOUNDARY:
War Zone

❁ ❁

JASON HEARD him out impassively, then got up and walked to the rear of the tent.

"Coffee, boyo? It's old, but the tea's older."

Val Con leaned back in the camp chair, weary, now that there was leisure. "Is there water?"

"That there is."

There was a slight clink and the sound of liquid running, then Jason settled again at the table, big hands curled around a steaming steel mug. Val Con raised his mug, closing his eyes and concentrating on the sweet feel of water along a parched throat.

Jason sighed, sudden in the silence.

"So, the 'trang're massing and they're facing this way. Not the best news we've had on the week, but not unexpected. Why else did you spend all that time with Erob's people, planting those little tokens of esteem around the grounds?"

Val Con opened his eyes. "It would be better, if they did not get this far."

"Can't argue with that," Jason conceded and raised the mug for a swallow of old coffee.

Val Con sipped at his water, and allowed himself for the first time in days to touch the place where Miri's song lived within him.

For a moment, he simply beheld her essence. His eyes filled and he closed them, bringing all of his attention to her, asleep and distant as—

He opened his eyes and put the mug down so suddenly it thumped on the table.

"Fact of the matter is, 'trang general has his nose outta joint because Kritoulkas and Redhead just threw a bunch of his crack kiddies out on their ears," Jason said, possibly to himself. "Not only that, but they lost the prize, and a bit of their own armor, to boot." He shook his head. "Small wonder we're up for special attention." He raised the mug, drained it and set it aside.

"We're as ready hereabouts as we're likely to get," he said, suddenly brisk. "Next good thing to do is make sure we've done our best down the hill." He pushed back from the table and paused, eyes suddenly speculative.

"You'll want to be with Redhead for this next bit, will you, lad?"

Miri had been in battle while he was away from her side. She might have died—Val Con shook his head sharply and glared into Jason's face.

"I certainly want to be with her so we might usefully plan the best defense," he said, more curtly than he had perhaps intended.

Jason merely nodded and stood up. "We're both on the same wavelength. Meet me at the flitter in fifteen minutes and we'll go on down together. I'll just call over the Big House and let the general know he's in charge."

THEY WERE MET by an improbably cheerful soldier with a newly healed gash on her chin. She ran a disinterested eye over Val Con and gave Jason a wide grin.

"Morning, Commander. You missed the party."

"That's right, Sandy, rub it in," Jason said mournfully. "I suppose I'm not taking it hard enough that you had such a good time t'other day when I was stuck up the hill with nothin' to do but watch the tyros train."

She laughed and turned, guiding them expertly through a series of interlocking trails.

As the lady's conversation was reserved for her commander, Val Con amused himself by identifying trenches and probable weapons caches, while he kept half an inner ear on the song that was Miri. She was very near now, he could tell from the flavor of the song. He discovered his heart was pounding, though the pace their guide had set was no more than brisk. Indeed, it was all he could do, not to leave his companions behind and run through the forest, into his lifemate's arms.

"Almost there," Sandy said, guiding them sharply right, then left, and abruptly there was a camp, and soldiers, and sky shielding strung over the whole.

The sentry went left without hesitation. Val Con, his attention on Miri's song, looked right, toward its emanation, hoping for a glimpse of copper braiding, or an edge of her face, but the way was filled with leather-clad strangers—

Val Con stumbled, heartbeat stalling. He found his feet instantly, heart slamming painfully into overaction. Breath returned with a shout.

"*Shan!*"

The white-haired man whipped around, pilot-fast, graceful in fighting leathers. His arms opened and Val Con hurtled into the embrace, hugging tight, his cheek against his brother's shoulder.

In that moment, he was a child again and Shan returning home at last from the long year of contract-marriage. He had been with his music tutor when he heard his brother's voice in the entry-hall and had leapt from the 'chora to fly down the stairway, into the ready embrace.

"Shan, *Shan* . . ."

"Hello, denubia."

Beloved voice and oh, gods, to hold his brother to him, to feel the heartbeat beneath his cheek and the lungs laboring so . . .

He eased his hold, leaning back in arms that seemed reluctant to lose him, raised eyes, and then shaking fingers to his brother's cheek.

"You're weeping."

Shan grinned, wavering. "So are you."

There was a sound quite close at hand, as possibly of a whetstone being drawn slowly down a blade: Jason Carmody clearing his throat.

"Take it you two know each other."

Val Con flicked a glance to Jason, noting the high color in those portions of the face not hidden by golden beard.

Blushing, he thought in astonishment. *We've embarrassed Jason Carmody, the man who has no shame.* Carefully, he went half a step back, releasing Shan with a reluctance that was echoed in his brother's withdrawal.

"Shan, this is Gyrfalks Junior Commander Jason Carmody, commanding the forces here." He lay his hand on the leather sleeve—*merciful gods, to once again touch kin*—gulped a breath and looked up into the big Terran's face.

"Jason, here is—here is my brother, Shan yos'Galan. Master Trader and—and . . ."

"And captain," Shan's voice smoothly covered his emotion, "of the battleship *Dutiful Passage*, in Lytaxin system. Perhaps, by now, in Lytaxin orbit."

The unnatural color was already leaving Jason's cheeks, though his eyes sharpened considerably.

"You don't say. Wouldn't be that you're the laddie brought that lifepod down into our quarry, would it?"

"Unfortunately, it would," Shan said soberly. "I do apologize, Commander, but there really was nothing for it. The pod was all but out of fuel. I had to come down somewhere."

"Well, and you're part of my reason for being here. We're bound for a bit of chat with Sub-Commander Kritoulkas and Captain Redhead, if you'd care to join us?"

Shan inclined his head and Val Con caught the flicker of a smile in his direction.

"I'd love to join you, Commander. You should be warned, however, that Sub-Commander Kritoulkas doesn't seem taken with me."

"Sub-Commander Kritoulkas," said Jason, turning to the left once again and motioning the patient sentry to move on, "isn't taken with most people. Count yourself approved though, laddie. After all, she let you live."

VAL CON had changed, Shan thought, settling next to him round the sub-commander's hastily cobbled conference table.

He had thought so, when the two of them had spoken mind-to-mind and Val Con issued the orders that ended with four of the line direct on or near Lytaxin, and in peril of all their lives. Mind-to-mind speaking, however, had claimed more of his attention than he had supposed. The larger pattern had matched the Val Con he had known, and he hadn't leisure, then, to peruse its subtleties.

Now, as Commander Carmody spoke apart with Sub-Commander Kritoulkas while they awaited the arrival of Val Con's lifemate, he had leisure.

Damage. With Healer's eyes he traced a swath of devastation through memory, heart, and thought. That there had been enough of the essence of Val Con yos'Phelium left after the storm of destruction to effect a Healing was nothing short of miraculous.

For Healing there had been. Shan traced that, too, along the brutal path of ruin. Whole segments had been regrown, others were still in process. Still other segments had been patched, strengthened, and reintegrated into the whole—a whole that was recognizably and indisputably Val Con.

Only—different.

And just now beginning to show the colors of tension and distress.

Shan blinked, brought his brother's face into focus, and reached out to touch his hand.

"Val Con. What befell you?"

The mobile mouth tightened and Shan heard anguish and something that tasted of—shame?—along the edge of his Inner Ear, but the green eyes did not falter.

"The Department of Interior befell me." He took a hard breath. "I'm sorry, Shan."

Sorry? Shan shook his head, extending Healer's senses and once more tracing the scars, the damage, so very—much—damage.

"How?"

Val Con smiled, humorless. "You don't want to know."

"Then at least tell me—with intent?" But even as he asked, his inner eyes found the pattern, among the layers of scarring and repair. Not a Healer's touch, no. But the touch of someone very certain of his effects, who had inflicted his tortures with foreknowing thoroughness.

He blinked and looked again into his brother's eyes.

"Balance will be—difficult."

"Balance by Code," Val Con told him, "is not an option."

Shan nodded, seeing that resonate through the darkness of the man who was now his brother. Formerly, Val Con's pattern had—sparked, flaring here and there with excess energy and passion. This revised person showed no such exuberance, yet passion was not dead. Merely, it was—consolidated—a hot, bright glow from the deep center of him, from that place one might call his soul.

From that lambent center, from Val Con's very soul, leapt a construct of living opalescent flame, arching strongly and entirely out of that which was Val Con, to find its equal and apposite root—in the scintillate, stubborn essence that was Miri Robertson.

"Hey, boss." Her voice brought him out of a contemplation of that astonishing structure and into the world that was. She slid into the vacant seat at Val Con's left hand and nodded cordially to Shan, her Yxtrang taking up guard behind her—No, Shan corrected himself, behind *them*.

"Found your brother, I see."

"Cha'trez." Val Con's smile was so tender Shan felt his stomach wrench, even as he saw the flames of the lifemate bridge ripple and flow, back and forth, from soul to soul.

"Nelirikk." Val Con had turned in his seat to address the Yxtrang. "I find you well?"

"Very well, Scout. We have won glory for the Troop on the field, and gained two flags which hang subservient to our own."

Val Con lifted an eyebrow and looked to his lady. "Have we a battle standard, I wonder?"

She grinned at him. "Piece of quality merchandise, too. Cultivate a little respect and we'll show it to you, after the jaw's done."

"When am I not respectful?"

"You want the whole list, or will a summary do?"

"OK, here she is." Jason Carmody broke off his conversation with the sub-commander and the two of them approached the table. He grinned.

"Redhead. Kritoulkas tells me your bunch worked like pros."

She shook her head. "We did OK," she said seriously. "Lost a lot of people, though."

"Happens, when you're running with volunteers and tyros," Jason said, matching her seriousness. "Important thing is, you seen action and got the job done. They'll know what to expect next time, which is fine, because the scout's brought news of a bigger party coming our way. Seems you and Kritoulkas have earned yourselves some admirers."

"Not just that," Kritoulkas said in her sour way. "This last bunch of 'em were after the captain's lifeboat. Expect they might have thought he was sent from this battleship of his down to the house. House looks like a command post. Hell, a month ago, it *was* a command post."

Jason Carmody nodded and looked over to Shan. "Want to bring me up to speed on that?"

So, for the second time in as many days, Shan told the story of the sabotaged pod, the Yxtrang attack, and his unplanned arrival on the planet surface.

"And I find since that I've made a rather serious error, Commander. I honestly did think it was best for everyone to detonate the lifeboat and stop the Yxtrang armor. However, the lifeboat contained a working space-link radio, which Sub-Commander Kritoulkas tells me is something of a local rarity at the moment."

Jase nodded. "'trang took out the satellite net first off. Standard operating procedure, according to Beautiful. We're gonna need to know what upstairs looked like, last you saw it. Grab you a computer outta—"

"That's done," Val Con's—*Miri*—spoke up. "Had him working

on it soon as we pulled back here." She reached in her jacket pocket, removed a disk and passed it over. Jason grinned.

"One step ahead of me, which is what I should have expected, my small!" He looked back to Shan, who lifted his eyebrows.

"An outline of my ship's capabilities and strengths is also on the disk."

"Hah! Your idea?"

"It did seem the sort of information you might find helpful," Shan said and Jason grinned again.

"Gonna retire and let the crowd of you run the war. Call me when it's over."

"Might want to reconsider," Miri said, her shoulder nestled companionably against Val Con's. "My experience is that retirement's a good way to get yourself into more trouble than you know the name of."

Jase nodded. "I'll hold off a bit, then. Not any too fond of trouble, myself." He looked around the table, abruptly serious.

"Here's what, people. We're as ready up the house as stubbornness and the scout's ingenuity can make us. Kritoulkas and me're gonna walk the area when we're done here, to see if we're missing anything the 'trang might want. But we're at a bad disadvantage when it comes to air support and cover. As in, 'trang got it, and we don't." He looked at Shan.

"Think that ship of yours can provide any cover?"

"We carry one space-to-world gun," Shan said slowly. "Which is good for offense, but not particularly outstanding for defense. Besides that, we have no radio . . ."

"Don't give up so easy," Jase advised him. "Very possible that we'll capture us a 'trang radio for the scout to coax into honesty. You're right, though, son. Space-to-world weapon's nice to have on the side of the angels, but it's no substitute for good local air cover, which is what we don't have, Erob's force having gone West when 'trang bombed the fields, coming in."

Val Con stirred. "Air cover. But would a bombing run—several bombing runs—against Yxtrang strategic targets be of just as much utility?"

Jason shrugged. "Sure. While we're wishing for pie-in-the-sky we might as well wish for ice cream, too."

Val Con shook his head and leaned forward across the table. "There is nothing fantastic in such a bombing run, Jason. We have here—" he pointed to Shan, to Nelirikk, and touched himself lightly on the chest—"three pilots of Master quality. We have there—" a point off to the southwest—"many dozens of aircraft."

Jason stared. "Yxtrang aircraft."

"True enough. However, Nelirikk is in a unique position to coach my brother and me in the fine points of an Yxtrang board. I promise you, we are both able learners. And with three planes in the air, we might do real damage. With the luck beside us, we might just possibly convince the 14th Conquest Corps that the prudent course is strategic withdrawal."

"Hmm." Jason stroked his beard.

"Bad plan," Miri said flatly. Val Con turned his head, both eyebrows up.

"Miri, if it lifts, we can fly it. Neither Shan nor I has yet found his limit in piloting." He tipped his head. "Truth, Miri."

"I don't doubt it. But unless you're planning on a real spurt of growth in the next half-hour or so, it ain't gonna work."

"I don't under—"

"Simple." She cut him off and pushed her chair back, motioning him to stand up with her. "Beautiful, plant yourself there. Boss, you stand right here." When the two of them were side by side, she stepped back, arms crossed, and hitched a hip onto the edge of the table.

"If Beautiful is standard-issue, and from what we seen, he is, you're about a foot-and-a-half shy of make-weight."

Shan had to admit she had a point. One did not usually think of Val Con as small, but set against the Yxtrang, he appeared almost fragile. Viewed thus, it seemed even more fantastic that Val Con had fought hand-to-hand against this giant—and *prevailed*, as both Miri and Nelirikk insisted was true.

Miri shifted abruptly, leaning forward as if she had seen the steel overlay Val Con's pattern—which, Shan thought suddenly, she might well have.

"Ain't no use getting stubborn," she snapped. "Won't change the fact that *you're too little*! Cockpit made to hold Beautiful is gonna have stuff set outta your reach."

"If the captain pleases," the Yxtrang said quietly. "There is some variation in height among the Troop. Cockpits of fighter craft are somewhat adjustable. A pilot the size of the scout's brother can easily fly."

Miri nodded. "That's good. Any Yxtrang pilots measure down to the scout?"

Hesitation. "Captain. No. Occasionally an—undergrown—Troop survives to adulthood. But they are never pilots."

"Hah." Val Con lifted an eyebrow, catching his lifemate's eye. "*Scruffy midget?*"

Her mouth twitched. "Point is—"

"The point *is*," Val Con interrupted, "that, if the cockpit can be made to accommodate Shan, then it can be adapted only a little more to accommodate me. We can certainly fabricate adaptations."

"Is that right, Beautiful?" Jason Carmody asked, across whatever might have been Miri's answer.

"Commander. I—I believe it possible."

"Then we go with it. Three in the sky, taking out the prime points, while the rest of us shred 'em on the ground. That should set 'em to re-thinking their position."

Sub-Commander Kritoulkas nodded. "You and Redhead want to walk the line with me now and get a feel for the situation while the pilots work out their differences? I got a feeling sooner's the way the smart money bets."

"Right you are." Jason loomed to his feet. "Meet us back here in a few hours, boyo," he said to Val Con. "We'll want to coordinate pretty close. Coming, Redhead?"

"In a sec." She waited until they were alone before pinning each with a glare in turn. Shan felt her will strike his and ring, like a blade off of hull plate.

"OK. The three of you work out the best way to run this gig. I understand you gotta take risks." She looked directly at Shan, which he hardly felt was fair. "What you ain't gotta take is *stupid* risks. Val Con."

"Captain."

She eyed him. "Figure your adaptations and test 'em out. When you've got things to where you think you can fly, I want you to think if you'd let Shan or Nelirikk or me fly with those arrangements. And if the answer comes up 'no,' I want you to back away from it, you hear me?"

"I hear you, Captain."

She shook her head. "For whatever that's worth." Once again, her eyes touched each of them in turn. "Nothing stupid, all right? It's an order."

"Captain," Nelirikk said. "We will bring glory to the Troop."

She sighed and slid from her perch on the edge of the table. "And here I thought you were listening to me."

SHIP'S ARCHIVE provided latitude and longitude of Erob's clanhouse and Priscilla ordered the *Passage* into a synchronous mid-orbit above that location. It was the least they could do for Korval's ally, she thought.

The very least.

Since the successful repulsion of the flea attack, the Yxtrang had offered them no more harm, though Lina reported a lively interest in the *Passage*, its heading and possible mission, in the messages she monitored. It was Rusty's particular frustration that he had not yet been able to establish a link with the planet, while listening in on Yxtrang radio chatter remained absurdly easy.

As she approached the bridge to relieve Ren Zel, she considered the problem of communication. Erob possessed a pinbeam, but ship's archive indicated that the in-house had simply been a booster station, by which messages were sent to a satellite-based transmitter/receiver. The Yxtrang destruction of Lytaxin's satellite defense had also taken the pinbeam, which meant that a 'beam sent from the *Passage* to the address of Erob's receiving station would never find its mark.

But, Erob's *in-house* might still be capable of receiving, if there were some way to deduce an address. Ren Zel argued that a broadbeam call to any and all listeners imperiled more than it might aid, but she was beginning to reconsider that. If they were clever . . .

The door to the bridge slid open and she stepped through, nodding to Thrina and Vilobar, who were going off-shift. They stopped for a moment, speaking to her with the warmth of old friends, but she read pity in them. That confused her for a moment until she recalled that, of course, they thought Shan was dead.

Silly friends. Shan wasn't dead. She would know if Shan were dead. Which she had told Gordy when he rushed to the bridge after the lifepod went off-grid. She saw him try to believe it and come half to terms with the fact that she would know. She could have helped him to full belief, but that would have required Healing and she didn't—quite—trust the edge of Healer sense that had been honed in the cold stone hall of weapons.

She made her way quietly to the command station and paused by Ren Zel's shoulder. He was a-hum with concentrated energy and she looked to the screens, seeking the reason.

"What is that?" she demanded, staring at the tangle of ships and IDs on his prime screen.

"I attempt to ascertain," he replied, without looking up. "They began releasing shuttle-craft about five hours ago, and now there are cutters, lighters, and work-boats away. Small craft, lightly armed; most have only meteor shielding; none, save the cutters, are planet-capable." He sat back and, most un-Ren Zel-like, ran a hand through his hair. "It makes no sense."

Priscilla frowned at the screen. The Yxtrang did indeed seem bent on sending as many poorly armed craft as possible into peril. Why? What gain? She felt something between her fingers, looked down, saw the red counter and idly walked it across her knuckles, her attention once again on *why*.

If the *Passage* were to pick off those defenseless craft one by one? The gain would be a measure of the range of her guns, as well as an understanding of the enemy: Would the *Passage* attack, waste power and supplies on pawns? Would a warrior chief, such as the commander of the Yxtrang battleship, trade materiel for that information?

No, she decided, the red counter warm in her palm. The trade was wrong—too many ships were fielded. His intent was otherwise.

Ren Zel's work screen showed a shifting, three-dimensional pattern—Maincomp's view of the situation. Taken in whole, the pattern bore a relation to the *Passage*'s own orbit, though it was obvious that they were in no peril from—

Priscilla froze, her eyes on Maincomp's pattern.

"Assume the current number of ships remains stable," she said, barely aware that she was speaking aloud. "Run calculations for six hours, twelve hours, twenty-four hours and display the results in sim."

Ren Zel's fingers were already moving across the board. The work screen blanked momentarily, then the simulation began.

The ships moved in strange ballet, revealing and hiding the Yxtrang battleship in coy display.

"Replay," Priscilla directed, "from the vantage of the battleship."

Once again, the ships danced, orbits intersected and diverged. Priscilla heard Ren Zel take a sharp breath.

"It opens. It closes," he murmured and Priscilla nodded.

"It's an eye. Those ships are shielding the battleship from us, and every—" she checked the sim—"every twenty-two hours, a path manifests in the shield-wall, from the battleship to the planet surface."

Ren Zel moved, demanding an elucidation of the point that passed beneath the Yxtrang battleship's position once every twenty-two world-hours, though she could have told him that—of course—it was Erob's clanhouse.

She leaned forward, reaching past him for the comm-switch.

"Tower, here."

"Rusty, I want you to send broadbeam to the planet surface, timed bursts thirty seconds in duration, three bursts over the next thirty minutes. The Tree-and-Dragon signature, if you please. Let's see who we wake up."

"Yes, ma'am." Keys clattered over the open line, then Rusty was back. "First burst away, Captain. Second and third on the timer."

"Thank you. Relay any reply to the command helm immediately."

"Will do. Tower out."

"Captain out." She flipped the switch and looked over to her first mate, noting the weariness in him. Smiling, she touched his sleeve.

"The shift passes, friend. Get some sleep. The next few shifts may be very long."

THE KEY was the start-up sequence.

Each pilot had fifty-five seconds to touch a prescribed series of keys, toggles, and pins, which simultaneously brought his fighter's various systems on-line, charged the engine and announced that the pilot was, indeed, of the Troop. Should the pilot miss or misplace a keystroke within the sequence, his plane would not only fail to start, but the defense computer would redirect the paths of two high voltage currents into the pilot's couch.

Encouraged toward excellence by Nelirikk's description of a failed sequence he had witnessed during his own training, neither Val Con nor Shan mislaid a stroke, from first run to last.

They moved from that to a generic description of an Elite Guard's personal armament—two to five hidden knives; a long arm with bullets carrying internal flechettes of pain-killer so a victim would not understand his wound, or fast-acting poison, or even hallucinogens; and an assortment of clubs, spikes, and such, and perhaps a hand gun as well—and a thorough lesson in the facial graphics of those most likely to be encountered one-on-one.

That done as thoroughly as might be on such short notice, Nelirikk had Shan go through the drill a dozen times more on the dummy board they had hastily constructed of scrap wood and one of Kritoulkas' conference chairs. When he pronounced himself satisfied with the performance, they set about modifying the "cockpit" to Val Con's dimensions.

The modifications included a broom handle, several shaped plastic grips, and a chock of wood to bring the brake pedal within reach of short legs. Val Con flew through the sequence, shaving time on each run, until Nelirikk called a halt.

"Scout, understand that if you fall below the allowed timing by a factor exceeding five, the defense computer assumes it has been subverted by an enemy robot and releases the electricity."

Strapped into the conference chair, Val Con sighed and pushed his hair out of his eyes. "Thank you. I will bear that in mind. Again?"

"Again," Nelirikk agreed. "Strive for fifty seconds."

And fifty seconds it was, perfectly done. Nelirikk nodded. "Enough."

Val Con unstrapped and came to his feet, leaning over the dummy to disengage his adaptations.

"And have you done as Captain Robertson commanded, brother?" Shan asked from behind him. "Have you considered whether you would allow her or myself or Nelirikk to fly with those mods?"

He knelt and pried the chock loose from the "brake pedal," then rose lightly and faced his brother.

"I have asked myself that question. And I must say that I would certainly never allow anyone who fell under my care to fly such a gerry-rig as we have here." He nodded toward the block of wood he held and look back to Shan, green eyes brilliant.

"Unless flying it held the best chance of their survival and the survival of kin."

"Necessity," the Yxtrang said surprisingly and Val Con nodded. "Necessity."

"Necessity," Shan agreed. "I only wonder if your lady will see it."

"Ah." Val Con moved his shoulders. "My lady may not. But I expect that my captain will."

THE CHANNEL LIGHT came on and Priscilla depressed the switch.

"Command helm."

"Captain, we got a reply from the broadbeam."

Such rapid reply could only mean a pinbeamed message. Priscilla smiled. *Good. We found Erob's in-house.*

"To my screen three, please, Rusty."

"Sent." The channel stayed open, which was odd. Priscilla looked to screen three.

"Pod seventy-seven?" she demanded, staring at the terse

announcement that this unlikely entity was on-line. "Rusty, did you get a fix on the origin of this?"

"It's coming out Erob's territory," he said and now she knew why he had left the line open. "Not the house. Mountain range toward the coast. Here."

Another window opened on her work screen, marking Pod 77's location on the planetary map. She upped the magnification, zooming in close, and called for place name display. The red counter was in her hand, alive with Shan's presence.

"Well," she said into the open channel. "Whatever it is, it lives on Dragon's Back Mountain." She sat back in the chair, feeling an electrical something, like a looming thunderstorm, stir the still ship air.

Dragon's Back Mountain. Priscilla drew a careful breath. Korval and Erob. Allies down the centuries. And a—pod?—situated on Dragon's Back Mountain. A gift, perhaps? Korval tended to protect its own interests closely, and Erob was seated upon an outworld, far from the homeworld's assistance, should it be attacked.

The counter blazed against her hand and she abruptly recalled yos'Galan's butler. A modified war robot, as Shan had told her, and, with its other duties, entrusted with the defense system surrounding Korval's valley.

Merciful Mother.

"Priscilla?" Rusty's voice carried concern. She shook her head, focused her thoughts.

"Yes. Rusty, do me the favor of sending to Pod seventy-seven in—in the code I will upload to you in a moment. Inquire into the state of its defenses."

"Defenses? Priscilla, how do we know it's not some wise-ass Yxtrang radio jockey, having himself a giggle?"

"We don't know that until it replies to us in our own code," she said, reaching to her board. Quickly, she ran her fingers over the sequence, accessing the captain's key file. She requested and received Korval's House code, uploading it to Rusty with a finger-tap.

"There. Send the message, please, Rusty. And wire the reply directly to me, whenever it comes in."

There was a momentary hesitation, then, "Will do. Tower out."

"Command helm out," she absently, her fingers moving once again across the board, requesting information available to the Captain's Key, relative to Pod 77 or Dragon's Back Mountain, Lytaxin.

THEY WERE MOVING OUT this evening, bound for the quarry and points beyond. Meet Yxtrang before they knocked on the door, that was the gig. Surprise them, maybe. Buy time.

Time for the rest of the defense forces to man the serious talking points. Time for Val Con and Shan and Beautiful to steal the fighters and start their runs.

It was the planes that decided her on Erob's ruined airfield for the Irregular's hold-tight.

"No use stealing the damn' things if you can't bring 'em home," she'd pointed out at the coordinating meeting. "We'll secure the airfield." She looked up and met Jase's eyes square across the table. "No problem."

He'd nodded after a second, and that was that. The only thing she had to do now was make good on her bet.

And not worry.

Walking toward her quarters to get her gear together and maybe grab an hour's nap, Miri snorted. It was funny how in the thick of things you never had time to worry. You dealt with whatever the gods of battle sent against you and mostly you weren't even scared.

Before and after—that was the time for nerves and terrors. Double, if you had a lifemate and a new brother and the man who'd guarded your back against his own laying their lives out in a cockamamie death-defying gamble.

She'd already come up with a dozen ways for them to die before they even got to the planes. Miri moved her head, shaking away the tally of possible destructions, but she couldn't shake away the knot in her gut or the cramp in her chest.

She turned right, nodded at the sentry and stepped into the dimness of her quarters.

Val Con got up from the edge of the cot, came two steps forward and opened his arms.

She flung forward, catching him in a hug as desperate as his own, thought to look at his pattern and felt the chill tingle of his fear in her blood even as she raised her head to meet a nearly savage kiss.

They made love like it was battle-practice, hard and silent and fierce, and when they were through, she held him tight against her still, one fist twisted in his hair.

"Damn you, don't die."

Warm breath exhaled into her ear. "I love you, too, Miri."

He pulled away and they straightened their clothes, found discarded weapons belts and buckled them into place. Val Con touched her cheek.

"I will meet you at Erob's airfield, tomorrow afternoon." He lay a finger across her lips and she felt a ripple of dark-edged humor go through him. "No problem, eh?" The finger lifted.

Miri smiled, though it was hard to see him through the tears.

"No problem."

TACTICAL DEFENSE PODS 72 to 83 were retired from the Korval fleet with the building of the *Felicitous Passage*, two hundred fifty Standard years ago, according to the sealed file the Captain's Key had accessed.

Red counter gripped tight in her hand, Priscilla learned decommissioned Pods 72 through 76 had been donated to the scouts.

Pods 79 through 83 were used as live target fire in a series of defense exercises during a period of heightened Yxtrang activity.

Pod 77 . . . She scrolled down the file. Theonna yos'Phelium, delm, had bestowed Pod 77 upon Korval's staunch ally, Clan Erob. Then ordered the report Priscilla now perused sealed. She frowned, leaned back, and then touched the scroll key again, searching—there.

Pod 78, the last entry stated simply, *is on Moonstruck. Refer to Plan B.*

Her frown deepened. Refer to Plan B? But surely—The screen

shimmered and a message box appeared in the bottom left corner, rapidly filling with text.

TACTICAL DEFENSE POD 77 ON-LINE.
WEAPONS CHECK.
INITIATE SCAN.
LONG GUN CHARGED.
SCAN CONCLUSION: MID-ORBIT HOSTILITIES.
INITIATING SECONDARY SCAN.
TARGETING COMPUTER ON-LINE.
TACTICAL COMPUTER ON-LINE.
SCAN CONCLUSION: INVASION CONDITIONS.
MANUAL OVERRIDE DISALLOWED.
ALL SYSTEMS ON-LINE.
ALL SYSTEMS ABLE.
AWAITING TARGET.

THE SCOUT'S PLAN was simple: Steal three fighter-bomber craft from those grounded at Field Headquarters, lift and destroy planes, ammunition, armor, and similar other targets before they could be brought against the defenders.

It was a plan somewhat short on detail, but Nelirikk never doubted it would succeed, to the glory of captain and Troop. It was much too audacious to fail.

For this venture, Nelirikk had sacrificed the mustache and the unsoldierly hair, and stood once again in Yxtrang uniform, the officer to whom it had belonged having no further need. He had modified the rank-marks, so that he became an Adjutant of the Inspectors Office, and the scout's brother had with wonderful skill painted the appropriate *vingtai* on his face.

"Remember to clean this nonsense off once you're safely away," Shan said, standing back to admire his handiwork. "You do look fierce, if I say it myself. One might very easily mistake you for an Yxtrang."

This was a pleasantry, such as Nelirikk was coming to expect from the scout's brother, who was by no means as imbecile as he sometimes spoke. Accordingly, he bared his teeth in a grin, displaying the *vingtai* to best effect.

"Terrifying," Shan announced, his face betraying no noticeable terror. "I may swoon in fright."

"Why not sit down, instead?" the scout asked from the doorway. "And allow Nelirikk to decorate you?"

"No need of that," Shan said, turning to put his brush by. He turned back and Nelirikk gasped, hand slapping his sidearm even as his brain told him that it was impossible that a major of inspectors should be standing before him when only a moment ago—

"*Hold!*" And that quickly it was the scout before him, face full of danger, poised on the balls of his feet, having taken up the position of shield to—

To who other than Shan yos'Galan?

Carefully, Nelirikk moved his hand from his gun. Carefully, he inclined his head.

"Forgive my error," he said in the full formality of the Liaden tongue. The scout settled, head cocked to a side.

"And yet it was not an error," he murmured in Terran. "Your whole body screamed astonishment and alarm. You went for the gun as defense. But, enlighten me—what did you see?"

Shan cleared his throat. The scout spun on a heel to face him.

"I suspect he may have seen a Inspector Major here among us. At least, that was the impression I was trying to convey." He looked up, silver eyes catching Nelirikk's gaze. "I gather the illusion was convincing? How gratifying."

"Convincing," Nelirikk agreed, hoarsely. The scout shook his head.

"I saw you turn to put the brush away," he said to his brother. "I saw you turn back and Nelirikk reacting to threat. There was no inspector major here."

"Ah." The silver eyes widened slightly. "Perhaps now?"

Nelirikk gulped, but this time managed to stand calm as the major loomed over the scout, face pitiless behind the tattoos of rank and accomplishment.

The scout shrugged, read Nelirikk's face with a quick green glance over the left shoulder, and looked back to the major.

"Nelirikk is convinced, in any case. I see only yourself."

Shan smiled and became once more a slim man of slightly less than middle height, slanting white eyebrows showing pretty against the smooth brown skin of his face.

"Recall that you were the only one of us who could curb Anthora when she was in a mood to have her way. It's doubtful that we'll meet with an Yxtrang of such discriminating will. And if we do," his mouth tightened. "If we do, I'm afraid I have other defenses."

"Do you?" The scout sighed. "These are new abilities, brother?"

Shan nodded. "I warn you that the explanation will be a thing devoid of sense. Though I am, of course, willing to try."

"Leave it for the present," said the scout, "if it's nonsense. When this is over, let us share a glass or two and tell each other fantastic stories."

"Done."

"Done," the scout echoed and stepped aside.

"So the two of you, fine-looking pilots, both, will proceed boldly across the field, pausing only to distribute explosives at likely looking Communications centers. You will then claim your planes and board. In the meantime, I will advance by a more circuitous route and stealthily steal my own. We will then proceed as discussed, each making at least one pass over the airfield before peeling off in his assigned direction. Questions?"

There were none. They had been through this before. And, after all, the plan was simple.

The scout nodded. "Good. It's time we were gone."

DUTIFUL PASSAGE:
Lytaxin Orbit

❁ ❁

IN ONE HOUR, Standard, the Yxtrang Eye would be fully open, at once clearing a firing path from the battleship to Erob's House and placing the thickest layer of shielding ships between the battleship and the *Passage*.

Priscilla had run the math a dozen times in the last few hours, assigned the tactical comp to find the means by which the *Passage* could divert, prevent, or minimize the Yxtrang's beam.

The answer came back negative.

She had copied their situation files and downloaded them to Pod 77. What, if anything, that ancient non-sentient made of those facts, she had no idea. Subsequent efforts to engage it in dialog had met with no response. Perhaps it had simply stopped functioning.

Ren Zel, hastily briefed on his return to the bridge, stood silent, his eyes on the screen displaying the movement of the Yxtrang shield.

"No answer whatsoever?"

"Nothing," Priscilla said. "I wonder if I've offended it."

"Overloaded it, possibly," he returned, eyes still on the screen.

294

"You say it is very old, and a defense logic. It would perhaps not be equipped to sift through such levels of data as the *Passage*—" He stopped and drew a slow, careful breath.

"Or perhaps it is."

Priscilla looked to the screen, saw the message window filling with words.

⚝　⚝　⚝

TACTICAL DEFENSE POD 77 ON-LINE.
DOWNLOAD DATA ANALYSIS COMPLETE.
DEFENSE PLAN FORMULATED.
PHASE ONE ENACTED.
UPLOADING TO MOBILE UNIT TARGETING COMP.

⚝　⚝　⚝

Ren Zel flung forward, clearing a tertiary screen and accessing the targeting computer in three rapid keystrokes. Priscilla sat rapt, the red counter in her hand, watching the words form on the screen.

⚝　⚝　⚝

ESTIMATED TIME UNTIL OFFENSIVE ACTION: 43 UNITS.
SYNCHRONIZING MOBILE UNIT TARGETING COMP.

⚝　⚝　⚝

"It's uploaded settings for guns seven and nine," Ren Zel told her, fingers moving across the board, "and instructions to fire to those coordinates in forty Standard minutes."

⚝　⚝　⚝

TACTICAL DEFENSE POD 77 ON STAND-BY,
CONDITION ORANGE.

⚝　⚝　⚝

The words stopped and Priscilla stirred at last.

"Remove Pod seventy-seven's instructions from the targeting command queue, please, First Mate."

He spun his chair around, showing her a face which was entirely devoid of emotion.

"I cannot," he said quietly, and she read the effort he expended to hold to calmness. "The file is sealed."

"Sealed, is it?" She reached to her own board. "I'll pull them—"

Ren Zel cleared his throat.

"Forgive me. I should have said that the instructions and the coords are under the seal of Delm Korval."

"Under delm's seal?" Priscilla felt a thrill not unlike terror. Theonna yos'Phelium had left the power to implement delm's seal resident in the ancient defense pod. Theonna yos'Phelium had been a far-seeing delm, indeed.

Or a frothing madwoman.

Priscilla took a breath, felt the red counter warm in her hand and looked to Ren Zel.

"So, we can see it, but we can't change it." As she said that her witch sense told her it was true: some ancient Korval necessity now ruled their fate. "Fine. To my screen two, please. Let's at least find out what we've gotten ourselves into."

"UNCLE WIN DEN!" Alys ran headlong out of the house as he was preparing to step into the flitter for an inspection of the outer ring defenses. He waited, remembering to frown.

"Well, niece? I thought you on duty at the core-comm."

"I was, Uncle. But there was a message . . ." she paused to gulp more air into her lungs. "A message on the telecoder—the old one, that never takes any messages?"

tel'Vosti froze, remembering late night fright stories told him by *his* uncle, too many years ago, and centering around that particular, always silent, telecoder.

"Go on," he urged Alys.

"Yes. The message says it's from the Planetary Defense Unit, and it—" her eyes lifted to his, baffled. "Uncle, it says that it's activated the meteor shielding over Erob Central Control."

LYTAXIN:
War Zone

✸ ❀ ✸ ❀ ✸ ❀ ✸ ❀ ✸ ❀ ✸ ❀ ✸ ❀ ✸ ❀ ✸ ❀ ✸ ❀ ✸ ❀ ✸

VAL CON MELTED AWAY at the edge of the field, taking his bag
of cockpit adaptations and another, similar to the one Nelirikk
carried with him. His target was the comm shed at the south end of
the field, which housed the back-up space-link. After setting the
charges contained in the second bag, he would choose a plane and
lift. The mark was one-half-hour.

Shan and Nelirikk walked openly across the field, Nelirikk
bearing his bag of explosives, the scout's brother swaggering
empty-handed, as befit the sort of officer he had found in Nelirikk's
undermind. *Their* targets were the radar support shack and back-up
communications.

The field was busy, but not overly so. They had arrived, so
Nelirikk thought, in the trough between the first wave moving out
and the second. Those who were abroad had duty to attend. No one
paid attention to two officers arrogantly and unhurriedly about
their own duty. They marched directly up to back-up comm, Shan
waiting with cold impatience while Nelirikk deftly jimmied the
lock, pushed the door open, stepped back and saluted smartly. In

character, he ignored the salute and stamped into the shed, Nelirikk in his wake, swinging the door closed behind them.

"Do not touch that," he said, pointing at a green striped panel. "Alarm circuit." He had dropped his bag and fished out two of the scout's devices.

Shan took one of the explosives, moved to the left, seated it and armed it as his brother had shown him, while Nelirikk did his part of the work on the opposite side of the shed.

Two minutes later, they were once again striding across the busy field.

At radar support, the door was unlocked. Nelirikk paused, threw a worried glance toward his companion and was answered with a vicious glower from the inspector major.

Well enough, thought Nelirikk. *We do what we have come to do.* He thrust the door open and brought his fist up in salute. The major tramped by him with no acknowledgment, into the radar shed.

A tech jumped up from behind the board, his face displaying surprise that quickly became chagrin as he read their *vingtai*.

"Inspectors . . ." The salute was hasty, the face pale behind the tattoos that showed him a specialist, confirmed twice at combat radar, a volunteer who had achieved success in a difficult mission, originally of Ornjal's Tech Troop. "I was not told you were to be here. I—"

Shan frowned, and the tech gulped. Slowly, the gesture filled with such menace that Nelirikk felt his own heart stutter, the scout's brother pointed at the door.

"Inspector Major." The tech saluted. "I received no notice of your coming. Duty demands that I ask to see your passes."

"We have no time for that!" Nelirikk snarled, moving forward. "There have been security failures at several locations! We must check this facility and certify it! Out, and leave us to duty!"

Despite the sweat beading on his upper lip and the definite paleness of his face, the tech was not so easy to rout. He took a hard breath and met Nelirikk's eyes squarely.

"I need some ID, sir. You understand. I am required to . . ."

They had given the scout's brother perhaps thirty words of the

Common Troop, without ever expecting he would have need of them.

"Fool!" he roared now, thrusting a hard hand under the tech's nose. "Papers, damn you!"

The tech jumped, saluted even more hastily, pulling his work orders, his day sheets, his meal cards, as the officer cursed him for a sluggard dog and seemed almost ready to strike him.

Shakily, the tech ordered his papers, offering them with yet another salute.

The scout's brother snatched them, looked them over contemptuously, with a special sneer for the coveted meal cards. Abruptly, he turned, shoved the offensive papers into Nelirikk's hands and stalked over to the screen bank.

"Troop!" barked Nelirikk. "Have you eyes?"

"Sir!" A shaky salute. "Yes, sir!"

"Good! Take them elsewhere if you ever wish to eat again!" He threw the papers and the tech caught them against his chest, his eyes on the meal cards Nelirikk still held in his hand.

"Yes, sir."

"Put yourself on half rations tonight," Nelirikk snapped, and pushed the cards into the tech's sweating face. "Dismissed!"

"Sir!" The tech saluted, threw a terrified glance at the major, who was now inspecting the lateral board, and all but ran from the shed.

Nelirikk pushed the door shut, dropped the sack and yanked it open.

"Quickly," he said, putting the bomb into the hands of the scout's brother. "We are off the mark."

CROUCHED in scant cover, Val Con waited while an officer dressed in what he had to believe was the original of the uniform Nelirikk had approximated for himself, face bearing *vingtai* eerily similar to Shan's artwork, performed what could only be an inspection.

Precious minutes ticked by and still the officer did not emerge from the comm shed.

Three minutes more, Val Con thought, belly down under a cable lorry. *If he is not gone in three minutes, I will set the charges against the shed's exterior and trust in the luck.*

Chancy enough under the best of conditions, the luck being notoriously fickle. Yet, what else could be done? This whole mad venture sat on the knees of the luck, born of the desperate necessity of success. They must succeed in routing the Yxtrang. Must. The cost of failure was too terrible to contemplate.

The door to the shed opened and Val Con tucked his face into the crook of an arm, watching sidewise as the inspector and his aide marched to the waiting armored car, entered and were driven away.

Close on the mark, Commander, he told himself, checking the area carefully. *Be quick, now, and all's well.*

Finding the immediate environs suitably empty, he left his cover, ghosted to the shed and let himself inside.

THE SCOUT'S BROTHER was safe in his chosen craft. Nelirikk continued further down the field, so that there should be some distance between the two of them on take-off.

From the corner of his eye, he saw an armored car make a wide turn and bear down on his position. There was no reason to assume that the driver of the vehicle was in any way interested in an adjutant inspector, but Nelirikk felt the newly shaved hairs lift on the back of his neck.

Taking care to betray no haste, he changed course, angling toward one of the newer, Raphix-class planes. The damned car came after and Nelirikk grit his teeth, marching on, soldierly, measuring the distance, if it came to a chase.

Behind him, the car accelerated. Over the engine's excitement, a voice shouted out in the language of the Troop, "You there! Halt for the Inspector Major!"

Nelirikk ran.

IT WAS WONDERFUL, Shan thought, what a little height did for one's perspective.

Snug in the cockpit of the quiescent Yxtrang fighter, trusting his projected suggestion to any and all passersby that this same cockpit was empty, he looked down the field of planes.

Some way down the field, lorries and refuellers were busy preparing the next pod of planes. Shan made a note of that.

Closer to home, he spied the broad shoulders and soldierly stride of Nelirikk Explorer, followed by an armored car bearing the Yxtrang graphic for "Inspection Office." Shan sat up, trying to get a reading on the occupants of the car. His touch fell short and he saw the car accelerate. Saw Nelirikk break stride and bolt for the ladder of a plane.

It lacked five minutes of the mark.

Shan engaged the shock webbing, hands moving—though he was careful not to be too quick—over the fighter's board.

VAL CON was running too close to the mark. Delayed and delayed again by the movement of maintenance vehicles and technical crews, he finally swung back, angling for the last of three planes that sat in pristine isolation at the very edge of the field.

It was chancy. The location was open, and the guards—three guards, he counted—suggested that these craft were meant to be flown by pilots of rank.

Chancy. He sank back into his sliver of shadow and tried to weigh how chancy. The cause was not served, if he died before he ever gained the air.

After all, he had promised Miri that he would meet her at Erob's field this noon.

He smiled a little then, feeling the tension in his face. A foolish promise on both sides, given what they both undertook. Still, she would expect him to exert himself to keep it.

A diversion was clearly required. If he could but entice the guards a few steps away from their posts, he would have Luken's oft-desired honest advantage that made a dash for the nearest craft possible.

As if his thought ignited it, thunder roared across the field, closely followed by a second boom, which was an air-to-ground cannon being fired. A second engine roared into life and the guards were running toward the sounds, rifles ready, and Val Con threw thought away, gathered his bag and his breath and ran.

He didn't look for the guards. He looked at nothing but the ladder, convenient enough for one of Nelirikk's length, but requiring a leap at the end of his race, and with the bag to hamper him—

A pellet hit the ground a pace ahead, gravel bits exploding, and he jumped, grabbed the ladder, heard another shot, but he was climbing, and it was a third shot and a fourth. His hand slipped and he snatched a recovery, felt the bag slide and let it go, swarming up, up, and falling into the cockpit, the left leg numb beneath him, but he flung forward, slapped the switch and the bubble rose up and over, sealing him into safety with a click.

THE ENGINE ROARED to life and the plane began to move. Shan applied the brake, carefully, found the control for the cannon, crossed hairs on the armored car's position and pushed the firing stud.

The plane lurched under him, the armored car went up in a hail of metal, and he eased off the brake, letting the engine have its way as he saw the plane Nelirikk had chosen, with the Yxtrang numbers 32 on the tail, begin to creep forward. Nodding, he took the lead, relinquished the brake entirely and let the engines pull the plane down the runway, pushing her a little now, hauling back on the stick the instant he was able.

Climbing, he looked down, saw Nelirikk's plane leap off the field, and quite a commotion on the ground. A finger's width above the tree-tops, he leveled out and banked hard, sweeping back the way he had come, using the belly guns to kill the planes sitting weak and defenseless, pulled back on the stick at the end of his line, saw 32 flying neck-or-nothing, lashing the field into shrapnel.

It was now thirty-five minutes since they had separated and there was no third fighter in the air. Shan bit his lip, banked again, searching—and saw a plane rising, a sleek affair with the numbers 03 painted high on its proud tail. He grinned. Trust Val Con to steal himself a beauty.

For an instant it seemed to him that the pretty plane faltered, then it was climbing, arrow-bright, leveled and banked smoothly right, sweeping in low over the field, guns blaring.

All according to plan, Shan, he told himself, ridiculously relieved. *With a phrase or two varied. We're all safe in the air, for whatever that's worth. Go east, young man, and finish things up. After which, I promise, you may go mad.*

He pulled on the stick and made his turn, still climbing, east, in search of targets.

HE'D BEEN HIT. The left leg, well above the knee. There was blood. A lot of blood. Not good.

There was also pain, now that he had seen the wound. He tried to shake it out of awareness, used the levers to shrink the cockpit to minimum, and discovered the shock webbing was too large for him, and then discovered that it didn't matter. He could not be webbed in and reach his instruments. Instead, he raised the pilot's couch to maximum and perched precariously on the edge. The pain . . .

The drill.

He stretched, took a breath and touched the first key, chanting the drill to focus his mind.

"Power check; external go. Internal, go. Clock set synchronize; clock reset to trip zero. Power on. External power stable. Internal stable. Release external cable."

He faltered, the pain chewing his thoughts. He ran the Rainbow, quickly, drawing the body away from the mind, continued to chant the drill.

"Drag brake on, mech brake on. Engine A start. Engine A positive, null thrust."

He was late on the mark. They would be worried, but he couldn't rush the drill, because . . .

Something would go wrong, if he rushed the drill.

"Engine B start. Engine B positive, null thrust. Clock check; timing positive. Annular pressure fifty percent, thrust positive. Scan positive. Weapon check; outboard cannon check."

There were soldiers, on the ground far below. They were

running toward him. He looked up and there was a soldier there, too, at the top of the ladder, looking down at him through the dome.

"Remove fuse sixteen. Cap fuse sixteen. Pull pin seven."

There was a truck headed his way, he saw the cannon in its bed and hurtled through the last of the drill.

"Drag brake off, mech brake off, inlets open, full power, on."

He was moving, as the drill said he should, scattering soldiers as he gained speed. He looked up, saw the soldier still clinging to the dome, then forgot him as the speed built and off to the right a building exploded, brilliant orange smoke spreading rapidly in the whipping wind.

The speed was building quickly and the pressure felt good against him, except his leg . . . and it took him a moment to find the dial that told him the plane was going fast enough so he pulled back hard on the stick, and didn't notice when the soldier finally slid off the dome.

Climbing, he saw another plane circling, but it didn't fire, so he banked to the right, setting up for his run over the field, like they'd planned.

He saw another building blow up as he came in low—incandescence, then heavy black smoke, rapidly thinning. He triggered the cannons, saw planes and men die under him, then he was climbing again, and the other fighter was banking, heading east and he remembered that was the plan, too. Shan would go east. Nelirikk would go south. He would go west.

Accordingly, he banked to the right—"*Ah!*"

He held onto consciousness, the agony receded. Stretching for the dial, he upped the oxygen content in cabin, enough, he hoped, to keep him from getting sleepy. Not enough, quite, to make him drunk.

Filling his lungs with richer air, he stretched again to the board, and increased the cabin pressure, which would help reduce the bleeding.

This craft was a beauty, wonderfully stable. He took advantage of that to remove both hands from the controls and cut the rest of the leather away from the wound. Then he bandaged it as well as he could, taking care to make the wrappings tight.

WAR ZONE

❋❋❋❋❋❋❋❋❋❋❋❋❋❋❋❋❋❋❋❋❋❋❋❋

"YOU WILL FORGIVE ME if I seem discourteous," Miri told the guy with the hatchet. "We are in train to engage the enemy and timing is vital. I suggest that you continue to the rear and remove your folk from active danger."

"Your concern does you credit," he replied, but not like he meant it. He gestured, showing her the rabble and the rakes, spears, pistols, pipes, knives and rocks that was the most of their gear.

"As you see, we are armed. We are prepared to fight. Forgive me if I notice that your troop is thin. We will bolster your numbers and increase the opportunity of success." His face was bleak, and not quite sane.

"We are before you now because we did fight, Captain, and we prevailed. All of us have dead in the city."

Last thing she needed, Miri thought. Buncha crazy civilians with no idea of discipline, half of them out on their feet and a short handful holding anything like useful weaponry.

She glared at the guy and he didn't flinch, there being something in the set of his mouth that reminded her, forcefully, of Val Con in his hell-or-high-water mode. She could move on without taking them, sure. But she couldn't stop them from following and making a mob scene on the field that would send discipline straight to hell and get needless numbers killed.

Damn it.

"Very well," she agreed, inclining her head at the angle that said she knew he had her over a barrel and she was letting him have his way, but not to push it.

"The sergeants will assign your people to existing squads. Understand me: you *will* follow the orders of the sergeants, from this moment until the enemy is defeated. In the meantime, I do not take children onto a battlefield."

She pointed at the nursery contingent—two dozen kids, none of them over eight or nine, guarded by three adults armed with hunting rifles, which were the closest thing to real weapons in the whole mob.

"Those will proceed, with their protectors, to the rear and beg grace of Erob."

"Captain, they will." He bowed then, deep and courtly, like she was doing him some kind of major favor, instead of inviting him to get massacred, and turned to relay her orders to the rabble.

"METEOR SHIELD?" Emrith Tiazan looked at her kinsman, saw neither madness nor levity in his face, and asked, steadily, "What meteor shield?"

"The one that our instruments assure us is even now in place, covering an area with Korval's Tree as its center."

Korval's Tree sat in the front garden and well for them that it did, Erob thought, sighing sharply.

"It appears that the Planetary Defense Unit is concerned that the Tree may come under attack from space." She eyed tel'Vosti. "I must assume that its concern has at least one leg in reality?"

"I think we have no option, Emrith."

"So." She moved behind the desk, accessed the delm's archive and keyed in a search for "Planetary Defense Unit." The answer came quickly enough, and when she had read it she sighed again. Gift of Korval. Gods protect them all from Korval's gifts.

"Here is something to amuse, Win Den," she said, scrolling to the end of the file. "In times when its attention is not diverted by the possibility of meteor strike, Planetary Defense Unit is none other than Dragon's Tooth, Korval's contract suite." She sat back, suddenly very tired indeed.

"The blood thins, Win Den. We should not have forgotten this."

"Peace dulls the senses," he said softly. "Give praise, Emrith, that Korval's Tooth has remained alive. Let us hope that it is also sharp."

TROOPS WERE MOVING, up from the south. Nelirikk identified the supply line, dropped the nose and used the cannon rather than squander the precious bombs nestled in the fighter's belly.

There was return fire on his second pass, and he spent a bomb to take out the anti-aircraft turret at the head of the column, then used the cannon again, killing a command vehicle before he was past it all and banking to the left, setting up for his final pass.

Two more bombs away from his hoard, and a foursome of land-armor destroyed. Nelirikk climbed and swung back to the course, well satisfied with his work thus far.

A STORM WAS BREWING and the rising wind was unexpectedly troublesome when the plane slowed in the aftermath of cannon fire. Shan held his altitude with brute force and swept back again, his cannon-fire concentrated on a line of slow-moving trucks.

The plane shuddered and lost forward speed rapidly. Shan gunned the engines and below him saw blossoms of flame as the ammo trucks exploded.

POD 77's instruction to *Dutiful Passage*'s guns seven and nine was to fire a broad, low-level magnetic beam directly into the Yxtrang shield, intensity to remain constant for five Standard minutes, increasing to maximum for one-half minute and cutting out.

Priscilla shook her head, fingers building the equation in screen two while Ren Zel fed data to Maincomp for simulation. A mag beam that low would deliver little more than a nudge to even the lightest of the shield boats. What possible defensive gain might accrue to such a—

Beside her, Ren Zel hissed, for all the worlds like an offended house cat. She gasped, startled out of her concentration, looked to the sim, and wondered at his restraint, that he had neither howled nor roared.

The mag beam fired, low and steady, off of gun seven for five Standard minutes into the mass of light craft, encountered in the third layer an extremely light pallet-skid. The beam pulsed, the skid moved. In the fifth layer, the skid encountered a workboat and the pressure of its shielding coupled with the steady push of the beam started that craft moving as well.

The sim for gun nine showed a similar phenomenon, each beam finally pushing a cluster of ten small ships, toward the center of the Eye.

When the first of the defenseless boats hit the edge of the Eye, the power simultaneously pulsed to full. The boats, impelled by the beams, skittered into the firing zone, and—

"They won't stop the beam," Priscilla whispered. "They don't have enough shielding. It will go right through them."

"Not entirely," Ren Zel said. "The beam will lose energy as it passes through the obstacles and will strike the on-world target with somewhat less intensity."

She felt ill, even as she approved the Pod 77's tactics. A defense logic, indeed. Once the battleship's weakened beam struck through atmosphere, the ancient weapon would have a clear return shot.

"How many," Ren Zel asked quietly. "How many of those things are at large?" He inclined his head, acknowledging her place in the line direct of a clan not his own. "If it may be told."

"Two," Priscilla told him, and felt his relief as sharply as her own. "Only two. This one, and one other."

THEY'D BEEN LUCKY. For one thing, Yxtrang hadn't been expecting them—not quite yet, anyhow. For another, they hadn't exactly been over-manned.

For a third thing, Miri thought as she waited for the last of the situation reports to come in, Yxtrang had thought they'd be going up against a professional fighting force.

What they got was the remaining Irregulars, whose ranks had been doubled and doubled again by the time they hit the airfield, by bands of desperate and vengeful civilians.

Miri wondered if the guy with the hatchet had managed to stay alive. Seemed like she owed the man an apology. *His* crew hadn't been rabble. She'd seen rabble, now.

The Irregulars launched the attack, hitting the Yxtrang mess tent with three rounds of mortar fire at half-through dinner. They'd followed up with an occupation of the ammo dump and turned the two captured field pieces against the disoriented Yxtrang.

It was the mob that attacked the remaining entrenched field piece in a wave. The soldiers there had faced knives, spears, rocks, and raw hatred. None had died easy, and there were an astonishing number of Yxtrang among the mass of corpses.

The last report came through and Miri sighed. Eleven Irregulars dead or missing. Hundreds of civilians, ditto. Yxtrang had spiked the fuel tanks with sand, damn their black hearts. She'd've done the same.

But, the airfield was theirs, theoretically, and a couple hundred meters in all directions, with a tenuous western connection.

Theory came in to it because the Yxtrang weren't being good losers. They hadn't thrown their guns away and run screaming from the field. They had retreated in as good order as possible, those who were left, and now they waited in the woods, maybe for dark, maybe for a dawn attack, but probably for reinforcements. Now and then, a couple would dance out onto the floor and throw a party favor, probing for weakness.

Miri, drawing on a stockpile of weaponry Yxtrang had forgotten to take with them when they vacated, called for occasional mortar fire to the south and east. To the west were the fringes of Kritoulkas' crew, and a couple pieces of modest merc armor.

She'd ordered the captured field artillery used for on-the-spot training—so far a quarter of the troop had been part of the drill. They were firing randomly on the valley trails most likely able to support incoming Yxtrang armor or supplies.

The civilians, with nothing nearby to murder, were in the way, milling around on the runway. That was no good. She called to one of her lieutenants to clear the field and a few minutes later a sergeant and a squad marched over to move the mob along.

Miri drank some water from her canteen and checked the time. Ought to be seeing planes, real soon. The wind was rising, and she could see heavy clouds on the horizon. Great. The piloting tapes Val Con had her learning weren't coy about the difficulties of flying in storms. The sooner she saw planes, the happier she'd be.

In fact . . . She tipped her head, frowning after the sound which might have been engine noise—but wasn't.

She listened with care. *Armor*, she decided. *Kritoulkas must've decided to advance herself a little while things're quie—*

She felt the rumble then, shouted, "Incoming!" and saw the Irregulars go for cover, and some of the brighter civilians.

Armor.

And it wasn't theirs.

HE HAD USED all his bombs, to the glory of the Troop and the mortification of the enemy. The 14th Conquest Corps had lost heavily this day, in arms, ammunition, equipment, and status.

They had lost pilots, too. Three of rank who rose against him had gone gloriously to duty's reward.

Nelirikk checked the fuel gauge, made one last mid-level pass over the wreckage and confusion that had been the 14th's southern stronghold, and set his course for Erob's airfield, where his captain and his arms-mates awaited him.

IT WAS POSSIBLE, Shan thought, that he had done lasting damage. Certainly, he'd played merry havoc with the heavy artillery, the armor, and the ammo.

And the planes.

Despite holding *Soldier Lore* deep in his bones, he was far too much Korval to kill ships without pain. Reason said that the ships of the enemy must be nullified.

But a pilot's heart wept for the pretties left dead or dying, never to know the sweet thrill of lift again.

The building storm was at his back as he came in toward the

agreed-upon airfield and saw, with a gasp of relief, that the Irregulars' flag was flying.

In the woods, as he passed over, half-a-dozen armored vehicles, closing rapidly toward the field.

He banked sharply and saw the storm straight-on, a wall of boiling black cloud, lanced with lightning and topped with miles of blazing white thunderheads; then he dropped the nose, caught a tank in the cross hairs and pushed the firing stud.

FIRST, THERE WERE NO PLANES. Then, there were two, from opposite directions.

Miri watched the first come in ahead of the racing storm, saw it slow, drop, then swing back over the woods, and the noises it was making promised enemy.

"Mark that!" she yelled to the crews. "Get the mortar and both pieces on that heading. Rapid fire!"

The second plane circled the field once, waggled its wings a couple times, and then came in low, flared out neatly and touched down with barely a sound, coming around in a wide circle until its nose was pointing at the woods.

The pilot cut power, but a whine remained in the air as the hatch went up and Nelirikk, his face showing faint marks like daubs of paint, dropped to the ground, ran to her and saluted.

"Count three rounds in the nose cannon, my Captain. No fuel to fly with."

She took his salute, wondering how someone so ugly could look so good. "Can't help you with the fuel. We got armor gonna come outta those woods pretty soon. Can you aim the cannon while you're grounded?"

"Yes, Captain."

"Do it."

He bolted for his plane and it was time for the first one to come back in, too fast, to Miri's eye, touching down and flaming out in the same instant, rolling uncontrolled toward the far end of the field. It came to her that the pilot was dead, or bad hit, and she reached inside her head for the comfort of Val Con's pattern.

The last thing she remembered seeing was the bright orange 'chute popping out of the tail of the rolling plane, dragging its speed down to nothing.

THE SHIP was on red alert, the crews responsible for guns seven and nine by the captain's order removed from their stations.

The timer in the corner of the main command screen counted to zero and faded. Targeting comp reported guns seven and nine on-line, magnetic beams, low.

Captain and first mate watched as actuality repeated simulation and the beams inexorably pushed defenseless ships into the maw of the Eye.

The Yxtrang battleship fired.

Shuttlecraft and workboats, pallet-skids and lighters, took the charge, expanded. And were gone.

"Beam energy leached by a factor of three, Captain," the first mate said quietly from his work screen. The captain nodded.

Targeting comp reported guns seven and nine off-line, targets destroyed.

THE WIND buffeted his ship. He corrected, nearly over corrected. The horizon was higher than it should be, surely. . . ? A long reach to the board and that was corrected, too.

He was approaching his first strike zone, the airfield far behind. Below, the enemy moved. He found the supply column and came in low.

These were hardened soldiers, familiar with the sounds of battle. Few even looked up as air cover streaked over.

Val Con dropped the nose of the ship, brought video cross hairs to bear on the streaming troops, and fired his cannon.

The sound was a long low moan; the plane shuddered and lost forward speed rapidly. The slower it went, the more the local winds tore and tossed it.

The run took just seconds, the return a hard right bank and he gasped as the injured leg was pressed by acceleration.

Back again, flying low, nose down . . .

These *were* seasoned troops. There was return fire, but the anti-aircraft gun wasn't in position yet.

Val Con brought the cross hairs to bear once more, ignoring the figures running for cover, concentrating on his target.

This time he scored a direct hit, and the surprising blast lifted the plane and bounced him around in the oversized cockpit. He rescued himself with a snatch at the instrument panel, his vision black at the edges and the pain was a carnivore, eating him alive . . .

It was instinct, a snatch at life no less vital than his grip on the instrument panel.

He reached into that portion of himself that had been most abused by the Department, and flipped a certain toggle-on.

The pain did not fade, it was simply no longer relevant data. He was aware that he was wounded, that the wetness down his leg was blood, and he bent to tighten the wrappings, for it would be inefficient to die of blood loss before the mission was done.

Very distantly, there was song. The song comforted him, though he could not stop right now to listen. There were targets below him and the mission was imperative. If he failed, the song would die, and he would not allow that.

HE HAD DONE with the moving troops and flown on, seeking other targets. He had tightened the wrapping on his leg again, and enriched the air supply. He cut a long strip of leather from his jacket and used that to tie himself, standing, against the board. The fuel gauge was fine. There were still many bombs in his belly.

He went over the field at mid-level, saw the shapes of space-worthy ships and knew he had found targets that merited his skill. He came back in, readying his guns, but they were alert here, they weren't a moving column that was vulnerable to air attack.

They fired missiles at him and he saw people on the ground, running for planes. He brought the nose down and fired at the planes, because it would be bad to have to fight them all in the air.

The rising missiles altered courses, seeking. Val Con saw one beside him, pacing him, it seemed. He veered toward it and it veered away. He laughed, veered toward it again, and watched it pull away.

Cannon-fire was not so coy. Bursts exploded just off his wing-tip and he banked right, braced hard against the board, and there was a song in his head and he wanted to listen, but he couldn't because there was an enemy plane coming against him and he had to uncap his wing cannon and fire.

He was nearly blinded by the explosion, felt his craft buffeted, heard the sound of metal shred bouncing off the high-strength skin.

Reflex took over and he banked sharply to the right, knowing that he shouldn't—sharply to the right, the leather tie held him up, and sharply to the right and now he was behind the plane that had been chasing him and if he pressed this switch again. . .

The cannon fire was pretty. He laughed at the explosion.

He'd gotten past the field, though, and he needed to kill the spaceships. He banked to the right, coming in low, and he'd always been good at this part. He knew how to almost touch the tops of the trees and he went over the big hump and remembered that he needed to have all the weapons live.

But the spaceships weren't sleeping anymore. One was awake and lifting, and people on the ground were shooting at him, two more missiles came by to look at him and veered off because the ship said he was an Yxtrang ace.

He fired his cannon at the rising target but he was too fast, and by it, and swept around to the right and pulled back on the stick because the target was climbing.

He needed to do something about that, he knew. This target—this target was *troop transport*. He couldn't let it get away and bring more soldiers down.

There was a song in his head. He'd heard it many times before. He banked right and saw the target above him, and pushed the power bar to full.

The target got slightly closer, but he knew it was faster than he was and could fly higher. He fired his cannon, but it didn't explode like the other targets.

It was hard to move with the power bar all the way up and the leather strap was holding him tight while his mount climbed directly under the target, but the target was getting smaller.

There was a song in his head and he wanted to listen, but the target had to be stopped. The sky was getting darker and the target getting smaller and he couldn't go much higher because it was the wrong kind of ship—

He fired his nose cannon and his wing cannon and his missiles all at once. He fired and thought maybe he'd hit the target and then thought maybe he hadn't because it kept moving and he couldn't go straight up anymore, anyway. His leg was hurting and he was very tired.

He closed his eyes and sagged against the board.

He remembered then that the song was named Miri and that he'd been very lucky to hear it.

EROB, what numbers of them were in the house rather than in troop with his astonishing and admirable niece, or on the grounds, had taken shelter in the deep cellars.

He had given warning, for whatever good that would do them, to the defenders locked outside the shield, and relayed an encoded situation report to Jason Carmody's last known position, down by the quarry encampment.

Duty done, Win Den tel'Vosti sat behind his desk in the back parlor that had become his war room, and waited for what might occur.

"Uncle?" Alys stood poised on the threshold, looking slightly rumpled in a tunic handed down from an older cousin, the weapons belt pulled snug 'round her waist, gun ready by her hand.

He sighed. "Child, you should be in the cellar with the rest."

"But you aren't," she replied, irrefutably. "Why came you here?"

He sighed again, feeling very old, indeed, and as if all his years had taught him nothing.

"Because I am a general, child. Duty requires me to be at my station, in case there should be need."

"Oh." She came lightly across the room and leaned against his side, one arm across his shoulders. He put his arm around her waist, careful of the gun.

"What will happen, Uncle?"

"I don't know," he said softly. "Perhaps nothing." But even Alys was too old to believe that.

"Dragon's Tooth would not have awakened," she told him, "if it were nothing. Clan Korval is our ally."

Wisdom and folly in one short utterance, tel'Vosti thought. As if to be Korval's ally placed one in anything like safety. He hugged her lightly.

"That's so."

The lights went out. The computers went off-line.

There was sound: the scream of ten thousand fingernails drawn simultaneously down ten thousand slate boards, going on and on.

The air was filled with static and the room was very warm. Alys gasped and flinched, caught herself and stood quiveringly still against his side, her arm like a bar of lead across his shoulder.

The sound stopped.

The lights came up. The computers beeped and rebooted. The air was gentle, pleasantly cool against the skin.

Alys sighed and slumped a little. tel'Vosti remembered to breathe.

The intercom on the desk chimed. He leaned forward and touched the key.

"Yes?"

"Uncle, it's Kol Vus. There's another message on the old telecoder. Planetary Defense Unit says that the shield has deflected an energy bolt. Shield power is down, it says here, by fifty-five percent." There was a pause.

"Planetary Defense Unit advises us that the shielding will not divert another strike. And then it says, 'Phase Two enabled, Phase Two confirmed, Phase Two in progress.'"

SHAN THREW HIMSELF DOWN the ladder and ran low across the field, pistol in hand, and flung to his belly next to the small leather-clad crumple.

His foray in the woods had stopped one Yxtrang tank, which left five more closing on the field. The Irregulars all seemed to be pointing in the right direction, the mortars and anti-armor guns in position. Nelirikk's plane, with the Yxtrang number 32 on the tail, was on standby power, which might well mean there were rounds left in the nose cannon. For the moment, the side of the airfield was as safe as any other position in the immediate vicinity, but it wasn't going to stay that way, and Miri. . .

She lay like one dead, face against the ground, the combat helmet askew, showing a bright gleam of hair.

That she was *not* dead or even wounded, he knew, though he barely knew what to make of the tangle of steel and fire that confounded his Inner Eyes.

The ground shook. A turret appeared at the end of the field, as the first of the Yxtrang armor cleared the trees. Shan came to his knees, pistol ready, heard the whine from Nelirikk's plane change pitch, and went down, covering Miri's body with his own.

Nelirikk's cannon roared, the ground steadied, Shan rocked back on his knees, holstered the pistol, gathered his brother's lifemate into his arms and ran.

SHE WAS SO TIRED. Opening her eyes was too much effort. But she had to open her eyes, because . . .

Damned if she knew why.

It was warm. She was tired. So . . . very . . . tired. Better to sleep and not to care . . .

Because there had been three planes and only two had landed. She needed to open her eyes and look for the other one, the most important one, to be sure that it got home safe.

She demanded sight with all her will and heavy eyelids lifted. The world was a blur.

It took her a second to realize that was because she'd fallen across the instrument panel and her cheek was against one of the dials. She exerted more will, and got herself upright, helped by the strap around her waist, that anchored her to the board.

That was better. She could see the instruments, the fuel gauge, the altimeter—*how* high?—and the compass. And through the windscreen she could see—

A slow drifting. And that was wrong, she knew from the tapes he had made her learn. Wrong, because it meant—

The plane wasn't level.

Her hands were heavy, but she got one around the joystick, found the horizon meter and slowly pushed on the stick, watching the horizon line crawl down from almost vertical toward level.

The stick was hard to move. She tried to shift her weight to the left, to bring more push into play—and would have fallen if the strap hadn't held her.

Still, she managed to inch it down until the dial finally displayed a clear horizontal bisection, the blue-white of sky on the top, the black that meant ground on the bottom.

Now, from side to side out the window, there was a horizon, distant and level. It rotated slowly. . .

And that wasn't wrong or right, just a fact, until she knew where—and the compass heading showed that. She found the sun and realized she was flying in the wrong direction, bent to work the stick again, and below her was a boiling cauldron of gray and white and she jumped, the leg went, but the strap held her up and his voice was murmuring, distant and almost too soft to hear . . .

"Storm. Below."

She reached out to touch his pattern, but it wasn't there—no, it *was* there, but *around* her and, fading, somehow, its colors attenuating into mist, the interlockings beginning, slowly, to untwine.

She bit her lip. "You're dying. Val Con—"

"Fly. The. Plane."

THE LIFEMATE BRIDGE swirled with energy and Shan could see Val Con's essence, very faint, and Miri's, much stronger—and an incomplete third that drew threads from each, spindle-dancing above, or below, or within the bridgework.

And he dared not touch any of it.

So he did what he could and sat guard over her body in the shell of what had been a hangar and eventually Nelirikk joined him there.

"The captain, I saw her fall." The blue eyes moved, registered the soft rise and fall of her breast and flicked up. "Not dead."

"Not dead," Shan agreed.

"The scout has not returned from his mission."

Shan nodded, his attention on the flow of the lifemate bridge. It had taken his father a full year to die of his lifemate's passing. But the connection between his parent's souls had been as slender as a thread of spider silk, compared to the conflagration that linked Val Con and Miri. If Val Con was dying . . .

"What ails the captain?" Nelirikk asked. Shan looked up.

"She's with the scout."

The blue eyes blinked, then Nelirikk nodded. "More armor comes. And soldiers."

Soldier Lore bestirred itself. "What's our situation?"

"We can prevail," stated another voice from the doorway, in rusty Trade. "With boldness."

A man strode forward—a Liaden male cradling an Yxtrang rifle in his arms like a child. A hatchet hung in a loop on his belt, stained red from edge to blunt.

Nelirikk rose to his towering height. The Liaden ignored him, walked past him and then stopped, looking down at Miri. After a moment, he turned and addressed himself to the Yxtrang.

"You fly for the captain? Eh? Kill enemy at her word?"

Nelirikk inclined his head. "Sir, I do."

"She allowed me and mine with her, on condition we obey the sergeants. The sergeant of my squad is dead and there are many others, who joined at the last, with no sergeant to order them, but who will fight with ferocity."

"You tell me this for a reason?" Nelirikk inquired and the man pulled his lips back from his teeth—a death's head grin.

"I tell you this because I desire you to lead us, Yxtrang-of-the-Captain."

"I do not—"

"My entire line is gone, damn you!" the Liaden shouted. "Will you take what I offer and use it well, or must my Balance fall short of my dead?"

A heartbeat of silence, no more. Nelirikk bowed.

"Soldier, I will lead you. For the glory of Troop and captain. Show me to your fighters."

SHE FLEW THE PLANE, dropped the nose and brought it down into the clouds ruthlessly, remembering ships she'd never flown and emergencies she'd never experienced.

The sky was a long time gray; the buffeting and noise of the winds amazed her. The ship went subsonic with an odd fluttering and she had to fight the controls, stretching too far to reach—and then she was below the clouds.

There was green all around, and a river to her left. The clouds sweeping by obscured her vision momentarily and then tore away.

In the distance she could see the airfield, the Irregular's flag flying high.

Lightning flashed off the left wing and the plane lurched as thunder boomed through the metal walls.

She was closing on the airfield fast and the winds were making it difficult, tossing the plane like it was no more substantial than a butterfly. It was hard to see properly, to understand direction from this perspective.

Down and ahead—Yxtrang armor in the trees.

She looked to the board, saw she had bombs to spend. She checked on the situation through the windscreen.

And saw the Yxtrang fighter, closing fast from the right and behind.

She veered the plane, brought it right down on the deck, and saw Val Con's pattern all around her, overlaying everything in tired, fading color.

She knew what to do, stretched to the board and did it, bringing the plane down, *down*, wingtips brushing the treetops, and the Yxtrang fighter was on her, but that wasn't important yet.

The Yxtrang on the ground had noticed her. She saw the turret on the anti-aircraft move, tracking, and she kept the speed steady, sweeping in low and insanely fast, waiting for it, waiting for it and the turret was on her and the plane behind had fired, but missed. She was directly over Yxtrang now, opened her belly and dropped the bombs, dumped what was left of her fuel and she was past and the other plane was still on her tail. The armor found its range and fired. Miri smacked the switch and the landing gear came down.

The fighter behind them blew up.

THEY WERE NOT SOLDIERS, but they were fierce and willing, in their hatred, to take orders.

Accordingly, Nelirikk had them wait, in the cover at the near edge of the airfield. Wait, until the first plane flashed over, dumping fuel and the last of its bombs onto the heads of the enemy. Wait, until the anti-aircraft fired and destroyed the pursuer.

Then, with the enemy disordered and dismayed, he rose up, roared the battle cry—"Revenge!"—and led the rabble to war as the wind rose and thunder out-sounded the cannons.

THE BEAM leapt up from the planet's surface, threaded the Yxtrang Eye and touched the battleship.

There was a flare, which would be the outer shields, Priscilla thought, and a second, which would be the inner.

She sighed and shook her head, for it had been a valiant effort, if ill-favored and—

That quickly the Yxtrang battleship broke and ran, accelerating, and rising—

"Position report, Captain."

Ren Zel's voice was level, betraying nothing. "Tactical report, Captain."

"Tactical?" Priscilla demanded and reached for her board, banishing the Eye and the battleship to a quarter screen, and saw the break-in noise of a dozen ships, IDs blossoming—Terran IDs. Terran troopships.

"Affiliation?"

"Tree-and-Dragon," Ren Zel said, as more ships phased in-system. "Gyrfalk." He paused. "Juntavas."

"Juntavas," she repeated and looked over to him. He met her eyes, blandly.

"Perhaps they consider the Yxtrang bad for commerce."

"I suppose that's possible." She looked back to her screen. Something strange was happening close in by the Yxtrang battleship. Space was behaving in a most unusual manner—pulsing—and there seemed to be something phasing in, phasing out—in, out, in, out—

In.

Priscilla drew a breath, staring at the big asteroid, that was behaving as no asteroid could.

"Priscilla!" Ren Zel said sharply and she put out a hand to touch his sleeve.

"Clutch," she said, projecting calmness into his agitation. "It's only a Clutch ship, friend. Captain yos'Galan's brother is—adopted—of a Turtle."

"Yes," he said, taking a breath. "Of course."

RIGHT RUDDER *and some left aileron. Crab into the wind, but not too much, and down two-thirds flaps to slow it. Keep the nose down and almost level and pop those leading slats right now to cut lift hard. Down flaps the rest of the way, don't bounce. Main wheels down. Crush thrust reverse, slight bounce, nose wheel down and guiding. The wind's up now and we're getting off center, didn't correct the crabbing enough and the rudder's fighting the wind hard and slam the brakes now with that wounded leg—*

The pain shot through her like jellyfish fire. She convulsed where she lay, back arching, and Shan swung over, holding her shoulders flat, reaching with Healer sense and then pulling back because their patterns were united in a beautiful alien arabesque, and Miri opened her eyes as the plane rolled by them, too fast, even if—

"*Val Con!*"

She screamed herself back into the plane, and fell onto the stick, pushing it forward with the last of her strength. The leather tether cut into her and she should be sure, but she knew she couldn't move, no more, never again. . .

"UNCLE," Alys said from the depth of the intercom. "Planetary

Defense Unit says it's taking down the meteor shield, following a successful strike at the enemy's targeting computer."

tel'Vosti stared. Sighed.

"Thank you, niece."

"Yes. It also says that reinforcements have arrived."

LIAD:
Department of Interior
Command Headquarters

❀ ❀

OF THE FOUR ASSIGNED to the detail at Jelaza Kazone, two were undergoing retraining. The report on the Commander's screen indicated that one of those would quite possibly re-attain his pre-catastrophe condition. The other would not, in the informed opinion of the departmental senior overseeing the process, re-achieve his former level of expertise. However, the senior remained sanguine concerning that one's eventual effectiveness as a first-line operative.

Not so, Agent yo'Zeamin, whom the Commander's second had been obliged to dispatch in the antechamber of the Commander's own office, nor Agent pel'Iso, fatally shot by a Solcintra Port security guard during an ill-conceived attempt to steal a Jumpship.

From the two presently undergoing retraining came a tale of horrific—nightmarish—event, alike in nothing save the overmastering sense of personal doom. One reported a disconnection with the physical world coinciding with an overriding need to flee.

The second stated that his head had begun to pain him and he had closed his eyes to ease the strain. When he opened his eyes, he found himself standing on the outside of Jelaza Kazone's perimeter, near the place where he and the others had crossed over the evening before. Disbelieving, he closed his eyes once more. And opened them to discover himself on the ridge that marked the boundary to Korval's Valley, with no memory of having walked there. He continued to function in this on-again, off-again manner until he was apprehended in Solcintra itself by a first-line operative, who took the precaution of locking him into a storeroom before placing the call to her cell-leader.

The most disturbing part of this unlikely occurrence, to the Commander's eye, was that the expert's report indicated the force in operation during the agent's lapses of perceptual sense was the raw will of the subordinated native personality.

It was this Agent whom the expert felt might be adequately retrained to basic operative. The Commander frowned, touched the button to activate the line to his second's desk.

"Commander?"

"Agent ven'Egut."

"Undergoing retraining, Commander."

"Yes. See to his termination. Unacceptable risk."

"Yes, Commander."

He cut the connection and swept the screen clear. Three Agents, lost to Korval. He would meditate upon the best answer to that. In the meanwhile, there was Agent yos'Phelium's pet Terran to consider.

A match program placing the gene-set known as Miri Robertson against the Book of Clans had yielded an—interesting— piece of data.

The genes of Miri Robertson closely matched the genes of Clan Erob, Korval's oldest ally.

This significantly altered the face of event—transforming an apparently chance meeting between yos'Phelium and a "Terran mercenary" into a bit of well-planned and long-standing subterfuge.

It also invested one place in all the wide galaxy with a reason for Val Con yos'Phelium's presence.

Commander of Agents touched the speaker-button once more.

"I will have four full Agents of Change in the mid-level meeting room in twelve hours precisely. Commander's Priority.

"I will also have the history, decision point records, and current clan and strength particulars on the planet Lytaxin. I need full loyalty-compliance reports on any Agent ever on Lytaxin."

"Immediately, Commander," said his second. "Is there more?"

The Commander hesitated, considering three Agents wasted and likely a Korval dramliza responsible. Especial study was required there, with one mistake already laid to his account.

"Yes. I will have an overview of the current strengths of the various dramliz on planet, and a comparison of reputed powers. Also . . ." Here he hesitated. It would not do to disturb the balances quite yet. But, if Anthora yos'Galan were to call due a debt from another dramliza. . .

"Also please refer to me, for tomorrow's morning briefing, our contingency plans for dealing with the guilds and halls.

"That will be all for this moment," he concluded, and closed the line.

LYTAXIN:
Erob's Clan House

THE ORDERS had come from the captain's own lips, and so, on the morning of the sixth day following the battle of the airfield, Nelirikk left the bunker-like infirmary beneath Erob's house and went out into the open air.

He marched with a steady step, eating one of the wonderful pastries the house cooks had brought to the captain's room. He wore a lieutenant's bar and captain's aide insignia, as well as the green scarf at his left shoulder—the troop-sign of The Irregulars—and a Tree-and-Dragon which the captain had very nearly been able to pin on him without assistance.

The orders. Orders. He was so pleased that she was able to give orders that he would have marched to every mountaintop on the planet for her.

"Get outta here," she'd rasped, pale against the pale pillows that supported her. "That's an order. Eat an extra dessert or two. That's an order. If you need something to do, go down the airfield and see what's cookin'. I don't want you back in this room before tomorrow unless you got a real good reason."

Her wounds were like unto a pilot's wounds. During those long hours of grief and waiting, when it was thought both would pass on to duty's reward, the Healer who was a star captain and a soldier had explained to him about wizards and the bond of lifemates. Yet, had not he seen the very real burns from the tie belts, the black eyes and pulled skin of high acceleration . . . Strange indeed were the lives of those who guarded Jela's Tree.

The world was strange now: Troops in good order patrolled, and while some looked on him warily, none barred his way. The air was good, the sun a pleasure, and he had elected to walk, as the captain's purpose had clearly been to insure his value to the troop and to preserve his health while she slowly regained her own.

The way he had chosen brought him to a ridge, and a view reminiscent of his not-so-long-ago vantage in the 14th Conquest Corps command shack when the courageous, silly plane had struck back with honorable intent against the Corps, and the scout's vessel had flung Jela's own challenge at the sky.

The valley was full of planes and ships of various sorts, for the mercenaries were taking no chance that the 15th would come to finish the campaign the 14th had started. There were missile units and fighters, and one odd small ship which he guessed to be the courier or personal vessel of a commander.

The blast crater where the scout's ship had been was already, and wisely, being recycled into a foundation for some new structure.

Was it a trick of his mind or was that not a scout ship dropping quickly into the valley?

His heart nearly crawled into his throat in admiration of those lines. One day, perhaps the captain would permit him inside such a vessel.

He finished the pastry in a gulp, watching as the scout ship set neatly down on the near edge of the field. In a moment he began to run.

THERE WERE THREE OF THEM standing by the ship in casual uniform when he arrived: a woman and two men, all Liaden, all pilots by their stance and alertness, speaking with a soft Erob official.

The official was pointing to a spot of trees and Nelirikk heard, "Fighters . . . only defense left . . ." as he slowly approached the group.

The two men were surely of the elder pilots. One carried a cane, the other grew a mustache on his face, as if he were Terran. Both showed gray in their hair. Both were weeping openly, as the woman stood sober-faced and watchful.

Her eyes widened when she saw him, and she moved a hand, gently and with purpose. The men turned to face him, instantly alert to threat.

Nelirikk saluted.

The Liaden with the mustache—surely the first Nelirikk had seen—stood as if under great strain, face wet with his recent tears. The other man was both more at ease and more dangerous: his eyes quickly touched lieutenant's bar, scarf, Tree-and-Dragon, then lifted to Nelirikk's face.

Momentarily Nelirikk felt as he had when the captain had first walked round him. This one could take his life in a moment if need be. This one, by Jela—

"Nelirikk Explorer, Lieutenant First Lytaxin Irregulars," he stated in the Liaden High Tongue. "May I be of service, scouts?"

The three looked between themselves, and as one, they bowed, equal to equal as he had learned it. The Erob official took this as a good sign and removed herself quickly from the scene.

"Shadia Ne'Zame, Scout Lieutenant, First-In," the woman said, laying her hand over her heart. "Clonak ter'Meulen, Scout Commander," said the man with the most tears. "Forgive my display, Lieutenant. I have heard just now that my daughter died here."

The third looked him over very carefully, and drew from some inner pocket a hand on which gleamed a single, silvery ring. He opened his palm, displaying a pin which was the twin of the Tree-and-Dragon Nelirikk wore.

"I, too, serve Tree-and-Dragon, Nelirikk Explorer, and am at some pains to recall your name among our lists."

Nelirikk stood rooted, as if he faced the very scout, the scout who—

"I am recently recruited, sir. I am personal aide to Captain Miri

Robertson, First Lytaxin Irregulars, who is lifemated to Val Con yos'Phelium, Clan Korval. I serve Line yos'Phelium."

Gently, the scout lieutenant sighed. The man with the mustache shook his head, Terran fashion, and looked piercingly at the man with the dragon in his hand.

"Clans revert to type, my friend. So here we have a true Soldier and if that ship over there isn't a Juntavas courier—a pirate, in plain speaking—I'll eat my coord book."

Ignoring his companion's speech, the nameless scout bowed deeply.

"Sir," he said to Nelirikk, "I must put myself in your hands and beg the grace of an introduction to your captain, she who lifemated Val Con yos'Phelium, for I, too, am pledged to line yos'Phelium. Where may she be found?"

"Sir, she is in the infirmary, recovering from wounds received in the recent glorious battle."

"Is she able to speak with me? Or perhaps her lifemate might speak with me."

"The captain is now allowed visitors. I think it likely that she would speak with scouts, although I cannot guarantee. Her lifemate . . ."

He paused, recalling what had been brought out of the Pilot Elite fighter.

There was sudden bleakness in the air, and the face he looked down upon was very close to one he knew in its bland intensity.

"Her lifemate, sir, is in the sealed autodoc. The medical technicians expect he may be able to speak next week, and perhaps in a month to walk."

The air warmed, the face before him all but smiled.

"Then I am persuaded you should take me to his lady with all speed." And abruptly the shift came, from High Liaden into the tongue of the Troop.

"Soldier, do your duty well, for your charge is a heavy one." He bowed, and the language was again Liaden, in the mode the scout's brother had taught him was called 'Comrade.'

"I am very pleased to see you, Nelirikk Explorer. My name is Daav yos'Phelium."

AUTHORIAL DENIAL

THE BOOK you have just finished reading is not our fault.

We freely admit that *Conflict of Honors*, *Agent of Change*, and *Carpe Diem*—the first stories in the Liaden Universe—were our fault. Yes, we committed those stories—and others. We're not ashamed.

But having committed those stories—and seen them published, back in the late 80's—we were told by our publisher that the numbers weren't there. No one had read our books, that means in Publish-Speak. And, since no one had read the first three, the outlined fourth—and the proposed fifth—would not be needed.

We don't pretend that this news wasn't a blow—even a severe blow. But life goes on. We had moved to Maine just before *Carpe Diem* came out; we busied ourselves exploring our new state, landing—and losing—gainful employment, buying a house, and adding cats to the household as appropriate. Amid it all, we wrote.

Steve wrote computer columns, features, book reviews, brochures, web pages, and advertising. Sharon did some of that, some of the other, some more of something else. That was for other people.

For ourselves, we wrote Liaden stories. Over dinner, during

drives in the country, one or the other of us would break out of conversation, or reverie, with, "Story stuff. What if. . . ?" We fine-tuned the Liaden Code of Proper Conduct, argued esoteric points of melant'i, painted in scenes, and met some wonderful characters.

Let's be clear here. The Liaden Universe is where our hearts are. Home. Yxtrang, DoI, Aunt Kareen, and all.

Sometime during all this life-going-on time, the rights to our novels reverted to us. Sometime a little later, the internet arrived in Maine and we—electronic communications addicts from the old days of neighborhood bulletin boards—drove on up to join the party.

Within days, we were deluged—a phenomenon that continues to this day, though it has slowed to a gentle shower—with e-mail. "*Are you the* Steve Miller? *The* Sharon Lee? When's the next Liaden book? When is *Plan B* coming out?"

One of our early correspondents put together an electronic list for discussion of things Liaden, and so the Friends of Liad were born. From them, we began to understand that people *had* read our books—and wanted more.

Without the encouragement and support of the Friends of Liad, *Plan B* would likely have never been written down.

But the blame for *Plan B* doesn't rest solely on the heads of the Friends of Liad; there's another party equally culpable.

Stephe Pagel.

※　※　※

A BOOK ISN'T DONE until it's published, and Stephe is the man who decides what—or if—Meisha Merlin will publish. He not only decided to make *Plan B* a reality, but he contracted to reissue the first three books as the omnibus *Partners in Necessity*, two prequels in the omnibus *Pilots Choice*, and the single-book *I Dare*. He's also been heard to say that a book about Clutch turtles would be really cool.

Clearly, this man merits watching.

Oh, and one more thing: True enough that a book isn't done until it's published, but a story—a story's not done until it's been read.

That's where you come in.

For reading our book, for completing the arc of wonder—thank you.

Sharon Lee and Steve Miller
October 1998

I DARE

A Liaden Universe® Novel

DAY 276

❧❧❧❧❧❧❧❧❧❧❧❧❧❧❧❧❧❧❧❧❧❧❧❧

Standard Year 1392
Master Jen's Workshop
Neglit

THEY HAD DOUBTED his skill. *Laughed* at him, by Erlady! Took leave to believe him a once-was—a ten-thumbed, aging Terran, half-blind; incapable of bringing the table silver to luster, never mind to copy a ring.

That had been before the Liadens.

They were Liadens, right enough, with the pretty cantra pieces dandled like candies 'tween their slender elvish fingers and sweet words of flattery in their mouths.

Truth owed Erlady, it were the cantra pieces spoke loudest. A man and his grandson, with three cantra pieces to draw against, lived well, for a year or six, here on backworld Neglit.

And they promised him three cantra more, when they came to collect the ring.

The ring. Now, there was a beautiful piece of work. In his young days, he would have snatched the job up for the challenge of it, no thought of payment in his head.

He'd aged out of that nonsense—paid he would be. *Well*-paid.

And still he had the delicate, brutal trial of the work, the result of which, polished and re-polished until the intarsia-work gleamed like water in the beam of his work-light, proved he was yet a master of his craft.

They'd sought *him* out, the canny Liadens. *Him*, Jen of Neglit Center, though they surely had all the fabled master jewelers of Solcintra to choose from. Yet they traveled to an outworld, sought out an old and fading *Terran* master, commissioned him to make—to remake—their ring. And why was that?

The tale they'd spun for Terran wits was simple enough. The original ring, a family heirloom, had gone missing, and must be replaced before certain elders of the house noticed its lack.

Such things happened, drain pipes and gambling games being universally hazardous to jewelry. And mayhap the jewel-masters of Solcintra gossiped 'mong themselves, and a whispered word might waft to the ear of the stern elder, to the dismay of his pretty patrons.

Mayhap.

He was canny enough not to question them too nearly. He had no ambition to risk his six cantra, though he might have balked, if they had wanted paste or light-gold or glass.

But they were keen in their instructions: he was to use only pure-gem, true-gold and emerald. A *replacement*, that's what they insisted on: full duplication of the ring that was lost.

A replacement, exact in every detail, is what he had made for them.

He picked the ring up, turning it this way and that, admiring the simple power of the design. Caught in fluid perfection, a bronze dragon hovered, wide-winged, above a tree in full green leaf. Smiling, he set it against the holopic they had given him of the original.

"I witness ye'd deceive the master who made yon," he told the copy fondly.

"Indeed, it is remarkable work," said a strongly accented voice at his elbow.

The master jeweler started badly and jerked around on his stool, frowning down at the pale-haired Liaden in his costly leather jacket. "Enough to give a body his death, sneak-footing behind one!" He caught himself up, looked from his visitor to the workroom door, with the bell hung above it, that jangled when one of his rare customers came in from the street.

He looked back to the Liaden's smooth, emotionless face. "How came ye?"

The Liaden gestured behind him, to where the inner door stood ajar. "Through the house."

Fear—the tiniest spark of fear—flickered in the master jeweler's heart. The boy was his last treasure. He did not think these were child-thieves, yet—

"I have distressed you," the Liaden said gently. "It was not my intention."

"Well." Mindful of the three cantra yet to come, the master jeweler moved his hand, smoothing the fear out of the air, and spoke moderately. "Understand ye, it's late. The boy needs his rest."

"Of course," said the Liaden and a shadow moved at his shoulder. The master jeweler looked up, meeting the still eyes of the female Liaden.

"The child was asleep," she said in her soft, emotionless voice. "We did not wake him."

He ducked his head, relieved to look away from her eyes. "Thank'ee."

"Surely," she said, then moved forward. Her partner stepped aside, giving her clear view of the worktable. She paused, face as ungiving as ever, studying holo and reality, sitting side by side in the work-light.

"Excellent," she said at last, no faintest lilt of appreciation in her voice. She raised her cold eyes to his face, and went toward the table, her path forcing him to turn somewhat on the stool. The male Liaden had vanished into the shadows of the shop.

"You are indeed a master jeweler," the woman said. She extended a hand and plucked the ring up, turning it under the light, then lowering it to compare against the holopic. Trapped on his stool, the master jeweler watched her, seeing neither pleasure nor relief on her cold, comely face.

"Yes," she said finally, and dropped the ring as if it were a common trinket into the pocket of her jacket. The holopic went to the other pocket, from out of which came three cantra coins, shining across her palm like moons.

"You have earned your fee, Master Jen," she said, extending her hand, the coins glowing, murmuring comfort and ease and schooling for the boy. He leaned forward, felt a sharp pain at the base of his skull.

The Liaden woman stepped back and let the body fall to the floor. Her companion took the polishing rag up from the worktable and used it to clean the gore from the wire-blade before slipping it away into an inner pocket. From another pocket he drew forth a vial, and anointed the corpse with its contents. Then he recapped the container, and wiped it, too, with the polishing rag before returning it to its place.

The woman raised her hand and turned, walking unhurriedly down the dim, cluttered room. He followed her back into the house, past the still figure in the small bed, through the forced door and out into the night.

They were five minutes gone when the first flames licked to life, feeding on the lines of accelerant left to nourish them. Five minutes more found house and workshop both engulfed in fire so fierce the water from the firefighter's cannon sizzled and evaporated before it ever touched flame.

Five hours from the start, the fire was out, having consumed house, shop and contents, leaving not so much as an ash on the scoured stone floor of the basement.

DAY 283

❀ ❀

Standard Year 1392
McGee Spaceport
Fortune's Reward

"HOW MANY TIMES you figure on firing me?"

Pat Rin yos'Phelium sighed. "Refresh my memory, Mr. McFarland. How many times have I succeeded in firing you thus far?"

The big man grinned. "OK, that's fair. But, see, I thought we had an understanding. I ain't only your pilot; I'm your backup. This idea of yours—to cash up and go to ground—not a thing wrong with it. In fact, it's a great idea, even considering how much you bothered to tell me, which I really ain't dumb enough to think is the whole story. Only thing wrong with it is you're planning on going in without backup, and that just ain't bright. How you go to ground— you go easy and smooth, making just as few ripples as you can. But you go with the certain knowledge that no matter how smart you are, or how low you keep your head, something's gonna happen— most likely having to do with blind stupid luck—and you're gonna be needing backup.

"You gotta suppose they're gonna find you, and be ready for it.

341

You go in thinking *anything* different and you might as well take a pistol right now and blow your own brains out. Save everybody some trouble."

Such eloquence. Pat Rin raised an eyebrow. "You intrigue me, Mr. McFarland. I wonder how you became such an expert in *going to ground.*"

"Someday I might tell you," the big man said, shortly.

It occurred to Pat Rin that he had annoyed his pilot quite as much as his pilot had annoyed him. He took a fresh hold on his temper and inclined his head.

"Forgive me, Pilot. I did not intend to cause you pain."

"You didn't," Cheever said, still tending toward short. "Unless you count a headache." He sighed, gustily. "Look, we been through this. Covering you is part of the deal between me and Shan. Do me the favor of believing I *ain't* dumb enough to go back on my word to a Liaden, OK? You got a problem with the arrangements, take it up with him next time you two are in the same room together."

"Ah." Pat Rin considered that. Such solicitude was . . . unusual; his cousins every one being younger than he, and accustomed all their lives to seeing him set his own course. What had persuaded Shan *this time* that Pat Rin might meet with difficulties large enough to warrant a Cheever McFarland? Unless . . .

Shan was a Healer, not a prognosticator. However, Shan's youngest sister, Pat Rin's cousin Anthora, was a dramliza of some note—including among her talents the ability to foretell event. Pat Rin had once witnessed Anthora in the throes of her gift, and did not doubt that the ability was genuine. Perhaps she had foreseen the cold shadow of the clan's danger even as he was preparing to leave planet, and whispered a word in her brother's ear?

And, in the end, what matter? Pilot McFarland was correct. It lay well outside the scope of Pat Rin yos'Phelium's melant'i to disturb an arrangement between Shan and another.

He sighed, and favored the pilot with a straight look.

"I am counted quite a good shot," he said, with what mildness he could muster. "I offer this as a point of information."

"Yessir, I don't doubt it. But you gotta sleep sometime."

And that, thought Pat Rin, *would appear to be that.* He inclined his head, granting the point as much to Shan as to Cheever McFarland.

"Very well," he said. "Since you insist upon remaining in my employ, I will tell you that I require a dawn departure."

The big man favored him with a stare. "You do."

"Yes, I do," Pat Rin said, rather sharply. "Have I made a demand which is impossible for you to meet?"

"No. Would've made things a easier on us both, though, if you'd've thought to call the tower and have us moved to a hotpad."

It was Pat Rin's turn to stare. "In order to accept a hotpad hook-up, I would have had to file my license number with the tower," he said, wondering if the pilot had returned from his leave just a little drunk, after all.

Cheever nodded. "Yeah, but my card's already on-line. You could've filed the request manually, direct into the queue, an' nobody'd known it wasn't me on the board."

"Pilot McFarland—"

"Cause you know the protocol for accepting the hook-up, right? Just like you know the rest of the board? I tell you what, it beats hell outta me why you won't sit second. I don't think I ever seen anybody as hungry for the boards as you are—and I sure could use the help. Backup, get it?"

"Mr. McFarland, I am not a pilot. Placing my hands upon that board—"

"What's the protocol for accepting a hotpad hook-up?" Cheever demanded.

Pat Rin glared, goaded. "The keys to accept the hotpad hook-up are twelve-green-right and the appropriate ship axis is north-south-east-west—that assumes one has a matching power-source, which we do else the power light would indicate blue-blue-red rather than the blue-blue-blue presently showing, and we would be using converters, at a cost of an additional half-cantra the Standard—pro-rated to the Terran minute—for the service." He drew a hard breath, and attempted once more to leash his temper. That a mere hireling should challenge him on so basic a drill! Did he *look* like a fool?

The Terran nodded. "Right. So you coulda done it, though they woulda likely hit you up for a higher charge unless you remembered to tell 'em to orient from ventral instead of dorsal, since this is a pre-1350 ship and they'd've mistook your protocol 'cause the lines look so new." He nodded again, possibly to himself.

"If you got that much, you can move us around when we're locked on to an outside bay in orbit somewhere. I'd right appreciate it if you'll sit second for me, 'case we might need an extra pair of hands or eyes somewhere down the road. *Boss.*"

Pat Rin sighed, chilly in the sudden absence of his anger.

"Mr. McFarland, I am not a pilot, and my hands on the board would be sufficient to frighten any honest ship-handler into an early retirement. Yes, I know the protocols. Nearly all my kin are pilots. I was myself tested for pilot. And I failed. Repeatedly. I am at a loss as to how I might make this circumstance any plainer to you."

"Done just fine," Cheever assured him. "You're wanting me to understand that you know what to do, you just don't do it fast enough. That it?"

"Yes."

"OK. But there's stuff you could be helping me out with—to both our benefits. You know your equations, don't you?"

Gods, but didn't he. When he was a child, he had thought it a game—Uncle Daav, Cousin Er Thom—even Luken!—would throw out a partial piloting sentence and applaud lavishly when he completed it properly. On those occasions when he missed his line—often, at first—they would gently recite the correct response, and applaud again when he told it back without error.

He had done the same with his own child; teaching him the nursery rhymes of pilots . . .

Pat Rin looked up at the bulk of Cheever McFarland. *Master Pilot*, he reminded himself, and sighed. "I know my equations, Mr. McFarland. Yes."

"Good. I can't force you to do it, but I think it'd be best for the ship—my judgment as Master Pilot, while we're being clear on stuff—if you'd sit second for me."

The best interest of the ship must carry all before it. Pilot or no, the care and keeping of ships was bred into his bones. Korval, after all, was ships.

Pat Rin bowed, novice to master.

"Very well, Mr. McFarland, as you feel it is a matter of ship's safety, I will sit in the second seat."

"Great," Cheever said, and stretched, arms over his head, hands brushing the ceiling of the ship. "I'm gonna go get a shower and some caffeine. Meanwhile, you call the tower and get us moved to a hotpad, OK? Don't forget to tell 'em about that orientation to ventral."

So saying he turned and exited the bridge, leaving Pat Rin glaring at nothing.

After a time, he sighed, and moved over to the board to input the request to the tower.

DAY 283

Standard Year 1392
Liad Department of Interior
Command Headquarters

SATISFIED, COMMANDER OF AGENTS closed the field report.

Korval's strengths—that it husbanded—one might say, hoarded—ships; that it valued the skills and reactions of pilots above any other skill a clanmember might possess; that they deliberately bred for pilots, thus propelling themselves to a pinnacle of the type . . .

Those strengths had hidden a notable weakness.

Pat Rin yos'Phelium, heir to Kareen, elder cousin to Val Con, who should by all right of blood and kinship, now stand as Korval Himself—excepting only that he was not a pilot.

Crippled, in Korval's eye, he had been cast aside, dismissed to a wastrel life of spoilt self-indulgence.

The Department of the Interior, however, knew just how to value Pat Rin yos'Phelium, and his place within the Plan.

Commander of Agents smiled slightly and lay his hand on the closed folder.

Despite that the Department found it necessary to its own

success to remove Korval from the board, yet it was true that the world, in some measure, required Korval. Lose a clan which held controlling interest in a triple-dozen industries on-planet, which controlled the pilots guild, funded the Scouts, which owned outright fifteen trading vessels and unnumbered smaller craft, not to speak of the yards which serviced them? The planetary economy trembled at the whisper of such calamity. Why, Korval owned the very dies from which cantra pieces were struck, only leasing them to the Moneyers Guild in twelve-year renewals stretching back to the time of the first Val Con yos'Phelium, Cantra's heir.

In any wise, it was no part of the Department's Plan that Liad should be made bankrupt. It was all to the Department's good that Liaden economy flourish and expand.

Thus, if the economy demanded a Korval, then a Korval there would be.

DAY 284

❀ ❀

Standard Year 1392
Departing McGee

CHEEVER MCFARLAND BULKED large over the controls of *Fortune's Reward*, hands delicate and sure, nearly caressing in their motions. Despite his size he sat comfortably in the pilot's chair, which was locked at the rearmost limits of its track. At this stage in the flight his attention was securely on the board—with its dozen of lights, meters, knobs, and switches—and on the screens ahead.

The pilot's choice of screens for the main board was sparse: centered was local space forward, with radar ranging imposed over the combined straight visual and near infrared view; rear view was a super wide angle in radar encompassing everything not on the front screen at half-size below it. Some few of the screens were surprising— especially the left corner screen, showing a double-deck transcription of the last 144 syllables of Com One's radio communication in Terran—incoming on top, outgoing on the bottom.

The co-pilot's board was live, and Pat Rin yos'Phelium sat, ill-at-ease, in the chair before it. He scrupulously avoided the controls, concentrating instead on the Jump equations he was engaged in framing for the pilot's approval. As if in testimony to the fact that he sat second by the pilot's whim alone, instead of the proper view of space outside the ship, the screen above his board showed a mosaic of thumbnails: every system on the ship represented in an order known only to the pilot.

Pat Rin finished his last calculation and filed it. Leaning back in his chair, as far away from the board as he could reasonably sit, he watched the screens as Cheever McFarland threaded *Fortune's Reward* through the crowded spaceways of near orbit.

From time to time Pat Rin saw a pause, a decision point, pass through the pilot's hands. At the third such he glanced up and saw a new window open on the left.

"I'm watching for long-range interception," the Terran said, calmly matter-of-fact, "cause in here, with all this mess, the normal thing to do is be worried about the next 72 seconds or so, then the next 720 seconds, and not much beyond because so many of the orbits are tight and the maneuvering's hectic. But if someone was looking for us to be Jumping from a particular point, more or less, they'd likely be close to an interception trajectory somewhere down the line, like three hours or so when a ship like ours might normally be expected to Jump."

A lesson in piloting, forsooth. Pat Rin moved a hand in acknowledgment.

"And so right now, there's a ship moving parallel, but that ain't a problem—I doubt anybody'd be trying to chase us with an ore-ship. There's also one summat behind that got underway from the repair docks about the time we hit orbit. Shows up fine on visual but the beacon on it's a bit funny and out of adjustment, I'd say. They been tuning their orbit something fierce, just like a ship right out of dock might."

Pat Rin moved his hand again as Cheever checked in with control once more, confirming by voice his destination and learning that, "due to heavy traffic," the Portmaster requested all ships add another quarter planetary diameter to Jump run-up.

"Damn," Cheever said under his breath and hit the com button.

"Control, can we stay on original schedule? I've got a novice here calculating that Jump for all he's worth and we'll be in your way all day if he's gotta start over!"

The delay might have been due to more than the crawl of light across space; the answer was a half-chuckle. "Oh, aye, that's a stet then, *Fortune's Reward*. And I'm to tell you your novice owes a drink to the submaster next trip through."

"To hear is to obey, Control. *Fortune's Reward* out."

Pat Rin glanced at his pilot quizzically.

"I could have recalculated those equations—the quarter diameter is scarcely a—"

A Terran headshake.

"Sure it ain't. But now we got an excuse when we Jump a bit ahead of time with all the wrong energy levels, just in case we're being snooped."

And so they were prudent, on the off-chance that Korval's enemy had found him. Cheever McFarland was a man who took his own advice, then, and built plans upon worst-case projections.

"Tell you what," the pilot was saying, "once we Jump I'll adjust that side and you can shadow me inbound to Teriste. I'll probably ask questions to see if you're paying attention."

Pat Rin bit back a sharp retort. It was never good luck to argue with an elder willing to teach what was needed—especially with Plan B in effect.

DAY 50

❀ ❀

Standard Year 1393
Lytaxin Erob's Medical Center

THE NAMES OF THEIR KIN had gained them entrance to the house and a rapid and willing guide to the place where their sister lay, recovering from her wounds.

It was well, Edger thought, following Alys Tiazan Clan Erob, Cousin to Miri Robertson Tiazan Lady yos'Phelium, that they had not tarried, but had descended to the planet surface with all haste and come directly to this dwelling-place.

Truth, it had been Sheather's disquiet that had spurred them to seek their kin so speedily. Yet Sheather had studied Miri Robertson to a depth that none other of the Clutch had yet studied an individual of the Clans of Men, and Edger had been willing to heed his brother's impatience.

Nor was this impatience found to be excessive, once the door to Clan Erob's house had been opened to them. The news given by Alys Tiazan was alarming in the extreme and Edger hoped most stringently that they had arrived with speed enough, and skill sufficient for the tasks which bore their names.

Before him, the impossibly frail person Alys Tiazan ran. Her red hair, so like his sister's, was made into double braids that lifted a little in the wind of her own passing. Walls barred her way, then slid silently and swiftly aside, allowing her, and, quickly after her, themselves, into a short, quiet hall, where a single man wearing the clothing and sidearm of a mercenary soldier stood at guard before a door.

He looked up as they bore down upon them, frowned and moved a few steps forward, holding up his many-fingered hand, palm turned to them.

"Hold it," he said to Alys Tiazan. "You ain't taking them in there, are you, kid?"

"Indeed, I am," she returned, somewhat breathlessly. "They have kin-right. My cousin will wish to see them immediately."

He was a well-grown male of the kind which named themselves "Terran," yet he did have to look up quite some distance to survey both Edger and Sheather.

"Kin right?" he repeated, eyes squinted a little.

"The child speaks truly," Edger answered. "Miri Robertson Tiazan, Lady yos'Phelium, Captain Redhead, as she is known here, is sister to myself and this my brother. We are likewise kin to he who is named here Val Con yos'Phelium Scout."

The soldier frowned down at Alys. "Orders was, kin visits only, and as few of them as possible. Cap'n Redhead ain't hardly eight hours outta the 'doc, kid. She gets too tired, the techs'll stick her back in the box, and you can depend on it she won't like that."

"In fact," Sheather spoke up, with a forcefulness much unlike his previous diffidence, "we are here precisely because we have heard alarming reports of our sister's health. It would ease us, could we see her, speak with her, and make our own evaluation of her condition."

"Oh." The soldier chewed his lip, then appeared to take a decision with a sharp nod of his head. "OK, I can see where you'd want to make sure she's on the mend. I can let you in for a quick look, but like I said, there ain't no profit to anybody in getting her tired out to where the techs take an interest. Especially not with her partner in the state he's in."

Edger blinked. "We have heard that our brother's situation is dire."

"Well," the soldier said judiciously, turning to lay his hand on the door-plate, "he ain't as bad as he was six days ago, but I sure wouldn't want to trade places with him." The door slid open and he stepped aside, waving a casual salute.

"There you go. Remember what I told you, now."

"We will remember," Sheather said, and followed his brother into the room where their sister lay, convalescent among the songless.

RED-HAIRED MIRI ROBERTSON, lately captain of the Lytaxin Irregulars, lay against a mountain range of pillows, eyes closed. The room was full of sound—usual sickroom stuff: the bubble and babble of the machinery; the occasional rustle from the med tech there to tend them—and her. Funny, she thought, somewhat muzzily, how sickrooms always sounded just the same, Terran or Liaden, planetside or space based.

Sighing—quietly, otherwise the tech would be after her to take a nap, like she just hadn't spent six Standard Days unconscious in an autodoc—sighing, she marshaled her attention, deliberately blocking out the too-familiar sounds of the sickroom, and focusing on the place inside her head where she'd gotten used to finding the—ah, hell, call it the life force, call it the soul-shadow, or just call it the pattern, of her lifemate.

Previously, this edifice had been scintillant, brilliant with color, cunning in its complexity. A little more recently, she had observed it fading, the clever interlacings unraveling with regal, horrifying precision. Val Con had been dying, then, of various wounds, the most serious being the bullet he'd taken off an Yxtrang Elite Guard while in the process of stealing an atmospheric fighter craft the guard had considered, reasonably enough, belonged to his outfit.

Elite Guards used bullets with a smorgasbord of loads—explosives, hallucinogens, and other not-so-goodies. The bullet that had nicked Val Con had carried nerve poison. He hadn't taken a full hit, which was the good news, a full hit being something that could drop a full-grown Yxtrang soldier, and probably melt your basic "a bit over average height—for a Liaden" on the spot.

So, Val Con hadn't died, though at that his luck was mixed on the day. They'd managed to share his other injuries between them so that she ended up in the 'doc for days, being healed of wounds she'd never taken, and he was still sealed in a crisis unit, not quite out of danger yet. Shan had explained it to her—all right, he'd tried to explain it to her, but she had a feeling she was going to have to get him to go over the tricky bits again, like how exactly she came up with acceleration injuries when her body had been passed out cold on the ground, miles away and below the plane she'd brought in when Val Con—

Never mind, Robertson, she told herself. *There ain't any way to make sense outta it. Just stipulate it happened, OK? No use banging your head against the impossible.*

Banging her head against the impossible was also getting in the way of checking up on Val Con. She ground her teeth together and concentrated, feeling the sweat break out on her face. Chest tight, she craned inward, seeing nothing but gray, nothing but—it hadn't used to be this hard!

Abruptly, she had it—the pattern flared, bright and coherent, burning away the swirling fog.

Miri swallowed.

No doubt that this was Val Con. No doubt that he was alive. But there was—a division—a rift—interlockings sundered, portions isolated from the whole; here and there colors fluttered, pale, while other patches showed nearly translucent.

"Oh, gods," she whispered and bit her lip again. She absolutely did not want the attention of the med tech for the next while. She needed time to study this, to try to figure out just exactly what she was seeing.

And what, if anything, she could do to fix it.

Carefully, she brought her whole attention to one flickering sector, noticing what seemed to be fault lines—

"Cousin Miri!" a young voice shrilled, which would've been enough to get her attention, without the med tech doing her bit for peace and quiet by snapping a High Liaden order to, "Remove yourselves at once!" while a voice big enough to rattle all the aching bones in her convalescing body boomed, "The songs are all of discord, brother!"

Miri opened her eyes, took in nine-almost-ten Standards old Alys Tiazan, hair neatly braided and hands on her barely-existent hips, glaring at the med tech, while two large, shelled people moved with ponderous purpose toward the wall of instruments.

"Remove them immediately," the tech ordered, but Alys was having none of it.

"They are kin and have the right to be here! Yon lady is my cousin by blood-tie and I myself will—"

"PIPE DOWN!" Miri yelled, or tried to yell. The 'pipe' was pretty good, though not up to her best. 'Down' suffered from her voice squeaking out into a cough. Still, she managed to achieve the desired effect: Everybody got real quiet and all faces turned to her. She glared at each in turn, trying to ignore the sweat running down the side of her face, and the way her pulse was pounding way too hard against her eardrums.

"What the hell's the matter with you people?" she snarled, somewhat faintly. "Don't you know there's a sick person in here?"

"Cousin . . ." Alys began.

"I said pipe down," Miri interrupted, then dropped into ragged Low Liaden, in case the kid hadn't caught it. "That means: Be still, child, and don't dispute your elders."

Alys looked stubborn, but managed a creditable bow. "Yes, cousin."

The med tech was sputtering. Miri ignored her for the moment and looked up at the tallest of the two tall non-humans.

Eight foot high and bottle-green, the room's soft light waking gleams of malachite and cobalt among the tiles of his magnificent shell, eyes as big as dinner plates, yellow and slitted, like a cat's; four hundred pounds, if he weighed an ounce—her brother, Twelfth Shell Fifth Hatched Knife Clan of Middle River's Spring Spawn of Farmer Greentrees of the Spearmaker's Den, The Edger. May the gods have mercy on her soul.

"Glad to see you, Edger," she said.

"Sister, the song of my heart achieves fullness in your presence."

Wow. She looked to the second, smaller, and less grandly shelled Turtle. It struck her that he looked worried, though she'd've been hard put to say how she had formed that opinion.

"Sheather. What's bugging you?" She moved a hand against the coverlet. She'd meant to lift it and give him a high sign, but it was too much effort.

"Sister. The songs within this room irritate me. More, they interfere with the progress of your healing. If kin may say so, and with apologies, should I speak too briefly—I fear most strongly for you, wounded as you have been, and surrounded by discord. More, I fear for our brother, the mate of your heart, for it has been told us that his wounds are more serious than your own, leaving him more greatly vulnerable to the ill effects of wrong singing."

She blinked at him, sagging back against her battalion of pillows, the breath burning in her chest like she'd run an obstacle course with a full field pack on her back. She closed her eyes and wearily, warily, looked inside her head, at the broken, flickering pattern that was Val Con. The mate of her heart.

"Lady yos'Phelium," the med tech said, "allow me to call the House to your assistance. These . . . persons . . . tire you dangerously and—"

"One must be the judge of one's own danger," Miri said, more-or-less hitting the High Liaden mode from boss to hired hand. She opened her eyes and looked from Sheather to Edger.

"You're telling me that you got a better way to heal Val Con than the autodocs and the monitors can do?"

"Sister," Edger said solemnly, "we do."

"OK," Miri said, and took a couple minutes to chew on that, not that Edger or Sheather would notice. The Clutch did not lie. Especially, they didn't lie to kin, and they had the same rule as Liadens did about the duty of kin caring for kin. Which didn't mean that they couldn't do as much damage as the next guy in, all from good intentions. She moved her head against the pillows and sighed.

"Can you gimme a demonstration, before we move on to

something life-and-death?" she asked. "Understand, I trust your word, but it seems to me there's room for reasonable doubt and honest error, especially since we're talking across species. Things just might not . . . match up," she finished, somewhat lamely.

"Our sister is prudent," said Sheather, and exchanged a longish, yellow-eyed stare with Edger, who eventually looked back to her and spoke.

"There are those among the clans of men who are more sightful than the common run," he boomed, his big voice shaking the bed she lay in. "These sighted ones may see into the soul of their fellows, touch the strands of their being and, sometimes, cure the ills that afflict the spirit. Should such a one be brought to us, we might show them our intention and our technique."

"That is quite ridiculous," stated the med tech.

"No it ain't," Miri said, way too tired now to deal with the tricksy modes of High Liaden. She managed to get her hand up and pointed at the kid. "Call Shan and get him down here."

Alys frowned while she worked her way through the Terran sentence, then she smiled, walked over to the house phone, and punched the call button.

LYTAXIN:
Erob's Grounds

🟦🟦🟦🟦🟦🟦🟦🟦🟦🟦🟦🟦🟦🟦🟦🟦🟦🟦🟦🟦🟦🟦🟦

THEY HAD PASSED the first sentry and were well on the way to raising the second, moving along the paths and wooded ways like the shades of dead soldiers. Not a leaf rustled, nor stone turned, not a branch broke by reason of their passing.

Nelirikk's heart soared with pride, that he walked at the head of such a group, equal, among peers. Swift and silent, that was how an explorer walked.

It was also, of course, how Liaden scouts walked, which his three companions were. They were an oddly matched trio, more gaggle than Troop, and very easy with banter among themselves—which reminded him forcefully of the manner often kept between the captain and the scout to whom he was sworn.

"How much farther to this house of yours, Explorer Nelirikk?" That was the shorter of the two elder scouts, called Clonak ter'Meulen, who wore a Terran-like mustache beneath his snub nose.

"We must be passed by one more sentry," Nelirikk told him. "Shortly after, the wood will surrender to field. From there, if we continue at the current pace, we will raise Erob's house in approximately twenty-five Standard minutes."

Clonak sighed gustily. "So far? Shadia, my delight, run ahead and beg the house to send a car. I am far too frail for all this traipsing about in gravity."

The youngest scout laughed. "Yes, of course. I can see the wobble in your gait. Poor old Clonak."

"Well, I don't know that I like that theme," the mustached scout commented. "I was thinking more along the lines of 'dear, delicate Clonak,' myself."

"I'm certain you were," Shadia said cordially, deftly ducking beneath a wickedly taloned branch.

"I don't see you running ahead to the house," Clonak pointed out.

"Nor will you," Shadia returned with spirit. "Send a car, indeed! Come, Clonak, it's a lovely day for a stroll. Even with the gravity."

He sighed. "What a desperate failure of discipline we see among the ranks of our juniors, eh, Daav?"

Daav yos'Phelium, he who bore the Tree-and-Dragon device that proved him in service to Clan Korval, raised an eyebrow. "Now, I'm puzzled. It seems to me that Shadia merely displays a—naturally regrettable!—lack of respect for an elder. How do you find a failure of discipline?"

"I outrank her," Clonak began—and between one step and the next fell both silent and still, the others doing the same, until they might have been three leather-clad boulders scattered along the pathway.

Likewise frozen, Nelirikk craned his ears, hearing the small sounds made by the sentry standing his post, just 'round the next bend in the trail. Nelirikk's regard for Clonak increased, even as he relaxed.

"It is well," he said, keeping his voice low. "Only the guard at his—"

"Halt!" the sentry shouted. "Who goes there?"

The brush to Nelirikk's left and slightly in advance of his position erupted into noise, as if some large animal was crashing back and forth, perhaps trying to free itself from one of the plentiful thorny bushes.

"Halt!" the sentry shouted again. "Give me the word or I shoot!"

The brush grew silent, then rustled more courteously, branches shivering as a large figure pushed through to stand in the very center of the path. He was holding a Soldiers General Duty Long-arm in two hands, aimed up into the blameless sky. Slowly, he bent and placed the weapon on the ground. He straightened with even more care, went back two steps, and held his hands, palm out, at belt-level.

"Capan Meery Roberzun," he said, and Nelirikk felt the hairs on the back of his neck lift.

"Captain Miri Robertson," Daav yos'Phelium said in a stage whisper, loud enough to be heard ahead.

"Identify yourselves!" the sentry snapped, wisely remaining at cover. Nelirikk stepped forward, hands visible and very empty, one eye on the Yxtrang soldier who stood, patient and open-handed, in the path.

"Lieutenant Nelirikk Explorer, Lytaxin Irregulars." The soldier in the road did not react to the Terran words, as of course he would not. Troop were not taught Terran. Only squad leaders were given Trade.

"Aide," Nelirikk finished, for the benefit of the hidden sentry, "to Captain Miri Robertson. The word is *sardonyx*. I escort three scouts to my captain."

Out of the edge of his vision, he saw the soldier's lips move, saw his eyes go wide.

"Capan Meery Roberzun!" he repeated, voice too loud with excitement. He pointed at the rifle on the ground, and his next words were in Common Troop. "Sir, we have come to offer the Hero Captain our weapons and our lives." He swallowed as Nelirikk faced him squarely, possibly unnerved by the lack of *vingtai* on a face so plainly of the Troop.

"Have I the—the honor to address the Hero Nelirikk Explorer?" he stammered.

"What's that guy want, Lieutenant?" the sentry asked, but before Nelirikk could reply, Daav yos'Phelium stepped forward, claiming the soldier's attention with a hand-wave.

"We?" he snapped in the tongue of the Troop, his accent only slightly more rancid than Val Con yos'Phelium's. "Produce this *we*! Immediately!"

"Sir!" The soldier's fist hit his shoulder with a will and he spun on his heel to address the bushes, from which there issued no immediate reply.

"Dammit!" the sentry abruptly shouted. "Where did you come from?"

"The airfield, most recently," Clonak ter'Meulen replied in cheery Terran. "Before that—well, you'll appreciate that I can't tell you everything, even though you are carrying some very impressive firepower. I'm one of the scouts being escorted to Captain Robertson by the Lieutenant over yonder."

"He really is," Nelirikk called over his shoulder, anticipating the sentry's next question.

"Yessir. But what is he *doing* here?" wailed the sentry.

Clonak *tsk'ed*. "Why, only making certain you don't decide that it would be best for all to shoot the charming young person asking after Captain Robertson's health. It happens that the scout standing next to dear Lieutenant Nelirikk is kin to Captain Robertson, and very tender of her possessions."

"Possessions!" the sentry sputtered.

On the path, Daav yos'Phelium moved.

"Well?" He snapped at the bushes, crossing his arms over his chest. "Am I blind? Am I a fool?"

The bushes offered up no reply.

The scout snorted.

"Hero Captain Miri Robertson has no use for cowards. Lieutenant?"

Nelirikk came to attention and glared into the soldier's stoic face. "Captain Miri Robertson accepts only the bravest and most skilled into her troop," he snarled, taking up his cue with a will. "This is the captain who attaches a scout to her troop! *This* is the captain who keeps an explorer as her aide! The captain who broke the back of the Fourteenth!"

"Show yourselves," Daav ordered the bushes, and swept

forward in a graceful lunge. He came up holding the long arm at ready. "Or die."

Still the bushes were silent, the branches melting away from the one who came forward, hands out and empty.

"There is one who is wounded," she said and looked over the scout's head to Nelirikk. He read the mark of an explorer on her cheek with a feeling of inevitability. Of course: A mere Rifle infiltrate the first line of guard, intent on giving his battle oath to Captain Miri Robertson? Common Troop did not behave—could not behave—in a manner so contrary to command. An explorer, however, like a scout, was required to think beyond the boundaries of the common. An explorer, like a scout, could easily claim the service of a Rifle, who would no more question her commands than he would the commands of any other officer.

"Hold!" he snapped at Daav, but the scout had already lain the rifle down.

"I do not shoot scouts," he said in calm Liaden. "Unless they give me cause."

The explorer looked down at him. "No cause," she returned, her Liaden halting and modeless. "Wounded, one's senior. Wounded—" She moved her hands in frustration and looked again to Nelirikk. "He is at glory's gate," she finished, in Troop tongue.

"Shadia?" Daav said quietly to the bushes.

"Here, Captain Daav," the youngest scout's voice came from the bushes at the explorer's back, a bit breathless in the Liaden mode called 'Comrade'. "He doesn't look the picture of health, truth told." There was a pause and a low groan. The explorer twitched, and stilled, her eyes down turned.

"Tell the sentry to send for a field 'doc," Shadia said flatly. "This man's dying."

"We need a 'doc, quicktime," Nelirikk heard Clonak tell the sentry. "There's a man down and critical."

"Mister, those're 'trang soldiers and all the 'trang I've seen lately *want* to die," the sentry argued.

"Yet you will observe that these particular Yxtrang soldiers appear to wish to live. They're behaving appropriately, aren't they?

They've put down their guns like good children and they're being very seemly, by my standards, at least," Clonak's voice hardened. "Call for an emergency team. Now. You really don't want the scout over there on the pathway angry with you."

"Embroider my legend, do," Daav called, over the sound of a comm unit being engaged.

Nelirikk watched the explorer, seeing her eyebrows pull tight as she strained to follow the conversation.

"Medical assistance is being called for your senior," he told her in the language of the Troop.

"Yes." She shot him a look of challenge. "You are Nelirikk Explorer, lieutenant in the troop captained by Miri Robertson. Will you take our oaths and receive us into the Troop in the captain's stead?"

Certain as he was that the captain—and most certainly the scout—would welcome explorers into their service, and as well as he understood the dilemma behind the question, it was beyond the scope of his duty to stand as oathtaker in the captain's place.

"I will not," he said, wishing the Common Tongue possessed even so minor a word as "alas".

"What's amiss?" That was Daav yos'Phelium, speaking yet in the mode used between comrades, his bright black eyes darting from the explorer's face to Nelirikk's.

Nelirikk sighed. "She—they—came to give an oath and be . . . welcomed . . . into a troop, with a proper captain, to give their lives form and, and duty. We—the 'doc . . ." He stammered to a halt. Both of Daav's eyebrows were well up, but he waited with explorer-like patience for the matter to be made plain.

"It is cultural," Nelirikk achieved at last. "A matter of— appropriate behavior. They wish to—they must—offer their oath only to the captain or one who stands oathtaker in her stead. I—I cannot take oaths in keeping for the captain. And they cannot accept anything from the enemy."

"Ah." The black eyes gleamed. "And your own oath—to Line yos'Phelium, was it?"

"Yes."

"Yes. I believe we may contrive." He stepped toward the watchful explorer.

"I will have your name," he snapped in his awful Yxtrang.

She lifted her chin, "Hazenthull Explorer."

"So." The language shifted to Trade. "Hazenthull Explorer, I offer you compromise. I am kin to the Hero Captain Robertson—blood ties, eh?"

Her mouth tightened, but she gave a short jerk of the head. "I understand."

"Good. Understand that Captain Robertson's duties are manifold, including a position of command over the kin unit of which I am a genetic member. The name of the kin unit is Line yos'Phelium. Captain Robertson accepted the oath of Nelirikk Explorer in *the name of this kin unit*." He tipped his head. "Do you understand this? I do not wish to trick you."

Once again, she jerked her head. "I understand."

"Excellent. Attend me closely, now: The customs of kin allow me to take from you an interim oath."

Hazenthull frowned. "Inter—a *temporary* oath?"

"Just so. In the service of your senior's life. The 'doc which has been called for is his only immediate chance of survival—Shadia does not use the word 'dying' lightly. I do not willingly watch scouts perish, as I believe I said. I require of you an oath that you and yours will serve Line yos'Phelium, in the person of Daav yos'Phelium—that is myself. In turn, I will give you my oath to bring you to Captain Robertson herself, so that she may make what judgment that a captain must, for the good of her troop." He paused, perhaps awaiting a question. Hazenthull remained silent.

"The term of our oaths," Daav continued, "shall be concluded when the captain has given her judgment. Can you agree to this?"

There was a long silence. Nelirikk saw the explorer's eyes narrow, as if she were turning the proposed oaths round in her mind, seeking the trap that she knew must be there.

Nelirikk could have pointed out the ambiguity attending the precise expiration of term, but it was to the Troop's benefit to acquire the services of other explorers, if it could be managed, and so he held his tongue.

Finally, Hazenthull Explorer gave another of her terse nods. "We are free to offer and to honor these oaths."

"Splendid." Daav waved at the patient soldier. "Explain the matter to him." He flicked a look to Nelirikk. "Assist her, please, Lieutenant."

"Scout." Nelirikk bowed slightly and stepped to Hazenthull Explorer's side.

Some distance up-trail, he heard the sound of a jitney engine, growing rapidly louder.

LYTAXIN:
Erob's House

❁ ❁

" . . . **GRACE OF THE MOTHER** we came through well and whole," Priscilla was saying.

The transmission was remarkably clear, considering that it was a jerry-rig replacement for the planetary communication net the Yxtrang had shredded. And it was beyond joy to be able to hear his lifemate's voice, after these long, eventful days of separation. Still, Shan thought, wistfully, it would have been ecstasy, to behold her face, to run his fingers into her curly black hair, to stroke her creamy cheek, to put his lips—

"Shan?"

He shook himself. *Do strive for some breeding, Shan*, he told himself, *will you scorn her voice because you may not have the rest?*

"Forgive me, Priscilla, I was entranced by the mental image of you doughty warriors, knives caught between your teeth—"

"Shan . . ."

"Priscilla, you really must spend less time with my sister," he told her earnestly. "You have her inflection exactly, there."

From their ship, high in Lytaxin orbit, she laughed. Shan,

seated at the desk in the guesting room Erob had ceded him, smiled wryly and stroked the comm's plastic face.

"Let us make plans for your stay on planet," he said. "Leave now and I'll be at the spaceport to greet you."

The beam hummed empty for a moment, then gave him Priscilla's sigh.

"Love, you know I need to be with the ship. Ren Zel is able, but—"

"But Ren Zel is not of Clan Korval," he finished, knowing the necessities as well as she. "Gordy of course is of Korval, and also possesses all of nineteen Standard years. Too young by a year or so to stand command of a starship orbiting a world enduring post-war conditions."

"True," she said, her voice soft across the distance that separated them. "And you cannot leave Miri and Val Con while they are so ill."

"Miri is out of the 'doc," he said, suddenly recalling that he had not told her that. "Weak as a kitten, of course. Val Con . . ." His throat closed and he shook his head, as if she could see him.

"The techs still believe he'll be . . . impaired?"

"Impaired." He grinned without humor. "Yes, they do believe that, and quite ill-natured I find them for it, if you will have the truth."

"I'm sure you do," she said gently. "I—when he is out of the 'doc and an evaluation is made, perhaps—"

Shockingly, the portacomm on his belt buzzed. Shan jumped, swore, and thumbed the receive.

"One moment, Priscilla—yos'Galan," he snapped into the portable.

"Shan—Lord yos'Galan—it is Alys Tiazan. I am in the recovery room with Miri my cousin and two of the Clutch who are her brothers."

Yes, of course, Shan thought. *The situation had only lacked eight foot turtles.*

"How delightful for us, to be sure. I shall be down directly to make—"

"Their Wisdoms," Alys interrupted, with a refreshing lack of deference for his station; "Their Wisdoms say that the songs of the machines are harming my cousin, your sister. They say that the autodoc may be preventing Val—preventing Lord yos'Phelium—from healing completely. The med tech is—" she paused, apparently decided that he could judge the med tech's state of mind for himself, and finished in a rush. "Cousin Miri says to *get you down here*." The last four words were in Terran, pronounced in tones so authentically Miri-like that Shan grinned, even as his heart trembled.

"One moment," he said to Alys, flicking the 'mute' toggle. He glanced at the desk unit. "Priscilla?"

Her answer came slowly. "It is possible," she said, "that the rhythm of the machinery is interfering with total healing. It has been known to happen. Rarely." She was silent, then burst out. "Who knows what may harm them? They are linked, heart and mind, by that—edifice!—no more simple humans than—than the Clutch are. No," she corrected herself, more calmly. "More human than the Clutch are. And the Clutch may see truly—for their own kind."

"Then it appears my task has been laid out for me," Shan said and flicked the portable on.

"Please allow my sister to know that I am on my way to her side," he told Alys Tiazan. "Ask her, as she loves me, to stay her hand from the med tech until I arrive."

There was a small snort, as if Alys had half-strangled a laugh, then a demure, "I will so inform my cousin, sir." The line cleared.

"Priscilla, my love . . ."

"Until soon, Shan."

"Until soon. May your Goddess send it *very* soon."

He thought he heard a soft sigh before the connection light went out. Sighing himself, he stood, and left the room at brisk walk.

A short time later, he turned smartly into the hallway containing Miri's room, and nodded to the guard on duty.

"I am summoned."

The merc shook his head as he turned to put his hand against the plate. "They call this rest? She might as well hire a band and call it a party."

The door slid open and the guard waved an impatient hand. Shan strolled across the threshold and—paused.

Immediately before him, two very tall, green persons wearing a truly impressive quantity of tilework across their shoulders and down their backs, confronted an average-sized Liaden woman—which is to say, her nose was not quite level with the equator of the shorter tile-bearing person. That the woman was in high temper was obvious even without the abrasion of her passion against his Healer sense. The Turtles—were invisible to his Healer sight, in contrast to the rather irrefutable physical evidence. Shan glanced aside, locating Alys Tiazan, strategically placed between the med tech and the bed in which Miri wilted against an oppression of pillows, long red hair snarled across one shoulder, eyes closed in a face as white as salt.

Ignoring the med tech's anger, Shan focused on Miri, catching the shine of mayhem along her pattern, and a fear bordering on terror.

"Cousin Miri," Alys said. "Lord yos'Galan is here."

The woman in the bed opened fierce gray eyes and gave him a ragged grin.

"What took you so long?"

"I had to shave."

The grin widened, briefly, then one hand wavered more or less horizontal, index finger almost pointing at the taller of the two green persons.

"Edger," she said, hoarsely. The finger moved perhaps the width of a thought. "Sheather." Her hand fell back to the coverlet. "This is Val Con's brother, Shan yos'Galan. He's a Healer. Tell him what you told me."

"What they told you," the med tech snapped in a mode perilously close to superior to inferior, "is arrant nonsense! The machines are needful! Your heartbeat must be monitored! Your air must be filtered! Your blood pressure and body temperature must be monitored! Shut down the machines and risk doing yourself needless, preventable harm, Lady. To even think of removing your lifemate, damaged as he is, from the catastrophe unit . . ."

"Quiet."

One word, quavering on the broken edge of a whisper—terrifying from a woman who could make herself heard amidst the pandemonium of a battlefield.

" . . . is to kill him outright!" the med tech continued unabated. "These—persons!—are not of Erob's house medical staff! They—"

"Silence!" Shan snarled, in all the force of Command. The tech's anger flared and he countered it, barely heeding what he did; merely casting out a glamour of cooling, like a handful of snowflakes. The med tech fell silent, passion melting, bowed and went over to sit in a chair.

"Very good." He transferred his attention to the turtles, who were yet standing patiently, watching him out of yellow cat eyes.

"Shan yos'Galan," the turtle on the right—Edger, Shan remembered—boomed in what was recognizably the Liaden High Tongue, though exactly which mode was a bit difficult to determine at this volume. "It is a joy to speak with the brother of my brother."

"It is an honor to meet one of whom one's kin has spoken, often and with affection," he responded in the ritual stiffness of the High Tongue, in the mode of meeting the kin of kin.

"Allow me, also," said the turtle named Sheather, in Terran, "to express my joy at making your acquaintance, Shan yos'Galan."

"I'm delighted to meet you, as well," Shan replied in the same tongue. He glanced over to the bed, saw Miri rigid against her pillows; once again caught the edge of her fear against his Healer sense.

"Please forgive me if I force the topic too quickly," he said to the turtles, in blessedly quick, modeless Terran, "but I cannot help but see my sister's distress. The med tech seems to believe that you would have her—and my brother as well—separated from the healing units."

"These devices are all in discord!" cried the turtle named Sheather. "They interfere with the truesong of my sister's self. We hear that our brother is more grievously damaged still. I fear—in my heart, I fear—that the machine which imprisons him, helpless and unable to communicate his own needs, may also slay him."

Shan frowned. "And yet our sister has come successfully out of a similar machine, healed of her injuries and only needing to regain her strength. Many—" What had Val Con said the Clutch called the family of humankind—aha! "Many of the Clans of Men do exactly that, every Standard Year. It is how we heal ourselves of physical wounds."

"Yet, as my younger brother will have it, we hear discord emanate from yon devices and know too well the damage that may be done. Our sister is surrounded by those things which leach her strength, and make her path to full vibrancy into a perilous journey, uncertain of a happy outcome." Edger blinked his eyes solemnly. "Our sister tells us that you are one who may see into the fabric of others, and who may reweave somewhat that which has become unwoven."

"I am a Healer," Shan said slowly. "But I have no skill in mending physical hurts—only common first aid, which this med tech will trump, without a single machine to aid her."

"It is your skill in seeing that we would harness, for the lives of our sister and our brother," said Sheather. "We have already observed the skill with which you silenced the medical technician and soothed her anger before she became a danger to herself."

He had *what*? Shan looked over to the med tech, sitting peacefully in her chair. Carefully, he extended his regard and brushed her pattern, encountering an overlay of cool patience, beneath which the rest of the woman's . . . essence . . . appeared to slumber.

Oh, gods, he thought in consternation. *Shan, you idiot, what have you done?*

"I will have to confess," he said, looking up into Sheather's enormous eyes, "that I am not entirely certain that . . . whatever . . . I've done to this person has been in her . . . best care."

Edger turned his massive head and—sang, one high, whispery note that was gone before Shan could quite—

"She takes no harm. She reposes in calmness and heals herself of her distress. It is well done," Edger stated.

"They said," Miri rasped from the bed, "that they could do a demo, like, and let you decide if what they thought was best would kill us or not."

He looked at her. "*I'm* to decide? How delightful for me! Val Con did mention to you that I'm his heir, didn't he? This is the perfect opportunity for me to murder you both and grasp Korval for myself."

"Sure it is," Miri said, agreeably. "Look, whyn't you turn off the monitors for a couple minutes while the tech's having her nap, and let Edger sing you a couple bars, OK?"

"My sister's plan has merit," Sheather said.

Miri turned her head on the pillow and addressed Alys, her voice almost steady in the mode between kin. "Cousin, you are wanted elsewhere. What we undertake now is Korval's affair, and nothing that should trouble the sleep of one who belongs to Erob."

For a moment it seemed that Alys would protest, then she bowed, as kin, to the woman in the bed—"Cousin Miri"—and as housechild to the turtles and Shan alike—"Wisdoms. Lord yos'Galan."—before walking away, with chilly dignity, and letting herself out into the hall.

Shan met Miri's eyes down the room. "You're certain you want to try this?"

She gave him a lopsided grin. "Hate to break it to you, but I've breathed unfiltered air before and didn't take no lasting harm."

He sighed. "I'll take that as a 'yes'." He moved over to the wall and threw the first switch, then the other five in quick succession. Across the room, the med tech sat, dream-eyed, in her chair.

The last unnatural hum faded from the air and the room filled up with quiet. Sheather filled his lungs, tasting the various scents on the confined air, soothed by the absence of discord. His work at the wall of instruments completed, Shan yos'Galan returned to them, his hair pale as the light of the homeworld's lesser moon; his eyes the color of the substance Men named silver.

"Very well," he said, his voice pleasing in its conservation of power. "I have a subject for a test, if you are willing, sirs."

One's brother blinked down at the man, tasting, Sheather was certain, of his power and his courage. "Say on, Shan yos'Galan."

The white-haired man bent and touched his right knee lightly. "I very foolishly wrenched my knee—it's too trivial a thing for the 'doc, but I will confess that it does irritate one." He straightened and looked from one to the other of them with his sightful silver eyes. "Is this the sort of thing one of you might put right, while I watch?"

One's elder brother signed that he would undertake this minor bit of healing. Thus released, Sheather moved away down the room, to stand by the bedside of his sister, Miri Robertson.

"Understand, this will be a very small thing, in comparison to what we propose on behalf of our brother and sister," Edger said.

"I understand perfectly, sir. What we wish to prove here is the concept. If my leg shatters under your care, it is an inconvenience, quickly put right by some time in the 'doc, and we have our answer without risk to either our brother or our sister, both of whom are as precious to me as I know they are to you." He paused and tipped his head. "I hope you won't be offended by my screams, if it should happen to occur that my leg does shatter."

"I believe you will not find it necessary to scream, Shan yos'Galan," Edger said solemnly. "I ask you now to open your eyes and hold yourself to silence."

Shan yos'Galan straightened and closed his outer eyes. Sheather heard the song of his power intensify even as Edger opened his mouth and sang the two notes required.

SHAN COMPOSED HIMSELF and dropped his inner shields, watching with Healer's eyes.

At this exposure, the turtles stood revealed as systems of all but intolerable complexity, informed by a method entirely outside of his understanding, stretching far beyond his ability to read, yet tantalizingly familiar, as if . . .

All at once he had it: Himself, just home from Healer Hall and quite vain of his new-trained powers, striding up to Korval's Tree, the redoubtable Jelaza Kazone, and flinging his shields down like a dare.

Immediately, he had been swept into a long, slow, greenness that spiraled on—forever, or so it seemed to his shortsighted eyes. Every turn of the spiral was unique, rich with nuance and surprise. Ensorcelled, Shan hung, and watched, and was delighted—until Val

Con knocked him into the sodden grass, and lay across his chest, shouting in his ear that it was " . . . *raining*, and our mother has been looking for you *every*where!"

Val Con.

Shan took another breath, deliberately imposing calm, sternly refusing the impulse to enclose himself in puny protections. This was for Val Con's life; he dared not make an error—of any kind. His knee ached, a little; Healer eyes saw the irritation as an angry red glow. He allowed the minor pain to remain within his consciousness.

Faintly, a note sounded. He heard it as the warm wash of rain against his naked skin; saw it as a bell tone, attenuating . . . The first note was joined, complimented, enlarged, by a second, inspiring the gentle shower to rain in earnest as the tone coalesced into a ball that grew dense, denser, dense to the point of implosion . . .

The music was ended. His knee was pain-free. A quick scan showed an entire absence of the angry glow of injury that had surrounded it.

Shan opened his eyes.

"Well?" Miri rasped.

He turned to look at her.

"Perfectly well," he said, and took a harder breath, deliberately strengthening his hold on the physical world. Slowly, he brought his protections up; and found himself saddened to lose sight of the turtles' vast incomprehensiveness.

If they can heal Val Con of the effects of the poison. If he can walk. If he can fly . . . he thought exuberantly; and then, more soberly. *If it fails, we may lose both.*

He stepped to the bed and bent down to take Miri's thin, cold hand between two of his.

"I give you the judgment of your thodelm, Korval," he said, in the mode used when addressing one's delm.

She blinked. "I ain't Korval."

"The Code teaches us that lifemates are one melant'i in two bodies. Val Con is nadelm—Korval-in-future. You are true lifemates, bound by the soul. My own father died of his lifemate's death-wound. You speak for both of your lives in this—and for Korval entire."

She paused, her eyes losing a little focus, as if she consulted her memory of the Code, which was ridicul—

Her gaze sharpened. "It is," she said, her voice pure and firm in the High Tongue, "as you have said. I decide as Korval in this, for the good of Korval. Let Thodelm yos'Galan render his judgment."

"I believe it to be—the best gamble for the clan, to allow these your brothers to attempt their peculiar form of healing. I say *gamble.* I have heard the judgment of the medical technicians; in best case, my brother will emerge from the 'doc able to care for himself, to speak, to reason, and to walk, for some limited distances. Your brothers offer a potential for a greater win—and a greater loss.

"I may not convey what I have seen, just now. However, as a Healer, I approve both the method and the results." He paused, then added in Terran.

"It could work."

She was utterly still for a moment, limp and white-faced against the pillows, then nodded.

"That's a go, then," she said in Terran.

Shan released her hand and straightened. "As Korval wishes."

"It is therefore decided," Edger proclaimed, and fixed Sheather in his eye. "This my brother will remain and sing our sister into harmony. Shan yos'Galan and I will make haste to the side of our brother and discover us the song we must craft for his whole good health."

"Sounds like a plan," Miri said, and gave Shan another of her ragged, heart-stopping grins. "Take the med tech with you, and drop her someplace to sleep it off, OK? I don't want her waking up halfway through the proceedings and getting her nose outta joint all over again."

DAY 50

⊛ ⊛

Standard Year 1393
Liad Department of Interior
Command Headquarters

COMMANDER OF AGENTS closed the file and leaned back in his chair.

He was not one to indulge optimism out of season; however, he allowed the plans lain for Clan Korval's confoundment to be . . . adequate.

Of necessity, the plans of action were several, for Korval presented several fronts to the offense.

There was, first, the on-going effort to recover Val Con yos'Phelium, rogue agent and Korval's delm-to-be. A breakthrough had been made on this front, in the form of a gene-match program run against the supposed "Terran mercenary," Miri Robertson. The odds that yos'Phelium was on Lytaxin, sheltering with Korval's oldest ally, Clan Erob, now approached certainty. Recent reports of Yxtrang activity near or on the planet, followed by a rumor of hurried retreat, and other rumors of a strangely behaving vessel seemingly carved from rock—these reports only added weight to the prediction of the odds.

So, a team of four full Agents of Change had been dispatched to Lytaxin, to recover Val Con yos'Phelium—alive. Alive, he yet had value to the Department he had betrayed. Alive, he would serve as both bait and bridle to the remainder of Korval, for surely his kin would do nothing to endanger the life of the one who would be delm? Surely, they would do all they were bidden, in trade for a guarantee of his safe return?

Commander of Agents was prepared to guarantee Val Con yos'Phelium's safe delivery back into the midst of his kin. Val Con yos'Phelium, after all, had been an Agent of Change, fully trained by the Department. And those who had once been trained could be retrained.

The second object of the Department's attention was Anthora yos'Galan, the sole member of Clan Korval remaining upon Liad. She had prudently withdrawn from yos'Galan's Line House, Trealla Fantrol, and established herself at Jelaza Kazone, Korval's ancient stronghold.

It was . . . daunting . . . that the masters of the dramliz, despite repeated testings, had failed to measure the limits of Anthora yos'Galan's abilities. According to one confidential guild report, she was not merely the best of the current depleted population of wizards, but the most puissant dramliza to manifest since Rool Tiazan's death, forty years after Cantra yos'Phelium brought her passengers safe to the planet they would name Liad.

Wizardly power, however, is but a matter of degree. The results of research done some years earlier and set aside for lack of relevance suddenly proved illuminating. It had been found then that certain modifications to a standard stasis box produced interesting reactions in a dramliza confined therein, not the least of which was an effective neutralization of wizardly abilities. Commander of Agents had ordered such a box constructed, and rendered mobile. It was even now in the final stages of testing. When it was completed, Anthora yos'Galan would give up her residence at Jelaza Kazone, from which base she might provide unknown, and potentially disastrous, assistance to her scattered kin, and live at the pleasure of the Department.

It was possible that Korval's wizard had value to the clan, though the clan left her alone and unguarded upon Liad while the rest fled to safety—somewhere. The Commander accepted that Anthora, too, might hold value as a hostage. It might be—should Val Con yos'Phelium not survive his recapture—that his half-Terran foster-sister would fulfill the roles intended for him, even to the ultimate destruction of the clan. Commander of Agents allowed himself some flexibility on this point of planning, pending clarity from the team sent to recover yos'Phelium.

Commander of Agents allowed himself a small smile before he pushed back from the desk and rose. Strike at the heart—once, twice, thrice—and Korval *would* fall.

It was well.

LYTAXIN:
Erob's Medical Center Catastrophe Unit

❀ ❀

MED TECH PER VEL sig'Zerba jumped to his feet as the door to the catastrophe unit slid open.

"Sir, I regret," he said to the white haired man who entered. "This area is forbidden to—" He stopped, staring quite open-mouthed at the second . . . person . . . to violate the area—all two-and-a-half meters of . . . it—magnificently shelled and bottle green, luminous eyes as round and as yellow as moons.

The door slid closed. The med tech, with difficulty, returned his attention to the white-haired man.

"Sir—Lord yos'Galan. We had discussed this matter, sir. The catastrophe room is forbidden to all but medical technicians. The instruments are very delicate and the life of your kinsman depends upon their unimpaired function. It is natural to wish to stand close to kin who are in such desperate case, but, truly, sir, he cannot know whether you are here or elsewhere. You best serve him now by recruiting your strength and preparing yourself to show him a calm face when he emerges from the unit."

"These machines, also, sing of discord," the large green person rumbled. "Where is the device which imprisons our brother?"

Med Tech sig'Zerba blinked. "The catastrophe unit is there." He moved a hand toward the black rectangle, its domed lid bristling with readouts, monitors, alarms, and regulators. He looked again to Shan yos'Galan and bowed slightly. "Since you are here, I will tell you that the latest data has been analyzed. Repair has been successful on many fronts. Cerebral function has been stabilized, so we may put the fear of seizures and random states of alt behind us. Blood systems and the functions of the organs are as they should be." He hesitated.

"And the damage to the nervous system?" Shan asked quietly, tasting the man's reluctance almost as his own. "How goes the repair there?"

The tech sighed. "Not well, alas. Repair may only occur where some system remains. Regeneration . . . has met with variable success. The latest analysis yields an estimate of forty-five percent function." He inclined his head.

"This means that your kinsman will not be able to pilot a spaceship, an airship, or a landcar. With practice, he will very likely regain his ability to walk, to grasp objects, and to throw them." He took a breath and met the white-haired man's intense silver gaze. "This is not so bad, if your Lordship will but recall the state in which his kinsman entered the unit. We had all despaired of his life, then. That he has regained so much is . . . cause for joy. That he has lost some things which he will never regain—that is . . ."

"Not to be tolerated," the large green person said, in a voice that made every dial in the room jiggle and jump.

Med Tech sig'Zerba jumped, too, and stared up into the huge, luminous eyes. "I . . . I beg your pardon, ah . . . ?"

"This is Twelfth Shell Fifth Hatched Knife Clan of Middle River's Spring Spawn of Farmer Greentrees of the Spearmaker's Den: The Edger," said Lord yos'Galan. "He also claims kin-right to your patient. He has heard distressing reports regarding our kinsman's course of treatment, which your latest analysis supports. We had come here because of those reports. There is a . . . Clutch healing . . . that we propose to try."

"Propose—" Per Vel sig'Zerba took a hard breath, and retained his hold on calmness. "Lord—Sirs. The condition of your kinsman is precarious. This is not the time to 'try' alternate healings, but to allow the known method to stay its course. The time for alternative healings is when we have brought the patient safely out of his crisis and back into daily life. Then, after study and analysis, a regimen of rehabilitation and additional measures will no doubt be prescribed. Now, however, we must bow to proven methods, for the best eventual health of your kin."

"With all respect to yourself and your craft," Edger said, while the instruments jittered in their places, "the method now employed dangerously leaches my brother's strength." The big head turned. "Open your eyes, Shan yos'Galan, and look at our brother. Does he seem to you to be mending as he should?"

Shan frowned and widened his perceptions, ignoring the orange and yellow flutterings of alarm that were beginning to infuse the med tech's pattern, and waited for the familiar and well-loved pattern of his brother to appear.

Moments passed. The med tech's alarm showed more orange, less yellow, and a spike or two of red.

Shan opened his shields wider still, caught a glimmer of Edger's seductive intricacy, but yet nothing remotely resembling Val Con's precise complexity or—

"Sir—" Med Tech sig'Zerba began and Shan held up a hand, hurling aside his shields entirely, desperate now to find his brother, his outer eyes on the readouts fixed into the roof of the sarcophagus, which told of him being alive . . .

Suddenly, he had it—a hint; nothing more than a faint touch of acerbic sweetness, as familiar to him as his brother's face. Sternly keeping himself to a Healer's discipline, he followed the hint, slowly, and with an eye to peril.

And found Val Con at last: diminished, lackluster and fragmented, surrounded by a sticky gray quag. Distantly, and engrayed, like a dirty rainbow, he could see the bridge that linked Val Con's soul to Miri's.

"No!"

"Sir! I really must insist that you both leave. Now. You are doing your kinsman no service by becoming overwrought on—"

"Stop." Shan opened his outer eyes and fixed them, with difficulty, on the med tech's face.

"What have you done to my brother—cerebral function has stabilized, you said. How was it found to be unstable?"

The tech blinked. "Why, there were—surges. One might almost say power surges. Also overactivity; extreme excitability, in what should have been an at-rest state. These anomalies led the seniors to suspect damage—not unexpectable, in light of other traumas. Steps were taken to normalize brain activity, and those efforts have been successful. We need no longer fear debilitating seizures or fatal lapses of attention."

"You . . ." Shan took a breath, for once at a loss for words.

"What distresses you, Shan yos'Galan? Does our brother not thrive beneath the known method of healing?"

"They have—In their care to normalize they have weakened the link between our brother and his lifemate—the same link which allowed him to survive his injuries until the field 'doc received him. They have—he is fragmented, without form . . ." He looked at the tech.

"I myself told the seniors that this man is lifemated," he said, his voice sounding thin in his own ears.

The tech inclined his head, nervously. "Indeed. It is so noted in the file. However, normal cerebration is not—"

"Out," said Shan.

The tech blinked. "Sir?"

"You will leave," Shan repeated and heard the power echoing within each word. "You will not return here until Val Con yos'Phelium has departed the area. You will not report this to your superiors. Go!"

The tech's face wavered, eyes going cloudy. He bowed, precisely, and walked briskly down the room and out the door.

Shan slapped the lock up as the door closed and strode back to the brooding black unit and the enormous, patient turtle.

"I am able to end the healing cycle," he told Edger. "Some time will elapse before our brother may be removed from the unit, for systems need to cycle down in an orderly manner."

"I understand you," Edger rumbled and looked about him. He raised one three-fingered hand and swept it toward the wall with its profusions of equipment. "And are you able to silence those, as well?"

"Yes." Shan was already at the unit's control panel, flicking switches, turning knobs; withdrawing sensors, shutting down the flows of drugs and nutrients, canceling the muscle toners. When every light on the panel was dark, saving the master, he went over the wall of instruments.

Gods, gods—normalizing cerebral function? Fools! And if Val Con were crippled because they had denied him his lifemate . . . Shan took a breath, deliberately leashing his anger, and threw the last switch, then cast about him for—there.

He rolled the cot over to the healing unit, shook out the blanket, and took a moment to master an urge to pick up the nearest heavy object and have at the delicate instruments lining the walls.

"While we await our brother's release," the Edger's voice rumbled him out of his thoughts of mayhem and despair, "there is a matter we must undertake."

Shan looked up at him. "Yes? And this matter is?"

"A thing—you might perhaps call it 'fine tuning'," Edger said. "Your sight, your love and your understanding will aid me in what work I undertake, for the best health of our brother. You will guide the song—and deny it, should it wander from its purpose or reach beyond its bounds. Before we meet together in the field of mutual labor, it is prudent to test our partnership and strengthen that which may not be as strong as will be required."

"A dry run," Shan said, and nodded. "I understand the concept. What would you have me do?"

"Only listen, while I sing, with the scales behind which you shield your seeing eyes put aside."

Yes, of course. Shan took a deep breath in preparation, focused and brought down his shields, completely, as Priscilla had warned him not to do, his inner self exposed entirely, so that any with eyes—or other senses—to see might find him revealed in all his faults.

"Ah." A sound like the purr of an impossibly large cat. "You are a blade to behold, Shan yos'Galan. Who crafted you may be justly proud of his work. Hear me now."

The first note was an iron-tipped bolt through the living core of his heart.

The second note was a dash of acid across his eyes.

The third note flung his essence out into the snarling winds of Fortune and Mischance. Harried by their teeth of ice and iron, he struck back, willed *walls* and walls there were—stone walls and a stone floor on which he knelt, doubled over and sobbing, making no sense of the hand held down to him, until a stern female voice scolded him.

"This is no safe haven—and well you know it! Rise now and return. Quickly!"

Long strong fingers closed around his wrist. He rose, whether by her will or his he could not have said, and stood looking into the chill blue eyes of a raw-cheeked blonde woman no longer in her youth.

"Priscilla." How he was certain that this woman was she—but certain he was. "Priscilla, the song is changing me."

Her face softened. She let go his wrist and cupped his face in her two hands.

"The song changes us all," she said softly. "Do not fear it. Now go." She kissed him, the stone walls faded, and he straightened, his face wet with tears and his mouth warm from her lips, to face Edger the Clutch turtle in the room of catastrophes.

The turtle blinked his enormous eyes, once, and inclined his body as far as the shell would allow.

"All honor to you, Shan yos'Galan."

Stiffly, Shan returned the bow, equal to equal. "May our work together return perfect health to our brother," he said, his voice chill in the High Tongue, and turned to open the lid of the sarcophagus.

The interior lit itself, dimly, casting cool blue shadows across the slender, naked body of a man. Shan unsnapped the locks and lowered the front wall of the box. The pallet slid out of twilight and into brightness; the man was revealed as gold-skinned and unscarred; lean muscled, and somewhat longer in the leg than the average run of Liadens. His chest rose and fell with the blessed, unhurried regularity of deep sleep. His face was smooth—achingly innocent, in repose—the well-marked brows at rest, firm mouth tightly closed, long dark lashes smudging golden cheeks. And Shan saw with an absurd feeling of relief that the gash which had disfigured his brother's face had been erased by the 'doc's scar-cancelling program.

"Time passes, Shan yos'Galan," a big voice rumbled behind him. "And I fear that haste must be made."

"Yes, of course." Blinking away tears, he slid his arms gently beneath his brother's shoulders and knees and lifted him from the pallet to the cot. Val Con sighed and nestled his cheek into the pillow, his lips relaxing into what Shan dared to call a smile, but did not approach true wakefulness. Shan spread the blanket tenderly over the slim body and looked up into Edger's eyes.

"Now what?"

"An excellent question," the turtle said. "Let us ascertain. Your whole attention is required in this time and place, Shan yos'Galan. Do you place your regard upon this our brother and guide me in my exploration."

"Guide?" Shan stared at him. "How am I going to guide you?"

"I subvert my will to yours: Should the song go beyond its bounds, only will me nay and I will contain it. Should it quicken that which is best left sleeping, your touch will give it back to hibernation. It must be so, for the best health of our brother."

Shan inclined his head, glanced down at Val Con's sleeping face and, for the third time in a single day dropped his shields completely, focusing his entire attention on the murky disorder of his brother's once scintillant pattern.

"First, we question," Edger boomed, and formed a series of three short, interlocking notes. Watching with Healer's eyes, Shan saw fires sequentially awake and die within the murk, illustrating a pattern both broken and feeble—the damaged nervous system.

Edger sang again, and Shan saw a quickening of color, a sparking of passion, fading almost immediately back into the ambient grayness, displaying the med tech's proudly achieved normalized cerebration.

A third time Edger sang and the lifemate bridge blazed in glory, alive with the force of two willful, passionate souls, joining each to the other in—muddy melancholy.

"What," Edger inquired, his voice approaching a decibel level that Shan thought might pass for a Clutch whisper, "was that last?"

"The bridge that connects our brother and our sister, soul to soul and heart to heart."

"Those who heal by machine dared tamper with *this*?" Edger demanded, albeit rhetorically. "They are fools, Shan yos'Galan."

"I'm inclined to agree," Shan said, more than half of his attention still on Val Con's mired pattern. "They have forgotten what 'lifemated' means—what it had meant, in the past."

"This joining is not . . . usual among the Clans of Men, I know. Is it more usual among your Clan Korval, or among my sister's human clan of Erob?"

"Erob bred mighty wizards, once," Shan said, dreamily. "Korval has always been—Korval. Wild cards, pirates, and random elements. The luck moves roughly about us."

There was a pause, long enough for Shan to register as too long, in his stretched state astride two worlds, and then a gusty sigh.

"I am ever more in awe of these my kin, who live with such passion, creating thereby an artwork the like of which has not been seen in my lifetime! I am—I will seek the words, betimes; they elude me at this present. Mayhap I must learn new words to describe new art and encompass new endeavor. In this time and place, however, we have before us a work of love and artistry. May we sing as truly and with passion akin to those we would serve. Are you able, Shan yos'Galan?"

Gods, was he? Was *anyone*?

A flash of panic fragmented his inner sight. He took a hard breath, fighting for balance, and heard his father's voice from years gone by, stern and sweet and beloved.

"We do the best that we are able, my child. We make the best decision we may, dependent upon our experience and our training. It is what we owe to kin and to those who reside under our care. If it were true, I would tell you that necessity makes us wise. What I will tell you is that we all do our best; that we all make errors; and that those who love us will forgive us."

Shan gasped, and deliberately drew a calming breath into his lungs; another; and a third. Centered once more, he opened his inner eyes and beheld his brother, injured as he was and with only Shan to stand between him and a Clutch turtle's fearsome singing.

"I am able," he said, keeping his regard upon Val Con; only upon Val Con, whose future depended upon his brother Shan, and who would forgive him, if he failed.

Edger began to sing.

MIRI LAY BACK on her damp pillows and looked up at Sheather.

"Guess we better get dancing, in case the med tech comes back with her boss."

Sheather blinked his eyes, first one, then the other, solemnly. "Perhaps we will dance in a future time, you and I. It occurs to me that I would learn much from such an exercise. But, for now, I ask that you merely listen to the song I have crafted for you."

Right. Miri bit her lip, trying to remember that Shan hadn't looked like anything had hurt during the little song that Edger had sung his knee. Hadn't looked anything but surprised, really, and kinda . . . dreamy, like Val Con looked when he was deep into playing the 'chora.

"You need have no fear," Sheather said, in what passed for soft from Clutch. "I am your brother. Your heart has spoken to my heart. I will not cause you pain."

Which, come to think of it, sounded suspiciously like a Liaden promise. Miri sighed. *What's wrong with you, Robertson? Gettin squeamish in your old age? If Sheather wants to cut your throat, his knife's way too sharp to hurt.*

"Sister?"

She grinned up at the long green length of him. "s'okay. You sing; I'll listen. Fair division of labor."

"Just so," said Sheather and paused. Miri sagged against her pillows and closed her eyes. Eventually, she heard something that might have been a note, or possibly just the wind, combing through leaves . . .

It was spring, and she was in a garden, strolling along a stone-lined pathway. It was a meandering path, all but overgrown in some places by effusions of flowers. In the branches just over her head, birds sang, oblivious to the passage of a stranger through their garden. The perfume of growing things was an intoxicant.

The path spiraled in, ending abruptly at a glade. She paused on the last stone, looking across a stretch of blue-green grass at the trunk of an enormous tree.

The glade was dim under the vast lattice work of branches, and she blinked, then grinned as her adjusting vision made out the slim form of a man leaning against the massive trunk. Unhesitating, grinning wide enough to crack her face, she started across the springy grass.

The man stepped away from the tree and came forward to meet her. He was wearing a beat-up black leather jacket open over a fine white shirt, soft dark trousers and comfortable boots. His hair was dark brown, his eyes were green, and the grin that split the beardless golden face was every bit as wide as hers.

"Cha'trez." The soft, beloved voice caressed her ears and she laughed for the sheer joy of hearing it.

"Val Con." She grabbed his hand and stood holding it like an idiot, too damn happy to think of anything to say.

"You look good," she did say, finally—which sounded funny until she remembered that she knew he was in the catastrophe 'doc, being healed of injuries that should have killed him.

"Looks deceive," Val Con murmured, which was a joke. He tugged on her hand, urging her to walk with him back to the base of the monumental tree. "I am very glad you came here, Miri."

"Yah?" She slanted a glance at the side of his face. "Mind telling me where here is?"

"Not at all," her lifemate said. He stepped right up to the tree and turned to face her, laying his free hand against the trunk.

"This is Jelaza Kazone—the safest place in the galaxy."

She'd've pegged that as another joke, normally, because neither one of them put much stock in "safe." But she felt a stroke of . . . certainty . . . come right out of the core of him and into the core of her.

It took her balance, as such things still did, though the gods knew the strands of them were so tangled together it was by no means certain which one would fall down, if either caught a pellet. She felt Val Con's fingers tighten on hers and she flung her free hand out to brace against the tree.

Welcoming gladness overfilled her, an embrace of green joyousness so vivid that she staggered, vision whiting, ears roaring— and might have fallen, except her partner was there to catch her and ease her down to sit with him on the soft grass, their backs against the Tree.

Slowly, the jubilation faded. Miri blinked the glade into focus, ears registering the racket of bird song once more. She sighed and closed her eyes, settling against the trunk that tangibly warmed her back in a sort of physical smile.

"Cha'trez?" Val Con's voice carried an edge of worry.

She shook her head and looked at him. "It behave like this often?"

His smile glimmered. "Only when it likes you."

"Lucky me," she said and leaned her head against the warm bark. "You know, of course," she said to Val Con's bright green eyes, "that all this is only a dream."

One eyebrow lifted. "As much as it must naturally pain me to disagree with my love and my lifemate—"

"A dream," Miri repeated, interrupting him ruthlessly. "I got out of the 'doc this morning. You—" She put her hand over his heart, feeling its firm beat against her palm.

"You're broke into six dozen pieces, Boss. They figure to get you outta the Last Hope sometime in the next week, Standard." She sighed.

"I wish you'd stop pulling these damn fool stunts," she said, trying to sound severe. "You're gonna get yourself killed."

"I'm sorry, Miri," he said meekly and she laughed, flinging forward suddenly to hug him.

"I'm sorry, too. Gods, I miss you. Miss you enough to dream you this hard . . ."

"This is not a dream, Miri," Val Con breathed in her ear, his arms tight around her. "This is Jelaza Kazone."

"The safest place in the galaxy," she said against his shoulder. "Right." She sighed and straightened out of the embrace. "We won, by the way."

He stared at her blankly for the beat of five before understanding dawned in the green eyes.

"Ah," he said, "the Yxtrang. That is good."

"You could say." She shook her head. "Happens reinforcements showed up in orbit just about the time we was finishing that business at the airfield. I ain't got all the details, but Shan and Beautiful sketched it in for me. Long and short—our backup is Suzuki and every merc who happened to be at liberty when the call came through, plus a Clutch rockship, captained by Edger." She grinned, remembering something else. "Edger and Sheather are here—there. Wherever. Got a serious problem with our course of treatment. Threw the tech outta my room and—hold it." She closed her eyes, trying to focus.

"Miri?"

"Wait, wait. I—" Her memory abruptly came through with the gruesome details of the last hour, and also a spike of pure terror. She opened her eyes and looked into his face, which she couldn't be doing, and there was more, worse, than him just being bust up . . .

"The techs say you're not going to be able to pilot," she said, hearing her voice waver. "They say—the nerve damage—you might not be able to walk, at first, and there's something the matter with—with my . . . seeing . . . you. They—"

"No." He caught her hands in his. "Miri, think: Edger and Sheather are come, and they have thrown the med techs out. And then?"

"Then . . ." Then what? Right, she had it. "They sung Shan's knee better and said they could fix us up all right and tight. Edger and Shan went off to sing at you. Sheather—Sheather must be singing to me right now." She sighed, sharply. "My head hurts."

He grinned at her. "No, it doesn't."

"Know all about it, do you?"

"More than I had used to do," Val Con said seriously. "I—whatever happened that . . . allowed you to pilot that craft after my body failed me . . ." He reached out and touched her cheek, eyes shadowed. "Miri, I don't know what we are become."

"Greater than the sum of our parts?" she asked and saw him frown.

"That is—?"

"The whole is greater than the sum of its parts," Miri recited. "Maybe what happened—however it happened—is that we built an *us-pattern* which is . . . stronger than either you or me alone."

The green eyes gleamed. "Together," he murmured, "we are hell on wheels."

Miri grinned. "Like that. Maybe. Least it gives us a theory to play with."

Val Con tipped his head. "It does not distress you, this . . . new intimacy?"

"Person can get used to the damnedest things," she said, shaking her head. "I wouldn't trade what we got—whatever it is—for a Class A Jumpship."

"There's no need to make that trade," Val Con commented. "Korval owns several Class A Jumps. Only tell me which you choose to reserve for your use and it is done."

She stared at him, then grinned, slightly lopsided. "I keep forgetting how rich you are."

"Now, there, you are out. yos'Phelium is not nearly so wealthy a line as yos'Galan—they being traders, you see, and yos'Phelium tied to administration."

"And mayhem," Miri added.

"From time to time," he agreed. "One must do something to relieve the tedium. However, Clan Korval itself is . . . influential. We own yards, and ships, houses, businesses . . . dea'Gauss will reveal all, when we are arrived home. My information is several years out of date, but I don't expect that Nova has run us off our legs."

"We going back to Liad?" Miri asked, watching him.

"Eventually, we must. The Department of the Interior—that must be Balanced, and not only on Korval's account. I have a duty, as the Captain's heir, to keep the passengers safe from peril. The Department preys on all of Liad, and on all Liadens. That will end."

Miri frowned. "Captain's heir? What captain?"

"Eh?" He blinked, then shook his head, rueful. "I have forgotten that you have not yet read the Diaries. The *Passage* carries a complete transcription. Ask Shan, when you are returned, to provide them to you. You will need to know our history and the decisions which have gone before ours, when we are delm."

Right. "We likely to be delm soon?"

He sighed and took her hand. "Soon, yes. Nova holds the Ring in trust, and has proved herself able on many paths. But she cannot Balance the Department of the Interior. That, cha'trez, is for us." He glanced up suddenly, brows pulled together, as if he had heard someone call his name.

"Ah. I must return." He stood, and bent to offer her a hand. She slid her fingers into his and rose smoothly, then stood looking into his eyes.

"Val Con—" Her throat closed, and it was all she could do to blink the tears away.

He stepped forward and slid his arms around her, hugging her tight as her arms slipped 'round his neck.

"It will be well, Miri," he whispered in her ear. "Gods, time runs—give me your kiss to bear away."

She raised her mouth, hungrily. Scant heartbeats later, they relinquished the embrace with equal reluctance, and Val Con turned toward the pathway.

"Until soon, Miri," he said.

"Until soon, Val Con," she whispered, and watched him move away across the grass, quick and silent and graceful. She turned her face aside for a moment, and when she looked up, he was gone.

Alone, she stood in the glade, listening to the birds and to the wind, gently combing the moist, spring leaves.

THEY HAD SEEDED the fragmented nervous system with a double-dozen crystalline notes, and turned to the larger problem of weaving the unraveled pattern whole. Shan saw himself within a gray, ill landscape, Edger's song ranging somewhat before him, seeking, as would a hunt-beast, and wherever it passed, color took root and began to glow.

Up ahead, the song snagged on a sullen, dusty outcropping, disturbing murky complaints of burnt sienna and umber. Shan extended himself and caught the note, holding it frozen while he examined this anomaly.

It had the taste of something constructed, yet it reacted when he put his will upon it, hissing in a febrile hostility that said *wrongness* to his Healer senses.

He widened his area of perception, seeing how it was laced, haphazard, into his brother's soul—laced *twice*, now that he looked more closely, with some of the original rough bindings broken and replaced by stuff somewhat finer and recognizable as the same material of which the rest of the pattern was formed.

Carefully, he put his will against the edifice, felt it snarl and jerk, like a half-tamed dog, straining against the newer, finer lacing. Wet red numbers flared, foretelling doom and dire consequence. Shan reached forth and shushed them.

Once more, he brought his attention to the newer bindings, recognizing Val Con in the knots and redoubled lacings. So. His brother valued this thing, whatever it was, but did not care to trust it. Well and good.

He cast his will over the edifice, calmed its hostility with a kiss, ran his hands along the shape of it, smoothing away the kinks of falsehood, closing the access ports of strangers, draining off the poison pooled at its core. Then he withdrew to the place where Edger's note reposed in patience and contemplated the results of his efforts.

Its color was better—richly topaz, with glints of copper—its shape more pleasing, less intrusive, nor did it snarl when he touched it with his will, but merely held itself in readiness. It would do.

He hoped.

He removed the compulsion from the note in progress, allowing it to swell forth and encompass the thing—whatever it was—and mold it irrevocably into the totality of Val Con.

DAY 286

❀ ❀

Standard Year 1392
Teriste MidPort
Panake House,
Field of Fire,
Speculator's Trust

AS IT TRANSPIRED, Cheever McFarland knew Teriste, though not the side that Pat Rin knew. Cheever knew the repair shops, both large and small, and had offered to arrange to have the modest Tree-and-Dragon sigil on the ship removed, or covered; which offer Pat Rin refused after some moments of consideration.

Fortune's Reward already appeared on the day-board, and was registered with the portmaster, and while it was true that it would very soon be desirable for it to become another ship entirely, registered to a fictional owner from a far outworld, it would perhaps be best to have those adjustments made in a place somewhat less . . . popular . . . than Teriste.

Pilot McFarland also knew numerous local eateries catering to Terran or mixed crews, and it was to one of those they repaired before they moved forward with the various tasks of the day.

At the Panake House, Cheever's jacket—or perhaps his face—won them entry into the roomy and more comfortable inner sanctum with a cheerful, "This way, pilots!" from the beaming host.

The menus were on the table and coffee poured before Pat Rin could refuse.

The offer to "stow those bags" was waved away, politely acknowledged, and followed by a "back in two" as the waiter hurried to refill the cups at another table.

The menu, for all that it was in Terran—a language Pat Rin read well—was next to incomprehensible. The "slabs" and "stacks" offered for his delectation were meaningless, as were the supposed qualifiers: *thick, short, full* . . .

He needn't have concerned himself. His companion intercepted the waiter with a wave of his big hand.

"Two Morning Specials; double medium slices, and c-juice."

This repast, when it arrived, proved to be a stack of flatbreads which one—taking Cheever McFarland as one's model—doused with various liquids and jams; recognizable eggs; and several patties of ground or pressed meat, each about the size of one the flatbreads.

Warily, Pat Rin sampled the various offerings. The juice drink was familiar enough; the other flavors pleasantly spicy. He had a bit more of each.

"This here," Cheever said, around a mouthful of flatbread. "This is a hard-working port. This place here is always open, and pilots always get the best tables. Take whatever they got on special and you'll get a good, cheap meal."

Pat Rin glanced up from his plate. "However, I am not a pilot."

McFarland forked a meat patty into his mouth and chewed thoughtfully.

"You can pass though," he said eventually. "We get you a jacket and nobody'll doubt you know Jump."

He emptied his coffee mug, waved it in the general direction of a waiter, then shook it gently at Pat Rin.

"If we're going low or something, you're gonna have to learn to drink this stuff like you mean it."

Pat Rin raised an eyebrow, looked at his nearly untouched mug, and smiled slightly.

"I see that I face greater hazards than I had thought," he said in quiet Terran. Deliberately, he picked the mug up and took a long slow sip of the dark beverage. He sighed slightly, wishing for some quiet morning tea, and sipped again as the waiter hove into view, bearing a oversized carafe.

"Nah, now this isn't too bad," said Cheever. "If we get to a place where *I* only drink a sip, you can pass . . ."

"Pilot, I see many lessons ahead for both of us!"

Cheever only nodded as the waiter warmed both their mugs from his pitcher, and offered news of fresh pastries and doughnuts to finish the meal.

PAT RIN'S NAME gained them entry at Field of Fire, where the hostess was pleased to find them a place in the members only section as guests of the house.

The hostess also offered to waive the range fee in return for his signature in the guest book. It was seldom that a Liaden shooter of his caliber called on a Terran establishment such as this, and the signature of the reigning champion of Tey Dor's would enhance the melant'i of the house. Whether he could afford to indulge the house in this, Pat Rin left for later, merely bowing polite acknowledgment of the offer.

They were then walked down a long, transparently walled hall, the hostess intent on convincing Pat Rin of the joys of the establishment. As they passed several dozens of lanes, some lighted and occupied, some lighted and empty, and some dark, all with a variety of targets visible, she continued her spiel, explaining that Field of Fire was not the largest range in number of shooting lanes on planet—no. But it was the best equipped, certainly, holding a complete set of house weapons from light to heavy, including dueling pistols of many calibers. There were also tuning and repair smiths on duty at all times, and instructors.

She paused there, recognizing a potential faux pas, and covered by extravagantly sliding a keycard into a section of wall marked "Club Members Only."

Beyond the door there was better lighting, upgraded carpeting, and a small canteen, manned by an alert looking young man. The individual lanes fanned away from this concourse, eight on each side of two small central shooting theaters capable of accommodating four marksmen at once.

Only one of the single lanes was occupied, and through the thick plastiglass a man could be seen laboriously packing an armored travel bag with an array of small pistols. On the floor next to the shooting stand was an identical bag, sealed.

Their hostess escorted them past the semi-circle of observer's seating to the theater on the left, activating the keyplate and lights with a card and—after the door slid soundlessly aside—motioning them down the ramped entranceway to the sunken shooting floor with its equipment benches and controls. She made no attempt to descend to the floor herself: only shooters were allowed in the fire-zone.

"I think you gentlemen will be comfortable here," she said. "The range isn't scheduled until this evening. You're cleared for up to three hours of shooting; the timer starts with the first shot or when you invoke the tracking computer, whichever comes first. Once again, we will be pleased to waive all charges, should Lord Pat Rin care to sign our guest book."

Pat Rin accepted the keycard and the code as she left, and in short order he and Cheever McFarland had arranged their equipment, donned the club-supplied ear protector headsets and began the straightforward testing-and-truing of what the Terran termed "the hardware".

On Cheever's bench sat two massive chemical LaDemeters and several dozen cartridges, a much smaller and also chemically powered double-barrel derringer-style boot-pistol with its bright shells next to it, and a brace of standard pellet pistols, three extra charges for each sitting by. In his hand was what appeared to be a large—even for a Terran of Cheever's not-inconsiderable size— survival knife. Before each of his three shots with it he turned and glanced over his shoulder to make sure no one was watching, and as soon as he finished the third shot he carefully reloaded it, sheathed it, and immediately slipped it back into his boot.

He moved on quickly, though not as stealthily, to the derringer, squeezing off shots quickly and accurately, the gun almost hidden in his big hands. The noise of its firing—like that of the knife-weapon— was a sharp *snick*, even through the ear protectors. The chemicals left a slightly smokey haze and an acrid odor, which was quickly cleared away by the air filtering system.

Pat Rin was still working with his first weapon, a standard caliber Liaden dea'Nobli pellet pistol. While the caliber may have been standard, the pistol itself was a work of art, with filigree metal work, a custom jay-bead quick-sight, and grips of lovingly hand-shaped kreel-horn. Each shot produced a quiet *whap* through the ear protectors, though the accompanying magnetic whine seeped through without hindrance. His "show gun," the dea'Nobli was more accurate than many clans' dueling pistols and more costly than most.

The targets varied from stationary bull's-eye, to gallery-like mythic creatures, to moving human silhouettes, chosen by the shooter's whim. Satisfied with the dea'Nobli against the bull's-eye, Pat Rin was about to bring up something more challenging when the rhythm of his companion's shots altered—and stopped.

The big man's hand motion was discreet but clear. Lowering his gun, Pat Rin turned and saw that they'd drawn a pair of observers, who were lounging in the chairs on the other side of the plastiglass, mugs and food on the table before them.

The man was certainly Terran—not quite perhaps of Cheever's size, but larger than the average male of the race, with the dark and beginning-to-wrinkle complexion of one who has been overexposed to solar radiation. An ex-mercenary perhaps, or a native of one of the back-worlds, his face was strong-featured, square jawed, and not overly intelligent.

The woman was . . . most likely . . . Terran, and also dark, though it appeared her complexion was of birth rather than burn. Her hair made a black silken cap 'round her neat head, her features were fine, and she had quick ebon eyes, which at the moment rested upon himself with more than casual interest.

"Just sat down," Cheever said, sotto voce. "He's muscle, but if she ain't a pilot I'll eat my license. They both got bags, but she's . . ."

"She is carrying a gun under her right arm," Pat Rin finished for him, "which is why the vest seems a bit bulkier than one might expect on so warm a day. The man is, as you say, a bodyguard."

The woman raised her hand, perhaps indicating that they should feel free to continue with their practice.

"I believe it is time to take a break, Mr. McFarland. Please do me the honor of saving our records. Then we shall see what we may discover of our visitors."

"Gotcha."

Pat Rin engaged the safety on the dea'Nobli and left the pretty gun lying ostentatiously on the bench, feeling the accustomed weight of the hideaway in his right sleeve as an unexpected comfort. Cheever McFarland at his back, he touched the keypad and stepped out into the concourse.

Cool air assailed them, and the increasingly familiar odor of coffee.

"There was no need to disturb yourselves on our account, Master," the woman said in lightly accented Liaden as they approached. Seated, she bowed, gracefully approximating the mode of novice to master, which was surely flattery. "We will be using the other theater in a moment, but it is rare for us to see such shooting here."

Pat Rin inclined his head. "We had not intended a demonstration, and I fear the shooting may not have been up to our best. We have been some time traveling."

"Ah, all the more impressive!" The dark eyes measured him, then she turned, motioning to her companion, bespeaking him in Terran no less mannered than her Liaden—"Julier, my manners have failed me. Please—fetch our guests coffee and a snack—or perhaps tea for the master."

Pat Rin eyed the woman speculatively, and held up a hand. "Allow me to send Mr. McFarland, as well," he said, following her into Terran. "He understands my taste in coffee."

She gave him a half-smile and shrugged a proper Terran shrug. "Of course you will wish to send someone to attend your interests."

Pat Rin glanced to Cheever.

The pilot nodded, waiting for the bodyguard to rise. They walked side-by-side to the canteen, not quite bristling, like two strange cats thrown together on unknown turf.

The woman leaned toward Pat Rin, inclined her head in a motion that became a formal bow.

"Master, it is urgent that we speak—alone. I am Natesa. I believe our interests coincide."

THE TWO BIG MEN fidgeted, uncomfortable in their sudden roles as spectators, as the door sealed with a slight hiss.

"They are nervous of this," Natesa said as she walked with him down the ramp to the shooting floor. "It speaks well of them."

"I suspect we all four have some concerns," Pat Rin murmured, picking the dea'Nobli up from the bench. "Mr. McFarland tells me that you are a professional shooter and likely a first class pilot."

"Ah, and my guardian informs me that you are a better shot than you appear."

Pat Rin sent an exasperated glance toward the two-man audience, and Natesa laughed, soft and musical.

"I thought you might appreciate the level of assistance I am equipped with when the locals insist. Julier is a good man in a barroom brawl—as I suspect Mr. McFarland is—but he is perhaps in the second tier, both of shooters and of intellects, unlike Mr. McFarland." She smiled, and pointed. "I shall take the blue side."

Pat Rin appraised her coolly as she finished unloading the weapons from her bag. These disposed to her satisfaction upon the bench, she turned to face him fully, raising one hand, fingers spread wide, in the old, old, gesture of peace.

"By your leave, Master. I should test these as well."

From beneath her vest she pulled a palm gun, laying it carefully on the bench, its muzzle aimed, without a doubt, down the lane. The design was not familiar; and it was unclear from its lines whether it was a chemical weapon. Natesa reached beneath her vest once more and brought forth a tiny and strange weapon—which was immediately recognizable, despite that he had held one only once, and that many Standards in the past.

He raised an eyebrow, and she inclined her head, not without irony.

"I thank you for your care; you may rest assured that I know this is *not* a toy. It is best that we be plain with each other. I am called Natesa the Assassin—among other things—and that"—she pointed—"is a triple caliber pellet weapon. A single shot. Very high energy. Perhaps the equivalent of one of Mr. McFarland's special loads."

So. Pat Rin drew a careful breath, conscious that the stakes had risen, though not, or so he thought, out of all reason.

"I am not," he said to the woman's intelligent dark eyes, "a professional. Certainly I carry nothing to . . ."

She raised her finger to her lips with a sibilant Terran *shush*.

"You are correct, of course," she said, with a brisk nod. "Neither of us can be expected to display all of our weapons and backups. However, you should know that I see two of your hideaways."

He inclined his head, coming the lofty lordling. "My thanks."

Her lips twitched, and she bowed once more.

"Shall we say best of fifty?" she asked. "Mixed targets? I have here a match in caliber for your pellet pistol."

"Of course." He checked the charge on his weapon as she checked hers.

"Shall we alternate? Use the same targets? Or shoot duo?" he asked, automatically looking at the floor to be sure of his footing.

"Duo," she said promptly, and moved a hand toward the targeting switch. "I choose this. You choose the targets."

And that, Pat Rin thought, was a gambit. The gamester in him rose to the challenge: the best refutation of a gambit is acceptance.

He reached to the controls, punched his choices in, and held his finger on the presstab as he looked over to her.

"We shall have duplicate heavy game. The pace to be energetic. The distances to vary identically. If you agree."

She nodded rather than bowed, her face merely comely. "Indeed, heavy game. An excellent choice."

He raised five fingers to indicate the delay to start, activated the presstab, and stepped back to the line.

Numbers flickered on the ceiling, counting down. The lights dimmed. The targets came up.

Heavy game.

The first target swung out of the floor, at the far end of the alley, a crouching image of a man bringing a sighted rifle to bear. Pat Rin's shot was quick, and automatic. One shoots between the arms, below the stock, as close to the throat as one can. The target spun away, replaced by something out of the left wall—two men, side by side, with pistols, followed by a young girl with pistol, skip the young boy with the flowers in his hand, try the head shot on the figure with a gun sheltering by a tree trunk.

He was aware that in the other lane the targets came out at the same time, and that it seemed the sound of her gun was overlaying his . . . but the targets came on.

Pat Rin was sweating, the dea'Nobli's charge near exhausted, the targets each taken down in their turn, allowing the boy with flowers, the old man with his broom, the couple with their ice-licks, and the two tiny creatures—perhaps they were dogs?—to hold their ground.

In a moment, the scores.

Natesa whistled lightly. Blue side: 297 points. Green side: 298.

"May I?" she asked, reaching toward the controls.

Pat Rin bowed, and the assassin brought up the fine scores.

"So, Master. We each have fifty live targets. We each score fifty respectable hits. My times were—see here—slightly faster. Your shots were exceedingly accurate, if slower. Mine were all good enough."

Pat Rin bowed. "Your shots were all quicker than mine, and with heavy game, this is important. I will tell you that I noticed you overcorrecting a drift to the left at the end. Without that, you would have certainly had the three hundred."

She laughed then, and bowed lightly.

"Master. You see well enough to watch both our targets. And why the drift to the left, if you can tell me?"

He looked at her carefully, raised a finger and indicated that she should spin about. She shrugged and did so, coming to rest facing him, dark eyes quizzical. He moved his finger again, miming a slower spin, which was perhaps an error: he was momentarily distracted by her shape; and the tilt of her shoulders and head made it plain that she had noticed.

"I believe it is clear," he said in Liaden—in the mode of master to master. "Your vest bound you slightly as you worked. It is that very flat item above your left kidney that is the problem."

"Ah." For an instant only was Natesa the Assassin nonplused, then she bowed, deeply, in the mode of novice to master. "I am instructed."

She straightened and gave him a serious look.

"Let us inspect weapons a moment," she said, "and speak looking down the alleyway so that none behind us may read our lips."

Now it was come. Whatever it was. Pat Rin bowed agreement and proceeded to field strip his pistol.

"Master of Tey Dor's," she said softly, her hands busy and sure at her own weapon, "please consider me at your disposal. If you have need of transport, or a safe house; for additional bodyguards, for a cash advance—" She shot him a quick, dark glance. "Understand, I have discretion. More. I have jurisdiction. Much may be contrived, if you have need."

"And you offer from the goodness of yourself, no doubt . . . ." he murmured, glancing across to her.

She raised her head and looked fully into his face.

"If you like, you may consider this a formal offer of the Juntavas—an extension of the aid-and-comfort you may perhaps have heard." She paused.

That she was a Juntava did not surprise him—he had supposed as much. That she came to him with this generous and open offer of aid was—distressing. Still, it was best to hear her out, so that he might know what protections he might need to find—elsewhere.

Bland-faced, hands steady on his weapon, he inclined his head—courteous invitation to continue.

Natesa sighed. "Ah. I feared you would see it thus. Master, hear me—I repeat it: *our interests coincide.* I know, I know—the old agreement. But many things are . . . not as they have been." She held up a hand, her face earnest.

"So, I will tell you: the Juntavas discovers that there is something very wrong on Liad. Korval-in-person disappears from the breadth of space, but for you—perhaps you are the bait in a trap?—and the silly young cousin. Korval ships ply their routes, but we note the changes in long-established patterns, the captains redistributed, the crew-members put ashore, the heavy weapon pods mounted.

"In other sectors, confusions begin to grow, which seem to our analysis related to the . . . alterations in Korval's behaviors. We hear of—certain people one is wise to avoid; of some of those who have dealt with particular Liadens turning up—not ruined or shamed—but dead."

Plan B, thought Pat Rin, and then said it, softly: "Plan B is in effect. Korval is beset, Natesa the Assassin. We have gone into hiding."

"Yes?" Her eyes gleamed. "But *you* have not gone into hiding, Master. And the Juntavas has made a study of Korval. We do not expect that the dragon is meek in its exile. We anticipate decisive action, from an unexpected quarter—and that soon." She paused, her eyes yet on his face.

"Understand me, Pat Rin yos'Phelium. As a Sector Judge I am able to provide what you may need. *Whatever* you may need. And if you should lead us to your kin, that the Clutch turtles may be satisfied that the Juntavas treats with honor, so much the better for us all."

"Sector Judge?" he repeated the unfamiliar title quietly, slowly fitting his gun back together.

"Yes, yes." Impatience was evident in her voice. "I am—a power. When there are disputes over territory, or of proper ownership of particular objects or properties, I am called in to find the answers, to make things smooth again. And if there is a problem which cannot be solved by discussion, I am empowered to solve it as I may." She paused as she concentrated on something finicky within her weapon.

"This is why I walk with Julier, who is a gift of the local boss while I am on planet. The boss wishes to be certain that I will agree with him when need be."

She glanced at him as the *snick-click* of the new charge going home broke the silence.

"The old agreement—that the Juntavas does not meddle with Korval. That Korval does not meddle with the Juntavas . . ." Pat Rin said, softly, so softly. "You counsel me to set it aside, you argue—persuasively!—that circumstances have altered so entirely that the boundaries of wisdom—the boundaries of mutual survival—have been re-drawn, placing the Juntavas and Korval side-by-side in the face of a common enemy." He moved his shoulders, of a sudden very weary.

"You know who I am. It is not within my scope to set aside clan policy. Certainly, not this, of all possible clan policies. No matter what the need."

She was silent. He stood and backed away from the work bench, his gun pointed specifically away from her. He glanced along the alley, and moved to the target console.

"Shall we shoot?" he asked, fiddling with the settings. "One hundred targets, descending from standard size and distance to one sixth size and double distance."

"You are certain?" she asked, and, indeed there was a tentative note in the soft, cultured voice.

Pat Rin glanced over his shoulder, saw her standing, gun reassembled and aimed at the innocent floor, slim and deadly and very comely, indeed. "Why should I not be certain?" he asked lightly. "A cantra to you, should you best my score."

She laughed then. "You *are* a gamester, aren't you? But no, I'll not put you out of pocket. Rather let us agree to part amicably." She bowed, lightly and with whimsy.

"And yes, Master, I would be very pleased to shoot again."

They disposed of the hundred targets in short order, failing yet again to find one of them ascendant over the other. Natesa had left him, then, with a graceful bow. He let her out of the theater to rejoin her gift bodyguard, and re-admitted Cheever McFarland.

"We will be departing Teriste earlier than anticipated, Mr.

McFarland," he said as the big man loaded his second LaDemeter and stepped up to the line. "When we finish here, I will call at the bank. It would be best if you take leave this evening."

The pilot looked at him, wearing an expression between a grin and a grimace. "Got a date?"

"Mr. McFarland, I do. I must to the casino, else we arrive at our destination without enough cash to buy into a game."

"Oh. Yeah. But she's something, ain't she, Boss?"

"Pilot?"

"That Natesa. A bit of a looker and she shoots like a champion. She ought to, 'cause she's the reigning champ in *this* club."

"I am informed, but not surprised." Pat Rin stepped up to the line and squeezed off his first shot.

"Juntavas, huh?"

"You are apparently aware."

"The boy she was with had a half-dozen tell-tales on 'em. Tattoo here, 'nother one there. Carries official Juntavas ordinance—what that Natesa *don't* do—even wears the damn ring! Got no style at all. I gotta tell you, if he's a friend of that lady I'll be surprised."

"Indeed. I believe her to hold you in much higher esteem than that enjoyed by Julier."

"I sure hope so. He's about as subtle as a drunk merc at a nude beach."

"Mr. McFarland, if you think to spoil my aim by distracting me or by making me laugh, you're quite off the mark."

"Well, a guy's got to try. You're two whole shots up on me with twenty to go."

"Shoot, Mr. McFarland. If you continue, you may match Natesa's score."

"Guess *she* was distracted, huh? I think she likes you, Boss."

"Mr. McFarland . . . ."

"Yeah. Right. Gotcha. My shot."

THE PRIVATE ACCOUNTS manager was new since the last time Pat Rin had accessed his funds at Teriste Speculator's Trust. The former manager had been male, soft-spoken and respectful.

The new manager was female, breathless and provoking.

"I very much beg your pardon, sir," she dithered, her fingers stuttering over her keyboard. "I don't seem to find that account. I—oh, here! Ah, no. No, that's not it."

Pat Rin swallowed a caustic comment, counted to twelve and pointed out that the paperwork he had provided listed not only his name and his account number, but the first of his two pass phrases, which really should be all she needed in order to locate his funds.

"Yes, yes, of course, you are quite correct, sir!" she babbled. "It is only that—well! I see that I will need to bring the branch manager in. Only a moment, sir, of your goodness. I will return immediately—" She leapt up from her chair and fled, the door sealing behind her.

Pat Rin bit down on his annoyance. Really, this was preposterous. There should not be the slightest difficulty in accessing his account. The manager had very likely miscoded the request; indeed, it was a rare wonder that she had been able to type at all, as badly as her hands had been shaking.

And why had her hands been shaking? he wondered abruptly. He was hardly a fearsome individual, after all; and his request had been merely commonplace.

Frowning, he got up and walked 'round the desk. The screen was still active, awash with red lines and danger-signals. In the center of it all was the code for his private account, showing a balance of some ninety-six cantra; followed by an unfamiliar code, also in red.

Just so.

Absolutely calm, he retrieved his paperwork from the desktop, folded it into the inside pocket of his jacket, rounded the desk and lay his hand against the door. It slid open at his touch, which surprised him somewhat, but he rather thought that the new manager was unused to dealing with dangerous clients.

Walking quickly, he went down the hall and through the discreet common office, heading for the door to the street. Behind him, he heard a clatter of heels and a gasped, "Sir? Sir, a moment, please!" He did not turn his head, but swept out the door.

Gaining the street, he strode on, despite the fact that his knees had developed a disconcerting wobble. He had scarcely gone six steps before he was joined by a large man carrying a pair of gun bags.

"Business concluded, Boss?" Cheever asked.

"Concluded," he said, rather breathlessly, "but not to our advantage. I was not able to withdraw funds. Worse . . . Mr. McFarland, I fear I may have alerted someone . . . unsavory . . . to my presence."

"Bound to happen, I guess," Cheever said philosophically. "Time to lift?"

Pat Rin walked on, somewhat less quickly now, and forced himself to focus. Panic was never a winning hand.

"No. I must attempt the casinos. With the ship's fund and my personal accounts beyond reach, the need for money becomes desperate."

"If they know you're here, they'll be watching the casinos," Cheever pointed out, reasonably enough.

Pat Rin moved a hand in agreement. "They will. But the casinos have security on-staff and an investment in maintaining the safety of their clients. I may be seen, but it is unlikely that I will be importuned." He sighed. "The risk must be accepted in any case. We must have cash."

There was a short pause, then a sigh.

"If that's the way it's gotta be, then we go with it," he said. "I'll be coming with you."

It was perhaps indicative of his state of mind that Pat Rin felt not annoyance at this presumption, but relief.

"Thank you, Mr. McFarland," he said. "I will be glad of your company."

TERISTE
Casino District
The Practical Statistician

❂ ❂

"LORD PAT RIN—a moment, if you will!"

The beautifully dressed gentleman did not look up at the hail. He received the dice, shook them briefly and threw with an expert's snap of the wrist, rings flashing richly in the table lights. The dice struck the felt-covered end wall, rebounded, rolled twice and stopped; the first and second die each showed one pip, while the third displayed five. The gentleman stood quietly, dark head tipped, calmly awaiting the House's judgment.

"Seven called and seven rolled!" the croupier announced, deftly separating three coins from the bank and placing them before the winner. "House pays three gold to the gentleman with the blue earring." The dice rattled to the cloth beside the coins. "Roll again, sir?"

The gentleman took a moment to consider, as well he might, gambling at gold level, with the House's three and his own two riding the toss.

Jewels flashed as shapely fingers spread above the coins. "Hold."

"The gentleman with the blue earring holds his line," the croupier cried. "Who rolls against the House?"

The dice passed to a brassy-haired lady in an inexcusable scarlet coat, who shook them with great energy. The gentleman with the blue earring deftly palmed his five gold and left the table, moving away from the area from which the most unwelcome hail had come, and toward the table at which Cheever McFarland had last been seen.

No sooner had he cleared the crowd surrounding the dice table than his sleeve was snatched and held by a sharp-faced man of extraordinarily nondescript dress.

"Lord Pat Rin?"

He lifted an eyebrow. "Yes?" he murmured, and glanced significantly down at his mangled sleeve.

Alas, his captor was wholly intent upon his own business and failed of taking the hint.

"Sir, there is one who would speak to you. Most urgently." The man's fingers tightened. Pat Rin frowned.

"You will," he said, softly, and yet unmistakably in the mode of Command, "release me."

Startled, the stranger did just that, dropping back a step, his dead eyes leaping to Pat Rin's face.

"Your pardon, sir. I meant no disrespect. But there is one who has—"

"Urgent need to speak with me," Pat Rin finished, all of his attention seemingly upon smoothing the creases out of his abused sleeve. "Just so. I do not desire to leave my amusement. If your—employer—must speak to me as urgently as that, he will come to me."

The stranger gaped, then bowed, abruptly and muddy of mode, spun on his heel and vanished into the crowd, leaving Pat Rin to stare at the place where he had been and damn himself three times for a fool.

Careful to display neither haste nor concern, he crossed the room to the Smaller Wheel and insinuated himself into the crowd 'round the table. There, sheltered on all sides by tall Terrans, he tried to think.

That the sharp-faced man belonged to the Juntavas, he doubted, though the possibility could not be rejected out of hand. It was conceivable that the local boss sought to gain advantage over the Sector Judge who had been thrust upon him. And yet . . .

The sharp-faced man had been Liaden. Plan B specifically warned him away from Liad—and from Liadens. And, truth told, there was that about his recent captor which made the Juntavas—most especially the Juntavas in the person of Natesa—show honorable, wholesome and foursquare for clan and kin.

There was a disruption in the crowd of spectators to his left. Pat Rin half-turned and looked up into the very welcome face of Cheever McFarland.

"Well met, Pilot," he murmured, for his companion's ear alone. "I believe it is time for us to leave."

They were not—not quite—taken unaware.

They left together by a side door, at Pilot McFarland's insistence, and made rapid progress toward the distant shine of a taxi stand.

The night was busy with wind, damp with the threat of rain; and it had taken Pat Rin a few moments to be certain that the small noises and the motions of shadows were concerted action and not simply the random pattern of people on the town.

And by then, it was clear that they were both shadowed and outnumbered. Cheever flipped his pocket lightly and Pat Rin muttered under his breath, "Not yet, we have no plan."

They had continued moving in the direction of the transport kiosk, hoping against the odds for the timely appearance of a taxi or a shuttle, but the interception went smoothly.

"This way, please," the pale-haired man who drifted in beside them said in Liaden, and then in accented Terran, "There is no need for alarm."

The place to which they were taken was not far from the casino district, down a windowless alleyway and into a court where several vehicles were parked. Surprisingly, there were a smattering of trees and bushes here, as if some effort at landscaping had been made.

They were ushered past the trees, into a somewhat smaller and dimmer alley. Several of their escort peeled off to take up what Pat

Rin thought must be guard points. A few more steps along the second alleyway and they came to a rough-walled building. The door stood open; the pale-haired man bowed them within. He entered after, his bodyguard sealing the door behind all.

The man led them down a thin and lowering hall, then, and into a sparsely lit, irregularly shaped room.

The room smelled of old dust and the floor was uneven, as if the building had shifted and created tectonic ridges in the tiles.

The leader motioned toward a rude table attended by two ruder chairs, set near the center of the gloom. He took for himself the chair nearest the door, his second standing behind him.

They took this as a model: Pat Rin in the chair; Cheever McFarland behind.

"We are messengers," the pale-haired man murmured, soothing the air between them with a gesture one might more reasonably expect to encounter at a High House dining board than at a rough plastic table in a badly lit, abandoned storeroom. "Merely messengers, sir. Bearing news from those who wish you, not harm, but only well."

"News," Pat Rin repeated, liking the matter no better, and fervently grateful for the formidable bulk of Cheever McFarland standing behind his chair. He took a breath, keeping his face calmly neutral—the old, the familiar, gambler's mask—and inclined his head.

"Of course," he said, matching the man's soft tone, "one welcomes news, when one has been heedless upon holiday."

The man across inclined his head gravely, his gun-sworn standing at stiff attention behind his chair.

"Of course," he agreed, and put his hands palm down against the table, meeting Pat Rin's eyes squarely.

"I bring news of your clan."

Yes? Pat Rin flicked a glance downward, looking for the Tree-and-Dragon token held discreetly between two of the man's quiet fingers. He was not . . . entirely . . . surprised to discover it invisible.

He looked again at the man's bland, mannerly face. "One is ever joyful to have news of one's kin," he said softly.

"As who is not?" the other replied according to the proper formula and leaned forward abruptly, his curiously flat eyes pinning Pat Rin's gaze.

"Your kin are dead," he said, as if it were the merest pleasantry; as if he imparted nothing more startling than an unlooked-for change in the weather.

Behind the gambler's mask of calm neutrality, Pat Rin froze, hearing again that calm, uninflected sentence, not quite making sense—His *kin*. His kin—*dead*? *All* his kin? Quin? Luken? Nova? Shan? His mother? Dead? Ridiculous.

"Ridiculous," he heard his own voice state, dispassionately.

The other man inclined his head. "I understand," he murmured. "So large a change in Korval's fortunes—in your own fortunes. Of course, so skilled a player as yourself would wish proof. As it happens, we have proof." He dropped his eyes deliberately to the tabletop.

Pat Rin followed his gaze, saw the sinewy golden hands lift up and away, leaving alone upon the scarred plastic a smallish thing that glittered even in light so low; a thing he had reason to know well, having seen it upon the hands of several of his kin, most lately on the hand of his cousin Nova, who held Korval in trust for Val Con.

And who would have surrendered Korval's Ring to the man who sat before him only in the extremity of her death.

He forced himself to blink, to look up from the impossibility on the table before him; forced himself to speak calmly to the man opposite, who sat watching with his flat, predator's eyes and his curiously immobile face.

"There are," he observed, as if the thing upon the table were the merest bauble, "others before me. Indeed, I believe that there are children not yet halfling and at least one Terran far-kin to whom the Ring would fall before ever it came to me."

The man smiled gently. "They no longer impede you. Nova yos'Galan, Anthora yos'Galan, Shan yos'Galan, Kareen yos'Phelium, Luken bel'Tarda, Val Con yos'Phelium, even Gordon Arbuthnot. All have been swept from the board."

Hearing the names of his kin—his *dead* kin—but the man had

not named the children! Pat Rin grasped that thought, insisting that his mind work. The pale-haired man had not named the children, but his mother and Luken—by every iteration of Plan B he had ever memorized, Luken bel'Tarda and Kareen yos'Phelium were responsible for the safety of the children. If his mother and Luken were—dead . . .

No. It—they could not—it was not possible . . .

Blindly, he reached out, plucked the Ring from the table and stared at it, eyes tracing the familiar lines of Korval's Tree-and-Dragon, the bright enamel-work, the perfect emeralds framing the boldly scripted *Flaran Cha'menthi*.

"Who did this?" he asked, eyes on the dragon, on the emeralds. Two *perfect* emeralds . . .

"It is necessary," the pale-haired man said in his soft, mannerly voice, "from time to time to remove from play those who impede the work of the Department of the Interior. Thus it was with those who had been your kin. And, now, through the efforts of the Department of the Interior, you rise to your proper estate."

With an effort, Pat Rin lifted his eyes to stare at the man opposite, who inclined his head deeply—a seated bow of profound respect.

"*Korval*," he said.

Pat Rin could not quite control the shudder as he placed the ring back in the center of the table. He took a breath.

"The Department of Interior will require some . . . service, in payment of its efforts on my behalf," he suggested gently.

The pale-haired man moved a hand in that curiously soothing gesture. "You need only mind the Department's interests with the Council of Clans. Advisories and information will be delivered to you at the appropriate times." He smiled. "Small enough payment. You will find the Department is a staunch defender of its allies."

"Ah." He took a hard, sudden breath, raised a hand as if to shield his face, and all at once recalled himself, snapping the arm down as he glanced aside. "Your pardon," he gasped, as the hideaway slid from his sleeve into his hand.

"Of course," said his enemy. "You will wish time to assimilate—"

Pat Rin brought the little gun up and shot him through the right eye. The body of the man collapsed forward, face flat on the table, his gun-sworn snatching at her sidearm as he fell. The boom of Cheever McFarland's weapon and the rain of blood from the gaping hole in her chest were simultaneous.

"You OK, sir?"

Pat Rin took a breath which failed to fill his lungs, and tried another, finding his voice at last, remarkably steady, though somewhat light.

"I am perfectly well, Mr. McFarland, thank you." Absently, he slid the hideaway back into his sleeve and stood.

"You'll have to leave your jacket," Cheever said apologetically. "The blood."

"Of course." He unfastened the seal and stripped the garment off, dropping it into the merciful shadows along the floor. For a moment, he stared uncomprehending at the square of cloth Cheever silently held out. Clean-silk. It came to him, then, that his face might not be . . . perfectly . . . clean. He plucked the cloth up and used it thoroughly, then dropped it, too, into the shadows.

"Is that Nova's ring?"

He looked up at the big pilot, then turned and plucked the thing off the table. Two *perfect* emeralds. Fools. And, yet . . .

"Mr. McFarland, I fear we're in a scrape." He held up the counterfeit. "This is *not* Korval's Ring, though those—" he swept his hand at the dead without looking at them—"claimed that it was. They also claimed that all of my kin are—are dead." His voice was not doing so well, after all. He swallowed and forced himself to go on.

"They named names, Mr. McFarland. And—we are neither of us children. Or fools. We both know that a man who tells one lie does not necessarily tell two."

Cheever's face in the dim light might have been hewn from wood.

Pat Rin inclined his head. "Just so. Balance is owing." He slid the bogus Ring onto his left hand—onto the *second finger* of his left hand—and held it up to catch the sullen light.

There was a brief silence before Cheever nodded his big head.

"Gotcha. Now, let's get outta here before their buddies wonder what all the noise was about."

At the door to the alleyway, Cheever held up his hand. Pat Rin obediently slipped into the shadows at the edge of the doorway, gun ready, as the big Terran moved silently out into the dark.

Shivering in his thin silk shirt, Pat Rin counted to twelve, to twenty-four—to thirty-six, and the alley gave up neither sound nor light nor Cheever McFarland. Forty-eight, and Pat Rin began to consider the likelihood of alternate exits and how they might be guarded. Fifty-seven—and gravel scraped in the alleyway, as if purposefully scuffed beneath the heel of a boot.

A heartbeat later, Cheever McFarland himself materialized, showing empty palms.

"We're clear, sir. The guards are accounted for."

Soundlessly and quickly. Pat Rin slipped his gun away. "Your work?"

Cheever grinned and lowered his hand. "I ain't that good." He jerked his head to the right. "Your girlfriend did us a favor."

Girlfriend? There was the very slightest of motions in the shadows at the right. Pat Rin turned, and Natesa the Assassin allowed him to see her, bowing profoundly in her dull black leathers.

Behind her Pat Rin caught glimpse of a face, a body in the weeds—the man who had accosted him at the casino . . .

"Master. I hear there was a disagreement inside. Perhaps we may assist you."

She straightened, showing him a face expertly darkened, in which her eyes shone like ebony waters.

"I understand that you have already assisted me," he replied, and bowed in acknowledgment of the debt. "Have you taken any harm from it?"

Amusement, rich and subtle, was conveyed in the curve of one leather-clad arm. "No harm in the least. They were unwatchful and arrogant."

He moved a hand, describing the building behind him. "There are two dead persons in the room at the end of that hallway. It would be best if they were not found."

"Housekeeping will deal with it," she said calmly, and bowed once more. "Again, I offer transport and whatever you might require." She straightened, eyes gleaming. "Master, there was no need for you to be in that room at all."

"There was every need," Pat Rin corrected, and raised his hand. What light there was skidded off the bright enamel work, and Korval's ancient sigil flared like a star in the alley. The assassin drew a breath, pulled the most obvious weapon from its holster and offered it to him across her two palms.

"Service, Korval. I would stand at your back."

Pat Rin closed his eyes. Cantra's own words, from the very Diaries of Korval, burned bright against the inside of his eyelids: *In an ally, considerations of house, clan, planet, race are insignificant beside two prime questions, which are: 1. Can he shoot? 2. Will he aim at your enemy?*

Pat Rin opened his eyes and bowed, acknowledging his receipt of her oath.

"Service accepted," he said, and turned to his pilot. "Mr. McFarland, we are enroute."

The big man nodded and touched the butt of the gun thrust through his belt. "Yessir. I see that we are."

DAY 287

❀❀❀❀❀❀❀❀❀❀❀❀❀❀❀❀❀❀❀❀❀❀❀❀

Standard Year 1392
Departing Teriste

THERE WAS A Juntavas safe-house somewhere on Teriste; Natesa had wished to take him there. Which offer he of course refused, insisting that they—or at least he—return to *Fortune's Reward*.

"I will not leave my ship untended when there are enemies to hand," he said, reasonably. At least, he thought he was speaking reasonably, survival dictating that one *ought* to speak reasonably—in fact, with all courtesy—to a Juntavas assassin.

She considered him for a moment in silence, black eyes unreadable in her darkened face. She bowed then, honor to the delm, and Pat Rin felt a frisson run his spine, which she certainly saw—and it would not do to show weakness before such a one, when he must display only strength and absolute certainty—when he must be ruthless in the pursuit of his Balance . . .

"After all," Natesa murmured, "Korval is ships." She looked to Cheever, who nodded.

And so they three had returned to *Fortune's Reward*, though in an order dictated by Cheever McFarland, who took to himself the task of ascertaining that enemies had neither subverted the ship-codes nor awaited them within the shadows of neighboring vessels. When the all-clear came, Pat Rin went forward, Natesa slightly behind and to his left, and thus they entered his ship.

Cheever was already at the board, chatting with the tower as if the entire universe had not been altered in its course over the last hour—but, of course, for Cheever, the universe maintained. The two of them had been beset by cut-throats, whom they had dispatched with speed and efficiency. They had thereby gained a rather . . . irregular . . . ally, but Cheever seemed to hold the Juntavas in neither awe nor loathing, regarding them simply as another fact of life. And life went on.

So it did.

Standing in the center of the piloting chamber, Pat Rin took a careful breath, and turned toward the waiting assassin. His oathsworn.

"I was unfortunately naive prior to raising this port," he said, speaking in the mode between equals. "I seek now to correct an error."

She inclined her head. "Master, I am at your service."

"Then you will tell me if it is possible—or when it will be possible—to alter the name, ID, and port of origin for this vessel."

She pursed her lips, considering; indicated the busy pilot with a subtle move of her head. "Pilot McFarland already files an amended flight. He is wise in this, I think. We have this evening discommoded a player of whom I am insufficiently knowledgeable. Ignorance being an active threat to survival, it is wisdom to retire to a less volatile location.

"So. If you will allow me, there is a station within this sector where the modifications you mention may be made, easily and professionally."

"And the price?" he asked, which was only prudent, when buying from the Juntavas.

Natesa's dark eyes gleamed with amusement. "I have jurisdiction there. The legitimate expenses of a Judge on assignment are charged on account."

"I see." He had taken her service, he reminded himself—

necessity. And if, through her, he had also taken service from the Juntavas entire?

Necessity.

He took a breath, deep and calming, and looked down at his hands. Bright and bogus on the second finger of his left hand—the finger on which Korval-pernard'i had worn the true Ring, and, gods willing, wore it still—his newest adornment quite cast his usual jewels into the shade, as if they were mere paste, instead of . . .

Instead of cash. Pat Rin shook himself, recalling that his earnings on the evening were slight, and all accounts closed to him. He looked up, to find Natesa watching him closely.

"Something else," he said, showing her his right hand, all a-glitter with gemstones.

She inclined her head. "It would be most profitable to sell those here. If you will, I may summon one to conduct the appropriate transactions. The money will await you at the service station we spoke of."

And he had only to trust her, he thought, and very nearly laughed.

"Of your kindness," he said, instead, and had the things off, jumbling them into her waiting palm. He hesitated, then, and raised a hand to the blue earring. His trademark, by which he would be known.

"Hold," the woman said, softly. "The rings are enough for now, Master. That—it is worth too little, if it must be sold without provenance."

He considered her, both eyebrows surprised into lift, but she only smiled, and bowed, and moved to the board, murmuring a request that the pilot open a comm line for her.

"We got lift scheduled inside the hour, sir," Cheever McFarland said over his shoulder, face as calm as always. "Any idea where we're going?"

"First, we must undertake certain renovations too long ignored—Natesa has the coords for the . . . preferred shop in the sector."

Unflapped, Cheever nodded. "And after that?"

Well? Pat Rin asked himself, interestedly. *And after that?* He looked at the big man steadily.

"After that shall depend upon necessity, pilot." He moved a hand toward the hall leading to his quarters. "If you have no need of me, I shall retire now, and meditate upon my . . . requirements."

"Right." Cheever nodded again. "I'll give you a heads-up when we raise the station."

"Thank you, Mr. McFarland," Pat Rin said, softly. He inclined his head, and walked away from the busyness of the piloting chamber, down the hall and into his quarters.

ASKED, IF ANY were bold enough to do so, Pat Rin would have said that he was not a fond man. Of course, one had preferred acquaintances—even preferred kin—but one was not, after all, clan-bound. Certainly, he was no such weeping heart as might overload his personal databank with images of his kin, in all their faces and seasons.

Indeed, a most thorough search of that same databank produced precisely six images, all unsatisfactory in the extreme.

Six.

Carefully, he arranged them on the screen, side-by-side, top-to-bottom; enlarging each as if he would read every line and nuance of the digital faces.

Here: Shan, Nova and Anthora grouped, laughing, around the ubiquitous Jeeves. The picture was not recent—Shan was wearing Korval's Ring in trust, which he had assumed upon Cousin Er Thom's death; Anthora looked the merest halfling, and Nova—Nova scarcely looked older.

Here was Quin, his own heir, caught in the midst of a race against his cousin Padi, Shan's daughter. This image was of more recent vintage, though still some years behind the calendar.

The next picture—that was recent, and Pat Rin spent some time looking into the faces of the two most dear to him in all the worlds. Luken bel'Tarda, his foster-father, sandy hair gone to gray, shoulders square in his second best coat, and Quin, who had gone from hooligan to young gentleman in the space of one image, standing before the hand-knotted Pasiryki carpet which was Luken's pride and sole extravagance. Fortunes had been offered Luken, in exchange for that rug. Alas, fortunes interested Luken—not at all. Quin was dressed in traveling clothes, his dark hair painfully neat, the opal blue eyes which were his legacy from his mother wide and guileless. A kit-bag sat at his feet. After the picture was taken, Pat Rin recalled, finding it suddenly difficult to breathe, he had escorted his son to the excellent private school that now—that had had him in its keeping.

Another: Not recent, though not as old as the image of his cousins and their housebot. His mother at study, various editions of the Code laid open on the table around her workstation; her face intent upon the screen.

Another: His cousin Val Con, slouched in a chair before the fireplace in Trealla Fantrol's family parlor, his legs thrust out before him and crossed at the ankle, a glass of wine held loosely in his left hand. He was looking directly into the camera, and gently smiling, eyes as brilliant as the emeralds in the counterfeit ring on Pat Rin's finger.

The last image was the oldest of all, blurry with the photographer's lack of skill. It showed four persons in formal tableau, paired two-by-two. On the left, tall Anne Davis, kind-faced and smiling, her hand resting on the shoulder of a yellow-haired man of extraordinary beauty—Er Thom, her lifemate. Beside Er Thom, lean and dark and diabolic—Uncle Daav himself, holding the hand of a slight and elegant lady, her tawny hair caught back from her face by a carven comb, her green eyes aglow with joy. Aelliana, Daav's lifemate. Val Con's mother. Dead—they were all four dead; had been dead long before Plan B had been called. It was a portrait of ghosts he studied so intently, and had been so for years . . .

Six images, incomplete and old—which, if the representative of the Department of the Interior was to be believed, was all that he had now, of his kin.

He sat for some time, staring sightlessly at the screen, trying to think of a way—any way—to gain news of his kin without endangering those who might yet remain unmurdered.

Fortune's Reward carried a pinbeam. He was in possession of a beam-code, meant for use in the irregularly scheduled roll calls, as well as other codes, which in happier times would rouse Luken; the *Dutiful Passage*; Nova; dea'Gauss; and the master computer at Jelaza Kazone.

He dared invoke none of them, he decided after a period of cold and close reasoning. The Department of the Interior had located him, offered their preposterous deal, and their messenger had died as a result of their impertinence. These facts in no way guaranteed that the Department's interest in himself had likewise died. Indeed, he rather thought that their interest might grow significantly warmer, when it was discovered why their messenger, and his team, had not reported in.

Certainly, the Department of the Interior was monitoring his accounts. Certainly, they monitored Korval's known bands and, perhaps, if only one adult had fallen to them, the lesser known bands, as well.

Pat Rin shivered, closing his eyes. He dared attempt to call—no one. More: he dared not be taken by the Department alive, to then be compelled to betray whomever yet remained at large.

And, above all, he must not allow his desperate desires to blind him to the possibility that the Department's messenger had indeed told him nothing more than the plain truth, and that he, Pat Rin yos'Phelium, was the last of his clan.

He opened his eyes, blinked several times to bring the faces of his kin into focus, and pulled the keyboard to him.

He left the images on the primary screen, opened a second screen and, typing uncertainly with fingers that were none too steady, began to compile a list of . . . Korval's . . . necessities.

THEY HEARD HIM OUT—the pilot and the assassin—as he outlined his requirements and his plan. When he had finished, the pilot whistled, long and low.

"So, you're gonna vanish, and build up reserves?"

Pat Rin inclined his head. "In essence."

"It is a bold plan—and difficult," the assassin said in her turn, her slim fingers woven together upon the table. "I wonder, Master, about the necessity of a working spaceport. I wonder—will a primitive port—even, a very primitive port—serve you? You might then shape it to your needs."

He thought about that. A spaceport was necessary—he would need ships; he would need to build, dock, and maintain ships. And yet, spaceports invited the galaxy, and it was equally imperative that he remain beneath the range of Korval's enemy. Until he should reveal himself, at a time and place of his choosing.

"A primitive spaceport has some advantage to us," he told her. "But not so primitive that it may be not be upgraded—quickly."

"I understand." She looked down at her hands, then into his eyes, her own as deep as starless space.

"Let us then posit a world which is primitive in many ways, yet its barbarism allows—opportunity for manipulation. A strong-willed person, capable of conceiving and implementing a plan, might do whatever he wished, eventually." She sighed, which he thought was not like her. "I know of such a world."

Pat Rin glanced at Cheever McFarland, who waved a big hand, indicating that he was attending the conversation, but had nothing to add.

So.

He considered Natesa the Assassin, her quiet hands and unquiet eyes.

"I believe you are not entirely pleased with this world," he said softly. "Why not?"

She moved her shoulders—closer to the fluid and ambiguous Liaden gesture than an honest Terran shrug. "I have—no jurisdiction there," she said, matching him soft for soft. "I—perhaps—have contacts there, tenuous contacts, at best. I know the language, as do you. I know of a . . . relatively secure landing place, so that we need not alert the port to our presence—but jurisdiction?" She met his eyes squarely. "*No one* has jurisdiction there."

"Ah." A world that was alike protected from the so-called Department of the Interior, and the Juntavas—perfect.

Pat Rin inclined his head.

"I believe that is—desirable."

She nodded, as if she had expected no other answer. As perhaps, Pat Rin thought, she had not.

"What's the name of this place?" Cheever asked from his corner of the table.

Natesa turned to look at him. "Why, Surebleak, pilot. Have you heard of it?"

Surprisingly, the big man threw back his head and laughed.

"Oh, I heard of it, OK." He transferred a wide grin to Pat Rin. "She's right, Boss. If there's a world where anything can get lost and never looked for, it's Surebleak."

"Good," Pat Rin said, and inclined his head to both. "Then it is settled."

DAY 50

Standard Year 1393
Dutiful Passage
Lytaxin Orbit

THE SHIFT WAS more than half done. First Mate Ren Zel dea'Judan finished the last report in the queue and leaned back in his chair, reflecting that it was odd that the paperwork of war and the paperwork of trade should be so similar.

Though, he thought, reaching for his cup, to be precise, they were no longer at war, but rather stalled in some halfling state between the usual and the unthinkable, waiting for the gods knew what.

Ren Zel sipped, found the tea tepid, sighed and drank it anyway.

The reports provided by the mercenary forces on the planet below spoke of the "mop up phase" of the on-going military operations, and indicated that the present hostilities between the mercenaries and those Yxtrang soldiers remaining were sporadic and disconnected, ranging over considerable geographic area. Clan Erob's airfield, which had been a point of contention before the Yxtrang warships had abruptly withdrawn from orbit, abandoning thousands of soldiers to their deaths, was secure. What was left of Lytaxin spaceport was also secure.

The captains and mates of the ships now surrounding the *Passage*—officers old in warfare—gave as their expert opinions that it was extremely unlikely that the departed Yxtrang would return with reinforcements to retrieve the soldiers they had left behind.

Ren Zel shuddered, and not because his tea was cold. To be abandoned by one's ship among hostile strangers, the last duty remaining one to die well . . .

It struck too close to the heart, that, and set uneasy memories snarling. To have one's death recorded and made fact before ever one had lain down and—

"Have done!" he told himself sharply and stood.

He wanted tea. Fresh, hot tea, and an end to the nattering of ill memory. He was clanless—dead to kin, outside the laws of Liad. Dead in truth, had Shan yos'Galan not put forth his hand, and declared that he and his crew welcomed pilots of ability and steady will. Here, on *Dutiful Passage*, Ren Zel dea'Judan, deceased of Clan Obrelt, had comrades, and a place, and work—as pilot and, now, as first mate, under Shan yos'Galan's lady lifemate, Priscilla Mendoza. His wealth exceeded, by many orders of magnitude, anything another clanless might hope to achieve—aye, and many who were clanned, as well.

Tea. He moved to the refreshment console—and the comm unit on his desk beeped.

Pilot-quick, he was across the room, finger on the button.

"First Mate."

"Hi there, First Mate," Radio Tech Rusty Morgenstern said brightly. "Got a call on the priority channel for the officer in charge. Want it now?"

Priority channel? "Certainly."

"All yours," Rusty said. There was a click as of a second line being opened, then Rusty's voice again, almost painfully respectful. "Here's Pilot dea'Judan, ma'am—officer on shift."

"Thank you, Mr. Morgenstern," said a cool feminine voice. "Pilot dea'Judan?"

"Yes, ma'am," Ren Zel agreed in his careful Terran. "May I know to whom I have the honor of speaking?"

There was a slight pause, as if the lady were taken aback to find one who did not know her.

"I have the honor," she said, abruptly and icily in the High Tongue, in the mode of announcement, "to be Korval-pernard'i. My personal name is Nova yos'Galan. I will be arriving at Docking Bay Two in one-half hour, Standard. My necessity is to meet with the captain immediately upon my arrival. Am I plain?"

"You are extremely plain, my lady," Ren Zel answered in the mode of oathbound to lord, which was precise, as even the laws of Liad must acknowledge, while disputing his right to speak at all to a living Liaden lady. "Arrangements will be made to welcome you at Bay Two in one-half hour, Standard."

"That is well," said Nova yos'Galan and signed off. Ren Zel frowned.

Nova yos'Galan, first speaker in trust for Clan Korval, was the sister of Shan yos'Galan. He had met the lady once, standing protected and anonymous within the shadow of his captain's melant'i. That same captain who casually brought his sister's reputation a whisper from ruin by introducing Ren Zel, in Terran— "Pilot dea'Judan, sister. Ren Zel, my sister Nova, also a pilot."

Now she came, Korval-pernard'i, riding a double wave of danger, and demanding to see the captain of *Dutiful Passage*. By whom she could only mean her brother, who was . . . no longer aboard.

Ren Zel leaned over the desk and punched in a quick sequence, barely glancing at the keypad. The second remote trill was cut off by the deep, resonate voice of Priscilla Mendoza, who had been first mate before him.

"Mendoza."

"Pray forgive me for disturbing your rest," he said in formal Liaden, scarcely heeding his own speech. "Circumstance requires."

"Appalling circumstance, apparently, to have kicked you back into the High Tongue," said Priscilla in light Terran. "What tragedy has overtaken us, friend?"

Ren Zel smiled slightly and amended his language. "I pray forgiveness," he said carefully. "One has just now closed conversation with a lady of high mode, indeed." He glanced at the clock on the wall beside the refreshment unit. "In precisely twenty-eight minutes, Standard, Nova yos'Galan, Korval-pernard'i, will arrive at Docking Station Two. Her desire is to enjoy an interview with the captain, immediately upon her arrival."

Priscilla said three hard-edged words in a language neither Terran nor Liaden. Ren Zel blinked.

"I beg your pardon," he said, as gently as Terran allowed him.

Her sigh came clearly out of the speaker. "No, I beg your pardon," she said, equally gentle, "for I must send you into peril alone, and for no better reason than I cannot face the upcoming interview with Korval-pernard'i on an empty stomach."

She sighed a second time. "Please do me the favor of meeting Lady Nova at Docking Bay Two and escorting her to my office."

"I?" Ren Zel bit his lip. "Priscilla, I am—"

"Pilot, first mate, and crewman of good standing on this ship," she interrupted. "Lady Nova knows how to value such things."

And he had, after all, Ren Zel reflected wryly, received his orders from his captain. He inclined his head, as if she could see him—and who knew that she could not, dramliza that she was? "I will meet Lady Nova and bring her to you in your office."

"Good," said Priscilla.

His hand moved toward the disconnect—and stopped as she spoke his name.

"Yes?"

"It will not be necessary," she said, "to tell Lady Nova that her brother is not presently aboard."

The ways of the dramliz were mysterious, Ren Zel thought, but the ways of Korval were stranger still. Again, he inclined his head.

"I understand," he said, and the connection light went out.

THE STATUS LIGHT went from red to green, and the hatch slid open, revealing a tall blond woman wearing the leather jacket of a Jump pilot over serviceable dark shirt and trousers. Her face was comely, as he had recalled, and fell easily into a frown, though he had taken care to be in place several minutes beforetime, so that she would find him neither tardy nor breathless.

He bowed, oathbound to lord, which might have waked a question in her mind, had she been less focused upon her own business. As it was, she returned his courtesy with an inclination of the head, and a brief, "Pilot."

"Lady," he murmured, straightening in proper time and keeping his gaze decently averted. "I am sent to bring you to the captain."

"So I surmised," she answered drily, the accent of fabled Solcintra gilding her words. "If the captain has likewise desired you to lead me the long dance, I pray you will allow yourself to be persuaded otherwise. I do know the shortest route, and will have no difficulty escorting myself."

Well, and Captain yos'Galan had been known, upon occasion, to issue such orders to those sent as escort, Ren Zel allowed, and bowed again.

"The captain was off shift," he offered, softly, "and required time to prepare."

"Of course," said Lady Nova and swept a slim hand toward the corridor. Korval's clan ring flared briefly in the light, silver and green. "My business with the captain is urgent."

"Certainly. If your ladyship will accompany me . . ."

ALL HONOR to the lady: She did not insist on the shortest route, through the narrow service corridors. However, the pace she set through the public corridors was swift enough to discourage conversation, which Ren Zel could only feel was to his benefit.

Soon enough, the bright red door of the captain's office came into sight. The lady broke her step, courteously allowing Ren Zel to lay his palm against the plate. The door slid silently open and he preceded the guest across the threshold, as protocol required, saw his captain sitting tall and proud behind the desk and swept a low bow as Nova yos'Galan stepped past him.

"I bring—" he began, and then halted, as Priscilla's voice overrode his, speaking mild Terran.

"Well met, sister. Will you have wine?"

Ren Zel straightened. *Sister*. What came next was between kin. He had no business here. He moved one careful step forward. Both women looked at him, but he kept his eyes on Priscilla's face.

"Captain, shall I take your place on the roster this shift?"

She smiled. "That will not be necessary, first mate. Please, pursue your rest shift."

He bowed—"Captain"—again—"Lady"—and resisted the impulse to back out of the office.

The door slid shut behind the brown-haired pilot. Nova took a deliberate breath, and glared at the woman behind the desk. "So. Sister and captain, is it? Where is my brother?"

"Planetside," Priscilla said in her deep, calm voice, and raised a hand as if she felt Nova's cry of protest rising. "It was an accident, I swear. We had taken damage and he insisted on being part of the repair crew. The enemy attacked and separated him from the ship." She paused, then added, "Seth Johnson gave his life to protect his captain and his ship in that action. I think you knew him."

Nova bowed her head, recalling with the vividness that was her gift and her curse the long, rat-faced Terran pilot. "Who are we, that people die for us? All honor to him."

"All honor to him," Priscilla repeated softly.

Nova looked up. "First mate rises to fill the void in command, when the captain is separated from the ship. It is understood. Now—sister?"

"Shan and I have declared lifemates."

Nova closed her eyes. "With recourse to neither law nor first speaker."

"The clan was scattered; our enemy in pursuit," Priscilla murmured. "I refused to leave the ship to be safe, and he was too wise a captain to order his first mate away."

Nova opened her eyes. "Ah, I understand! A sacrifice upon the altar of duty! How like Shan, to be sure!"

Priscilla threw back her head and laughed. After a moment, Nova sighed and moved forward to take a chair. "I believe I will have a glass of the white, if you please. Sister. And then you may tell me how my brothers fare, planetside."

"Shan," said Priscilla, moving gracefully across the room to the bar. "Fares well. Val Con fares . . . less well." She poured two glasses of white wine and carried them to the desk. She handed Nova a glass and sat again behind the desk, her own glass cradled in long, slender fingers.

Nova's mouth tightened. "How much . . . less well . . . stands my younger brother?"

Priscilla raised her glass and almost laughed again, to catch herself employing one of Shan's delaying tactics.

"Val Con was desperately wounded in the strike that broke the back of the Yxtrang on-world. He remains in the catastrophe unit at Erob's medical facility. The med techs there are divided in their predictions of the final percentage of his disability."

The color drained from Nova's face, leaving it a sticky beige color; her distress slammed across Priscilla's inner senses with the shrill force of a scream.

"Nova—"

Her lifemate's sister raised a slim, golden hand, and turned her face aside. "A moment, of your kindness. Val Con—" Her breath caught. "If he is not able to fly . . ."

If Val Con were not able to fly, Priscilla thought, following Nova's logic effortlessly, then he could not, by Korval's own law, be delm. And Korval needed its delm now as never before, with Plan B in effect, and enemies on all sides.

"Val Con's lifemate is out of the 'doc and by all reports will make a full recovery," she said to Nova's stricken eyes. "She will be able to fly. Korval has its delm."

"Lifemate," Nova repeated flatly, and had recourse to her glass, eyes half-closed.

"Lifemate," Priscilla asserted. "Shan says—lifemates in the fullest sense, shadowing the link that your parents shared."

Nova closed her eyes. "Gods be merciful," she murmured. She had another sip of wine and opened her eyes. "I will be leaving for the planet surface as soon as I have cleared descent with the appropriate commanders," she said, with a forced and brittle calm.

"There are Yxtrang on the planet surface," Priscilla pointed out, though she had very little hope of turning Nova from her course. "You will be placing yourself in peril."

The other woman stared at her for a long moment, violet eyes unreadable.

"I acknowledge the possibility of peril," she said, slowly. "However, the report I have from the mercenaries is that Erob's House is no longer in immediate danger of attack and that the Yxtrang have lost heart. I am Korval-pernard'i. Necessity exists."

And that, Priscilla thought with an inward sigh, *was that.* She knew better than to try to talk any Liaden out of an action that had been found, by some fey balancing of duty, desire, and melant'i, to be "necessary."

"May I ask you a thing," Nova said suddenly, "as captain of this vessel?"

What now? Priscilla wondered, but kept her face and voice serene. "Yes."

"I wonder how you came to name a clanless first mate?"

"Ah." Priscilla leaned back and sipped her own wine, her eyes drawn upward, to the glittery frivolous mobile Anthora yos'Galan had given her brother Shan. "Ren Zel is able; mere hours away from master pilot. He is respected by his shipmates, and—" She brought her eyes down to meet Nova's gaze. "And, he is not . . . entirely . . . clanless. This ship—this crew—are his kin. He will fight to keep both safe, with his last gasp of life."

Nova sat for a moment, then inclined her head. "It is well-reasoned. I thank you." She stood, leaving her empty glass on the corner of Priscilla's desk. "If I may have the use of a comm?"

Priscilla rose. "You may use this one, and welcome," she said. "I am wanted on the bridge."

"Thank you. Sister." She smiled, then, sudden and genuine. "I am glad to be able to say it."

LIAD
Department of Interior
Command Headquarters

❋ ❋

THE BOX WAS approximately five foot square, matte black and, on casual inspection, seamless.

Commander of Agents, completing an inspection that was not at all casual, paused before the door and looked to the hovering technician.

"I would examine the interior."

"Certainly, Commander." The tech removed a cylinder no longer than his forefinger from a pocket and depressed a section of its black surface. There was no sound, but when Commander of Agents again faced the box, it was to discover that one wall had slid away. The interior was very dark. Commander of Agents produced a hand light from his pocket, flicked it on and stepped into the box.

Its interior dimension was somewhat less than the outside led one to expect; the ceiling short enough that Commander of Agents needed to duck his head and round his shoulders. A taller person would not have been able to stand at all, but would need to kneel upon the ungiving metal floor.

"The apparatus," the technician murmured from the doorway, "is enclosed in the floor and the sidewalls. If one braces oneself against a wall, or kneels or lies down on the floor—the lethargic affect is far greater. The test subject has been able to experience the weakening of his abilities, which was not expected, but which may prove useful. In the short term, the perceptible ebb of power has been observed to awaken panic to the verge of hysteria in the test subject."

Commander of Agents played his light around the interior of the box, noting with satisfaction the smooth, nearly featureless metal walls. There were a series of small vents—33 holes altogether, the report had said—on the immovable wall. These were for ventilation, or for the introduction of gasses, as necessary. On the very center of the "ceiling" were several indentations—these the microphone and speakers for communicating with the inmate, or for introducing sounds as might be required. An uncomfortable place, altogether, in the normal way of things, but for those of the dramliz—a torture.

"You lost a subject, I believe?" he said over his shoulder to the technician.

"Commander, we did. The first dramliza understood her circumstance very quickly and was able to raise sufficient power to hurl a fireball at the apparatus beneath the floor."

The Commander's little beam of light danced across the floor, found a black smear rather like a grease stain on the floor nearly at his feet; a similar stain ran half-way down the wall he faced.

"Did the mechanism take harm?"

"Tests immediately after the incident indicated that the apparatus remained fully functional," the technician said. "The material, you see, is highly reflective of that energy utilized by the dramliz. The bolt was thus sent back to the subject from the floor and all the walls, immolating her. An unfortunate loss of an interesting subject. I very much regret the waste."

"There is some waste in all experiments. You have found the second subject less volatile, I understand."

"It was understood that proper testing required that we utilize dramliza of greater rather than lesser ability, and the present subject, like the first, is very strong. He is, however, young; and we hold his cha'leket hostage to his cooperation. Also, I took care to show him the stains you have found, sir, and explain in depth how they came to be there." The technician paused. "There was, of course, some danger that he would attempt to suicide, using this proven means, but he is, as I have said, young, fond of his cha'leket, and inclined to believe in the possibility of rescue."

Hunched, the Commander backed out of the box and flicked off his light. Straightening his cramped shoulders, he looked again to the technician.

"You planted the belief that he might expect a rescue?"

The tech inclined his head. "It seemed the best strategy, given the need to conceal our development from the dramliz."

The Commander took a moment to consider this. Ordinarily, he did not tolerate such innovations from mere technicians. In this case, however, given, as had been said, the need to conserve resources . . . He inclined his head.

"You have done well," he said. The technician bowed profoundly. "I will wish to speak with the subject in"—he glanced as his chronometer—"four hours, Standard. I suggest he spend the time before our meeting in there." He flicked a negligent hand at the box.

The tech bowed again.

"Commander, it shall be done."

LYTAXIN:
Mercenary Encampment

❁ ❁

CLONAK WAS ON the camp, engaging in poker with as disreputable a half-dozen card sharps as Daav had been privileged to behold in at least twenty years. He hoped, though without much optimism, that Clonak would allow them to retain their dignity, if not their pay.

Shadia, sensible woman that she was, had retired immediately after their release from Commander Carmody's dinner party.

Nelirikk—or Beautiful, as Commander Carmody had it—had chosen to remain with the fearsome duo he referred to, with no irony that Daav could detect, as "the recruits". The Rifle—one Diglon— appeared of a phlegmatic nature and would very likely follow Shadia's sensible schedule. However, the winsome and biddable Hazenthull had been another kindle of kittens entirely. She had been most displeased to find that she was not to be allowed to sit sentinel by the autodoc enclosing—and gods have mercy, healing—her senior, and had only reluctantly accompanied Nelirikk and Diglon to quarters.

Which left Daav, wide awake and content to be alone, sitting cross-legged on the bench by the 'doc containing the wounded explorer, eyes closed against the darkness.

It was at times like this that he could feel her sitting next to him, her knee companionably pressing his; her silence sanctifying his disinclination to talk. Aelliana, his lifemate. Dead these last twenty-five Standard years.

Daav sighed in the dark, and felt Aelliana lay her hand, comfortingly, on his thigh.

It came to him that he was as much a ghost as she: his brother was dead, and his brother's lifemate. Who of Clan Korval would remember Daav yos'Phelium, so long absent from kin and hearth? Certainly not the so-formidable son referred to, by explorer and mercenary commander alike, as "the scout"—as if there were only one in all the galaxy. The small boy he had given, weeping, into the care of his cha'leket had in some way become a man revered as a lesser god by the Yxtrang soldier he had bested in single combat; lifemate of a red-haired rakehell no less beloved of Jason Carmody.

"What may we bring to these feral children, our kin?" he murmured into the darkness.

"Why a working Rifle," Aelliana answered, her voice warm inside the whorlings of his ears, "and a brace of explorers. It seems a gift they will know how to value."

Daav smiled and resisted the temptation to pat the hand that could not be touching him. "Why, so it does. And how fortuitous to have met them upon the road, to be sure."

Aelliana laughed softly and it was all he could do, not to open his eyes and turn to look at her. Instead, he smiled for her, and sighed, just a little.

"Commander Carmody has promised to send a message to our son's lady, desiring her to visit at her earliest convenience," he said. "Perhaps we may meet her soon."

"Will she accept the Yxtrang, do you think?" asked Aelliana.

Daav sighed again. "Commander Carmody thinks it. . . . possible. And we see that she has allowed our son to persuade her to one Yxtrang already . . ."

"Singularly persuasive, this scout of yours," she teased him.

"You will hardly blame him whole cloth upon me," he said, with mock severity. "Not only did I find you an enthusiastic participant during construction, but saw you thoroughly besotted with the result."

"You, of course, never named him 'Little Dragon', nor recited nonsense verses for hours on end to lull him to sleep."

"A man of my honors and position? I should think not."

"False, oh false, van'chela! A man of your dignity, indeed."

"Oh, and now I have no dignity?" He forgot himself and spoke aloud, rousing the tech on duty.

"Everything OK over there?" she called.

"Yes—" Daav began, opening his eyes, and then came to his feet, staring at the 'doc, which ought to be—which had been—aglow with readouts, and status lights.

"Something's wrong," he called to the tech.

She ran to his side, took one look at the somber 'doc and shook her head with a sigh.

"Nothing wrong," she said. "He's just dead, is all."

Things that Go Bump in the Night

THE HOUSE LAY shrouded in pre-dawn, its rooms at rest. Abovestairs, a woman slept uneasily in a bed beneath a silvering skylight, her hair a dark wing across the pillows. A gray cat, his pre-dawn nap disrupted by the lady's restive habit, sat at the foot of the bed, meticulously washing his whiskers.

"Necessity," the woman said clearly, her voice full of unshed tears. The cat paused in his ablutions, paw poised by cheek, ears ticked forward, as if reserving judgment on the truth of her assertion until he had heard the whole.

"Necessity, captain," Anthora yos'Galan moaned, twisting beneath the knotted blankets. She gasped and abruptly sat up, silver eyes wide, staring toward the cat, but seeing something entirely else.

"Yxtrang," she gasped. "Suicide craft. Gods, oh gods—the *Passage* . . ." She blinked, eyes focusing at last on the cat, who met her gaze, looked away, and completed the suspended pass at his whiskers.

Anthora threw back the blankets and swung to the floor, the ribbons of her bed shirt fluttering with the speed of her movements.

Barefoot, she went across the room, snatched up a white silk robe and shrugged it on, knotting the sash as she moved.

"Lord Merlin," she called as she passed from the room.

The cat shook out his paw, jumped to the floor and followed.

HE HAD BARELY closed his eyes when the battle-dream formed, horrific as ever, shaking him out of slumber, as it did every third or fourth sleep shift. Lina, the ship's Healer, assured him that the memory would fade in time and leave him in peace. Until that time, however, Ren Zel was left to devise his own strategies for outwitting the demon and gaining his rest.

With the room lights cycled to their brightest, he pulled a bound book of Terran poetry from the cache next to his bed.

The volume was a collection of lyrical poetry on the theme of sensual delight; a gift from one Selain Gudder, with whom he had enjoyed a liaison of pleasure three trade trips back. He smiled with remembered fondness and, opening the book at random, soon lost himself in the rich, evocative language.

Eventually, lulled by images at once alien and comfortable, he caught himself nodding and waved a hand to extinguish the light.

He fell immediately into sleep. At once his sleeve was snatched by—well, he was not precisely certain who, save that the touch and the voice seemed—familiar—and whose evident distress had root in the same horrific incident which haunted his own sleep.

"Peace, peace," he soothed her, for she was crew—she must be crew, mustn't she, who had such a memory upon her? It was no less than his duty as first mate to ease her.

"Peace," he said a third time, as she thrust the dream forward, shrilling a warning of disaster to come.

That brought him up for a moment, then he saw that she must be caught yet in the throes of the thing, where past and present were as one.

"We are beyond it," he told her, in the mode of Comrade. "We are safe. The battle is over. The war is ending. All is well." He extended a hand and touched her shoulder, lightly, as a comrade might. "Sleep now; you have no cause for worry." And with gentle firmness, he pushed her away.

He half-woke, then, sighed, and subsided into dreamlessness, the book slipping from his fingers to the floor. A few hours later, he drifted toward wakefulness once more, roused enough to feel the cat kneading his chest. Drowsily, he raised a hand and stroked the creature, feeling the plush fur warm against his palm, and the vibration of a purr—his eyes sprang open in shock.

"*Cat?*"

The room lights came up at the sound of his voice. There was no cat on his chest; no cat glaring at him reproachfully from the floor, or the comm shelf or the desk. There was, however, a long white whisker caught in the weave of the coverlet. Ren Zel worked it loose and stared at it for several heartbeats before throwing back the covers and swinging out of bed.

There was no cat under the bunk. There was no cat in the 'fresher. Truly, his cabin was catless. As it should be.

And yet . . .

He held the whisker up to the light, admiring its length and its sturdiness, then went over to his locker. A moment's rummage produced a thin glass sampling vial—another reminder of Selain—with a re-sealing top. The whisker slipped easily into the vial. He resealed it with care and glanced ruefully at the clock.

Two hours 'til the start of his shift; too late to court sleep a third time. Well, then, a shower and an early start, he thought philosophically, moving toward the 'fresher.

He showered longer than was usual for him, invoking the cold, needling cycle twice, but the cat whisker was still in its vial when he emerged.

THE SONG WAS EVERYWHERE; it filled the room, the planet, the infinite cup of space itself. At once a single note and wholly aside the song, Shan observed the bold, improbable and eminently *correct* pattern that was Val Con yos'Phelium.

In the course of the Healing, they had come across other leavings of the interloper responsible for the insertion of the calculation program. When they did, Shan had reached forth his will and made the interloper subservient to the greater pattern of his brother. Now, as the song rested within itself, he inspected the work, tested the bindings and the connections, observed the brilliant shine of integration, and was satisfied.

Shifting his regard, he considered the arc of living power flowing in unending waves of iridescence to and from the guarded center of the pattern, where Val Con kept his soul—and found it beyond anything he had ever before observed.

The thing is done, he decided; and it is good.

Gently, he brought his attention to the song, signaling completion. The note stretched, altered, quickened, and stopped.

Shan shook his head and blinked his eyes, focusing first on Val Con, covered with a thin blanket and deeply asleep, and then across and up, into the luminous eyes of the enormously old being called Edger.

"It is done," he said, feeling his voice rasp in a dry throat.

"It is done," Edger returned, and lifted a three-fingered hand in what seemed a salute. "And done well. All honor to you, Shan yos'Galan." He blinked. "Our brother sleeps now and will wake when the time is appropriate. We two should likewise seek our beds."

"That," Shan said, abruptly aware of aching back and the grate of exhaustion immediately behind his eyes, "is a wonderful idea." He hesitated, glancing at the figure asleep upon the gurney. "Should we—?"

"I believe we may leave him here in all safety," Edger boomed, moving toward the door. Shan hesitated a moment before bending and kissing his brother on the cheek.

"Sleep well, denubia," he murmured, and followed the turtle down the room.

ONCE, IN A TEASING MOMENT, Anthora had asked her brother Val Con how scouts were able to persuade savage persons to divulge sometimes quite secret information about their world and culture, all without being ritually murdered and eaten.

"Oh, there's nothing to that," Val Con had assured her, green eyes dancing. "It's only a matter of asking the right questions."

She had laughed then, as she had been meant to do. And it had only come to her slowly, over a course of years, just how often success in any endeavor hinged upon asking the right questions. Even when one was a dramliza at the height of her not-inconsiderable powers.

Especially when one was dramliza.

Now, as she sped along the path to the garden's center, horrific visions of the *Passage* beset by countless numbers of mine-bearing Yxtrang in tiny craft, she berated herself for her stupidity. Every evening since she had removed to Jelaza Kazone, just before retiring, she had gone out to the heart of the garden. Leaning thus cosily against the Tree, she had, bumblebrained, asked the question, "Are those most dear to my heart alive?" and flung her mind out into the void.

Every evening, she counted the fragile, brilliant flames of her kin, and was thereby comforted.

And never once had it occurred to her to ask who—if any—reposed in danger, who was their enemy and if there were any means known to the dramliz, or hidden in her own untapped talents, to aid them.

Of course, it was true that they all reposed in danger, with Plan B in effect. To Anthora's mind, however, there was danger and there was *danger*, into which latter category attacks by armed and desperate Yxtrang plainly fell.

The stone pathway ended at a glade dimly illuminated by the night-blooming friatha. Anthora did not slacken her pace, but sped across grass that chilled her feet and soaked the hem of her robe, straight to the faintly phosphorescent enormity of the Tree. She lay her hand against the warm bark.

"Good morning, Elder," she said, though she hardly needed to speak aloud. "I'm an idiot."

Above her head, leaves rustled in a light chuckle, though the air elsewhere in the glade was still. Anthora sighed.

"Yes, all very well. But the *Passage* will be—or perhaps already has been!—under attack by an Yxtrang force. I must warn them, or—" She broke off, biting her lip. What if the attack were past? If the *Passage* was already an Yxtrang war prize; Shan—and his Priscilla, too—dead or dying of unspeakable tortures?

She felt a soft, reassuring pressure against her shin and glanced down, finding Merlin in the shadows at her feet. She looked up into the dark, attentive leaves.

"I must warn them," she said again to the Tree. The leaves directly over her head were still, though there was a commotion higher up, as if a squirrel had thrown a small stone forcefully groundward. Anthora stepped back and a seedpod struck the turf by her right foot.

"Thank you," she murmured, warmed. Bending, she gathered up the gift, skritched Merlin's ear and straightened. She cracked open the nut and ate the kernel, savoring the minty taste. Then, she set her back firmly against the trunk of the Tree, closed her eyes, and brought before her Inner Eye the construct of emotion, intelligence, and power that was uniquely in this galaxy known as Priscilla Delacroix y Mendoza. Priscilla was a Witch, with talents and abilities uncannily close to those Anthora held, as one of Liad's few remaining wizards. If any on the *Passage* had the ears to hear her message, Anthora thought, it would be Priscilla.

Thought was swept away in the tide that drew her from herself into timelessness. Light flickered in tongues like flame, and there was wind, upon which souls strange and unsought swirled like so many alien leaves. Within the maelstrom, Priscilla's pattern flared, brilliant.

Anthora exerted control—but, instead of making the expected contact, she hurtled past her target, tumbling out of control—no. Control was there, abrupt and rather startled, as if she had someway stumbled and landed in the arms of a stranger, who now took care to set her gently upon her own feet. Puzzlement emanated from the one who had caught her; puzzlement and a dim, sweaty horror, doubtless the residue of an ill dream.

Anthora snatched at that hint, trapped it, wove it to her own dream—and even as she wove saw it shaken into another image entirely, accompanied by a brief, warm touch of comfort.

Contact was broken then, and not by her will. Blackness swirled, thick and comforting as a favorite blanket.

Anthora sighed, opened her eyes and discovered herself all a-tangle at the base of the Tree, her head resting on a moss-covered root, and Merlin staring down into her face.

Painfully, she sorted her limbs into seemliness and sat up, her back against the Tree. Across the glade, sunlight touched the bank of night-bloomers, which were folded tight in daytime slumber.

She had been asleep, Anthora thought in disbelief. Asleep for *hours.*

Beside her, Merlin settled, chicken-fashion, atop the moss-covered root, his eyes slitted in satisfaction.

Anthora let her head fall back against the Tree and spoke aloud, her voice breathless.

"It was not a foretelling—it was a memory. I don't know who—held like a babe!" She bit her lip, hard, curbing her baffled indignation. To be held like the merest novice, and then dismissed—*put to sleep*—as if her will were nothing—

"The battle is over," she continued, more or less calmly. "The enemy has been vanquished. The *Passage* is safe, and I—" Her voice broke here and not even she was certain if the cause was hysteria or fury—"I am not to *worry!*"

LYTAXIN:
Mercenary Encampment

◉ ◉

THEY WERE GRANTED quarters by Commander Carmody; good quarters, with a shower in one corner and a corporal before the door.

Nelirikk, who knew the order of the Gyrfalks and how the soldiers were distributed in camp, understood that they were well-contained, surrounded by watchers, in case there should be trouble.

He did not anticipate trouble, himself. Less so, after watching the gusto with which the recruits wolfed the sandwiches sent from the mess tent—explorer no less ravenous than Rifle.

It was, largely, a silent meal. After, the recruits made use of the shower, brushed out and put on their battle leathers.

Clean and fed, Diglon Rifle sat unconcernedly on the floor, his back against a cot, and rolled out his kit, preparatory to stripping and cleaning his weapon. Nelirikk approved—it was a common soldier's duty to care for his weapons, as much among Terrans as among the Troop. More, the familiar task would soothe the Rifle, who must know as well as Nelirikk did that he was a single soldier, surrounded on all sides by those not of his troop, who had no reason to trust him.

No, thought Nelirikk, sitting on his own bunk, a piece of fancy-work in his hands, the Rifle was not his most pressing problem. His problem was Hazenthull Explorer.

She had argued against Daav yos'Phelium's order that she bunk with her troop, leaving her senior alone and vulnerable, in the care of those who had been their enemies. It spoke much for the abilities of the scout's father, that he had been able to enforce his will and see his order carried out, however reluctantly, while raising neither his hand nor his voice.

Now, denying herself the simple solace of caring for her weapons—or even of sleep, though he could read exhaustion in the muscles of her face—Hazenthull Explorer, dressed and ready for combat, prowled the quarters from end to end and corner to corner.

On her third circuit Diglon Rifle looked up from his task, tension growing. "Explorer?" he said, respectful and soldierly. "Duty?"

Hazenthull checked.

Head bent above his work, watching from the side of his eye, Nelirikk saw her understand the danger. Surrounded by those who had defeated them in battle, oathbound to a Liaden, soon to offer oath to another—it was unthinkable that these things be so. And yet, incredibly, they were so. It was the duty of command to accept these impossibilities as commonplace, with no breath of unease. For the good of the troop—large or small.

So. "At ease, Rifle," she said, firmly, but not too firmly.

Comforted, he saluted, and returned to his weapon.

From the corner of his eye, Nelirikk saw the explorer take a breath, turn cleanly on her heel and walk down the room, to where he sat, setting careful stitches in the gift he was making for Alys Tiazan.

For seven or eight heartbeats, she stood over him. Nelirikk continued his work without looking up. At last, she moved sound-lessly back, folded her legs and sat on the floor before him. He raised his head and met her eyes.

Surrounded by the tattoos describing her honors and accomplishments, her eyes were dark brown; the shade, Nelirikk thought, of his captain's favorite beverage. She jerked her chin at his hands.

"What work?" she demanded, in the tongue of the Troop.

Nelirikk smoothed it on his knee before holding it up for her to see. Her eyes widened as she recognized the device he was working into the patch—the device of the troop that had broken the back of the Fourteenth Conquest Corps.

"There is a young soldier in the House of the captain," he said, also in the Troop tongue, "who is worthy of this."

Hazenthull's mouth thinned. "Soldier."

Nelirikk returned to his work, plying the needle with care. "As much as I am. Or you are." He glanced up, switching to the dialect of explorers, in consideration of Diglon Rifle's comfort. "Why do explorers march with common troop?"

Her eyes shifted. "Command had left planet. We fell in—"

Nelirikk tied off the green thread. "I meant," he said, interrupting her ruthlessly, "why were explorers fighting alongside common troop?"

She glared at him. "That is for the senior to tell."

As chain of command went, she was correct, Nelirikk allowed, threading his needle with crimson. It was . . . useful . . . that soldierly behavior made it impossible for Hazenthull to answer a question she would rather not; explorers not being always at one with soldierly behavior. Still, Nelirikk did not begrudge her the stratagem.

Needle at the ready, he glanced up.

"The captain will require things. Things that run counter to the order you know." He moved his head, a short jerk toward the busy Rifle. "Far out of the order that one knows."

Hazenthull sighed. "She will take us out of context," she said, sounding as weary as she looked. "She is fortunate. Half her work has been done for her."

For what context was there, Nelirikk thought, for being abandoned to the enemy—the *victorious* enemy—while Command ran to save itself? He bent a moment to his work, concentrating on keeping his stitches small and even.

"The captain will require that the *vingtai* be erased." He raised his head again, giving her a plain sight of his naked face. "As you see. The healing units have an erasure program." He stopped short of telling her that the procedure was painless, though that was the truth as he knew it. Acquiring *vingtai* was excruciating; it seemed somehow wrong that they could be effortlessly and painlessly wiped away during the course of one brief sleep inside the healing unit.

"The captain requires this because her troop is the enemy of Yxtrang," Hazenthull said slowly, working out the process of Command's thought, as explorers were taught to do. "Soldiers who think they are Yxtrang, who wear the rank marks and hold the traditions of the Troop, will not fight strongly against Yxtrang." She frowned.

"Explorers can backtrack the captain's thought and understand the requirement. But, he—" she cocked her head toward her Troop—"he is only a Rifle. He will not understand."

"You are second in command," Nelirikk told her ruthlessly. "It is your duty—or the duty of your senior, if he is able—to make him understand. I suggest that the best strategy is to lead by example." He saw her draw a sharp breath, but did not allow her to speak.

"Captain Miri Robertson does not accept mediocrity. She expects superior performance. Occasionally, she demands more. You will adapt—"

"Or die," Hazenthull snarled, as if it were a challenge, and not a truth they both knew in their bones.

"Or die," Nelirikk repeated, calmly.

Hazenthull looked down, possibly at her hands, folded tightly together on her knee.

"The senior . . ." she began, and paused, throat working. "Protocol linked us, junior and senior—you know how it is done. Before it did, he had been twice across the sea of stars, marking many worlds for the future conquest of the Troop."

"He brought much glory to the Troop," Nelirikk said, when he had set an entire row of stitches and she had not spoken again.

"Much glory . . ." she repeated. "I am junior to him in all ways—in glory, in knowledge, in understanding. When the order came down that we should accompany the Fourteenth as . . . when we had the order, he first sharpened his grace blade, and had me sharpen mine, and while we sat together over this task that we hold in common with all soldiers, from creche to command, he talked to me of battle. He said that a soldier must always be prepared to die, that—that duty demanded that the death not be wasted, but served the living good of the Troop." Another silence, not as long as the first, then a rapid burst of words.

"The senior—that he has not received the Starburst—regardless, he is a Hero. To allow him to . . . just die, when Command had betrayed us, would be to go against everything he had taught me. It is not to the good of the Troop that such a soldier die, uselessly and in defeat, when there is so much more . . ."

From outside the door came the sound of the corporal's voice, issuing challenge.

"Scout Captain Daav yos'Phelium," came the reply.

Hazenthull came to her feet, face toward the door, muscles betraying eagerness. Nelirikk put his work aside and had also risen by the time the scout's father entered.

His face was bland; his muscles betraying nothing more than a reasonable alertness, yet Nelirikk felt compelled of a sudden to move within restraining distance of Hazenthull Explorer.

The scout paused, and looked up into Hazenthull's face, his hands folded together at belt level.

"I'm sorry, child," he said, in Terran. "He's dead."

DAY 307

❀❀❀❀❀❀❀❀❀❀❀❀❀❀❀❀❀❀❀❀❀❀❀❀❀❀

Standard 1392
Blair Road
Surebleak

IT WAS INSURANCE DAY in Boss Moran's streets, and Jim
Snyder, the boss' new second-hand man, made it a point to hit the
pavement early, collar turned up against the cold morning wind.
He'd been third-hand man last Insurance Day and while the events
of that day had resulted in Jim's elevation, he was determined to
learn from the downfall of his predecessor.

And what he had learned, first and above everything, was that
the boss expected Insurance Day to go easy and smooth, no problems,
no short-pays, and no excuses.

Bosses in general were a touchy breed, which only made sense,
when you thought about it. Bosses had all the responsibility of
keeping order on their turf, collecting the insurance, putting the
bouncers on the borders, setting the tolls—*and* seeing that collected
tolls was turned in—it was a job of work being a boss, no argument
there, and anybody took it on, in Jim's opinion, had a right to be a
touch irritable.

It could be that Boss Moran was a thought touchier than most.

Jim couldn't precisely say: he'd been just a tad when Boss Tourin owned these streets, and Boss Randall hadn't lasted long enough to make much of an impression. Boss Vindal had held on couple, four years—Jim'd run a toll-booth under Boss Vindal. It hadn't been bad; he couldn't off-hand remember her shooting anybody for shorting on the tolls. But, push come to shove, maybe she hadn't been such a good boss, 'cause when the smoke cleared off their meeting, it was Boss Moran standing and the late Boss Vindal being carted off to the crematory.

Sometimes, all the fatcats would meet on neutral ground and rework the boundaries, trading around this business street for that manufacturing block. It was important to have a strong boss protecting your interests when that happened—even though it hadn't happened lately. Give her a couple beers and Jim's Aunt Carla could tell stories that would raise your hair right straight up on your head, about the days when *she'd* been just a tad and lived on Boss Henrick's turf. That was before the fatcats had one of their meetings. Boss Tourin had got made at that meeting, and everything from Blair Road over to Carney—part territories from Boss Henrick and Boss Tiede—got swopped out and called his turf. There'd been a period of shakedown, and one of the bosses—Aunt Carla switched between Henrick and Tiede when she told it, depending on how much beer she'd had—got to thinking he'd been cheated when he sat down after the meeting to do the math. Lot of guns on the streets back then, as Aunt Carla had it, and the crematory'd done real well.

But they didn't have them kind of problems no more. Not on these streets. Boss Moran had held the turf for going on three years and if he occasionally shot his second-hand for a minor screw-up in addition, or made a public example of some shopkeeper who'd got behind on his insurance payment—well, that showed he was a strong boss. And you needed a strong boss to protect your interests, else some other boss would make a move on the turf—and there wasn't no percentage for anybody in that.

First stop on the morning was Wilmet's grocery. Jim opened the door with a shove, and the bell hung on the wire overtop clanged in protest. Old Wilmet came hurrying out from the back, and stood twisting his fingers together while Jim made a leisurely circuit of the place, on the spy for any improvements to the premises, or new equipment. He helped himself to a pretty good apple, and kept on inspecting, til he'd eaten all the fruit except the brown spots. He dropped the core to the floor and nodded at Wilmet like he'd just noticed him.

"Insurance day," he said, hooking his hands in his belt. He saw the other man's eyes dart down, following the motion, saw him look real hard at the gun on Jim's belt, before he looked up and nodded, quick and sort of jerky.

"So it is," he said, and his voice sounded a little jerky, too, Jim thought. That was good. It was important that the streeters kept a healthy respect for the boss—and for the boss' 'hands.

Making a show about it—stretching it out just a little—Jim reached into his pocket and pulled out the Book. The grocer was looking a little grey around the mouth. Jim licked his finger and leisurely leafed through to the right page. It took him a couple minutes to review the payment schedule—Jim could read, but it wasn't a strong point—nodded, and looked up. The grocer was sweating now. Jim let himself smile on one side of his mouth, like the boss did when he wanted to make you squirm. Useful tactic; and Jim knew personally that it worked a treat.

"So," he said to Wilmet. "'at's twelve, cash, this month, and the boss'll have the rest in chocolate, sugar, 'toot, and pot meat. Case lots—you know the play."

The grocer's face was so gray now that Jim kind of wondered if the man was going to pass out. He did pull a stained rag out of his pocket and mop his forehead with it.

"Twelve cash, sure, yeah. Just a sec." He scurried into the back. Jim helped himself to another apple, not as good as the first one, but the best he could find in the basket.

Wilmet was back, bills clutched in his hand, and counted them out, one through twelve, right there between the carrots and the potatoes.

"The kid'll take the goods to the boss' house," he said, looking down at his money. "Everything delivered before lunch, Mr. Snyder."

Jim nodded, dropped the unfinished apple to the floor, fished the pencil out of his other pocket, and made a tick-mark on Wilmet's page. Then, he put the book and the pencil away, picked up the cash and stowed it in the folder the boss had given him, slid that away, gave the trembling grocer a cheery nod.

"You're covered 'til next month, Wilmet. Profit to the boss."

"Profit to the boss," the man repeated, at a whisper.

Jim grinned and strolled out, slamming the door so hard the bell tore off its wire.

By mid-morning, Jim had called on and collected from all the streeters listed in the Book, except for the hardware store, which he'd deliberately left 'til last because it was just a couple doors up from Tobi's, where he figured he'd grab a bite and a brew before taking the day's receipts back to the boss.

In no real hurry, feeling kind of warm and peaceful in the pit of his belly, Jim strolled 'round the corner, heading on down to the hardware store.

Something bright and colorful pulled at the edge of his vision and he glanced across the street, expecting to see maybe one of Audrey's Scarlet Beauties, out on an early job.

What he did see rooted his feet to the ground and left him staring.

It was—a store. Jim guessed it was a store. But it was like no other store he'd seen in his life. The big front window was not only unshuttered, it was clean, so you could see right into the brightly lit insides, and count—one, three, eight, nine, *twelve* rugs, some hanging around the walls, some laying down on the scrubbed plastic floor. Rugs in colors Jim had no name for. Rugs woven in patterns so complex his eyes crossed trying to look at them.

As if that big, bright, risky window wasn't enough, the door to the joint stood wide open and a thin little rug showing vines and flowers in dark red, bright blue and yellow was laying half on the store's floor and half on the crumbling walkway, where anybody who went into the store would walk on it. Standing just inside the doorway was a man Jim might have mistaken for one of Audrey's, if he'd seen him maybe at Tobi's: Darkhaired and on the short side, almost girl-slender, he was dressed in a pretty blue jacket, with a gleaming white shirt under it. His britches were a darker blue than his jacket and fell smoothly to the break of his shiny black boots. He was standing with his hands behind his back, gazing out at the street as if the view of the crumbling tarmac and shuttered, dusty storefronts was—interesting.

Looking at him, Jim found himself counting backwards, trying to remember exactly when he'd changed his shirt last.

As if he'd felt the incredulous weight of the stare on him, the little man looked up, meeting Jim's eyes across the street. Jim clamped his jaw and glared, so the guy would know he was lookin' at somebody important on the turf.

The little man—he sort of bowed, inclining from the waist an inch or two, then turned and walked into his store.

His impossible store.

"How the sleet long has *that* been there?" Jim demanded of Al, the hardware guy, a couple minutes later, jerking his thumb over his shoulder in the general direction of the rug store.

Al shrugged. "Couple days."

"Couple *days*?" Jim boggled, remembering the storefront as he had last seen it—empty, 'course, its previous occupant having been a streeter Boss Moran had used as a public example, three, maybe four Insurance Days ago. As third-hand man, Jim had been in charge of the clean-up crew that stripped the joint—shoe store, it had been. He remembered, now. He glowered at Al, trying to regain some of the vanished feeling of warm accomplishment.

Al shrugged again, and looked up at the ceiling, like maybe the date the rug store had opened was written on one of blackened beams above Jim's head.

"Yeah, let's see. Day before yesterday, him and the big guy come in right while I was opening. Needed board, hammers, nails, paint, brooms, soap, buckets, wet mops, cleaning cloths, heavy gauge wire—didn't I have a time digging that out!—and a buncha eye-hole bolts. Talked soft, paid cash. Went back over there and started in. Looked out around lunchtime and they had the shutters off the window and he was out there with a wet mop an' a bucket of soapy water, scrubbin' away. Heard some hammerin' from inside and saw a couple of the extras in and out—guess he had 'em runnin' errands for him. Anyhow, they was still at it when I locked up. And when I come in yesterday morning—well, there it was, just like you see it now, and the big guy, he was out front sweeping the sidewalk."

Sweeping the sidewalk. Jim closed his eyes.

Now, strictly speaking, the situation was out of his hands, the rug store not being notated down in the Insurance Book. Jim having come up through Toll, instead of Insurance, he'd never even seen a store set up, much less done it himself. But one of the couple hundred things that Boss Moran didn't have no patience with was 'hands who were light on *initiative*. Set a high price on initiative, did Boss Moran, and as Jim was as eager to show well to the Boss as he was to *not* follow the previous second-hand man to his final ash-pile, he considered that he had no choice but to cross the street after he had concluded his business with Al, and demonstrate to the fancy little man in his pretty blue jacket just *who* was a big dog on the turf.

So thinking, he pulled out the Book and read off Al's premium—fifty, cash, and nothing in goods. Al pulled the bills outta his drawer and paid without comment.

Jim made the tick-mark in the Book, folded it and the pencil and the money away, turned—and turned back.

"So, what's his name?" he asked.

Al shrugged for the third time on the visit, trying for deadpan, but Jim thought he saw the man smile.

"The big guy calls him 'boss'," he said.

The bright-lit showroom was empty when Jim swaggered in through the open door a couple minutes later. He had just enough time to figure out that the big rug hanging on the back wall showed a bunch of naked people, doing things to each other that Jim felt pretty confident even Audrey's Specials hadn't mastered, when it was pushed aside, revealing a doorway, and the pretty man, entering the main room with a slight smile on his face.

"Good-morning, sir!" he said, and his voice was soft, like Al'd said it was, but clear, for all of that, and not at all jerky. "Doubtless you have come to take advantage of our grand opening sale."

Jim stared at him hard, and hooked his hand in his belt near the gun. The man glanced at the gun, but didn't seem exactly bothered, which a man who was naked—that is, who wasn't carrying—really oughta been. Up close, his blue jacket showed a nubbiness that Jim vaguely associated with silk, having seen a silk pillow upstairs at Audrey's, once. The shirt beneath was white enough to hurt a man's eyes, and he was wearing a blue stone in one ear—it matched the color of his jacket.

"In what way may I serve you?" he asked, and there was something funny about the way he talked. Not that he was hard to understand, or anything like that, but there was smooth kind of feel to the way he said the words, like he'd carefully polished each one and taken all the burrs and sharp edges off.

Jim frowned and did his best to harden his glare.

"It's Insurance Day," he said. "You owe Boss Moran for the month."

The man inclined his head, gravely courteous. "Thank you, but I have my own insurance." He moved a hand that glittered from the big ring on his second finger, showing Jim the cluster-fuck rug. "I see that you have some admiration for this specimen, here. Now, this is a very interesting carpet, of a type not normally found beyond the world of its weaving."

Following him to the back wall, Jim stared up at the frolicking people. "Why not?" he asked.

"Ah, because they are done as penance, you see. The weaving of the carpet is imposed by temple upon adjudged sinners, who are required to weave in an open square, where all may see them and know their shame. After the carpet is completed—and a value affixed to it by the temple—the penitent is required to purchase it and display it in the public room of their home for the rest of their life. So, you see how rare it is to come across one of these. Look!" He lifted the edge of the rug, and turned it over to display the underside.

"See these knots? One hundred twenty to the inch! Truly, sir, this is a carpet that will give you many years of enjoyment." He flipped the edge right-side-up and ran his fingertips over the projecting backside of an amazingly curvaceous lady.

"Feel this nap. Imagine walking barefoot on this carpet."

Jim extended a hand—and jerked it back, pulling his glare on, big-time.

"I ain't here to buy no rugs. This is Insurance Day. You're on Boss Moran's turf and you owe on the month."

"No, no, please," the little man said, rubbing his fingertips over the lady's bottom once more before looking up at Jim. "Put yourself at ease on that account, sir. My insurance is entirely adequate." He moved a hand, drawing Jim's eye to the corner of the room. Jim looked—and blinked.

He thought he knew every pro gun in the surrounding three territories, but she wasn't nobody he'd ever seen before. Not all that much taller than the guy, she was slim, except for some really interesting curves, her skin dusky and soft-looking. She wore a dark vest, dark shirt and dark trousers. A pistol with silver-chased grips showed in the holster on her belt—and she stared at him outta black eyes as cold and as pitiless as a dead winter night.

It took some effort to look away from those eyes and back to the guy, but Jim managed it.

"Boss Moran don't let nobody else sell Insurance on his turf."

The man inclined his head. "I understand. There is no difficulty. This lady is in my employ."

What that had to do with the way business was done, Jim couldn't have said. He was beginning to think maybe the little guy was a couple snowflakes short of a blizzard. Not that it mattered. Insurance was Insurance, and it had to be paid, every first of the month. That was how business was done under Boss Moran, no exceptions, no problems, no short-pays, and no excuses. Unless somebody had an ambition to be made a public example of.

Any case, the situation was outta Jim's hands. He'd tried—even the boss would have to admit that—and done as much good as anybody could, trying to reason with a nut-case. It was up to the boss to decide what to do with the little guy now.

Jim frowned regally down at him. "I'll be reporting to Boss Moran right after I leave here," he said. "You got a present or something you wanna send along?"

A good present—say, something along the lines of that amazing rug on the back wall—might actually help keep the boss' temper down to a non-life-threatening level. Which you'd think even a nut-case could figure out.

Not this one, though. He wriggled his shoulders under his pretty blue jacket and murmured.

"Alas, I have nothing that would be . . . appropriate, I think."

Jim shook his head.

"OK," he said, ominously. "If that's how you wanna play it, it ain't no skin off my butt."

It struck him that this was a pretty good exit line, so he did, stamping hard on the little rug in the doorway. Once on the sidewalk, he turned right, toward the boss' place, rather than going down to Tobi's for lunch, like he'd planned.

Somehow, he wasn't real hungry.

From behind him came a sound remarkably like a hiss. Pat Rin turned and looked at Natesa, both eyebrows up in inquiry.

She shook her head, black eyes snapping.

"There was no need to provoke him."

"No? But, as I understand it, our whole mission here is one of provocation, with violence as the pay-off."

That Natesa knew this, he had no doubt. They had planned as best as they were able, choosing the victim and the turf with care. For Pat Rin to succeed—for his Balance to succeed—he must establish himself as a power—a "fatcat"—and the territory he annexed must be on the Port Road.

There were two paths by which one might arrive at the pinnacle of fatcat. One might, for instance, perform a service for an existing boss which required territory and status to balance it. This was a potentially bloodless path, but time-consuming.

Natesa herself had argued, persuasively, for the quicker way— elevation by assassination. This was the traditional path, and one of the primary sources of Surebleak's multitude of ills. Cheever McFarland had offered it as his opinion that the sooner Pat Rin established himself, the quicker the real job could get done, which had also been persuasive—and so Pat Rin had allowed himself to be persuaded.

Now, however, the Juntava appeared to be having second thoughts. Pat Rin spread his hands, averting his gaze from the false glitter on his left hand.

"We will shortly have callers, if all goes according to plan," he said, softly. "We have provoked, wisely or no, following the plan— wisely or no. If you have found a flaw in my intentions, now is the time to speak."

For a moment, Natesa stood silent, her eyes on his face. Then, she bowed in the mode of student to master.

"I would ask that you not expose yourself," she said, slipping into High Liaden. "Master, it is not needful. There are Mr. McFarland and myself to receive and . . . entertain . . . these callers."

"Ah, I see. My oathsworn are expendable, but I am not."

Again, she bowed. "Master, it is so."

"I disagree," he returned, his tone rather more acidic than the mode allowed. He sighed, and moved his hand, soothingly.

"Come," he said, going back into Terran, "let us not argue. The trap has been set, and we as much as Boss Moran are caught in its unfolding."

She appeared to consider this, sleek head slightly to one side, then shrugged.

"As you say." Light as a dancer, she glided out of her corner, using her chin to point at the rug hanging on the back wall.

"Is the manufacture of this carpet truly as you described it to the boss' hand?" She asked.

"Of course," Pat Rin said, walking toward it with her. "Surely, you don't think I would misinform a customer regarding the value of his potential purchase."

"But . . ." her brows pulled together. "How did it come to be at Bazaar?"

"I suspect that someone who did not like warmth retired from the kitchen," he murmured, extending his hand to sample the pleasant nap again. "I paid a cantra for this carpet. Were we selling out of Solcintra—and with certification from a merchant more experienced than myself . . . There are customers of—that I know, who would offer twenty cantra, sight unseen—not because of its subject matter, but because of its rarity." He moved his shoulders, considering what he had thus far seen of Surebleak. "Here, we will be fortunate to recover our cantra."

He stood for a moment, the Juntava—his oathsworn—at his side, considering the thing that had come to him, over the weeks of their association, weighing his necessity against the likelihood of erring against custom. He had performed this exercise more than once, over the last few days, and had learned that his necessity was greater than his natural wariness of Juntavas custom.

So.

"I am doubtless lacking in courtesy," he said, very gently, "but I wonder if you will tell me your name."

Beside him, he felt her shift, and quickly turned to face her, schooling himself so that he neither stepped back nor went for his weapon, but only faced her, and met her eyes, equal to equal.

Her face was composed, her eyes bottomless.

"You know my name, Master," she said, matching his gentle tone.

"I believe I know your gun name," he replied, wondering at the strength of his need to know this thing. "I ask that you honor me with your personal name."

There was a brief silence; the composure of her face unbroken, then, a quiet, "Why?"

He inclined his head. "I hold your oath, which means that I have certain obligations toward you. As I am certain you know. The path we embark upon is chancy. Should there be need, I would wish to . . . properly inform your kin."

"Why, as to that," she said, lightly—too lightly. "You need merely inform the Juntavas that Sector Judge Natesa, called The Assassin, has ended her career under conditions described hereunder." She extended a hand, as he had done, and stroked the nap of the Sinner's Carpet. "To file such a report is to fulfill your obligation as oath-holder, completely and with honor."

So he was rebuffed, Pat Rin thought, as he might have known he would be—and very gently answered in his impertinence, too.

"Very well." He bowed slightly, to show that the subject was closed. "Will you join me in a cup of tea before our visitors arrive?"

Boss Moran counted the take while he listened to Jim's report. He put the bills down when Jim got to the sudden new store and the streeter who had his own Insurance, and sat staring at him, his face starting to take on that purple tinge that meant somebody, somewhere, was gonna get hurt.

"Who's the Insurance?" he asked; Jim shook his head.

"Don't know her. Pro, though." He frowned, trying to remember what the little guy'd said.

"Told the streeter he couldn't buy nobody else's Insurance, but he said everything was warm, 'cause she worked for him." Jim remembered something else. "Hardware guy says the rug-man's 'hand calls him 'boss'."

"Yeah?" The boss' face was the shade it had been when he'd up and shot his former second-hand, his eyes all glittery and narrow. Just about the time Jim started to have some serious concerns about the length of his own lifetime, the boss slammed both hands down flat on the table and shouted for Tony.

Jim relaxed. Tony was head of the publicity committee.

The pretty little man—and his pretty little store—was about to become a public example.

FIVE OF THEM walked across the red-yellow-and-blue rug and into the brightly lit store, Jim and Tony first, then the boss, then Veena and Lew. Barth and Gwince took up position outside, showing serious weaponry.

The store was empty, just like it had been earlier in the day. The boss looked around, walked over to the rug hanging on the right-hand wall, picked up a corner, and let it drop.

"Rugs," he said, and shook his head. "How much is he sellin' these things for?"

Jim bit his lip, suddenly aware that not having asked the little man this question demonstrated a lack of initiative on his part. He was about to blurt out a number—four hundred cash seemed expensive enough—but the smooth, rounded voice of the streeter who owned the joint cut him off.

"That particular carpet is a little worn toward the center, as I am sure you have noticed," he murmured, walking forward with his empty hands in plain sight. "However, such wearing must not be thought a defect, rather, it is a badge of authenticity. We do, of course, have its papers on file. So, this carpet," he extended a hand and stroked his palm across the material, like he was gentling a restless dog. "This carpet, I am able to sell to you for one thousand cash."

"One thou—" Boss Moran stared at the little guy, who stared right back, cool as a water-ice despite the presence of five armed people any one of who was bigger, heavier and meaner than he was.

"You know who I am?" the boss asked. The guy moved his shoulders in that snaky shrug of his.

"Alas. However, I feel certain that you are about to tell me."

"Damn straight." The boss used his extended fingers to hit him, hard, in the shoulder. "I'm Moran. I'm the boss from Blair clear on over to Carney. You set up on my streets, you follow my rules. Got that?"

"I confess to having had a similar tale from this gentleman, here—" The hand sporting the big, flashy ring swept gracefully towards Jim. "I believe he also wished to sell me insurance. I was unfortunately not able to accommodate him, as I have my own insurance, which is entirely adequate to my needs."

"You set up on my streets, you take my Insurance," the boss told him, and brought a rolled weed out of his pocket. He snapped his fingers and Jim jumped forward to light it with the industrial strength flame-stick the publicity committee had loaned him.

The boss drew in a deep lung full of smoke and blew it down into the little man's face. Give the guy credit, Jim thought, remembering his first face full of the boss' smoke, he didn't flinch and he didn't cough, though he did fold his hands, neatly, in front of him.

"Could be you don't unnerstand about Insurance," the boss was saying, conversational-like. "Lemme 'splain it to you." He waved the weed at the thousand-cash rug, its business end hovering above the cloth by no more than a baby's hair. "Now, see, without Insurance, somethin' terrible might happen to your stock, here. You got nice stuff—it'd be too bad if it all burned up, say, in a fire."

The little guy inclined his head. "Thank you, I understand the concept of insurance very well."

"Good," said the boss. "That's good. But there's worse things could happen, if you wasn't to have Insurance. You—you could get hurt. Happens alla time—guy falls, breaks his leg. Or his neck." He brought the weed up and had another long draw. The smoke this time missed the little man's face, though Jim couldn't have exactly said how—or when—he'd moved.

The boss looked around, eyes squinted at the rugs on the wall, on the floor, counting . . .

"I'm figuring your insurance payment is ten thousand cash. Per month. You can pay Mr. Snyder, there."

The little guy spread his hands. "Regretfully, I must once again point out that I hold my own insurance, with which I am perfectly satisfied."

The boss nodded, looking serious. "Right, you did say that. Not a problem. Bring her out. I'll get rid of her for you."

"Ah." He turned his head slightly and spoke over his shoulder. "Natesa."

"Sir?"

Jim whipped around, staring—and sure enough, there she was, all in black, like before, the fancy gun glittering in its holster. Behind her, standing just in front of the clusterfuck rug, was a big, rugged looking guy, his arms crossed over his chest, eyes half-closed, looking slow and sleepy and stupid, like really big guys usually were. If he was armed, his vest was covering the weapon.

"Natesa," the little guy was saying, moving his hand to show her the boss. "Here is Mr. Moran. He represents himself as someone able to be rid of you."

"He is," she said composedly, "in error."

"Are you certain?" the little guy asked. "I wish us to be plain, Natesa. I had understood that our contract was exclusive. If I find that you are also in the employ of Mr. Moran, I shall be most displeased."

"I have never seen Mr. Moran in my life," the pro answered, still in that completely composed voice. "Nor do I wish to see him again."

The boss' face went purple, but he only nodded again, and said to her, real serious, "We can deal. Tony."

Tony was the quickest shot on the boss' staff. Jim saw him go for his business piece—and way too many guns went off.

There wasn't any time to draw, no time to really understand what had happened, before it was all over.

Jim was standing, arms held out from his sides. Natesa the pro was standing, too; her pretty pistol pointed at him. The big guy was standing, not sleepy-looking at all, holding a cannon in one hand, the business end covering the street door. The pretty man with the blue earring was standing, palm gun also pointed at Jim. There wasn't a mark on any of 'em—the little guy's jacket wasn't even wrinkled.

The publicity committee hadn't done so good.

Tony was on the floor at Jim's right. There was a neat little hole centered between his eyes. His gun was still in the holster.

Boss Moran—former Boss Moran—was in a heap under the rug he'd threatened to burn. His weed was crushed, like somebody'd stepped on it, a couple sad little curls of smoke twisting up from it.

Jim swivelled his eyes, made out an arm and a loose gun on the floor, which was probably all that was left of Veena and Lew.

"Your compatriots are dead, Mr. Snyder," the little guy said, and his voice was kinda breathless, like maybe he'd run a couple blocks. The gun, though, that stayed steady, and even if it hadn't, the pro wasn't havin' no trouble at all with her aim. "If you attempt to draw a weapon, you will join them. Am I plain?"

Jim licked his lips. "Yessir."

"Good. Now, I have a proposition for you—"

"Company," the big guy interrupted quietly. Jim turned his head cautiously, and saw Gwince in the doorway. It didn't take her long to figure out what'd happened. Jim saw her take stock of the three holding guns, her own pointed peaceably at the floor. She nodded at the big guy.

"Boss?" she said.

He jerked his head to the left. "He's the boss."

If Gwince thought she'd never seen anything in her life lookin' less like a boss than the fancy guy in the blue jacket, she didn't say so. Instead, she nodded to him, and said again, real respectful.

"Boss. I'm Gwince." She frowned at the mess on the floor. "You want we should get rid of that for you?"

"Shortly, perhaps." The boss' voice was back on the smooth, not breathless at all. "First, however, you and your partner have a choice to make. Please bring him inside and close the door. Take care not to rumple my carpet."

"Yessir," she said, and leaned outside, keeping one foot in the store. "Hey, Barth! Boss wants ya!"

He came quick enough, which is how you stay alive, in the employ of bosses, checked on the edge of the doorway, eyes flickering around the room while Gwince moved behind him, closing the door real slow, so as not to muss the boss' rug.

Gwince was no dummy, and Barth was some quicker than her. He wasn't in the room two heartbeats before he had the situation scoped and the little guy pegged, with a nod and a soft, "Boss."

"Barth," the boss returned, softer. Then, considerably sharper. "Please tell me if any of the deceased had kin."

Barth's forehead rumpled and he shot a look at Gwince. "Kin?"

"Family," the boss said, even sharper. "Brothers, sisters, mothers, fathers, children—anyone who valued them—and who will miss them, when they are discovered to be absent."

"Well . . . ," said Barth, "Tony had a girl, I think . . ."

"Not anymore," Gwince interrupted. "Smacked her around once too often, and she went and found somebody else to pay the rent." She frowned down at the bodies on the floor.

"Veena—unnerstand, I don't know if it's her or her money he'll miss—but she always sent some of her draw to her brother. Lew—" she shrugged. "Lew ain't got nobody that I ever heard about. The boss . . ." Her eyes flicked to the little guy's face. "Beg pardon, sir. I meant to say, Moran—might be some of the other fatcats'll miss him. I don't run at that level."

"I see," the boss said. "Do you know how to contact Veena's brother?"

"Yeah, I do. You want I should break the news to him?"

"Eventually, perhaps I shall. We will also wish to take her possessions to him and to discover the sum he was accustomed to receiving from her, so that a payment schedule may be arranged."

Gwince blinked. "Payment schedule? Boss, unless I read this wrong, Veena went down shooting at you and your crew, here."

"Indeed. She died in performance of her duty. Her pension shall be assigned to her brother, as her surviving kin. These others . . ." The boss glanced to Natesa, who inclined her head. "We shall publish their names in the newspaper, and also an announcement of the . . . change of administration."

"Newspaper?" Jim shook his head, keeping a careful eye on Natesa's gun. "We ain't got a newspaper."

"We did though," Barth said, excited. "Sleet, musta been eight, nine years ago. Only thing Randall did before Vindal come along and promoted herself was shut down the gab-rag and make the guy who owned the print shop into a public example. Vindal, she got busy with building up the border guards an' all . . ."

The boss held up a slim, pretty hand, his big ring glittering like something alive. Barth gulped into silence.

"Is there a printer in this territory?"

"Oh, well, sure," Barth said, nodding. "Sure, there is, Boss. Just she ain't never done a gab-rag, is all."

"But she may be able to adapt herself to the concept. Very well." The boss lowered his hand, and moved his eyes. "Mr. Snyder."

Here it come. Jim squared his shoulders and tried not to look at the pro holding the gun on him. "Yessir."

"I believe that you are a man who values his life, Mr. Snyder. Am I correct?"

It took Jim a second to figure out what he was hearing, but once he did, he nodded enthusiastically.

"Good. Then this is what we shall do. You and I are going

into the back room. I will ask you questions and you will give me truthful answers. When my questions are satisfied, I will arrange for you to be escorted across the border."

Jim goggled. "You're sending me outta the territory?"

"I am. I don't wish to seem discourteous, but, since the two of us are dealing in truth, I must confess that you are not at all the caliber of citizen I wish to tenant my streets. However, you did not draw on us, and so you have earned your life. Conditionally."

The boss sure did talk a twist. Frowning, Jim worked out his meaning, and arrived at the theory that the new boss valued *initiative* just like the old boss had, and that Jim hadn't shown all that well.

"Hey, it ain't so bad over on Deacon's turf," Gwince said cheerfully. "You'll do just fine, Mr. Snyder."

Easy for her to say, Jim thought. Nobody was talkin' about throwin' her off the turf she'd grown up in. On the other hand, looking at Natesa's gun and cold, patient face, it didn't look like he had much of a choice.

"OK," he said to the boss, trying to sound like moving turf was nothing. "We can deal."

"I am delighted to find it so," the boss said, and pointed at the back wall. "Please go with Natesa. I will join you very soon."

Natesa moved her gun, inviting him to walk ahead of her. He did that, and the big guy lifted the rug away from the door so they could pass.

"Mr. McFarland," the boss said when the big man had dropped the carpet back across the doorway.

"Sir?"

"You will please ascertain if Gwince and Barth have value to my administration. If they do not, or if they choose not to remain in my employ, they may also be escorted to the border and passed without toll. If they wish to remain, and you find them valuable, please consider them attached to your department."

"Yessir," the big man said easily. "I'll get right on it."

"Thank you, Mr. McFarland," the boss said, and left them.

"OK," the big guy said. "My name's McFarland, like you heard. Which of you don't wanna stay on? Sing out, now; don't be shy."

Gwince looked at Barth and Barth looked at Gwince. They both looked at the deaders on the floor and then back to big Mr. McFarland. Neither one said anything.

"Right, then." He put his hand-cannon away in its holster and nodded at the floor. "First job we got is to clean out those pockets. Then, we'll straighten up and put everything back neat, the way the boss likes it."

"Yessir!" they said in unison, and in matching tones of relief, and moved forward to tackle their first job for the new boss.

The woman Gwince was the key that gained them entry into the late Mr. Moran's so-called 'mansion', much more than those on the ring retrieved for him from the dead man's pocket.

By the time Pat Rin had met and taken provisional allegiance from the house staff; spoken to the printer, hastily summoned from her shop, covered over with ink and ill-concealed terror, regarding the necessity of a newssheet and the contents of the first issue, which would—"yessir, Boss, no problem at all"—be available on the street tomorrow at no later than one hour beyond dawn; and located the boss' private office, it was dark on the—on *his*—streets. Natesa and Cheever McFarland were engaged in other parts of the house—Natesa on a "security check" and Cheever interviewing others of the staff. Well enough: Duty awaited him as well.

The office was on the second floor, a dank and dismal chamber—cold, as it was cold everywhere on this wretched planet—the walls of which had once, perhaps, been painted white. The desk was rust-colored plastic, the filing cabinet was red plastic, the two chairs—one behind the desk, one in front of it—were blue plastic and yellow, respectively. The floor was also plastic, and in need of a scrubbing. The rug—for there was a rug in this room that otherwise showed him neither books, nor comm unit, nor teapot, nor potted plant, nor any other human comfort—the rug was nothing short of astonishing. Merely, it was a primitive of tied and woven rag, rectangular in shape, yet made with some artistry, so that it was cheerful without being over-bright; pleasant and easeful on the eye.

Pat Rin gasped, his vision suddenly clouded. There was someone—someone within the few ghastly blocks of this wretched, filthy city that he was now pleased to call *his*—some one of his people had heart enough to have produced a thing of beauty. He shook his head, banishing ridiculous tears, and walked, somewhat unsteadily, over to the file cabinet.

He pulled open the top drawer with difficulty, and stood staring, confronted not with a row of neatly labeled files, nor even a disorderly mess of papers. No, the top drawer of Boss Moran's cheap, unlocked filing cabinet was filled to capacity with cash of every denomination, mixed all helter-skelter, as if it had just been flung within, and the door slammed shut.

The second drawer held a similar outrage. The bottom drawer held coins.

Pat Rin closed it and straightened. *Idiot*, he thought. *Not even a safe?* Sighing, he crossed the room to the desk

The blue chair was grubby, the plastic mesh seat stretched, the plastic legs bowed alarmingly. Pat Rin pushed it to one side.

There was a small book lying in the center of the desk; for one mad instant he thought he had discovered Moran's personal debt-book—but, there, Terrans did not keep debt-books. Most especially, he suspected, recalling his researches into the place— not to mention the tales he had from Natesa and Cheever—did the worthy citizens of the planet Surebleak fail of keeping debt-books.

He picked the thing up and opened it, frowning as he riffled the pages. Very quickly, he ascertained that what he held was Moran's Insurance Book, listing all the businesses in the territory, what they owed and what they had paid.

It was a singularly frustrating document, written with some blurred and blurry charcoal-like substance; the notations ranging from barely lettered to indecipherable. Pat Rin emerged from his study not much informed on the topic of the profit to be had from Insurance sales on Surebleak, and with a nasty ache over his eyes.

Sighing, he rubbed his forehead and deliberately sought out the cheery, unassuming little rug on the dirty plastic floor.

The pain in his head flared, and he was seeing—not the floor in the office of the vanquished Moran, but the floor of his store in the aftermath of the gunplay, the gleaming plastic surface littered with the bodies of—the bodies of his kin.

There—Anthora, her arm blown off at the shoulder; here, Shan, a pellet hole between his frost-colored eyebrows; there again! Quin, half of his face torn away—

Retching, Pat Rin raised his hands before his eyes, blocking out the horrific sight; and hearing again the pale-haired man's inflexible, emotionless voice: "Your kin are dead. Nova yos'Galan, Anthora yos'Galan, Shan yos'Galan, Kareen yos'Phelium, Luken bel'Tarda . . ."

There was a sound in the doorway, audible even over the voice of his enemy, chanting the names of his dead. Pat Rin spun, the gun coming neatly into his hand, and in one smooth motion, he raised it, aiming—

At Juntavas Sector Judge Natesa, called The Assassin.

It spoke well of her skill, that she neither went for a weapon nor drew his fire by assuming the attitude of prey. Merely, she paused in the doorway, black eyebrows arched above black eyes, and inclined her head.

"Master," she murmured in the mode of student to teacher. "It pleases me to find you so well guarded, as I was just now coming to scold you for deserting your oathsworn."

Pat Rin lowered the gun, heartbeat roaring in his ears, stomach roiling. He fussed over the placement of the palm gun in his sleeve, and answered her without looking up, in Terran.

"I had thought my oathsworn intent upon their own business."

"Certainly, Mr. McFarland and I were performing our various duties, to insure that the house would keep you safe," she said, keeping to the High Tongue. "Yet Mr. McFarland tells me he had left Gwince at your back."

Another word from her in the language of home and he would—he would do something irreparable. Pat Rin took a deep breath and found the courage to meet her eyes.

"If you please. I prefer to converse in Terran."

Something moved in the black eyes; she inclined her head before he could identify it and murmured. "As you wish."

"Yes." Pat Rin cleared his throat. "Gwince stood her duty well.

When I had done speaking with the staff and with the printer, I dismissed her to her meal, and perhaps to her bed." He glanced away, resting his eyes cautiously on the rag rug. "She has taken losses today."

"To hear her tell it, perhaps not," Natesa said drily. "However, you may be pleased to learn that she rose to meet Mr. McFarland's expectations of her. It could not be expected that she would refuse a direct order from the boss, but she did seek out her department head to inform him of her dismissal."

"Whereupon you were dispatched to scold me," Pat Rin concluded, and moved his shoulders. "Well, I am pleased that Gwince proves herself able. But I do not intend to live with a constant guard at my back."

"Then you do not intend to live," she said, leaning gracefully against the doorframe and crossing her arms beneath her breasts. "I am disappointed."

He inclined his head, eloquently ironic. "I am, of course, grieved to hear it."

Natesa sighed, sharply. "Illuminate my error, that you draw on me twice inside a single conversation."

And it was not, he thought, her error, but his own. Error understood too late, with his feet irrevocably upon a path that demanded he deal violent death to people who had never heard of Liad, or Clan Korval; Plan B, nor even the Department of the Interior. People who had brothers. People who might live well for several years on the profit made in selling the piece of trumpery he wore upon his finger— provided they weren't murdered for gain in the meanwhile.

"I beg your pardon," he said to his oathsworn, being certain that his tone was inoffensive in offering the unaccustomed Terran phrase.

"That is no answer, Master," she chided, her eyes intent upon his face.

Indeed, it was not—and Natesa was wise enough in custom to know he owed his oathsworn more than pettiness and ill-temper. And yet, what might he tell her that would not reveal he who held her honor in his hands as the madman he undoubtedly was?

Sighing, he showed her empty palms. "I beg your pardon," he

said again. "I—people have lost their lives today, for nothing more than my necessity. Shall my Balance go forth as it must, more will die—and those before ever I lay hand upon my enemy." He moved, suddenly restless, pacing 'round the desk to stand staring down at the rag rug. From Natesa he felt a vast patience, which soothed him oddly, and moved him to speak more fully.

"Balance—you understand that Balance *must* go forth. This—Department—must be answered."

"Certainly they must," she said, softly, from the doorway. "Your kin have died at their hands."

Almost, he laughed.

"Yes. But that is not why the Department must be stopped," he said to the rug and looked up to meet Natesa's eyes.

"I am old enough to know that Balance does not bring back the dead. If I murder worlds—slay the galaxy—yet my kin will not arise—" Tears, however, were arising, and he had been—must continue to be—very careful not to weep before his oathsworn. He closed his eyes, breathed deeply and calmingly, and again met Natesa's black gaze.

"However, Korval has—a contract. An ancient and explicit contract, which requires the one who wears this—" he showed her the ring on his finger, "to protect the population of Liad. Such assumptions as the representative of the Department of the Interior made, such policies and procedures as he revealed to me—Liad is in danger. If Balance does not go forth—and that with precision—innocents will be enslaved or worse." He found it somewhat easier to breathe, thus retracing the chain of duty and right action he had laboriously forged in the aftermath of the Department's . . . offer . . . to himself.

The silence stretched, not uncomfortably, then Natesa spoke in her quiet, sumptuous voice.

"I understand—and I thank you." She straightened, and stretched, cat-like and supple.

"Last seen, Mr. McFarland was attempting to convey the notion of *vegetable* to the cook," she said. "I doubt he succeeded, but it is not unlikely that we have some sort of meal awaiting us."

Food. Pat Rin's stomach clenched—and yet he must eat and remain healthy, so that he might see his Balance precisely placed. Once again, he looked up at Natesa.

"I have taken your point regarding the necessity of a guard. I bow to the wisdom of my oathsworn."

"Ah." She smiled. "We will endeavor not to leave you too often with strangers." She moved an arm, gracefully inviting him to proceed her out of the room. "We mustn't keep the cook waiting."

There were vegetables—a mess of indeterminate green leaves boiled with a piece of fat. As a dish, it was a failure—even Cheever McFarland scarce ate more than a fork full—yet at that it was not the worst of the offerings brought forth for the new boss' delectation.

The meat was old—a fact that the cook attempted to disguise by using a heavy hand with hot-tasting spices. Cheever didn't even manage a fork-full there, and neither Pat Rin nor Natesa bothered to take a portion onto their plates.

On the other hand, the rice was quite good, and the butter not, as Pat Rin had certainly expected it to be, rancid. He satisfied himself with a plate of rice, well-buttered, smiling as he saw Natesa do the same. Cheever manfully worked his way through the table, a fork-full here, a half-spoon there.

The choice of beverages were three: a uniquely undrinkable hot brew that the serving girl had whispered was, "Tea, Boss;" beer, which Cheever drank without gusto; and plain cold water. After one disbelieving sip of "tea," Pat Rin had water; Natesa again following his lead.

"What they're calling coffee ain't no better," Cheever said. "Worst excuse for 'toot I ever smelled in my life. Didn't even bother to try and drink it." He shook his head at Natesa. "We're gonna have to figure out something about provisions."

"Security first," she said, and he grinned at her, good-humoredly.

"Boss, this woman don't know how to live high. OK—security." His big face got serious.

"We ain't in too bad a shape, everything considered. The old boss put a high price on his hide, so we inherited some good systems." He used his fork to point at Natesa. "Not as good as she can do for

us, but we don't got to be worried about being overrun while she's
doing the upgrades. People . . ." He put the fork down and reached
across the table to break off a piece of hard brown bread, the meal's
other outstanding success.

"Got some decent people. What I mean by that is, they can be
trained. Old boss doesn't seem to have made himself real popular
with the hired-ons, so we're going in with them feeling grateful to us
for doing them a favor. Gwince has the instincts of a pro. Barth's
probably steady as long as we don't ask him to do too much work."
He buttered his bread.

"Any one of 'em'll sell us out to a high bidder, 'course—that's
the way they do business here. But we ain't gonna see a high bidder
'til folks catch their breath—longer, if we don't give 'em any reason
to feel abused." He grinned. "Which Boss Moran also made real easy
for us."

Pat Rin pushed his empty plate away and reached for his water
glass. "How—" he began, and the door opened to reveal the doorman—one Filmin—and a young red-haired woman enclosed from
throat to ankles by a tolerably good black velvet cloak. To her feet were
strapped the daintiest of silver sandals.

"Girl's here, Boss," Filmin announced, and, obviously feeling
that he had fulfilled his duty with utmost propriety, departed,
closing the door loudly behind him.

The girl, rather quicker than Filmin, checked, her eyes sweeping
the room. Pat Rin raised his hand, the ring glittering in the dull light.

"I am the boss," he said. "May I know your name?"

Her eyes were ginger brown, her gaze straightforward and not
at all afraid. "I'm Bilinda, Boss. From Audrey's House."

Audrey, so he had gathered from the excellent Gwince, was the
owner of the most profitable business in Pat Rin's new territory. He
thought that whorehouses were often so.

"I see," he said gently. "But, do you know, I did not request a
companion for this evening."

"No, that's OK," Bilinda told him easily. "It's all written down on
the schedule. I can write it out for you, if you wa—" She stopped, her
rather pale face suddenly ablaze, and her gaze not—quite—so fearless.

Pat Rin frowned at her, wondering what the difficulty might be, then recalled the unlettered entries in the book he had found above stairs.

"I can read," he told Bilinda, and saw the fear edge out of her eyes.

"However," he continued, "I am not thin of company this evening. Nor do I foresee a need to follow the former boss' schedule."

Bilinda frowned. "You don't want me?"

Pat Rin raised his hands soothingly. "It is a matter of business," he said gently, "and nothing whatsoever to do with you, yourself. I regret that I did not know of the existence of the schedule and thus exposed you to the dangers of traveling at night." He glanced at Cheever, who was sitting almost absurdly still.

"Mr. McFarland will escort you to Audrey's House. Also, if there is a fee—"

Bilinda blinked. "Fee? For me? Nossir, Boss. That's all part of the arrangement. This is how Ms. Audrey pays her Insurance." She hesitated, then said, rather breathlessly, "I don't mean no offense, but—if you ain't gonna hold with the arrangement, does that mean Ms. Audrey's outta business?"

Across the table, he heard a slight sound, as if Natesa had sneezed. Pat Rin gave the girl a slight frown. "That is between Ms. Audrey and myself." He inclined his head. "I apologize for the inconvenience, to yourself and to Ms. Audrey. Have a pleasant evening, Bilinda. Mr. McFarland?"

"On my way." Cheever came to his feet and grinned at the girl. "OK, Bilinda, time to go home."

There was, as the vernacular went, no percentage in arguing, which Bilinda was quick enough to understand. She gave Pat Rin a nod, and, on reflection, Natesa, too, and allowed Cheever to usher her out. The door closed—softly—behind them.

Pat Rin closed his eyes, abruptly very, very tired.

"Master?"

He opened his eyes. "I believe I will retire for the evening," he said with a languid wave of the hand. "The exertions of the day have quite exhausted me."

It was meant to ape the manner of the more insular and annoying High Houselings, but Natesa did not smile. Merely, she inclined her head and rose.

"I will escort you to your bedroom and make certain that all is secure."

Someone had been at the bedroom. Here, as nowhere else in Boss Moran's narrow, tawdry house, the floor was clean, the walls washed, the bed linens spotless. There was a rag rug akin to the one in his office next to the bed. He stood near it, watching Natesa make her circuit about the room.

When at last she was satisfied, she moved to the door, paused on the threshold and inclined her head. "Master. Sleep well. One of us will be close by."

"Do not cheat yourself of sleep to guard mine," he said, and she did smile, then, by which he knew she would not obey him.

"Sleep well," she said again, and stepped into the hall, pulling the door behind her. Within an inch of closing entire, the panel paused, and her voice wafted to his ear.

"My name is Inas Bhar."

DAY 50

❀ ❀

Standard Year 1393
Lytaxin
Erob's House

THE BREEZE SUBSIDED so gradually she couldn't have said when it quit completely. She noted its absence; in so noting decided she had slept long enough—and awoke.

For a moment she lay, eyes closed, listening to the silence, feeling the jubilant singing of blood through her veins, the sweet passage of air through her lungs. She stretched, luxuriating in the smooth slide of well-toned muscles. Sensuously, she stretched her mind as well, reaching out in that undefinable, definite way, to the pattern that was her perception of Val Con's self.

The pattern blazed with lucent purity, its byways and inroads fully integrated, absolutely, entirely and unmistakably Val Con; joyously intact. Throat tight with the beauty of him, Miri extended herself and stroked him, raising a crackle of startled lust, and a flicker of the particular bright green she understood to be laughter. Then, slowly—very slowly, as if relishing every instant of contact, she felt his fingers stroke down her cheek, and across her lips. Miri sighed, reached—and found him abruptly absent, though she saw his pattern as plainly as she ever had.

Regretfully, she opened her eyes to Erob's sickroom. The wall of medical gizmos was dark and silent; the tech's noteboard standing blank and ready in its place, though no tech was in evidence. Nor was there any sign of the large-ish green person known to them both as her brother Sheather.

Throwing back the quilt, Miri bounced out of bed and strode over to the door to check the lock. Locked, all right, and from the inside, too. She tried to figure out if that worried her, or ought to, then decided the hell with it: The door was locked from the inside, and Sheather, who had presumably arranged for that circumstance, was conclusively not in the room with her. Therefore, Sheather was on his own inside a Liaden clanhouse. That might've been worrisome, had the House in question not recently survived both a civil uprising and an Yxtrang invasion. At this stage in the proceedings, nobody was likely to get too upset about a little thing like a Clutch turtle wandering the halls.

Which, come to think of it, sounded a whole lot more entertaining than sticking around a deserted sickroom. She wasn't sick. If she'd ever felt better in her life, she couldn't at the moment recall the occasion.

She did feel a trifle grubby, which could be remedied by a shower, after which she intended to go for a walk, unless somebody came up with a compelling reason why she shouldn't.

Decision taken, she moved briskly in the direction of the 'fresher, stripping off her nightshirt as she went.

THE SHIFT had thus far been quiet. Ren Zel had run routine systems checks, and done some general housekeeping. His mind did wander, now and again, to the impossibility of the cat in his cabin and the irrefutable evidence of that long, white whisker. At last, knowing what he would find, he pulled up the current roster of the pet library.

As he had expected, there were no cats currently on file in the library. Certainly, there was no ship's cat, free to wander the vessel, earning its passage by dispatching vermin. Useful as such creatures were, they had a tendency to get into unchancy places, resulting in fouled machinery and, more often than not, a dead cat.

And even if the *Passage* did harbor a cat, who had let the creature into his quarters?

He sighed and closed the roster.

It was a puzzle, certain enough, and the only other possibility that occurred to him was that a crew member had smuggled a pet aboard. Though how they had kept it secret from all was another, just as knotty, puzzle.

He sighed again and considered taking the whisker to the ship's Healer, to see what she might scry from it. Lina was a Healer of no small skill, her lack of success with himself having to do with some sort of 'natural shielding' that he possessed. He understood that this was not entirely unknown. Unhappily, the shielding prevented him being Healed of the nightmares of battle, and the pain of his dying. Though he thought he was healing of that last wound on his own, if slowly.

So, then, he thought. At shift-end, he would take the whisker to Lina. That was the best course, surely.

SOMEONE HAD BEEN KIND ENOUGH to lay in a couple shirts in her size. The same someone, Miri supposed, newly showered and thoroughly air-dried, who had been forethoughtful enough to shine her boots and make sure that her leathers were clean.

The arrangements had a certain feel of Beautiful to them—the Compleat Captain's Aide, Miri thought with wry gratitude, sealing the cuffs of her shirt. She stamped into her boots, put her hand against the plate and left the dressing room. Half a step into the main room, she checked, turned and frowned at the man lounging in the chair next to the tech's station, his legs thrust out before him and crossed neatly at the ankle. He was dressed like she was, in working leathers, and boots buffed to a mirror finish. One irrepressible eyebrow rose at her frown.

"The door," she said, trying to sound severe, "was locked."

"It was," Val Con admitted. "And it is locked now. I hope you don't think me lax in such matters."

It took a major effort of will not to laugh out loud, which was, of course, what he wanted. Instead, Miri managed quite a credible sigh while she surveyed him.

He looked like his pattern, she thought—new-made and shiny; so beautiful it made a body's throat close up and her heart start acting funny. In fact, he looked miraculously well for a man she'd been told was going to have to devote some considerable time to relearning how to walk. Val Con raised his other eyebrow.

"Is there something wrong, cha'trez?"

"Depends," she said. "We having another one of those dream sequences?"

"Dream—Ah. Jelaza Kazone." He smiled. "I believe it safe to assume that we are now both present in . . . contiguous reality." He tipped his head, considering. "Mostly contiguous reality."

"Mostly's more than we had last time," she allowed, drifting over to his side. She cleared her throat. "You don't happen to know where Edger and Shan are, do you?"

"Alas. Must we locate them immediately?"

She looked down into his face. "You got anything better to do?"

"Yes," he said. She saw familiar lightning weave through his pattern, and shivered.

"Yes, is it?" Her hand rose, not entirely on her order. Softly, she stroked the well-marked, mobile eyebrows, ran her fingertips along the high line of his cheek . . .

"Cha'trez?" His voice was not quite steady. Miri stroked his cheek again.

"Scar's gone, boss," she murmured, tracing the place where it had been.

"Many scars are gone. I am—Miri . . ." He took a hard breath. "Miri, let us make love."

"Here?" she asked, teasing him, like her own blood wasn't hot with desire.

He reached up and captured her hand. "Why not?" he murmured, and kissed her fingertips before slanting a glance of pure mischief into her eyes. "The door is locked."

IT WAS THE CUSTOM of Emrith Tiazan, Erob Herself, to take a turn or two through the atrium prior to seeking her bed. As this had also been the custom of her father who had been delm before her, the room's cycle had long been set opposite the day-night cycle of the outside garden, where the seedling of Korval's Tree held dominion.

Here, there were more convenable plants, mild-mannered and conducive of an easy sleep. Korval's Tree promoted madcap dreaming, of a kind unsuitable in old women who had lost a third of her House in the late warlike disturbances.

Alone with her thoughts and her dead, she ambled along the sweet-smelling ways, pausing now and again to admire the progress of certain favorites. Her shoulder muscles began to loosen under the suasion of the mock sunlight; her houseboots made a soft shuffling sound against the shredded bark path; the first notes from the singing waters wafted 'round the next curve, teasing her ears. Comforted by all that was gentle and usual, Emrith Tiazan's face relaxed into a smile.

She followed the path around, and the full song of the waters rushed to greet her. She paused, as she always did, face turned up toward the false sun, eyes closed in pleasure, before moving across the little stone bridge to her especial spot, a stone nook, surrounded by simple rock plants, enchanted by the joyous waters.

Which was this evening filled very nearly to overflowing by two large, green . . . things.

Emrith at first thought them twin boulders, brought in and disposed by some well-meaning but mad gardener. Then she saw the extended foreleg of the smaller, culminating in a three-fingered hand. She walked closer, discovering other details—beaked faces with nostril slits, horny green hides, and a shell-like substance partially encasing each large torso. Both appeared asleep. Or dead. Emrith Tiazan stared at them a long time, by her lights. She didn't even wonder where they had come from—to whose orbit, after all, did any of the strange, uncomfortable or dangerous oddities of the universe attach themselves?

Eventually, she sighed and did something that she had done only once before in this garden—she reached in her pocket and thumbed on the remote.

"My delm?" An Der sounded startled, as well he might, she thought, sourly.

"Find Shan yos'Galan," she said, striving for an appropriate calmness. "Bring him to the singing waters in the atrium. I believe I have found that which belongs to his House."

AS AGREED, the majority of their party waited in the side garden while Nelirikk went ahead to alert his captain to the presence of both scouts and recruits.

The hour was far advanced, and he was certain that the medical technician currently in a position of authority over the captain would find his visit unseemly. Had he been in pursuit of an Yxtrang commander in similar straits, Nelirikk would simply have put the technician aside and given his report; a soldier's duty came before all: illness, pleasure, sleep, or food.

Liadens held to another ordering of duties, and the necessities of soldiers were not always at the top of the list. Which is how it came to pass that a mere medical technician could order a captain.

Nor was it appropriate, according to the complex net of rule and custom in which Liadens ensnared themselves, for a captain's aide to lay hands on a med tech for the purpose of gaining his captain's side.

It was thus necessary to have a reason for speaking to the captain *at once* that the tech would accept as sufficiently urgent to disturb her rest.

Wrestling with this conundrum, Nelirikk turned a corner—and slammed to a halt, staring.

Two people were walking toward him—two people he had reason to know well. The woman was none other than his captain, who he had last seen that morning, lying pale and weak against pillows; med tech on the hover. The man was no one less than the scout himself, who certainly should not be walking—not so soon, if ever again.

Regardless, here they came, strolling hand-in-hand down the center of the hallway, to the uninformed eye, as vulnerable and as guileless as children. Nelirikk frankly stared.

"Hey, Beautiful," the captain called. "How was your walk?"

"Captain." He recalled himself and came to attention, saluting. "My walk was . . . interesting."

"Yeah? You didn't seen any Clutch turtles, did you?"

Clutch turtles? Nelirikk managed to stifle the shiver, while fervently hoping never in his lifetime to see a Clutch turtle, enemy of the Troop, slayer of fleets.

"Captain," he replied, somewhat stiffly, "I have not. I have, however, seen scouts, and together we have—"

"Scouts?" the man murmured. "Are you certain?"

Nelirikk frowned. "Are there others among Liadens who walk silent and woodwise and arrive on-world in a scout class ship?"

"Actually," the scout said surprisingly, "there are."

Nelirikk thought about that, then looked to the captain, who was watching him out of ironic grey eyes.

"Two represent themselves as scouts: Clonak ter'Meulen, scout commander; Shadia Ne'Zame, scout lieutenant, first in. The third . . ." He looked from grey eyes to green. "The third did not say he was a scout, though the others treat him as a peer—and at times defer to him. The lieutenant addresses him as 'captain'. He bears a Tree-and-Dragon—" He touched the matching symbol on his collar, "and gives his name as Daav yos'Phelium."

The scout's eyebrows rose. "Does he?" He glanced at the captain.

"Odds he's the genuine article?" she asked. He moved his shoulders.

"It would be difficult to fool Clonak, even at this remove; he and my father trained together. Later, he was a member of the survey team of which my father was captain. Uncle Er Thom said the two of them were great friends—even though Clonak had been in love with my mother." Again, he moved his shoulders, and smiled into the captain's eyes. "If it's *odds* you're after, my lady—then I am compelled to say that I have too little data and must see the man for myself."

"Sure you are," she said resignedly. The scout grinned and Nelirikk gave a start, the sense of wrongness about the other man's face crystalizing all at once. The green eyes moved; pinning him.

"Yes?"

"I—" Nelirikk cleared his throat. "Scout, your *nchaka* is— gone."

"Ah." The smaller man inclined his head. "The Troop remembers."

"The Troop remembers," Nelirikk affirmed and looked back to his captain.

"Captain. In addition to scouts, my walk produced recruits."

She shook her head. "The Irregulars are outta business; ain't taking recruits. Point 'em at Commander Carmody."

"Commander Carmody has given medical care, food and quarters, so winning himself a place in the camp-tales. However, if the captain pleases, these recruits will give their oaths and their weapons only to Hero Captain Miri Robertson, who vanquished the Fourteenth."

She sighed. "You're talking about *Yxtrang* recruits?"

"Tales of your prowess echo throughout the ranks of two armies," the scout murmured. "A hero to Yxtrang and mercenary alike, you—"

"Can it," she told him and frowned up at Nelirikk.

"How many?"

"If the captain pleases. One Rifle and an explorer—two in total. The third—a senior explorer—has gone to glory's reward."

"Yeah? Two of you have an argument?"

"Captain. I had not the honor to know Gernchik Explorer before he died. He was wounded in a rear-holding action, to allow the officers time to escape. Seeing that his condition was serious, and unwilling to use the grace blade, his junior—Hazenthull Explorer—attached Diglon Rifle to her command, and marched the three of them here, to present their weapons and offer you their oaths."

"And to get her senior into an autodoc, quicktime." She nodded. "How's she taking his death?"

This was the joy of serving a captain wise in the way of the common troop. Nelirikk saluted. "Captain. She is at the moment . . . docile. Daav yos'Phelium gives it as his opinion that this condition might change, quickly and catastrophically."

"He does, huh? Then I hope you got her someplace where she can't do too much damage."

"Captain. She is in the garden attached to the side of this wing."

The captain blinked. She looked at the scout, who lifted an eyebrow.

"Nelirikk," she said, mildly.

He swallowed and came to full attention. "Captain."

"Have you lost your mind?"

"No, Captain."

"You're sure about that?"

"Yes, Captain."

"Right." She looked up at him. "You want to tell me what you was thinking?"

"Captain. It was the thought of Daav yos'Phelium that Hazenthull Explorer should be brought immediately to give full battle-oath to the captain. He fears that the interim oath he holds from her is not strong enough to bind, if her grief overcomes her reason. He was supported in this by the scouts."

"Daav yos'Phelium holds temporary oaths from an Yxtrang common trooper and an explorer?" she asked

"Yes, Captain."

She shook her head and looked again at the scout. "This has got to be your father."

"He does appear to have something of the familial sense of humor." His face was bland.

"Is that what you call it?" She sighed. "What else, Beautiful? Might as well spill it all."

"Captain, there is no more. Your recruits await you, accompanied by scouts."

"The Irregulars're out of business," she repeated, but it was scout she was speaking to. "I don't guess it would be good form for Line yos'Phelium to hold a private troop."

"There is," murmured the scout, "some precedent."

"Great. I suppose the House routinely hires Yxtrang soldiers to guard its piggy-bank. No—" she raised a hand—"*don't* tell me."

"As the captain wishes."

"No respect, that's your problem." She fell silent then, frowning at a space somewhere between Nelirikk's left elbow and infinity. Eventually, she looked up.

"OK. Get on back. We'll be there soon."

Nelirikk saluted. "Captain. Thank you, Captain."

"Think you'd know better than to thank me by now," she said, and her voice sharpened. "If the explorer decides her oath ain't binding, shoot her dead. If her trooper's reasonable, you can stop there and wait for me. If hell breaks, I expect you and the scouts to be standing when it's done. This is an order."

Nelirikk saluted once more. "Yes, Captain."

"Right. Get outta here."

Another salute and he was gone.

Miri waited until the sound of his footsteps had faded to nothing before looking into her partner's speculative green eyes.

"How much precedent?" she asked.

THE CHILD IS GOING to break, Daav thought, stifling a sigh. Behind his eyes, he felt Aelliana stir, though she offered no comment.

To casual—that was to say, non-scout—eyes, Hazenthull was the picture of well-mannered docility. She sat where she had been directed, on a wide stone bench beneath a fragrant tree laced with fairy lights, Diglon Rifle at her side.

The garden was largely shrouded in night, pierced gently here and there by the spangle of decorative lights. Shadia was invisible between the bench and the outside gate, on the alert for trouble. Clonak had disappeared into the shadows nearer the house, guarding the door against the possibility of an Yxtrang rush.

As oath-holder, Daav occupied the position of greater peril, leaning against an artfully place boulder directly before the stone bench occupied by his oathsworn. He crossed his arms over his chest, which put his right hand on the butt of the pistol riding hidden in his vest.

Gods, he thought, *I don't want to waste a scout.*

"Nor ought we to endanger the House." Aelliana's tone was more than a little acerbic, which was, Daav owned, no less than he deserved, who had placed Erob's House in peril by insisting upon this mad course.

If the captain comes quickly . . . he thought. Yes, and if

Hazenthull could but hold scout-sense against the rising tide of rage—that the solution which was to have bought her senior's life had failed, leaving her and her dependent trapped and in the power of the enemy . . .

"She depended upon her senior to find the way clear, once he was healed," Aelliana said. "She did not plan fully."

How could she? he replied, reading the change in Hazenthull's muscles, malleable under the growing warmth of her rage. *His survival was the essence of her plan.*

On the stone bench, Hazenthull shifted, her muscles bunching as if for the charge. Daav's hand closed around the hidden pistol.

"Explorer." Unexpectedly, Diglon Rifle leaned forward. "Explorer, the captain comes."

She turned on him, face set in a snarl, and started badly when the house door snapped open, admitting the person—and the voice—of Nelirikk Explorer.

"Prepare for inspection!" he commanded, in the Yxtrang common tongue.

Diglon Rifle rose at once, marched over to the pool of light spilling from the open door and dropped into parade rest.

Hazenthull Explorer sat, as a woman turned to stone, staring, her face beneath the tattoo work beginning to crumble.

"Explorers kept discipline, when I was in the corps," Nelirikk said, acidic in the extreme; and then snarled, "Prepare for inspection!"

The command voice sent a little thrill even along Daav's scout-trained nerves. Diminished as she was, Hazenthull was in no condition to resist.

Sullen, but obedient, she stood, walked out into the light and assumed parade rest slightly in advance of Diglon Rifle, as befit her higher rank. Nelirikk placed himself to the right and slightly forward of both, eyes front.

Daav sighed and stood away from the boulder, hands at his side, pistol nestled yet in its secret pocket, and wondered how soon the captain might arrive.

Wonder was speedily answered.

"Troop! Attention!" Nelirikk bellowed, and all three

straightened as the empty doorway framed a slender woman in working leathers, her white shirt laced with silver cord, her red hair neatly braided and wrapped three times around her head, like the crown of a barbarian princess. At her back, not immediately noticeable, walked a man, dressed as she was, in working leathers, his shirt black, his hair dark.

Daav took a careful, quiet breath. *The scout, is it?* he thought. *Aelliana, behold our son.*

His vision slipped, the images going ghostly, as it did when she was actively using his eyes, rather than merely depending upon the data he gathered for both of them.

"A scout sublime," she murmured. "No more substantive than a thought, and the edges of him so sharp he fairly glows. Though I think that he would not be quite so invisible if his lady did not deliberately draw the eye to herself." She paused. "A formidable pair of children, to be sure, van'chela—and aptly joined, leaf and root." His eyesight blurred; became his own once more. "We may be proud."

Or terrified, Daav amended, and heard her laugh before she vanished from his awareness.

Straight up to the waiting troops walked the red-haired lady, and stood before them, hands behind her back, chin up. She took her time considering them; the man at her side glanced casually 'round the garden, unerringly picking out the positions of the three scouts.

Apparently satisfied with what she saw, the lady deigned to speak. "I am Captain Miri Robertson, field name Redhead." Her voice was firm, her Yxtrang slow, but robust, her accent, Daav noted wryly, neither native nor quite as ghastly as his own. "I am in command here. Lieutenant, present the recruits."

"Captain." Nelirikk saluted, showily, and barked out. "Candidate Hazenthull Explorer, stand forward for inspection!"

For a marvel, she did so, and saluted, somewhat faintly, her stance eloquent of disbelief as she gazed down upon a captain two-thirds her height and less than half her mass.

"Captain," she said, warily.

"Explorer." The captain's tone was cool

"Candidate Diglon Rifle!" Nelirikk ordered. "Stand forward for inspection!"

He did, saluting with energy. "Captain!"

"Rifle." Slightly warmer, there, accompanied by an infinitesimal nod of the head. "Why do you want to enlist under me?"

"Captain." He saluted, looking bewildered, as well he might, thought Daav. *Why* was not the concern of mere Rifles.

"Captain, soldiers need command. We are . . . abandoned in place, without orders, except to resist the enemy until we die." He paused, brow furrowed, tattoos rumpling. "Captain, I would rather live than die."

Captain Miri Robertson, field name Redhead, smiled. "So would I." The smile faded.

"Hazenthull Explorer."

"Captain."

"Why do you want to enlist under me?"

There was a pause, possibly longer than was quite considerate of the captain's honor.

"Captain. Soldiers need command."

The captain shook her head, Terran-style. "But explorers—like scouts—chafe under too much command. As I well know." She paused, then snapped in full command mode.

"Explain!"

Hazenthull jerked, and saluted, hastily. "Captain. It was known that the Hero of the Battle for the Airfield had recruited an explorer. It was thought that such a captain might attach more explorers to her unit. The Fourteenth Conquest Corps has deserted us. Without command we are dead and without honor. Under a Hero captain we may serve with honor and die with glory. For the good of the Troop."

There was a small silence before the captain nodded. "Better." She glanced at the silent scout, perhaps gaining some information from his face that was invisible to Daav. She brought her gaze back to the two Yxtrang.

"Before I ask for your oaths," she said slowly, "I will tell you that the troop you came to join, the Lytaxin Irregulars, was a field troop,

I DARE   493

its ranks filled by survivors from the first wave of the invasion and a
few old soldiers who had been separated from their home troops.
Having done duty, the Irregulars have—honorably and without
prejudice—been disbanded. The survivors have returned to rebuild
their homes. The old soldiers, many of them, have been reattached
to their home troops, which came in as part of the counterattack.
Those who have not are temporarily attached to mercenary units
here. They will take transport when the mercenary forces lift and
will rendezvous with their home troop out of headquarters.
Understand this. I hold rank as a captain of mercenary soldiers,
commissioned by Commander Carmody himself, but at this time, I
have no command."

She paused. Neither recruit made a sound.

"In addition to my rank as captain," she continued, "I owe
allegiance to a kin-group—Clan Korval. This kin-group has
acquired a worthy and cunning enemy. In order to fight this enemy,
we will need soldiers. The sub-group Line yos'Phelium stands ready
to receive your oaths, if you wish to give them, but you must understand that this service will be different. You will be required to learn
languages other than the tongue of the Troop; cultural study will be
required. I expect this of explorer and Rifle, alike. Worse, you will
serve not one captain, but the leaders of the sub-kin-group, who are
two and equal." She put her hand, palm flat, against her chest; then
likewise touched the man beside her.

"This is Val Con yos'Phelium Clan Korval. He is, among many
other things, a Liaden scout and my lifemate." She tipped her head,
and asked a question in Liaden. "Do you understand 'lifemate',
Hazenthull Explorer?"

"If the captain pleases. As we are taught, it is an arrangement of
sexual convenience, with implications of exclusivity."

"Oh, my," Aelliana murmured.

She's young, Daav countered. *And I will own, my lady, were we
both embodied . . .*

"True."

The captain's eyebrows had lifted. She glanced at the man
beside her.

"Hear that?" she said in Terran. "*Convenient.*"

He moved his shoulders. "The interpretation of custom is uniquely subject to error, as even the most careful scholar will confess."

Hazenthull stirred. "If the captain pleases," she managed in her ragged Terran. "Does this mean that 'lifemate' is not a sexual architecture?"

"In general, it is," the captain said slowly. "In specific, it's a lot more. Nelirikk'll fill you in, and you can mince it up into Rifle-size pieces. If you wanna go through with it, that is. I wouldn't blame you if you didn't want to have nothing to do with swearing to Line yos'Phelium. Nelirikk can fill you in on that, too."

Hazenthull's eyes moved, questioning.

"The scout who stands beside the captain is of Jela's own blood," Nelirikk said in the tongue of the Troop. Daav saw Diglon start and lean forward, face intent.

"The Line the captain asks you to give oath to is the Line to which I have myself given oath. When the captain and the scout go against the enemy of their blood, I will be at their backs. If there is a place or a service of greater glory in all the galaxy, I have not heard of it."

There was silence. Hazenthull looked to Diglon Rifle, not as if she were seeing him, Daav thought, but as if she were weighing the burden on her soul. She sighed, and saluted.

"Captain. We came to offer ourselves and our weapons to Captain Miri Robertson. That has not changed. If a captain so wise in war will accept our oaths and weapons, we will serve her until our last bullet is spent."

The captain nodded, glanced aside—and Daav found himself pinned in a feral gray glance.

"If Scout yos'Phelium will relinquish the short-oaths he holds in my name, this man and I will take your oaths to Line yos'Phelium."

YOS'GALAN HAD BEEN ROUSED from his bed, Emrith Tiazan surmised, not without a certain satisfaction. Not that he was rumpled, mis-buttoned, clumsy, or in any way unseemly; but the silver eyes were heavy, and the charade of the voluble fool was missing entirely. Indeed, one might almost say the bow he accorded her was . . . terse.

"Erob."

"yos'Galan." She inclined her head, merely, not bothering to rise from her seat on the edge of the stone bridge; and pointed at the giants slumbering in her quiet place.

"Those are yours, I believe?"

He sighed. "In fact, they are not, though they stand kin to my brother and his lifemate."

She sighed in her turn. "How else? Well, no matter. Korval's kin-lines are not mine to tend. Thank the gods. Remove them. Immediately."

The thin white eyebrows lifted. "I failed to notice the location of the pneumatic hoist when I came in. Perhaps you would be good enough—?"

"Or perhaps I would not. *Wake* them, yos'Galan, and remove them. Understand me, I would not require it of you, were your cha'leket or his lifemate able. However, my information is that both are convalescent, so the duty falls to near-kin."

"They are," he said slowly, "guests of your House."

She stared at him. "I beg your pardon? Who admitted them?"

"Surely that information is in the door-log."

Well, and so it would be—later just as much as now. And she was far too wily an old woman to be found in doubt of an assertion made by one of Korval. She sighed again and looked at the large, unmoving bulks of them, sprawled all over her comfort place.

"And I suppose this is just like home?" She raised a hand. "No, leave it. Only tell me how long they will sleep."

"Forgive me, but I am ignorant of their customs and their habits. It may that my brother's lifemate will know the length of their sleep cycle, though I hesitate to disturb her own rest."

"Yes. Well." Creakily, she began to rise from her seat on the edge of the bridge, and was agreeably surprised to find a large brown hand extended to her service. She slid her hand into his and allowed him to help her rise, then walked with him, companionably side-by-side back across the bridge and toward the door.

"This is a pleasant garden," yos'Galan said, smiling at a colorful bank of gladoli.

Well, and it was that, Emrith allowed, when it wasn't being invaded by giant turtles. She inclined her head.

"I thank you," she said calmly. "It is one of the joys of—"

The remote in her pocket gave tongue. She snatched it out, thumbed 'receive' and snarled, "Who dares?"

There was a moment of terrified silence, or so she devoutly hoped, before An Der spoke, respectfully.

"Your pardon, my delm. I relay a message from the door. Lady Nova yos'Galan has arrived claiming guest-right and requesting the comfort of her close-kin."

"Has she," said Erob, and directed a glare at the lady's brother. "Pray conduct Lady Nova to the guesting suite in the garden wing. Her brother will be with her shortly. Should she have any other requirements, the House exists to serve her." She closed the connection.

yos'Galan spread his big hands. "Surely you can't blame me?"

"Oh, can I not?" Emrith Tiazan snapped. "She is your sister!"

"But more than that," he said soothingly, "she is Korval-pernard'i, in which face she strongly represents a force of nature. A brother—a mere thodelm!—hardly commands her arrivals and departures."

She drew a deep breath, but he was bowing, gracefully, and with more than a touch of irony.

"However, since the House has promised my sister the comfort of her close-kin, I should betake myself to the guesting suite in the garden wing with no further delay. Good evening, ma'am." And so he left her, seething.

"LIEUTENANT, please take the troops to the staff cafeteria inside and wait for me there," Captain Robertson ordered. She turned her head, looking out across the dark garden.

"Shadia Ne'Zame."

The darkness shifted, and coalesced into a woman in scout leathers, bowing the bow between equals. "Captain Redhead?"

"Do me the favor of lending your countenance to the troop," the captain said, and her Liaden bore the very accent of Solcintra. She switched to Terran. "Stay out of trouble, got it?"

Shadia grinned. "Got it." She waved a hand at Nelirikk. "After you, Lieutenant."

"Troop, about! Single file! Follow me!" Nelirikk marched into the House of Erob, followed by an explorer, a Rifle, and, lastly, skipping, a scout, who lightly touched the control as she passed over the threshold. The door slid shut behind her.

Daav shifted, and found himself caught in the regard of two pair of eyes—one gray, one green.

"Clonak," the scout said, without turning his head. "Grant us half-an-hour."

There was no reply, merely a subtle disturbance in the air, then the slight sound of the gate at the end of the garden, opening—and closing.

Daav waited.

Surprisingly, it was Miri Robertson who spoke.

"Any ideas what we ought do with you?"

The tone was more than a little ironic; the dialect street-rat Terran. Daav shrugged, deliberately Terran.

"I don't know that you need to *do* anything with me," he said, in his most finicking, professorial accents.

She snorted. "Got the proper respect for command," she told the green-eyed man at her left shoulder.

"Ah," he said, eyes and face bland. She shook her head and looked back to Daav, an expression of mingled exasperation and amusement informing her mobile features.

"Wanna tell me under what authority you took those oaths?"

"Blood kin," he said, more sharply than he had intended. "I couldn't very well take oaths for the House, you know—especially as I rather think my name has been written out of the roster of lives and into the lists of Korval's dead."

"No," the scout said in his soft, murmuring voice, "it has not."

Daav met the green gaze and waited.

The scout's left eyebrow slipped upward a fraction. "Surely, you don't think your brother gave over hope of your eventual return—or that your son did?"

"My brother," Daav said slowly, "perhaps not. What my son might do is—alas—beyond my ability to predict. He was so young when we parted, you see."

"Precisely," the boy murmured. "It will perhaps amuse you to know that your son did not strike your name from the book of the living, nor did he ever give over hope of your eventual return. He had several pointed questions to ask you, as I am certain you will understand."

"My understanding is perfectly engaged," Daav assured him, "since it was the very need to ask pointed questions which drew me out of my Balance and sent me back toward Liad."

Something flickered in the green eyes. The boy inclined his head. "I regret to inform you that Er Thom your brother has died during your absence. He survived his lifemate by only a Standard."

It still sent an electric chill along his veins, the knowledge that Er Thom was gone; that he would never again see his brother's face, or hear the rare, sweet music of his laughter. Daav took a hard breath, inclined his head in turn, and dropped into High Liaden for the perfectly correct response.

"I thank you. Clonak had previously informed me of these things, but I had not yet had it from kin."

He straightened to find the captain looking over her shoulder at the scout.

"Well?"

"Well," he returned.

"Right." She looked at Daav, gray eyes serious now. "You want back in or is this just a visit?"

He had discussed this very choice with Aelliana, several times. *She* was of a mind to become re-clanned, pointing out that he could not reasonably expect to resurrect Professor Kiladi on Delgado and would thus need to establish another character elsewhere, over another period of years, before he might take up his Balance once more.

"And truly, van'chela," she had said, "I believe this phase of

Balance complete. Now it is time to gather allies and to pool what is known."

Sound advice it was, and well-argued, yet there was a certain disinclination to return to the confines of Liad after having for so many years enjoyed the easy customs of the Terran worlds.

Miri Robertson grinned. "Tough call, ain't it?"

"Surprisingly so." He smiled at her. "I am guided in this by my lifemate, who I am persuaded would wish me safe among kin."

"Safe among kin ain't what we're offering this quarter," she told him, very serious indeed. "Be sure you know that."

Daav raised his eyebrows. "I know it now, I thank you. The condition is not so different from my life away."

"OK, then. First things first." She moved one step back, which put her shoulder-to-shoulder with her lifemate.

Daav took a sharp breath, and felt Aelliana, awake and aware, and very interested in the matter at hand.

Miri Robertson lifted her chin and looked him in the eye before spreading her arms in the ritual gesture.

"We see you, Daav yos'Phelium," she said, the High Liaden phrase ringing against the darkness. "Come forward and be reunited with your House."

Throat tight, and eyes misted, he stepped forward. He had to bend a trifle to accept his Thodelmae's kiss; not at all to receive the Thodelm's. He did not entirely anticipate the embrace that followed— as perhaps his son had not, judging by its abruptness and the rough, anguished whisper in his ear:

"Father, where the *hell* have you been?"

DAY 308

❋ ❋

Standard Year 1392
Blair Road
Surebleak

DESPITE A NATURAL desire to please one's oathsworn, Pat Rin
did not sleep well. Indeed, his exertions toward a restful slumber
were so little rewarded that he arose from his celibate, sagging bed
after only a few hours of tossing and turning, and made hasty use of
a shower which could at best be coaxed to produce tepid water.
Thereafter, Natesa at his back in defiance of a direct order to seek
her own couch, he had another tour of his new property, yanking
open every drawer in every room, ending—unfulfilled, frustrated,
but considerably warmer for the exercise—in the so-called "parlor,"
where he was in good time to greet the printer.

That worthy came, as she had last evening, ink-stained and
breathless, with the addition this morning of a fistful of flimsy gray
sheets, which she thrust at Pat Rin with a broad grin.

"On the street, Boss. Got a couple of mine from the shop and
some of Audrey's on the corners, reading 'em out, with extras to
give the ones who can read themselves."

"Well done." Pat Rin shook one sheet loose and passed it to

500

Natesa, took another for himself, and put the rest atop the chest of drawers he had been, fruitlessly, exploring.

It was, he saw at once, the paper that was gray; the printing itself was remarkably crisp and resisted smudging. The announcement of the change in administration was set top-and-center, with no alteration in his original text. That was good. At the bottom of the page was a boxed advertisement, announcing the grand opening sale at the Carpet Emporium on Blair Road, directly across from Al's Hardware.

"We will want one of these put out every morning," he said to the printer. "I will give you news from the boss' office. It would please me, however, if this effort were to develop into an . . . honest . . . publication, imparting news of interest and importance to everyone who lives on these streets."

The printer nodded. "I was talking to one of mine last night, while we was setting the type on this. Old fella. He remembers way back, and he says we usta have a—a daily gab-rag. Told me how to set it up. We're gonna need couple people on the street, finding out what's up and who's doin' which. They'd write it up and we'd set it—and every morning, early, it's on the street, free. *Free*," she said again, emphatically, though Pat Rin had made no demur. "Reason we can give it away, is we sell these boxes like you got here to the joint-owners—like Al and Tobi and, hell, Ms. Audrey. Sounded weird to me, but Laird—that's the old guy—Laird says the owners paid up, and were glad to do it. The percentage is that they got more traffic through their joints, especially if they'd do a—a *special* on something everybody needs—sugar, say. Sell it low instead of high to—"

Pat Rin raised a hand, and the printer chopped off in mid-sentence, eyes showing white in her ink-smudged face.

"I am familiar with the concept. It is precisely what I propose and I am delighted that you have an advisor to hand. Do you find yourself able to undertake this project?"

"I'm in," she told him. "I need to know what your piece is so we can price up the boxes right."

Pat Rin frowned. "My . . . piece. I—Ah." It was expected that he take a profit from the printer's endeavor, while absorbing nothing of the risk. Gods, what a hideous place. He sighed.

"My piece will be taken in advertising space," he said, showing her the flimsy sheet. "A box, precisely as you have it here, with words that will alter at my discretion. Three times a week, I will have such an advertisement from you."

She blinked. "That's it?"

He lifted his eyebrows, consciously adapting a High House hauteur. "It is sufficient."

"Yessir," she said hastily, and cleared her throat, looking around her. "Well, if you're not—"

"Hold." He extended a hand, and she froze as if he had turned her to stone. "There may be another service you may perform for me. I will pay," he said sternly, "for this service."

The printer glanced aside, possibly trying to gain something from Natesa's face. In this, she was apparently frustrated, for she looked back to Pat Rin with a jerky nod. "Sure, Boss. What can I do for you?"

"Pens," he said.

"Pens?"

"To write with. Ink pens. Black ink, by preference, or blue. But any color will do—I apprehend that I may not be able to afford to be proud. Have you such access to such things?"

She swallowed, her eyes sliding toward Natesa again, before being forcibly brought back to his face. "Yessir. I can get you pens. Black ink *and* blue. Got red, too, and green. Purple . . ."

"Black," he said firmly, and added, after taking thought. "And red. A dozen each, if you have them in such quantity. If not, as many as you can bring me today, with the balance due when they are available."

She nodded, jerkily. "Right, Boss," she said, her feet sliding against the plastic floor, preparatory to taking her leave—and froze once again when Pat Rin raised his hand.

"One last thing," he said. "A—a logbook."

"Logbook, Boss?" There was genuine puzzlement on the woman's face.

503

Pat Rin sighed. "A bound book, with the interior pages blank, so that one may—may make notations. Of a good size . . ." His hands moved, squaring it out in the air between them. "The binding of some durable material—leather, perhaps or—"

"Got it!" The printer's face lit. "Can do, Boss. Got just what you need. I'll send it over with the pens."

"And an invoice," Pat Rin cautioned her. "I *will* purchase these from you."

"Sure, Boss. Whatever you say." She moved her feet again, clearly aching to be gone.

"Thank you," Pat Rin told her. "You have done well. Natesa will see you out."

"Right. Uh—you're welcome. Boss." She darted after Natesa and Pat Rin closed his eyes, wishing most heartily for a cup of tea.

Pat Rin put the tin down on the kitchen table, not quite able to repress the shudder, and stood, head bent, striving for patience. Once, the tin before him had contained a perfectly unexceptional blend of afternoon tea. Now . . .

The cook, who had been hovering, hands twisting in his apron, sighed.

"Bad, huh?" He said it almost wistfully.

"On several counts," Pat Rin told him, with really commendable calmness. "First, it is old. Second, it is damp. This sort is a dry leaf tea." He took a careful breath. "Well. We shall have to purchase more. When—"

The cook was shaking his head vigorously. "No, sir. Or, at least, not if you're after more that look like that tin there. Got a bunch of 'em in the pantry."

"Which are of like age?" Natesa murmured.

Pat Rin moved a shoulder. "The age perhaps does not matter so much," he said. "This tin had been stasis-sealed. If the others have not been breached, there may actually be something in this house worth drinking." He waved a languid hand at the cook. "Take me to the pantry."

The man blinked. "Ain't no need of that, Boss. Won't take me a minute to fetch 'em out for you."

"Yes, but you see," Pat Rin explained gently, "eventually I will wish to partake of a meal, and I am afraid that the quality displayed last evening must improve. Rapidly. So, I am interested in what else might be in the pantry in addition to tea; and if any of it is eatable, or may be made to be eatable." He fixed the man in his eye and frowned. "In short, I wish to ascertain whether I need a new pantry or a new cook."

"Oh," the cook said. "Gotcha." He unwrapped his hands from his apron, and pointed. "Right this way, Boss."

Pat Rin followed, Natesa at his back. The pantry was at the end of a narrow hallway, behind a heavy wooden door. The cook pushed this portal open and brought up the lights, revealing half-a-dozen orderly shelves of tinned stuffs, and bags that announced their contents in letters and pictograph: salt, sugar, flour, rice. To the right of these were a few bins, covered over with old blankets. Above, suspended by cords from the center beam, were perhaps a dozen round, waxy balls.

The cook stood respectfully aside as Pat Rin toured the room. There were more empty shelves than full, which struck him as odd in the house of a supposed Power—but, then, much about the late Boss Moran's house struck him as odd. He perused the stocks leisurely, finding first ten stasis sealed tins of the same unexceptional blend as that which had been spoilt. He picked one up and stood with it cradled in his hand, reading the labels of the other tins.

It appeared that he was wealthy in tinned fish, tinned crackers, and two or three varieties of tinned soup. Next to these things were perhaps half-a-dozen glass jars, vacuum-sealed, each bearing a hand-lettered label: *Jam*. He took one of those, too, and carried it and the tea-tin in the crook of his arm as he moved over to inspect the contents of the bins, Natesa to his right, and a step behind.

Further to the right, within the shadows cast by of a row of empty shelves, something moved; at the door, the cook gasped, and stiffened. Beside him, Natesa drew, fierce and fluid—

"Do not!" He flung a hand out, and she whirled, staring at him out of obsidian eyes that must surely have done damage—*had* done damage . . . He shook away the wound and pointed. "It is only a cat."

She looked down the line of his finger and the cat obliged him by strolling out into the greater light, sparing the two of them a yellow-eyed glance of utter boredom before trotting off down the room, to be lost once more in the shadows.

"I . . . see," Natesa said, on a long sigh, slipping her weapon away. She looked back at him, eyes considerably less sharp, and inclined her head. "Master."

"Surely, merely lucky?" he responded, deliberately flippant, and looked over to the cook, standing clenched and slightly pale by the door. "I have some . . . familiarity . . . with cats."

"Yessir, Boss. Boss Moran, he liked to shoot cats."

"Yes, well. I prefer not to have mice." Taking a deep breath, he continued to the bins.

Leaning over, he flicked back the blankets. Bin One contained a goodly number of some sort of tuber, still wearing their native soil. Bin Two was wholly given over to pungent-smelling bulbs—possibly the local equivalent of onion. Bin Three was filled near to overflowing with large orange fruits, which appeared to be of a robust habit.

Pat Rin turned to face the cook, and pointed up at the center beam.

"Cheese?"

"Right you are, Boss. Best cheese in the city."

"Ah. As it happens, I am partial to cheese."

The cook smiled. "We'll getcha a slice off the one in the kitchen, when we go back. Man who likes cheese'll find it a friend."

Pat Rin eyed him. "I infer from this that Mr. Moran did not care for cheese?"

"Nossir. Boss Moran, he didn't like much, 'cept to hoard his money. And makin' his 'hands crawl—he did get a heapin' cup o'pleasure outta that."

"I wonder that you stayed with so unsatisfactory a master," Pat Rin commented, but the man only stared at him. Sighing, he jerked his head toward the bins.

"Those tubers—are they a local specialty?"

The cook nodded. "Jonni grows 'em up on the roof. He takes care of 'most all the vegetables."

"I see. Yet when Mr. McFarland particularly desired vegetables for last evening's meal, you sent in a mess of leaves. I wonder why?"

"After *greens*, is what he told me. We're too early in the season for greens. Froze some stuff, end of last growin' season, but it's gone now, too."

"I see," Pat Rin said again, and used his free hand to motion the cook out into the hallway. "Let us repair to the kitchen. I am very much in need of tea, and perhaps some of your excellent bread, with jam on it."

They were seated 'round the kitchen table sometime later when Cheever McFarland arrived, all three supplied with a beer tankard filled with a gently steaming pale green liquid. Plates before each bore the sticky remains of toast-and-jam sandwiches. Pat Rin and the cook had their heads together, apparently engaged in producing a grocery list, while Natesa looked on, her eyes heavy, and faintly amused.

"Mornin'," he said to her, and pointed at the wreckage. "Any more of any of that left?"

She moved her head in a subtle nod toward the counter. "There is tea, and there is jam, and there is bread. Toast is made on the grill."

"Right." He considered her. "Long night?"

The fingers of her left hand flickered in the sign-language known as Old Trade, letting him know the boss hadn't slept—and neither had she.

"Right," he said again. "I'm on shift now. Get some rest. I'll sit on him."

She smiled faintly. "I wish you good fortune, but I believe you will find yourself bested," she murmured, easing out of her chair. At the sink, she emptied what was left of her tea, rinsed the beer mug and set it to be washed.

She looked back as she left the kitchen. Pat Rin yos'Phelium and the cook were still deep in their plans; the cook laboriously writing down the boss' suggestions.

"DON'T LOOK LIKE THE AD'S drawing so good," Cheever

commented at about half-past lunch. "What say we shut the store for an hour and go on down to Tobi's for bite?"

Pat Rin glanced up from the battered notebook he'd been studying for most of the morning. "We do not appear to be awash in customers," he allowed, courteously. "Nor have I properly attended the hour. By all means, Mr. McFarland, provide yourself with lunch."

Cheever sighed mightily and shook his head. "I thought we'd got the concept of 'security' through to you. I ain't leavin' you here on your own, even if you probably are the best shot on the planet." He swung a hand around, impatiently. "Think about it! What if five guns come in through the front door right now and you was alone?"

The Liaden smiled, politely, like Cheever'd maybe told him a slightly off-color joke. "Why, then, Mr. McFarland, I should immediately be out the back door."

"If I believed that—which I don't—how'd you plan on dealin' with the two they sent 'round to watch the alley?" He frowned, as ugly as he knew how. "You ain't making things easy for your security, Boss. My copy of the plan don't include the part where your head gets blown off."

"Ah." He closed his eyes. Cheever considered him, letting the frown go, and allowed as how he was worried. The plan—because there was one, hammered out between the three of them long before they raised Surebleak—was only good to a point. Taking over Moran's territory—that had been according to plan. They had to have a planetary base, and while Moran's streets weren't exactly convenient to the spaceport, they had been the nearest most accessible target. From here, they could consolidate, and figure out how to get past the more powerful fatcats who controlled the territories surrounding the port.

He'd considered that they'd be using their guns more than once, 'cause that was how business was done on Surebleak, and didn't think much more about it.

Since yesterday, though, he'd thought about it a lot.

Pat Rin . . . Pat Rin wasn't a pro. Oh, he was a good shot; he walked the walk, and that cool, pretty face of his didn't give away much, but that was gambler bravado—plus a measure of pure cussedness, give the boy his due—and nothing like what marked Natesa out as a gun to fear.

Pat Rin had a revenge to accomplish. Cheever understood that. In fact, he sanctioned it. And he didn't doubt—if the boss had to personally shoot every fatcat and loyal 'hand on Surebleak to do it, that the job would get done. What worried him, considerable, was the question of what would be left of Pat Rin yos'Phelium at the end of the campaign. He'd already taken a hit that would've unhinged most Liadens, as Cheever understood it. Pat Rin hadn't come unhinged—at least, not so you'd notice—but he was starting to show some strain. Even as he sat there in his chair, eyes closed and restful looking, Cheever could see the tension in his muscles, and new lines starting to etch in around his mouth. The success of the game depended on this man, Cheever thought—and came suddenly to the realization that nobody—maybe not even Pat Rin himself— knew what Pat Rin would do next.

"Well." The Liaden opened his eyes and slipped the little book away into his jacket. "One does not build an entire day's labor upon a jam sandwich." He stood, a shade less graceful than his usual, which Cheever thought was the sleepless night starting to show.

"Let us have lunch, Mr. McFarland."

Come down to it, Cheever hadn't expected to win the argument, and he wasn't sure he liked the idea of the boss in Tobi's surrounded by workaday streeters, now that he had the victory. Still, they had to show their faces around town—that was the point of the rug store, after all. As if to enforce this line of reasoning, Cheever felt his stomach rumble an order for a brew and a sandwich.

That being settled, he followed the boss into the store proper just as the first customer on the day walked in off the street.

She was a sight to behold—on first glance as out of place on the street as Pat Rin himself. Second glance found the silk to be second-grade synthetic; the jewelry light-gold set with mine-cut stones. Still, she bore herself as would a person of melant'i, come to call upon an equal.

Accordingly, Pat Rin bowed.

The lady considered him out of clever blue eyes, and shook her pale, elaborately coiffed head.

"I won't even try to duplicate that," she said, and her voice was high and sweet. "Let's just consider that I done what was polite."

"Indeed," Pat Rin said, smiling. "Let us do so. Have I pleasure of addressing Ms. Audrey?"

She nodded, unsurprised. "Expecting me, were you? Well, I guess you shoulda been, after last night. I was out on business, or I'd've tried to set things straight then. I'm hoping we can come to an accommodation today, if you got time?"

"Mr. McFarland and I were on our way to lunch. If you would care to join us . . . ?"

"Great minds think alike," she said, with a grin. "I was hoping you'd see your way clear to having a bite at my place. Not as public as Tobi's, and the food's better."

Pat Rin considered her, noting a certain tension—which was certainly expectable in one come to call upon the new and unknown quantity to whom one owed allegiance—as well as a certainty of her own worth. The clever eyes met his with frankness, which was rare in this place where he found himself. She was not by any means in her first youth, and struck him as both competent and commanding.

In fact, she was just such a one as he would need by him, if they were able to forge an alliance built on mutual profit.

He inclined his head. "Almost, you persuade me," he murmured. "Mr. McFarland?"

He felt, rather than heard the big man sigh. "Sounds great," he said. "Tobi's ain't the kind of place to do business, Boss."

So, Pat Rin thought grumpily, *I have cleared the matter with 'security.' Behold me, virtuous.*

"Well, now, that's—" the lady began, and cut herself off, frank gaze going over Pat Rin's shoulder.

"Will you *look* at that," she breathed, reverently. "I ain't *ever* . . ." She brought her eyes back to Pat Rin's face with a visible effort.

"That is one hell of a rug."

"So it is," he agreed smoothly, slipping into his merchant's role. He moved a hand, inviting her to make a closer inspection. Nothing could have been more to her liking.

At his direction, she sampled the nap, her fingers as reverent as her voice, and obediently inspected the underside, admiring the precious, hand-tied knots.

"Who'd make something like this?" she asked, when he had done and stepped back to allow her to commune with the carpet.

"Certain . . . members . . . of a particular sect," he replied, with perfect truth. "It is very rare to find such things for sale."

She looked at him, blue eyes shrewd. "Why's that?"

"Because, upon its world of origin, this carpet is a religious artifact, and the rules of the sect did not allow of them being sold."

"So, how'd you get this one?"

He smiled, liking her more and more. "Naturally, I must protect my suppliers. Let us say that it was offered for sale from a licensed dealer, who had paperwork sufficient to convince me of the carpet's authenticity."

She sighed, stroked the carpet one last time and moved a regretful step back, her eyes still on the pattern of the joyous revelers.

"How much does something like that put a body back?"

"That carpet—being a uniquity, you understand—may be purchased for eight thousand cash—" He raised a hand, smoothing away the protest he saw rising to her lips. "Or, it may be leased, by the Standard month, or the Standard year."

"Leased." She frowned, the clever eyes showing puzzlement. "What's that?"

"Ah. It is an arrangement whereby a customer will agree to pay a set sum which is significantly lower than the cost of the carpet, plus a refundable amount of earnest money, in order to have the use of a particular carpet for a month, two months—a year." He moved his shoulders, and raised his hands, showing her empty palms. "In that case, there are papers to be executed—agreements to be made. The customer would pledge to protect the carpet from spoilage, to keep it safe from theft, and to return it, intact, upon the day specified.

If the customer failed of meeting the terms, he would be seen to have purchased the carpet, and the full retail price would then be due."

Audrey considered him with interest. "So, how much to lease it, say, for a month?"

Pat Rin frowned slightly while he did several lightning calculations. *Of all the mad starts*, he scolded himself—and yet he was certain that he needed this woman's goodwill. Not that he would buy her—in fact, he doubted that he could buy her—but that he would show good faith, and a willingness to negotiate—yes, that he must do. Equal to equal. So . . .

"I ask two thousand cash, plus earnest money of an equal amount. But, you see, it is not efficient—for either of us—to lease for a month. I must ask a higher rate, because I must move it, twice, in a very short time. The most efficient arrangement for both is one that allows the carpet to rest in one place for a period of a few months. Should you wish to contract for three months, for instance, the monthly rate falls to one thousand cash; six months, and the rate falls again—to eight hundred cash. A year's lease may be had for a mere six hundred cash per month, plus the deposit of earnest money."

She grinned at him. "That's quite a scheme. Let's see . . ." She was quick at her numbers. "If I lease from you for a year, you'll see a return of seventy-eight hundred cash—two-hundred cash less'n the full selling price."

"Precisely so. However, the carpet will not be available as an item for sale during the period of its lease, and I must cover my potential loss."

It was a laugh this time, full-bodied and attractive. "Sure you do! And you get the rug back at the end of it to sell. Or lease. Seems to me that leasing's more profitable."

"On certain items, of course it is. I am fortunate that the carpet under discussion is durable as well as difficult to stain or to singe. However, it *is* a unique item and thus vulnerable to theft. And if it were stolen, I should not have it to sell ever again."

"There's that." She looked at him thoughtfully. "OK, I came to invite you to lunch, and your 'hand there's lookin' about ready to eat one of the rugs, which *can't* be good for business. Let's go over to my place, and talk."

"Certainly," he inclined his head. "After you."

Smiling, she turned and led the way out, though she did pause for a moment on the threshold, to look back over her shoulder at the Sinner's Carpet, and sigh.

MS. AUDREY'S HOUSE quite cast the late Boss Moran's "mansion" into the shade. Most likely, Pat Rin thought, as he followed his hostess through wide rooms and broad hallways, before embarking upon its career as a whorehouse, it had been three connected houses, and had required extensive remodeling to achieve its present state of relative sumptuousness.

It was a well-occupied residence, to judge by the number of brightly dressed young people they passed on the way to the "private dining room." The urge to understand it as a clanhouse was very nearly overmastering—and a temptation that he must at all costs resist.

The "private dining room," achieved at last, proved to be a cozy interior chamber. A long table at the far wall supported various tureens and platters. A smaller, round, table sat on a rag rug of a kind he was coming to know well, in the center of the room. Three places were set with what appeared to be silk napkins and silver utensils. A glass at each place was filled with a faintly amber liquid. In the middle of the table sat an artful and modest bowl of flowers.

"Here we are," Audrey said, cheerfully. "Gotta serve ourselves, but we can talk private."

She ushered them to the buffet, removed the lids from the tureens, and proceeded to serve herself, which was certainly her right, in her own house. Pat Rin picked up a plate, as she had, and followed her down the table, taking a mite from every unfamiliar dish. When he reached an end, he followed his hostess to the round table, situated his plate, pulled out his chair and sat.

"Elegant little thing, ain't you?" she said wistfully.

In the act of unfolding his napkin, Pat Rin froze. *How dare*— Slowly, leisurely, he turned his head, and met her eyes, frowning.

It could not precisely be said that a frown of disapproval from Pat Rin yos'Phelium caused seasoned gamers to swoon. However, it was generally agreed among those who had reason to know that it was no easy thing to bear, that frown, nor that it brought forcibly to mind the recollection that Lord Pat Rin shot first at Tey Dor's—and had done so for a number of years.

Ms. Audrey laughed, quite merrily, and shook her napkin out.

"Now, no offense meant—it's a habit of business, like you doing a quick-and-dirty assess on my poor old rag rug, first thing you walk in the room." She sighed, and looked up to bestow her pleasant smile on Cheever McFarland and his well-filled plate.

"That's right," she said comfortably. "Man your size has got to have his food. Enjoy yourself."

"I intend to, ma'am, thank you," Cheever answered easily. He shook his napkin onto his knee, picked up a fork and fell to.

Not entirely mollified, Pat Rin finished with his own napkin, extended a hand to his glass, raised it and essayed a exploratory sip.

It was a new wine, and a sweet one, with a faint, enchanting note of something reminiscent of ginger beneath. Pat Rin had a second sip and set the glass aside.

"The wine is pleasant," he said to his hostess. "May I know the vintage?"

Audrey smiled. "We just call it Autumn Wine. It comes in from the country in lots of six, and I generally buy a couple dozen, if that many pass through. Some of our clients are partial, and some of the staff. We've got a few left from last season's buy; I'll be pleased to give you a bottle."

A gift of wine. Pat Rin felt absurdly pleased as he inclined his head. "Thank you, I would like that."

She nodded, and had an appreciative sip from her own glass. "That's good," she murmured, and shook her head. "Understand, this wine'll turn, if you keep it too long into spring, and what you'll have then is some nice smellin' paint remover."

"Ah, then I will remember to enjoy it soon, with warm memories of your hospitality."

For a heartbeat, she stared at him, her mouth half-smiling, then she shook her head and returned to her meal.

At long last did Pat Rin address his own plate, and found the unfamiliar viands good—even very good. Nor did he wonder when Cheever McFarland rose from his place to refill his own plate.

"I wonder," Pat Rin said softly, "if you know who makes the rag rugs. I have several in . . . my . . . house, and would be pleased to have more—or even to purchase some for trade."

"Well, for that, Ajay Naylor makes 'em—has for years. But buying 'em for trade—there's no profit there, Boss. The rugs is how she pays. Strictly barter, is Ajay."

"Is she? But the trade I had meant was not necessarily local."

"Gonna sell 'em at the port?" Audrey frowned at her plate consideringly. "Might do, I guess."

"Do no ships come through the port?" Pat Rin murmured.

"Oh, well, ships. Sure they do. Once in a summer snowstorm. The trouble with trying to sell things to the *ships* is you gotta deliver the full order on time. Which means you need a safe road from here to there. Which you ain't got."

"And yet there is the Port Road, which runs through this territory and straight to the port," Pat Rin pointed out.

"That's right. And there's six different territories between here and there. That's a lot of toll—and assuming there ain't a turf war goin' on in one—or more!—when you gotta pass—*not* the way to bet, not with that bunch. Also assuming that somebody up an' comin' don't decided to knock you over and make your profit his."

"I see." Pat Rin sipped his wine. "Then we will need to work to secure the Port Road, so that all may have equal access to trade."

Audrey blinked at him. "Sure we will," she said politely, and Cheever McFarland laughed.

"Don't egg him on, ma'am," he said, pushing his plate aside and reaching for his glass. "He'll do it just to prove you wrong."

"Thank you, Mr. McFarland," Pat Rin said coolly, and turned back to his hostess.

"You will understand that I have not had much time to go over such records as I have . . . inherited . . . from the late Mr. Moran, so I wonder if you might tell me if there is a bank within my territory?"

Her eyebrows pulled together in a puzzled frown. "Bank?"

It was seldom that Pat Rin had cause to question his abilities in Terran, but she was so plainly at a loss, and that over an inquiry after an institution that must surely be well known to so astute a businessperson . . . Hurriedly, he sifted his vocabulary for the correct word to convey his meaning—and the word was "bank".

"Bank," he said again, softly, certainly—but her puzzlement did not abate. "Forgive me. An . . . institution . . . which keeps large sums of cash in trust for customers, which makes capital loans, receives collateral, pays out interest—"

"Oh!" Understanding dawned. "Gotcha. Pawn shops. Sure, you got two established and one making a start." She frowned, briefly. "Pays *out* interest, now—that's opposite the way it's been done. The shop charges you interest, see, to keep your item instead of selling it. No percentage in them paying *out* interest, when they gotta store the stuff, too."

Beside him, Cheever McFarland shifted, but when Pat Rin looked, the pilot was found to be gazing raptly at the artful arrangement of flowers.

"A pawn shop is a different enterprise entirely," Pat Rin said carefully. "The institution that I envision holds cash in trust for members, and loans cash to other members, to whom it charges interest. The institution then pays interest to its depositor-members, in payment for its use of their funds." He was about to go on to elucidate the more arcane functions of banks, but he saw from her face that he had said quite enough. Audrey obviously thought he was raving.

She had recourse to her glass, and sat holding it in her hand, looking at him out of considering blue eyes.

"OK," she said at last. "Just who would be running this joint—this *bank*?"

Pat Rin raised an eyebrow. "A board of trustees."

"Uh-huh. And the reason they don't take all the free money and leg it for Deacon's turf would be?"

Ah. *You have forgotten where you are*, he told himself, and sighed ruefully.

"Ordinarily," he answered Audrey, "I would say, because of the contracts and laws binding upon them. I quite see that such contracts and laws would be unenforceable under . . . present circumstances."

"It'd be tough," she allowed. "We don't have much to do with contracts and laws—not here, an' not on any other turf I ever heard of." She frowned and had a bit more of her wine.

"I like the idea," she said slowly. "I can see how it could work. But these trustees of yours—they'd have to be people who weren't tempted by big stacks of cash, and that ain't anybody I ever met."

"Many people are tempted by large sums of money." Pat Rin frowned. Surely, he thought, there was something, some *mechanism*, aside from law and honor, which would insure the safety of the investors, and the honesty of the trustees?

"How if," he murmured, his eyes now on the flower arrangement as well, but seeing something rather different—Mr. dea'Gauss seated in his office, holding forth on the structure of a particular fund that Pat Rin had wished to invest in, outlining the various failsafes and protocols . . .

"How if the procedures required the keys of at least three trustees in order to access the money itself? If the trustees are all businesspeople of consequence . . ."

"And, better yet, if they all hate each other," Audrey said, suddenly smiling. "This could work. It *could* work. It'll take some planning and some finagling, but it might be possible." Her smile widened into a grin. "Just moved from the Impossible pile to the Maybe pile. You'll be a trustee, yourself?"

"Indeed I will not. The bank—best call it a—a *mercantile association*—it should have nothing to do with the boss or the boss' office. Ideally, it should be a separate entity, protected by those laws and contracts we have both agreed are unenforceable at the moment."

She stared, then laughed, and looked aside to Cheever McFarland. "He like this all the time?"

"No, ma'am," Cheever said seriously. "Some days he's downright ornery. He sleeps, occasional. And, from time to time, he likes a game."

"Does he?" She looked back to Pat Rin with interest. "Cards?" she asked, then corrected herself, "No, you're a boxman, ain't you? Dice."

Pat Rin sighed, and spared a glare for Cheever McFarland, who was once again studying the flowers. To Audrey, he inclined his head, slightly.

"I am . . . familiar . . . with most types of gaming and gambling practiced in the galaxy."

"Well." She finished her wine and put the glass down. "What're you doing here?"

He raised an eyebrow. "Rusticating."

She didn't smile. "Plan on sticking around?"

"Surely that's my business."

"Was," she said, her voice almost stern. "But then you set yourself up as boss. That changes the rule of play." She raised a hand, as if she'd felt his outrage.

"Hear me out, just hear me out. Nort Moran was a stupid, selfish animal, and the whole territory's best off without him. Vindal—that was the boss before—she was smart, but she wasn't tough. Word was she didn't even try to pull when Moran walked in on her. You—you're smart *and* you're tough—and we need you. You're gonna be good for business—this bank idea of yours, for one; and putting the gab-rag back on the street. That's for day one. Who knows what you'll come up with by the time you're on the street a week?"

"Who, indeed," Pat Rin said politely, sternly suppressing the shiver. For the second time in his life, he was being offered a Ring. Gods. At least, this offer was made with honor—or so he thought—perhaps leavened with a healthy dose of fear.

Audrey nodded. "Right. Right. You're the boss. An' I'm outta line." She sighed, and pushed back from the table. "Just—think about it, OK?"

Apparently, their luncheon business was concluded. Pat Rin

inclined his head and rose. "I will think about it. My thanks for a most delicious and convivial meal."

"You're welcome," Audrey said, matching his formality. "I hope it'll be the first of many." She glanced up to Cheever McFarland. "Mr. McFarland, my pleasure."

"No, ma'am. *My* pleasure," the pilot assured her, gallantly, which won him an easy laugh before she led them back through the hallways and spacious rooms to the main entranceway.

There were rather more people about now, the clients obvious by their less grand—and more concealing—clothing. That several of the clients took him for a new addition to the house was plain from the stares of interest he intercepted. He sighed to himself, and followed his hostess, coming up to her side when she stopped a sleek young man dressed only in a pair of scarlet synth-silk trousers, and a purple sash. The young man favored him with a wide smile.

"Villy, love, run down to the pantry and bring a bottle of Autumn Wine up for the boss," Audrey said, quite loudly enough to be heard across the room. In fact, several heads turned in their direction—clients and residents alike.

The young man's smiled dimmed considerably, but he nodded briskly enough. "Sure thing, Ms. Audrey. Back in a sec." He was gone, running lightly on bare feet.

"He's a good boy," Audrey said comfortably to Pat Rin. "Your wine will be here in a flash."

"Ms. Audrey," he said, softly, but with genuine feeling. "You must remind me never to dice with you."

She laughed, and patted his arm. "Let them get a good look at you," she said, her voice as soft as his. "Your security's right behind you. Besides, it's been a long time since anybody was stupid enough to draw in *my* house."

There was a light patter of feet against floorboard, and Villy was back, bottle in hand. He presented it to Ms. Audrey with a flourish and prudently faded away.

"OK." Audrey presented the bottle with a similar flourish, smiling as he took it from her hands.

"Thank you," he said, pitching his voice to be heard.

"Glad to be able to oblige," Audrey assured him, also in carrying tones. She smiled impartially around the room and they went on.

In the entrance hall, Cheever opened the door and examined the street.

"Clear," he said, over his shoulder. Pat Rin bowed to Ms. Audrey—the bow between equals—turned.

"Oh," she said. "One more thing."

He looked back, eyebrow up.

"I'll lease that rug from you for six months. Can you have it here tomorrow?"

THROUGHOUT THE AFTERNOON they entertained a steady trickle of customers—most, so Pat Rin thought, come to look the new boss over. It was peculiarly unnerving, to be thus on display, and it required every bit of his considerable address to carry through, moving unhurriedly among his customers, answering questions with gentle and attentive courtesy.

Beside himself, the Sinners Carpet was the item of most intense interest. He lost count of how many times he displayed the knots; elucidated the fabric; told over its curious history—and revealed that, beginning on the morrow, it was on lease to Ms. Audrey, for a period of six months, Standard. Often enough, this led to a discussion of the concept of "lease," as it had with Audrey.

When at last Barth arrived to take up his post as night guard, Pat Rin felt he had been, in the idiom of Shan's mother, *spin washed and hung out to dry*. His head ached, and he wanted the study of his house in Solcintra, with its comforts of books, and comm screen, and a chair that cherished the contours of his body—wanted it so fiercely that his sight misted and he bent his head, biting his lip.

It is gone, he told himself, grimly. *Everything and everyone— gone, dead, destroyed, unmade. Believe it. Make your Balance your focus, or you will surely go mad.*

"You all right, sir?" Cheever McFarland's voice was soft, for a wonder, and carried a strong note of concern.

Pat Rin straightened. He must not display weakness before his oathsworn. He took a breath. "I am perfectly fine, Mr. McFarland," he said coolly and strode up the sidewalk, toward the "mansion" he called his home.

The door was opened to them by Gwince, grinning good-naturedly.

"Evening, Boss. Mr. McFarland. Natesa said to tell you, Boss, that the work you wanted done is in process. Cook asks when you want to eat supper. Printer's boy brought a package for you. Natesa put it in your office."

Pat Rin closed his eyes, there in the tiny vestibule of his house, and tried to recall what tasks he had particularly wished Natesa to accomplish. Ah. That would be the upgrading of Boss Moran's security arrangements. Very good. News of the delivery from the printer was also welcome—he had two persons of honor on the day, which surely found him richer than yesterday. What had been the—yes. Supper.

"Please tell the cook that Mr. McFarland, Natesa and I will dine in one Standard Hour. Mr. McFarland has a bottle of wine, which we will wish to drink with the meal."

She took the bottle from Cheever, eyebrows twitching in what might have been surprise, but she merely murmured a respectful, "Yessir, will do."

"Thank you, Gwince," he said and began to turn away, then swung back. "I wonder, do you know Ajay Naylor?"

Gwince looked surprised. "Sure, Boss. Everybody knows Ajay."

"Alas, not everyone," Pat Rin murmured. "I have not had the honor, an oversight that I wish to rectify. Do you think you might ask her to call on me at the store tomorrow, mid-morning?"

Now, Gwince looked puzzled, even faintly alarmed. "Sure, I can do that." She sent a glance into Cheever McFarland's face, but apparently found nothing there to ease her distress.

"Um, Boss—just so you know. Ajay's like four hunnert years old. She ain't—well, she ain't—" Gwince stumbled to a halt, regrouped, and produced a rather faint, "She makes rugs, see? And trades 'em out for stuff she needs."

Gods, what a filthy place! Pat Rin thought, furiously. *As if I would murder an old woman*—His fury flamed out, leaving him cold and shaken. While it was true that he had not yet murdered an old woman, who could say where the necessities of his Balance might take him? Gwince was within her rights to be wary of his reasons for wanting Ajay Naylor. He sighed and met her eyes.

"I have business to discuss with Ajay Naylor," he said, mildly, and was absurdly pleased to see the alarm fade from her eyes.

"Right," she said, briskly. "Mid-morning tomorrow, at the rug store. I'll tell her, sir."

"Thank you," he said again, and walked down the short hallway, Cheever McFarland a large and ridiculously comforting presence at his back—and paused on the threshold of the front parlor.

Last seen, this chamber had been very nearly as grubby as the printer he had interviewed there. This evening, while the furnishings must still dismay any person of taste, other matters had undergone a change for the better.

The floor, for instance. This morning, it had been a dull and slightly sticky gray. It now flaunted its true color for all to see—a pale, and not unbecoming blue—and showed a small, repeating pattern of a darker blue—flowers, perhaps, or some sort of decorative insect.

The walls, which had this morning been of a dinginess in competition with the floor, had been washed, revealing that they had, at some all but forgotten time in the past, been painted a blue to match the floor. The ceiling, likewise relieved of several years of grime, was discovered to be white, the central globe-shaped light fixture yellow. The effect was unexpectedly pleasant—rather like walking into a sunlit sky.

"Well," he murmured, and heard Cheever McFarland grunt behind him.

"Thought she was going to sleep."

Pat Rin glanced at the big man, eyebrows up. "You think Natesa did this?"

"Well, sure, don't you?"

"No," said Pat Rin, looking 'round the room and considering its possibilities. "I think she had it done. I wonder what else has gone forth, as we were whiling our hours in pleasure?"

"Guess we could take the tour and find out."

"We could," Pat Rin conceded. "Or we could ask Natesa, which would be much less fatiguing." He turned to look up the big man.

"Mr. McFarland, I am going to prepare for dinner. I don't doubt that you are heartily sick of the sight of me and wish a few moments to yourself. I give you my word that I will not be assassinated before the dinner hour."

Surprisingly, Cheever grinned. "Dismissed!" he said cheerfully and nodded. "See you at dinner."

Blessedly alone, Pat Rin took one more look at the blue room, reminding himself to congratulate Natesa on the result, and went upstairs to dress for dinner.

THE MEAL ARRIVED in a surprising two courses. The first consisted of a plate of tinned soup for each, and a communal platter of crackers and cheese. This was removed by a main course of baked tubers under a spicy brown sauce accompanied by thin slices of meat braised with onion; fresh bread, butter, tea, and Autumn Wine.

"Much improved," Pat Rin murmured, and heard Cheever McFarland chuckle.

"Improved ain't the word. I'm thinking that the cook was after poisoning us last night, eh, Natesa?"

"Possibly," she answered. "Just as possibly, he was frightened enough to have been thrown off his skill." She sipped the wine cautiously, and Pat Rin saw her eyebrows lift.

"This is pleasant," she said. "Have we a winery?"

"Alas. The bottle is a gift. And we are instructed that it is a fragile thing, not to be held far into the spring." He moved his shoulders. "We are further told that this vintage originates in the country, and that sometimes as many as two dozen bottles make it into this territory, whereupon they are purchased by Ms. Audrey."

"Ah." Her face lit. "You called upon Ms. Audrey?"

"Rather, she called upon us. We had a very pleasant discussion over lunch in her house."

"Where the boss here sweet-talked her into startin' a bank—no, hold it, a mercantile association—since pawn shops ain't good enough for him, and she tried to get him to promise to be boss for life." Cheever forked a slice of tuber and looked at it meditatively. "'Course, that's how it works here, anyhow, but she seemed of the opinion that his life was gonna be longer than most. Right taken with him, she was. Thought he was elegant."

Natesa laughed.

"We have also," Pat Rin murmured, "placed the Sinner's Carpet at lease for six months', Standard, at a rate of eight hundred cash per month."

"Ms. Audrey, of course," Natesa said. "No one else could afford it." She paused, her head slightly to one side. "Indeed, I am surprised to hear that *she* can afford it."

"A test of trust," he said softly, finishing the last of his meal with real regret. "She must know if we can work together—which is what I must know, as well. Also, I believe that her smuggling operation is profitable." He moved his shoulders. "So, we have progress upon the day." He pushed his plate aside and reached for his wine.

"I have noticed the improvement in the front parlor," he said, which phrase would have been entirely appropriate in the High Tongue, but struck the ear oddly in Terran, almost as an accusation.

However, Natesa, who spoke Liaden, seemed to have heard the commendation he intended to convey. She inclined her head politely and murmured that she would inform the staff of his approval.

"How's house security?" Cheever asked then.

Natesa turned to him. "Like the meal, much improved. We are not impregnable, of course, but we are difficult . If tomorrow's work goes as well, we will be formidable."

"That's good. What about the overheads? I can help out tonight, if you need it."

"Thank you; assistance would be most welcome. There is also a . . . device . . . in the sub-cellar that I would like to have your—"

The door to the dining room opened just enough to admit a thin person dressed in what appeared to be the street standard: Ill-fitting trousers and shirt, with a second shirt worn over the first, as

Sharon Lee & Steve Miller

a jacket. This particular specimen also had a shapeless cap crammed down over his ears. He came two steps into the room, a flicker of shadow at his heels, and froze, eyes stretched wide in a pointed brown face.

Pat Rin tipped his head, considering this apparition. He was young—a boy only; at a guess, several Standards younger than Quin—and bore himself with the tentativeness one might expect of a smaller and weaker "extra"—those who loitered in crowds on street corners, and were available for such day-labor as might manifest.

"Good evening," he said gently to the wide, frightened eyes. "I am the boss."

The boy nodded vigorously, and abruptly reached into his pocket. Pat Rin tensed and forced himself to relax, which was wisdom, for what came out of the pocket was a tuber. The boy held it up, and then touched it to his chest.

"What the—" began Cheever, but Pat Rin held up a hand, watching the wide eyes watch him, watch his *face*, with such intensity that—

"Wait," he said. "I think that this is Jonni, who gardens on the roof."

The boy nodded so vigorously this time that his cap came off his head and tumbled to the floor between his boots. He made no move to pick it up.

"And I also think," Pat Rin continued, "that Jonni is deaf."

The boy nodded again, his snarled black hair, released from captivity, flopped in his face.

"Deaf?" Cheever blinked. "But they can implant—" He cut himself off on a sharp sigh. "Right. Surebleak."

"Indeed." Pat Rin frowned. There was something he had heard, once—perhaps from Val Con?—that the deaf on low-tech worlds often developed a sign language for use among themselves, which, while diverse as to culture, were each built along the lines of Old Trade, with its emphasis on the concrete over the philosophical.

Tentatively, he moved a hand in the ritual greeting.

Jonni cocked his head, his eyes suddenly on Pat Rin's hands, rather than his face. His own hand—the one not holding the tuber—rose, touching fingertips to lips and descending, palm up, and stopping at chest level.

Not the sign he had used—not quite. He repeated the boy's truncated version, and earned himself another enthusiastic nod.

"So." He sighed, and moved his hand again, showing first Cheever and then Natesa. He said their names, clearly, keeping his face turned toward Jonni, so the boy could read his lips, then drew a circle in the air with his index finger, signing "protection".

Jonni frowned briefly at that, then suddenly grinned. He dropped the tuber into his pocket and used both hands to mimic pistols.

Diverse as to culture, indeed, Pat Rin thought, and tried the sign for "service".

But this proved beyond Jonni's ability to translate; and after a few frowning moments, he gave it up with an exaggerated shrug.

"Just so," Pat Rin said, slowly and distinctly. "Why have you come to me?"

That met with comprehension, and produced a veritable storm of signs, the single one Pat Rin recognized having to do with growing—or growing things. Quite possibly the unfamiliar signs were technical terms, invented to describe specific plants.

Pat Rin held up a hand, palm out. Jonni's hands faltered; fell.

"Tomorrow morning," he said. "We will go to the garden and you will show me. Is that soon enough?"

Jonni nodded.

"Good. Tomorrow morning at . . ." He ticked the time off on his fingers and heard Natesa sigh behind him.

Once more, Jonni nodded, then offered what was apparently his version of "good-bye"—a mere reversal of "hello"—recaptured his cap with a swoop, and vanished out the door before Pat Rin could return the courtesy.

"Tomorrow morning at two hours past dawn?" Natesa asked, resigned.

"It would be best to tend to it before I leave for the store," he told her earnestly. "And tomorrow will be an early day because of the necessity to deliver the Sinner's Carpet to Ms. Audrey's house."

He tipped his head. "You needn't come with me, you know. He scarcely looks able—or inclined—to hurl me off the roof."

"True. However, he may easily have friends who are very able and desperately inclined." She rose, and sent a meaningful glance at Cheever. "Mr. McFarland, if we are to tend the overheads, now is the hour."

"Yes'm, I see that's so." He frowned at Pat Rin. "Gwince is your security this shift. Try not to do anything to scare her, OK?"

Pat Rin inclined his head, stiffly. "I will do my humble best, Mr. McFarland. Within reason."

The big Terran just shook his head, and followed Natesa out of the room.

On the verge of following, Pat Rin paused, his eye drawn . . .

The cat was sitting upright beneath one of the extra plastic chairs, tail wrapped neatly 'round its toes, ears forward-pointing and interested, eyes glowing like molten gold.

"Well," said Pat Rin and went gracefully to one knee, extending a finger in greeting.

The cat considered options, leisurely, and at precisely the moment Pat Rin thought to withdraw his hand, stretched up onto its toes, walked from beneath the chair and touched the proffered finger with a flower pink nose.

It was, Pat Rin saw, the precise cat that had startled Natesa in the pantry that morning: Brown, with several broad, uneven stripes of black down its washboard sides, and another down its spine. Its tail was slightly fluffy, as was the rest of the cat, and also striped brown-and-black. It was not by any means a handsome cat; rather a brawler, if its ears were to be believed, and Pat Rin all but wept with joy to behold it.

"Well," he said again. "I don't doubt but that you've come to thank me for protecting you from Natesa's skill."

The cat blinked, strolled forward and stropped forcibly against Pat Rin's knee. Lightly, prepared to snatch his hand back at the suggestion of a claw, he stroked the brown-and-black back. The tail went up, the cat arched into the second stroke, and there was heard a momentary grinding sound, as if someone were drawing a whetstone down a blade. Pat Rin smiled, stroked the cat a third time and, reluctantly, arose. The cat looked up at him, yellow eyes molten.

"Duty calls, and her voice is stern," Pat Rin told it. "I must to the office. You may come with me, if you like, or you may return to your own duties, in the pantry."

So saying, he departed the dining room, collected Gwince from the other side of the door and went upstairs to his office, where Natesa found him, some few hours later, having resolved both the overheads and the matter of the device in the sub-cellar.

He was slumped over the desk, his head resting on an open book, pen fallen from lax fingers, an ugly brown and black cat curled on the floor by his knee, eyes slitted and yellow. Natesa drew a sharp breath, heart squeezing, then saw his brows pull together in a frown at some upstart dream, and sighed. He was asleep, nothing more. Silent as an assassin, she went forward.

He had been writing—black ink across the grayish pages of his so-called log-book. She glanced at the left-hand page, expecting to see code-words, or some arcane language of symbol and nuance . . .

He had chosen to write in Trade, very simply, the smooth lines of his hand drawing her eye even as she told herself that this was not hers to read.

Surebleak, Day 308, Standard Year 1392

My name is Pat Rin yos'Phelium Clan Korval. I write in Common Trade because I do not know who you will be, or from what world you will hail, who will come after me. I will begin by describing the circumstances immediately preceding my residence upon this planet. I will delineate the Balance that must go forth, and the reasons for its going forth. I will put down, as best as I am able, those things from other log books and diaries that may illuminate my actions and necessities.

Let it begin.

On the planet Teriste, in Standard Year 1392, Day 286, a messenger of the Department of the Interior brought me word that the entirety of my kin were killed—murdered by agents of this Department.

I will herein name the names of my kin, lest they are forgot, and I will say to you, whoever and whenever you may be, that it is only I, Pat Rin, the least of us all, who is left now to carry Balance to fruition . . .

DAY 50

❈❈❈❈❈❈❈❈❈❈❈❈❈❈❈❈❈❈❈❈❈❈❈❈

Standard Year 1393
Dutiful Passage
Lytaxin Orbit

LINA HAD AGREED to meet him over tea in the library at the end of his piloting shift. The necessity of retrieving the whisker from his quarters put Ren Zel a few moments behind the appointed time, and he found her at table ahead of him, teapot steaming and two cups standing ready.

"Well-met, shipmate," she said with a smile, that having become a joke between them, over the years of their acquaintance. Despite the concerns he brought with him from his shift, Ren Zel felt his mouth curve upward in response.

"Shipmate," he responded, slipping into the chair opposite her, and inhaling the fragrance of the tea. "Ah." His smile grew wider. "Shall I pour?"

"If you please. I find myself remarkably indolent this hour."

To find Lina indolent was to find an impossibility. Ren Zel filled a cup, and passed it to her. She cradled it in her hands and lifted it to sample the aroma. Ren Zel poured a cup for himself, and leaned back in his chair, likewise enjoying the sweet steam, and then taking a bare sip, teasing his tastebuds with the complex notes of the beverage.

"So," said Lina eventually, putting her cup aside. "How may I assist you, shipmate? Have you been dreaming again?"

"In fact, I have," Ren Zel murmured, setting aside his own cup and reaching into his pocket for the sampling tube. "And, when I woke, I found that dreaming had produced—this." He placed the tube before her on the table, then sat back, with an effort.

"I . . . see." She picked the tube up and turned it this way and that in the light. "A singularly handsome specimen. Found in a dream, you say?"

"In the aftermath of a dream," Ren Zel said, slowly. "I woke— or dreamed I woke—and felt the weight of a cat on my chest. I raised a hand to stroke it—and realized of a sudden that a cat was—not possible, so that I woke in truth." He waved a hand at the tube. "And found that whisker caught in the coverlet."

"I see," Lina said again, her eyes on the whisker. "And was there a dream before the dream of the cat?"

"Two," he said promptly. "First was the battle-dream. I woke from that and read until I nodded. There was another dream, then. Within it, a . . . shipmate had come to me with the same dream, of the fleas and the—solution we undertook to save ourselves. I soothed her as best I might and sent her to her own rest. And then—"

Lina raised a hand. "Did you recognize this shipmate?"

Ren Zel considered that, then shook his head, Terran-wise. "Indeed, it was only that she had the memory upon her, and stood so very distressed, for ship and crew . . ." He moved a shoulder. "But, after all, it was a dream."

"Just so." Lina touched the tip of her forefinger to the tube's seal. "May I?"

"Certainly."

And so she had the whisker out, and settled back in her chair with it held close between her two palms, and her eyes closed.

Momentarily ignored, Ren Zel retrieved his teacup and sipped, recruiting himself to patience.

"I know this cat . . ." Lina murmured, her voice slightly slurred, as if she spoke in her sleep. Ren Zel froze, cup halfway to his lips, unwilling to break the Healer's trance.

"I know this cat," she said again, barely more than a whisper. "It is . . ." Her face changed, tightened; her eyelids flickered, flew open. She sighed and shook her head gently. "To my knowledge, this cat has never been on the *Passage*."

With which, she picked up the tube, reinserted the whisker, resealed the top, and leaned forward to place the whole before him.

Ren Zel lowered his teacup, looking from her careful face and opaque eyes to the tube and its captive wonder.

"It had seemed," he said eventually, and with utmost care. "that . . . trance had produced more information regarding this cat."

"Had it?" Lina recovered her cup and sipped.

And whatever that information might have been, Ren Zel dea'Judan was not to be made a gift of it. He bit his lip, staring down at the tube, concentrating on breathing. He had counted Lina among his friends . . .

"You think me cruel," she said. "Friend, acquit me."

He looked up, saw sympathy in her eyes and raised a hand. "Then, why—?"

She shifted, setting her cup down. "Tell me, has there been a return of that phenomenon such as Shan reported, when he found you on Casiaport?"

He blinked, bought a moment of thought by putting his cup down.

"Certainly not. Why should there have been?"

She moved a hand, soothing the air between them. "Forgive me; I meant no offense. It was merely that Shan had said you were in trance, and foretelling . . ."

"I was wounded," he said, more sharply than he had intended, "and raving."

She was still for a moment, then inclined her head. "As you say, Pilot."

Ren Zel flinched. "Lina . . ."

"Ah, no—" She bent forward and put her hand over his where it rested next to the damned tube. "Peace . . . peace. Friend, you must understand that it is . . . difficult to know the correct path to take with you. We have on this ship three not-inconsiderable Healers—one a full dramliza—and you remain beyond the touch of all, shielded so well that none of us may so much as reach forth and give you ease of ill dreaming." Gently, she patted his hand and withdrew.

"With you, we must—we must pilot blind, trusting our training and an honest regard for yourself to win us through to safe landing." She sighed and picked up her teacup to sip. Ren Zel, curiously breathless, did the same.

"So," Lina continued. "I will tell you that the trance did produce more information. Not," she said wryly, "as much as I would have desired. Yet more than I will give to you. My training—and my sincere regard for yourself—tells me that it would be best to allow you to proceed . . . unencumbered by preconception. The cat may never come to you again—or it may reappear often, at the times it chooses. Cats are like that, after all."

"So they are." He picked up the sampling tube and slid it into a pocket, rose and bowed, respect to a master. "My thanks, Healer."

She smiled, wistfully, and inclined her head. "Pilot. Good lift."

"Safe landing," he answered, that being the well-wish pilots exchanged before a journey.

He walked back to his quarters slowly, wondering what sort of journey Lina supposed him to be on.

DAY 309

❀❀❀❀❀❀❀❀❀❀❀❀❀❀❀❀❀❀❀❀❀❀❀❀

Standard Year 1392
Blair Road
Surebleak

NATESA HAD PERHAPS been correct to protest his choice of hour for this meeting, Pat Rin thought, as he followed Jonni on a tour of the rooftop garden. The air was frigid, and the light breeze soon had him a-shiver and longing for the temperate climate he had been born to.

Well, he would have a cup of tea soon enough, and in the meanwhile he was in a fair way to learning the sign-names for rather a number of vegetables.

It appeared that Jonni's purpose in the tour was to elicit Pat Rin's advice on the crops to be planted this season. The unraveling of this would doubtless have proven tedious, if not impossible, as the beds had lain fallow over the winter beneath tarpaulin shrouds, long since stripped of their visual aids to communication. But here Jonni revealed unexpected resources.

Showing Natesa empty hands with fingers spread wide, he opened a plastic tool chest and pulled out an object inexpertly wrapped in oilcloth. A few moments later, Pat Rin was holding a spine-shot paper book entitled *How to Grow Food in Small Spaces*, and trying to simultaneously read the descriptions appended to the pictures Jonni pointed out and attend the boy's hand-talk and pantomime.

So, in the end the planning was only laborious, leaving Pat Rin feeling that he had personally turned every bed and hand-set every seed.

"That is good then," he told Jonni, closing the book. "With care, we will be comfortably supplied through next winter. I depend upon you to do well for us."

The boy smiled and nodded, and reached rather anxiously for the book Pat Rin cradled in his arm.

"A moment." He held up a hand, and the boy stopped, smile vanished and eyes anxious.

Pat Rin sighed. "Only a question, child. Can you read?"

The pert nose wrinkled, and the right hand wobbled in a sign which was most perfectly plain: *So-so.*

"Ah." He glanced to Natesa. "I suppose it is too much to hope that there is a school in this territory?" He asked, foreknowing the answer.

But she surprised him. "Gwince tells me she learned to read at Ms. Audrey's house. I do not believe that she was ever employed as a Scarlet Beauty, so it seems at least possible that Audrey sponsors a school." Her mouth twitched in a faint smile. "For some definition of school."

"Well, since I will be seeing Ms. Audrey today, I will make inquiries." He held the book out. Jonni pounced on it with visible relief and went over to stow it in the tool chest, first re-wrapping it in its sheet of waterproofing.

A blade of wind sliced across the rooftop; Pat Rin gasped, shivering renewed, and turned toward the rather fearsome metal staircase which ascended from the attic to the garden.

"Come," he said to Natesa. "There will be tea in the kitchen."

"BEAUTIFUL," Audrey breathed, some hours later, gazing raptly at the Sinner's Carpet.

It did look well, Pat Rin thought, standing at survey by her side. He had been at pains to impress upon the extras hired to carry and lay it that it did indeed matter how the carpet was oriented in the room, that the edges be straight, and that there be no unsightly wrinkles. In fact, it had taken rather longer than he had estimated to finish the thing properly. But the result was well worth the labor.

"I got it all planned out," Audrey was saying, with what sounded to be genuine happiness. "Real special deal, only for the, you know—connoisseur."

"I hope that it brings you profit," he murmured politely and she chuckled.

"Oh, it will. That rug is gonna be *good* for business." She turned to him with a smile. "Thank you. Now, let's step along to my office and I'll hand over the deposit and the first month's rent."

"I wonder if you might assist me," he murmured, as they walked through halls and rooms much less busy than yesterday. Audrey threw him a quick blue glance.

"Well, I can try," she said, with appropriate caution. "What's up?"

"There is a child of my house who requires tutoring. He reads, but poorly. I would have his skill increase."

Both of Audrey's eyebrows were up. "If he reads at all, he's better off than most of the streeters."

"True. However, he bears the burden of being deaf, and thus it is doubly important that he learn to read and write well." He tipped his head, considering. "It would also be good if he were able to learn basic mathematics."

She snorted, half a laugh. "What d'ya think this is, a nursery school? Who's the kid?"

"His name is Jonni. He is employed as my gardener."

She stopped, there in the middle of the hall, and turned to stare at him. Perforce, Pat Rin also stopped, wondering.

"Kid about—what?—thirteen? fourteen?—with a kinda pointy face and a head full of black hair that just makes you itch to take a comb and a pair of scissors to it?"

A fair description. Pat Rin inclined his head. "It sounds the very child."

Perhaps she heard him, perhaps not. Certainly, she continued on as if she had not—"And deaf. Blizzard, it's gotta be the same kid!"

"I am to understand," Pat Rin ventured when several moments had passed and she said nothing more, "that Jonni is known to you?"

"Known—" She looked at him, her face set in grim lines. "Look, that kid used to live here—we taught him what he knows about reading, and he used to be pretty good at his numbers, too. Not that he cared about the reading or the sums—but he did care about growing things, and so he learned what he needed for that. Then— it's been maybe two years ago, now—an'—well, you don't need the details. Short of it is a customer walked in here one night higher'n a spaceship on somethin' that wasn't doin' him no good, and when the smoke cleared, he was dead, which he deserved—and so was two of mine, which they didn't." She sighed. "An' o'course one was Jonni's mom. Kid come strollin' in from somewhere, took one look and screamed—first time I ever heard him make a sound—turned 'round and ran out the front door. A couple of the boys went out after him, but they lost him in the dark. And, you know, we thought he'd come back, after he got himself in hand." She sighed. "Hasn't yet."

A bitter tale, indeed, and if the boy could not bear to return to the place of his mother's murder, who was Pat Rin yos'Phelium to call him a coward? Yet, he must have his letters and his sums, if he were to profitably make his way into adulthood. He looked up at Audrey.

"I will speak with him," he said, and saw her brows lift slightly, possibly in amusement. "If he will not come here for lessons, perhaps lessons may come to him." He tipped his head. "If, of course, you are agreeable to providing tutoring for this child, in return for a reasonable fee."

She waved her hand, a shapeless, meaningless gesture. "Oh, sure—got a pregnant girl right now who reads like a house afire. She'd be glad of the work and the cash. Don't know how she is with her numbers, but there's Villy to do it, if she ain't able. Patient as glass, Villy, and real good with the kids."

"Then it is decided in principle," Pat Rin said, with a feeling of entirely ridiculous relief. "That is good. I will speak with Jonni this evening and see if I might persuade him here tomorrow. If not, I will send word and you may dispatch his tutor."

"Suits," she said, and suddenly grinned her wide, infectious grin. "There you go again, pitching changes into the wind! Let's make that settlement before you decide it's too cold and install central heatin' on the streets!"

IT WAS MID-MORNING when he and Cheever McFarland returned to the store to find a bent and tattered person at the front window, her hands and nose flattened against the glass.

So rapt was she that Cheever McFarland needed to clear his throat three times before she stirred and looked up, blinking, but unafraid.

"I'm Ajay Naylor, Boss. Gwince said you wanted to talk to me."

Cheever shook his head. "I ain't the boss," he said, and pointed. "He's the boss."

She peered along the line of his finger, and there came over her face an expression Pat Rin was beginning to know well—raw astonishment mixed with disbelief.

He inclined his head. "Indeed, I am the boss. Thank you, for taking the time to come to me. Will you step inside, so that we may talk in comfort?"

Disbelief increased by a factor of six. She turned back to Cheever.

"This is for real? He's the boss? The one took Moran and the publicity committee out, like Gwince was tellin' me?"

"This is for real," Cheever assured her. "He's the boss. I'm one of his 'hands."

She shook her head. "Damn." Her gaze drifted back to the window. "Pretty things you got there. Boss."

"Thank you. Would you like to examine them more closely? As a rug-maker, yourself, you will perhaps be interested."

She grinned at that, showing toothless gums. "I'm interested, OK. Though you can't hardly put my rugs in the same room with them."

"Ah, but I intend to," Pat Rin said, moving to unlock the door. "If the two of us are able to reach an agreement."

GWINCE OPENED the door with a grin and a nod.

"Evening, Boss. Mr. McFarland. Natesa sends that the work progresses, Boss. Cook asks when you want to eat supper."

"We shall dine in an hour," Pat Rin answered. "Please ask Jonni to attend me in my office in three hours."

"Yessir, will do."

"Thank you, Gwince." He moved down the hall, and paused to look up at Cheever, who grinned.

"Got it. See you in an hour." He strode off, whistling. Pat Rin continued, more slowly.

The business with Ajay Naylor had been concluded to mutual satisfaction; she was not adverse to providing him rugs on commission, though she was less sanguine, even, than Audrey regarding the possibility of shipping off-planet. The road was the thing, as he understood it. As recently as Ajay's young womanhood, the Port Road had been neutral territory, and free passage guaranteed. That was not to say safe passage, even then, but caravans had regularly formed to bear items for sale or trade to the Port and most, if not all, won through.

On the subject of what had changed, Ajay was unclear. There had been a rumored falling out among several of the bosses of the larger territories, which resulted in the road being closed, and abandoned to bandits. Another rumor had the Port itself closing, the ships withdrawing entirely. But that rumor, Ajay had allowed, with a certain dryness, had likely been air-dreams—as he doubtless knew better than she.

Ajay departed, and there had come Al, the keeper of the hardware store, and their near neighbor. He had chatted for awhile, admired the carpets without displaying the least desire to understand them, and finally brought the conversation around to Pat Rin's proposed Insurance rate structure.

Upon being informed that Insurance payments were for the meanwhile suspended, Al looked less pleased than one might have supposed, and pulled his long chin thoughtfully.

"Gotta have a scheme for makin' money," he said. "No offense meant, Boss."

"Nor any taken," Pat Rin assured him. "My scheme for making money is entirely straightforward—I intend to sell carpets. For cash."

"Yeah, OK," the man said. "Though you might wanna get in some low-end stuff—I'm not sayin' cheap, just affordable to some-body—well, sleet, to somebody like me. These 'uns are pretty, but they're pricey. But that's just the store. You're the boss—need to get cash somehow."

"For what should I receive funding?" Pat Rin had demanded, rather heatedly. "Does the boss mend the holes in the street? Does he fund clinics? Libraries? Schools?"

"Well, no. Not lately. Audrey, she grabbed what she could of Vindal's clinic and library before Moran torched 'em. You get nicked, or break a leg or an arm—like that—go to Audrey's house; they'll take care of you. Can't do much if you're sick with something high-end, but they're pretty good with the usual. Same way, you wanna learn how to read—go to Audrey's. Somebody there'll teach you."

"It appears to me," Pat Rin commented, "that if there is Insurance—or street tax—to be paid, that it ought to be paid to Ms. Audrey, who is doing more for the residents of this territory than any boss."

"Naw, naw, that ain't fair. See—done right, now—forget Moran; he was a pig—done right, the boss is the one who fixes the problems. Say I got a problem with Tobi and we ain't been able to work it out. So we come to you and we say, Boss, we got this problem and we can't fix it—tell us what to do. And you maybe study on the case for awhile and then you tell us what to do. Oughta get something for havin' to do everybody else's thinkin' for 'em. Right? An' then, see, the boss is the one who keeps the turf together, and makes sure no other bosses annex us. Ought to get something for that, too. An', if you was thinkin' about bringing a clinic, or maybe a library out on the street, to kinda ease the load on Ms. Audrey—you oughta get cash for that, too." He'd paused here, perhaps a little startled at his own eloquence, then did his summing up.

"Tell you what, Boss—this little store ain't gonna support alla that."

Nor would it, Pat Rin thought now, climbing the long, chilly stairway to his room. Properly done, as Al described it, a boss on Surebleak was near enough to delm. He sighed, irritated with himself. He had allowed the information that this was a Terran backworld, brutish and barely-governed, to blind him to the fact that persons of honor naturally strove to form into clans, if not precisely kin-groups.

Sighing again, he pushed open the door to his room, saw a shadow move and heard a burble the instant before the brown-and-black cat hurled itself into his legs, tail high and purring fit to deafen him.

Smiling, Pat Rin bent down and stroked the animal. Impossibly, the purrs increased, and the cat threw itself against Pat Rin's legs in an ecstacy of welcome.

"All very well," he said with mock sternness. "I suppose you've been lying abed all day, neglecting your duties to the cook?"

The cat burbled again, shifting from side to side and it lifted first the left front paw and then the right, kneading air.

Pat Rin laughed softly and straightened. "Flatterer. Now, by your leave, I must prepare for dinner."

DINNER WAS SIMPLER this evening—a jam pastry removed by a casserole which took advantage of the pantry's abundance of tinned fish. Despite its lowly beginnings, the dish pleased.

The conversation was mostly between his oathsworn, on the arcane lore of security. Pat Rin listened closely, astonished at those things they considered merely prudent, and marveled at the tale of protocols and devices that had been put into place, solely for the purpose of protecting his life.

Pushing his plate aside, he sat quietly sipping tea. There was eventually a lull in the discussion of protections and defenses, offensives and attacks, and Natesa turned to him, her eyes dark and luminous, her face subtle in shadow and nuance.

"Has Ms. Audrey a place in her school for Jonni?" she asked, with every appearance of interest.

"Curiously, she does, though she doubts he will come to her. He had used to live in Ms. Audrey's house, until his mother got her death there, whereupon he ran away. We left it that I shall speak with him, and if he will not go to her, she will send a tutor here."

"That is well, then," she said, approvingly.

"Well enough," he agreed, and hesitated on the edge of mentioning his conversation with Al. But—no. That was something he wished to examine thoroughly himself, weighing his melant'i well, before he sought the opinion of a Juntavas Sector Judge.

So. "We have a contract with Ajay Naylor for rugs on commission. She doubts the spaceport, as well, though she tells me the Port Road had been open and neutral in her youth."

"It had been, until several concurrent tragedies changed the rule," said Natesa. "First, there was a turf war between two neighboring bosses, which ended, not as might be expected—in one boss annexing the other's territory—but in the subdivision—in the several subdivisions—of both territories. From there grew chaos, which might have eventually settled, had it not been for the arrival of an epidemic virus. There was a vaccine at the Port—Surebleak belonged to the Health Net in those days, too—and it was to be delivered by Port personnel. But the Port was short-handed, and, rather than sending Port personnel, in an armored car, with appropriate weaponry, they sent several natives, who were employed at the Port, with a list of territories and the number of vaccines to be left with each boss."

Pat Rin put his mug down. "They were robbed?"

"Ah, no. But that was only because they sold the entire shipment to the boss just next the spaceport, and disappeared." She moved her shoulders, eloquent as a Liaden. "Perhaps they were clever enough to keep vaccines for themselves. One rather hopes they forgot that detail. It was, by all reports, a horrible disease, and thousands died for lack of the cash to purchase the cure."

He closed his eyes. Gods. What sort of world produced such people? And yet, Al and Audrey, Gwince, Jonni, Ajay, Villy . . .

"Master?"

He opened his eyes, seeing what appeared to be honest concern for himself reflected in her face.

"I wonder," he said, changing the subject brutally. "What are our options of communication devices? I find no radio, for instance, among Mr. Moran's former possessions. How do the bosses keep contact among themselves? Worse, I find no local radios, so that we might communicate between ourselves—myself to you from the store, for instance."

Cheever grunted. "Been tryin' to crack that nut," he said. "Got a couple people on staff who say there's a native equivalent of a portacomm, but the trade's controlled by one of the bosses out from here. I'm going down to check on the ship, day after tomorrow. Thinking about making a side trip to check out the portacomm trade while I'm over that way." He paused. "Speakin' of which, the emergency talkies off the ship'll do fine to keep us three in touch. I'll bring them on back, if you want."

"Yes, do that," Pat Rin murmured. He finished his tea, put the mug down, and looked up to find Natesa's eyes yet upon him.

"*Do* the bosses communicate between themselves?" he asked her.

Her eyes narrowed slightly. "My information indicated that the more powerful bosses, who control larger territories—that there had been communication between them, arrangements of trade, alliances. Whether this is still so . . . I doubt. Matters seem to have deteriorated badly since the report was written." She sighed, sharply, and leaned forward, eyes and face intense.

"The difficulty with Surebleak is that the boss system is rotting from the core. There is no orderly transfer of authority when bosses are often murdered by a wild gun who aspires only to their power. Such guns rarely have any notion of responsibility, or of administration, never mind compromise and mutual profit. So, the territories are proliferating in number while they dwindle in size, and chaos is become the order of the day."

"Chaos is what we wanted," Cheever pointed out from his end of the table.

Natesa nodded. "Indeed, chaos serves us very well in what we propose to do. But it hardly serves those who live here, and who cling to survival amidst the slow disintegration of their world. Nor is it good for business."

Juntavas business, that would be. Pat Rin considered her.

"I would think the Juntavas a supporter of chaos."

"Not so—not so, Master. The Juntavas is a champion of order. We require certain things so that business may go forth: safe and easy access; safe and easy egress; steady supply; an economy. And a consistent structure of command, with which profitable associations may be forged. Surebleak offers none of these things. It is a bitter waste—and not only for the Juntavas."

"But if a boss arose who was able to consolidate and hold the territories—and train a successor to do likewise?" Pat Rin asked.

"Perhaps the rot might be excised," she said slowly. "Perhaps. But we must first ask if Surebleak is able to produce such a boss."

"Surely, there are honorable people in other territories, as we have found here?" he said.

"Surely, there are," she agreed. "But, consider the present system, if we may dignify it so. Did a person of honor and integrity arise, yet she must take the path to power which is open to her—cold murder. To unite all—even most—of the territories, she will need to murder much more than once. And, upon achieving her goal of one cohesive territory, she must transform herself into a statesman, capable of compromise, slow to slay even the most intractable dissident." She shook her head. "I do not know that one individual could successfully encompass both roles, and yet they are inseparable."

"Yet, you are yourself both judge and assassin."

She smiled. "I am *called* Assassin," she said, amusement rippling her voice. "Would you like to know why?"

"Yes," Pat Rin said seriously. "I would."

But Natesa merely laughed and came lightly to her feet.

"Perhaps I will tell you one day." She glanced aside. "Mr. McFarland, if I may have a few moments of your time?"

"Sure thing." The big man got to his feet, and looked at Pat Rin, who raised a hand.

"Gwince. I will try not to frighten her. Thank you, Mr. McFarland."

"Good-night, Boss."

Alone in the dining room, Pat Rin sighed, closed his eyes and simply sat for the space of a dozen heartbeats. He was tired, gods. Already he was tired—and there was so much yet that he must do.

"The shortest way to finish is through begun," he murmured, which was what Uncle Daav had used to say. The Liaden words felt odd in his mouth, after even so few days of speaking only Terran. Would he be able to speak Liaden at all, when he at last returned to the homeworld to destroy Korval's enemy?

Well. One thing at a time—and that was Anne Davis advising him now. "Er Thom's Terran," according to his mother, but never in Uncle Daav or in Cousin Er Thom's hearing.

Pat Rin pushed back from the table, gathered Gwince from her post at the door and went down to the kitchen.

The cook was polishing a soup pot; he set both rag and pot aside when Pat Rin walked in and nodded politely.

"Evening, Boss. What can I get you?"

"Nothing just now, I thank you. I merely wished to tell you that I am pleased with the standard of cooking displayed since yesterday's dinner."

The man grinned, and shuffled one foot. "That's—thank you, Boss. I mean to keep the standards high."

"I am delighted to hear you say so," Pat Rin assured him, and turned to go, his mission accomplished.

Two steps toward the door, he recalled something else and turned back.

"The brown and black cat," he said to the cook's suddenly anxious face.

The anxiety deepened. "Yessir. He ain't bothering you, is he?"

"Not at all. I merely wished to know his name."

"Name?" the cook repeated, hands twisting in his apron. "Well . . . Cat, I guess. I mean—who names cats?"

Pat Rin paused, then inclined his head. "A personal idiosyncrasy. Good evening."

"See ya," said the cook.

The office was the next order of business. He left Gwince guarding the door and went over to the file cabinet to retrieve his log book.

He had written perhaps three pages when Gwince put her head in the door.

"Jonni's here, Boss."

He glanced up. "That is well. Send him in, please."

She vanished, and a moment later Jonni stepped tentatively within, his pointed face showing wariness.

"I'm not going to eat you, you know," Pat Rin said mildly, and motioned at the yellow plastic chair. "Sit a moment. I have a proposition for you."

Still tentative, Jonni sat.

"Thank you. Ms. Audrey has said that she will teach you to read better, to do sums and to write. I wish that you will undertake these things. Do you understand me?"

The boy nodded, insufficiently exuberant—his cap remained on his head.

"That is good. Now. Ms. Audrey tells me that you may not wish to go to her house for lessons. If this is so, then she will send a teacher, and you will have your lessons in this house." He fixed the child with a stern eye, much as he had done with Quin, by way of enforcing his filial authority. "The lessons are not negotiable, but the location is. Which do you choose?"

The boy held up a hand, fingers rippling—*wait*.

Fair enough; it was bound to be a weighty choice, between honor and horror. Pat Rin leaned cautiously back in his own chair, prepared to wait for some time, if necessary.

It was unnecessary. Jonni sat for several moments with his head bent, contemplating, perhaps, the hole in the right knee of his trousers, then looked up, eyes bright. He made a sign as appropriate as it was lewd.

"You will go to Ms. Audrey?" Pat Rin asked, to be certain.

Jonni nodded, placing his cap in peril of a tumble.

Pat Rin smiled. "I am pleased. Be in the front hallway when I leave tomorrow morning, and you may walk with me as far as Ms. Audrey's house."

The boy grinned, and nodded again.

"Good. Is there anything else?"

A headshake, grin unabated.

"Then our business is concluded. Good night." He made the sign that he knew as "farewell".

The boy rose, hesitated and—bowed. It was in no discernible mode, though it was done with grace and good intent—and surprised entirely.

Before Pat Rin could clear his throat, Jonni was gone, ghosting out the door.

Another victory upon the day, he thought, picking up his pen and returning his attention to the log book.

It was well.

HE WAS RUNNING down cold and twisting hallways, gun in hand. The ones who pursued him also had guns—as he knew to his dismay—and there were many more of them than his pellets could account for. He could not do this on his own. He needed help. He needed kin.

The hallway twisted, right, left, right, and spilled him into a dingy gray room, where a lone man sat in a chair, legs thrust out before him, holding a glass of wine. Pat Rin's heart leaped and he ran forward.

"Val Con! Cousin, you must help me—" He extended a hand, touched his cousin's shoulder—and leapt back, an unvoiced scream choking him.

The man in the chair was a skeleton, grinning death into his eyes.

Gasping, Pat Rin awoke. Slowly, he oriented himself, and

brought his labored breathing down. He turned somewhat in his twisted nest of blankets, and his knee bumped something solid.

Carefully, he put his hand down—felt warm fur and the beginning vibration of a purr—the nameless brown and black cat.

Smiling, he put his head back down on the flat pillow, his hand still on the cat.

The rest of his night passed, dreamless.

DAY 310

※ ※

Standard Year 1392
Blair Road
Surebleak

THE CAT DOGGED his heels from the bedroom to the kitchen, sat
by his knee while he broke his fast with bread, cheese, and tea; and
trotted, tail high and jaunty, at his side down the hallway to the
vestibule.

It was a strangely crowded vestibule. In addition to Cheever
McFarland, who was entirely capable of filling the small space
without assistance, there was Jonni, and the slender subtlety that
was Natesa.

"Good morning," Pat Rin said to his oathsworn, simultaneously
offering the same greeting in sign to the child.

"Mornin', Boss."

"Good-day, Master."

The child likewise returned his greeting; paused and signed
something else, not, Pat Rin thought, to himself, but to—

The cat.

"Good morning, Boss Silk," he murmured, reading—and
captured Jonni's attention with an interrogative wave.

548

"The cat's name is Silk?" he asked, imitating the soft, smoothly flowing sign.

The boy nodded, grinning, and tossed a spangle of sign off his fingers.

"Ah, did he so? I had thought him a cat of discernment."

"What does he say?" Natesa wondered softly.

Pat Rin shook himself. "Why only that this cat—this Silk—had the good sense to scratch the late Boss Moran very thoroughly not too long ago, to the vast amusement of one barbaric and blood-thirsty child." He tipped his head. "Forgive me if I pry, but am I to understand that you will be accompanying us today?"

"My business today is on the street, and I thought to walk with you and Mr. McFarland—and one bloodthirsty child—until my way turns from yours." She bent her head gracefully, suggesting a full bow in her favorite mode of student to master.

"Perhaps I am inconvenient."

"Or perhaps you are not," he said dryly. "One merely inquired."

"Cat comin', Boss?" Cheever asked lazily from his lean against the door.

"I believe that his duties keep him at home," Pat Rin replied, and looked sternly down at his attendant feline. Silk blinked molten gold eyes, then turned and flowed away down the hall toward the kitchen.

"Now is the hour," Pat Rin said. "Mr. McFarland, the door, of your goodness." He moved a hand as he spoke, alerting Jonni to the door's opening, and they exited the house a veritable army: Cheever, then Pat Rin, the boy at his side, and Natesa, silent and graceful, walking slightly to the rear and the right.

He heard the pellet sing by his ear and Natesa's shouted "*Down*" in the same instant, and dropped to the street, gun to hand, a target in his eye.

It was target practice then—heavy game, and when the targets stopped showing, he blinked, disoriented, and with a high buzzing in his ears.

"Stay down," Natesa hissed, from somewhere behind him. "Do not move. We are awaiting Mr. McFarland's sign."

It was the word "sign" that jerked him back to the reality of the street, where he lay in the half-frozen mud, staring at the dead man crumpled at the base of the wall opposite, his blood shockingly bright on the dingy walk.

"Where . . ." he began, but Natesa's voice came again, louder this time.

"We have the sign. I will stand first. Count slowly to twelve. If I have drawn no fire, stand, but hold your weapon ready."

He sensed her movement and counted to twelve, slowly. Silence reposed upon the street. Pat Rin rose, gun held ready.

Across the street, a door somewhat down from the dead man opened, and a woman peered out, then hastily withdrew, the door slamming into place.

More action across the way. Cheever McFarland slipped out of an alley that should have been too thin for him, and waved.

"All clear," he shouted and strode toward their position.

Released, Pat Rin spun, looking first at the ground near at hand, but there was nothing there, save the mud.

"Master?"

"The child," he said, remembering the pellet whine and Natesa shouting—and of course Jonni could not have heard either. Though, surely, seeing all of his house going to the ground, he would—

"The child," he said again, to Natesa's black, black eyes. "*Where is the child?*"

Her gaze shifted over his shoulder. He turned and saw the ragged huddle of cloth, not so very far away, really.

"Gods."

He knelt next to the still, small body; and turned the boy in his arms. No breath, no heartbeat, no wide, glad smile. *Gods, gods . . . no.*

"Master?"

"Who did this?" The High Tongue felt like ice in his mouth.

"Master, Mr. McFarland has found Jim Snyder among the fallen," she answered softly. "He believes the others come from Boss Deacon's turf."

Pat Rin knelt, holding the dead child in his arms, and if he wept

now before his oathsworn, he was lost to shame; lost to all but a vast
and frightening coldness.

*This ends, and ends now. No more of mine will be shot down in
the streets.*

He raised his face to Natesa, and saw her eyes widen.

"Fetch Audrey," he said. He heard his voice shake—and did not
care. "I will know the name of my enemy. They will answer me.
Fully."

NATESA HESITATED AT THE ENTRANCE to the garden, an
unaccustomed shyness rooting her feet to the top stair. Mid-way
across the roof, she saw him, silhouetted against the starry glow of
Surebleak's nighttime sky; seated on the edge of a shrouded garden
patch, shoulders bowed, the cat crouched at his side. Neither
seemed to note the wind, intermittent from planetary north, which
added to the evening's chill.

The child's death—she recalled the face he had shown her then,
mud-streaked and slick with tears, icy with a purpose that surpassed
mere revenge by an order of magnitude, and shivered with something more than the cold.

"Inas, why are you come?" His voice was soft and mannerly. He
did not turn his head. And who knew what the invocation of her
personal name might mean?

Natesa gathered her courage, lifted her feet and entered the
garden.

"It is cold," she said, matching his tone. "I have come to bring
you a blanket."

"Ah."

Gently, she moved among the shadows of the dormant beds,
and came to stand before him, the blanket draped over one arm.

He looked up at her, his face a golden mask in the starshine.

"Thank you," he said, but made no move to take the blanket
from her. Beside him, the cat straightened from its crouch and
settled into a sit, fuzzy tail wrapped neatly 'round its toes.

Natesa sighed lightly. "Ms. Audrey bade me say that her house
is open to you."

The golden mask displayed no emotion. "I am grateful to Ms. Audrey, but I do not seek distraction."

The wind gusted, bitter enough to dismay her, though she had taken care to don a jacket. This close, she could see that he was shivering, though she doubted he knew that himself.

"Pat Rin." Surely, she might dare his name, when he had established the mode himself? "Pat Rin, you are cold. The night is not temperate. At least the blanket, if I cannot persuade you to go inside." She bit her lip. "You serve no one, if you sicken."

"Very true," he said politely, yet still he made no move to take the blanket.

Wondering at her own temerity, she stepped forward and draped it around his shoulders. The cat Silk, sitting tall at his side, blinked golden eyes in approval.

Something moved in his face. Indeed, he sighed, and lifted a hand on which Korval's Ring glittered, to touch the fabric of the blanket and pull it more snugly about him.

"Thank you," he said again, and it seemed to her that there was more than mere ritual in the phrase. "I am grateful for your care."

"You are welcome." She hesitated, unsure of what now she should offer, reluctant to leave him here, alone, but for his cat and his dead, inside the freezing night.

"You will wish to know," he said surprisingly, "that I have decided to take up the roles you doubt may be acted by a single individual."

She frowned. "I beg your pardon?"

"I will unite the territories," he said, sounding altogether sane. "We shall have laws and contracts. We shall have free and easy travel between streets, even to the spaceport itself. We shall rejoin the Health Net. There will be schools, libraries and clinics. Children and adults will take advantage of these benefits without fear for their lives. I will accomplish this thing."

"Pat Rin . . ."

"We will begin by annexing Boss Deacon's territory."

Natesa shook her head, torn between impatience and pity. "Pat

Rin, Boss Deacon is well-protected. More, his territory lies in the opposite direction of our goals."

"You have not attended," he chided her gently. "I will unite the territories. Thus, we will take first he who has dared to deal death to one of mine. It shall serve as a lesson, and bring us to the attention of those others with whom we will need to treat."

"And, having done so," she said with asperity, "you will receive even more assassins into your presence, until one of them succeeds."

"Inas, we can prevail—not without blood, no. And perhaps we shall entertain more assassins before we win through. But it can be done. I see it. I know how to proceed."

Pity overruled impatience. His mind had broken beneath the burden of his griefs. Had she been other than a Sector Judge, she might well have cast herself to her knees and sent up a wail to the heedless gods, which was how one grieved for the dead and the demented on the distant, unlamented world of her birth.

Instead, she extended a hand and touched his shoulder, lightly, companionably.

"It is good that you have a plan. Mr. McFarland is below stairs. Let us go to him and discuss procedures over tea and cheese."

She had not expected to so easily persuade him, but he rose at her word, slipping the blanket from his shoulders and folding it neatly over his arm.

"Let us do that," he said, still in that soft, oh-so-sane voice. "Silk—we descend." He inclined his head, courtesy itself. "Inas, after you."

DAY 50

❁ ❁

Standard Year 1393
Lytaxin
Erob's Clanhouse and Gardens

DESPITE HIS LACK of haste, Shan reached the proper suite rather sooner than he would have liked, and, stifling a sigh, put his palm against the plate.

A chime sounded, faint on the far side of the door. The last note had not quite faded from the ear when the door whipped open, revealing a Liaden woman of exceptional beauty, golden hair sweeping her stiff shoulders, violet eyes wide in a face so rigidly calm it seemed a sculpture, audaciously formed from pure, pale gold, rather than living flesh. Shan's ravaged Healer senses perceived the expected anger, twined with equal parts terror and relief—a volatile combination which did not bode well for calm discourse between siblings.

Well, nothing for it but to begin, he thought, and swept an elder brother's affectionate bow.

"Good evening, sister," he said, choosing the Low Tongue, which was Nova's preferred language, rather than Terran, which was his. "How delightful to find you here! I trust you had a pleasant journey?"

Nova's mouth tightened. "A pleasant journey," she repeated, so flatly as to be entirely modeless. She took a breath and stepped back, moving her hand in the gesture of welcome. "Pray enter, brother."

Perforce, he entered and wandered down the room to the wine table. He picked up a glass and poured a portion of Erob's agreeable, everyday red into it, which really was too bad of him. The Code dictated that he wait until he was offered refreshment, but, then, the Code also taught that informality among kin was acceptable. In any case, it offered Nova opportunity to be irritated in a minor chord, and perhaps would leach off a measure of that explosive mix of emotion.

"Wine, sister?" he inquired over his shoulder. "Erob's red is quite passable. The canary is a touch sweet and I found the jade musty the other day—though perhaps that was merely a bad bottle."

"The red, of your kindness," Nova said, calmly, beside him. Shan sighed inwardly. Well, he had survived the full lash of Nova's temper more times than he could count; he could doubtless survive it now. He poured a second glass of red, and handed it to his sister, who inclined her head and took one small sip.

Shan sipped his wine and counted, slowly, toward twelve.

He had reached *nine* when Nova abruptly put her glass on the table, and brought her eyes up to meet his.

"I had occasion to trade news with Priscilla Mendoza just recently," she said, conversationally. "She tells me that our brother and Miri Robertson rejoice in a true lifemating."

"Oh, it's a wizard's match, plain enough," Shan said with false good cheer. "I can see the linkage clearly—any Healer may, who cares to risk having their Sight dazzled for hours."

"I see." She paused, tension screaming in every line of her. Still, her voice was calm and even when she spoke again.

"Priscilla now calls herself captain of *Dutiful Passage* and allows me to know that she is come into yos'Galan as a thodelm's lifemate."

Shan grinned. "Never have I held Priscilla's courage in higher esteem!"

Nova sighed. "Another true lifemating, brother? One would . . . dislike to believe that you set aside your first speaker's word from mere willfulness."

"*Mere* willfulness?" He raised his eyebrows. "Are we or are we not of Korval? We are never *merely* willful. Surely your study of the Diaries has revealed that to you!"

"Shan."

He sighed and rubbed the tip of his nose. "I cannot judge. The only measures I have are what I see between Val Con and Miri—and what I saw between our parents. I—we—are something—other. Though what manner of other, I am at a loss to know." Another sigh, sharper. "I need to see Priscilla." And that, he thought, was a piece of understatement worthy of Val Con himself.

"She expressed a similar need." Nova picked up her glass and drank off some wine as if it were a not-very-tasty tonic. "So, I find both of my brothers lifemated with recourse to neither Code nor first speaker. We will inaugurate a vogue, and bring runaway matings into fashion."

She finished the wine in a snap and put the glass back on the table.

"Priscilla's other news concerned Val Con's health," she said, calm, so calm, while the flames of her dismay and fury suddenly leaped, fair scorching him. "I am to know that he is desperately wounded, barely escaping his death, and that he may arise from the catastrophe unit unable to fly."

Oh, Shan thought. *Oh, damn.*

"The med techs have," he said carefully, "expressed differing opinions. Some believe that Val Con will at first be all but entirely disabled, but that he will, over time, improve, even learning to walk again. That is the extreme view." He paused.

Nova's face had paled considerably, but she waved at him to continue.

"The less extreme view is that Val Con will emerge able in almost every way, except in his possession of the reaction times necessary to a master pilot, much less a scout pilot. These also believe that his health will remain fragile for some years, if not for the remainder of his life."

Nova was now pale to the lips, but she watched his face unwaveringly, and for a second time waved at him to go on.

"The most optimistic," he said, neglecting to add that this group was comprised entirely of himself, two Clutch turtles, now soundly asleep in Erob's atrium, and Miri Robertson Tiazan. "The most optimistic believe that our brother will awaken to himself complete and unimpaired."

Nova blinked.

"How can opinions diverge by so much?" she demanded. "The first and the second are consistent in affect, merely different in degree. But—that he awaken completely healed? How—"

Shan sipped his wine, deliberately buying time. Nova was going to like the risk they had taken with Val Con's life even less than the med techs had. And yet, to deny her hope, when he felt her terror for Val Con almost as his own . . .

"You must understand that there are . . . variables," he said slowly. "Did Priscilla tell you anything of the nature of Val Con's injuries?"

Nova blinked. "She had said he was grievously wounded. I had assumed—piloting injuries . . ."

"There were some of those," Shan allowed. "Acceleration injuries, broken bones gotten by bouncing around in a cockpit built for someone twice his size—in every direction . . ." He sighed and rubbed his forehead; a headache was building, blast it. "You understand, there were no ships, so it fell to Val Con and myself and—another pilot—to take them from the Yxtrang. In the process of acquiring his ship, Val Con was nicked by an Yxtrang pellet carrying a load of nerve poison. A full hit would have killed him more-or-less instantly, as I understand it. The effects of the smaller dose over a longer time are . . . not well documented. Additionally, there are . . . . variant methodologies . . ." He eyed her, wondering if she was swaying or if his vision was wavering. "Sister?"

"You—and Val Con," Nova repeated, voice shaking, "*stole* ships from the Yxtrang?"

"Well, they had so many, you see," he said apologetically. "It was necessary to mount an air strike, so naturally—"

"You could have been killed!" Nova interrupted.

Shan sipped wine. "It was war," he said, striving for patience. "I *would* have been killed had I huddled in House with the infirm and the children. And if you think me capable of turning Val Con from necessary action by an appeal to common sense, you vastly overrate my powers of persuasion!"

She stared at him for another heartbeat, then inclined her head, allowing him the point. "Just so. Now—'variant methodologies'?"

Here it came. He finished his wine and set the glass aside.

"In consultation with Clutch turtles Edger and Sheather, Val Con's lifemate became convinced that there was more effective healing available—a Clutch healing. I offered myself up as a test subject and found the healing . . . remarkably efficacious. Miri then decided—as Val Con's lifemate and for Korval—that he and she would undergo this healing. Edger and I labored some hours over Val Con, and left him sleeping easily, his condition much improved from when we had him out of the 'doc—"

"Out of the 'doc?" Nova demanded. Shan sighed. Well, and he had known she wouldn't like it.

"You dared to dice with the life of Korval Himself? When the medics—when you yourself!—admit that the long-term effects of the poison are unknown, that—"

"Nadelmae Korval decided," Shan interrupted, somewhat louder than he had meant to do, "for herself, for her lifemate, and for Korval entire."

"Nadelmae Korval," Nova spat, "is a Terran-raised mercenary, ignorant of clan and of Code—"

"No, she's not."

Nova stared. "Explain."

He rubbed his forehead. Gods, he was *tired*. Quickly, he accessed a Healer's energizing routine. The expected jolt of vigor was more like a faint tremble of nervousness, but it would suffice. For a while.

"Miri and Val Con rejoice in a true lifemating—recall it? I'll wager cantra to kittens that you'll find her just as Code-wise as—why, as Val Con! And I'll further wager that she's found to fly like a scout. She knew very well what her decision might mean, and she did not make it lightly."

I Dare 559

There was a long silence, while terror, fury, hope, and exasperation warred behind Nova's eyes. Finally, she sighed.

"I will see our brother."

Shan shook his head. "That would not be wise. We left him sleeping, in a state . . . somewhat akin to trance. He will wake himself, when he is ready."

"I will *see* him," she repeated, with barely leashed violence. "If he is entranced, he will not heed me, and I will have had some ease of heart." Her eyes glinted. "Surely, I am allowed kin-right?"

Surely, she was allowed kin-right, Shan thought, and truth told, it would ease his own heart to know that Val Con still slept sweetly, Healed and removed from all danger.

"Very well," he said. "But a glance, only, and then I will need to seek my own bed."

Nova inclined her head and turned toward the door.

"LADY YOS'PHELIUM?" The med tech scrambled to her feet. She was showing a little white around the eye, for which Miri blamed her not at all, and doing pretty good—after the first, incredulous gape—about not staring at the patients. Miri inclined her head, trying for a sort of matter-of-fact haughtiness.

"These, my oathsworn," she said, choosing the High Liaden mode of employer to employee—which was close enough to true, considering that she was blood-and-genes of Erob, "require optimization. They have been underfed of late, and are doubtless in need of supplements. Also, the tattoo work will be removed. The med techs attached to the mercenary unit have an erasure program. Pray contact them and request its transmittal, in the name of Captain Robertson."

The tech swallowed, hard, and managed a fairly credible bow of acquiescence.

"It shall be done." She looked up—at Nelirikk, at Hazenthull, at Diglon—and down—at Shadia, and back to Miri. "Forgive me, but one is not able in the language of the—of the subjects. One would forestall an . . . unfortunate situation, my lady."

"I understand," Miri assured her, and moved a hand, bringing both Nelirikk and Shadia to the tech's attention. "Scout Lieutenant Shadia Ne'Zame, and my aide, Lieutenant Nelirikk Explorer, will stay here to assist you in any way required."

The tech actually looked relieved to hear it, which probably showed how little experience she had with scouts, bowed again and moved over to the first 'doc of the three in the infirmary.

"If the . . . elder soldier . . . will come forward?"

Nelirikk translated it in terms of an order and Diglon Rifle stepped smartly forward.

Miri exchanged a look with Shadia, who grinned and gave her a Terran thumbs-up. "We have everything under control, Captain Redhead."

"Why don't that make me feel better?" Miri asked, rhetorically, and went away to find Emrith Tiazan, to tell her what was going on in her medical center.

MIRI HAD GONE to the med center to attend the needs of yos'Phelium's newest dependents, leaving Val Con alone with his father.

When he was a boy, he had used to dream of this meeting: His father would arrive unannounced, and swing him up into strong arms; his father would be sitting at his bedside one morning when he woke; he would be called from his studies to attend Uncle Er Thom in his office, and his father would be waiting for him there . . .

Child-dreams, which had nothing to do with this moment, in which he, grown and lifemated, stood in a garden far away from home, in the presence of a stranger, who smiled at him faintly and said, "Well."

In appearance, Val Con thought, one's father was the antithesis of one's foster-father. Nor had the holos of Daav in his youth prepared one, entirely, for the elder scout standing, serene and patient, before him in the pre-dawn garden. The holos had been of a man at the height of his powers, whip-thin and sharp-featured; his plentiful dark hair confined into a tail; black eyes looking boldly out of the image.

This man had thickened a little beyond slenderness; his hair more gray than brown, cut close to the head in a manner subtly Terran. His face, never beautiful, even in youth, had yet a certain austere charm, startlingly like Uncle Er Thom; and the black eyes assessed one with all of a scout's directness.

And, Val Con thought suddenly, *he has deliberately engineered this pause to allow me time to study him*. Almost, he grinned in welcome of this oldest of scout tricks.

Daav raised an eyebrow. "You had some pointed questions to ask me, I believe?"

"The most pointed I had asked: What have you been about all these years?" *While I waited for you, and Uncle Er Thom did . . .*

Daav's eyebrows lifted slightly. "Surely I made an entry in the Diaries? Yes, I'm certain of it. I distinctly recall your presence at the event—there's a blot on the page, where you jostled the pen."

And the other blots, thought Val Con, who knew the page well, *are tearstains*.

"However," said Daav, "since the substance of the entry appears to have slipped your mind—I was about the Balancing of my lifemate's death."

"But," Val Con heard himself, with no little astonishment, state, "your lifemate is not dead."

Daav appeared to experience no corresponding astonishment upon hearing this assertion. He merely raised a hand; the old silver puzzle-ring flashing like a zag of lightning 'round his finger.

"It was some time before that became clear to me," he said. "Our arrangement had been . . . flawed. And—forgive me—I had *seen* her die. It was far more reasonable to think I had gone mad from grief than to believe I was truly hearing her voice." He lowered his hand.

"In any case, since the assassin—say, rather, the one who had employed the assassin—so earnestly wished me to look to Terra for my villain, I could scarcely do less than accommodate him."

"Though perhaps," Val Con murmured, "not in quite the way he had wished."

"Well, what would you? Aelliana would never have wanted me

to start a war in her name—even had it been absolutely certain that her death was called by Terra. Which it was by no means. The Code quite clearly states that, in matters of life-Balance, the wishes of the Balancer are secondary to the wishes honorably imputed to his dead." He lifted his shoulders in a common Terran shrug.

"My lady would have said that Terra struck because it was afraid, and that fear arises from ignorance. So, I have been teaching cultural genetics. To Terrans."

"Ah," Val Con said softly.

"Ah, indeed," his father returned. He tipped his head. "Your lady captain speaks common Yxtrang very like a scout—or perhaps she speaks it like *the* scout."

"I really ought to teach Nelirikk my personal name," Val Con said, musingly. He moved his shoulders, *not* a shrug. "I concede that the Common Troop had not been among Miri's languages before— recent events."

"Ah, yes! The heroic flight of captured Yxtrang fighters against the over-advantaged foe, in which action you were wounded unto death! Pray, do not be coy, sir—tales of your prowess precede you. Commander Carmody holds you as an object of awe, and appears to consider you thoroughly deranged."

Val Con laughed.

"Yes, well." Daav shifted a step or two aside and stretched, carefully, Val Con thought, as would a man who was concerned that his back muscles might protest.

"Tell me, if you would," he said, settling back from his stretch, "who is this puissant enemy with which Captain Robertson has beguiled my poor Yxtrang?"

Val Con lifted a brow. "I thought they were yos'Phelium's Yxtrang?"

"One feels a lingering tenderness," Daav told him earnestly. "They are such good children."

"You relieve me," he said. "As for the enemy—" He paused, head cocked; saw his father stiffen, and turn his head. The gate at the end of the garden swung on its hinges; and very shortly the shadows relinquished Clonak ter'Meulen.

"Half-an-hour and then some," he said, smoothing his mustache with loving fingertips. "Morning, Shadow."

"Good morning, Clonak," Val Con replied, considering the pudgy scout. Something was . . . shifting . . . at the edge of his mind, as if the pieces to an old, old puzzle were snapping, at last and inevitably, into their proper places.

"Clonak," he said again, hating what he was seeing; knowing that it must be true; "my father wishes to know the name of Korval's great enemy, that murdered his brother and his brother's lifemate. You can tell him that, can't you?"

The older scout tipped his head. "Already did, but I don't mind repeating it: Department of the Interior. You remember that, don't you, Daav? Though I'm not certain I'd write Er Thom against their account; what I heard from Shan was that he had died of his lifemate's dying."

"Which he would not have done," Daav pointed out quietly, "had Anne remained among us."

"True . . ."

Val Con took a step forward, drawing the eyes of both men.

"You fed me to them," he said, and his voice was, perhaps, not quite steady. "The scouts *gave* me to the Department."

Clonak stared at him as if he'd taken leave of his wits. "Well, of *course* we gave you to them, Shadow! Who else did we have more likely to trump them than a first-in, pure-blood yos'Phelium scout *commander*? Concentrated random action. Would we waste such a weapon? Would you? I didn't think so. Besides," he finished, crossing his arms over his chest. "It's the duty of the Captain to protect the passengers. Er Thom *can't* have missed telling you that!"

"As close-kin, I ask that you not kill him," Daav said into the silence that followed this. "I allow him to be twelve times an idiot. But he is also my oldest friend, and I value him."

Val Con closed his eyes, ran the rainbow, sighed—and opened his eyes.

"Very well," he said, imposing neutrality, if not calm, on his voice. "It was my duty and I was suited to the need. But the plan has gone awry. The Department continues."

"Yes, it does," Clonak said, as if to a half-wit, "but you are no longer its creature, eh? I see our weapon returned to us, increased three-fold; a Captain with an intimate understanding of the danger from which the passengers stand at peril." He flung a hand out, palm up. "And scarcely a heartbeat too soon, all doom having broken loose. The scouts hold themselves ready to receive your orders, Commander."

Val Con shook his head. "Amuse yourself elsewhere. I've no patience for it."

"Now, Shadow," the pudgy scout said sternly, "do not, I beg you, come the kitten. I took losses at Nev'Lorn—and so did you."

Val Con blinked. "Nev'Lorn?"

"Clonak, the lad's been ill and away from the news," Daav's deep voice was perfectly serious. "He hasn't heard that the Department of the Interior mounted an armed attack against a scout base and that dozens of his comrades are dead of it."

The Department had openly attacked scouts? Val Con blinked again. The thing made no sense. The Department flourished precisely because it operated along hidden avenues, far removed from the ken of honest folk, and made no large, overt moves.

"Why?" he asked Clonak.

"Why? Why else but out of concern for yourself!" He sighed, suddenly and sharply. "Shadia found the mark of a scout in a derelict orbiting an interdicted world, and filed the report, all according to regs. She didn't make the connection between yourself and the mystery scout, though others of us did. The Department caught the report off our bands and moved in, apparently having performed the same leap of logic." He shrugged. "They were that desperate to have you back, Shadow. Or, at least, they were desperate lest someone *else* have you."

"You rate me high," Val Con said drily. "Certainly, the Commander would wish to recover—or neutralize—me before I became a threat to the Department. But to risk everything in an open strike against the scouts—" He shook his head. "That is not how the Commander does his math."

"Might have gotten a new tutor," Clonak offered. "Or perhaps he finds himself strong enough to commence upon a second phase, and begins to be bold."

Cold feet ran down Val Con's spine. *That*, now, was all too likely. The Department's Plan called for expansion, after all, and it might well seem the time to move, with Korval scattered to its various safeplaces. He was about to say as much to Clonak when a soft sound caught his ear, anomalous in the stillness of the pre-dawn garden. He cocked an ear, waiting for a repetition, and raised his left hand in the scout's sign for *wait*.

NOVA SET THEM a brisk pace down the quiet pre-dawn halls of Erob's clanhouse. Indeed, they were moving so swiftly as they rounded the corner into the main hallway that they very nearly knocked over the red-haired woman in working leathers who was striding in the opposite direction.

Shan checked, boot heel skidding on the waxed wooden floor. "Miri?"

She grinned. "Hey, Shan. Worked a treat!"

He eyed her, astonished; Healer senses brought him a second astonishment in the luminosity of her pattern, by which time Nova had recovered both her balance and her glare.

"I'm speechless," he told Miri, "which my sister will tell you is no common occurrence. Nova, here is Miri Robertson Tiazan, Lady yos'Phelium."

Nova's glare solidified into disbelief. "*You* are Miri Robertson?"

"'fraid so," Miri said, not without a measure of sympathy. She nodded, easily. "Pleased to meet you."

"I—" Nova began. Shan, deciding that bad manners were the lesser part of disaster, interrupted her ruthlessly.

"We're on our way to see how Val Con does," he said to Miri's amused gray eyes. "Would you like to accompany us?"

"Can't—gotta find Aunt Emrith and give her some good news. Tell you what, though, if you're looking for Val Con, you'll find him in the garden at the end of the wing. He's having a talk with his father."

"His father?" Shan blinked. "Miri—"

"Daav yos'Phelium is dead," Nova, not to be outdone in any mode, including rudeness, interrupted.

"No, he ain't. We just did the whole welcome-back-to-the-Line thing an'—" Her eyes lost focus somewhat, and then widened.

"Something's wrong," she said, and was gone, running back the way she had come.

Shan was after her in the next heartbeat, Nova at his side.

WRONG WASN'T the beginning of it.

Miri ran, her head full of gunfire, deadly shadows in the garden and Daav was down, Clonak beside him, and Val Con— Val Con . . .

She slapped the doorplate and dove through the opening, hitting the ground and rolling for the cover of the hedge to the right. Gun ready, she surveyed the enclosure.

Three dark, utterly still lumps in three widely spaced locations 'round the garden were deaders. A single huddle near the ornamental boulder in the center was the scout named Clonak ter'Meulen, working with rapid ferocity over another leather-clad form. At the opposite end of the garden, the gate swung open on its hinges.

Heart in her mouth, she walked over to the busy scout.

"How bad?" she asked, as the door cycled behind her. She spun in time to see Shan and Nova whipping through, neck and neck, for all the worlds like they were running a race.

"Nothing a 'doc won't put right," Clonak said, sitting back on his heels, and sighing in plain relief.

"Right. Shan'll help you get him down to the med center." Spinning on her heel, she checked her inner sense of Val Con, locating him some distance from where she stood, his pattern a muddle of horror, stubbornness and sheer crazed adrenaline.

"The Department of the Interior," Clonak said, and she didn't stop to hear anything else, but ran, ran as she had never run, not even when Klamath was coming apart around her, out the gate and after him.

DAY 345

❀ ❀

Standard Year 1392
Hamilton Street
Surebleak

"BOSS CONRAD'S HERE to see you, Penn."

Penn—Boss Penn Kalhoon, actually—frowned down at the balance sheet he'd been working on, and waited for the roaring in his ears to subside.

Boss Conrad was here. He'd hoped—never mind now what he'd hoped; it was too late for hope. Reality was that the man who'd come blazing out of Moran's territory less than a Standard Month ago—the man the streeters called Boss Killer—was in his territory—in his *house*—and suddenly Penn Kalhoon was looking at ending the day early.

Thera . . . Thera'd be OK, he told himself. Conrad targeted bosses; streeters and staff attached to a particular boss' household were, by report, safe as anybody ever was, so long as they had the good sense not to draw on Conrad or one of his 'hands.

The exception to that'd been Deacon. Conrad blew the house, there, boss and crew—but did it so neither of the houses next to it blew, or took fire. They'd shimmied a little, maybe, when Deacon's crumbled down into its own cellar-hole.

And, according to Penn's sources, Deacon had bought that special bit of attention fair and square by doing something stupid even by his standards, and sending a team onto Conrad's turf to take him out. The team never made it back to Deacon's territory, but they managed to screw up good before they all got shot dead: They killed Conrad's kid.

After consideration, Penn had finally allowed that Conrad'd done just what he needed to do to Deacon, and not one bit less than Penn might've done himself, if it'd been *his* kid killed.

He just wished the guy hadn't gone off his head and decided to wipe out every other boss on the planet, too.

"Penn?" That was Marj, his second, still standing by the door and not exactly sounding calm. He sighed, capped his pen, closed the notebook, settled his glasses on his nose, and looked up.

"OK," he said, voice steady. "Please show Boss Conrad in, and have Dani bring us some hot tea—I hear he likes tea."

Marj was looking distinctly white around the mouth. "Penn, this is the guy who—"

"Yeah, I know who he is," he cut her off. "And what I want you to do—no matter what happens—is cooperate with Boss Conrad. Got that? You level with him—explain how you're my second and you'll be glad to show him whatever he needs to see. Be *smart*, OK? You seen the reports—the only one he wants is me. He'll be good for the streets—you seen those reports, too. Be smart, Marj. Tell me."

She swallowed, eyes wet. "I'll be smart, Penn."

"Great." He nodded. "Now go get him. It ain't polite to keep a guest waitin'."

THE REPORTS all had Boss Conrad peaking at the lower end of average tall, with brown hair and brown eyes, a blue earring, a glittery hand-ring, and a liking for pretty clothes. All that was true, but Penn was still unprepared for the slim and elegant person who followed Marj into the office, his 'hand walking quiet and solemn at his back.

The 'hand—it was the woman. Natesa. Penn felt one of the knots in his gut loosen. Natesa was a pro; he didn't have to worry about a botched job. She'd be quick and she'd be clean. Not that the big guy's hand-cannons wouldn't've done the needful, but there'd been an awful mess left to add to Thera's upset.

Much relieved, he stood up from behind his desk, keeping his hands in plain sight, and nodded politely.

"'afternoon, sir. I'm Penn Kalhoon."

Dark brown eyes considered him gravely from an ageless golden face. The reports put him in his thirties, which he probably wasn't any younger than. But he could've just as easy been ten, fifteen, even twenty years older. He inclined his head, more formal, somehow, than a standard nod of greeting.

"Good afternoon, Penn Kalhoon. I am called Conrad. Please forgive me for disturbing you at your work." His voice was soft and pitched in the mid-range, real easy on the ear.

"That's OK, sir. I've sorta been expecting you."

The well-marked dark brows pulled slightly together. "Ah, have you? I wonder why."

Penn shrugged. "My sources said you was tending in this direction." That was the truth—wasn't no use lying to the man. He was gonna need to know the state of things, and best he had it straight from the one who knew it best. Penn pointed.

"I'd be pleased if you'd sit. Dani'll be up real soon with some tea."

The eyebrows moved again, upward this time. "Tea would be most welcome," he murmured and did sit, graceful as a girl. His 'hand took up her post behind him.

Penn sank down into his own chair, wondering what to say now, and was saved from making an immediate decision by the arrival of Dani with a tray full of cups, pot, and cookies. She got everything down on the desk with no spills, which was pretty good, considering how bad her hands were shaking, and shot him a look from wide, scared eyes.

"Thanks, Dani," he said easily, like he was having lunch with Thera. "We'll take it from here."

"Yessir, Boss," she whispered, and fled, closing the door a little too hard behind her.

Carefully, Penn poured tea into one of the cups, sipped it, and bit into a cookie.

Having demonstrated his good will, he filled another cup and passed it across the desk.

"I thank you," Boss Conrad murmured and took a sip, then favored Penn with a straight look. "I hope that you will forgive me if I come quickly to the purpose of my call," he said.

Penn swallowed the rest of his cookie.

"Sure," he said, and his voice sounded a little edgy to himself. "You're a busy man."

"As you are," Conrad said. "So, then—quickly: I am here to offer you an opportunity to enter into a partnership with me."

Penn blinked, thinking he'd heard it wrong, and dared a quick look up at the pro. She smiled slightly, and inclined her head.

"Um," Penn said, and had another swallow of tea to clear the sawdust out of his mouth. "What kind of partnership?"

"A perfectly unexceptional sort of partnership—or so I persist in believing, despite those who have felt they would rather die than accept it." Conrad sipped his tea. "I envision free passage and trade between my territories and your own, and a pooling of our various resources, for the betterment of all. You will continue to administer your streets, as you have been doing so ably for these last ten Standards. I will administer my streets, and hope to do as well."

Penn blinked again, then shook his head with a half-laugh. "I'm sorry. See, when you walked in here, I knew my day was done. Gonna take me a sec to focus." Something struck him and he looked into Conrad's smooth, calm face.

"You didn't offer this deal to all the—all the other bosses, did you?"

"In fact, I did not. The late Boss Deacon did not impress me as someone with whom it would be advantageous to associate. The rest, however—yes. I offered them this precise deal."

"And they turned you down?" Penn rubbed his nose. "How dumb are these guys?" He waved a hand. "I know, I know. Dumb enough." He closed his eyes, turning the deal around in his head, looking at it from this angle and that, seeing profit, growth, and—a snag.

"I worked hard to make my streets safe," he said carefully.

"Some of those turfs you picked up are pretty rugged, according to my sources. The tollbooths don't keep all the trouble out, but they keep it down."

"True enough. We are in the process of developing a street patrol, which will eventually work to keep trouble to a minimum. In the meanwhile, we may leave the tollbooths in place, as checkpoints only. Travelers would be required to stop and submit to a search, as they are now, but no cash would change hands."

"OK, that's a workaround—we can do that."

"Good. I wonder how you feel about trading people as well?"

Penn froze. "Trading *people*?"

Boss Conrad moved his hand; his big ring sparkling. "Gently. I only meant that it might profit you if—for an instance—I were to ask a master brewer who lives inside my territory to come to you for a time, to teach the craft to one of yours. Likewise, I am in need of assistance in the matter of inaugurating schools, such as you maintain. Now, we have a system of . . . itinerant teachers, who wander from street to street, teaching those who would learn how to read. I wish to do better than this, but I must be taught how."

"I get it," Penn grinned, excited now. "An' if your master brewer, say, didn't want to leave home, maybe I could send my student over to him for a while."

Conrad smiled, faintly. "Precisely."

"OK, so far this is easy." Penn looked at the other man seriously. "What's the catch?"

Another smile, slightly less faint than the first. "The catch is that I wish to secure the entire length of the Port Road, and I will require you to guarantee safe passage for all along that portion which runs through your territory. I will undertake likewise."

The Port Road ran more-or-less through the middle of Penn's turf, and it was as safe as the rest of his streets. But . . .

"We're cut off by Ivernet to the north, and Whitman, on the east. I can hold my piece of road, OK, but there ain't nobody gonna come walkin' out of Ivernet's turf. Whitman—I can talk to Whitman, if you want. She's not somebody who snubs a profit, if you know what I mean. But Ivernet—sleet, Ivernet's crazy."

"Ah. Nonetheless, I will be calling upon Boss Ivernet and offering him the deal. If the deal is not acceptable, then measures will be taken."

Penn shook his head. "You're a braver man than I am," he said.

"Merely foolhardy, I believe." Conrad leaned forward to put his cup on the desk, and came to his feet, smooth and graceful. Penn stood, too, feeling like his whole body was grinning.

"It seems we agree in principle," Conrad said, inclining his head. "Natesa."

The woman moved. Penn had time for one sharp spike of terror before he saw that it wasn't a gun in her hand at all, but a portable radio.

Shakily, he took it.

"If you need to speak with me—a consultation, an emergency— simply push the 'four' key. If I need to speak with you for similar reasons, I will use my radio and yours will emit three tones, from low to high. Is this acceptable?"

"Acceptable," Penn croaked.

"That is good. And now, I will take my leave and allow you to return to your work. Good-day, Penn Kalhoon. It is . . . a pleasure to do business with you."

"Good-day, sir. Ma'am." He raised his voice, "Marj!"

The door popped open so fast he knew she'd been listening at the knob. Her face was white all the way to the hairline, but she was grinning fit to beat all.

"Marj, Boss Conrad and his 'hand are leavin' now. Please take them down to the door."

"Yessir!" she said snappily, and turned her grin on the man and the woman. "Right this way, Mr. Conrad."

They followed her without a backward look between them and Penn sank back into his chair, taking pleasure in the simple act of breathing.

After a while, though, his brain started in, like it always did, and he shook his head. Going to call on Ivernet, was he? That Natesa'd better be a *damn* good shot.

DAY 345

❋ ❋

Standard Year 1392
Jolie's House of Joy
Surebleak

"HOUSES ON IVERNET'S turf?" Wyn, their host for the evening, shook his head regretfully. "There ain't no houses on Ivernet's turf, Mr. Conrad. We hear there ain't much on Ivernet's turf—least ways, not much anybody else'd want. Now, if you was going over to Whitman's territory, we'd be right pleased to direct you to Mirabell's House."

"Alas," Pat Rin murmured. "My fancy is quite set upon visiting Boss Ivernet."

Wyn looked over to his partner, the Jolie from whom the House took its name. She sighed.

"Mr. Conrad, Wyn's right—there ain't anything on Ivernet's turf you'd want. We had—when was it, Wyn? Two years ago? Three? When them kids come through?"

His broad forehead rumpled in thought. "Oh, hell, yeah, I remember them. Three years, it musta been—in the flat middle of winter."

Jolie nodded, leaned forward and touched Pat Rin's sleeve lightly with pale fingers.

"Two kids, it was. They made it outta Ivernet's territory just like Wyn says, in the middle of winter, their feet wrapped in rags and not a whole piece of clothing between 'em. How they got past the tollbooths, we never did find out. Lost one right off—she wasn't nothin' but skin over bone, an' so cold—we couldn't get her warm, and I'll tell you, we covered her over with every blanket in the house, with Nuce and Silbey one to a side. Nothin' we did was any good—she was that worn out with the drugs and bad food and then running through the snow to get away. To get safe." She turned her face aside, for all the worlds like a proper Liaden lady attempting to recover from a too-intimate display of emotion.

"So," she said after a moment, looking back to him, her blue eyes damp. "The second one hung on a while longer—long enough that we thought she'd make it. Long enough to tell us how it is over there." She pressed her fingers more firmly onto his sleeve, and withdrew.

"Mr. Conrad, it's a hell-hole over there. Saying Ivernet's crazy don't begin to cover it. There's drugs—something they call 'nirf'— and most take it because it cuts down on the empty feelin' of not havin' no food. There ain't no houses, just like Wyn told you. Some work for whatever they can get—an' mostly what they get is nirf. Nor ain't there much in the way of business, like we got here in Boss Penn's territory—or like you got yourself, sir, in your turfs!—'cause nobody knows when Ivernet'll blow a gasket and him and his 'hands'll come out on the streets, lookin' to go huntin', like they call it, and burn themselves down a buncha houses so they got enough light to see by."

It seemed an apt description of a hell-hole, Pat Rin allowed, grateful for the patient presence of Natesa, silently supping at his right hand. Apt enough that, had it been possible, he would have allowed himself to be persuaded to visit Boss Whitman instead.

Necessity, however, existed.

"I am forewarned," he murmured. "But, as it happens, there is one thing that Boss Ivernet holds that is of interest to me. The Port Road runs through his territory."

"Yeah, it does," Wyn said, sitting up a bit straighter, eyes bright with interest. "You after securin' the Road?"

"I am," Pat Rin said, well-pleased with him. "I intend to have it open from the center-land to the spaceport, safeheld, with free passage to all."

Wyn whistled. "You talk to Penn about this?"

"Indeed, it was the purpose of my visit. Mr. Kalhoon and I discussed the matter this afternoon, and were able to reach a mutually advantageous agreement," Pat Rin said, and felt Natesa shift beside him. "Please do speak with him, yourselves, and ask what questions you may have. I am certain that a boss who administers as well as does Mr. Kalhoon must speak often with his people."

"Penn's the best boss in nine territories," Wyn assured him warmly, and shook his head. "Audrey told us you was a change-maker," he continued, glancing over to his partner. "We tried, Jolie. Audrey said he was stubborn, too."

"Yeah. Yeah, she did. *And* she said he was good for business, which he won't be, if he gets killed on Ivernet's turf." She glanced at him, a blush mantling her cheeks. "Not that it's my decision, really, or to say that Ms. Natesa ain't a pro . . ."

"I thank you for your care," Pat Rin said, sincerely, "but my plans are firm."

"And that's why he's a boss," Wyn finished, slapping the table, and grinning, wide and pleased. "Tell you what, stop over with us again on your way back out. We'll be happy to see the both of you."

Warmed, Pat Rin inclined his head. Audrey, of course, had provided the introduction to the house of Jolie and Wyn, as she had provided introductions to the other six whorehouses in the six territories that were now either his or allied to his. All the heads of household had been cordial, but none save Audrey—and now these—had shown any personal concern in himself. Indeed, why should they? Bosses came and bosses went, and even a boss who was good for business was bound to be murdered one day.

"I thank you," he said again, inclining his head. "It will be a pleasure to renew our acquaintance on my return."

"That's fine, then," said Wyn, coming to his feet, with Jolie at his side. Pat Rin stood, in respect of the host, and Natesa did, as well.

"It's time for us to go on the floor and make sure everybody stays calm," Jolie said. "If you want company, just choose who you like—on the house. There's a morning buffet laid out for the early guests and the one's who're late going home—you're welcome to that, too."

"You are gracious," Pat Rin murmured. "I do not myself desire a companion this evening, though perhaps Natesa might wish to avail herself."

"Whatever suits," Wyn said. "I'll take you on up to your room and make sure the doormen know who you are. Staff quarters, up the back of the house. We don't get much trouble here, but sometimes a customer'll take a shine to one of the staff and make a little bit o' noise." He waved a hand, indicating that Pat Rin should walk with him.

He complied, being very careful not to look back at Natesa, who after all deserved what joy she might take, here in a place which was as safe as Surebleak came, on the eve of an enterprise of surpassing danger, if not outright stupidity.

Which is how he happened to miss the subtle gleam in the night black eyes thoughtfully considering him as he quit the room.

SHE CAME TO HIM naked, which she had not done in his several dreams upon the subject, bearing a bottle of wine and two glasses.

Pat Rin, roused from his labors with the log book, himself divested of jacket and most of his weapons, opened the door to her knock and stood, quite plainly staring.

"Is something amiss?" Natesa's rich voice held an unsubtle note of laughter.

"Not in the least," he assured her, recovering his address with a quick mental shake. "I was merely trying to recall if I have ever before seen you stand weaponless."

"Ah," she smiled this time, and showed him the glasses. "May I come in? Jolie believes this to be quite drinkable."

"Does she?" He stepped back, allowing her to pass, and watched her walk to the table, marveling at the subtle beauty of her, slim and far too alluring in her creamy, soft shirt and form-fitting black trousers. Forcefully, he moved his eyes, and closed the door.

When he joined her at the table, she had already closed the log book and put it to one side, making room for the glasses and the wine.

"But I am not entirely unarmed," she murmured as he came to her side, "as you are not entirely unarmed." She slanted an amused glance into his face. "Even in the presence of friends, we are vigilant. Certainly, we are deplorable."

"And very likely deplored," he agreed, as she produced a wine knife from her waistband and addressed the cork.

"I wonder why you are here," he said then, watching her long, clever fingers ply the knife. "Do not mistake me—I am pleased to share wine with you! It is only that I had thought you destined this evening for the pleasures of the house."

"Ah, yes." A sparkling glance from black eyes as she extracted the cork and set the wine to breathe. "That was not well done of you."

"Was it not?" he asked, which was simple idiocy. Better to have denied having taken any action. *Much* better to have failed to understand her.

"No," she asserted. "It was not." She reached for a glass; her sleeve brushing his—the veriest whisper of cloth against cloth, and nothing to answer for the bright flicker along his nerves.

The wine was poured, neatly and without fuss. Natesa handed him a glass. She held the other, but did not yet drink, only stood there looking at him, her face serious.

"You deny yourself the pleasures of the house, do you not?"

He inclined his head, allowing amusement to show. "Certainly. I am the boss and there is ever work awaiting me."

"Yes, of course." She raised her glass—a Terran toast—and he followed suit.

"To our success upon the morrow."

"To our success upon the morrow," he repeated, and they drank.

"Do you have concerns of tomorrow's outcome?" he asked her, after they had sipped again, savoring the vintage, for true wine it surely was, and nothing like the mis-named if pleasant Autumn Wine.

She laughed lightly, and sat, all grace and elegance, in the room's only chair. Pat Rin leaned a hip against the table, and looked down into her face. His fingers itched with the desire to stroke her soft cheek—which was beyond idiocy and well into madness. He had another small sip of wine, recruiting what sanity remained to him.

"Success is never assured," Natesa said, speaking seriously, for all her seeming gaiety. "And tomorrow we go against an opponent who is neither predictable nor trained, which mixes in additional danger."

"We have known these things," he pointed out, "and made plans accordingly. We do not go to Boss Ivernet naked; and there will be back-up within reach."

"All true—and yet we are well-advised to go lightly. Indeed, was I not already certain of your answer, I would ask you to reconsider and remain at holiday here while Mr. McFarland and I, with a small team, go in to smooth the way."

He did not immediately reply, being engaged in a thoughtful study of her face. She returned his regard, widening her eyes a little, her lips curving into a slight and unmistakably seductive smile.

He understood then that she meant to punish him for his temerity in leaving her to the pleasures of the house. He breathed in, deep and careful, deliberately cooling the growing warmth of his blood. Balance was her right, as it seemed she considered that he had transgressed. But Balance did not require him to act the fool.

So, business: "We had gone over this. It is my intention to offer to deal with every boss; extreme force being reserved for those who violently refuse. We cannot simply murder a man on his reputation. It may be that he is . . . misunderstood—although I grant that seems unlikely. However, we cannot discount that it *may* be possible. Shall we try to number between us those who now believe that Jonni was my true-son, his dead mother my wife, from whom I was long separated by malicious circumstance?"

She inclined her head. "True. Yet I would not see you put yourself in unnecessary danger. If Boss Ivernet is harmless and maligned, then no harm is done to him by sending an emissary first.

If he is as has been reported, sending a forward team means that your life is preserved."

She finished her wine and stood. Gently, she set the glass on the table, and turned to face him, resolution in her eyes.

Pat Rin put his glass down, straightening away from the table—too late, she had swayed one step and was close, her hip grazing his side, her hand rising, slowly and stringently in sight, toward his cheek.

So much for Balance, he thought. So much for honor and right action. Desire electrified his blood. He looked up into her eyes, and knew he was lost—knew that he *must not* lose.

"Inas," he whispered. "Inas, do not."

Her hand paused. "Why?"

"Because—because I hold your oath," he managed, though his voice shook shamefully. "I would not dishonor you."

Something moved in her face; in his distress, he could not have said what.

"Ah," she said, softly, her breath warm against his cheek. "I see." Her hand moved; a light finger touched the gemstone in his ear, then she stepped back, bowing in the Terran mode, innocent of nuance.

"Pat Rin, goodnight. Sleep deeply. Dream well."

"Sleep well, Inas," he returned, and watched her go lightly away from him, and let herself out of his room.

DAY 346

🌀🌀🌀🌀🌀🌀🌀🌀🌀🌀🌀🌀🌀🌀🌀🌀🌀🌀🌀🌀🌀🌀🌀🌀🌀

Standard Year 1392
Industry Street
Surebleak

GWINCE GUIDED the car to what passed for a curb, set the brake
and looked up. Pat Rin could see her worried frown in the reflection
of the rear view mirror.

"Boss, I ain't likin' this street too much."

Which only proved her a woman of superior sense, Pat Rin
thought. In his recent travels, he had seen bad streets—even very
bad streets.

This street was—an affront to the honorable, a blight upon the
eye; a dismay upon the soul.

Burned out buildings lined both sides of the pitted road, broken
windows gaping like fanged entrances to black and bottomless
gullets. There were no trees, nor flowers, as there had been seen on
some of the streets under Penn Kalhoon's care; there were no
people; no vehicles on the street, saving their own.

One house stood, unburned and unbroken, along the whole
doleful thoroughfare: A glowering gray pile, protected by a rusty
fence which had been draped with a glittering net of metallic spikes.

"Very well," he said, steeling himself, and turned to meet Natesa's eye. She inclined her head, novice to master, with no discernible irony.

"Gwince, please contact Mr. McFarland and have him bring his team in close. Natesa and I will see if Boss Ivernet is at home."

Gwince bit her lip. "Boss, it might be a good idea to wait 'til Mr. McFarland gets here."

"Call now," he said, patient in the face of her concern. "Surely, they will not open fire without first discovering who we are."

He was wrong.

He had taken precisely fifteen steps up the shattered walkway toward the house, Natesa at his back, when the first pellet snarled past his ear. He found his target, fired and leapt in the same instant, coming down heavily on his shoulder behind a pile of broken concrete that might once have been part of a wall.

The air was full of pellets, snarling and whining, pinging off his scant cover. Pat Rin leaned out, found a target, fired and ducked back, face dusted with concrete. He leaned out again—and froze.

Natesa lay, exposed and unmoving, on the walkway leading to the house. Even as he stared, disbelieving, a pellet chipped the stone by her head. He could not tell if she were alive—no, her hand! Surely, her fingers had twitched toward her fallen weapon?

More pellets stormed and he ducked again, measuring the distance with his eyes, ignoring the old, self-taunting voice telling him he was too slow, far too slow. He would not fail in this. He would not leave her out there to die.

Carefully, he holstered his gun. Carefully, he got his feet under him. The storm of pellet fire lessened; he focused on the still figure lying on the broken pavement, took a breath—and ran.

Fleet and desperate, he reached her side, lifted her in his arms and hurtled back toward the dubious shelter of broken concrete.

He almost made it.

DAY 51

❁❁❁❁❁❁❁❁❁❁❁❁❁❁❁❁❁❁❁❁❁❁❁❁❁❁❁

Standard Year 1393
Lytaxin
Erob's Grounds

HE WAS TOO LATE.

Swearing, Val Con went to his knees beside the still form huddled beneath the curtain edge of the forest. Carefully, he turned her over, wincing as he uncovered the contorted face. Beldyn chel'Mara. She had been a scout, once.

The wound she had taken in the firefight was serious enough, though not by any means a death-wound. No, the agony recorded in the dead face told the tale: Agent chel'Mara had understood that she was being followed—and by whom. Her Loop would have presented the calculation demonstrating that he would catch her before ever she reached her ship; and would further have elucidated her odds of winning an encounter with him, depleted and panicked as she was.

So she had obeyed the implanted orders, and accepted the Loop's Final Routine, suiciding to avoid capture.

Damning the Commander to the torments of twelve dozen hells was futile from this distance—and he had no spare seconds to waste.

Quickly, fingers swift and steady, he went through the dead

582

Agent's pockets, belt and hidden pouches, stripping out everything, even the coins and her licenses. Cramming his harvest helter-skelter into the pocket of his vest, he rose and backed away. Any moment now . . .

"Who is it?" Miri's voice was breathless. He held up a hand, warning her away, counting: *One, two, three, four, five—*

Beldyn chel'Mara's body blazed into white radiance. Val Con threw an arm over his eyes, felt the heat and the stench of burning flesh wash his face, heard the roar of incineration, and—nothing.

Cautiously, he lowered his arm.

The thin grass upon which the Agent's body had lain was lightly scorched. Nothing else remained.

"Who," Miri repeated, from the approximate vicinity of his elbow, "was that?"

He looked down into frowning gray eyes.

"Agent of Change Beldyn chel'Mara."

"Suicide?"

He nodded, and hesitated before he asked his own question, seeing once more in his mind's eye the gate slamming open, hearing the first shots snarl over his head as he hit the ground, rolling; the long body crumpling . . .

"My father?"

"Clonak's got him in a 'doc by this time. Didn't seem too worried. My turn to worry, I guess." She used her sleeve to mop her damp face.

"If we're gonna have this lifemate link—and I ain't saying it's a bad thing, necessarily—then we need to fine tune some stuff. All I knew is you was scared, you was mad, and you was gone. Clonak said it was the Department, and I lit out, thinking they'd managed to snatch you."

"That argues for fine-tuning, indeed. We have a project to embark upon during our unencumbered hours."

"Of which it don't look like we're gonna have that many for a while. These people ain't gonna give up, are they?"

"No," he said, slipping his arm around her waist in a brief, absurdly comforting hug. "In fact, Clonak's news indicates that, far from giving up, the Department is moving into Phase Two of the Plan."

"Phase Two? What's that?"

"They move more openly, dispose of their enemies, disband the Council of Clans, and establish themselves as a government."

Miri's eyes widened. "Are they serious?"

"Very serious," Val Con assured her. "And—much worse—the odds are good that they will succeed." He stepped back and pulled the assorted jumble of Beldyn chel'Mara's belongings from his pocket. "And somewhere in this is . . . ah." He held it up; Miri squinted, and sighed.

"Ship key. Great. Now all we gotta do is find the ship."

"That is not a difficulty," he said, depressing the appropriate button. The device came alive in his hand, quivering with the desire to be re-united with its ship. Val Con closed his fingers loosely around it, and spun, very slowly, on one heel. Three-quarters of the way through his revolution, the key lunged against the prison of his fingers.

"This way," he said softly, and moved off, the key bouncing in his hand, Miri walking silent at his side.

"NO," SHAN SAID FIRMLY. "We are not going after them."

"Shan, the nadelm and nadelmae of Korval are—"

"What you don't seem to grasp," he said, raising his voice to interrupt his sister and his First Speaker for the second time in an hour. "Is that the nadelm and nadelmae of Korval are *extremely fierce individuals*. Miri Robertson is a captain of mercenary soldiers. She has within recent memory led soldiers into war, survived several battles, retaken an airfield held by a hostile force—oh, and attached an Yxtrang explorer to her command.

"You will recall that Nadelm Korval holds rank as a scout commander. While this is not of itself a guarantee of ferocity, I will tell you that I have it on his authority and on the authority of that same Yxtrang explorer that Val Con yos'Phelium bested a soldier twice his size, and desperate besides, in single combat, each of them armed with a knife."

"Shan—"

"All of which means," he swept on, making his third interruption on the night, "that the universe is more in peril from them than they are from the universe; and that the enemies they cannot vanquish with a glare and a wave of the hand are no one that we want to meet, out strolling in the dawning forest. Furthermore, Erob has dispatched actual soldiers in pursuit of the remainder of this enemy—who and how many they might be. *And* I will remind you that you are Korval-pernard'i. As your subject thodelm, referencing Chapter Eight, Paragraph 15 of the *Code of Proper Conduct*, I *forbid you* to risk yourself while the nadelm is unavailable to us."

He took a deep breath, in preparation of even more forceful arguments, if need be, but she stood silent, staring at him out of a face rather paler than usual.

However, if Nova was speechless, there were others present who were not.

"Bravo!" Clonak ter'Meulen brought his palms together in appreciative applause. "Well acted, sir! Yes! *Well* acted! I'll have the tape, by the gods!"

"Clonak," Shan said, warningly. "I am—"

"No, no, darling, don't speak! You have delivered yourself of a masterful performance. Recruit your strength. Allow me to carry on in your stead." He came forward and bowed, all correct and very High House: Honor to a delm not one's own.

"Lady Nova, how delightful to see you again! Did you enjoy the war?"

She glared, which deflated Clonak not one bit. "Alas, that I missed the more robust episodes. I arrived only hours ago."

"Is that so? Then you will not have met dear Lieutenant Nelirikk! A jewel of the first water, is Lieutenant Nelirikk. I am persuaded that you will like him extremely. As you have heard, he was defeated by your foster brother, the inestimable Shadow, in hand-to-hand combat, winning, thereby, a place of service to your House. A man of many excellencies—and so fortunate that he was with us, when we picked up the others yesternoon. It is of course too soon to predict their own worth to the House of Korval, but I feel certain that they will strive to give good service."

"Others?" Shan repeated, stomach suddenly cold. "What *others*?"

Clonak turned a beatific smile upon him. "Why Hazenthull Explorer and Diglon Rifle, none other, who have only an hour ago given their oaths of service to Lord and Lady yos'Phelium."

Shan closed his eyes.

"Tired, darling?"

"Exhausted, if you will have it," he said, and sighed. "Line yos'Phelium holds service oaths of *three* Yxtrang?"

"I don't doubt but they'll be found useful to have about the house. Indeed, Captain Robertson waxed eloquent upon the point." He paused to smooth his mustache. "I doubt it's occurred to Shadow as yet, though it will—awake upon suits as yet undiscovered, your foster brother!—but I'm certain Daav had the possibility of a breeding pair in his eye." He moved his shoulders. "Well, he would, you know. We are all but products of our training."

"A breeding pair," Shan repeated faintly, but Nova was after other game.

"If you believe for one moment that I will accept that man as Daav yos'Phelium, no matter what sort of hoax you and he have been able to foist upon my brother—"

"Ah!" Clonak cried, slapping his hand to his forehead. "Forgive me! You put me in mind of why I had come to seek you out. Wait, I know I have it here . . ." He made a show of searching his pockets, and eventually produced, with a flourish, a much folded sheet of printout.

"While they had him in the 'doc, I asked the techs to do a gene match. I knew you would care, dear Lady Nova, and sought only to put your mind at rest."

Frowning, Nova all but snatched the proffered paper, unfolded it—

"Korval," she read. "Out of Line yos'Phelium."

"Which is precisely as it ought to be," Clonak said, and turned toward the door. "It has been delightful chatting with you, children, but I must be off now, to find how Shadia goes on. Ta!"

The door slid closed behind him.

❈   ❈   ❈

"JUST A LITTLE arrogant, ain't they?" Miri asked, settling on her belly under the bush they'd chosen for cover. "No guards, no whistles, no man-traps. Just . . ." She waved a hand at the ship nestled against the wooded hillside, in full sight of anybody who cared to look for it, now that Val Con had puzzled out the key combo and turned off the invisibility routine.

"They depended upon the cloaking device to hide it," he murmured. "And there are no guarantees that the ship itself is free of traps."

"Huh." She glanced at him. "It's probably set up to report back to base, ain't it?"

"There will certainly be a trans-light locator, as had been hidden on Agent sig'Alda's ship," he said, brows pulled together in a frown. "Also, it will be programmed to dispatch a distress call, if it is left too long alone. The Commander is not a fool. He will doubtless have discovered by now that Agent sig'Alda's ship never was in orbit about Waymart. It may be expected that he has caused this ship to carry . . . upgraded security."

"Terrific." Miri glared at the ship, but it refused to dissolve like a bad dream in the brightening sunlight. "We can't just let the damn thing sit there—it's a bomb waiting to go off."

"Agreed." He nestled his chin onto his folded arms, eyes on the ship. "It might be possible to disarm it," he said eventually. "I have Beldyn's license. Using it, I should easily be able to access maincomp and initiate a complete systems shutdown."

"The word 'easily' is bothering me, here."

He turned his head to smile at her. "Of course it is. However, I cannot *easily* envision another course of action, given that the ship is here, four of its Agents are dead, and it is almost certainly going to apply to the Department for assistance when its countdown is done and no one has reported in." He looked back to the ship.

"I suggest that you await me here, with the most of Beldyn's belongings. I will use her license to access maincomp. If I cannot trigger a systems shutdown—if maincomp requires two or more licenses to validate the order—perhaps I can at least reset the timer."

"And give us time to get the other licenses and come back to try again," Miri said. Silently, she went over the plan. It was a nice, simple plan; it had some play in it, and a built-in contingency scheme, which the gods knew wasn't standard for either of them. Still, she didn't like it much and said so.

"Alternatives?" Val Con asked, which she might've known he would. She sighed and shook her head.

"I can't even think of a good argument to support us going in together, instead of splitting up," she said. "Must be getting old."

He smiled. "We are decided, then." He looked at her, green eyes serious. "I will be very careful, cha'trez."

"You always say that," she complained, and sat up, wary of tangling her hair in the near branches. "Guess we better move on it, then."

"Indeed. The best path to finish is through begun."

He came to his knees, fishing in his vest for the stuff he had taken off the dead Agent. Most of it, he handed to her, reserving for himself the ship key, a metal card that was the late Beldyn's piloting license, and a flatish, notched piece of long metal.

"Interior key," he murmured. "For unlocking chests and inner hatches in times of disrupted power."

"Right," she said, and pocketed the jumble as Val Con ghosted out from under their bush and moved toward the Agents' ship.

THE HATCH ROSE in response to the key's command, and Val Con entered the ship of the Department.

The cabin lights came up as he proceeded, alert for traps and trip-beams. He achieved the center of the piloting chamber without mishap, and paused there to look about himself.

The board was locked down, screens blanked; the status lights showed all systems at first level standby—primed to leap into complete wakefulness at the touch of a pilot's hand. A prudent measure, Val Con thought, for a pilot who had chosen not to land at a port, where he might command the luxury of a hotpad, and who could not know if he would depart hotly pursued by enemies, or at leisure and in his own good time.

Well. Quick and silent, he went through the rest of the ship, satisfying himself that he was alone, then returned to the piloting chamber, pulling Beldyn chel'Mara's piloting license out of his pocket.

MIRI SHIFTED under the bush, her eyes on the ship. The hatch had come up without any fireworks going off and Val Con had walked on in. Inside her head, she saw the particular pattern that meant he was being careful, and thinking in small, tight steps. There was no sense that he saw anything that struck him as odd, or dangerous, or—

Silhouetted against the wooded hill, the ship's hatch descended, inevitably and with dignity. Miri flung herself to her feet, heedless of the scratches inflicted by her passage through the bush, her shout swallowed by the accelerating whine of engaged gyros.

The Agents' ship hurtled into the sky.

HIS HANDS flashed across the board, calling for an abort. The ship ignored him.

He slapped up navcomp, which obligingly displayed the laid-in and locked course, the coords of which were all too familiar.

The Department's ship was taking him to Headquarters.

Val Con bit his lip, letting the force of the ship's rising press him into the pilot's chair. His hands on the board—the very keys had recognized his fingerprints, he thought, and gave a wry mental bow to the Commander, who was, after all, no fool.

The ship hurtled upward. Maincomp allowed him to activate the screens, so that he could see the ground falling away beneath him, the bush where he had left Miri already indistinguishable in the blur of green.

Headquarters, he thought, and then thought of the Commander, and of the likely fate of one who had broken training, to the several-times loss of the Department.

Returning to Headquarters was not an option.

Val Con reached to the board and opened a comm line.

A CHIME SOUNDED. Priscilla, more than half of her attention on the systems report cluttering her main screen, reached absently across the board to hit the toggle.

"Mendoza."

"Priscilla, this is Val Con." His voice came out of the speaker, calm and clear, immediately recognizable, though she had not heard it for more than three Standards. She sat up, staring.

"Already?" she demanded. "Shan said it would be days yet—"

"Shan was mistaken," he interrupted. "Attend me now. There is a ship rising from Lytaxin at longitude 76.51.33 west, 39.24.17 north, at an acceleration of 7.8 local gravities. Acquire it, please."

Her fingers danced over the board. "I have it."

"Good. Destroy it."

She blinked; checked her instruments. "Val Con, you're on that ship."

"Indeed I am. Fire at will."

"No."

"Priscilla, if you refuse, you will destroy the clan. The ship will not obey me and the course laid in will deliver me into the hands of our enemy." Calm, so calm, his voice. It was his very calmness that convinced her that his order was right and necessary, though, Goddess, what she would say to Shan . . .

"It would be best," he said. "If you fire while we are in atmosphere."

She smiled. "Yes, of course it would." Her fingers moved on the board again, unhesitant and certain. "Beam up," she murmured. "Target locked."

MIRI CRANED UP INTO THE BRIGHTENING SKY, watching the ship that was taking him away from her. It was at the edge of her vision, now, a speck against the white clouds of morning. Soon—

Slashing through the white clouds came a slender radiant beam. It touched the speck, surrounded it, pulsed.

The ship blew up.

Miri screamed.

✄   ✄   ✄

REN ZEL WOKE, suddenly and entirely.

A glance across the dark room at the glowing ice-blue digits of the clock proved that he had been asleep just over an hour. Despite this, he felt extraordinarily alert, even a bit restless. A walk, he thought, would be just the thing to put him restful once more.

So thinking, he arose from his bed and dressed rapidly in the near darkness. Stamping into his boots, he reached out and plucked his pilot's jacket from its hook. His fingers caressed the worn, scarred leather, running over the tiny seams that each marked a place where the leather had been torn and, later, mended.

He smiled, there in the darkness, and swung the jacket up and on. The next instant, he stepped into the hallway beyond his door and strode off toward the right.

The hall bent sharply to the left, then to the right. Ren Zel moved out with a will, senses wide open, more energetic with every step.

The hall bent again to the right. He rounded the corner and walked into a garden, stepping from carpet to grass and pausing at last, his face turned up to a sky silvered with starlight. He took a deep breath of fragrant air—and felt something bump against his shin.

Carefully, he looked down, his vision tainted with silver, so that the large gray cat making a second, even more robust, pass at his leg seemed for a moment to be outlined in light.

"Gently," Ren Zel murmured, bending down to offer a forefinger in greeting. "That leg has already been broken once—and very thoroughly, too."

The cat blinked up at him and touched its nose, dainty, and slightly damp, to the offered finger. The demands of courtesy having thus been satisfied, it pushed its head hard against Ren Zel's hand, startling the man into a soft laugh, as he obligingly rubbed the sturdy gray ears.

A small wind moved among the leafy things, bearing sweet, unaccustomed scents. Ren Zel drew another deep breath, and straightened with a final chuck of the cat's chin.

"Come now, let me walk through this garden. I have been— long away—from gardens."

He strolled forward, boots whispering across the grass, smiling as his sleeve brushed the leaf of a misty night bloomer and released a scent as sharp and as satisfying as cinnamon. Precisely such a small treasure might have been found in the garden maintained by the House into which he had been born, years and worlds away.

Directly ahead, the grassy route he followed dead ended in an opulent sweep of greenery, but before one reached that, one came across the roots, and then the trunk, of a monumental tree.

Ren Zel picked his way across the surface roots. Glancing down to be certain of his footing, he saw that the cat companioned him still, gliding silently over the irregular ground.

Arriving at the tree itself, Ren Zel steadied himself with one hand flat against remarkably warm wood, and craned upward.

Above him, he saw shadow, sketching, perhaps, the shapes of leaf and branch. The stars were quite obscured, and the brilliant, silvery sky. He squinted into the vastness of the shadow in vain; details eluded him, though he gained a vivid impression of strength, of . . . age . . . and . . . warm regard.

From the high branches came a sound, as of something come loose and falling swiftly groundward. Pilot reactions flung Ren Zel back half a dozen paces, which was well, else the small plummeting object would have struck him squarely on the head.

Instead, it smacked in to the dark grass and was immediately leapt upon by the cat, who planted both white front feet firmly on its prize and looked up at Ren Zel with unmistakable challenge, as if to say, *Well? I've caught it for you, Master Timid. Are you too faint-hearted even to look at what it is?*

Ren Zel stepped forward and bent down, not without a certain amount of wariness, recalling the antics of tree-toads in the garden of his youth. The cat stepped back, tail high, and flicked out a negligent paw, moving the object sufficiently for his eye to find it.

No tree-toad here. Frowning slightly, Ren Zel bent and picked up what proved to be a seedpod—*two* seedpods, connected by a thin branchlet. He looked at the cat, sitting primly, tail around toes, its gaze very much on Ren Zel's face.

"Your tree is throwing things at me, eh? Am I to infer that I am unwelcome?"

One quicksilver paw came out, passing lightly over the whiskers, then the cat was walking away, tail high. Ren Zel moved his shoulders, thought to drop the seedpods, and then did not: they felt warm and comfortable in his hand and it came to him that he would have need of them, later.

Halfway across the glade, the cat paused in its purposeful perambulation and looked over its shoulder. Again, Ren Zel had the distinct impression that, if the animal could speak, it would this moment be saying something rather sharp to one Master Timid Sandfeet and urging him to come along quickly, now.

Thus gently persuaded, Ren Zel stepped forward. The cat watched him for a moment, then, apparently satisfied that he would do as he was bid, took up the lead.

PIECES OF WHAT had once been a ship fell, tumbling, out of the sky.

Miri, stirring beneath the shelter she did not remember taking, watched them fall, and gingerly, ready to snatch back at the first cold shock of emptiness, extended her thought to the place where his pattern should have been.

It was—there. Pre-occupied right this second, but displaying no signs of attenuation like she'd seen when he'd been dying on the Yxtrang fighter. In fact, he seemed quite amazingly busy for a man who ought to have been vaporized when the beam pierced his ship.

Carefully, not wanting to disturb his concentration, she pushed her thought a little deeper into his pattern. Her vision side-slipped crazily, and she was seeing the ground from high above, turning gently and rising slowly beneath her as—as?

Escape kite, Val Con murmured in her ear. *The manual key opened the emergency drawer, and triggered the escape hatch.*

She closed her eyes, which didn't quite get rid of the disorienting far-view of the ground. Even more carefully, she withdrew her thought from his pattern, and opened her eyes to the sky.

High up against the clouds, she saw a long, black wing, spiraling lazily downward.

❊   ❊   ❊

THE PATH culminated in a door. The cat stopped and looked at him over its shoulder.

Ren Zel surveyed the situation. The door was set into a section of wall. The section of wall was part of a greater wall, which formed, so he was persuaded, part of the first story of a clanhouse. He glanced down at the cat.

"I am afraid I'm no use to you. My print will not open this."

The cat yawned, sauntered over to the door, stood on its back feet, braced itself with one paw against the lower door and stretched toward the latch with the other. Ren Zel sighed sharply.

"Understand me, it's useless! This is a clanhouse—I am clanless. There is no door on all the worlds of Liad which will open to my hand."

The cat stretched higher, its paw questing well below the latch.

"Merely disobliging, am I? Well, the proof is easy enough." He went forward two steps and snatched at the knob, already hearing in his mind's ear the blare of bells as the house took alarm from the touch of an intruder.

The knob turned easily in his hand. The door swung wide, silent on well-oiled hinges. The cat strolled inside, then stopped and looked over its shoulder in a way grown far too familiar.

"No." Ren Zel stared down into glowing eyes. "I cannot."

The cat came back, stropped itself one way and the other, soft and caressing, against his legs, then moved on again, down the dim hallway.

It was risky—even given the malfunction which had allowed him to open a coded door. He did know the risk. Yet the house lured him, with its promised glimpses of the life he had been denied. Surely, he thought, just a short stroll down the hall, a glance into a room or two—surely there was no harm in that?

Knowing his peril, Ren Zel stepped inside, closing the door carefully behind him, and being quite certain that the lock had caught before he followed the cat into the deeps of the house.

Time and route blurred. He thought they might have crossed a dark, deserted kitchen, he and the cat, and gone up a thin flight of stairs insufficiently illuminated by night-dims, and down another hall, or possibly two . . .

Time righted itself. They stood before another door. The cat stroked, long and sensuous, across Ren Zel's legs, then stretched high on back feet, reaching for the palmplate set far above its head.

"This is the private apartment of someone who belongs to this house," Ren Zel said, his voice barely a whisper. "*Surely*, my hands are useless to you here."

The cat did not even deign to turn its head. Ren Zel sighed, stepped forward and put his hand with absolute certainty against the coded plate. His palm tingled as the house scanned him. His shoulders stiffened beneath his many-times mended jacket, as if tensed against the grip of a hostile hand.

Silent and stately, the door slid back on its groove. The cat made a pleased burble and all but leapt within, tail held tall, fairly quivering with joy.

Ren Zel took a step back. That is, he *meant* to take a step back, to retrace the half-remembered path through private, richly carpeted corridors, to descend the back stairway, cross the kitchen, and gain, first, the starlit garden, and shortly thereafter the familiar, beloved halls of *Dutiful Passage*.

He went forward another step, clearing the beam, and heard the door slide shut behind him.

It occurred to him, somewhat belatedly, that he had lost his mind.

Mad or sane, his traitor feet kept on, walking him softly and without haste through a pleasantly cluttered parlor, 'til he crossed yet another forbidden threshold, into the very sleeping room of one who was clanheld, alive, and joyous.

The inner room was spacious, the center held by a bed of noble proportion, set directly beneath a skylight, from which silver beams illuminated the rumpled coverlet, and wove stars into the long, dark hair of the woman asleep against the pillows, one rounded arm flung high over her head, a frown disturbing the smooth expanse of her brow.

Sanity returned, quick and cold, freezing his feet to the carpet.

They would kill him, the people who belonged to this house. Truly, they would kill him—and justly so—a stranger who had forced himself, alone and uninvited, into the very sleeping room of one of the clan's precious children.

Biting his lip, he half turned to go—which was the moment the cat chose to leap upward from the floor, landing solidly on the stomach of the sleeping woman.

"Ooof!" The lady jack-knifed into a sitting position, snatching the cat into her arms. "Horrid creature! First, you refuse to share my sleep and now you refuse me solitary slumber! Unhandsome, Lord Merlin! I had thought you for the garden all the night—" She stopped, hearing her own words, so Ren Zel thought, and put the cat gently to one side, staring across the rumpled blankets to—himself.

"Oh," she said, and tipped her head to a side, as one puzzled, but in no wise terrified to find a stranger standing at the very foot of her bed. "Good evening, Pilot." Her voice was slow, the tone oddly reverberant. She spoke in the mode between equals.

By the Code, he should throw himself on his face and despoil her no further while she got on with the business of screaming for her agemates, or her elders, or her delm to come quickly and dispose of him.

Ren Zel inclined his head, matching her grave, unfluttered attitude. "Good evening, Lady."

In the starlight, she smiled, and tossed the coverlet aside, sliding out of bed and coming toward him on silent, naked feet, her bed shirt floating 'round her knees.

"Now, *you*," she said. "I confess I had not expected you. May I know your name?"

He did bow then, very gently, in the mode of introduction. "Ren Zel."

She smiled again, and shook her hair back. He thought it threw off sparks in the starlight.

"A brief name, but well enough." She paused, standing so close that he could see the color of her eyes beneath the winsome dark brows—silver, like the starlight.

"My name," she said, "is Anthora." She held out a hand, the lace of her sleeve falling gracefully back along her arm. "May I hang your jacket away? We are all pilots here."

"I—" His throat closed. He took a breath. "I should not stay."

"What—when you have come so far? At least take your ease for an hour before the exertions of the journey back."

She swayed forward another half-step, the silver eyes wide in a face not precisely beautiful, with its sharp cheekbones and pointed chin. It came to him, as if from a distance, that he had seen a like face—then lost the thought in horror as he found his hand rising, drawn as if by a magnet toward her silken cheek.

Her eyes flickered, following the motion, and he used the moment to go back a step and to lift his hand higher, displaying the twin seedpods, still attached by their branchlet.

"A gift," he managed, his voice sounding unsteady in his own ears. "If the lady pleases."

"A gift?" For an instant she merely stared, then threw back her head and laughed, fully and without artifice. Ren Zel felt his mouth curving into a smile, his eyes following the perfect curve of her throat down to the rounded thrust of her breasts against the thin stuff of her shirt—his breath caught, blood heating; and in that moment she met his eye, still grinning, and reached out to pluck up the pods.

"A handsome gift, I own, and perfectly suited to the occasion! Come, let us share."

He blinked at her, tongue-tangled with mingled desire and dismay. "Lady, I do not—"

"No, have a care!" She raised an admonishing finger. "You have brought the gift; our duty is plain. So!" She broke one of the pods from the branchlet. It lay for a moment on her open palm, then neatly halved itself, showing a plump, sweet-smelling kernel.

"Thus, for the guest." She extended her palm, and perforce he took up the offered nut. "And now for me." Again, the pod lay quiet for an instant before falling apart in perfect halves. Daintily, she plucked the kernel from its nest, raised it to her lips, and paused. Silver eyes slanted up at him, mischievous and gentle, as if she perfectly comprehended his dismay—and his desire. "Eat, denubia. I swear that you will find it good."

Denubia. She should not call him so, he thought, plucking the kernel free of its nut-half. He was no proper recipient of a Liaden lady's endearments. Carefully, he slipped the kernel into his mouth—and gasped as a riot of taste exploded along his tongue, and exploded a second time—and yet again, so that his eyes perceived strange patterns in the aether and his ears heard music behind the silence, and his treacherous, traitor body cried out against its incompleteness.

He gasped again as the sensations faded, though they did not dissipate entirely. It seemed to him that he could still see lines of power and probability intersecting in the air all about; and that the low hum of music trembled just inside his ears.

"Gently . . ." Her voice was—and her hand was on his arm, which should *not* be.

"Lady, cry you mercy . . ." He could not allow this, whatever *this* was, to go on. If he was a-dreaming, he would wake. Now. Closing his eyes, he drew on—why, in someway on the lines he perceived about him, pulling this one *thus*, and this other one *so* . . .

"Sit the board serene, Pilot. Sometimes, it is wisdom to do nothing." She stroked his arm, tracing lines of fire on his skin through the much-mended leather. He made the error of opening his eyes and beheld her face before him, silver eyes worried and teasing at once. The threads he had gathered slipped from his grasp; the building surge of music settled back to a sweet hum. Anthora smiled.

"It is well," she said and stepped back, holding out both hands. "Your jacket, Pilot. You do not need it here."

True enough, he thought, and had it off, placing it in her hands with a lingering touch.

She held it for a moment, as if considering the weight of the leather, then looked back to him, her brow knit in puzzlement.

"This jacket carries many wounds."

"Healed," he told her, striving for some measure of lightness. "Both of us healed, well enough. That jacket saved my life, Lady."

"All honor to it," she said, silver eyes solemn, and shook it sharply, as if she snapped a rug free of dust, and moved away to drape it over the edge of a chair.

She was back in the next instant, and it came to him that the room was growing lighter, for he could see the full curves of her body plainly through the pale shirt.

"Time grows short," she said, moving close and smiling into his eyes. "May I have your kiss, Ren Zel?"

He had been born for no other purpose than to give her his kiss. And he came to her too late: dead and beyond them both to heal it. He shook his head, realized that she might not understand the Terran gesture, and murmured.

"No. Lady—I am clanless. You are—I should not be here . . ." he finished, helplessly.

"Poppycock," she said in plain Terran and grinned, lopsided and adorable. "Well. Let us try another face of the fortress. You will see that I am quite without shame—so: Since I am a lady and may mind my own melant'i—Would you spurn *my* kiss?"

He looked into silver eyes and knew that he should lie.

"Never."

Her grin softened as she closed the final distance between them, setting her naked feet carefully beside his boots. They were much of a height, and she easily lay her arms about his shoulders. Her breath was warm against his cheek and he held her waist between his two hands, cradling her closer still as their lips touched—

And the universe took fire.

DAY 349

❈ ❈

Standard Year 1392
Hamilton Street
Surebleak

HE WOKE with the echo of gunfire in his ears, and a searing sense of loss.

"Natesa!"

Someone nearby whispered her name, the voice unfamiliar—thin and ragged—and yet if there were a friend of hers nearby . . .

"Dammit, don't you start that again!" *That* voice was immediately identifiable: Cheever McFarland, and in something of a pet, to judge by the volume.

Pat Rin opened his eyes, gaining an immediate view up into the big Terran's face, which showed more worry than temper, despite the volume—and, just now, a profound and dawning relief.

"Now, why didn't I think of doin' that before?"

"Doing what?" Pat Rin asked, and heard the unfamiliar ragged whisper emerge from his own mouth. Other details of his condition were beginning to emerge: He hurt, comprehensively; and his left arm was immobilized.

"Never occurred to me to just tell you to shut up," Cheever was

600

continuing. "Well, o'course, it wouldn't—when in your life have you ever done what you were told?" He frowned, trying for ferocious.

"You been layin' here for the better part of two days, out cold, and feverish—which would've been worrisome enough—*and* you been talkin' Liaden non-stop, except for the occasional hour when you'd yell for Natesa. Which is what happened to your voice. What happened to the rest of you is you took a pellet in the arm and another one in the thigh, and you're in Penn Kalhoon's personal house, being taken care of by his personal staff, none of who speak Liaden, by the way, which is probably a good thing, considering the little bit of it I could scan."

He did have some memories of . . . conversations; long, intimate talks with his dead kin, of the sort they had rarely engaged in. There had been those things that he had wished to say—most especially to his son; and also to Shan, with whom he had so often been out of charity, so often for such little cause . . .

"It was not my intention to disturb the staff," he managed now, his ragged voice waking the discomfort of a raw throat. He drew a breath, which also was also painful, but not beyond his ability to endure.

"Natesa."

Cheever grimaced and Pat Rin felt again the fiery pain of loss, as the pilot's face dissolved in a shameful wash of tears.

"Naw, now, don't go jumping to endings." The other man's voice was unexpectedly gentle. Pat Rin closed his eyes; the tears leaked beneath his lashes and left cold, wet trails down his cheeks.

"Listen, Boss, she's gonna be fine. Caught a pellet in the shoulder—the jacket took most of it. If it hadn't been a custom load, it wouldn't've stopped her at all. As it is, she's gonna be outta bed and raisin' hell before what passes for the doctor 'round here lets you eat better'n oatmeal." He paused, then added, thoughtfully.

"Thing is, Natesa's some peeved about you putting yourself on the line like that—I ain't exactly happy about it, myself. We're your security—I'm sure we told you this, couple dozen times, maybe. We take the chances while you get under cover—which this time, you did, according to Gwince, but then what'd you have to do but *leave* cover and set yourself up as a target nobody who wasn't drugged outta their brains—which Ivernet's were, your luck—coulda missed."

"My oathsworn," Pat Rin whispered, eyes closed against the slow leak of tears, "are not expendable."

"*Yes, we are,*" Cheever said, plainly exasperated. "That's the point—ahh, never mind. I'll let Natesa pound it into your head. Maybe she'll have better luck."

He lay there, letting the sense of it sink into his bones. Natesa was alive. She would be fine. Life went on.

"And Boss Ivernet?" he asked, recalling at last the why of placing himself and his—gods pity him—his beloved, into such danger.

"Wasn't enough of Boss Ivernet left to take to the crematory after the mob got through with him." There was a certain grim satisfaction in the Terran pilot's voice. Pat Rin opened his eyes and stared up into his face.

"Mob?"

"Right. See, after you went in and practically got yourself killed over this, wasn't much Penn Kalhoon could do but back you, not to mention Ivernet's own streeters suddenly understanding that there might be a way out and joining in . . ." He shook his head. "Wasn't pretty. Quick, though—it was that. Especially with the bosses on the other side of Ivernet comin' in to lend a hand. Turns out everybody wanted him outta there, but none of 'em could figure out how to go about it 'til you come along." He shrugged.

"So, you got the turf. Penn's second—Marj Fender—she's sittin' in the Boss Chair, temporary-like, tryin' to get everything sorted out and stable. Penn wanted me to make sure you knew they was just holding it temp, and not making a turf-grab. You bled for it—it's yours. That's his words."

"All honor to him," Pat Rin whispered, closing his eyes again. He was, ridiculously, exhausted, his face wet with more than the unabated run of tears.

"We will need to send word to our other territories and—"

"Done," Cheever interrupted. "*Some* of us been workin'."

And all honor to Cheever McFarland, who held the course, as a pilot should, despite near catastrophe.

His ears registered a sudden bustle across the room, and a brisk female voice, borne closer on the clatter of heels against tile.

"Mr. McFarland! You promised!"

"Sorry, ma'am. Got to talkin'."

"Well, you can get to talkin' with Chim, downstairs," the unknown woman scolded, "and leave Mr. Conrad to rest up. Even bosses get timeout for gunshots and fever!" A sharp sound, as if she had brought her palms forcefully together. "Go on, now—out! That's enough damage for one day!"

"Yes'm. Boss, I'm within range if you want me, got it?"

"Yes," his voice was barely audible, even to himself. "Thank you, Mr. McFarland."

The bed shook slightly, echoing Cheever's path across the tiles. Pat Rin opened his eyes by a raw application of will, and found himself looking up into the round face of a smiling woman of about his own age.

"I'm Kazi," she said. "Mr. McFarland says, 'the doctor, so-called.'" She lay one cool, plump hand against his forehead, *tsk'd* and brushed his hair back, as if he were a fractious child.

"Wore you right down to nerves, didn't he? I don't know why, but people think bosses ain't human, somehow. Well. Let's wash your face, then I'll check your progress. You were lucky, if Mr. McFarland didn't tell you—the thigh shot missed the artery and the bone; it's a nice, clean wound. No problems there. The arm's a little trickier, but I think you're gonna to be just fine, so long as you're sensible. Can you be sensible?"

She had produced a bowl and a cloth from somewhere. He watched her through slitted eyes as she dipped the cloth in the bowl and wrung it out.

"Perhaps . . . I . . . can," he whispered. "I have . . . not attempted . . . recently."

Kazi smiled, leaned forward and used the cool cloth to wipe his face. "There, that feels better, doesn't it?" She dropped the cloth into the bowl and put it aside.

"OK, now I'll check the wounds. You can have a nap after—or if you fall asleep while I'm poking you, I won't be offended. I do want you to have some broth a little later, but the nap comes first." She folded the coverlet back from his left side and reached forward. "This might hurt you some. Feel free to yell and swear."

Indeed, it hurt amazingly, though her hands were light and certain. Pat Rin closed his eyes and gave his attention wholly to recalling the order in which the books were shelved in his mother's study, starting from the topmost of the floor-to-ceiling shelves. He was just starting on the second shelf when Kazi spoke again.

"They both look good." He opened his eyes to her face. She smiled and nodded. "Whyn't you go to sleep now? I'll be back in a while with something like dinner."

Sleep. His weighty eyelids closed. "Thank you," he said—meant to say—and let the black velvet tide of sleep bear him away.

DAY 355

❀❀❀❀❀❀❀❀❀❀❀❀❀❀❀❀❀❀❀❀❀❀❀❀❀

Year 1392
Hamilton Street
Surebleak

"BOSS?" GWINCE PAUSED in the threshold of the parlor Penn Kalhoon had set aside for Pat Rin's use. "Boss Melina Sherton's here to see you."

He looked up from the book he had been reading—a bow to Kazi's insistence that he "rest" between entertaining callers. Melina Sherton held a large territory considerably out from his present location; bordering on the almost-mythic "country", with its fresh vegetables, fields and wineries.

"Pray show Ms. Sherton in," he said, putting his book aside; "and ask Dani to bring refreshments."

"Yessir."

Pat Rin straightened in his chair, careful of the arm in its awkward rigid bindings. A cane leaned against the table at his side, another concession to the doctor's list of instructions.

He had not, of course, been able to acquiesce to all of her demands, though he did make a push to be *sensible*. Behold him, for an instance, guesting yet in Penn Kalhoon's household, rather than returning to his home turf, or going on tour with Cheever McFarland.

Light footsteps sounded in the hall. Pat Rin turned his face toward the doorway, and inclined his head as his guest came through the door.

"I hope that you will forgive me if I remain seated," he murmured. "I mean no disrespect to yourself."

Thin reddish eyebrows arched above tan eyes.

"I think a man who went down with a couple pellets in him six days ago has a right to stay seated for as long as he wants," she said. Her voice was strong and emphatic; her person thin of flesh; her face long and bony. She nodded.

"Melina Sherton. I hold the territory behind Ira Gabriel."

Boss Gabriel had called on Pat Rin yesterday afternoon, one of three on the day, as opposed to two, the day before. He had proven himself to be a sensible man, and willing to deal. They had parted amicably, Ira clenching his portacomm in one outsized fist.

"I have met Boss Gabriel," he said to Melina Sherton. "An excellent individual."

"He knows what's good for business," she allowed, moving forward and seating herself in the chair facing him. "I've been dealing with Ira for almost eight years; he's a man believes in that Road, same like you do. I guess you talked about that."

"Indeed, we did. And yourself?"

She blinked. "Me?"

"Yes. Do you believe in the Road? I anticipate that holding it open might cause difficulties for you, with your territory situated as it is."

"Because a road goes both ways, you mean." She tipped her head to a side, considering him. "I thought about that—thought about it a lot, if you want to know, because I got an interest in the border farms, and some trade further in. And what I decided . . ."

Here, Dani appeared with the tray, which she disposed quickly and quietly on the table. Hands steady and sure, she poured—for Pat Rin, who took a sip to demonstrate that the beverage was undrugged—and for the guest. She departed, also quickly, but without seeming in haste, leaving the door slightly ajar behind her, as per his standing instructions.

Pat Rin sipped again and put his cup on the table. "Forgive me," he said to the other boss, "we had been discussing your decision regarding the freedom of the Port Road through your territories."

"Right." She held her cup against her knee, and leaned forward, tan eyes intense. "I decided that it's OK for the Road to go to the Port and to the country. Sleet, I started in trying to figure out how we could have more of them—a safe-road out to the coast and back! Another one up into the hills and back!" She laughed.

"Same sorta thinking that got me in trouble eight years ago, when I decided the only way to protect our farms was to set up as boss of the turf next in—act as a kinda buffer zone. That's what it was gonna be, a safety zone between the rest of the city and the holdings. Then I got to looking around my streets, seeing what was needed and who was where. Got in touch with Ira and found him to be of the same general tendencies . . ." She shook her head. "Ancient history. What I'm trying to tell you is, if you're still offering that deal like you got with Penn, I'll be pleased to sign on and hold the Road clear, share out info and help settin' up schools and clinics. Might be some of mine could teach some of yours to grow eatables in little land-patches, or up on the roofs."

Memory's eye provided a vivid picture of a garden shrouded on a rooftop, awaiting the touch of the gardener who would never come again . . .

Carefully, he took a breath; another—and met Melina Sherton's eyes.

"That is precisely the sort of partnership we wish to form—a cooperative of skill and knowledge, which will benefit everyone."

She nodded. "Sure would. And if anybody can hold that kind of cooperative open, it's you. A boss who ain't afraid to put his life down on what he believes to be best? I'll team with him."

"Thank you," Pat Rin murmured, reaching for his tea cup. He sipped at leisure, and turned the conversation to the particulars of her turf. Sometime later, they found themselves in agreement, with a date set on which Pat Rin would call on her at home. She received her portacomm gravely, and Gwince showed her out, closing the door gently behind her.

Pat Rin wilted against the back of his chair, and closed his eyes. He could feel the trembling in his legs and in his unbound arm. Though he was much improved in health, yet even seated negotiation had the ability to exhaust him, and Melina Sherton had been his fourth interview on *this* day.

Seated thus, he might have dozed. In fact, given his weakened condition, it was inevitable that he doze. The next thing he was aware of was the light *snick* of the door being pushed to.

He opened his eyes and beheld Natesa.

Their paths had crossed but seldom in past days. As Cheever had predicted, she had risen from her sickbed while he was yet confined by weakness, and set herself to whatever tasks had need of her skill. It did occur to him that it was anger which kept her from his side; a notion he had tried—without much success—to put down to the morbid affect of ill-health.

And now, she was here, having sought him out of her own desire, whether to throttle him or to mock him remained to be discovered.

"Master." She bowed, elegance itself, and straightened, her black eyes and grave, sweet face unreadable.

He inclined his head, approximating the bow between equals as best he might, seated and awkward as he was.

"Natesa. I am pleased to see you, well and dancing."

"I am pleased to see you, also, Master, though it must on the mend, with the dance yet before you."

He smiled, rueful. "Both Mr. McFarland and Doctor Kazi allow me to know that I am fortunate to be able to hear the music."

Natesa inclined her head. "You did a very foolish thing; that is so. Very brave and very foolish. I have often marked how frequently courage and foolhardiness make partners. I am persuaded that you have made this same observation."

"Alas, mine has not been an existence where courage is commonly found, although certainly I have seen fools. The most recent, in my mirror."

A frown disturbed the serenity of her brow. "No," she said eventually, as one who had given the matter due consideration. "No, I would not have it so, though you must, of course, please yourself." She paused, then bowed once more—oathsworn to oathholder— and Pat Rin felt his blood chill.

"Master, I have come to ask you for a thing. I hope that you will be able to accommodate me."

He inclined his head. "I would not be so churlish as to refuse you anything," he said softly, while he felt his chest muscles tighten, as if in anticipation of a blow.

"Ah." Another grave inclination of the head, before she looked directly into his eyes.

"I would have my oath returned to me."

The familiar flames of loss blew high, taking his breath, and his voice; incinerating what was left of his heart.

He bought time with a stately, seated bow, straightened and raised his one good hand, palm up, in the gesture of release.

"Your oath is returned to you, honored and unsullied," he said, and it was the High Tongue that came off of his lips, though he had not willed it so. "Pray accept my gratitude, for service given well and without stint."

Deeply, she bowed. "I receive my oath with joy," she said, which was the proper beginning of the ritual phrase, properly spoken in the High Tongue. She straightened, and finished, in Terran: "I do not want your gratitude, Pat Rin yos'Phelium."

He had thought himself beyond any further hurt—thrice a fool! Gasping, he averted his face, his cheeks stinging as if she had struck him—and felt her fingers in truth against his cheeks, cool and soft and soothing.

"Gently," she murmured. "Pat Rin, hear the rest."

He allowed her strong, cool fingers to turn his face, so he looked into her eyes, inches away from his own.

"I do not want your gratitude," she repeated, the vicious words transformed by her voice into a caress. "I want your love."

Shivering, he raised his hand and touched her satin cheek. "You have it, always."

She laughed, softly. "And he asks for nothing in return! Very well, sir, I will give you a gift."

She bent closer, her breath warm and sweet against his face.

"I love you, Pat Rin," she said, in the mode between intimates. And kissed him on the lips.

DAY 51

֍ ֍

Standard Year 1393
Lytaxin
Erob's Clanhouse

SHAN SAT ON A CHAIR in the hallway outside the room where his long-absent uncle Daav was reported to be in the care of the autodoc. Nova had gone to Erob, in order to offer what assistance an allied clan might in the aftermath of the discovery of murderous intruders in a protected garden.

Having begged off this duty, Shan closed his eyes and meticulously went through several levels of exercise designed to raise his energy levels, clear his thinking, and sharpen his flagging Healer senses. He would of course pay for this indulgence later, and he would be well-served indeed if he fell flat on his nose just when he was needed most.

And whether that would be when he was called to identify the dead, broken bodies of his brother and his brother's lifemate, the gods alone knew.

Really, Shan, have some sense, he told himself, opening his eyes with a sigh. *Didn't you just explain to Nova that they are very fierce individuals?*

Which in no way meant they were invincible.

Beside him, the door swished open. He turned in his seat and found himself doubly netted by a straight black glance and the heart-stoppingly familiar glitter of a pattern that he had last seen in his childhood.

"Shannie?" The deep, grainy voice was precisely the same. He came to his feet, feeling his mouth stretch into an idiot smile.

"Uncle Daav. Where have you been?"

He held up a hand on which a ring flickered silver lightnings. "Now, do not, I beg you, begin! I have done quite enough explaining to your cha'leket. Apply to him for details."

"If he shows himself, I will," Shan said, suddenly somber. "He and Miri are missing in the aftermath of your little fracas in Erob's garden." He tipped his head, Healer senses tracing an anomaly.

"Will my brother also explain the very odd . . . resonance that I find in your pattern?"

"Ah, you did come a Healer! Excellent." Daav smiled. "He might very well explain it, as he deduced both its presence and its cause with what I would have said was extremely scanty evidence. However, as you *are* a Healer, a practical demonstration might be of benefit to you . . ." He closed his eyes, and said, quite distinctly, in the mode between lovers.

"Aelliana, here is Shan, wishing to make his bow to you."

There was a pause; a sense of something shifting. Healer sense processed the change as a fading and a solidifying; not at all the expected manifestation of a completely new pattern.

The person before him opened black eyes and smiled—a sweet and somewhat tentative smile, entirely different from the lightly edged expression he had been offered moments before. The muscles of the face were used differently; the shoulders less square, and more rounded. Healer though he was, Shan felt the fine hairs lift along the back of his neck. Manifestly, absolutely, evidentially, the person before him was *not* Daav yos'Phelium.

He was seeing a ghost.

The soft black eyes widened, and the smile did, too. "Shannie!" The deep voice was lighter, the graininess softened by the burr of a

Chonselta accent. "Now, shall I come the flutterhead and exclaim over your gains in height?"

"Aunt Aelli," he smiled at her, as gently as he knew how. "You were never a flutterhead. Even I knew that."

She gave a peal of appreciative laughter. "Well done! But if you wish to make a bow, you know, you must do so quickly. It would be too bad of me to give Daav a headache, which he will have, if I linger overlong."

"I see." He bowed, affectionately. "Aunt Aelliana, it is good to see you again."

She extended a hand to touch his cheek. "Thank you, Shannie. I am glad to see you, too. Take good care, now." She closed her eyes.

"Well." The voice had returned to its proper depth, the accent of Solcintra highlighting the grain, rather than softening it. The eyes opened, black and incisive. "That was a quick chat, for kin so long apart."

"She wished not to be the cause of a headache."

The smile was soft, but not in the least tentative. "She guards my health closely." He paused, as one considering the issue from all sides. "Someone should, I suppose." He moved his shoulders, something of experiment, or so Shan thought, and nodded, Terran-fashion.

"Well enough, for an old scout," he said. "Now, what news? Your brother and his formidable lady have not yet returned from their pursuit of our enemy, you said. Have they been long away?"

"A few hours. What's worrisome is that the soldiers dispatched by Erob have not as yet picked them up in their sweep."

"Which only means they've gone beyond, or gone aside, or stayed within," Uncle Daav pointed out. "A scout commander, as I hardly need to tell you, is no inconsiderable force in his own right. A scout commander seconded by Miri Robertson Tiazan . . ." He shook his head. "My imagination trembles."

Shan grinned. "Would you like some tales from the late war?"

"I have had tales from Jason Carmody, and from Nelirikk Explorer, enough to fray the nerves of even an old scout who is well-accustomed to Clonak ter'Meulen." He lifted an eyebrow. "I suppose that Clonak is with Line yos'Phelium's newest dependents?"

Shan shook his head. "Last seen, he was off to confer with the techs who had charge of the dead, leaving Scout Ne'Zame and Nelirikk to wait for the others to emerge from the 'docs. When I looked in, the scout was coaching the explorer on the finer points of Terran poker. The tech let me know that the two in the 'docs had fallen on poor times of late and were in need of supplements, in addition to the cancellation of their *vingtai*." He paused. "In all fairness, you should also know that my sister Nova is to house. Just now, she's with Erob—"

"Which is where we should be," Val Con said.

Shan spun, gasping. "How many times did father ask you *not* to do that?"

His brother grinned, and shook the renegade lock of hair back from his face. "My deplorable manners."

"He forgot," his lifemate said earnestly from his side. "He's never at his best right after he's blown up a ship."

"I'll remember that." He blinked. "Blew up what ship?"

"Surely, the Department's ship?" Daav murmured.

Val Con nodded, and looked seriously to Shan. "Brother, will you bear us company? Father?"

"Certainly," Daav said, quietly.

Shan sighed. "I've been doing my utmost to stay out of Erob's path—and you'd be wise to do the same. The moment you meet her, she'll be demanding that you remove the Clutch turtles from her garden."

"Yes? Could she not simply ask them to go? Edger is a courteous man, and Sheather only one step from timid."

"They're asleep."

"Ah. That does put another face on it." He looked at Miri.

She grinned and shrugged. "Have to risk it, I guess."

"Indeed." He tipped his head. "Hazenthull and Diglon?"

"Still in the 'doc. Now that she has them, the tech refuses to let them go until they have reached perfection."

"An artist. That is good. Now, which way to Erob?"

"I AM TO UNDERSTAND that these outlaws, then, were in pursuit of Nadelm Korval?"

Nova inclined her head. "Erob, it is so. Scout ter'Meulen had performed a preliminary identification of the three who were . . . dispatched on-site. Nadelm Korval and his lady are thought to be in pursuit of the fourth."

"Scarcely healed and already in turmoil." The old woman sighed. "If it were not unworthy of an ally, I should insist that you depart, Korval-pernard'i. This planet has lately endured two military actions. We need no more peril, just now."

A rebuke, Nova thought, and a just one. She inclined her head. "Indeed, it was not our intention to burden Erob with our unseemly disputations."

"However, the dispute in question is not merely Korval's, but of all Liadens."

Heart in mouth, Nova turned in her chair.

There were four walking into the conference room, but she had eyes only for one.

Dark hair overlong and a little mussed, as if he had been out in the wind, the errant forelock falling, as it always had, across the smooth forehead and almost into the brilliant green eyes, her brother Val Con stood tall on his own two legs, one hand hooked in his belt, the other finger-woven with the red-haired woman at his side.

He might have been a shade too thin for a sister's comfort; the high curve of his cheekbones a thought too sharp, but he was Val Con, alive, walking—and even now one well-marked eyebrow was rising, as it certainly should, with her gawking at him like a half-wit.

"Sister ain't talking to you?" Miri Robertson asked him, while Shan and a grizzled man in scout leathers paused behind them.

"Alas," he said softly. "I fear I am in disgrace." The eyebrow was well up, now; the green eyes quizzical. "Come, Nova, cry friends."

"Frien—" the word died in her throat. She took a deliberate breath, and made another attempt.

"Friends," she said, and then, more sharply than she had intended—*much* more sharply, gods, but it was such a relief just to behold him—"Where the devil have you been?"

Val Con laughed, and bowed, jauntily, still holding hands with the red haired woman. "A theme, in fact! I fear that a complete answer will need to wait upon current business." He looked to the woman at his side.

"Cha'trez, have you met my sister Nova?"

"Real quick, in the hall, right before the little dust-up in the garden," she said. She produced a nod and a grin. "Hi, Nova."

"Good morning," Nova told her, quellingly, and was not at all comforted to see Miri's grin grow wider.

"Good." Val Con moved a hand and the elder scout stepped forward. "And here is my father, Daav yos'Phelium, joyously returned to us, and accepted of his thodelm."

Thus introduced, Daav yos'Phelium inclined his head and smiled. "Good morning, child," he said, gravely. "You resemble your father extremely."

"So do you," she said, which was true, in some way that she could not quite quantify.

"Hah. An artifact of our upbringing, perhaps." The black eyes moved. "Good morning, Emrith," he said to Delm Erob.

"Daav yos'Phelium." She sighed and leaned back in her chair. "It needed only you."

His eyes gleamed. "I hold neither Ring nor rank. What possible harm can I do?"

"Do you know," she said dryly, "I was only just asking myself that same question."

He laughed. She did not.

"Win Den will want to see you. He owes you a cantra, I believe."

"So much? I will be certain to look him up immediately."

"Yes, do that." She looked to Val Con. "So, Korval, what is this danger which threatens all Liadens?"

"It is called the Department of the Interior," he said, softly. "Four of its Agents came into your garden last night."

Erob moved a hand. "Korval-pernard'i allows me to know that those persons were in pursuit of yourself."

He inclined his head. "On this occasion, they were. However, the Department has taken from every clan. Pilots, scouts, accountants, scholars—if the Department has a use for someone of talent, it matters not to which clan that one belongs. The Department subverts and makes them their own." He paused, green eyes thoughtful.

"The odds that the Department of the Interior was instrumental in engineering the domestic dispute which preceded the Yxtrang invasion borders on certainty. Erob became a target because of its ties with Korval. I do not hide that from you. They will try again to cripple you—I do not hide that, either."

She considered him, silently, for some few moments. "You can, of course," she said eventually, "provide proofs for these assertions."

He bowed. "Proofs may be obtained, yes."

"So. And what is the great House of Korval doing to stop this terrible enemy of all Liadens? I believe protection of all Liadens falls within your contract of hire?"

"Indeed it does." Once more he bowed—employee to employer, as Miri read it, with a movement of the hand indicating both irony and dedication to duty.

"Korval plans a return to Liad," he said, straightening and looking directly into her eyes. "We shall take the war to our enemy in his home."

"We certainly shall not!" Nova surged to her feet, staring at him in horror. "Have you taken leave of your senses? Plan B is in effect—do you know it? I refuse to sanction any such madness." She raised her hand, showing him Korval's Ring. "As Korval-pernard'i—I forbid it."

"Oops," Miri Robertson said, into the absolute silence that followed this.

"Precisely," Val Con agreed. Hand-linked, they walked forward, until they were two paces from where Nova stood, rigid and outraged.

Together, they bowed honor to the trust-holder. Together, they straightened. It was Val Con who said the words—his right and his duty, as delm genetic.

"The Ring passes."

What Nova should have done next, according to the Code Miri had sleep-learned, was bow in exactly the same mode, repeat "The Ring passes," and hand the thing over, no muss, no fuss.

Nova shook her head, bright hair swinging around her shoulders.

"The Ring does not pass merely because you have taken a pet," she said, scolding, in the mode between kin.

Shan moved forward a step. "Nova . . ." he began—and stopped when Val Con raised a hand.

"Sister," he said, very softly, "we are facing an enemy that I know all too well. I *am* the Captain Genetic, truly lifemated. We have made promises and taken oaths, on behalf of Korval and of the passengers. The Ring passes now because it must. I will tell you plainly that I wish it fell into any hands but ours."

Nova hesitated for a heartbeat longer while she searched first Val Con's face, then Miri's. Finally, she bowed as the Code set forth. Straightening, she announced, "The Ring passes," removed it from the second finger of her left hand, and held it out in her palm. It was a massive thing, heavy with enamel-work, taking fire from the room's dim lighting.

Solemnly, Val Con received it, turned and held it out. "Cha'trez, please familiarize yourself with this object."

Blinking, Miri took the Ring, and stood frowning down at it.

Brilliant it might be, but up close, it showed its age. There was a runkle in top of the band, as if somebody had used the edge to strip wire, or maybe to scratch a message into hull plate. And while the intarsia work depicting Korval's Tree-and-Dragon was intact, one of the two emeralds framing the carved *Flaran Cha'menthi* showed a dark crack at its heart, and the other, whole, held more than a tinge of yellow.

"Emerald's bust, boss," she said, turning the Ring around and peering inside the band for an engraving.

"It has been so for . . . quite some time," Val Con said.

The inside of the band was smooth; any engraving that might have been there had probably been worn away by generations of Korval fingers.

She gave it one more hard stare, then handed it back to Val Con.

"Got it."

"Good." He stood for a moment, his eyes on the thing cupped in his palm. Then, with an air of decision, he slid it onto the third finger of his left hand. In her head, Miri heard a *snap*, as if a something had been locked tight into place.

There was a funny couple seconds, then, as if nobody was sure of what to do next.

It was Daav who finally moved, stepping forward and sweeping a profound bow to the delm's honor, beautifully timed and directed precisely between the two of them.

"*Korval.*"

They bowed together, delm to clanmember.

"Korval Sees Daav yos'Phelium," Val Con murmured, which was what the Code stipulated he had to say.

Shan was next, face stern and silver eyes austere. His bow, deliberate and eloquent of more than mere duty, was in the mode of thodelm to delm.

"Korval. yos'Galan is yours."

Beside her, she felt Val Con sigh, and then they both bowed, as they had to, from delm to thodelm.

"Korval Sees Shan yos'Galan, thodelm," Val Con said.

Shan went back a step and it was Nova's turn, bowing simply as clanmember to delm.

"Korval," she said, softly.

For a third time, they bowed together, delm to clanmember. Miri caught the shoulder-twitch on the way up, and took her turn.

"Korval Sees Nova yos'Galan," she said, with a seriousness that went clean through to her soul. Nova had just given them life-and-death over her and hers—and they had just accepted. Miri didn't know how Nova felt about it—the other woman's face was a cool, golden mask—but she felt like bawling.

Nova stepped to Shan's side, and Daav stepped forward once more, bowing honor to the delm.

It was, Miri thought, a much different bow than his first—plainer by several degrees of flamboyance, and considerably less bold. When he straightened, she saw that his face was also considerably less bold; the eyes wide and soft.

"Korval," he stated, and his accent was different, too.

Biting her lip, she bowed with Val Con, caught the signal again as they came up and hoped she was right.

"Korval Sees Aelliana Caylon," she said, and Daav went back to his place beside Nova.

Emrith Tiazan rose from her chair at the table, and bowed the bow between equals.

"Finally," she said.

DUTIFUL PASSAGE:
Lytaxin Orbit

❄ ❄

IN RECEIPT of his delm's order, Shan lost no time in repairing to the spaceport and hiring a lift to *Dutiful Passage*. Ostensibly, he was dispatched to insure that all was in readiness for departure, a detail that could have been retired by a short comm call to the captain of the vessel. However, his delm had most particularly desired him to attend to this task personally.

His brother had asked that his affection be conveyed to Priscilla, which Shan certainly intended to do—directly after he had assured the lady of his own passionate regard.

In the passenger section of the hired ship, Shan reclined his chair. He was well asleep before they cleared atmosphere; and woke, as he had primed himself to do, when they docked.

He sat up, eyes on the amber caution light over the hatch. The instant it turned green, he was on his feet.

"My thanks," he called to the pilot, and hit the bar, passing from the shuttle into the blessed familiarity of Docking Bay Six.

Three long strides and he was through the second door and into the alcove beyond, where she waited for him: tall, beautiful and stern—a goddess. Almost, he fell to his knees before her.

Even as his stride faltered, the goddess vanished, and it was a woman before him, her black eyes overflowing with tears given the lie by her smile, and by the arrow of joy that blazed from her heart to his.

She came into his arms—or he into hers. What did it matter? They embraced, neither speaking, allowing the tides of emotion to sweep between them, open as they were Healer to Healer—and, somehow, more.

And when the emotion had found its level and the joyful tears had stopped, Priscilla stirred in his arms, and lifted her hands to cup his face, her eyes searching his, puzzled, and perhaps a little afraid.

"Shan?" she said, in her deep, thrilling voice. "What have you done to yourself?"

MIRI AND HER LIFEMATE were on their way to the atrium, along with Daav and his. Daav claimed never to have seen a Clutch turtle before, a confidence Miri took with a cellar of salt.

"OK," she said. "Turtles out of the garden, then what? Jase?"

"Clonak," Val Con murmured. "Since he is to house. Also, we should find how Hazenthull and Diglon go on—for that matter, we should find how Nelirikk goes on. Then, certainly, Jason." He pushed his hair out of his eyes. "Haste is necessary. The ship—were I the Commander, I would have arranged for a direct beam to headquarters the instant the ship recognized me. We must assume that they know the trap was sprung—and that the ship has died. They will assume four Agents dead or out of commission."

"And they'll send an army right here to Lytaxin," Miri finished, because they'd hammered all this out 'round the conference table. "Which is why we gotta grab their interest and keep them busy. I got all that. What about Edger?"

"An excellent question," Val Con allowed. "I wonder if our father might be willing to undertake an ambassadorial mission on behalf of his clan?"

Daav glanced at him, one eyebrow up. "I will of course undertake any task my delm requires of me. Am I allowed to know what it is that the Clutch might bring to the effort, in light of the need for haste?"

"You are sent at a tangent, if you will, on behalf of an ally which may require . . . alternative quarters."

There was a slight silence. "You speak of Jelaza Kazone."

"I do. You know our case is desperate—not only does the Department target Korval, it targets all of Korval's works. If we lose this throw—which is all too possible—the Department will not rest until we are eradicated. Even should some of us survive, it would be chancy in the extreme to attempt to remove the Tree."

"I would call an attempt to remove the Tree from Liad in times of peace and placid harmony chancy in the extreme," Daav commented drily.

Val Con smiled. "Which is why you go as our emissary to the Clutch. I believe that the Elders will find the project appeals—and falls within their ability to accomplish." He paused, one eyebrow up. "There must be a scout in it, you know."

"And so there must be," Daav agreed. Silence, and a sense, Miri'd swear, of him consulting with an advisor. Or a lifemate.

"We are able to negotiate on behalf of the clan's ancient ally, Jelaza Kazone, with the Elders of the Clutch," Daav said eventually. "My lifemate wishes it known as her heart-wish that any arrangements for the removal of the Tree from Liad will be found—unnecessary."

"Yah, we do, too," Miri said, as they passed through the door into Erob's inner garden. "But hope don't win the war."

"SOLDIER LORE."

They were in the captain's office, wine to hand and a ravished tray of eatables on the side table. Shan had told the story of Weapon Hall, and his meeting there with his other self.

"The most dangerous thing in the Hall," Priscilla said now. "What possessed you to take it?"

"Lute gave it me—he said I'd need it, and that it wouldn't weigh very much." He sipped wine. "I believe my reasoning may have run along the lines of, 'Well, am I likely to lie to myself except for a very good reason?'"

Priscilla closed her eyes, and it *was* fear he saw, in her face and in her pattern—fear of the man he had allowed himself to become.

"I can put it back," he said, tentatively.

She shook her head. "No," she said, her sorrow tugging at his own heart. "You can't."

IT WAS RARE YOU SAW TWO CREATURES so completely asleep, Miri thought, considering the somnolent bulk of them, tucked all tidy and peaceful into a pretty little cave that was 'way too small for them.

"They can sleep for months," she said, as if Val Con maybe didn't know that.

"Yes."

"Do you know how to wake them up?"

"No."

"Great," she said, and stared at them some more, a certifiably dumb idea tickling at the back of her brain.

Well, she thought, *can't hurt anything. And then it'll be outta your system.*

So thinking, she took one step forward, cleared her throat and said, clear, but not particularly loud.

"Edger, wake up. We need you."

Nothing happened. *Of course nothing happened, Robertson*, she scolded herself. *You didn't think anything would happen, remember?*

She was just turning to Val Con to let him know that she'd taken her shot and it was his turn now, when a shudder rippled Edger's skin—and then another one, more pronounced.

The green eyelids flickered—and drew back, disclosing eyes as round and as yellow as moons.

"Sister," Edger said, at about a quarter of his usual boom. "How may I serve you?"

LIAD
Jelaza Kazone

❀ ❀

THE KITCHEN WAS awash with morning sun before the cat and the robot detected, each in its own manner, the sound of light, quick footsteps upon the back stair.

The robot slid the waiting muffin into the heating unit, and was pouring tea into a pale porcelain cup when the lady herself danced into the room, silver eyes sparkling, her hair a-crackle with power.

"Good morning, Jeeves!" she greeted the robot, her usually slow voice nearly brisk with merriness. She paused at the stool by the window and bent down to offer her finger to the cat sitting there. "Lord Merlin. You're looking very pleased with yourself this morning, sirrah."

The cat touched her finger with his nose and turned his head to gaze out the window. Anthora laughed and danced over to the counter, where her place was laid: teacup gently steaming, a single crimson flower in a tall, simple vase, napkin and jampot to hand. She slid lightly onto the tall chair, shook out the napkin—and gave a crow of laughter.

"Oh, no! Jeeves, where did you find this?"

"In the linen press, with twenty-three others exactly like it," the robot replied, slipping the muffin from the heating unit onto a plate and rolling across the floor to her side. "I thought it appropriate to your station."

"Good gods." She blinked, first at the robot, and once more at the napkin and its intricately embroidered tree-and-dragon, which she yet held at arm's length before her. "Two dozen of them, you say? It must have been done as a joke." She tipped her head, considering. "Or perhaps Cousin Kareen had them made. *She* would think them no less than needful."

The robot placed the plate before her and she dropped the napkin to her knee.

"Thank you," she said, and reached for the teacup.

"You're welcome," said Jeeves, rolling back a respectful distance. The orange sphere at his apex—his "head," as Val Con would have it, though it was no such thing; Jeeves' computational unit was enclosed by his stainless steel mid-part—the orange sphere flickered gently.

"Did you sleep well, Ms. Anthora?"

"Do you know," she said, setting the cup down and neatly breaking the muffin, "I do believe I slept most profoundly during the first half of the night, which, as it transpired, was a good thing, eh, Lord Merlin?"

The cat flicked an ear, but did not deign to turn from his study of the birds in the bush outside his window. Anthora smiled and bit into the muffin. There was silence for a time then—an easy silence, they three being well accustomed to each other's oddities.

The cat watched out the window; the woman ate and drank; the robot cast his awareness wide, downloading data from the perimeter points and initiating a security check of the house computer.

"Did you know," Anthora said at last, leaning back and pushing the plate away, "that, on Casiaport, there is a teashop on the same street as the Pilots Guildhall, where one might find the best winter soup on all the world?"

The robot's orange head flickered. "No, Miss Anthora, I did not know that. Shall I archive the information?"

She shook her hair back. "I don't think that will be necessary. Though perhaps you should find their recipe for winter soup. We will wish to feed Ren Zel what he likes best."

"This would be Ren Zel dea'Judan, first class piloting license re-issued out of the Terran Guild, countersigned by Shan yos'Galan and Seth Johnson; five hours certified test flight short of master class?"

Anthora straightened on the stool and looked thoughtfully at the flickering orange ball. "It sounds very like him. Has he been here before?"

"I have no record of the pilot before last evening," Jeeves said. "His palm-print is on-file in the house computer. He has access on all levels."

"Perfectly correct," she said, and looked over her shoulder toward the window. "*Really*, Lord Merlin."

The very tip of the cat's tail twitched; stilled.

Anthora shook her head. "Record Ren Zel dea'Judan as my lifemate, please, Jeeves." She paused, frowning lightly, then nodded. "Send the announcement to the *Gazette*. List his rank in place of clan—First Mate, *Dutiful Passage*."

The light in Jeeves' headball steadied. "Yes, Miss Anthora."

"Good," she said, slipping off the stool and moving purposefully down the room. "I will call Mr. dea'Gauss."

LYTAXIN:
Erob's Clanhouse

❈❈❈❈❈❈❈❈❈❈❈❈❈❈❈❈❈❈❈❈❈❈❈❈❈❈❈

ORDERS WERE TO await the captain's word. The captain's word being some time in coming, Nelirikk and Shadia set about exposing the Troop's newest recruits to the intricacies of poker.

Diglon Rifle grasped the rules of play with a speed that would have been notable in an explorer, and was presiding over a solid wall of money-chips when Nelirikk heard the cadence of a familiar voice in the hall.

"Attention!" He slapped his cards face down onto the table and surged to his feet, Hazenthull and Diglon scarcely a breath behind him. Shadia turned in her chair, the better to see the door.

Came the captain and the scout—well enough. And behind them . . . Nelirikk swallowed, heart slamming into overdrive.

Behind his captain walked one of *them*—a Clutch turtle, slayer of soldiers, destroyer of fleets, despoiler of worlds.

Beside him, Nelirikk heard a small, breathless sound, and dared to move his head the fraction necessary for him to see the recruits.

Hazenthull's naked brown face was stiff, her eyes wide, her lips compressed into a thin pale line. Diglon Rifle had the appearance of a foot soldier ordered to hold the rear against the approaching line of enemy war-wagons.

Scout Shadia, seated and at her ease, inclined her head. "Commander Shadow, Captain Redhead. Your Wisdom. Be welcome."

"Gently said," the slayer boomed in a voice that rattled the brain inside the skull. "May I know your name?"

The scout inclined her head once more. "Scout Lieutenant First-In Shadia Ne'Zame—in the short form. In the shortest available form, I am called Shadia."

"Yet another scout!" the creature exclaimed. "One's elder brother is even now conferring with the scout who is the direct ancestor of our own brother—he whom you this instant greeted as Shadow, which I had not known was a part of his name."

"Only," the scout murmured, "when Scout ter'Meulen is on-world."

Shadia grinned. "That's so, Clonak being an inspiration to us all. I should mind my manners more closely—but truly, sir, it's so *apt* a naming!"

"Others have remarked upon it as well," the scout said, not without a sigh, and glanced up into Nelirikk's face.

He expected something, then—an explanation, a raised eyebrow, the offer of the scout's own crystal grace blade with which he might honorably cut his throat before the shelled one bit his legs off and left him to die in agony.

It was not, however, the scout who spoke, but the captain. She came forward some few paces, hands behind her back.

"Beautiful. What's wrong with you and the recruits?"

"Captain." He hesitated, his eyes drawn irresistibly to the Clutch turtle. The old battle reports had not overstated the enemy: The horny and impervious hide, the shell that covered the back and the soft, vulnerable belly, the pitiless and unblinking yellow eyes.

"If the captain pleases," he managed, and was ashamed to hear that his voice was not . . . completely . . . soldierly. "Many, many years ago, Clutch turtles handed overwhelming losses across several battle zones to the Troop. The conditions of defeat state that the Troop will, from that time on, be considered the fair and just prey of the victors."

"That so?"

Nelirikk met her eyes. "Yes, captain. It is so."

"OK. You wanna explain what that has to do with you?"

He stared at her, then looked to the scout, who returned him a glance that was blandness itself.

"Captain, it has to do with me and with these recruits that—" He stopped, inwardly cursing himself for an unblooded crechling. Carefully, he saluted.

"Captain. The treaties between Yxtrang and Clutch have nothing to do with those who serve as soldiers in Jela's line."

She nodded. "That's what I thought, too." She pointed, over her shoulder and up, and continued in the tongue of the Common Troop.

"Soldiers, attend me! This is Seventh Shell Third Hatched Knife Clan of Middle River's Spring Spawn of Farmer Greentrees of the Spearmakers Den: The Sheather; field name Sheather. He is the brother-by-oath of myself and the scout. You will serve him and also his brother, who you will meet, as members of Line yos'Phelium. Am I understood?"

They all three saluted. "Yes, Captain!" rang in unison.

"Good. We will shortly be moving on the enemy of our Line." She looked at Nelirikk, and spoke next in Liaden, oathholder to oathbound. "Prepare them as befit those in the service of yos'Phelium," she said and dropped into Terran. "Draw leathers and arms outta the Gyrfalks stores. Give Diglon a short sleep-learn in Trade, and lay a base in Terran, if there's time. Drill 'em both in the signs and calls. You'll be called when it's time to board ship."

Once more, Nelirikk saluted. "Captain," he said, and then, "If the captain pleases."

"Now what?"

"What is our destination, Captain?"

"Had to ask it, didn't you?" She glanced at the scout, who inclined his head, ironically.

"Liad is our destination, Explorer."

Nelirikk allowed himself a grin before he again saluted his captain and turned to give orders to the recruits

DAY 376

❋ ❋

Standard Year 1392
Spaceport
Surebleak

ETIENNE BORDEN, Surebleak nightside portmaster, leaned back in the duty chair and grinned up at dayside 'master Claren Liu.

"Another exciting shift at Surebleak Port," he said, stretching the kinks out of his long arms. "Read all about it in the night log!"

Claren snorted. "If you've written 'Nothing happened during night shift. Nothing ever happens during night shift. Why is there a nightside portmaster here? Why is there a port here?' again," she said, crossing the room to the dispensing unit and punching up coffee and a bun, "you're going to call yourself to the attention of the guild, which just might pull you and send you someplace worse."

"Produce this someplace worse!" he challenged.

She paused in the act of removing her cup from the dispenser, and looked at him. "There must be someplace worse," she said eventually.

"Hah! I say hah! If there is any other world in the galaxy more backward or barbaric than Surebleak—notice the use of the word *if*—it cannot possibly support a spaceport. By this logic—*therefore*,

Madam Dayside—Surebleak is on the last rung of the great ladder of worlds, poised to topple into the roiling pit of chaos below it—and *any* other world in the galaxy—*any other world*—must, by an extension of pure, emotionless logic, be a better, cleaner saner world."

"Or maybe not," said Claren, and took a bite of her pastry. "Mithlyn was pretty bad."

"Mithlyn is a paradise," Etienne proclaimed. "I woo it! I embrace it! I make love to it!"

"Try, and you'll find you've lost some equipment in the process," she returned. "They're pretty strict about that kind of thing on Mithlyn." She sipped coffee and pointed at the master board with her bun.

"You signing out, or what? I want my dose of excitement."

"Excitement!" He spun in the chair, signed out with a flourish and surged to his feet. "The chair is yours, Madam Dayside!"

"Great." She approached it, unhurried, leaned over the board to put her coffee cup in the slot and her thumb on the scan-plate, glanced at the main screen—and stared.

"What the—" She brought the image up, diddled with the resolution—and stared some more. "There's a line of cars," she said over her shoulder to Etienne, "seven, nine—twelve cars coming in through the main gate."

"What?" He was next to her, blinking at the screen like an idiot. "We are invaded, Madam Dayside. The natives have come to claim the spaceport, that they may profit by selling the tugs for scrap."

"Could be, I guess," Claren said absently, watching the long, stately, *well-behaved* progress of the caravan, as it passed along the row of empty storefronts and vacant repair shops. "Anything strike you as funny about this?" she asked.

"Funny?" he repeated. "You mean, besides the fact that we are about to die in a farce engineered—no, I see. They came through the main gate. They came in by the Road."

"They did. And look at the cars—those aren't jalopies. Those are—" she stopped.

"What?" he demanded. "Those are *what*?"

"Fatcat cars," she said, having recognized the one belonging to Boss Vine, who held the territory outside the main gate. "Etienne, we've got twelve different bosses coming in here."

He gaped at her. "But—why?"

She sighed, straightened and crossed the room to take her jacket down from its peg. "Guess I'd better go find out," she said, looking at him over her shoulder. "You up for some overtime?"

BY THE TIME she reached the yard, the cars were parked in neat lines of three under the shadow of the tower, their noses pointed at the main gate.

Claren stopped a couple strides out from the door, firmly squelching the urge to walk up to one of the men or women disembarking from their vehicles and ask them what the hell they were doing. She was Dayside Portmaster, after all; a post of some dignity, even on Surebleak. She straightened her jacket, so the portmaster beacon stitched onto the breast could be seen.

The crowd had sorted itself out and was moving toward her as a unit, headed up by a man in a blue jacket, leaning lightly on a cane, his left arm in a sling, the empty sleeve neatly pinned up.

He halted a comfortable four paces out, the rest ranging 'round him. All of them, Claren saw now, carried something—one woman held a basket filled with shiny green fruits; the man next to the leader held a bouquet of red, gold and white flowers in his arms; another, very large man, held what appeared to be a roll of multicolored fabric on one broad shoulder.

The leader inclined his head—something more formal than the local nod and less formal than a full-mode Liaden bow.

"I am called Conrad," he said, his voice melodious and cultured. "And these are my associates. We have come to inform you that the Port Road stands open from the main gate to the inland farms, and to solicit the assistance of the portmaster in matters of off-world trade."

"Off-world trade?" She stared at him, and was returned a bland and velvet brown glance. "This is Surebleak," she said, sternly. "Just because the Road's open today doesn't mean it'll be open tomorrow. If one boss in line gets assassinated, the Road goes down again."

"Not necessarily," he replied, softly. "We are crafting ways in which chaos may be avoided in the future." He once again inclined his head in that curiously formal gesture. "Please, allow us to name ourselves to you, and to give the gifts we have brought."

There wasn't much use in telling him no, Claren thought, looking at the crowd of faces. Some looked cocky and tough; most were poised, with a touch of tentativeness, as if they weren't quite sure what she'd do. It was the realization that they were as nervous of her as she was of them that led her to bend her head, trying to match Conrad's style.

"I'd be pleased to learn the names of your associates, Mr. Conrad," she said, and was rewarded with a slight, charming smile.

"Very good," he said and used his chin to point at the man holding the flowers. "This is Penn Kalhoon, of Hamilton Street."

He came forward a step—a thin, bookish looking man, wearing a pair of steel eyeglasses, his pale yellow hair brushed painfully flat—and offered the bouquet. She took it, trying not to think how hard it was going to be now to get at the pistol under her arm, and nodded.

"A pleasure, Penn Kalhoon. I'm Claren Liu, Dayside Port."

He smiled, which did nice things to his face. "A pleasure, Portmaster," he said and stepped back, making room for the next one in line.

It went pretty quickly, and much smoother than she would have thought possible, and then there was only the tall man with the fabric over his shoulder left to be introduced.

"This," Conrad said, in his soft, cultured voice, "is Mr. McFarland, who is in my employ. Recent injuries make it . . . difficult . . . for me to carry my own gift. I hope you will receive it with pleasure."

McFarland stepped forward, shrugging the roll off his shoulder, catching it in deft hands and unrolling it on the tarmac at her feet: A simple and cheery little rug, made out of tied and woven scraps of cloth. Claren smiled—it was that kind of rug.

"So." Another faint smile. "We are delighted that you were able to speak with us this morning. We do not wish to keep you longer from the duties of your day. May we set a time when three of our number may come to you for a discussion of opening trade—and also, perhaps, to offer some franchise business in port."

This was a man who knew what a port should look like, Claren thought, and made a mental note to ask him, sometime, where he was from.

For now, she had another try at that formal nod of the head, and offered a time six days in the future as well-suited for a meeting between herself and the representatives of Conrad's "association". That should give her enough time to get some background and guidance from the guild.

"Excellent," he said, softly. "Our representatives will be with you upon that day and hour." One last inclination of the head, with the rest of the bunch giving the standard nod, and they were moving away, back toward their cars, leaving their rug, baskets, and bottles on the tarmac at her feet, and Conrad's 'hand, McFarland, rising up like a mountain in front of her, holding one hand out and empty, reaching into his pocket with the other.

"Thought you'd like to see today's newspaper, ma'am," he said easily, and displayed it—a single broadsheet, folded in quarters. He bent and put it on the rug, gave her a nod, and moved off after his boss.

Claren stood there, holding the flowers, and watched them get into their cars and pull out. When the last had disappeared down to the main gate, she turned around and gave Etienne the all-clear.

DAY 376

❀ ❀

Standard Year 1392
Blair Road
Surebleak

IN HIS FORMER LIFE, Pat Rin had often given parties.

Indeed, he had enjoyed a small reputation as a superlative host, whose most casual morning-gather was a jewel of charming companionship and graceful conversation. Despite the considerable effort he put forth to ensure the worthiness these affairs, he had never experienced the slightest tremor of nerves regarding their outcomes, and had observed with puzzlement the agonies of uncertainty borne by other, very gifted, hosts prior to the brilliant success of their latest soiree.

He had always supposed this lack of delicate feeling to be further testimony of the general impairment of his warmer emotions. Certainly, a man who, upon searching his heart, had once declared that he truly loved but two creatures in all the universe could hardly be expected to lavish a great deal of passion upon a ball.

Well, and the universe had changed, and he with it.

There was to be a gathering this evening in his own house, where he would host not only those associated bosses who felt comfortable leaving their turfs in the hands of their seconds for one more day, but several as yet unassociated bosses of territories removed from the Road.

He expected perhaps fifteen guests on the evening—certainly not a party of any size, though at that more bosses than had been together in one room on Surebleak in many a long year. He had satisfied himself that his cook was up to the challenge of providing a buffet meal and deserts for the expected few, and decreed that neither beer nor whiskey would be among the beverages. They would offer instead an array of fruit juices provided by Melina Sherton, tea, and coffeetoot. He might have gone a bit further and advised upon the particulars of the sweets being baked, but saw that his presence was hindering progress in the kitchen, rather than helping, and had retreated, nerves a-jangle, to his private parlor.

This chamber was adjacent to his newly painted and appointed office, and was, in truth, a wonder and a marvel.

A former storage room, it had been cleared of rubbish, the walls painted a soft and restful green, the scrubbed floor treasuring one of Ajay's large oval rugs. A shelf had been hung on the right wall, and held six bound books, none new, or familiar. He had not given them more than a perfunctory examination, merely running his hand down the spines and opening one or two at their beginning, but he found their presence soothing in some small way, much as the few modest flowers in the vase upon the lamp table.

This afternoon, he found the room occupied before him; Silk the cat was asleep on the astonishment of a genuine wooden rocking chair—a gift from Audrey, or so he was given to understand. He rather thought that the chair, like the parlor itself, was a gift from his lady; certainly, her hand was obvious, and because that was so, he smiled.

Bending, he picked Silk up, awkwardly one-handed, and sat in the rocker, draping the cat across his knee. Surprisingly, the creature stayed where he was placed, sputtering a few sleepy purrs. Pat Rin sighed, put his hand on the soft flank, and leaned back in the chair.

His leg ached, a little; his wounded arm, rather more. Perhaps, once trade was established, they might acquire an autodoc. He sighed. First, they needed to rejoin the Health Net. He would make a point of introducing the subject during his conversations with his guests this evening—planting the seed, Uncle Daav would have said. And something very much needed to be done about that ghastly and moribund port. A gaming house, perhaps. Certainly, a greengrocer, a trade store . . .

A light step interrupted these ruminations.

"Pat Rin." A soft voice murmured in his ear. Strong hands came down on his shoulders, kneading. "You promised that you would rest this afternoon, denubia."

He smiled and leaned back into her hands.

"I am resting," he murmured. "I am sitting in a comfortable chair, with my cat on my lap, and my beloved by me. Were I any more restful, I would be asleep."

"Ah. But there remain some hours until the first guests arrive. Perhaps a nap would not be entirely out of order." He felt her fingers against his hair. "Not entirely out of order," she repeated, her fingers moving in long, soothing strokes.

He felt his eyelids growing heavy, and the cat curled on his lap began to purr in earnest.

"I am surrounded and overpowered," he complained, forcing his eyes open—just. "Wretch—you have attached a potent ally."

She laughed, low, and came 'round to offer him her hand. "Come, upstairs with you! Silk and I will engage to sit on you, if that is necessary to making you rest."

"I scarcely think I *would* rest under such conditions," he commented, shifting his knees. Silk woke with a long, sensuous stretch, leapt to the floor and strolled off. Pat Rin put his hand into the hand of his love and allowed her to help him to his feet.

"We shall mount an investigation," she said, slipping his arm through hers. "And, then, perhaps both of us will rest."

THEY RECEIVED TWENTY, in the final count, with rather more of the associated bosses in attendance than Pat Rin had anticipated. It seemed that, despite the commonly held goals, there remained some, certainly understandable, rivalry between the allies, and none wished to quit the floor to the potential advantage of another.

He mentioned this to Penn Kalhoon when his hostly duties brought him at last to that gentleman's side; the other man nodded, unsurprised.

"We gotta expect that. I mean, most of the long-holders—Ira, Whit, Melina, me—we shot for boss because we thought we could do it better'n it was being done. And mostly, we were right. Not to say we didn't make mistakes." He sipped his juice and sighed. "That's good. I need to talk to Melina about getting some of this into my turf, now the Road's open." He grinned suddenly.

"See? Boss-think. You got it yourself, only bigger, better, flashier. None of *us* figured out how to open the Road, and I gotta tell you I been kicking myself about it daily since the day you come into my office and offered to deal." He had another sip of juice, and glanced up, light shining off the lenses of his spectacles. "That newspaper of yours—you know it's feeding the jealousy, don't you?"

Pat Rin frowned. "Is it? I had no notion. My thought had been to . . . inform . . . the residents of my own streets on subjects of interest to themselves. It was a severe shock, if you will have the truth, when Ira showed me the copy that had been brought into his territory. It was long out of date, but . . ." He hesitated on the edge of a possible indiscretion.

"But he was all warm to know that Deacon'd had a water-filtering plant in his turf, and that you was sponsoring free reading lessons to all comers. Now the Road's open, and news is easier to spread, we're all gonna find out pretty quick that Melina has a winery, and Ira's got six clinics, and Penn's got a school system—and everyone of us is gonna want what we're short of."

"Well, then." Pat Rin had recourse to his own glass—grape cider, according to Melina, and very pleasant, indeed. "If that is the case, then we must discover how to bring improvements to all territories, each according to their needs."

Penn laughed.

"Bigger, better, flashier. Count me in, whatever you come up with. Meantime, this is a—a *triumph*, in case you don't know it. Twenty bosses in the same room—bosses *only*, no 'hands to cover 'em, and their personal guns on file downstairs with your people?"

He shook his head. "Never thought I'd see it. Sleet, never even thought of the idea. Something else to kick myself for."

"Surely," Pat Rin murmured, "you have had enough to occupy you in keeping your territory stable for ten years?"

"Yeah, but see, I *knew* keeping my streets clean wasn't enough. What I didn't know was how to expand without—well, without starting a war. Now I seen it, and I learned something."

"Ah," Pat Rin said, and turned the conversation, gracefully, to Penn's wife and children, whom he had met during his convalescence.

Later, moving among his guests, he was stopped by a young person scarcely beyond halfling, her dark eyes darting nervously from side to side.

"Boss Conrad?" Her voice was high and louder than necessary.

He admitted it and she nodded, jerkily. "Voral Jene. Gough Street turf."

"Ah, yes." One of the unallied bosses. He inclined his head, remembering to smile. "I am pleased that you were able to come this evening."

"No problem," she said. "I wanted to talk to you about—I mean, couple the other bosses here say the Road's really open, that I can walk end to end, from the port to the farms, an' nobody'll stop me or make me pay a toll."

"That is correct."

Her busy eyes searched his face. "Why?" she asked, voice keying higher. "Why'd you do that?"

Something was wrong, here, Pat Rin thought, considering the frantic young face. Perhaps she had partaken of one of the all-too-common street drugs, which had now turned on her. He glanced casually to one side, saw Melina Sherton over by the buffet table, talking to Ira Gabriel.

"Why?" Voral Jene demanded.

Pat Rin frowned. "Because the trade is important," he said, keeping his voice soft and reasonable. "Both between territories and between the world and the greater galaxy. The trade will—"

"The plague come from the spaceport," she interrupted, very loudly, now. "You know that, don't you? It come outta the spaceport and damn' near killed everybody! I was just a kid, but I remember it! And you went and opened up the Road again! You're trying to kill us!"

The room was alerted now. From the edge of his eye, he saw Melina moving in, and Penn Kalhoon, too. Many of the other bosses were staring at them, their conversations interrupted by Voral Jene's shouted accusations.

Something else moved—out of place and stealthy—behind Melina. Pat Rin turned his head at the motion and the girl grabbed his wounded arm, shouting now. "You're going to kill us! We're all going to die!"

Gasping, he shook her loose and saw the man behind the buffet pull an outsized gun from beneath his jacket.

"'Ware!" Pat Rin shouted, and Melina spun.

Her first kick destroyed the gunman's aim, sending the pellet into the blameless ceiling; her second knocked his legs out from under him. Ira Gabriel was there in a rush, first kicking the weapon out of the man's hand, then kicking him in the ribs. The gun skittered a few paces across the floor before being snatched up by Penn Kalhoon.

Two other bosses were holding Voral Jene by her arms, despite her cries and struggles. The door burst open, admitting Natesa, Cheever, Gwince and Filmin.

Cheever was at the buffet in two strides, and had the downed gunman by the collar. Scarcely less quick, Natesa gained Pat Rin's side, her eyes cold, and her mouth tight.

"Search her," she directed Gwince, and the two bosses obligingly escorted Voral Jene to the nearer wall.

A few steps away, Penn reversed the gun he had captured and handed it peaceably to Filmin.

Cries of "Kill him!" "Kill them both!" were rising as Cheever hauled the erstwhile gunman to his feet. The man moaned and shook his head, and Pat Rin recognized him as Victor Armhaut, of Conklin turf.

Pat Rin took a breath. "Silence!" he snapped, the command mode ringing against the shattered ceiling.

Silence there was.

"Is anyone hurt?"

Against the wall, Voral Jene was sobbing, while Victor Armhaut reeled in Cheever McFarland's grasp, shivering and panting for breath.

Save for the ceiling, there were no injuries.

"What do we do now, Boss?" Cheever asked, shaking his captive a little.

Pat Rin raised a hand, drawing all eyes to himself. "An excellent question. We have gathered for a party, not an execution." He eyed the assembled multitude. His associates, all of whom had been in danger of the gunman; all of whom had some right to Balance.

"It is in my mind to fling these two into the street so that we might continue our evening," he said to his associates, acutely aware of Natesa's presence at his side. "What to you think?"

The room filled immediately with voices, and opinions.

"Can't just let them get away with . . ."

"Ought to shoot 'em both . . . ."

"Kick 'em in the head . . ."

"No, wait! Conrad—I know!"

"Josh Cruthers," Pat Rin said, raising his voice to be heard above the din. "What is your solution?"

The angry shouts died back to a bass rumble, then fell into silence as a thin bald man scarcely taller than Pat Rin himself stepped into the center of the room.

"Josh Cruthers, boss of Arcadja Alleys," he said, looking around at the assembled bosses. "Look, Conrad's right—we come here to get to know each other, not for a killin' . . . ."

"They drew on the man in his own house!" somebody shouted from the back of the room.

Josh Cruthers held up a hand. "Hear me out. Just hear me out, and if it don't make sense, well, then we ain't no worse off, right?"

There was a mutter of approval, and he continued.

"So, what I'm thinkin' is, I'll have my car drive these two back to Gough Street and let 'em out—so we ain't gotta see 'em. Then, tomorrow, the gab-rag puts out the news on 'em. Let everybody know Boss Jene and Boss Armhaut ain't gonna be allowed to join the Affiliation 'cause they pulled a gun on Conrad in his house, while we was all here on his invite. Ain't none of us wants to deal with 'em—so Gough and Conklin turfs won't get no help with clinics, or school tutors, or gardens, or nothin'—not till they got themselves bosses willin' to see there's a better way to get stuff done. . . ."

Pat Rin heard Penn Kalhoon's "They won't last a week!" amid a chorus of agreement.

Privately, he thought that the two renegade bosses would do well to last a week, but the Balance was no more than precise. Pat Rin inclined his head.

"With Boss Cruther's loan of a car and Mr. McFarland's assistance as an escort, I believe that our party may continue. Please—take them away."

He looked 'round the room, remembering to smile, and set about putting his guests at ease, which was the duty of a host.

"My apologies for the disturbance," he said to the room at large. "I direct everyone's attention to the buffet, where we still have many delights to share! Please, friends, party on!"

DAY 51

✿ ✿

Standard Year 1393
Departing Lytaxin

DAAV HAD BEEN taught patience, years and worlds away, at the tent of an expert, but he had never learned to delight in its practice.

Therefore, he waited, patiently, at the airfield with a small kit-bag composed mostly of necessities others thought he needed. Before he had departed Erob's house, young Alys Tiazan had come to him with a tin of tea, as well as a surprise: A flatpic of Val Con and Miri, captured, so Alys said, on the night Miri was acknowledged kin to Erob. Miri's expression was grave to the point of grimness, as she stood very close to full attention, as if her dinner dress were a particularly uncomfortable uniform. Val Con stood easier, as a scout would, bland-faced and non-committal.

Daav had thanked the child for her gifts, and was rewarded with a beguiling smile and a bow so accurate in its complexity that he thought she must have practiced for hours—a bow to the parents of one's most admired mentor.

Now, rather than pace—which would not have been patient— or taking the offered observer's seat at the temporary control tower, where he might have been diverted by this or that happenstance,

Daav lounged on a small hummock, with the airfield, the Truax Liftmaster Plus which was the Clutch turtle's idea of a world-to-space shuttle, and his kit-bag all in view.

The kit was, as he well knew, inadequate. Even dangerously inadequate. Beyond the gifts, and a few odds and end of toiletries, he had packed several changes of clothes, a pocket recorder, extra ammunition . . .

"Daav, don't fret so," her voice murmured in his ear.

"Well enough for you to say it;" he responded, glaring at the kit as if he might transmute its contents by will alone into the appropriate and needful equipment—aye, and a working team of scout specialists, too. "I'm merely waiting for the Honorable to arrive—and doing quite a creditable job of it, too."

Aelliana's voice carried an undercurrent of amusement. "Ah, yes. I see you being patient, patient, patient. Truly, van'chela, if you become any more patient you will kick your poor bag down the hill and—"

He laughed, half-hearted, for all that she was right; and ran a quick rainbow to center himself—and perhaps to buy some real patience.

"I am concerned of this mission, too," Aelliana continued. "But I cannot see how we might have altered event in order to accompany those returning to Liad—not when Korval Themselves gave us the task."

"Light-witted, ill-conceived . . ." Daav began and heard his lifemate chuckle.

"Yes, as much you like," she said, soothingly. "Of course we cannot create from thin air a proper scout diplomatic mission, outfitted with experts of protocol, biology, language, and geology. Nor could our delm. We are the cards they had to hand—and so they play us. You know very well that you had done just the same, when you stood Korval! And while we are *not* a scout team, we are certainly better than thin air. Besides, the Tree of Erob has gifted us at our new daughter's bidding, and so we are doubly fortified!"

"That," Daav admitted, "was unexpected. For her to calmly hold out her hand and expect to catch such gifts as if she had been born

beneath a Tree and spent her childhood at home in its branches—
and for the Tree to so willingly comply . . ."

"Here," Miri had said, handing the two seedpods to Daav. "One
for each of you. Eat 'em when Edger shows you to your cave."

"See," Aelliana murmured, at the near edge of memory, "she too
masters thin air!"

Daav laughed again, more fully this time.

"How not? Our son and our daughter expect that all of us are
the masters of thin air—and we cannot disappoint."

"Just so," she agreed. "And, now, you have been patient long
enough—the Honorable approaches his ship."

Startled, he looked down to the field, saw the large, green shape,
striding ponderously toward the Truax, and swept forward to pick
up his kit.

"Do you think we will truly have a cave to call our own?" he
asked as he walked down the hill, but Aelliana was elsewhere, and
did not answer.

BRACED IN a custom-built gel-stand, Edger flew the Liftmaster
like a scout. Designed to take compact, heavy objects into orbit, it
was a most perfect ship for its purpose, a Clutch turtle being no
one's light packet. Daav noted the ship's near-new condition with
nothing more than the twitch of an eyebrow, yet Edger made
answer, as if he had expressed his surprise aloud.

"When my brother, your egg-son, required the use of the clan's
vessel in an earlier phrase of this artwork, I perceived that I was
challenged to provide proper access to all human ports. Many of the
smaller ports-in-space cannot receive the clan's vessel, for its mass
is much greater than theirs; likewise, our vessel cannot access planetary ports without risking grievous damage to the facilities. In the
past, we had merely by-passed those ports and dockings which
could not accommodate us, reasoning that we could not trade with
those who could not receive our ships. However, the possibility that
my brother the dragonslayer might require the services of the vessel
of the clan and be unable to board—this is not how kin care for kin.
And so we have acquired a solution."

Aelliana remained quiescent, gone to wherever it was she went when she was absent from his awareness. Daav, strapped in to what would have been the observer's seat in a normally configured Truax piloting chamber, found the pattern of the lift so reassuring that he very nearly fell asleep during the zero-g phase.

"I would be honored," Edger boomed, breaking him out of his doze, "if you will scan the frequencies of which I might not be aware, or which those who have aligned themselves with scouts might find informative. We will dock very soon, now."

You should have thought of that, Daav scolded himself silently.

"Of course," he said, reaching for the board. "The honor is mine."

While there was some chatter on bands Edger was not otherwise listening to, neither its quantity nor its quality was worthy of note, excepting that it was so very earnestly normal. An uninformed listener might well suppose that all was well; the Clutch transport rising from the surface the merest commonplace; the mop-up phase of Erob's little difficulty stabilized; and that nothing was in the least out of order.

In the interests of thoroughness, Daav assayed an excursion through the side bands, which were also achingly normal. His explorations had brought him fully awake and he watched with interest as "the clan's vessel" made its debut on the screen, looking like nothing so much as an asteroid, sitting tamely in orbit about Lytaxin. Of course it was, as near as Daav understood the matter, precisely an asteroid, from which the Clutch had carved a space-going vessel adequate to their standards and needs, filled with whatever strange machinery was necessary to make a ship work the way Clutch vessels worked.

Daav had read technical analyses of the Clutch's so-called Electron Substitution Drive. Human research into the drive had been given up hundreds of years gone-by as its peculiarities resisted control and its necessities warred with common sense.

In short form, the ESD took advantage of the amusing tendency of electrons to show up in orbit elsewhere before they quite leave the orbit they are departing. Left to behave naturally during alterations in energy levels, this eccentricity goes unremarked by the larger universe, the trick being omni-directional.

However, it had been found that motion could be induced in certain plasmas and fields—and, by extension, to entire macroscopic bodies—simply by imposing *direction* upon the electron's absurd little dance.

Terran and Liaden researchers had struggled mightily, and had at last managed, by dint of applying outrageous amounts of energy to a test object about the size of a human head, to propel said object for very short distances. Having achieved this double-edged success, they had then thrown up their hands and conceded that the drive was less than cost-effective. For humans.

In the meanwhile, the Clutch had solved the scale problem, and effortlessly moved worldlets through space, one electron at a time.

The Clutch ship filled the viewscreen, now. Daav held his breath as Edger brought the Truax in at a speed nothing less than breakneck, plying the board nimbly with his three-fingered hands. Daav scarcely had time to note the new metal mated to native rock, and the lock hubs braced against pitted stone, before the shuttle latched solidly home.

AS FAMILIAR as he was with spacecraft, stations, and even moon-based research colonies, yet Daav was unprepared for the scale of things inside the asteroid ship. The piloting chamber could easily accommodate the expansive main control room of *Dutiful Passage*; the primary corridors wide enough for twelve battle-ready Terran mercs to march abreast; high enough that they might each stand upon the shoulders of a comrade and never scrape helmet along ceiling rock.

Even the "guesting room" where he and Edger carried the various boxes of supplies hastily culled from a stone-clad storeroom, might easily sleep a squad of soldiers.

Trotting along at the turtle's heels, feeling positively buoyant in the slightly-lighter-than-Lytaxin gravity, Daav idly did the math. Estimating the size of the "ship," he assumed that only an inner core approximately forty percent in diameter of the whole was habitable.

Of that forty percent, non-trivial portions must house power sources, machinery, shielding . . . All of which meant that—conservatively speaking and with no real number in sight—that "the vessel of the clan" encompassed a living space roughly equivalent to the entire inside area of the twenty-nine story building where he had taught on Delgado.

"If you will attend me now," Edger said, as the last carton was stowed. "We shall walk through those areas of the vessel that are most likely to be of need or interest to you. I fear that we are but an eyeblink away from commission of a grand and hasty side work. In celebration of the haste that will soon come upon us, then, I would ask that we address each other in the shortest form possible. As you are aware, the short-form of my name is Edger."

Daav had inclined his head, wondering what sort of haste might be coaxed from such a vessel.

"I am honored if you will use my personal name," he murmured, gravely.

"I thank you, Daav," Edger rumbled and fell silent, huge, cat-slit eyes looking down upon him.

The silence stretched, becoming uncomfortable even for one who had prospered as a scout. Daav was begin to wonder if he had perhaps missed a cue, when Edger said, as delicately as his big voice would allow . . .

"Might I ask the short form best used for the other pilot?"

Daav felt the familiar stirring. His vision faded somewhat, as he heard his voice—though not *quite* his voice, really—reply, with suitable gravity. "Forgive me, Edger; I was reposing at a distance. My favorite sister had sometimes called me Aelli, and so does my nephew, Shan. It would please me if you would use it."

The turtle sighed, great eyes blinking once, twice. "Aelli is a name rich in vibrations. I shall speak it with great pleasure."

It was a quick tour, then, with Daav aware of his lifemate, awake and receptive just behind his eyes. It seemed to him as though she walked at his right hand, though he was well aware that she did not. Following Edger, they passed several garden rooms—one remarkably similar to Erob's inner garden—and an area for swimming and taking one's ease beneath sun-bright lamps. Edger displayed a rather startling book room, several large empty spaces, the purpose of which he apparently assumed was self-evident, by-passed yet another pool-room, cut through the cathedral-like piloting chamber, and returned by a secondary corridor to the "guesting room," with the supply boxes and his kit bag stacked neatly along the far wall, and the lighting which was adjusted for human eyes.

"I leave you now to nourish and rest yourselves," Edger said. "We will become underway as closely as I am able to approximate 'immediately', and will be utilizing our vessel in the upper ranges of its capacity. A gong will sound to warn you of impending motion. If you are standing or walking, it would be wise to immediately sit upon the floor with your back against the wall. A second, lesser, gong will signal when it has become possible to perambulate. Should you elect to rest, please engage the webbing over the bed." There was a pause, not nearly so long as the previous pause.

"We three here—we understand that haste is of the essence. Therefore, it will be necessary that the journey be taken in several episodes. These are not the Jumps of which your ships partake with such elegance, and it is possible that you will experience altered conditions—even discomfort. It is my understanding that any feelings of disorientation are but passing, neither harmful to the body nor the song. However, if you experience difficulties, merely speak my name in the direction of this object—" He put a three fingered hand against what appeared to be a sculpture of red stone—"and I shall hear you."

He bowed then, surprising, and very nearly nuance-perfect: "From one who is honored to be permitted to act for a master of the art," Aelliana read—and left them, moving with quite fearful haste down the stone corridor, toward the piloting room.

Daav shook his head and turned on a heel to survey their quarters once more.

"It seems we should have invited a dozen of our closest friends!" Aelliana commented, as their eye fell upon the Clutch-sized bed.

He grinned and flung them onto the thing, laughing aloud when the low gravity rewarded them with a high, gentle bounce.

The quilt, when they were on it again, proved to be handmade, of a material Daav thought might be real cotton, and showing the precious irregularities of hand-sewing.

Acceleration webbing hung at the foot of the bed, to prevent rest-period lifts to the high ceiling, and a pair of what proved, upon experimentation, to be nothing more exotic than light plates were set into the rocky headboard.

Daav climbed out of the bed—no easy task, lacking a piton and ropes—and gazed meditatively at the carefully stowed supplies.

"Do you suppose we have been hoodwinked, Aelliana? That our delm has sent us off on this quiet, safe little mission to keep us out of harm's way? I begin to think that we might have remained on Delgado, oblivious and content, and left the proper ordering of the universe to our children."

"Had you not become just a trifle bored," she asked, "since Theo left us?"

He snorted. "That was not boredom, my lady. That was relaxation. Doubtless you misunderstood the state, having seen it so seldom these last twenty years."

Aelliana laughed.

"My own beloved lady mocks me," Daav said mournfully, crossing the room to the sculpture of red rock which their host had indicated was a communication device.

The structure proved to be an amazement, for it was not, as he had first thought, bonded to the stone floor, but grew out of it, as if some natural vein of rock had been purposefully and carefully mined out from the more common rock of the walls, then faceted and polished into a pleasant work of art. Daav ran his fingers along each of the seven faceted sides, marveling at the texture of the stone . . .

"I believe we have the cave we were promised," Aelliana said. "It pleases, odd though it is. Shall we honor our daughter's wishes?"

"Why not?" Daav returned, abandoning his contemplation of the red rock. "Though I warn you, she will never believe us so obedient."

※　　※　　※

THE SEED PODS became desert to a snack foraged from the assembled supplies. Aelliana concurred in the wine, and in the crackers-with-cheese-spread from a commercial camping pack. Daav opened the bottle with his utility tool, and sipped slowly.

It was his belief that Aelliana and he tasted different essences; that when she wished to put herself forward wines were slightly more complex. This hour she was alert—even playful—and he found the wine very good, indeed. The crackers were amusing, like a return to some childhood picnic, a theme that the seed pods continued, for how long had it been?

Daav sighed. Why, only since he had fled Liad, seeking Balance, sanity, and heart's ease.

In the dark days just after her death, he had been concerned— overly concerned—for his sanity in everything he did, for Aelliana had yet to find a way to let him know she was truly with him. Well he knew the power of habit and wishful thinking; and the willingness of the heart to cling to hope, despite whatever brutal facts the mind might wearily recite down the endless hours of grief-filled nights.

He refused to believe that he heard her voice. He *knew better* than to believe. Had not Master Healer Kestra herself assured him that theirs was a lifemating of uncertain prognosis? Was it not true, and despite all their efforts and wishes to make it otherwise, that Daav had never once rejoiced at the touch of his lifemate's thought against his own? Aelliana—she had some small bit of that: Touching him, she could read him. He had never envied her the gift—gods knew, she had few enough joys in her life—but the gift had been *hers*, not his. And she was dead.

He would never hear her voice again.

Desolate, he perversely attempted to embrace yet more desolation—deliberately refusing the Tree's urge that he take seedpods with him; refusing to tell Er Thom his plan; refusing to contemplate a return. Refusing to believe with every bit of his will that he heard his beloved's voice, until desolation itself betrayed him, and Aelliana caught him nodding in exhaustion before a computer screen . . .

"Daav? Shall we share?"

He smiled. "Indeed we shall." Taking a pod in each hand, he offered—and Aelliana accepted—the first bite.

THEIR SNACK FINISHED, Aelliana was pleased to accompany him on another tour of the strange vessel on which they found themselves. Daav wandered them leisurely back along the path of the tour Edger had given them, the tantalizingly glimpsed library the first goal.

Path was a more accurate description than corridor, Daav thought. There were irregularities in the stone beneath his feet, and apparently random turnings in the way, which put one in mind of a forest walk, rather than a tame hallway. Strolling along, he indulged himself in a scout-like amusement: in his mind's eye, he attempted to connect several of the rooms in a straight line. Perhaps it could have been done, but there seemed a certain shape for doorways, and an alignment—or perhaps lack of alignment—in a pattern he could not quite understand.

Aelliana offered the opinion that the water rooms—which she counted as rooms containing open pools or flowing water—of which they had passed at least four, appeared to be situated at a mathematically constant distance from the ship's core.

"I suspect we have a combination of the technical and the aesthetic at work, Daav," she said, excitedly, as such discoveries invariably excited her. "Closer to center there would be no whirlpool pattern to the drains—water would flow directly in from all sides. Situated as they are, the pools and brooklets follow a rhythm and flow more natural to a spinning world."

Very likely, she was right, Daav thought. Gods knew, *he* was no authority on Clutch aesthetics.

Ambling, they passed periodic gaps in the stone walls, and the gleam of fittings for a metal door. Otherwise, the ship was very much the cavern Miri had promised them—a cavern shaped by an intelligence far from human.

Daav ran his fingers along the wall as they walked, discovering patterns—or perhaps merely the marks of ancient chisels—and sighed. At every turn, he was reminded of the difficulty of the task his delm had set him. Negotiate with the Elders, forsooth! Convince a council of beings unimaginably old to offer refuge to a sentient tree as old, or even older, than they.

If the Clutch Elders are wise, he thought sourly, *they will decline the honor, with speed and force.*

"Daav." Aelliana's voice was urgent in his ear. "The ship . . ."

He paused. Indeed, he did feel something change in the rock beneath his feet—the briefest vibration, as if someone had slammed a door on the far side of a large building.

"Perhaps Edger is adjusting our orbit—" he began—and his voice was overwhelmed by the voice of the gong.

The entire ship rang with the sound; disorienting him for a fragment of a second. He made a pilot's quick recover and dropped to the stone floor, sitting with his back pressed against the rock wall, distantly amused at the new vogue in acceleration couches.

He leaned his head against the wall, closed his eyes and waited for transition.

Another vibration, so low he felt the long waves of it sweep up his legs and body, through his chin, and over his head.

He opened his eyes.

The walls were full of color; shot with veins of gold and silver, coruscating, so that he felt that he—that they!—were deep inside a quartz meteor revolving around a star of lambent blue.

He realized almost immediately that he should not have opened his eyes, for the busyness of the light disturbed his sense of direction. He looked down, bracing a hand against a floor streaming with pearl pink and aqua. His hand sank into the stone—he *felt* it; felt the textures of the colors—and now his equilibrium was disturbed, the stone hallway stretching up into the filaments of the blue-toned quartz . . .

The ship—or the universe—lurched; his inner ear protested; and he was seeing *through* dozens of layers of rock, threatening to reveal cold space . . .

Aelliana was with him, he could feel her presence, as if she too were amazed and appalled at the spectacle before them.

He twisted against the wall, trying to recover his shattered balance, but his body did not properly obey him. It was as if he were twinned, with two right arms to move, using two sets of muscles, superimposed . . .

"Daav!" Aelliana mirrored his panic, her voice echoing sweetly off the stone corridors.

"Aelliana!"

Briefly, disorientingly, he *did* see two right arms, braced by two ghostly right hands leaning on and into the flowing colors. There was fog boiling out of the rock floor, the air thick with motes of light . . .

He winced, lost that vision—lost everything but the confusion of trying to move an arm following someone else's orders—and her voice.

"Daav! Daav, I am—*here!*"

He took a breath, imposing discipline. "Aelliana, *where* are you?"

Somewhere beyond the chaos of color, a gong sounded, vibrating into his very soul. His vision cleared, and there again was the rock wall, bleeding color into the foggy floor, and the whole corridor was vibrating, as if the rocks themselves were singing, and the light thickened air was as lascivious as silk and Aelliana was beside him, her hand was on his shoulder, and he turned his face into her kiss—

No. She was not there. Rather—she was everywhere. He could feel the flow of her thoughts, feel her deciding where to look, feel her adjusting her balance against the wall she braced against—

His eyes—her eyes—focused on the wall opposite, shimmering with bolts of gold and green, but more solid, now, no longer threatening to fade into transparency.

"Daav," his beloved said in his ear. "I can see that this will need work!"

He half-gasped a laugh, as she lifted his right hand and caressed his face.

"I think the worst is over," she murmured. "Let us return to our cave."

"An excellent idea," he said. "A glass of wine would be most

welcome. And a nap, if you will have it. Edger should be more considerate of an old man's frailties."

"To Edger, you are the veriest babe," Aelliana retorted. "But,
yes, a nap—and then we must talk."

EDGER STOOD with his intricately shelled back to them, engaged
in a close study of the control board built into a rock buttress. He
was also, Daav realized, humming, or possibly singing, as he
touched first this, then that, on the board—

The tune altered, and though he did not turn to look at them he
raised a bit from the board as he spoke.

"Please, Aelli and Daav, if you will but tarry for five or six more
moments I will join you. I have news of interest to you both."

So saying, Edger returned to his hum; leaving Daav and
Aelliana to continue exploring this new, higher-level melding.

It was, of course, the lifemate-bond, but somehow expanded,
broadened, deepened beyond anything they had thought possible.
Daav, wary of joy unleavened, proposed it to be an effect of the
drive, which would fade upon the return to normal space. Aelliana
considered that the drive was a factor in the . . . speed . . . of their
joining, but offered the possibility that the seeds they had eaten were
the motivating force.

The exchange was far faster and far fuller than their usual, even
the pleasant after-effect of the wine had not dulled the transfers.
Occasionally, one or the other might be distracted by this memory
or that sudden bit of information . . . .

Aelliana had sensed the change coming first, for the images and
information she had been receiving through Daav had sharpened all
at once—as if she were seeing with her own eyes—and she was able
to conceive of moving an arm. Later, she proved herself capable of
walking, without Daav's active assistance.

The nap had been not quite that—instead they had relaxed with
eyes closed and shared: thoughts, emotions, *essence* . . .

There were some few of Daav's memories which Aelliana could
not properly access, nor could he grasp all of hers—but in every
case, those tended to be memories each had done the most to forget.

And there were certainly enough tantalizing—and sometimes dismaying—glimpses to beguile them both. For Daav, of her brother Ran Eld and his friend; of a marriage full of taunts and pain; of his own young and subtle face. For Aelliana, of planets she had never seen; and the tender tuitions in patience . . .

New to Daav was his ability to access a larger part of Aelliana's intuitive understandings of mathematics; new to her was sharing Daav's immediate and nuanced interpretations of the motivations of people. New, too, for her, was the surprising overlay of the Diaries, richly illustrating and informing her altered realization of her beloved, of Korval, and of Liaden history.

It had taken effort—a willful exchange of thoughts rather than the subconscious communication they had allowed themselves to be enveloped by—to go to Edger.

"Aelliana, my love, we cannot stare into this mirror until the stars cool. I do believe that this will, as you say, take some work. And perhaps the assistance of a master."

So, they had gone to find Edger, with Daav, like a youngster learning to trust the way a simple lean could take advantage of a duocycle's momentum, accepting Aelliana's direction of their hike.

"I will miss this," she said, "if you are right, and it is solely an artifact of the drive."

"I know," he whispered, and felt her feeling his regret—and his fear.

The gong sounded once more. Here in the control room it rang through them foot to head . . .

Edger turned, sweeping into a full bow and speaking in a booming, formal voice.

"True elders of your clan! I am humbled to be the first to see you thus."

He straightened, and continued in what passed for a more conversational tone. "The art of your children, my kin, has strong roots; stronger than I knew. Already their names are spoken among the Elders—and your names, as well. My request was that the Elders act in unprecedented haste and see you immediately, in the human sense.

"I am informed that the outer chamber will be open when we arrive, and that I might bring you directly there. The Elders make haste—surely, this is a work of art like none before! They will see you, I think, very quickly."

There was a pause, which Daav allowed to stretch.

"The Elders will see us," Aelliana breathed, for him alone. "Van'chela, can you imagine it?"

"I can," he answered, in the same way, "and it concerns me greatly. Recall that I know the Tree very well indeed, and I know what Jela's bargain has cost us . . ."

Before them, Edger bowed slightly, as if rousing from some deep process of thought.

"It would be pleasant if you would walk with me to the waterfall park. There, we may enjoy a small repast, and an hour of talk."

"It sounds a good plan," Daav admitted. "Might I know the ship's schedule—and your own? If we are to travel the next weeks with you . . ."

Edger blinked his huge yellow eyes, one, then the other.

"I see that you have studied the affect of our ships at low drive," he said. "For a task of such moment and urgency, I have utilized the higher drives." He turned, widely, motioning them to follow.

"We will enter my home atmosphere shortly after your next sleep period. You will be in the outer chamber, awaiting permission of the Elders to enter, in sixteen Standard Hours."

LYTAXIN:
Erob's House

❀ ❀

"WHAT ELSE?" Miri asked Val Con, after the last late meeting was done and they were alone in the sitting room of their suite.

He turned from the wine table, bottle and glass in hand, eyebrow well up. "We have put such things into motion as may be put into motion. All that remains us is to defeat the Department, vanquish the Commander, and reclaim the Agents."

"Piece of cake." She moved across the rug toward him. "Can the Agents be reclaimed?"

"The Healers will know," he said softly, pouring. "If I was able to break training, perhaps others may do so, as well."

"Or maybe not." She took the glass he handed her, and stood sipping, staring at nothing in particular, going over the plans they had laid. It was, she thought, going to be dicey.

To say the least.

"The kids?" she asked, that being a detail left in flux.

Val Con raised his glass. Korval's Ring gleamed on his finger, big and flashy and flawed.

"Do you think we should dispatch the *Passage* to the children? Shan and Priscilla are able, and the ship now runs as a battlewagon."

She frowned, weighing it.

"It'd draw attention—"

The comm buzzed. Shaking her head, she crossed to it and pushed the button.

"Robertson."

"Cousin, it is Kol Vus. A person has called for yourself and for your lifemate. He awaits your pleasure in the public parlor."

Miri's brows drew together in a small frown. "I thank you, cousin," she said, dropping effortlessly into the High Tongue. "Has our guest a name?"

"He produces Greenshaw Porter. He says it with remarkable ease."

Her frown deepened slightly. "I see. Pray allow Mr. Porter to know that we are on our way to him."

"Very good." The line went dead. Miri glanced up.

"Odds that Greenshaw Porter's another one of ours? Who ain't here yet?"

"Of the adult males? Luken bel'Tarda—and Pat Rin. Luken's duty under Plan B lies with the children, and I cannot this moment conceive of a circumstance that would cause him to abandon it. Pat Rin . . ." He moved his shoulders, abruptly aware of an uncomfortable home truth. "I cannot predict what Pat Rin might do, though I would not *expect* him to adopt a Terran persona. Certainly, not on a Liaden-held world."

"Well, something's got Kol Vus' hair up." She shook her head, and regretfully put her wine aside. "Guess we'd better find out what."

Greenshaw Porter was on his feet in the public parlor, which was only reasonable, the available chairs being much too short to accommodate his lanky frame. The House had provided him with neither tea or wine.

He was a long-faced man, unmistakably Terran, his tan-colored hair short and bristling, his eyes gray and alert, and Val Con felt a curious sense of relief that, after all, it was *not* Pat Rin, come to add yet another Korval life to the tale of those present upon Lytaxin.

Their visitor bowed as they entered the room, entirely in the

Terran mode, then straightened and stated, in the staccato accents of Standard Terran, "Greenshaw Porter, Juntavas courier. Miri Robertson and Val Con yos'Phelium?"

"That's right," Miri said easily.

"Yes." Val Con assured him, noting the position of at least two guns and a blade distributed about the courier's person.

The man nodded, apparently unsurprised. "The Juntavas has been looking for you. The offer is aid and comfort. We cooperate with Clutch turtles Edger and Sheather. I have verification."

"Ah, do you?" Val Con murmured.

The Juntava cocked a sapient eye. "Turtles thought you'd want it." He raised his hands, fingers spread wide. "I saw the rock in orbit. I heard there are turtles on planet. Order from Headquarters is proceed according to plan. Verification in my right outside pocket. You can take it, or I can give it."

Inside his head, Val Con heard Miri's song, alert and watchful. Deliberately, not really certain that it would work, he looked at the places where the Juntava carried his concealed weapons—one, two, three—and heard her song shift. Almost, he thought he heard her murmur "gotcha".

He raised his hands, fingers spread, returning the offered gesture of peace.

"Please," he murmured, "feel free to display your verification."

"Right." Slowly, fingers still held wide, he slipped his right hand into the outside pocket of his long jacket, and withdrew something so sharply luminous it seemed that he held a star between his thumb and first finger.

Still moving deliberately, he extended the brilliant token. Val Con held his hand out, fingers cupped. The crystal hit his palm, unexpectedly heavy, warm, its edges sharp, but not sharpened. He glanced down, eyes narrowed against the whiteness of it, saw without surprise that it was luminous at its core.

"Flashlight?" Miri asked from beside him.

"Exactly," he murmured, and handed it to her, returning his attention to Greenshaw Porter.

"We have received verification," he said, carefully. "More, we have only lately seen Clutch turtles Edger and Sheather, who know us to be well and at liberty. Please inform Headquarters that the Juntavas is quit in this matter."

"Not exactly," the Juntava said, and Val Con raised an eyebrow, feeling Miri come to full alert beside him.

"Explain."

"The Juntavas is missing a Sector Judge."

"Ah. I commiserate with the Juntavas upon its loss."

Greenshaw Porter grimaced. "Supplemental data. I'm attached to the Justice Department. High Judge himself petitions Korval for info. The missing Judge put herself on detached duty. Last known to be in company with Pat Rin yos'Phelium." His forehead wrinkled slightly. "Your brother, maybe?"

"Cousin," Val Con said absently, trying to reconcile Pat Rin with a Juntavas Sector Judge. And, yet, how *could* he predict what Pat Rin might do? He and his cousin were scarcely intimate. Indeed, Val Con had gathered that Pat Rin had few intimates. His foster-father, perhaps. And surely Luken bel'Tarda had taught his foster-ling to give the Juntavas wide clearance.

"Cousin," the Juntava repeated and nodded. "Questions from the High Judge: Does Korval know the location of Sector Judge Natesa? If yes, as a personal favor to the High Judge, who values his judges as a delm values his kin, will Korval divulge her location? Follow-up: If something happened to her, the High Judge asks for that info, too. No rage, no Balance. But he would like to recover the body." He hesitated before adding: "Myself, I know that Judge. She'd be hard to kill."

"I am desolate to disappoint the High Judge," Val Con murmured, "but his inquiry marks the first time I have heard of Sector Judge Natesa."

"You said she's on detached duty," Miri broke in. "Maybe she decided to quit the judging business?"

Greenshaw Porter shook his head. "No'm. Judges put them-selves on detached duty at will. They have discretion. Only Judges tell another Judge what to do. Or how to do it."

She threw a glance at Val Con. "Sounds a lot like being a scout."

"Perhaps," he returned, and looked to the Juntava. "Has my cousin been seen since Judge Natesa exercised her discretion?"

"Nossir. Both were in a dust-up—gunplay, unidentified deaders— then went off-grid simultaneous. Neither one resurfaced."

Gods, if it didn't scan like a Departmental "dust up", Val Con thought. *And never think that an Agent was less than the match of a Sector Judge, no matter how hard she was to kill.*

As for Pat Rin . . . Let it be known that Pat Rin was not an idiot. Let it further be known that he was a wizard with his pistols, and that he had once killed a man. And against whatever the Department might wish to inflict upon him—from mere death to menticide—he would hold no defenses whatsoever.

He looked up at the Juntavas courier.

"I am hardly in a position to trade fairly with the High Judge," he said carefully, feeling Miri drawing closer to his side. "However, I would be honored, were the Juntavas to allow me to know the time and the place where my cousin and Sector Judge Natesa were last seen."

Greenshaw Porter nodded. "I'm cleared for that. I have the report from Housekeeping. I'm cleared to share that, too."

"Thank you. That would be most helpful."

"I'll transfer it from my ship. Need a comm address."

Val Con recited the code for the unit in their upstairs rooms.

The courier repeated the address, nodded and bowed once more in the Terran mode.

"I'll asap that. I'm on-planet until tomorrow mid-day. Aid-and-comfort is in force until I lift."

"Thank you," Val Con said again. "I do not believe it will be needed."

REN ZEL STIRRED, stretched, smiled, opened his eyes—and stifled a curse. The clock across the room was adamant: three minutes until the start of his shift on the bridge. He rolled out of bed, realized abruptly that he was fully clothed and not a little rumpled; his boots showing smudges of what might have been grass stains. To appear on-shift so . . . He looked again at the clock. *Two* minutes until he was wanted on the bridge—and far worse to be late than untidy.

Ren Zel ran.

THEY READ the reports from the Juntavas together, Miri sitting on the arm of the chair, her hip against his shoulder.

There was a short bio of Sector Judge Natesa, accompanied by an image of a slender lady of good countenance, dark-skinned and sloe-eyed, her hair a silky black cap 'round her neat head.

Miri gave a low whistle, and leaned forward to tap the screen over the bio. "This girl can cook, boss. No wonder they miss her."

"She appears competent in the extreme," he agreed, scrolling down through a surprising number of missions completed on behalf of the Juntavas, most at the upper echelons of power.

Sector Judges might well be able to declare themselves on detached duty at will, but it appeared that Judge Natesa had been happy in her work, and had only thrice previously removed herself from duty—twice on recuperative vacations and one comprehensive disappearance, from which she reappeared within a relumma.

"First class pilot," he murmured, going through the remainder of her accomplishments, "master shooter; explosives expert. Yes—a lady of many competencies."

Who had very competently disappeared, so the next, extremely brief report stated, on Day 289, Standard Year 1392, from a Juntavas maintained yard, after filing the appropriate intention with her office.

Gods, so long ago? Val Con shivered and hit the key for the next file.

The report from Housekeeping, prepared by order of Sector Judge Natesa, was admirably detailed, listing descriptions of the dead, contents of pockets, wallets, pouches; types and numbers of weapons. A blue evening jacket, well-splattered with blood, but whole, was noted, and a square of cleansilk, its virtue destroyed by the blood.

"Note the guns," he murmured. "Note the other items inventoried . . ."

"Picks, garrotes, pipettes of acid, poison." She sighed. "You're thinking the Department."

"I am. The jacket is . . . distressing. Pat Rin often wears blue."

"Yeah, but there's no pellet holes in this one. Whoever was wearing it probably ditched it on account of it ain't polite to wear bloodstains on the street." Miri said sensibly. "Unless you got a match further up?"

He shook his head, unrelieved. Death was certainly preferable to the living agonies the Department was capable of inflicting. Kin might wish a clean death for kin, against so terrible an alternative.

"No," he said, aloud. "No, he is not listed among the dead."

"But that ain't making you feel any better." She frowned down at him. "In fact, it's making you feel worse."

He met her eyes. "I would not willingly remand my direst enemy to the Department's care, much less kin." He sighed. "Even kin scarcely known."

She blinked, then turned back to the screen, leaning forward to manipulate the keys, scrolling back up through Natesa's last filed contact with her office.

"She don't say anything about him being with her," she muttered. "Shit, she don't even say why she was in it in the first place."

"Aid and comfort," Val Con said, staring over the screen, seeing Pat Rin as he had last seen him, years ago: a creature of grace and poise, assuredly, with a needling wit and a languorous manner which could be put on and dispensed with in the flicker of an eyelash.

Vulnerable; so very vulnerable, did he fall into the hands of the Department. Which would, almost certainly, remake him into a bomb.

"*What*?" Miri turned to stare at him, her eyes wide with alarm. "What's wrong?"

He took a breath, trying to think it through, to get past the horror, to put himself in the place of the Commander, sworn to bring the Department's Plan to fruition. Which Plan included Korval's annihilation.

"Miri . . ."

"Don't say it—I think I just got the download." She closed her eyes, and in his mind's eye Val Con saw a blurring spin of color— redyelloworangegreenblueviolet—followed by a warming sense of calm.

"OK. So the Department might've got Pat Rin, either at this massacre, here, or sometime real soon after, and the Judge might be on the lam to save her skin, she being no dummy in a big way. And if the Department's got Pat Rin, they're gonna rework him." She bit her lip.

"How long's it take?"

He moved his shoulders, snapped to his feet and stalked down the room. "Eternity." He came to the window and stopped, staring out over Erob's nighttime gardens. The silence at his back was tangible. He sighed.

"Forgive me, cha'trez. The length of the process depends in large part upon the reserves of the candidate. Certainly, if the Department has had Pat Rin in their care for nearly two relumma, they will have completed their work long since. Especially as they will not be constructing an Agent of Change, but something far simpler."

"Q-ship. Got it. But we're forewarned."

"Not all of us," he said, turning from the window. "Pat Rin's foster-father and true-mother have the duty of protecting the clan's children. I do not believe either would deny him entrance to their safeplace." He reached up and pushed his hair out of his eyes. "Jelaza Kazone would admit him. Anthora would perhaps understand that there was something amiss—but she might not understand it in time to prevent him killing her."

"OK." Miri stood up, showing him palms in the gesture of peace. "OK. This is all might-have. We don't know where Pat Rin is. He might be holed up cozy on an outworld, waiting for the all-clear."

"True. Though that might-have does not tell us why the Sector Judge has run away."

"Might've taken a lover. Might've needed time out. Might've got drunk, fell down and broke her neck. We don't know she's hiding because of the business in the warehouse. We don't even *know* that she's hiding."

"And we do not know that she isn't."

Silence.

"Another might-have," Val Con said, slowly, hating it, and gods, if it were true . . .

"Go."

"The Department has acquired *both* Korval's child Pat Rin and Juntavas Sector Judge Natesa."

She blinked at him. "She's Agent material."

"Indeed she is. More, she has access to the highest levels within the Juntavas. The Commander might put such a tool to very good use."

"I bet he could." She shook her head. "We still got no proof."

"We have no proof," he repeated, looking not at her, so much as through her. "We do, however, owe the High Judge some *info*."

He came back to himself with a visible start and moved across the room to the comm unit. Miri sighed and went over to pour them each a glass of wine.

DAY 52

Standard Year 1393
Department of Interior Headquarters Liad

COMMANDER OF AGENTS was not one to allow the natural losses of warfare to overly dismay him. It was understood that there would be casualties—even, many casualties—as the Plan unfolded and the Department met with the resistance of small minds and imbedded interests. Thus, while he did not view his losses lightly, the Commander was able to maintain the dispassion necessary to ultimate success in those instances when the Department was momentarily thwarted.

The loss of a ship of the Department and four full Agents of Change on the planet Lytaxin—that was a different matter entirely. Very nearly, in fact, could the Commander be said to be—angry.

The ship had reported Val Con yos'Phelium on-board some time after the fourth Agent's implanted monitor went off-line. The ship itself had exploded some few minutes after lift-off. Commander of Agents was not so naive as to believe that Val Con yos'Phelium had died with the vessel.

So: Four Agents, lost on Lytaxin. One Agent, lost on Interdicted World I-2796-893-44, his ship captured and then destroyed. Three more Agents lost to the bitch half-breed . . .

Lost thus far: eight Agents and two ships. And what profit did the Department show from so great and widespread an expenditure?

Sand and ashes. Val Con yos'Phelium remained at liberty; Anthora yos'Galan slept secure behind the formidable walls of Jelaza Kazone.

Commander of Agents rose from behind his desk. He paced his office from end to end and side to side. At the beginning of his fourth pass, he checked, and deliberately called to mind the calming exercise he had first been taught as an Agent-in-Training, many years ago.

Slowly, he brought his heartbeat down, normalized his breathing, bled off the unneeded adrenaline. When he had done, he stood yet another few heartbeats, eyes closed; meditative.

Eventually, he opened his eyes and returned to his desk, ordered the hardcopy which he had in his agitation flung down, and set it to one side while he accessed his screen.

Alas, that ill news stalked the hour, the latest in the form of a memorandum from the financial department chair. Another of the Department's bleed-off funds had been uncovered, the program destroyed by the Masters of the Accountants Guild.

Commander of Agents flicked through the report, until he found the name of the Master in charge of the investigation.

dea'Gauss.

Very softly, Commander of Agents sighed.

dea'Gauss. Korval's man of business.

Commander of Agents extended an arm and touched the switch on his console.

"Commander?" His second's voice betrayed an edge of startlement.

"That matter we wished to place before the Council of Clans."

"Yes, Commander. We have been awaiting the most appropriate moment."

"So we had. I advise you that the moment has arrived."

"Yes, Commander."

"On another matter—I will wish to meet with a squad leader in . . ." He glanced over at the chronometered wall. "In fifteen Standard minutes, in the Level A meeting room. That is all."

"Yes, Commander." The connection light went out.

DAY 31

❋❋❋❋❋❋❋❋❋❋❋❋❋❋❋❋❋❋❋❋❋❋❋❋❋❋

Standard Year 1393
Surebleak Spaceport

VILLY BENT OVER the table, black pick held delicately, hook properly extended, between thumb and forefinger, eyes narrowed in concentration.

The pick hovered over the jumbled pile of brightly colored sticks, flicked out and deftly flipped a silver from the tangle onto the counting cloth. The boy took a careful breath, and the pick stabbed out again, three times, placing a red, an orange and a blue stick next to the silver on the cloth.

Pat Rin, viewing the performance with an expert's eye, saw the tell-tale quiver of a purple stick three layers down in the tangle, but Villy, in pursuit of the gold, either ignored the tremor or had determined that boldness would win the day.

He extended the pick, delicate—so delicate—touched the gold stick . . . lifted it . . .

"Oh, *sleet!*" he exclaimed as the sticks broke from their self-described formation and went rolling and tumbling every-which-way. He looked up, shamefaced.

"Sorry, sir."

Pat Rin raised an eyebrow. "Not entirely. Indeed, I see that you have been working. Your touch is much improved. Now, you must sharpen your eye. Attend me."

He swept the twenty-four brightly colored sticks up in a practiced motion, tamped them, placed them on end in the yellow-tiled circle which had been set into the table-top for just this purpose—and let go.

Obedient to gravity, the sticks fell, creating a satisfyingly complex multi-colored tangle.

"So," he said, receiving the black pick from Villy. "We have a dreadful mess, here, do we not? I will wager you twenty cash that all of those sticks may be extracted and placed on the cloth while disturbing no other in the formation. Have we a bet?"

Villy shook his head. "I know better than to bet against you."

"Youth today," Pat Rin mused aloud, while his eyes traced the intricate pattern created by the sticks; "lack the adventurous spirit." It was, he decided, a difficult fall. He could easily see his way clear to acquiring sixteen, even eighteen, of the twenty-four. The rest . . . well.

"Only twenty cash?" a rich voice asked from near at hand. "Why not a wager worthy of your skill?"

Calmly, he looked up and met Natesa's amused black eyes.

"What would you wager, my lady?"

"Let us consider." She tipped her head to one side, a finger over her lips as she ostentatiously considered the matter.

"I know," she said at last. "If you miss the twenty-four, I will have the Sinner's Carpet out of Ms. Audrey's house."

"Ah, will you?" He looked at her appreciatively. "And what is my prize, should I succeed?"

She smiled at him, slow and seductive. "Why, something very nice."

He laughed.

"Done," he said, fingering the pick into the proper hold. "Attend now, child," he said to Villy; "this may be the last time you see me play."

He looked down to the bright jumble, and let the room fade out of his consciousness, until it was only himself, the sticks, and the necessity to win.

The pick flashed out.

The first eight were simple liberations, after which the challenge began in earnest.

Quickly, he proceeded, dexterously avoiding anchor-sticks and rolling traps, while with every cunning infiltration of the pick another stick fell to the counting cloth.

It came at last to three, lying one against the other.

Pat Rin reversed the pick, inserted the flat tail in the whisker-wide space between the yellow stick and the blue, rolled the yellow, reversed the pick, and caught the stick in the hook to flip it, with a showy snap of the wrist, to the cloth.

The blue stick was likewise appropriated, and then the final orange, delivered to the cloth in a toss that sent it spinning high, turning over three times on its descent to the cloth.

Pat Rin placed the pick on the cloth next to the sticks, and smiled at Villy.

"That is how it is done, do you see?"

The boy shook his head. "I see that I'm gonna hafta practice a *lot* more."

"I did not say it would be easy, working in the casino," Pat Rin reminded him. "Perhaps, you would rather Sheyn took the sticks table?"

Sheyn was Villy's chief rival in popularity at Audrey's house, and though the rivalry was mostly friendly, still Villy would not easily bear having a task taken from him and given to the other boy.

"Nossir, Mr. Conrad! I'll practice."

"Good," said Pat Rin, stepping back from the table. "I will return later today."

He walked away, Natesa at his side.

"So," he said to her softly. "When may I collect my winnings?"

"Youth today," she said, calmly, "lack patience."

"Ah, but I am far beyond my youth. What you choose to see as impatience is merely the necessity of man with too few hours left him."

She looked at him gravely. "Yes, exactly so."

"I was certain that you must see it eventually," he murmured, allowing her to proceed him through the door and into the port proper.

The day was cool and bright—Surebleak high summer—and the port itself displayed a gratifying amount of activity. Work was going forth on several collaborative efforts, notably the duty-free shop—boldly named The Planetary Cooperative—and situated in the space formerly occupied, according to the ancient signage, by a Learning Shop; a fresh fruit, vegetable, and flower stall; and no less than two repair stations. Individual efforts included a beverage bar, featuring local fruit ciders; and a pastry shop. And, of course, the casino.

Pat Rin had hopes of a restaurant in the future, as well as a gem-stone and spice exchange. But, for the moment, progress was made. And it was good.

Side by side, they proceeded, slowed considerably by the numerous, "Morning, Boss." "Mr. Conrad, sir. Ms. Natesa. Good to see you both." One of the mechanics called out that the concordance books had arrived; and plastic cups of cider were pressed into their hands, with a smiling, "Just in from the farms this morning. Boss Sherton's compliments, Mr. Conrad."

"You are well-loved," Natesa remarked as they went on.

"So well-loved that you yet insist upon tasting my drink ahead of me," he said ironically. "When shall you give over security, Inas?"

Black eyebrows arched. "Why, I have done so. If my care now seems more particular, it is because I have a personal stake in your continued good health."

He looked at her consideringly. "I see that I have done ill, then, in returning you your oath."

"Not at all. I asked for its return because my interest had grown beyond mere business. You complied because the request was reasonable." She inclined her head, formally. "Thus, we comported ourselves with honor. What lies before us is a different game entirely."

"Which cannot be won," he said, soberly. "Attend me, my lady. This is Surebleak; I may be murdered in the next hour—and you, at my side. And if that fails, there are always those other enemies of my clan, who may discover me at any moment, and likewise slay us both."

"That is," she said in her calm way, "acceptable." She sipped from her own cup. "But not likely. The cider is good."

"You amaze me," he said, and sipped, finding it very good, indeed. So good, in fact, that it was quite gone by the time they reached the portmaster's office, a scant stroll from the new juice stand.

"Good morning, Mr. Conrad—Ms. Natesa." Claren Liu nodded easily as they entered.

"Portmaster. A pleasant day to you."

"It has been so far." She waved a hand at the main screen. "Never thought I'd see Surebleak Port so busy. If it keeps up like this, we'll be in competition with Terraport!"

"Never so large as Terraport," Pat Rin said softly. "Will you settle, I wonder, for a small, rustic jewel of a port?"

Portmaster Liu laughed. "Sure, I'll take that." She pushed out of her chair and went to her desk, pulling some few sheets of hardcopy from a file.

"'beam came through for you last night. I knew you were gonna be here today, or I'd've sent it in to you."

"Thank you." He glanced at the papers, saw the Health Net logo, and folded them into his pocket for later perusal.

"Other thing we're gonna want," she said abruptly, "is traffic. Fine as it is to have a small rustic gem of a port, if nobody lands, what we got is no better'n what we had."

"True enough. My associates and I have been considering that. There are trade bands, are there not? And pilot frequencies, where the goods and services of this or that port may be advertised?"

She blinked. "Well . . . sure. You're thinking about *advertising* Surebleak?"

"What harm can it do?" Pat Rin asked reasonably, feeling Natesa's presence at his shoulder as a comfort. "A few small advertisements only—perhaps in praise of our ciders and—our handmade rugs. We are not so out of the way that ships *may not* stop, if given good cause. That they *have not* been stopping has been due to our . . . reputation as a dangerous and backward world, served by—forgive me—a port of the lower tier."

"Nothing to forgive in the truth," Claren Liu said, brusquely, and stared off over his head for a long moment, before coming to herself with a nod.

"Tell you what. The port'll go in half with whatever the association comes up with for advertisement. We got a promo budget. Up 'til this second, I didn't have the barest idea of what to do with it." She grinned, self-mocking. "Add Surebleak to your pay-route! It's cold and they'll break your neck, too!"

At his shoulder, Natesa laughed.

"And now we may say—Stop at Surebleak, and enjoy the play."

"Not bad," Claren Liu told her, the grin somewhat less mocking. "Hold on a sec—I've got the rate book here." She bent again to the desk, rummaged briefly and emerged triumphant, waving a tattered brown booklet.

"Here you are," she said, handing it to Pat Rin. He glanced at the cover, found the rates in force until Day 96, Standard Year 1393, and slipped it away, too, for later study.

"Thank you," he said, inclining his head. "As always, it has been a fruitful visit. One of my house will be on the port in two days' time. If you have need of me before—"

"I'll call," she said, interrupting good-naturedly. "Those talkies were a good idea. Yeah, like you've had a bad one." She attempted the formal nod—at which she was slowly gaining proficiency, Pat Rin allowed—and straightened.

"Good to see you, then, sir—ma'am. Hope to see you again soon."

"Good-day, Portmaster," Pat Rin murmured.

"Good-day," Natesa echoed and the two of them departed, heading for the casino, a second training session, and an afternoon meeting in Elva Whitmore's territory.

"STILL AWAKE, Boss?" Cheever McFarland's big voice preceded him into the room.

Pat Rin glanced up from a frowning study of the Health Net papers.

"As you see, Mr. McFarland, I am not only awake, but irritable."

"Long hours'll do that," Cheever said cheerfully. "I've got a report, if you want it."

Pat Rin pushed the papers aside. "Indeed, I do." He considered the man, noting the subtle signs of weariness. "However, I would not keep you from your bed. Tomorrow is soon enough, if you are in need of rest."

Cheever shook his head. "Too wound up to sleep. What I'm after right now is a sandwich and a beer. What say we compromise and hit the kitchen?"

"Very well." He rose, leaving the papers on his desk.

"It's comin' along fine," Cheever said some minutes later, around a truly formidable sandwich constructed of cheese, greens, and onion between thick slices of the cook's homemade bread. "Got the rubbish cleared out. Got a couple of the local techs through the sleep-learner and put 'em to work fabricating the equipment. Got a couple building squads throwing us up some bays and dorms. Talked to somebody just 'fore I left this morning—sharp one, name of Perl—anyhow, she's been studying on the schematics for the cradle and thinks she's got a line on the how-to. Ain't gonna be pretty, right at first, but we'll have us a working yard that ain't dependent on the port."

He took a bite of sandwich and washed it down with a mighty swallow of beer. Pat Rin sipped his fruit cider. The warehouse district they had taken over for Korval's first ship yard on Surebleak had been burned out in some long-forgotten riot, and remained unclaimed by any current boss. Pat Rin had annexed it by the simple expedient of sending Cheever McFarland and a work crew to the area with the goal of cleaning it up.

"Where we're gonna get in trouble—soon—is cash," Cheever was saying. "Labor's cheap enough, but materials is high—and a lot of the equipment's just gotta be made, ground up." Another bite, another swallow.

"Where we're gonna get in trouble later—assuming we can get the rest of the job funded and online—is pilots, supplies and derelicts."

"The derelicts," Pat Rin murmured, "are, as we discussed, possible."

"Yah, OK, you got a line on the spaceship graveyard," Cheever said, grudgingly. "If it ain't watched. If it's still there. If the codes're still good. If, if if."

"There is a risk, but not, I think, a major one."

"So you said. All right, we assume you can deliver the ships," he grinned, wolfish. "Next problem's pilots."

"We are at work on that problem," Pat Rin told him. "Only today have we received from the hand of Surebleak Portmaster the book listing all public piloting and trade frequencies. Our plan is to advertise Surebleak's charms, and thus beguile pilots to us."

"Yeah?" Cheever said interestedly. "That's an assist. But, then you're gonna need a hiring hall on the port."

Pat Rin inclined his head. "I thank you—I had not thought of that."

"Would've, though. Think too damn' much, if you want my opinion—which you don't." He finished his sandwich and leaned back, nursing what was left of his beer.

"Keep in mind you'll have to pay risk money, for anybody bringing in a ship from the graveyard."

"Well." Pat Rin finished his cider, set the mug down, and sat gazing into its empty depths.

"Well," he said again. "It appears we are at a stand, Mr. McFarland. In addition to the necessity of . . . Korval's yard, there is upstairs a notice from the HealthNet, informing me of the current membership rates and citing a substantial sum due in penalties, as Surebleak's previous departure from the 'Net was in violation of several conditions of contract."

"The other bosses are s'posed to give us a percentage," Cheever commented after a few moments had passed in silence.

Pat Rin looked up. "So they are. And the funds thus far received have immediately gone into increasing the numbers of clinics and schools, and training for the medical personnel."

"So called." Cheever sighed gustily before quaffing the dregs of his beer.

"We're gonna need cash, or the gold-plated promise of cash within the next—fifteen, twenty days, or it's gonna get ugly. An' if we lose 'em because we ain't paid 'em, they'll never come back, if we was paying hard cantra. Better to shut down now, while we can settle everybody and tell 'em we'll do a recall in a month or so."

Pat Rin frowned. Of course, one did not solicit labor and then fail to pay. But it was hard, very hard, to contemplate halting the project so recently and so well begun . . .

"Let us delay decision until tomorrow," he said to Cheever. "Will you be with us, or must you return at once?"

"Figured on going back tomorrow afternoon. Wanted to check in with you. Should oughta talk to Natesa and Gwince; maybe do an inspect of house security, just to throw the fear of cold space into 'em and make sure they stay honest."

"Ah." He smiled. "Your vigilance is appreciated."

"Sure it is." Cheever thumped the empty mug to the table and stood. "I'm for a nap. You look like you could use the same, if you don't mind my saying so. Or even if you do."

"Yes." Weariness suddenly weighed upon him, waking the ghost of an ache in the arm that had been wounded. He rose, and put his mug in the sink to be washed. "Good-night, Mr. McFarland. We will talk tomorrow."

"We sure will. 'Night, sir."

Pat Rin climbed the stairs, and slipped as silently as he was able into the bedroom.

"Good morning, denubia," her voice was soft, barely blurred with sleep.

"There, I had not meant to wake you," he murmured. "I shall need to learn to walk like a scout."

"Only like Silk—who has appropriated your pillow."

He smiled in the dark, and undressed quickly, slipping into the bed beside her. Silk put up a brief defense of the pillow—for honor's sake—before stomping down to the foot of the bed.

"Victory is yours," she whispered, and moved near, entwining him in warm silken limbs, and nestling her head on his shoulder.

"Only until the morrow," he said, feeling muzzier by the moment; the ill news of the evening fading into a warm glow of contentment.

Sighing gently, he lay his cheek against her hair and slid, seamlessly, into sleep.

DAY 32

❈ ❈

Standard Year 1393
Blair Road
Surebleak

NATESA lay the HealthNet report on the desk and picked up her teacup.

"Three cantra in penalties. Three cantra earnest money, based on previous violations. Two cantra to rejoin." She sipped and shook her head. "The penalties are two cantra too high, and we can certainly force the earnest money down by a cantra. Yet, in our current state of budget, five cantra is as difficult as eight."

"Add Mr. McFarland's little matter," Pat Rin murmured, from his perch on the corner of the desk, "and we discover ourselves run entirely off our legs, with no hope of a quick recover." He moved his shoulders, irritated.

"And all the while, there are more than enough cantra to do the work, if I could but dare access them!"

Natesa stared at him, teacup arrested. "Is that so?"

Pat Rin met her eyes, frowning at her astonishment. "Is what so? That there are cantra sufficient to the task—and more—held on my accounts? Did you think you had joined with a pauper, lady?"

"It was not a consideration," she said composedly. "But, Pat Rin, this other—why do you not dare access your funds?"

He bit back a sharp retort. It was rare enough, after all, to find Natesa at half wit.

"You will see that I am not clever," he said mildly. "When I was about arranging the details of my former life, it never occurred to me that, some day in my future, I might very much wish for hidden funds. All of my accounts are woefully in sight, and the Department of the Interior will be watching every one. They will trace any transfer immediately, and follow it to us."

She sipped her tea, then put the cup down on the desk.

"Here is where the Juntavas is uniquely placed to serve you," she said. "Merely hire a courier."

"Yes, certainly!" he cried, descending into sarcasm. "Tell someone else where we are, so that they may sell the information to the Department!"

"Not so," she contradicted. "If we broke our contracts, who would deal with us?"

He sighed. "In fact, breaking contracts is bad for business."

"Precisely." She frowned, staring off into the middle air. Pat Rin reached for his cup and sipped, awaiting the outcome of her thought.

"It will be," she said eventually, "expensive. More so, for I cannot waive my fee in the matter. You will, however, retain between seventy and seventy-five percent of the total deliverable funds."

"The Juntavas takes one-quarter?" He raised a hand, signifying peace. "I make no quibble, if we have guarantee of anonymity."

"The fees cover several things—anonymity of the client is one. Discretion, timely delivery, real costs. My fee—is insurance. The Juntavas guarantees delivery, from our own accounts. Once the money is identified, and the transfer made to our various accounts, why, we do nothing but deliver the funds from our own nearest bank. No need to have couriers bounding to and fro like grasshoppers. If our courier is robbed of your funds, still we will deliver to you the agreed amount upon the specified date. So, you see why my fee must be taken."

"I do." He took his own turn at thought, weighing danger against necessity.

"Guaranteed anonymity," he said again. "The Department of the Interior, if we are to believe its agents—and I have predicated the subjugation of an entire world upon that belief—is no dismissible opponent."

"Allow us to know our business," Natesa murmured, retrieving her teacup. She sipped, black eyes considering him over the rim.

"There is no guaranteed safety," she said eventually. "However— if you will accept my advice—I think this course offers us more safety than any other; and gains us access to needed funding."

"My funds are in cantra," he said. "No more than twelve per cent of the delivery should be in cantra—the rest must be in Terran bits or regional currencies."

She shrugged. "A detail only. For such affairs, where the client pays a percentage, we calculate the conversion using the daily exchange tables published by the Bank of Solcintra." She inclined her head, ironic. "Unless the client requires another source be used."

"The Bank of Solcintra conversions are adequate, I thank you."

"Ah. You should also know that the flex in the fee structure has to do with the degree of difficulty in accessing the funds."

"I can provide pass-codes and ID numbers," he said.

"Good. Assume the deliverable will be closer to seventy-five percent; though there may be a hazard surcharge." A subtle smile. "Thus, the Department of the Interior is accorded the respect that it deserves."

"That is well." He finished his tea while considering other details. "So. I will take delivery at the Port . . ."

"I beg to disagree. Mr. McFarland will take delivery at the Port, with Gwince and myself as his back-up. You, my love, will remain well-guarded in your house, or perhaps you will visit Melina Sherton."

"Surely you and Mr. McFarland are of more value—" he began and stopped when she held up her hand.

"There will be no contract," she said, with an austerity one rarely had from Natesa, "unless this is done as I say."

He looked at her. "What shall I do if you are slain?"

"Avenge me." She lowered her hand. "Will it be as I have said?"

He slid to his feet. "Since the plan now involves Mr. McFarland risking his life, we will ask for his assessment. If he agrees, then we go forward."

Natesa smiled. "That is acceptable."

DAY 38

❁ ❁

Standard Year 1393
Liad Department of Interior
Command Headquarters

THE RADIO MUTTERED in the background, whispering of ships, of trade goods, and of scheduling changes. Commander of Agents paid it no heed; his attention squarely on the file before him.

The campaign against the Juntavas, which had unwisely involved itself in Departmental business, was well under way. Given the opportunity to choose his battle, the Commander would not have attempted the Juntavas. Not yet. Alas, the Juntavas itself had forced the matter by interfering with the Department's attempt to attach Pat Rin yos'Phelium.

That Pat Rin yos'Phelium had grasped the opportunity created by confusion to slip through the Department's net—that he remained unrecovered to this day—was both unfortunate and unexpected.

The search continued, of course. Pat Rin yos'Phelium—a creature of self-indulgence, a slave to play and pleasure—was certain to err, soon or late. And when he did, the Department would move.

In the meanwhile, the Juntavas was being dealt—

" . . . Surebleak Port!" The radio chirped.

Commander of Agents froze, and turned to stare at the tiny device. "Our duty free shop boasts a variety of local fresh fruit ciders and jams; made-by-hand rugs; pigup sticks made from local woods, and much more! And while you're on port, don't forget to visit the Emerald Casino. It's all here at pilot-friendly Surebleak Port!"

Surebleak, the supposed homeworld of Tiazan's so-called Miri Robertson. *Pilot-friendly* Surebleak Port.

Commander of Agents allowed himself a smile.

DAY 53

❈ ❈

Standard Year 1393
Dutiful Passage
Lytaxin Orbit

RUNNING, he cut the corner into the main hall close, skidded and threw himself into a somersault in order to avoid the collision.

He landed on his feet by the opposite wall, and only then saw who he had very nearly run down.

"Captain." He bowed deeply, feeling his face heat.

"Alas, no longer," Shan yos'Galan said calmly. "But don't, I beg you, be cast into despondency on my account! The truth is that I am perfectly well-satisfied to retire to the rank of master trader and laze through every shift while Priscilla and yourself accomplish the hard work between you."

This was a pleasantry, as Ren Zel well knew, and felt relief, that the cap—that Master Trader yos'Galan's experience of war had not altered him out of recognition.

"But tell me, do! Wherever were you rushing off to at such a pace?"

He bit his lip. "I am late to my shift on the bridge."

"A grievous thing, I agree." The silver eyes considered him, and there was something—someone . . .

685

"I wonder," Shan said, interrupting his line of thought, "not that it's any business of mine, of course! But, still, I do wonder what has happened to your jacket?"

"My—" He looked down at his arm, blinking. Why in the names of the gods had he been sleeping in his jacket? "I—" he began again and tentatively, unbelievingly, ran his hand down the unmarred leather sleeve. Memory stirred and he saw her again in the starlight, taking his jacket—*All honor to it*—and shaking it, shaking it *out . . .*

He looked up and met Shan yos'Galan's silver eyes and it came to him all at once where he had seen the like.

Ren Zel took a deep breath. "I had—a dream," he said, knowing that it explained nothing.

"I would say that you had quite a marvelous dream," Shan said, straightening from his lean against the wall. He beckoned, the master trader's ring blazing purple fires.

"Come along, child. We'd best sort this out."

"WILL YOU HAVE wine, friend?" Shan yos'Galan asked, some few moments later in the captain's private office.

Ren Zel hesitated, thinking of wine on an empty stomach after an evening, or so his memory insisted, rich in exercise.

"I think," he said carefully, "that I would rather—tea."

"And something with which to break your fast," Shan said, leaning to the comm unit. Priscilla was standing near the sofa, Ren Zel's mysteriously healed jacket held in her two hands, her eyes intent and her face peculiarly unfocussed.

"Thank you, BillyJo," Shan said into the comm. "It's good to hear your voice again, too."

Priscilla blinked, and sighed, as if the jacket were too heavy for her. Ren Zel stepped forward to take it out of her hands, his fingers delighting in the supple new feel of the leather.

"Well?" Shan asked, leaning a hip against the desk.

"Anthora," she said, "definitely Anthora. She's the only wizard I know who might have done something like this so seamlessly." She sighed once more. "Breakfast?"

"On the way."

"Good." She looked to Ren Zel and moved a hand, inviting him to take one of the two easy chairs as she sank down onto the sofa.

"I think you had better tell us about this—dream."

BREAKFAST ARRIVED as he was describing the garden with its massive tree and welcoming cat. He made a detour there, to summarize the previous dream and the impossible whisker caught in his coverlet. Shan put a plate in his hand, and he ate, not really attending, his mind on the memory of the dream, straining for every nuance, every description.

They listened silently, captain and master trader. At some point in the narration the comm buzzed, and by silent agreement it was the master trader who rose to answer.

Finally, he reached an end, and looked down into a teacup he did not recall emptying, and back to Priscilla's brilliant, dramliza eyes.

"It was a dream," he said, for perhaps the dozenth time.

"I don't believe that it was just a dream," Priscilla said gently.

"Other parties are likewise unconvinced," Shan added, lounging beside her on the couch. "That comm call was an encoded pinbeam from Jelaza Kazone." He looked at Ren Zel, slanting brows high, silver eyes—amused?

"My sister Anthora wishes to advise her elder and her thodelm of the fact of her lifemating with Ren Zel dea'Judan, first mate of *Dutiful Passage*. Very proper of her, don't you agree?"

EROB'S CLANHOUSE: Lytaxin

"HAVE I HEARD from Pat Rin?" Nova's golden brows pulled together, and she shook her head. "But I have been off-grid, you know, brother, and involved in other matters. It is true that I have not heard from Pat Rin, but it is equally true that I have not heard from Anthora."

They'd invited Nova to a dawn breakfast, after which they would escort her to the spaceport and the shuttle that would take her up to the *Passage*. For now, they sat on the balcony of their guesting suite, eating warm rolls, soft cheese and fresh fruit, beneath an orange-and-silver sky.

"Well enough," Val Con murmured, breaking open a roll. "But am I correct in recalling that there is a check-in protocol? For instance, had we been less engaged elsewhere, we might have accessed the pirate's band and sent an all's well."

"Pirate band?" Miri asked, spreading cheese on her roll.

"It is not really a pirate band," Nova said. "Shan began calling it that to irritate our father, and I believe—although I am certain he will correct me if I am in error—that Val Con began using it to irritate Cousin Kareen." She moved her shoulders. "In any case, it's simply a private clan-held frequency."

"As if I would ever *wish* to irritate my Aunt Kareen," Val Con said softly, and glanced over, green eyes warm. "We must get thee to a library, my lady. You have quite a lot of reading to do."

"Suits. Call me when the war's over."

Nova frowned, which she seemed to do a lot. "We are *not* going to war!"

Miri blinked at her, looked to Val Con. "We ain't?"

"It is like the pirate's band," he explained kindly. "If we call it a war, we will annoy Nova."

She grinned. "Got it."

"Val Con—"

"Is there a way to access the log," he interrupted, softly. "To see who has and has not checked in?"

"Yes, certainly. I can do so from Erob's comm room, if you wish. Indeed, you should have the new codes. Sit with me and I will give them you." She hesitated, and the frown this time seemed more worried than irritated, to Miri's sharpening eye.

"I wonder, brother—have you had ill-news of Pat Rin?"

"Ill-news—no," he said slowly, and Miri felt him picking his words with careful precision. "Say rather that we have . . . inconclusive news, and wish to assure ourselves that he is well." He extended a hand and lay it briefly over Nova's where it lay fisted beside her plate.

"I do not wish to distress you—I know that you and he are friends."

"Insofar as Pat Rin allows himself to be anyone's friend," she said, sharply.

"But truly," she said, after a long moment, probably to reassure herself, "he should be well. Pat Rin is very far from a fool—and Shan had hired him an extremely portwise pilot."

"*Shan* hired Pat Rin's pilot?" Val Con said, incredulously. "Matters must be very changed between them."

"Say rather that it was Shan's idea to place Mr. McFarland as Pat Rin's pilot, when he came to us with the message from Edger. It was in the clan's interest that Mr. McFarland not return . . . immediately to his usual rounds, and Pat Rin was preparing for one of his tours. Mr. McFarland was willing to be hired, and Pat Rin was willing—after I spoke to him, for I will not hide from you, brother, that *of course* Shan put his back up—to hire. So it was done. I checked Mr. McFarland's credentials myself—and Anthora pronounced him an honorable man."

"Well, then, it sounds as if our cousin is both well-served and well-protected," Val Con said, after a moment, being so careful Miri felt an ache starting between her eyebrows. "Doubtless our check of the roll will establish him in comfortable safety, and only a little bored."

"As to that," Nova murmured, "he had used to say that he would welcome being marooned on a backward world for a relumma or two, so that he might catch up on his reading."

There didn't seem much to say to that, Miri thought, polishing off the last bit of roll with mingled relish and regret.

Apparently Val Con thought the same.

"Tell me," he said, reaching for his teacup. "Have you found all the citations you require to make our case before Council?"

"Not all, certainly, but a good start has been made," Nova answered, pushing her plate aside. "The *Passage* carries the full text of the Diaries, as well as the Council book. I will be able to conclude my research en route and be ready to stand before Council the day we raise Liad."

Val Con looked at her, one eyebrow up. "But you will not do so," he suggested. "Until you have had word from your delm."

She sighed. "I will, of course, await the delm's word."

"Good," Val Con smiled, though to Miri he felt more wary than approving, and drank his tea.

ANTHORA LEANED BACK IN HER CHAIR, silver eyes focused on a point just above and light years beyond the top of the comm unit.

Mr. dea'Gauss had her instructions regarding the settlements, which he was to send to Ren Zel, for approval or adjustment. She had herself 'beamed the *Passage* with the proper announcement to her thodelm, which might very well amuse Shan, but for Ren Zel one *would* behave well and do everything that was proper. He should not suffer wounds on her account—he had wounds enough.

That she knew his wounds as her own was—piquant. That he would have acquired a similarly intimate knowledge of herself was—not harrowing; not quite that. She was, after all, of the dramliz, and accustomed to interfacing with her fellows and with some of the stronger Healers. Those interfacings were of necessity less absolute than the immediate and complete merging which had joined her to Ren Zel last evening; and while there was no help for it now—and while she would not trade this morning for last—she did rather wish that she had been . . . more decorous at some times in the past.

That Ren Zel would forgive her transgressions, she knew. Had he lived other than an exemplary and blameless life, she would have freely forgiven him all his sins. They could neither do otherwise, as closely as they were joined—in all but body.

Anthora sighed. She had felt his absence keenly this morning, when she had woken from her second sleep to find herself solitary in the tumbled bed. More than that, she had felt some alarm. Surely, he had expended enormous amounts of energy in his walk from the *Passage* to her bedroom. To make a like expenditure so soon after the first, and, moreover, a half-night of enthusiastic lovemaking, was foolhardy in the extreme. She would not have wished to undertake such a course, and she knew herself for a wizard of stamina, and will.

In fact, she thought, how *had* he managed that walk? She could quite understand the process—it was, after all, very similar to a piloting problem—but she was not persuaded that she could reproduce the effect . . .

She straightened in her chair, frowning as she tried to reconcile the equation.

The comm unit chimed.

Anthora jumped, blinked, and leaned forward to accept the call.

She blinked again as the screen coalesced into an image of a dark-haired woman in the uniform of a Clerk of the Council of

Clans. The woman bowed, from greater to lesser, by which Anthora understood that the Clerk was speaking on behalf of the entire Council of Clans, by order of the Speaker.

"Do I address Anthora yos'Galan Clan Korval?"

Anthora inclined her head a fraction, striving for Nova's air of cool competence.

"You do."

"Speaker for Council requires Korval's presence at a full meeting of the clans scheduled tomorrow for the hour after midday. Korval has been called upon to answer certain very serious charges."

"What charges?" Anthora demanded. "And who accuses us?"

"I am not authorized to divulge that information. Because of the seriousness of the charges, Speaker for Council will assess Korval one Class A Jump ship for every day it fails to send a representative to answer."

Anthora glared at her, which the Clerk bore with patience. Behind the glare, her mind raced.

The Council was empowered to levy penalties for a failure to comply with its rule. The weight of this threatened levy argued the presence of serious charges indeed, though what they might be—

Really, she thought, there was no choice. She could hardly explain that with Plan B in effect there was quite simply no way that she could authorize turning a ship—any ship, down to the meanest two-place shuttle—over to the Council. dea'Gauss himself could not order it done. She considered quickly. The Council knew Korval would not relish the loss of ship, so she must let them believe that their threat was potent. To tell them that Korval would resist any such attempt was folly. . . .

And, surely, she thought, she would be safe in the very Council hall.

Once again, she inclined her head that austere and irritating inch.

"I thank Speaker for Council, but there is no need to descend to threats. I will attend the meeting scheduled for the hour after midday tomorrow and will answer all charges then."

❆   ❆   ❆

REN ZEL had been excused from his shift on the bridge; another pilot set, by the captain's word, to cover his board. Truly, he would have rather been allowed to escape back into routine, to explore the strange dream that was not a dream in his own way and come to terms with his . . . with his lifemating.

For it seemed he was no longer clanless, outcast—dead. Abruptly, he had kin to care for—Shan yos'Galan was his brother, Priscilla Mendoza, his sister. He found another sister in Nova yos'Galan—she who was no longer Korval-pernard'i, for the news from the planet was that Val Con yos'Phelium had taken up the Ring and his rightful melant'i as Korval. Which was well for the clan, Ren Zel thought, distractedly—clans should be properly led by the delm, rather than held in trust, year upon long year . . .

In a daze, he had received the kiss of his thodelm and thodelmae; immediately thereafter, Priscilla had accessed the ship's roll and amended his file. *Dutiful Passage* had previously known him as a pilot; now it knew him as a *pilot of Korval*.

"You look shell-shocked, child," Shan said to him, sometime after the second pinbeam arrived from Liad, this from a certain dea'Gauss, directed to Ren Zel dea'Judan Clan Korval. Printed, this document occupied several sheets and proved, to his horrified eyes, to be a list of the properties, funds, and quartershare settled upon him.

"I—it is too much," he had managed, not quite certain himself if he was referring to the settlements—offered his choice of no less than *three* Class A Jumps!—or the abrupt and . . . irregular . . . alteration in his melant'i.

"Yes, I can understand how it might be. Anthora's a minx, and never fear that I will tell her so at my earliest opportunity."

Memory showed him the lady in question, her breasts heavy in his hands as she poised teasingly above him, her hair woven with starlight . . .

Face hot, he looked down at the printout.

"Perhaps," he whispered, "not entirely a minx."

There was a small pause. "Well, I am glad to hear you say so. For I will not scruple to tell *you* that—as much as I enter into your entirely reasonable dismay of the process—I wish you will accommodate yourself to these new arrangements, and allow us to embrace you fully. The clan can only be richer by your lifemating. Certainly, yos'Galan *does* rejoice in receiving you, and I am delighted in my new brother."

The printout smeared out of sense, as tears rose, and—shame to him—spilled over. In the act of throwing his arm up to shield his face, he recalled that it was no shame at all to share one's joy with . . . kin.

Nor was it useful to water the printout beyond readability. He made some shift to bring himself under control, and looked up to meet Shan's serious silver eyes.

"I wonder if I might have some time to . . . myself," he said tentatively. "I wish to relocate center, so that I may accommodate myself—and serve the clan usefully."

Shan grinned. "As to that, I have no fear at all. But, go, rest yourself, settle your mind. Come to us for prime, eh? And after that, I swear we will allow you to return to the comforts of your schedule."

And so Ren Zel had escaped, at least to the familiarity of his own cabin. Now, showered, and fulfilled by one of BillyJo's sandwiches, he lay himself down to sleep—and, in sleeping, dreamed.

He dreamed a starmap—*the* starmap: *Balent'i tru'vad*, the starweb of all creation. Vast, awesome in its balances and harmony, it lay revealed before him: suns, stars, worlds, lives, glittering, busy and inevitable. And throughout it all, woven into the very fabric of the universe, golden lines of power, such as he had first beheld in Anthora yos'Galan's chamber.

He bent his attention to those lines, apprehending the ebb and flow of their substance, the tectonic intricacies, the cohesion of their purpose. As he had in Anthora's chamber, he extended his hand and very carefully gathered two glowing lines to himself.

Far off in the starweb, a cluster of lines constricted about a lesser sun. Ren Zel released his hold; the lines relaxed, the flow of power resumed.

So. Once again, he extended his attention, this time in an attitude of seeking, rather than command.

He heard a tone, as if a council-bell had been lightly struck, and in the next heartbeat, *Balent'i tru'vad* was lost, and his sight filled entirely with pulsing golden light.

IT HAD BEEN CHI YOS'PHELIUM who had insisted, upon his succession to his mother's position as qe'andra to Korval, that the office defenses be upgraded to a standard she referred to as "adequate", and which Mr. dea'Gauss, in those younger days, had privately considered to be . . . draconian.

Today, reading the message in the lights of the "control board" she had caused to be installed in his office, he very much wished that he could return to those forever vanished days of his youth and most humbly beg her pardon. For it was truly said that delm's eyes see far—and the eyes of Korval see farthest of all.

Time-travel not being an option, the best way to atone for his doubts was to ensure that her care had not been in vain.

Carefully, adhering to a protocol altered and memorized every Quarterday, Mr. dea'Gauss pushed three buttons in sequence, alerting his staff and apprentices to the approach of danger. They would now, according to drill—for Chi had also insisted that there be drills, and routine practice of drills—close their work, touch the key sequence that would simultaneously download the information in their computers to the house computer at Jelaza Kazone, and scrub their own systems. That done, they would exit the building using one of the three "escape routes."

They had twelve minutes to accomplish these things.

At twelve-minutes-point-one, the building would seal itself. Since the walls and windows had years ago been reinforced with hullplate and blast-glass, Mr. dea'Gauss was comfortable in his belief that it would take both effort and time for the approaching enemy to gain entry.

His own task required some time—a little. Merely the retrieval of two letters, written long ago at the outrageous suggestion of that same Chi yos'Phelium; a moment to copy and address them as appropriate; the touch of a key to send. That done, he typed in the sequence that would initiate the download and wipe of his own records, and bent to retrieve the gun from the right-hand drawer of his desk.

❈ ❈ ❈

THEY'D THROWN the Erob comm tech out for a tea break she was more than willing to have, once it was explained to her that the pinbeam was needed for private Korval business.

Now, Val Con was seated beside Nova at a console in the inner bridge, Miri on his knee, both watching her fingers move, and taking note of the new access codes.

"Your codes would have worked, of course," Nova told Val Con, "but as a bounce to Jeeves. I set it up that way when you had been gone so long and had not . . ." Her voice faded, then strengthened. "Of course, I could not compromise our integrity, but Jeeves has your voice-map on file and he is very discreet."

"In fact," Val Con said, for Miri's benefit, "he has the ability to spread himself over eight different frequencies, re-routing on the fly, which makes him remarkably difficult to trace."

"Just so," Nova said coolly, and fed in the last string of code. "There, that should . . . yes."

A datalog shimmered into being on the center screen, displaying the call-ins for Day 52, Standard Year 1393. Nova scrolled upward.

"Luken, Padi, Shindi . . ."

"Shindi?"

Nova glanced at him. "Did not Shan—well," she caught herself with a shrug. "You would have been otherwise occupied, I suppose. The clan rejoices in fraternal twins, heirs to Anthora yos'Galan. Their names are Shindi and Mik."

"Ah." He smiled, and put his hand on Miri's knee. "The clan increases, cha'trez. We are doubly fortunate in twins."

She looked down at him. "Twice as much trouble, you mean?"

He laughed, and had the pleasure of seeing a cool smile pass over Nova's features before she turned back to the screen, scrolling ever upward through the long list of dates and names.

She reached an end, and waved her hand wordlessly. Foreknowing, Miri sitting tense on his knee, still he took a turn, scrolling downward through the names of his kin.

Excepting only one.

DAY 54

❧❧❧❧❧❧❧❧❧❧❧❧❧❧❧❧❧❧❧❧❧❧❧❧

Standard Year 1393
The Clutch Homeworld

THEY HAD BEEN made known to Handler, of Edger's clan, who sat with them quietly through the hours of waiting. Occasionally he would speak; if asked a question, he would answer, most courteously; but in general he worked silent, alternating between the handles of several knives.

The food they had packed in was adequate, and Daav was permitted a few moments outside every few hours, which he used to circumnavigate the asteroid they'd come in on. Otherwise, he—and Aelliana—awaited their summons.

Also in the chamber was a vast and silent member of the Clutch, lightly shelled, withal, and holding a naked crystal blade reminiscent of spear or sword. Daav had first thought the creature a statue, until Handler, upon hearing a gong from within the chamber, addressed a quick word to it. The guard-Clutch had answered with a brief whistle and a slight bow, thence returning to silence.

The waiting room was carved from rock, with three visible tunnels running off, and, as far as Daav was able to deduce, down. Edger had gone into the middle tunnel, to the meeting room of the Elders, many hours ago.

So they whiled the hours. Daav talked with himself, or wrote in his notepad, while inwardly he and Aelliana played games of discovery, sharing memories of kin, and of friends.

Too often Daav found himself projecting comfort, or worse, disdain—and once heard himself say, "For that, yes, we may have some Balance, for I am sure we still own some stock there, and I never liked the fellow . . ."

"Daav, so long ago, and so—"

"Knowing what I know, I can do nothing but this—would you have our children's children exposed to a clan permitting this?"

At other times, Aelliana showed Daav what it looked like, what it felt like, to explore the beauty of numbers; to see something as simple as a ship's course, or as complex as a star system, object by object . . . .

And then Edger was returned to them.

"Come," he said, and his big voice reverberated with weariness. "They will listen. You must tell them of the Tree and the necessities of my brother and sister. You will need speak, each of you, father and mother, and you will needs speak as elders. You must hold nothing aside, for the truth of things invests the walls of this place. What questions you may be asked I cannot say, nor may I offer comfort, for within are those who watched the stars and slew dragons and ruled clans before my first shell was dry."

DAY 44

※ ※

Standard Year 1393
Surebleak

THE PORTACOMM on his belt beeped for attention—an increasingly ordinary, not to say annoying, event. Pat Rin frowned. He had rather been enjoying the ride back from Melina Sherton's country territory, sharing the large back seat of his car with half-a-dozen bottles of Upcountry Canary; watching the peaceful streets of the Affiliation roll by his window. The pace Gwince set was rapid enough to make progress, yet slow enough that he could be seen, and have an opportunity to return the waves of those he passed.

The comm's beep changed from the single, 'attention' beep to the three-toned phrase belonging to calls from Security—Natesa or Cheever McFarland, that would be. Both of whom were at Surebleak Port, awaiting the contracted delivery from the Juntavas. He snatched the unit free.

"Conrad," he said, terse; no longer hesitating over the assumed name.

"Our shipment has arrived in good order," came Natesa's musical voice, unstrained and unsurprised. "Transhipping is well under way. I must admit to an error, however, in scheduling your visit to the country. It appears that certain matters have run ahead of us and your countenance is required at port, rather sooner than later. The portmasters themselves make the request."

Pat Rin sighed—for both portmasters to be on duty together was not a good sign.

"No news without complexity, eh, Natesa? Shall I rush?"

"Yes, denubia. It would be best."

Silently, Pat Rin damned the device for its lack of visual screen—or even a speaker capable of transmitting nuance.

"Soonest, then," he said, briefly, discreetly. "I will be there."

He thumbed the comm off, leaned forward and spoke to the driver.

"Gwince, if you please, we are in need of the banshee. Take me to the portmaster's office quickly."

She nodded. "Right, Boss. To the port!"

The siren wailed into life, startling the peaceful street outside his window into chaos. Lesser vehicles pulled quickly aside. Pedestrians, reflexes honed by years of violence, jumped for the meager protection of doors and alleyways. Some few, bolder, stood their ground, staring wide-eyed as the big car surged forward, pressing Pat Rin deep into the comfort of the big back seat.

"WHAT WE HAVE here is a conundrum," Dayside Portmaster Claren Liu said, from the head of the hastily cleared conference table. "The port has taken the report of First Class Pilot Bhupendra Darteshek—" This was, Pat Rin had learned, the name of the very tall, very thin, very dark-skinned Juntavas pilot—"and the corroborating report of First Class Pilot Vilma Karapov—" Pilot Darteshek's co-pilot, a well-muscled blonde with skin so pale it seemed tinged with blue—"that we've got what might be pirates in the system. They say that they were shadowed into Port—and they've provided instrument verification."

As the ability to come and go like shadows themselves was the claim the Juntavas—through Natesa—had made for their couriers, this hardly seemed auspicious. Pat Rin spoke across the table to Pilot Darteshek.

"How is that you allowed yourselves to be followed?"

White teeth gleamed in a thin, feral grin. "We don't be followed. They was here when we Jump in."

Pat Rin felt a chill run his spine, and inclined his head courteously. "That does put a different face on the matter. Thank you, pilot."

"Right," said Portmaster Liu, and looked 'round the table to be sure she had everyone's attention—everyone being the two courier pilots, Pat Rin, Natesa, Cheever McFarland, and nightside portmaster Etienne Borden—before proceeding.

"We all know that Surebleak is a low tier port. We do have two guild portmasters; we've got a few hands and two back-up volunteer portmasters who're on call in case of an emergency. We have two weather satellites to back up comm traffic and a comm satellite that backs up the weather satellites. We've got one space-going tug. What we don't have is defense." She shook her head.

"Why this is so . . ." she made a wry mouth and sipped from a dispenser cup of coffee.

"History lesson," she said apologetically. "See, Surebleak is a corporate world. It belongs—belonged—to something called the Gilmour Agency, which was set up to develop the planetary timonium deposits. They were pretty good-sized deposits, and the planet itself was near enough to habitable that they had some big plans for it—the designs for the orbiting mirrors they were going to use to eventually bring the temperature up a few degrees are on file in the port 'base." She shrugged. "The assumption was that there'd be a real economy here. Timonium and by-products going out, with maybe some specialty ores, gemstones, local lumber, and such to sweeten the load. Incoming would be supplies for the mines and the miners. In addition to development rights, Gilmour Agency was empowered to establish a local government corporation, which would have the responsibility of upgrading and maintaining the port." She had another sip of coffee and continued.

"Gilmour had barely gotten started here when their competitors located Tanzir's System two light years to galactic west. Three big airless rocks of not much else but high-grade timonium left over from the same event that helped make Surebleak the garden spot of the galaxy that it is. Gilmour Agency folded—defaulted on everything—and the local government never did get established—" She looked sharply down-table.

"I hope I'm not boring you, Boss Conrad."

Pat Rin bowed slightly in his seat. "Not at all. In fact, I expect that I will be needing as much of the formal history of Surebleak as you have . . . ."

"Right," she interrupted. "You will. Because all this comes down to the reason why we don't have weapons or defense. It's because the local planetary government has to approve, authorize, certify, and assist in providing all planetary or system defenses. And until just lately, Surebleak hasn't had a planetary government."

Pat Rin stared at her, deliberately haughty, while his mind raced. He was, by a vote of the Affiliated Bosses, Head Boss, empowered to speak for all if the need arose. His proposed structure had been somewhat different, modeled, as it had been, on the Council of Clans. His fellow bosses, however, had insisted that there must be one Head Boss—"Boss Boss," Penn Kalhoon had joked—and he had bowed to that, seeing that this was the model they understood. He had then appointed Penn Kalhoon Second Boss, and between them they had begun to match the tasks that needed to be done with those who had the talents to accomplish them. Which in effect meant . . .

He looked up to find Claren Liu looking at him with grim amusement.

"Boss Conrad," she said, with a formal nod of the head. "As Surebleak portmaster, I request your approval to begin planetary defense planning, your permission to act in the name of Surebleak in the case of incident, and your agreement to assist in developing an on-going security net." She paused. "Without your OK, all I can do is pass a note to the guild, saying I've got possible pirates in-system."

Pat Rin glanced out the window. The second level port office was bathed in sunlight, and overlooked the tarmac to the east, and with a portion of a road that connected to the Port Road. On the tarmac sat two ships—the port's tug and the courier's surprisingly large vessel.

"I assume that I must regard this as an official request?" he finally asked, facing the portmaster once more.

"That's right. It has to be witnessed by two master pilots or a master pilot and three first class." She offered him a sympathetic grin.

"We can't have ships running around shadowing our incoming now that we have an ad out," she said. "It'd be—"

"Bad for business," Pat Rin finished gently along with her.

He rose, and inclined his head.

"I acknowledge your proposal, Portmaster, and I hereby approve your request to begin planetary defense planning. I give you permission to act for Surebleak in case of incident. As for a planetary security net—" he glanced aside, catching Cheever McFarland's eye. "I may be able to provide assistance, especially if there are pilots to hand."

Cheever's eyes widened, then closed. Pat Rin suppressed a smile and sat down.

"I will sign documents, if that is required," he told the portmaster. "Mr. McFarland, if you would do me the favor of going to the car and bringing up the contents of the back seat. Portmaster, I propose a working lunch."

She grinned at him merrily. "Right you are. I'll send for food— and there's a couple others we'll want here, if you'll let me call them in?"

He inclined his head. "Certainly."

DAY 45

❁ ❁

Standard Year 1393
Sherzer System

"TOLD YOU THERE was something spooky about them 'quations, Shugg. I must know something deep down . . ." that was Andy Mack—the Colonel, so-called—idly stropping a credit chit along the flowing silver hair falling across the front of his leather jacket as he leaned against the back of second board's acceleration couch.

"Well, the screwy thing is it ain't exactly obvious, no matter how much you think about it . . . ." Shugg agreed.

The grizzled and short-haired Shugg—Flyer Shugg to his Surebleak acquaintances—sat second board at the moment, with Cheever McFarland at first. Crowding behind them were the other seven members of the expedition: Boss Conrad, Natesa, Etienne Borden, Juntavas pilots Darteshek and Karapov, Andy Mack, and "call me Dostie," the taciturn pilot of the port's official tug, whose hair—today at least—matched the electric pink tunic she wore beneath her jump jacket.

They had all sat second at one point or another during the trip. Pat Rin's glare had been ignored by the master pilot when his name came around on the roster; perforce, he had taken the seat warmed by Dostie, who had had it after the Colonel, who had it after Natesa, and had run his board with a cool aplomb he was very far from feeling. Now Shugg sat second, his grin slow and easy as he played with the screens.

"Lookit. We got a brown dwarf as primary and one-two-three neat as a pin stepping stone blue-and-green gas cousins with halos and then little Miss Blue running a bit askew in an outside orbit. Me, I'd like to know what happened to the missing planet!"

"Oh, hain't *missing*, Shugg!" Andy Mack scolded him genially. "You always want to find something *missing*. Check the resonance and you'll see . . . ."

Natesa smiled and raised her eyes; Pat Rin smiled in answer. He had, quite unexpectedly, *enjoyed* the trip, despite the crowding and the lack of opportunity to be private with his lady. But truly, he'd not found a group this convivial since . . . well . . . ever.

"Might be some rocks out beyond," Dostie offered. "But the Colonel's right, anything bigger than grains will get swept out of that gap because the mass ratio's almost a perfect 9, 5, 4, 3 . . . and with orbital periods being what they are—might be your Miss Blue *is* what's missing!"

"Now," Cheever said, raising his voice to be heard over the chatter, "we get to the fun part. If you were looking for a ship-stack out in the middle of this nowhere, where would you look?"

It was, of course, a joke, and Pat Rin was relieved to hear Pilot McFarland refer to their destination as other than a "ship grave-yard"—an image not conducive to hope, which had so delighted the pilot that he had used it in every other sentence. Likewise, he had dropped the word "derelicts," which the ships they sought assuredly would *not* be, from his vocabulary.

"Shall we ask them where they are, Mr. McFarland?" Pat Rin murmured.

Cheever, careful of watchful eyes, keyed in the call phrase, shrank the info screen to thumbnail on the second's board, and said, "I'll take bets. Who'd care to name time—minutes and seconds—before we get an answer from the beacon? Boss, you sit out, OK?"

The assembled pilots laughed, placed their bets, and settled into an animated exploration of the Sherzer system by instrument.

THE UNIVERSE WAS NOT SOMETHING Pat Rin yos'Phelium contemplated often, he being too much in it to feel apart from it. Now, however, he sat at the second board of *Fortune's Reward*, listening to its systems chuckling wistfully against the sudden silence of a ship with no one else in it, and shivered.

He had been to the brown drawf's system only once before. Cousin Er Thom had brought him—as surly and as graceless a halfling as one might ever wish to drown—insisting first that he memorize the coords, the call phrase, and the gate codes.

He had not, of course, wasted his time with Er Thom contemplating the universe. Instead, he had with cold dignity refused the shuttle's controls when they were offered, having already failed his piloting test for the fourth time. The terms of his refusal must have distressed his cousin, but Er Thom had merely nodded and changed the subject, filling the hours of the trip with stories of Clanmother Cantra, tales of Uncle Daav, arcane bits of ship lore; and, as they approached their goal more nearly, he had told of the strange mechanism which kept this collection of ships and ship parts together, for the use of Korval—and those whom Korval allowed.

Unwillingly, Pat Rin had listened, and despite his firm intention, found himself charmed out of surliness, so that he actually enjoyed sharing the picnic lunch Er Thom had brought along. After, and in closer accord, they crossed to the automated office, where he was shown the keys and the folders, and had his palmprint filed with the guardian computers.

That done, Er Thom had taken him on a tour of the stacks, showing him the controls and several ancient ships—one of which was still spaceworthy some six centuries after it was built!

Eventually, they had returned to the shuttle. As the ship-stack dwindled behind them, Cousin Er Thom had spoken to him seriously of his future, offering several alternative courses of education—all of them based away from the homeworld—borne his clumsy, halfling scorn with patience, and taken him back to the *Passage* as if all were well.

Now Pat Rin—perhaps the last of his clan; perhaps Korval-in-

Truth—had returned to mine the ship-stack, for the defense and preservation of the clan. He had been astonished that the access numbers he had memorized so long ago still worked; that the robot guardian recalled his palmprint; that the system of key and folder was precisely as the ill-tempered halfling had recalled it . . .

Around him, the ship burbled, and the familiar cycling of the air system failed to disturb his patient consideration of the past.

It was, truth told, the first time Pat Rin had ever been quite so alone. He had never—as his younger cousins had—done a solo run; and, though he not infrequently traveled alone, there had never been a time in his life when he had been more than a moment or two away from another human; even in space he had always had a pilot of superb skill to depend upon.

Now, the person nearest him was a pilot he'd barely met—Dostie. She, too, sat alone in a ship, more than two dozen Standard Minutes away from him. Natesa—alone in her vessel—was approximately three dozen Standard Minutes away, while Cheever McFarland, Flyer Shugg, and the nightside portmaster oversaw the checking and selection of the last of their potential fleet, lashed neatly together nearly four dozen minutes away.

To beguile himself, Pat Rin sat at second board, and began to tentatively explore the Sherzer system with instruments and screens. Sherzer II loomed in front of him; one long range screen showed the remaining cluster of ships to be explored, as well as the seventeen other "ship-stacks"—some no more than a collection of parts—with the limb of the planet and a distant view of the multi-hued planetary ring beyond. *Fortune's Reward* was in effect orbiting in formation with all of these ships, in the trailing LaGrange point of Sherzer II.

It was a lovely place for a junkyard, and Pat Rin found himself absorbed in the shimmer of the innermost ring; the colors of the storms swirling across the planet's surface; and the beautiful tracery of the lightning flashes—

"Boss?"

Cheever McFarland's voice boomed into the quiet ship, startling Pat Rin out of his reverie.

"Yes?" he snapped. There was a delay, longer than could be accounted for by the relative nearness of their ships.

"Um, yeah," Pilot McFarland said. "Sorry to bother you. But anyhow, we might have ourselves a problem, a kind of decision problem, if you know what I mean?"

Pat Rin shook his head, a habit which his mother had deplored in his cousins, and to which he had finally succumbed on Surebleak.

"Pilot, I am destined for *problems of decision* on this project," he said, making a conscious effort to lighten his tone. "If you can explain the situation in non-technical terms I will hear it and contribute what I may to the solving."

Again, he shook his head. The decisions. First had been the decision of which cluster of ships was most promising; then, after nearly two days, the decision to abandon them in favor of a potentially more . . . useful . . . solution.

The first cluster chosen had been a mixed collection of ships, all operable, but with visible problems ranging from missing space-suits to thruster fuel supplies too ancient to be reliable. A notation in the folder indicated that they had been for sale and were awaiting inspection of a potential buyer—fifteen Standards before. Apparently they had been passed over, and for good cause.

The possibly more useful solution came in the form of a pod of vessels of strange design and even stranger decor. Passed over in the first glance because they were parked among what looked to be random parts of two or three space stations, they proved on second glance to be asteroid miners. One side of each ship was painted flat black, the other a white so bright that it was nearly silver. And gaudily adorning each side—in white on the black side, in green on the white side—was the tree-and-dragon shield in so large a size that it could easily be seen before the true shape of the ships.

There was no way, of course, to quickly alter the look of the fleet, and because they were non-standard ships, checking them for utility was more difficult. Morever, their keys had been filed in a folder marked "reserved," though for whom Pat Rin had been unable to discover. Thus, each vessel was serially inspected and tested, and proved to be in remarkably good repair for ships left on their own in deep space. So far of the dozen, five had been found unfit.

Cheever McFarland cleared his throat. "Boss, this boat here is the queen. Call it a command ship. We got the complete package running and everything looks to be in great shape. Got a test program right here on the board that lets me check out the other ships remotely."

Pat Rin considered. This hardly seemed to be a problem . . . but the other man was continuing without waiting for an answer.

"Thing is, we got eight ships here that are in great shape. Got a lot of power, a lot of shields—these things are set for heavy duty asteroid belt mining!—Shugg says we can modify some of the rock drills and blasting charges—set 'em up as weapons."

Again, thought Pat Rin, this was good news, and not a problem at all. Eight ships and eight pilots was perfect.

"So, I'm thinking that the best thing is for us the bring these back and for you to fly that one home," Cheever McFarland finished.

Pat Rin froze; the words "I cannot!" stuck edgewise in his throat, caught up somehow with the lightnings across Sherzer II. With memory's ear, he heard Cousin Er Thom's soft, sweet voice, explaining why it was that Korval bought used ships, out-of-date ships, ships that had been foreclosed on—and why it was that they invested in repair yards, gave scholarships to pilots, and paid a good percentage of the Scout's maintenance bills.

"Your mother—she lives for the Code. Its study has become her life, and she excels at it. But, Korval—Korval is not the Code. Korval is *ships*. Always remember: Korval is ships."

He was brought to himself by Cheever McFarland's voice. "Boss? Other thing we could do is leave that one here and come back for it later."

Pat Rin blinked. Leave his ship? "No," he snapped, and took a deep breath.

"I will bring *Fortune's Reward* home, Mr. McFarland," he said, deliberately calm.

There was a slight pause, then, "Right. That's settled, then."

✳ ✳ ✳

"WELCOME PILOT." The words were warm amber against a dark screen. "Please log in."

Taking a deep breath, Pat Rin leaned forward, gingerly set his fingers against First Board's keypad and typed *Pat Rin yos'Phelium Clan Korval.*

"Please insert license."

Pat Rin glanced at the place in the board where a true pilot would slot his license for the ship's perusal, then back to the screen.

As he watched, the amber letters faded; reformed into another query.

"License available?"

Lower lip caught between his teeth, he typed *No.*

Astonishingly, the ship remained undismayed. "Palmscan, please," the next screen directed.

He placed his left hand on the pad, felt the tingle of the scan . . .

"Confirmed. Full access available."

Something *clicked* nearly beneath his fingers, loud in the silence of the piloting chamber. Pat Rin snatched his hand back as a section of the control board to his left parted neatly at the seam and an auxiliary panel rose, locking into place with a snap.

For a long moment, he stared at it. Full access, indeed, now that the weapons were available to him.

"Autodefense?" his ship inquired. "Autoshield?"

What did he know of such things? He touched a key, accepting both.

That quickly the board came fully back to life, with lights blinking and switches setting or resetting themselves. The screen layout went from Cheever McFarland's idiosyncratic groupings to default—and stabilized into a pattern familiar to him from childhood: this was the layout Uncle Daav and Cousin Er Thom had preferred; he himself had drilled on a dummy board set up just this way . . .

Low on the screen to the right was radar and sensor scan forward, low on the left was radar and sensor aft; low in the center was Jump status, and what—according to Cousin Er Thom—Uncle Daav had called the go-dial, a graph showing the balanced Jump potentials of the three strongest nearby gravity wells.

Above—and largest—was the "forward" visible view, with the aft view smaller to the left; ship status reports sat to the right, all cheerfully green: air supply, backup air supply, sensor power checks, weapons functions (green for the particle beam, green for the missiles: eight marked *short*, eight marked *mid*, four marked *long*; and one green for something marked chaff-bomb), and multi-channel receiver and back-up.

"Boss?" Cheever McFarland's voice came, quietly, over tight band. "Problems?"

Pat Rin sighed, gently. "I am acclimating myself, Pilot. The view from first board is somewhat larger than that from second."

There was a brief delay. "That's all adjustable—" the pilot began, and broke off. "Yeah, OK," he said after a moment, and somewhat sheepishly. "I think I know what you mean. But really, Boss, there ain't gonna be any problems. All you gotta do is tell the ship where you're going—check it against the book, you got plenty of time. Hell, after you put in the coords, set the auto-count, and sit back and snooze 'til it's time to punch the 'fresh scan' button for the sensors when you pop out."

"Which is why most pilots rejoice in having someone of wide experience sitting second for their first few dozen hours of flight, if I recall correctly." Pat Rin could hear himself getting testy with his absent stalwart, and authorized a complete systems check to take his mind off his tension.

After a moment, Cheever McFarland's voice re-emerged from the speaker, sounding suspiciously as if the pilot were suppressing a sneeze, or perhaps a chuckle.

"Right. On the other hand, you done right well for yourself with the jump in and kick butt approach—and we both know you got the math cold. But listen, while you been sitting there talking to yourself, we've been getting ourselves together out here. We're all sitting within sight of each other, and we're setting up a Jump plan. I'm figurin' we can take this whole shebang outta here in about three hours. As it comes to happen, Natesa don't have a whole lot to do—won't for another hour or two. You want I should have her walk you through the check-out procedures a couple times?"

Pat Rin looked down, saw the ring on his hand, the tree-and-dragon bold and new—and bowed slightly toward the unseen speaker.

"Indeed, pilot, that sounds like an excellent idea. I will await her signals with anticipation."

DAY 47

◈◈◈◈◈◈◈◈◈◈◈◈◈◈◈◈◈◈◈◈◈◈◈

Standard Year 1393
Surebleak Space

JUMP HAD CONSUMED seventeen Standard hours, forty-four minutes, twenty-seven and numerous odd-bits of seconds, during which time Pat Rin did what he always did in Jump: He read and studied.

This time, however, he read not of the whimsical philosophy of Harshaw, nor the patient rhymes of yos'Sandow, nor even from the Code—which, until lately, he had studied several hours a week.

No, during this historic and unlikely Jump he had studied tactical manuals and piloting theory, and technical manuals, as he had not since was a halfling. He studied the dozen pre-logged destinations in the ship's computer, laughing at the ironies of Liad and Lytaxin; puzzling over the one marked with a symbol from a Terran card deck, until he suddenly understood what the venerable *ace of spades* had to do with a Liaden pleasure-yacht.

The pre-logged Jumps were all what Cousin Er Thom would have called "dirty Jumps," calculated for broad energy levels and without updating for current mass or velocity. Emergency runs, all of them, for use in times of dire trouble, pilot injury, or the tragedy that put the ship into the hands of one who was no proper pilot at all . . .

He checked weapons—both the ship's armament and his various pistols. Gods, he was bringing a small fleet into Surebleak, each double marked visually as belonging to Korval. Yet, what choice had he?

And so with an hour to go he brought himself again to the pilot's seat and molded it and the board to him as best he might. He had become accustomed to seeing the transmission recordings, and added them above the main forward view. Pulling the chair up to the second stop, he locked it at an angle slightly less rakish than that required by Cheever McFarland's frame; raised it, turned the seat temperature down several degrees, then set it to automatic. The board he moved down, then brought it back to its original position. He engaged the shock webbing and sat back, eyes on the Jump grayed screens.

Carefully, deliberately, he reviewed those things Inas-called-Natesa had told him, both the quiet love-talk—which had been a comfort and a distraction in his isolation—and the practical matters that pilots share between themselves.

"Let the ship tell you if there is a problem," she had murmured, for his ears alone. "Your eyes will be quicker than your fingers in the first seconds of breakout. Place defense on automatic, and bring up your shields. Be in the seat well ahead of time, and always strap in when you sit first board, even in quiet orbit about a friendly world. Test the alarm levels because alarms should warn, not frighten or distract. Be certain that you can easily reach the controls and be certain that your ring will not hamper you nor catch on a toggle. I love you . . . .

"You will Jump first, denubia; and we will come in around you. We will be no more than a minute or two behind, and within a tenth-sec or closer on radio. I expect you to pilot like you shoot . . ."

Breakout.

Fortune's Reward announced itself around its Jump glare as *Bitty Kitty*, out of Fron Du Lac; the ship's air system purred, and his hand moved as if of its own accord, slapping "refresh scan." A glance at his screens oriented him wonderfully: Surebleak's port beacon was located and centered. There was no sign yet of his fleet, the Jump gauge was moving toward ready, and the gravity well indicator showed he was in tight. A good Jump, in fact. Pat Rin smiled.

"Pilot Cheever McFarland and Owner Pat Rin yos'Phelium," the voice snarled in Trade over the broadband. "You will maintain course and prepare to match locks in three Standard minutes. This is the Department of the Interior. Repeat: Maintain course and prepare to match locks. Disobey at your peril."

Pat Rin jerked forward, brought up short by the webbing. The scans showed nothing, and then several small bursts of energy—a ship maneuvering, perhaps. Or two—

An alarm warbled to life, and the aft radar scan showed him the signature of a ship, closing rapidly.

"*Fortune's Reward*, you are in our sights. The Department of the Interior is authorized to fire on you if you fail to comply. Your reply is mandatory."

Warning lights were flashing now, rippling across the board in waves of yellow. The scans showed him a second ship, starboard— and a third, hanging back, to port.

Natesa had walked him through the firing procedure, accepting the fact that his ship was now armed with her usual serenity.

Now, as she had taught him, he sighted on a ship, touched the acquire key, waited for the flash; moved to the next. And again. *Fortune's Reward* recorded its enemies, and he glanced to the status bar. The coils were recharged. Good.

Quickly, quickly, he brought the coils up, armed his weapons with a snap of a toggle, and pulled up the screen of dirty Jumps. He snatched the local coords with a slap of his hand, and took a deep breath.

Then he played the ace of spades, the gambler's best friend.

REALITY SHIFTED.

Jump glare. *Bitty Kitty* automatically declared itself to the universe. The snatched coords of his departure point were locked in, and the ship's Jump gauge showed a slow-building energy. Surebleak was a cloudy, distant, disk.

There was an eternity to wait, then, knowing that any second Natesa would be Jumping in, all of his would be Jumping in—vulnerable and unwarned . . .

His hand moved, slapping up the hailing frequency.

"Intruder alert! Port Surebleak, beware! Boss Conrad declares the highest alert!"

And, finally, coils were ready. He held his breath, touched the button—

Reality shifted.

He broke in just a few minutes from his departure location, the Jump glare of four other incoming ships blossoming at the corners of a great square before him. Also before him, on courses at tangent to his—the ships of his enemy.

"In the name of Port Surebleak," he broadcast on the hailing band, his hands busy on their own errands across the board. "I demand your immediate surrender!"

He glanced down to see what his fingers had wrought; saw an interception course charted and locked; and a digit poised above the acceleration stud. He pressed it. *Fortune's Reward* answered, pushing him into the cocoon of the pilot's chair.

Across the open bands, Korval ship *Patience of Stone* announced itself. Korval ship *Handtruck II* announced itself. Korval ships *Timonium Core* and *Survey Nine* announced themselves.

The screens flared as three more ships broke Jump in a tight, triangular formation, directly into the path of the closing enemy.

"Boss Conrad requires an answer!" It took him a heartbeat to recognize the voice that lashed across the frequencies. Natesa. Chest tight, he looked to his scans; found her ship—as surely the ships of the Department would find it . . .

Korval ships *Diamond Duty*, *Crystalia*, and *Pebble Probe* announced themselves.

Natesa repeated her demand, and the three enemy ships were rotating, as if seeking targets . . . .

Glare and noise. A single ship broke Jump dead ahead of Pat

Rin, turning the four, three, one configuration into a cone shaped gauntlet for the enemy ships.

Korval ship *Survey One* announced itself.

The enemy ship closest to Pat Rin increased its rotation; and a voice blared across all possible bands: "Pat Rin yos'Phelium, you are declared outlaw by Liad. Surrender or we fire!"

Surrender. Yes, certainly. He bit his lip, fingers sure and quick as he pressed acceleration, engaged the weapons comp and brought up the stored configurations.

"Flaran cha'menthi," he said quietly to the open band, and pressed the launch button.

FORTUNE'S REWARD'S first missiles spread out toward the enemy. The ships of the Department, neatly contained by the oncoming Tree-and-Dragon ships, returned fire in all directions at once.

The whir and thump of the missile launch unnerved him—he knew his ship's sounds and this was new to him. Then a whir again and the ship sounded normal.

He realized that he should have been in his spacesuit *before* engaging the enemy when his shields took a hit from an energy weapon. Fortunately, the shields—like the missiles his enemy may have been surprised to find launched from a supposedly unarmed ship—were late model, of a type most usually carried by those accustomed to going into harm's way, and easily up to the task of fending off a glancing shot.

His screens had multiplied, showing him missile tracks and beam markers, energy levels and a variety of ranges. A light came up on the board and abruptly there was chatter—his small fleet talking among themselves—

"Way to go, Boss! We're on 'em now. Just let me—" Shugg.

"I'm warmed and ready on the main cutter, Cheever."—Dostie.

"I'm closing on the lead . . ."—Natesa!

He wanted to shout, to warn her off, but his throat was too tight to admit the words and his quarry had fired again and the screens showed him things he had never needed to know before and he loosed two more missiles at the computer's prompting.

"It's the perfect globe—we'll get them all!" shouted the Colonel.

"Fire on the shields," Bhupendra Darteshek said quietly. "Going to yellow."

On screen, Pat Rin saw the first of his missiles disappear—intercepted. The tracking computer reported the second and third still on course, and—

Cheever McFarland's voice came across the tight band, as easy and calm as if he were suggesting wine before dinner:

"Let's break the middle rock. If you're not engaged, hit button number four on your red board. If you can't mesh, tell me."

The range guide was fluctuating rapidly as he closed on his enemy. *Fortune's Reward* prompted him to fire two more missiles. The circle over the enemy ship was a bright, blinking green—not ready, not ready.

The ship in the forward screen changed abruptly, as if sections were peeling away . . .

It took him too long to understand what had happened, but *Fortune's Reward* was quicker. Yet another screen flashed "evasive action" and he felt the ship take itself out of his hands, and he was pressed back into the chair, while numbers begin to decrease on the weapons board. The newest of his screens flashed "autodefense."

Fortune's Reward showed him the path of the nine missiles his quarry had launched, and then beeped at him.

The blinking green circle was now a dull red, firmly centered on the ship he was pursuing. He depressed the stud. The red circle changed to blinking yellow briefly, then back to ready. He fired again, eyes as much on the incoming missiles as anything else.

The ship's shield gauge went red; around him strange blossoms on the screens, around him silent explosions, around him missile tracks skating away—and then sound on the hull, as if rats ran across it, and more, dull bangs and clinks—missile debris.

The board beeped. He blinked the screen into focus, saw the question: "Acquire new target?"

The radio was filled with static and the forward screen showed empty. His enemy must have Jumped, he thought dazedly—but no, not that.

He had killed a ship.

A cheer arose from the radio.

"Boss got 'em!" yelled the Colonel. "Let's go to town!"

Pat Rin shook his head and leaned to his scans, searching out the signature of Natesa's ship, heart in mouth and fingers shaking . . .

Another cheer erupted; Pat Rin saw the second enemy ship evaporate on his aft screen, but Natesa—

Her ship sat quietly in orbit, with none to oppose her, and her voice came wearily into the midst of yet a third round of cheering.

"I could not close quickly enough. They Jumped out."

DAY 54

❀ ❀

Standard Year 1393
Solcintra
Liad

SHE WENT AS QUICKLY and as safely as she knew how. She carried
a hidden pellet gun, because Nova would have wished her to, and, in
truth, she was a fair shot—even Pat Rin said so.

That her sister—and quite possibly her brothers—would not
have wished her to leave the safety of Jelaza Kazone for any reason
whatsoever, she did not allow to weigh with her. Even in childhood
games, her elder siblings had always desired her to stand behind
them in moments of danger, or to run away and hide herself from
whichever pursuing monster might have walked out of the pages of
novel or log-book, as if she were not capable of dealing with such
apparitions, as well as the realities that spawned them.

And, truly, her melant'i was clear, as she had explained to
Jeeves. She was Korval's representative on planet, and it fell to her to
protect the material resources of the clan, as well as its melant'i,
insofar as she could.

Certainly, she had pointed out, she could not in conscience
allow the Council of Clans to attempt to strip Korval of its

Jumpships, one by one, in accumulated "penalties." Whether the Council's goal was to strip Korval of its ships, she could not have said. But any attempt to attach a ship would be resisted by Korval's employees and allies, with violence, if required. Thus, it was safer for all that the Council not be given any reason to make the attempt.

In keeping with her resolution to be just as prudent as Nova would wish, Anthora bowed to Jeeves in the matter of transportation, and thus found herself arriving at Solcintra in a ground car chauffeured, long-distance, by himself. She did not discover the second passenger until the car pulled to the busy sidewalk in front of the Council building.

"Really, Lord Merlin, this is the outside of enough!" she said in half-amused exasperation. "I should think *you* at least would understand my competencies."

Merlin flicked an ear and jumped out the car with her when the door opened. Anthora paused, disconcerted for the first time since taking the decision to obey the summons of the Council.

"I believe it would be best for all if you remained with the car," she said to the cat, heedless of the people who were forced to detour around her.

Tail up, Merlin went down the walk, across a lush strip of lawn and vanished into a bank of ornamental shrubs.

"Merlin!" Anthora cried, opening her Inner Eyes, which was of course useless. If Merlin did not want her to See him, she might search fruitlessly until Liad's star cooled. Behind her, she heard the purr of an engine and turned around in time to see her car pulling into traffic. Too late, now, to return Merlin to the robot's care, even if she could find him.

"Well, then," she told the shrubbery, with a good attempt at nonchalance. "I hope you know the way home."

She waited a heartbeat or two, in case Merlin chose of his own will to reappear. He did not so choose, however. Anthora bit her lip, then moved her shoulders in an attempt to cast off concern. Merlin had his own resources, gods knew. Doubtless she would find him asleep in the middle of her bed when she returned from her imminent adventure.

Squaring her shoulders under the stiff silk of the formal Council jacket, she went up the walk and through the ornamental wooden doors, and then the security doors, made of hullplate. She crossed the common room, with its domed ceiling painted with galaxies, suns and ships, and its stone floor, worn treacherously smooth by the traffic of centuries.

At the reception desk, set before the carved metal door to the Council Chamber itself, she bowed.

"Anthora yos'Galan Clan Korval," she said. "Korval's name has been called."

She straightened, looked defiantly into the retinal scanner, and moved forward. The door swung open, slowly, before her.

The Chamber was already full; the delms of Liad in their tiered seats, some silently doing paperwork, others talking between themselves. There were no dark screens, no flags of absence. Every seat was occupied; saving only one, which indicated a concerted effort by *someone* to fill the hall.

Unusually, there were a pair of guards flanking the door; another pair on the next tier down, and two more pairs along the stone side-walls.

At the bottom of the Chamber, Speaker for Council sat behind her high desk. She looked up as the door opened and leaned slightly forward, her amplified voice colder, even, than the High Tongue could account for.

"Anthora yos'Galan Clan Korval, stand forward and face this Council."

Slowly, with what she hoped was dignity, Anthora walked down the long aisle to the floor. Around her, she felt the sharpening of attention; conversations died as she passed; her inner senses processed the climate of the room as frigid, with a stiff, damp wind a-building.

Head up, shoulders square, unhurried and deliberate, she walked down the aisle that had grown miles since the last time she had accompanied Nova to Council. Finally, she passed Korval's empty station. Twelve more steps along a blessedly flat surface brought her into proper proximity of the high desk.

Anthora stopped, bowed gently into the bitter gale of the Speaker's contempt, and turned to face the Council.

Row after row of faces; many of them people she had known all her life; cool, formal faces, looking down upon her. Deliberately, she sought out Korval's known allies and friends: Justus, Guayar, Ixin, Reptor, Mizel . . . No smiles, no bows of welcome, no gestures of support. Waiting; all of them, waiting for her to answer a question she had yet to hear.

From the nearest row, where sat the delms of the High Houses, one arose and bowed. Anthora's heart sank. Aragon was not a friend of Korval.

"Aragon calls upon Korval to answer charges of kin-stealing, and of murder. How does Korval make answer?"

It was on the end of her tongue to make answer by telling him he had taken leave of his sanity, but she could See that he had not. Aragon did not pose this question lightly; and he believed in his heart that Korval had committed these crimes. The taste of *proof* slid across her senses, which was . . . terrifying.

She bowed, with courtesy, allowing the puzzlement she felt to be seen.

"Honored Aragon has the advantage of me. Who has Korval stolen? Who has Korval slain?"

His mouth thinned. "Aragon calls upon Korval to provide the location of—"

The door at the pinnacle of the Chamber swung open and a man descended the long aisle, running, though he was far from young, making no bid for dignity at all.

"Precedence!" he shouted, breathless and out of mode. "I claim precedence!"

"You are out of order!" Speaker roared, her amplified voice a thunderclap. "The Council sits in Judgment, which is of the highest precedence!"

"I claim precedence," the man repeated, arriving on the floor. Thus close, Anthora could see that he was sweating, and trembling, with the effects of exertion, yes, but also with fear.

"Who are you?" Speaker demanded.

He bowed, in the mode of introduction merely. "Har Par dea'Liss Clan Tuxent. I sit as one of seven equal Masters of the Accountant's Guild. I claim precedence, based on planetary security."

There was a short silence. Anthora, staring up at the wall of faces, saw frowns, and puzzled glances; saw delms leaning to their nearer neighbors, heard the swelling wave of whispering.

"Explain," Speaker ordered Har Par dea'Liss.

"Yes. I and five of my colleagues have received from the seventh of our colleagues—Mr. dea'Gauss—a communication indicating that his office was under attack by enemies of Liad. He informs us that he has taken certain measures, on behalf of the planet. These include having the dies for our currency removed from the treasury to a place of safety."

The whispering delms stopped whispering, and sat staring, shock making an electric tingle in the air. The Chamber was silent.

Speaker for Council cleared her throat. "This is, of course, fabrication. The honored dea'Gauss has fallen ill and is suffering delusions. Come, Master dea'Liss, call the treasury and assure yourself that—"

"I have called the treasury," he interrupted. "Two of my colleagues have gone to the treasury. The dies are no longer there. They were removed some hours ago, by unknown persons, who showed an order from Mr. dea'Gauss." He took a hard breath. "Two more of my colleagues went immediately to the offices of dea'Gauss in the city. It is abandoned and ransacked. There are dead men in the upper halls, near what had been the private offices of the dea'Gauss. They have been shot. None carry identification. Of dea'Gauss, there is no sign." He bowed.

"I repeat: I have precedence, based upon planetary security."

Mr. dea'Gauss had been attacked in his office? Anthora shivered, and threw forth her thought. It was difficult, with so many other signatures nearby, many of them noisy with growing agitation . . .

"Aragon demands to know Korval's place in this outrage!"

She turned and looked at him, read his loathing and loaded her words with absolute certainty.

"Korval knows nothing, and demands that the Council bend all efforts to recover Mr. dea'Gauss, who has obviously fallen into the hands of brigands."

Aragon blinked, and bowed, very slightly.

"By what right does dea'Gauss remove the dies from the treasury?" someone in the mid-tier called. "Those dies belong to Liad."

Master dea'Liss turned. "The dies belong to Korval," he said flatly. "They are leased to Liad, now as from the first striking. As Korval's qe'andra, dea'Gauss has every right—indeed, it is no less than his duty—to remove the dies to safety, if he has cause to believe they are at risk. His letter makes clear that he had ample cause. The dead men in his office underscore his point."

There was an outbreak of talk at that. Behind Anthora, Speaker for Council touched her chime. The talk quieted.

Anthora saw the Speaker glance in several directions, felt the multi-leveled tension as the glance turned into a survey of the room, and then the snap of a decision taken, as if from someone in the back of the room.

"Master dea'Liss rightly claims precedence. As Anthora yos'Galan is not empowered as a member of Council she will await the Council's attention in the Clerk's Retiring Room." She touched the chime.

As if the sound had conjured her, a Clerk appeared at Anthora's elbow.

"If Lady Anthora will accompany me?" she murmured, and led the way across the front of the room, to the discreet doorway. Anthora felt the weight of eyes on her back, and felt, too, the movement of several of those guards . . . . The Clerk pressed her palm against the plate and stepped back as the door swung open.

"Please await the Speaker's word here. There are refreshments, and a screen."

In the chamber behind them, several voices vied at once for the chance to be heard.

The Retiring Room was pleasant enough, with an open window overlooking the famous sunken formal Council gardens.

Anthora glanced over her shoulder as she stepped through the doorway, seeing Aragon still on his feet, with Bindan and also Etgora—and two guards falling in directly behind her, no doubt to flank the door. The Clerk pushed gently on her shoulder, hurrying her, guiding—and Anthora felt a quick, sharp prick as of a needle—

Anger flared, even as she felt the drug begin its work, seeking to slow her, to dull her senses—Idiots! Didn't they know she could turn any drug in a matter of seconds if she could but . . . .

The two guards entered the room, crowding her, distracting her, as she tried to locate the mental template to match the drug— and a hard hand slammed between her shoulder-blades sending her reeling into a tiny chamber, seemingly filled with fog. She bumped her head, staggered, and went to her knees, gagging, continuity shattering. Fiercely, she re-established center, while the drug set up a high buzzing in her ears—and she had it! Bellaquesa and cytaline: someone had wanted her very docile, indeed.

In a heartbeat, she had neutralized the drugs; though she felt a residual queasiness. She forced her eyes open.

The door was sliding closed. She lurched to her feet and threw herself forward, hitting it full-force, bouncing backward. She twist-ed in mid-air, meeting the floor with hands and knees, four-square and ready, rather than flat on her back and stunned.

She had landed on a curious, sooty stain. She blinked as the information leached into her consciousness. Zena tel'Woda had died here, by her own will, rather than allow the ones who had built this device to make her into their creature.

Her inner eyes were useless; all she saw was silver, cold and reflective; her other senses were fogged in, obliterated, useless. Worse, she felt ill, weak; her thoughts fragmenting. It was not the drug at work now, but some fey power the like of which she had never imagined. It felt—it felt as if her very blood was draining into the floor she knelt upon.

Anthora screamed.

DAY 47

Standard Year 1393
Surebleak Port

FORTUNE'S REWARD landed itself neatly and with no unseemly assistance from its pilot, who then busied himself with end-of-run checks and the orderly shutdown of systems with one eye on the hull light.

Mercifully, the routines were new to him and eventually engaged his full attention. When everything was locked down to his own and his ship's satisfaction, the hull was cool enough to allow egress.

He stepped out onto the field, shivering in the ice-toothed wind, and looked about him.

Eight mining ships were grounded nearby, their tree-and-dragon emblems a-glow in the wavering dawnlight. Gravely, he bowed to them—gratitude for service well given.

"They are warriors," she murmured from just behind his right shoulder. "All honor to them."

Turning, he saw her eyes widen, though he had no time to wonder at it. "Inas." He lifted a hand, fingers silking along her dusky cheek. She smiled, extended one finger to touch his earring, and leaned forward. He caught her mouth on his.

"You terrify me," he whispered into her hair, some time later.

"We are in balance," she replied, her arms tightening about his waist. "Whatever possessed you to engage that ship?"

He stirred. "It was the ship of our enemy and it lay within my means to stop it."

"Ah." Her arms tightened painfully, then she released him and stood away, smiling ruefully.

"Come, denubia, I have turned you from the course of duty. Did the portmaster not wish you to come to her immediately?"

"So she did," he said, and offered her his arm. "Best she know me for a rag-mannered dog at once."

Natesa laughed and slid her arm through his. "Yes, I am certain she will know just that."

"I confess that I am comforted by one thing," he commented, as they strolled arm in arm toward the tower.

"What is that?"

"Why, despite having broken what I am certain are many dozens of regulations, I need not suffer the indignity of having my license pulled."

"YOU." PORTMASTER Liu sat in official state behind her desk, a professional frown on her face. Pat Rin, seated across from her in a plastic chair with one short leg, steeled himself for the impending scold.

They were alone, Natesa having been waved into the conference room, where the rest of the pilots were talking at volume, replaying the recent battle. Pat Rin folded his hands on his knee, and gazed down at the counterfeit ring, reminding himself once more that the worst the portmaster might do was read him the long form of what Anne Davis would have termed "the riot act".

"You," Claren Liu repeated. "Deploying weapons within planetary space. Firing upon and destroying a ship within planetary space. Employing non-standard Jump technique. Failure to clear Jump with this station—*twice*. Violating established space lanes. Inappropriate acceleration within planetary space. Flying without a license."

Pat Rin looked up.

The portmaster shook her head. "Why in the hell don't you have a license? Sir."

He raised an eyebrow. "Because I am not a pilot. Ma'am."

She snorted. "Best imitation I've seen in a while, then. Defend your actions—it's required for the incident report."

Pat Rin glared at her. She glared back. He shifted in his chair, which rocked unpleasantly off its short leg, and sighed.

"The ship on which I had fired was intent on performing an act of piracy. I fired to protect my ship, myself, and this port. Certainly, I would not broadcast my piloting decisions under such circumstances."

The portmaster nodded. "OK. We got the tape—that'll go with the report." She cocked an eyebrow at him. "There's names on the tape—nothing I can do about it. Just like I can't help but notice how that ring of yours has the same design as those mining ships. Should've seen it before, I guess. I've worked on bigger ports. I've seen Tree-and-Dragon tradeships."

He inclined his head, and after a moment she sighed.

"Flyer Shugg tells me he can convert those things to defense units."

"He has said the same to me," Pat Rin acknowledged, "and I fear he will need to work quickly. For you also know that one of the three pirates escaped." He met her eyes squarely. "We must assume that they will return, with reinforcements. Of the eight mining ships, four will remain here as planetary defense."

Claren Liu frowned at him. "Where are the other four going?"

"The other four—and my private vessel," Pat Rin said, softly, "are going to take the quarrel home."

THE CONVERSATION snapped off as Pat Rin followed the portmaster into the conference room, and eight pair of pilot eyes pinned him.

"Well, here's the man hisself," Andy Mack said from his lean against the far wall. "Dressed up in his nice blue jacket, just like he ain't nothin' but a dirt-hog." He looked pointedly at Claren Liu. "Thought you was gonna take care of that."

"By the book, Colonel," she said, with edged patience. "We're doing it by the book." She looked around. "Master Pilot McFarland."

The big Terran stepped forward. "Yes, ma'am."

She pointed at Pat Rin, who mustered a glare for his pilot. Cheever smiled and nodded. "Morning, Boss."

"Mr. McFarland," the portmaster insisted. "You've said that this man sat second for you, and that you'll vouch for his board skill and his knowledge of the basic piloting equations. Is that correct?"

"Basic piloting 'quations?" howled Flyer Shugg. "Portmaster, that boy pulled a smuggler's ace outta his sleeve just as pretty as any of us ever seen and you're askin' does he know his *math*?"

"Quiet!" the portmaster snapped. "Mr. McFarland?"

"Yes, ma'am, I vouch for him. He knows his math and he knows his board. Bit thin on flight time, but there ain't no doubt he's a Jump pilot." His smile grew to a grin. "I'll be pleased to sign his card."

She nodded. "I'll countersign," she said, and turned to Pat Rin. "What name do you want on your license, pilot?"

Pat Rin took a breath, sought out Natesa's face in the crowd.

"This is a farce," he said.

She shook her head. "Indeed, it is in verymost earnest." She moved a hand, showing him the portable viewer on the table. "If you wish, you may review the tape, as we have done. It plainly shows that your ship was under the hand of a pilot of skill and daring."

"Son," Andy Mack added, "ever' single one of us here saw you in action and ever' single one of us watched the tape, too. No use sayin' you ain't a pilot—we know better. Now, tell the portmaster what you want your card to call you and let Cheever here sign you up. This port needs all the pilots it can fly." He shook his head, long silver hair moving over his shoulders like fog, disreputable face unwontedly serious. "Or don't you think that feller bolted right back home, yellin' for help all the way?"

Pat Rin moved his shoulders, throwing off tension, and met the Colonel's eyes. "I think he did exactly that," he said; and looked to the portmaster.

"The name on the license should be Conrad," he said steadily. "Jonni Conrad."

Across the room, Natesa smiled. Closer to hand, Cheever McFarland nodded.

"Jonni Conrad," the portmaster repeated, and it seemed to Pat Rin that she was trying to suppress a smile of her own. "OK. It'll take a couple minutes—and I want you to know that I'm putting a limit on you. First Class, grade S—that's "small ship." The S'll drop off as soon as you complete the required flight time across all classes of Jump ship. Understood?"

Yes, as if he would live long enough to master the intricacies of moving a passenger liner—or a tradeship—through Jump. Pat Rin inclined his head. "I understand."

"Good." She pointed at Dostie, who stood up from her place at the table, cradling something supple and dark in her arms. Cheever took it from her, shook it, and held it out.

Pat Rin swallowed, hard, in a throat gone dry. The license—it was true that he had been sitting first board, though he had only used the ship's programs, punching buttons at the computer's prompting. Still, he could allow the license, technically. But this— no. He had no right to a Jump pilot's jacket.

"Natesa," Cheever McFarland called over his shoulder. "Boss here needs some help with his jacket."

"Certainly," she said, and stepped forward.

"Natesa . . ." he breathed, as she came to his side. "It was the ship, not me."

"Very well," she said, in her calm, soothing voice. "When we have done with the present emergency, we will lift, you and I—and you will show me. In the meanwhile, we here are all, as the Colonel has said, seasoned pilots, and we must accept the evidence of our eyes and our experience." She took hold of his jacket and perforce he slipped out of it, remembering too late the gun in its hidden pocket.

"OK," Cheever said. "Now the new one."

He held it out—a jacket in black spaceleather, of a style perhaps not recent, lined in satiny black wickaway. Hesitantly, Pat Rin slid his arms into the sleeves, felt the weight of the thing settle across his shoulders . . .

"*Yes!*" Dostie yelled.

Shugg and the Colonel howled and stamped their feet. Juntavas courier Karparov clapped politely; Pilot Darteshek bared his teeth and shook a fist in the air. Etienne Borden shouted, "A brother! We increase!" Cheever McFarland winked and gave him a broad thumbs' up while Claren Liu nodded, no longer trying to hide her grin.

Natesa hugged him and kissed his cheek, which set up another round of hooting and stamping from Shugg and Mack, and gently slipped his pistol into the new jacket's inside pocket.

DAY 54

※ ※

Standard Year 1393
Passage Jump

REN ZEL AWOKE in good time to ready himself to take prime
meal with his sister and brother. As he dressed, he considered his
new estate with a good deal more calm than he had been able to
bring previously. Certainly, it was no ill thing to be enclanned.
Lifemated into Korval—that was . . . peculiar, certainly, and nothing
that the son of an outworld mid-House might ever had aspired to,
even had he not been made outcast. He wished, rather, that he might
speak to the lady with whom he had shared so very much pleasure,
to find what she thought of their mating, and to plan with her the
best structure for their lives. Would it suit her if he remained a-ship,
returning to her one relumma out of six? Was she perhaps a ship-
master in her own name, and—

He paused in the act of sealing his sleeves, blinking thoughtfully at nothing, as he recalled that Anthora taught at the College of the
Dramliz in Solcintra. She held a first class license, and had completed
some hours toward her master's. However, she had allowed her
piloting to languish while she pursued her wizardly studies.

That there should be aught for so a powerful wizard to study at such length and depth astonished him, but there was no doubt that his recollection was correct.

And what might he bring, he thought, shaking himself free of recollection and finishing with his sleeves, to a lifemating with one of the dramliz? Shan seemed to believe that his sister had chosen him as her mate, but Ren Zel doubted that. She had not been expecting him—and she had not known his name. Therefore, some other agency was at work in the matter—the cat, perhaps; or its enormous ally, the Tree?

Well. Soon enough to ask these things when he might have actual speech with his lifemate. He only hoped that she would not repent the choice, no matter how it had been made.

He glanced at his reflection—brown hair, brown eyes, symmetrical, unexceptional face—and then at the clock. Time to make his way to the captain's office, to partake of prime with his . . . family.

THE HATCH CAME UP, silent and slow, revealing the lean length of the Juntavas courier. He nodded and stepped back, waving them inside.

"We're set to lift as soon as you're strapped in."

Val Con went first, Miri at his back, her song edged with wariness. The entry corridor was thin and short, blossoming into a piloting chamber of less than spacious proportion. The board was, unusually, tiered, screens set close in a semi-circle at what would be eye-level for a pilot of Terran height. A Liaden-sized pilot would need to do something about lifting the chair, or put painful strain on her neck muscles.

"Like I said, we're cozy here," Greenshaw Porter said, leading them to the far side of the chamber. A door slid away at his touch, revealing two acceleration couches, one over the other, webbing retracted.

"This is it—first class accommodations."

Val Con inclined his head. "We thank you."

"My job," the Juntava told him, with a shrug. "I'm to say: The High Judge is grateful for the info."

"May he make good use of it."

The man grinned at that—amused savagery. "No doubt there." He slapped the upper couch, and turned away. "Make yourselves comfortable. I'll let the Tower know we're gone."

A passenger. Val Con looked at the couches, trying to remember the last time he had been a *passenger* . . .

"Well," said Miri, from his shoulder. "Which do you want? Up or down?"

THE DOOR SLID open to his palm; he stepped over the threshold and caught up short, face to face with she who had been Korval-pernard'i—his sister, Nova.

It could not be said that she smiled, but at least she refrained from frowning, and inclined her head with calm cordiality.

"Pilot," she said—her usual greeting to him, but given now in the Low Tongue, in the mode between kin. "I hear I am to wish you happy."

"Pilot," he said, matching her mode with only a tiny flutter of panic. "I thank you for your good wishes."

A moment longer she stood, studying him, or so he thought, out of bland violet eyes. Almost, it seemed that she would speak again, but she lost the opportunity in the arrival of her—their—brother.

"There, now, that wasn't so bad, was it?" Shan asked brightly, though of whom he asked it was not entirely clear. "Sister, don't eat him! I swear he's better behaved than any of us here—including Priscilla—and will gain Korval entry to Houses long since closed to us by reason of our dreadful manners."

"I make no doubt," she murmured, and of a sudden *did* smile—faintly, but with real warmth. "I feel for you most strongly, new-brother—joined to a clan as outlaw as it is odd!" She glanced aside. "Shan, surely he wants some wine."

"Surely he does, as he's hardly a lackwit," their brother replied, and put a big hand on Ren Zel's shoulder, urging him gently toward the bar. "Come along, child, let us fortify you. Red? White? Brandy?"

"Red, if I may."

Shan extended a long arm and held the decanter high, apparently considering its all-but-full state.

"This seems sufficient to fill your glass, and mine, too. Though I fear we're out if Priscilla is drinking red."

"White, please," her deep voice said.

Ren Zel turned in time to see the door to the innermost chamber—the quarters she shared with her lifemate—slide shut behind her. She smiled.

"Good shift, brother. Have you resigned yourself to your fate?"

He felt his mouth curve into an answering smile. "As fates go, it appears . . . less tiresome than some," he told her. "I do look forward to a conversation with my lady. There are those things that we must settle between us."

There was a sound to the right, as if Nova had sneezed, but Priscilla merely nodded gravely.

"You may then rejoice in the news that our sister brings us," Shan said, putting a glass of the red in his hand. "We are returning to Liad, immediately!"

"Do not allow Shan to persuade you that you will be with your lady *immediately*," Nova cautioned, stepping forward. "The delm's word is that we are to raise Liad, yes. But there we will hang in orbit until he releases us to the planet."

"Weeks, months, years!" Shan intoned, with mock dismay, handing Priscilla her glass.

"Very likely," his sister said gravely, though Ren Zel thought he saw the glimmer of her faint smile.

"Well, in that case, we do what we can to strengthen our spirits. I see a feast has been laid for us, and the only thing that keeps us from enjoying it is Gordy." Shan raised his glass, silver eyes quizzical over the rim. "Or, shall I say, lack of Gordy?"

Priscilla smiled. "He'll be here—soon."

The request for entry chime sounded.

"Or even at once," Shan said and called, "Come!"

The door slid away to admit Gordy Arbuthnot, foster-son of Shan and Priscilla, as well as Shan's true-cousin, on the Terran side.

"Cousin Nova." He bowed, correctly, as between kin, and then walked straight up to Ren Zel, face and eyes serious, shoulders, just a little, stiff.

"Hi, Ren Zel."

"Hello, Gordy," he said, gently, careful of the moods and manners of a halfling. It was not impossible, after all, that Gordy held his cousin Anthora in . . . esteem—and who was Ren Zel dea'Judan to call him a fool?

"Priscilla says you're lifemated—truly lifemated—to Anthora. Is that true?"

"Yes."

The young face relaxed into a smile. "That's great. I'm really glad." He bowed, jauntily. "Ge'shada, pilot. I wish you and yours a life of joy."

Ren Zel felt tears rise, hid them with his own bow. "My thanks."

"And now," said Shan, "we can eat."

THE MEAL was rather less boisterous than the informal reception, for Nova bore news of yet another kinsman. It seemed that Pat Rin yos'Phelium had not followed protocol in terms of reporting in. Nova was inclined to find this disturbing, and solicited the advice of kin. The conversation turning on where Cousin Pat Rin might most reasonably be supposed to have taken himself, and strategies for finding him, Ren Zel was left to listen, and watch, and grow acquainted with these who were now his family.

Listening, he reached for his glass—and froze as his ears became filled with a roaring, not unlike wind, and a voice edged with panic rang inside his skull.

"Ren Zel! I need you!"

There was a moment of heart-numbing cold, and a sensation not unlike passing through a bank of particularly tenacious fog. Ren Zel shook his head, banishing the mist, and discovered himself kneeling on an icy metal floor. Beside him was Anthora, on hands and knees above a char mark.

"Ren Zel?" she whispered.

"Here." He stood—say, he tried to stand, but the ceiling was too low to allow him to do so in comfort; he must need round his

738 Sharon Lee & Steve Miller

shoulders and duck his head. Uncomfortably bent, he looked around him, taking in the hard silver walls, seeing the bright lines of fire bent and twisted back upon themselves, warped and pale, excepting only the conflagration that streamed from the kneeling woman down into the cold floor, for all the worlds like blood rushing from a wound.

"Anthora!" He dared to use the mode of Command. "You must stand."

"Yes." Clumsily, she gained her feet, to stand bent as he was, her hair draggled and limp around a face that was shockingly pale.

"What place is this?" he demanded, moving to her side, crabwise, and slipping an arm around her waist.

"I don't know. I—it is drinking me. The walls—they reflect any ripple of power back, at double—quadruple!—strength. I dare not force the door . . ." She made a breathless sound he scarcely recognized as a laugh. "If I could." She swallowed and pushed her head against his hunched shoulder. She was trembling. He raised a hand and stroked her cold hair.

"Then we open it another way. There must be a control box . . ." He frowned at the featureless walls, the bitter floor, but all was—

"There!"

Anthora stirred, lifted her head a fraction and shook her hair away from her eyes. "Where?"

"Below the decking, there, do you see?" He released her and hunkered down, studying the various relays and switches in the box below the floor. He felt her hand on his shoulder as she lowered herself beside him, peering.

"Yes, I see it," she breathed. "But, beloved, it's on the other side of the floor."

"Hmm," he said, tracing wires with his eyes. "I believe . . ." He pointed. "Do you see that connection? If that were bent aside, the door would open and we could walk away."

"Ren Zel, I cannot reach those elements, and neither can you." Her voice caught. "We're going to die."

"No." He spun on a heel, nearly bowling her over. "We are *not* going to die. Believe it and you do their work for them!"

For one heartbeat—two—she stared at him, eyes wide. Then, she extended a hand to touch his cheek. "I see. Forgive me, denubia. I'll not be so fainthearted again." Her eyes dropped and there was the control box, plainly visible to Ren Zel, and through him, to her. The connection he had pointed out was a fragile thing; why, a cat might bend it aside . . .

"Yes!" Ren Zel whispered. He bent forward and she lost contact. The floor solidified; her inner vision fogged. She grabbed his shoulder.

There, beneath the floor plate, the connection. Hooked around the connection were four pearlescent claws adorning a large and rather furry white foot. The foot pulled, down and sideways. The connection bent, twisted—broke.

Across the tiny silvered room, the door slid open.

Anthora half-rose, staggered, vision whiting, and felt strong arms around her waist, sweeping her off her feet . . .

"RUN!" REN ZEL SHOUTED, his voice already shredded by distance.

She tucked, and hit the floor of the antechamber rolling. She heard a shout; felt hands on her shoulders and wrenched out of the guard's grip, slamming into the legs of a chair, the hidden pistol falling into her hand. The guard lunged, trying to grab her; trying to throw her back into the box.

She fell sideways, and fired point-blank into his face.

The room was quiet; bird song wafting in the open window. Anthora lay on the floor, her back against the chair legs, retching, unable to escape the sight of the guard's head exploding, though her eyes were closed.

Something furry slapped her cheek. She opened her eyes to slits and encountered a familiar furry face very close to her own.

"Merlin." Clumsily, she disentangled herself from the chair and clawed her way to her feet. The door leading to the Council Chamber had an ancient mechanical lock on it, which she snapped into place, singing the praises of whichever god or goddess held soundproofing among their honors.

Door locked, she leaned her back against it, feeling Merlin

pressed against her leg. A pleasant breeze informed the room, spiced with the scent of the tripina tree shading the open window. After the draining silver horror of the box, she felt entirely safe and secure here.

And that, she told herself sternly, *is illusion. Look to reality, dramliza!*

Unwillingly she moved from the door; forced herself to approach her former cell, and look within. Empty. That was good. Ren Zel had indeed escaped to safety.

Which she should do—and that quickly. For surely whoever had set the trap would return to remove it. She attempted a scan; wincing as the din from the Chamber slammed into her abused senses.

"We must leave," she whispered. "Merlin . . ."

But the cat was already moving, purposefully, away from the door to the Council Chambers and the misshapen black box, its door gaping open on horror. Anthora turned her face away and followed, averting her eyes as she edged past the body of the guard.

Merlin set a brutal pace through the service corridors. She was soaked with sweat and shaking badly by the time they gained the door that opened to the outside. At that, the luck had held; they'd met no one else on their escape route.

The luck changed when they hit the sidewalk.

"Wait!" She heard a man's voice shout, quite close at hand. "That's her!"

Anthora ran, the sound of pursuit too close behind; caught a glimpse of gray to her right and slightly ahead.

Dodging respectable pedestrians, she turned a corner, and heard the roar of a familiar motor.

"Jeeves!"

The car accelerated, door rising.

"There she is!" came the shout from behind. Involuntarily, Anthora glanced over her shoulder, saw her two pursuers round the corner, saw the guns in their hands—and the streak of gray, which was Merlin, launching himself, claws extended into the face of the lead gunman.

Roaring, Jeeves arrived, Anthora threw herself into the open hatchway. "Merlin! Come quickly!"

The cat leapt—not for the safe haven, but for the second gunman. He hit the man's shoulder, claws sunk deep.

"Merlin!" Anthora screamed, acceleration pressing her into the seat. The door began to drop. "No! Jeeves, we cannot leave Merlin!"

Implacably, the door fell, locked; the car surged forward, braked, back end swinging 'round and they were hurtling forward into the everyday traffic of a Solcintran afternoon, considerably exceeding the public safety speed, leaving her pursuers, and a large gray cat, behind.

Anthora began to cry.

"RUN!" HE SHOUTED. "The door is open!"

Gasping, he fell, his shoulder slamming against the hard floor, his vision a chaos of images, overlain by fiery threads. He concentrated, saw her hit the floor rolling, as a pilot would, gun in hand as she fired and—and lost that image entirely, replaced by a bright-lit room and the unmistakable taste of ship's air. An arm came 'round his shoulders, easing him up; a squeeze bottle was forced into his hand.

"Drink," said Priscilla Mendoza. "Electrolytes."

He managed to get the bottle to his lips, squeezed a healthy mouthful and swallowed with a shudder. He felt the vile stuff hit his stomach, mixing uneasily with dinner and terror.

"Easy." Priscilla's hand was firm and sisterly on his shoulder; squinting through the haze of golden lines, he made out Nova standing above him; purple eyes holding an emotion he identified as astonishment.

"Drink again," Priscilla told him. "Then food."

"And at some point, when you feel it proper," said Nova, "you will tell us what just happened to you."

"Nova, let be," Shan said sternly, from beyond Ren Zel's vision.

"Let be? Did he or did he not sit there—frozen and scarcely breathing—for the best part of half-an-hour? Does he have these fits often? I wonder what will go forth, should he have one at the board."

"Nova . . ." A clear warning note, there.

Ren Zel finished the stuff in the squeeze bottle, concentrated and set it carefully on the floor. He looked up into Priscilla's face, squinting a little to bring her into focus among all the pulsating golden threads . . .

"Better?" she asked.

"There is a device," he said, "that eats dramliz."

Her face hardened. "There have been several such, throughout history."

"This one is new," he told her. "It—they caught Anthora."

"What?" Nova drew nearer. "Anthora is at Jelaza Kazone. Not even she would be so shattered-brained as to—"

"Wait." He held up a hand, agitated. "Wait, I . . ." He closed his eyes, and memory flowed.

"The Council—Korval is called to answer—to answer for kinstealing, for murder—and dea'Gauss—dea'Gauss is missing, and he has hidden the dies. They asked her to wait in a Clerk's room and the trap—the trap was there."

"In a room off the Council Chamber?" That was Shan again, his voice as serious as Ren Zel had ever heard it. "Sister, if the Council itself is hunting us, I doubt the delm's wisdom in returning to Liad."

"We must," Nova said, but she hardly sounded certain. "At least to orbit—but Anthora is a prisoner!"

"No, she's not," Priscilla said coolly. "The door was open—you heard him say so."

"The door opened," he agreed. "But I could not stay with her. I do not know . . ." It came to him that he might use those glowing lines of power to his own ends. He might, in fact, go back to her, stand at her side and work with her to the destruction of their enemies. He—

"Gently, friend," Shan said, dropping into his range of vision in a veritable burst of gold. "You have done much this hour. Eat first." He held out a sandwich. Ren Zel took it, suddenly ravenous, despite the food he had already eaten, and wolfed it in three bites. A second sandwich appeared and he accorded it the same treatment, then drained the glass of tea that came after.

He sighed. "I am glad," he murmured, "to find the gridwork so strong here. Inside the box, one could hardly see the threads, and those that could be seen were pale and fragmented."

There was a pause.

"You of course," Nova said to Priscilla—or possibly to Shan, "know what he is talking about."

"Not . . . entirely." Priscilla cleared her throat. "Ren Zel, what threads are these?"

He blinked up at her, seeing the lines so crowded about her that she fairly shone.

"Why, the lines," he said, somewhat baffled, for surely *she* could see them, dramliza that she was? "The lines that tie everything together."

"Oh," she said softly. "Those lines." She exchanged a glance with her lifemate.

"Can you see these . . . lines?" demanded Nova.

"No," Priscilla said, still soft. "No, I can't. But I have it on the authority of those who can that they do indeed exist and perform exactly the function Ren Zel describes."

"The only difficulty," he said, in an effort to be as clear as possible, and not in any way to complain, "is that they are so plentiful and vibrant here that it is difficult to see beyond them to—to everyday things. I fear that I might put my teacup down on a line and have it smash against the floor . . ."

"Now that," said Shan, "I can help with." He leaned forward and held up a broad brown finger. "Focus on my finger, if you please—no, *not* that way—use your outer eyes! Look as nearly as you like, but only at my finger."

After a brief struggle, he was able to manage it—and felt something click, as if a relay had snapped into place. The lines of power vanished from his awareness and the totality of the captain's office snapped into being.

He sighed, as did Nova yos'Galan.

"Dramliza?" she said.

"There was never any doubt," Shan said, rising and reaching a hand down to Ren Zel. "Up you go, Pilot."

✳ ✳ ✳

THE CAR FISHTAILED 'round a corner, and fled down an alleyway at a speed that was far from considerate of human sensibilities— even when the human in question was a pilot.

Anthora had long since stopped crying, and now sat, tense, her hands fisted on her lap. Four times had Jeeves struck out for Jelaza Kazone. Four times, they had been blocked, and nearly surrounded, hounded back into the city.

"Go to the port," she said quietly.

"Ms. Anthora, you are Korval's presence on Liad." The robot's voice was shockingly calm as the car careered madly down an alleyway, and swung into another, more narrow, speed, if anything, increasing.

"If you leave Liad, Korval's claim to its material goods and properties is forfeit."

"Go to the port," she repeated. "*I* abandon nothing."

There was a pause—short for her, long for Jeeves—then a respectful. "Yes, I see. The port."

Even traveling at speed and with stealth, they arrived at Binjali's barely ahead of their pursuers.

Anthora had dared one call, and Master Trilla was expecting them. The gate began to open as they came into the approach, and closed after them with a clang. Jeeves gunned the motor, fair flying down the yard to the singleship on its hotpad and the woman in working leathers standing by.

The door rose, and Anthora leaned forward.

"Go," she told the robot. "Leave the car."

"Yes," said Jeeves.

The control panel went dark as the car rolled to a serene stop. Anthora stepped out onto the tarmac and inclined her head.

"Master Trilla."

"Anthora," Binjali's owner said, in her outworld accent. "Ship's ready when you are."

"Thank you," she said. "Be warned. They are directly behind us."

Trilla grinned, feral. "We've some surprises, never fear it. Go on, now. Good lift."

"Safe landing," Anthora returned properly, and entered the ship.

The ship rose swiftly, breaking a dozen regs in the first six seconds of flight. Grimly, Anthora flew on, ignoring the outraged demands of the Tower, flying by hand, so there was nothing to spill and be captured by Korval's enemy.

Up, up, very nearly straight up, then a sharp roll, and down, as swiftly as she dared, not quite a scout descent, not quite—but swift enough, as the luck willed it.

In her screens was the Tree, rapidly growing to enormity. The house screens were active, a blue crackle along the edge of her inner vision. She keyed the short sequence in, sent along the pirate band.

The blue crackle died, the ship fell through and she slammed on the retros, fighting gravity now—and winning, as the singleship touched nicely down in the center Jelaza Kazone's formal public gardens.

IT HAD BEEN a grand and busy several days of transit; so busy that Hazenthull Explorer had been able to immerse herself in the various learnings of language and custom—and forget for long hours together that the senior was dead. And why.

But it came at last that Commander Angela-call-me-Liz Lizardi, to whom the troop had been detached for this portion of the venture, had ordered them to ready themselves for departure. Reluctantly, Hazenthull folded away her studies, found Diglon Rifle in the rec hall listening, with four tens other of the merc common troop, to the turtle Sheather tell of his campaign against the Juntavas upon the world called Shaltren.

Returned to the quarters they kept in common, Diglon set about an efficient and orderly weapons check. Hazenthull undertook the same, and likewise made a review of the plan as they had been allowed to know it.

It was a simple enough plan, on its surface, but Hazenthull believed that a man who had engineered the theft of three Yxtrang fighter craft from the very fields of the Fourteenth, envisioned a more complex undertaking than she, in her youth and ignorance, could apprehend. Still, it would be a welcome thing to close with an enemy—and the scout's plan, simple or complex, promised action.

Weapons checked and plan reviewed, Hazenthull hesitated on the edge of her next duty—but it was a duty, and one she had shirked, for reasons she did not care to study too closely.

Squaring her shoulders, she walked across the room, to where Nelirikk Explorer, Hero and aide to Captain Miri Robertson, sworn to the descendants of Jela's blood, sat over a piece of fancy work.

He looked up as she came forward, his eyes blue and non-committal, as befit a Hero. Hazenthull hesitated—which was her weakness—steeled herself and spoke in the explorer's dialect.

"You asked a question, before, and I gave you no answer. We are on the edge of action and I may find glory upon the morrow. I would tell you, now, between ourselves, why explorers marched with the common troop."

He used his chin to point at the chair opposite him. "Sit and speak."

Sit she did. Speak—that was more difficult.

She mustered discipline, aimed her eyes forward and just over Nelirikk Explorer's right shoulder.

"We—Gernchik Explorer and Hazenthull Explorer—were assigned to march with the common troop in a disciplinary action following Hazenthull Explorer's field report in which Major Shevnir Quartermaster was named as keeping slack discipline, which had lost for us several interesting and irreplaceable specimens. Gernchik—would have written a different report. I believed that an explorer's duty outranked a major's pride."

She stopped, then finished it, though the section of wall she had been staring at was starting to blur.

"The senior died because I am a fool, and not worthy—never worthy—of his teaching."

Silence followed this, which was oddly comforting, though she would not have hesitated if Nelirikk had ordered her to draw her sidearm and shoot herself through the ear.

"Your answer is heard," he said, which was the old, familiar explorer's acknowledgment. "Now that your senior has gone to glory's reward, it comes to you, as his junior, to perform your duty as he would have performed it. It is no light charge, for Gernchik was an explorer of the first rank."

Hazenthull blinked. "He was that," she said hoarsely.

"Go now," Nelirikk Explorer told her. "There is an hour for rest before Commander Lizardi calls us."

She did not feel like resting, but Gernchik would not have argued the point. Hazenthull stood, saluted and went over to her bunk, where she stretched out beside her weapons and her pack, and closed her eyes to think.

"YOU LEFT HIM!" Anthora shouted.

On days other than this one, her emotion was such that teacups would have trembled against their saucers and wine glasses chimed their cheeks against each other. It was not entirely impossible that a stool might have become spontaneously airborne.

Today was a day like no other. Anthora stood in the middle of Jelaza Kazone's back kitchen, dirty and draggled; tears of anguish and of fury cutting rivulets of cleanliness down her grimy cheeks, and was reduced to stamping a foot for emphasis.

"You left Merlin among our enemies and I ordered you to stop!"

Jeeves' head-ball flickered soft orange lightnings; his wheels rumbled against the floor as he rolled over to put a kettle on for tea.

"Miss Anthora, you are aware that I have priorities. The highest of those is the protection of the human lives of Clan Korval. I must insure your safety at any cost, no matter how high."

Anthora scrubbed at her face, widening the muddy streaks. "But you and Merlin are—friends."

"Old friends," Jeeves agreed. "Merlin was among the first to make me welcome when I came to be yos'Galan's butler." There was a pause, the flickerings in his head-ball increased in rapidity—and all at once ceased.

"Perhaps it will ease you to learn," the robot said slowly, "that Merlin has undertaken a task in coordination with Jelaza Kazone. In essence it is a guerilla action, which carry a high factor of risk. But Merlin is old and skillful. I have confidence that he will succeed in taking the war to the enemy."

Anthora closed her eyes. "You say that Merlin goes ahead, to pinpoint our enemy's location so that more . . . concerted action may be brought against them."

"That is the core of our strategy, yes."

"We have no army to call upon, Jeeves. Only yourself, and me— and the Tree."

"Well," said Jeeves, lifting the kettle from its ring and pouring tea into a tall, workmanlike mug, "that's a start—and you must not discount your lifemate, who seems, if you will allow me to say so, a wizard to reckon with."

She blinked, and fell suddenly still, the way of Ren Zel's walking through hyperspace suddenly and most shockingly clear.

"Yes," she said, softly. "He is a wizard to reckon with. And so, of course, is the Tree."

ALONE IN HIS CABIN, Ren Zel staggered and grabbed the wall.

It came again—a cool, green rippling across his vision, longer this time, deeper, almost displacing the reality of the walls around him. He closed his eyes, and the green resolved into an image of the vast Tree in Korval's garden, seen as if he were looking up into the branches from below.

Good evening, elder, he heard her voice in his mind's ear. *I wish to undertake a journey.*

"Anthora," he whispered, and had the sense that she heard him—though it was impossible that she could, with the *Passage* in hyperspace and her standing in the free air of her garden. "Anthora, what are you doing?"

Beloved. Jeeves tells me that Merlin has been sent ahead into the heart of our enemy's territory, to act as our scout and our trojan. I go to his side, to rescue our servant, and to confound our enemy.

"Our enemy? Who is—" Memory rose and spilled over, flooding him for a moment or a lifetime, and when he at last shook his head free and gasped a deep lungful of air, he knew everything that she knew of the Department of the Interior, of Merlin's probable whereabouts—and dea'Gauss', too.

Yes, he heard her in his mind's ear, *now*.

"No!" Ren Zel yelled, waking echoes from the metal walls, but he was too late.

The image of the garden and the Tree faded, leaving only gray.

CLUTCH HOMEWORLD

AELLIANA WALKED the circumference of the ship in company with Handler as Daav searched his memories of Diary and scout lore and went over, again, and again, what they had said to the Elders. She admired the home star on the horizon and calculated orbits and probabilities, considered the carefully placed moons, and considered, too, the new crystal knife worn at their hip . . . .

"Go," the voice had come up from the depths of that strange room buried six thousand paces deep in the hillside. The room's shape was such that whispers could be heard, one end to the other, and half-a-dozen flickering flames enough to give each of the dozens of Elders substance as they . . . sat . . . motionless the while. How long that while had been . . . was difficult to fathom.

They had asked. They had asked of clan, they had asked of the nature of lifemates, they had asked of the Tree, and of Jela, and of the Tree and Jela, from the Diaries, about Daav's suppositions regarding Jela, about Val Con and Miri, about the Tree, about the seed pods and, once again, the Tree and how it shared—and then they asked about Aelliana and Daav.

Finally, they had asked about seed pod distributions and the known locations of the children of the Tree . . .

And then, they had said, "Go. Thank you for the gift of your time, Elders of Korval. Go."

"Daav, one comes—"

It was Edger, moving quickly.

"Aelli and Daav, you must come with me, " he said. "The Elders have decided."

DAY 53

※ ※

Standard Year 1393
Surebleak

IT WAS LATE. His household, saving the night guards, slumbered about him. He had risen from his own bed some hours ago, taking great care not to awaken his lady. Now, he sat behind his desk, Silk the cat a coiled, heavy warmth against his belly, writing in the log book.

He had long since given over trying to reproduce the original Diaries—his memory was too desperately incomplete. Rather, he had summarized what he knew of the crisis which had brought Korval-pernard'i to invoke Plan B, related his encounter with the agents of the Department of the Interior; and then meticulously noted down the minutia of Boss Conrad's days, taking great care to show how these actions had bearing upon the finality of the clan's Balance. He was disciplined, and wrote every day, so the book was fully caught up to event.

Indeed, it was somewhat in advance of event, as he had already written of the departure of four mining ships and a pleasure yacht for the homeworld, there to exact Balance from the enemy.

He had recorded the names of the pilots who were sworn to fly in this mad venture: Master Pilot Cheever McFarland, First Class Pilot Bhupendra Darteshek, First Class Pilot Andrew Mack, First Class Pilot Dostie Welsin, First Class Pilot Jonni Conrad. He also listed the names of their ships: *Diamond Duty*, *Timonium Core*, *Crystalia*, *Survey Nine*, *Fortune's Reward*. He had paused a moment, then, listening to the cat purring sleepily on his lap, and meditating over the list of stalwarts.

Pilot Darteshek had been a surprise enlistee; Pat Rin had expected him to return to the Juntavas, now that he had delivered his package and satisfied his curiosity. But, no. He had stayed behind while Vilma Karparov returned to their employer, and Pat Rin's inquiry into the matter had won him the pilot's thin smile— and nothing else.

He had no doubt it was Natesa who had arranged for the courier pilot's presence among what Cheever McFarland had dubbed, with no apparent irony, the "strike team." He had not found it necessary to ask. If it comforted her to know that there would be a Juntavas pilot by him during the upcoming affair, then surely it was no more than simple kindness to accept both her talisman and her hope.

For himself, he saw . . . some hope. That his hand had been forced and his timing thrown askew—well, what choice had he? The Department of the Interior had located him easily. He did not do them the disservice of believing that they would hesitate for an instant to hold Surebleak at hostage. He preferred to go to them on his own terms, using what advantage might come from consternation.

He closed his eyes, going over his arrangements once more.

"Pat Rin?"

He opened his eyes and turned his head, finding her, a shadow in the shadowed doorway.

"Inas," he said, feeling Silk shift against him in protest. "You should be asleep."

"And you should not?" She came forward, shadow taking substance, the flame-stitched gauze robe blazing as she crossed into the light. "*I* do not lift in six hours. Indeed, should it suit me, I may sleep the day away."

"Indeed you might," he said cordially. "And did you say that you would do so, I should certainly put off my lift in order to observe this miracle for myself."

She laughed, low and musical; and leaned against the desk at his side. The gaudy robe illuminated her dark beauty, and flowed tantalizingly along her slender shape. The sash was done but loosely at her waist, and her dainty feet were bare.

"You will freeze," he told her, but she shook her head lightly.

"Not if you come back to bed and warm me."

He raised an eyebrow. "Underdealt, my lady."

"Do you think so? I merely wish to bid you a proper farewell. How am I in error?"

It was the word 'farewell' that caught his ear and sent his glance to the log book, sitting open in its pool of light, pen ready to hand beside it.

"No error at all," he said slowly, and lifted his eyes to hers. "Inas . . ."

She returned his gaze calmly. "Yes, beloved. What has gone amiss?"

"Amiss . . ." He looked away, and bent forward to lay his hand on the book. The movement disturbed Silk, who leapt to the floor with a sleepy protest.

"This becomes yours—as my—as my lifemate and—my heir. If I do not return . . ." He shook his head. "In the back of the book, I have written . . . somewhat . . . of our kin. If any should come here, calling for aid, they must be cared for . . ."

She placed her hand over his on the book. "As your lifemate—and your heir—I will honor the book and study it. I will write in it every day, as you do, for the instruction of those to come. And in the meanwhile, should any of our kin find their way here, I will care for them as best I am able, until your return."

Pat Rin cleared his throat. "The dice may fall with whimsy," he softly. "I may not return."

"That is not acceptable," she replied, and lifted her hand from his, sliding her fingers caressingly under his chin and turning his face up to hers.

"You will return," she said. "Swear it."

Tears filled his eyes. He blinked them away and smiled for her.

"You hold my heart," he said. "If I am able, I will return to you. I swear it."

She smiled then, knowingly. "Liaden," she murmured, and kissed him, not at all gently.

DAY 54

❀ ❀

Standard Year 1393
Solcintra
Liad

THE DISTRESS SIGNAL blasted through the Tower, bringing the technical crew scrambling back from its tea-break, slapping up emergency screens, pulling in satellite feeds—and swearing, softly, and in several different languages.

"*Kynak-on-the-Rocks*, we have you located," the traffic controller murmured, her hands busy across her keyboard. "State the nature of the problem, and whether you are able to assume orbit."

"Shit no, we can't assume orbit!" Irascible Terran erupted out of the speakers. "We're holed, damn you! Nothing other than plain and fancy piracy. I call upon the Department of the Interior to Balance the damage it has deliberately dealt to Mercenary Unit Higdon's Howlers. I want a representative of that Department to meet me when we land—and we *are* landing, Tower! Give us an approach!"

There was a hurried consultation between the scan tech and the assistant Port Master on Duty—

"We've got leakage," he muttered, upping the magnification of his scans so the rest of the crew could see it.

"We've got a ship approaching Port on a dangerous course, claiming damage and an oxygen emergency," the traffic controller snarled, fingers flying over her board. "They're coming in, no matter what. I'm giving them to Mid-Port general yard. Comm-tech, call the proctors and get a squad over there! Who knows what this Department of the Interior is? Call them, too!" She subsided into silence then, excepting the occasional mutter featuring mercenary ships landing in Solcintra Mid-Port and that had better be two squads of proctors . . .

The comm-tech swung 'round to her board, alerted the proctors; then accessed the planetary directory. Department of the Interior was not listed. The tech bit her lip, and shot a query to the incoming Terran.

"How the bloody hell do *I* know how to get hold of them?" the same hugely annoyed voice snarled. "All I know is that they claim to be in charge of Liad and that they've holed my ship, damn their eyes, and they *will* pay for it—and pay handsome well!"

Proper enough, thought the comm-tech, if the Department—whatever it was—had damaged the Terran's ship, as he seemed certain. And the Department claimed to be "in charge" of Liad? The comm-tech was Liaden, and knew of only one entity that could remotely be supposed to be "in charge" of Liad.

She punched in the code for the Speaker of the Council of Clans.

"THE DEPARTMENT of the Interior is not represented by this Council," Speaker for Council told the port comm-tech testily.

"Request assistance in locating this Department, Speaker," the tech sent back, one eye on her screen, where the Terran transport was growing larger and more dismaying by the moment. "Incoming ship cites a matter of Balance with the Department of the Interior. I allow it to be Terran, ma'am, but the captain further informs us that the Department of the Interior is 'in charge' of Liad."

"That is absurd," Speaker stated. "Its wits are wandering."

"Yes ma'am, possibly so. However, it is crying Balance. Someone must answer, else they may sit here for as long as they like, using port resources and paying nothing, contingent upon receiving an answer."

There was a pause, long enough for the comm-tech to reconsider the wisdom of teaching law to Speaker for Council.

"Very well," Speaker said. "Please convey to the captain of the Terran vessel the compliments of the Council and inform him that, in order to pursue his claim of Balance we must know the name of an individual representing the Department of the Interior."

"Yes, Speaker," said the comm-tech, with no small amount of relief. "I will pass that message."

"They want a name, do they?" the Terran demanded of the comm-tech. "Fine, here's a name you can give them: Bar Vad yo'Tornier. He calls himself Commander of Agents."

SOLCINTRA
Liad

❋❋❋❋❋❋❋❋❋❋❋❋❋❋❋❋❋❋❋❋❋❋❋❋

THE PRISONER WAS NOT YOUNG. He was not Scout-trained. He was—no longer—armed. He inspired neither fear nor the premonition that he was both a danger and a threat to the organization—and to the completion of the Plan.

In fact, the prisoner was old. He sat quietly in the tiny holding cell, the dim blue light casting strange shadows along his face. From time to time, he spoke—numbers, most often. Sums. Account identifiers. Dates. Followed by such elucidations as, "account confiscated," "permissions rescinded," "account inactive." There were few surprises, there.

Prompted, he made other statements, not entirely understood by his auditors: "Phase Two begins when the fourth roll-call is missed."

"Phase Three begins when the fifth roll-call is missed."

"The Exchange declares a trading holiday when the sixth roll-call is missed."

Commander of Agents allowed himself a sigh. This was the second set of drugs. Neither it nor the first had elicited information regarding Korval's effective and surprising defense of the planet

Surebleak. The prisoner was likewise ignorant of the locations of Korval's hidey-holes and safeplaces; and resistive of the suggestion that Surebleak might be such a place.

The Commander moved a hand, calling for the third and most potent drug.

The technician hesitated.

The Commander turned his head to look at her.

"Forgive me," she bowed as one to the ultimate authority. "It merely occurs to me, Commander—if this man does indeed hold information vital to our success . . . He is an old man, in good general health, but lately subjected to several severe systemic shocks. There is the possibility of an overload, should we introduce the next drug before this dose has run the system."

"Understood."

The Commander considered the prisoner. Did he hold information vital to the Plan? Surely, he did. And, just as surely, he would be made to give that information into the Department's keeping. The third drug—the third drug was ruthless. Possibly, it should have been administered at once, despite the unfortunate side-effects. The Commander had reasoned that the lesser drugs would leave the prisoner largely intact, and that there might well be need for him sooner than an . . . amended . . . personality could be stabilized.

The need for the information he held was greater than any nebulous future usefulness. After all, it was not unusual for old men to die.

He felt a vibration run up his right arm and glanced down at his wrist-comm; noting at once the "most urgent" tag, and the request that he return to his office.

"Call me before you administer the next drug," he told the tech, and moved toward the door.

"GR17-67. GR17-68," the prisoner said, tonelessly. "Drawing rights invalidated."

The Commander checked, dismayed—for, here, at last, was information, plain, unambiguous—and crippling. If the prisoner was to be believed, the Department had lost access to two of its most lucrative funding sources.

"Check that!" he snapped at the agent standing silently at the prisoner's back.

"Commander."

"GR 24-89," the prisoner said. "Drawing rights invalidated."

The Commander turned and stared at him, seeing an old man slumped in a chair, the dim blue light accentuating the weary lines of his face, eyes unfocussed and dull.

"Check that," he directed the agent, and let himself out of the holding cell.

The loss of funding source GR 24-89 would be . . . catastrophic. The Commander held himself to a walk, allowing no taint of turmoil to touch his face. It would have to be checked. It would all have to be checked. Possibly the prisoner had lied—but when had the dea'Gauss ever lied?

FUNNY, how familiar it was: The gravity, the taste of the air, the smell of the grass, the green-tinged sky, the warmth of the sunlight against her hair—all of it said, "Welcome home."

Of course, this wasn't her home—not even close. The feeling of welcoming familiarity came straight from Val Con, just like the "memory" of the path she was walking to Jelaza Kazone, and the access codes tingling in the tips of her fingers.

She paused on the top of the last hill sloping down into Dragon's Valley, and turned to look back. Squinting, she could make out the Tower at Solcintra Port, stretching tall and black into the greenish sky. Val Con'd be well out of the port by now, she reckoned, resisting the impulse to find out for sure.

Don't jog the man's elbow, Robertson, she told herself severely, and turned to look out over the valley.

There was the Tree, dark green, dark brown, and way too high, its branches tangling with clouds . . .

Welcome.

It was the same sense of warm green joy that had overwhelmed her in her dream—only days ago? She smiled, more wry than not, and nodded toward its mile-high form.

"Jelaza Kazone," she said. "The safest place in the galaxy."

Right.

She brought her sights down, and got her first look at the clan seat, Jelaza Kazone, the house. Distance and the looming Tree worked to make the building seem small—a scale model, maybe, or a toy. She knew better. She could've recited the number of rooms, drawn a map of the public halls—and the private ones—and a map of the inner garden, too.

All from Val Con's knowledge of the place.

"I grew up at Trealla Fantrol," he told her, softly, from memory, "but I was born to be Korval. Uncle Er Thom had been fostered at Jelaza Kazone. He made certain that I knew it as well as he did."

Miri sighed.

Standin' here, gawkin' like a tourist, she scolded herself. *Get a move on, Captain; you got work to do.*

Not to mention explaining herself to Val Con's sister Anthora. She took a breath, feeling Korval's Ring move between her breasts. The last thing Val Con had done was put the Ring on the cord from his shirt, and knot the cord 'round her neck—that, and kiss her—before he went his way and she went hers.

She understood the reasoning—he was going inside enemy lines—against her best, most vehement, objections. If he was taken—her blood started freezing up, just to think it—or if he was killed, the Ring would be free, and she would be Korval Herself.

Next target, please, she thought wryly, remembering Daav and Aelliana, likely tied up for months on the Clutch homeworld, like a trump held hidden in a sleeve. If everything bad went down, there were two more yos'Phelium pilots in reserve, to tend for what was left of the clan. Or carry Balance to its fullest.

She wondered if they'd figured out yet that they'd been had.

Get moving, Robertson.

She took one step down the hill, toward the house of the clan—and dropped flat.

The grass was high here, though not high enough to hide her from a determined look-see. Fortunately, the guy she'd spotted had his back to her; his attention on the house. The movement she'd caught had been him taking a pair of field glasses off his belt.

He put the glasses up and got still again. Real still. Scout still. *Agent* still.

Miri nestled her chin on her arm, watching him watch. Eventually, there was another flash as he snapped the glasses back onto their hook, then a smooth rustle of movement, as he came up into a crouch, and eased down the hill, toward the house.

Her house, currently occupied by a young woman acknowledged to be, by those who loved her best, more than a little featherbrained, an old war 'bot—and some cats.

Oh, and, yeah—the Tree.

Down the hill, the grass shivered as if a light wind had combed through it—the Agent, moving closer to the house.

Knowing it was stupid, Miri rose into a crouch and went after him.

HIS SECOND bowed, and waited until he was seated.

"News from the port, Commander," he murmured and touched the appropriate button.

" . . . a name, do they?" An uncouth Terran voice snarled out of the speaker. "Fine, here's a name you can give them: Bar Vad yo'Tornier. He calls himself Commander of Agents."

The Commander folded his hands deliberately atop his desk, closed his eyes and indulged himself in a breathing exercise. When he opened his eyes again, a cup of his favorite blend sat, steaming, at his right hand, and his second was gone. A prudent man, his second.

Commander of Agents sipped his tea.

Bar Vad yo'Tornier. His name. His personal name, that he had taken care to hide and hide well, in the filthy mouth of a Terran—

A Terran what?

One-handed, he reached to the console, touched a series of keys and listened, impassive, from time to time sipping his tea, to the tale of the holed ship, the conversations between Solcintra Port and the Council, and once more to his name, shouted along the open bands by a heedless, idiot barbarian who—

Had no reason to know—or means to discover—such a thing.

Commander of Agents put aside the teacup, and brought his screen live. His second had, of course, compiled the necessary information, which the Commander read once, rapidly; then again, more slowly.

There was no doubt that the ship, Mercenary Transport *Kynak-on-the-Rocks*, wholly owned by Higdon's Howlers, Inc., displayed signs of damage on both the orbital scans and the schematic. That it was actually *holed*—well, perhaps it was, or perhaps it was not, and the portion of Solcintra Port was clear. The mercenaries had been cleared to land.

In the interests of thoroughness, Commander of Agents opened the file on the Surebleak incident. He had not expected *Kynak-on-the-Rocks* to match the specs for Surebleak's defenders, nor did it—still, it would have been tidy, and provided a link between Korval and this ship, this barbarian commander, who knew his name.

Mercenary Sergeant Miri Robertson . . .

The Commander blinked at the thought.

Could it be so simple? Val Con yos'Phelium—the Commander could believe that former Agent of Change yos'Phelium might ferret out even the most deeply buried secret, as nothing more than an exercise to pass a slow hour.

Both subtle and ambitious, Val Con yos'Phelium. And given to flights of unadulterated madness, before the training provided by the Department had normalized him.

yos'Phelium's last known location was Lytaxin, where mercenary units in the employ of Erob had recently turned back an Yxtrang invasion.

Methodical, Commander of Agents checked the lists of units known to have been on Lytaxin—and very nearly smiled.

Higdon's Howlers, commanded by one Octavius Higdon, had been on Lytaxin, one of several units hired by Erob to quell the war which the Department had nurtured.

The Commander's smile faded. Simple enough to suppose that Val Con yos'Phelium had hired Higdon's Howlers in turn, providing them with a drama, a name, and a port of call. Simple enough . . .

And yet yos'Phelium was not a simple man, nor was he a fool. He would suppose that the Department would access just this information—and draw just this conclusion.

Commander of Agents flipped through the files open on his screen, glancing at the profiles of the odd vessels that had defended Surebleak. A positive identification of those vessels had not yet been made, though the tactical report on *Fortune's Reward* was thorough. To find a Korval fleet there, obviously in the midst of maneuvers— and now, here, this other ship, carrying mercenaries and cleared to land, crying Balance owed by the Department of the Interior, invoking his own personal name . . .

Commander of Agents felt a sudden light chill crawl down his arms.

Val Con yos'Phelium was on Liad. And he meant the Department to know it.

SHE'D LOST the trail a dozen times, found it again in a bent stem, the outline of a boot-print in a patch of soft soil, a solitary scattering of unripened grass seeds.

On some level, she was aware that she, Miri Robertson, had never been trained to track like this, moving like a wisp among the high, rustling grass, in deadly pursuit of deadly prey.

The prey stopped some distance ahead. Miri crouched, consulted her—Val Con's—mental map of the territory, and sighed.

She was very near one of the perimeter access points—in fact, the gate she'd been making for herself before she took it into her head to stalk wild waterfowl.

Miri bit her lip. The perimeter was guarded and coded. The gate wouldn't open for a bogus code, though it would deliver a shock, progressively nastier, if anybody was stupid enough to keep trying in the hope of hitting the winning combination. Any attempt to force the gate—also won a shock. The beam was nice and wide, too, which made jumping the fence an equally bad idea.

Which fortifications and failsafes were all so much fairy dust, if the man she'd been tracking had good access codes—like Pat Rin's, for instance.

Miri swallowed around a cold surge of horror that felt more like Val Con's than hers, and made her decision.

Silently, she eased forward, pistol in hand, though she needn't have worried, her prey—sighted barely one hundred paces from her previous position—was completely intent on a project of his own.

She watched while he worked with a remote unit, apparently keying in pass-code after pass-code, with no success—and without receiving a tangible token of the gate's esteem, either. He'd managed to sync the remote to the gate's keypad, and was apparently committed to tapping in codes til the heat death of the universe.

Or the gate opened.

Miri closed her eyes briefly, ridiculously elated, as if the lack of access codes was an excuse for a party.

Can it, she snarled at herself. *His not having the codes don't prove Pat Rin's at liberty the same way his having them would prove the opposite. Loobelli.*

She opened her eyes, bringing the gun up, easing the safety off. She could hardly miss at this range; especially when she wasn't trying nothing fancy, only a simple kill.

She squeezed the trigger, the *snick* of the pellet simultaneous with the larger click of the gate opening.

Miri came up in a rush, running forward. The guy was down and he wasn't moving. She dropped to one knee beside him, confirming that her aim had been good, and reached for the fallen remote.

"Drop your gun and surrender!" a voice snarled.

Miri jerked around, saw the woman, the business-like set of her pistol. Behind her, she heard a click. The gate closing, that would be.

"Drop the gun," the woman repeated. "Or lose a hand."

"Wouldn't want that," Miri said, softly, feeling the weight of the weapon in her hand. She shifted into a crouch. The woman's finger tightened on the trigger of her gun.

Miri spun sideways, throwing her gun, punched a button on the remote, her finger guided by blind, stupid luck.

The gunwoman grunted, her shot in the air, and Miri was up and through the gate, running low; there was a shout, a second shot, and the sound of the gate going home.

Miri staggered, feet tangling; stumbled and went down, rolling. She fetched up against something hard and gritty, and lay there, heart pounding.

Her right arm was on fire—she'd probably caught the second pellet. A quick inventory discovered nothing else worse than bruises. She opened her eyes.

The hard, gritty thing was a goodish-sized rock. She used it to pull herself, swearing, to her feet, and looked around.

The good news was that she was now well inside Korval's perimeter. The bad news—that there was at least one enemy, probably more—and more remote lock-picks, too—around the perimeter, doing their all to get it. And the arm—that was bad; she didn't need the evidence of the blood-dyed sleeve to know she'd already lost too much.

Not in much shape to go hiking around the countryside, Robertson, she thought, snapping open her pouch and pulling out the first aid tape—and quietly crumbled to the ground.

HERE AT LAST was the place.

Val Con breathed a quiet sigh of relief. The distance from the rendezvous site had been somewhat longer than he had estimated— long enough that he had begun to doubt his memory. But, here it was, at last: overgrown, tumble-down, and, gods willing, forgotten . . .

He held up a hand, halting the rest of the small troop, and turned to catch Liz Lizardi's eye.

"We part company here, Commander."

"Here?" She glanced around at the vine covered walls, scrub trees and broken blocks of stone.

"Here," he repeated, suppressing a smile. Miri's fostermother was not a woman to spend three words where a gesture would serve. "Have you questions regarding the part of yourself and your troops?"

"Nope, sounds like a paid vacation to me," Liz said. "Bout a klick to the north, we'll find us a park and a street and a door. We guard the door. Anybody tries to go in, we stop them. Anybody tries to go out, we stop them, too." She shrugged. "Higdon sending backup— that a go?"

"Yes."

"Then we're set." She looked over her shoulder at her troop of two. "OK, let's take a walk."

"Commander." Diglon Rifle saluted with alacrity, his demeanor closely resembling that of a child given run of a sweet shop.

Hazenthull Explorer's salute was more sedate, her face properly devoid of expression, but Val Con could not help noticing the alert set of her shoulders. Nor did he miss the glance she sent to Nelirikk before following her commander down the path to the north—quite a speaking glance it was, too, for all it fell upon a face as giving as stone.

Ah, youth. Perhaps after . . .

If there was an after, which was by no means assured. Val Con closed his eyes briefly, thinking of Miri, going overland to Korval's Valley—to *home*—where she would be safe—or at least safer. This— it was mad, what he proposed to do. Capture the Commander in his own warren? Stop the unfolding of the Plan with a word? Rescue the passengers—oh, aye, just that. And who remembered the old contract—never canceled, never bought out, that tied Korval to Liad—and to honor—down the long years from Cantra to himself?

They have murdered us—us and ours. It ends, and ends now. No more of mine will be shot down in the streets.

"Scout?"

Val Con blinked and looked up into the stern brown face of Nelirikk Explorer.

"A quick nap," he said lightly. "Pay it no mind."

"A soldier fights best when he has rested well before battle," the big man agreed.

"Just so." He looked over to the third of their party, standing a little apart, gazing about himself with—perhaps it was wonder—the tile work of his shell showing pale ripples of purple in the shadowed light.

"Brother."

Sheather turned, his big eyes inward-lit.

"Brother," he said courteously. "Is the time of our departure upon us?"

Val Con walked forward, showing open palms. "Certainly, the time draws near. Forgive me that I come to you once more and say—it is not necessary that you accompany us after you have assisted in the opening of the door. Stay and watch, if you will. Return to the ship, by my preference. But, to come within—it is more than my heart can bear, brother, that you might be slain in the course of a hasty and ill-considered human quarrel."

"Your feelings do you great honor," Sheather said solemnly. "Certainly, kin wish to do all within their scope to preserve kin from harm. Just as certainly, we are bound to the word of the T'carais, who has bid me accompany you upon this vendetta, in which you will fully answer those who have slain others of your kin and keeping. This is your duty, as you have told us, and it is a duty the Clutch know as well. The T'carais sends me to his brother, the Deim of Korval, to fight, and to prevail."

He blinked, one eye after the other.

"The T'carais has done me the honor of adding to my name. As time is short, I will refrain from speaking it to you in fullness. However, I will tell you that my name now includes a phrase roughly equivalent to 'student of men'." He blinked again, both eyes in tandem.

"I am the first of our clan to undertake this scholarship. I began because my heart would know certain things. I continue because my T'carais would know in fullness—and my heart is not adverse."

Val Con bowed, deeply and with sincere respect. "Scholarship is a heady and dangerous undertaking," he murmured. "And of course the T'carais may not be gainsaid."

Which was true enough, he thought—no word of his would prevent Sheather from following, if the word of the T'carais sent him on.

He straightened.

"Attend me, then, brother, if you will. Explorer, guard us—and monitor the broadband. Our signal should find us soon."

THE ANCIENT and weary locking mechanism scarcely resisted Sheather's song: a note, another—and the thing was done. And done not a moment too soon.

"Scout," Nelirikk said quietly, "the signal arrives." He paused, head cocked, listening to the tiny comm-link behind his ear.

"Third repeat."

Val Con swallowed, thinking of Miri, safe at home.

Go on then, he told himself. *The time is come.*

Dutiful Passage was in orbit.

MIRI WOKE with no memory of having fallen asleep, and blinked lazily up at the orange cat sitting on her chest, solemn green eyes fixed on her face as if it sat sentry to her awakening.

"Hey, cat," she said.

The animal blinked its eyes, and a voice spoke from across the room—a male voice, talking up-scale Terran.

"Good afternoon, Korval," he said, over a sound like wheels across planking. "Are you feeling well?"

She turned her head on the pillow, but there wasn't anybody there, unless he was hiding behind the heavy-looking metal cylinder, fully equipped with three articulated arms, topped by a lighted orange globe, which was itself weirdly familiar, in a not-her-own-memory kind of way.

"Jeeves?" she asked, but it had to be it—him.

"Yes," he said, the orange ball flickering slightly.

"Great." She pushed herself up, forgetting the cat, which jumped sideways off her chest to the floor, venting a small, peevish hiss. "Plug into the perimeter's brains, there's people trying to get inside the valley."

The ball flickered—*he's thinking*, Miri caught from Val Con's memories, and swung her legs over the side of the cot she'd been laying on, unsurprised to find that it was part of a field doc.

"The interlopers have been dispatched, ma'am," the robot said. "Though I expect there will be more. Perimeter protections have been intensified.

"I must apologize for allowing you to be wounded. My attention was engaged by concerted assaults at the south and east gates. The lesser attempt at the north gate was hidden beneath the noise. I sent transport immediately I had your direction from Jelaza Kazone, and brought you in to the 'doc."

She moved her right arm, experimentally. It hurt like hell.

"Again, I apologize if I misunderstood your necessities. Extrapolating from Plan B, however, I merely initiated a quick-heal."

"You did exactly right," Miri told him, standing up. "I'm Miri Robertson, by the way."

"I had surmised as much," Jeeves replied. "How shall I address you?"

"Miri's fine," she said, wincing as her first step jogged the half-healed arm. "Look, I need the control room, quicktime. There's stuff I gotta be doing, especially if I shot the timing by being an hour in the 'doc."

"You were in the 'doc for no longer than a quarter hour," the war 'bot told her calmly. "You must try not to strain your wound." He rolled forward, wheels rumbling over the floorboards.

"Follow me, please, and I will take you to the control room."

"Right," she said, stretching her legs to keep up with the pace he set down the hallway. "Tell Anthora I'm here, and where she can find me, OK? I'll need her to fill me in on what's been going on here."

"Miss Anthora," said Jeeves, "is not to home."

"Not home?" She looked at him, but the orange ball gave her no clues. "Where is she?"

"I believe," he said, as they took a sharp turn into a narrow hallway, "she is at the headquarters of the Department of the Interior."

THEY HAD FOUND out soon enough what the more cryptic of dea'Gauss' drugged mouthings had referred to. As payment accounts were shut down, so too were the services and supplies they purchased.

Commander of Agents sat in an office lit by emergency dims, and glared at his screen. Behind him, the radio mumbled along on back-up power, whispering the names and the business of ships.

The power problems had been resolved. For the moment. The facility was running—as could be told by the noise of the intermittent fans attempting to move sluggish air about, at considerably less than half-efficiency—on its own emergency generation system. This situation would change for the better once the prisoner was under control and functioning on behalf of the Department.

But the man would have to survive.

The prisoner's health was—not good. The third drug, rather than inducing the desired state of submissive obedience, had elicited a strong allergic reaction. On advice of the drug-tech, he had been removed to the infirmary, where he remained stable, but feeble, guarded by a full Agent of Change.

Perusing the roster in his dim-lit office, the Commander reconsidered that assignment: Agents were in short supply. Surely a lesser operative might be set to guard one ill old man?

But no. dea'Gauss had deprived the Department of three Agents, each dispatched with a precise shot to the head. Records belatedly obtained from Tey Dor's demonstrated that dea'Gauss had been a regular at the club for fifty years; that he maintained several weapons and match-pistols, list appended; that he often shot with other of Tey Dor's patrons, list appended. Indeed, Tey Dor's records held all that one would wish, save the man's marksman rating. They also failed to note—though this was scarcely an area where Tey Dor's could be expected to concern itself—that the old man in question had worn clothing made of anti-pulse and anti-pellet materials; and that he had turned his office into a fortress.

No, the Commander decided; the dea'Gauss had won the honor of having an Agent at his bedside.

Which left the diminished roster and the rather longer number of tasks to be done.

A team of Agents had been sent to the Council of Clans, with orders to arm the devices in place. Likewise at the Council of Clans, the Protocol Officer, long ago subverted by the Department, consulted with the Speaker on the precise placing of Balance against Anthora yos'Galan, who had casually and brutally murdered an unarmed Council Proctor.

A second team of Agents, augmented by Departmental sharp-shooters, was en route to Low Port, explosives and coordinates to hand. Another full team of Agents was attempting to invest Korval's valley, while others undertook the infiltration of Higdon's Howlers.

The Commander blinked, bringing the screen before him into focus. Shipping stats. There were no Tree-and-Dragon ships currently orbiting Liad, which was odd. Scout ships were likewise in short supply—though that was less odd. One would expect Val Con yos'Phelium to have ships in support, whatever his plans. The absence of ships was . . . unnerving.

As yos'Phelium no doubt intended.

Commander of Agents extended a hand, calling up the list of secondary operatives. Surely, some use might be made—

"*Dutiful Passage,*" the radio blared so loudly the Commander missed his key.

"*Dutiful Passage*, Solcintra, Liad, Captain Priscilla Mendoza. Stand clear. Stand clear! We are on business of Korval and we are armed."

SILENCE WAS AS IMPORTANT as haste, and haste they made: Scout, explorer and Clutch turtle. The pipe easily accommodated the larger members of the party, though boots and claws alike some-times failed to find purchase on the water-smoothed surface.

Sheather, with his dark-seeing eyes, led the way, Val Con following, carrying a mini-torch to aid his poorer eyesight. Nelirikk brought up the rear, burdened with explosives, extra firearms and ammunition.

The *Passage* was in orbit, Val Con reminded himself. Soon, it would be joined by allies. Soon, they would know whether this bold strike at the heart of the enemy was lunacy or genius.

Speed-marching, they had covered distance, passing three gates at roughly equal intervals. When the aqueduct had been in use, the gates had functioned as flow control devices. They rested at each for five short minutes, then resumed the march.

"Ahead lies another gate, my brother," Sheather said in a remarkably quiet voice. "It appears to be both new and locked."

Val Con sighed. So quickly. He closed his eyes, allowing her song to fill his head, his heart, his soul. Deliberately, he extended his will, and sang a new phrase into the song. Then, he opened his eyes and stepped forward.

The warrens the Department had taken for their own had been carved out of sub-surface limestone to create tremendous storage bays for low-pressure gasses. Portions of the original waterworks were marked out as points of historic interest, somewhere overhead. But down here, far beneath the planet surface, the aqueducts had also fed underground pressurizing reservoirs in off-peak moments. Eventually abandoned as Solcintra's needs grew beyond the water offered by the River Kainbek, and as the necessity for a safer location for storing volatile energy than beneath the city itself became understood, the underground maze was a natural place to house a secret headquarters.

This door, now. This was the airlock; the interface between the old pipes and the new facility. Val Con inspected the controls, understanding them with a sense of relief twined irrevocably with terror.

"I had intended to use my blade here," he said to Sheather, "and on the other side, speed. That is still an option. But I ask, is there a note or two known to you, which will unlock the way for us with less danger?"

Sheather blinked his enormous eyes. "My brother is wise, to prefer a stealthy entrance to the cave of his enemy. I believe the key to this door may be discovered, if I am allowed a moment of study."

"Certainly," Val Con said, and fell back to Nelirikk's side. The explorer looked down at him with a grin and gave him a very Terran thumb's up.

LIT BY EMERGENCY dims, only the most essential of machinery online, the infirmary was a place of shadows, enemies and storybook monsters on the lurk for the fanciful.

Agent ter'Fendil was neither fanciful nor inclined to simile. He kept guard over the old man, as ordered, equally alert for signs of treachery or waking. Neither manifested, as the weary hours crept along—nor did the old man die, and release Agent ter'Fendil to duties more worthy of him.

That there were such duties, Agent ter'Fendil knew, having been present when the full team was called to attend to the future needs of the Council hall. He had awaited his own orders with anticipation, for surely the Commander would not fail to recall those treasures which Agent ter'Fendil, extrapolating from studies he had made as a scout, had recovered and delivered to the Department. He dared hope that the Commander would place the controls in his hand, allowing him the honor of deploying those treasures against the enemies of the Department.

Yet, here he stood, on guard at the bedside of an accountant, while he might be—no. The Commander was not one to forget past service; nor to fail of using what weapons came to his hand. That he was assigned this minor duty, now, did not mean he was forgotten.

The Department taught that all duties furthered the Plan, and Agent ter'Fendil had been well taught. Yet—

A shadow moved among the shadows, and vanished, into shadow.

Agent ter'Fendil frowned.

The shadows flickered again, fluid and quick.

Agent ter'Fendil blinked, and ran a quick diagnostic. Finding that he was slightly, though not by any means dangerously, low on energy, he accessed the Loop's energizing routine, feeling an immediate sharpening of his senses.

Straightening, he deliberately turned his gaze to the place he had last seen the shadows waver.

Something . . . moved.

Agent ter'Fendil walked forward.

The shadow solidified, taking shape as it strolled across a dim strip of illumination, gray tail held high and jaunty, white feet soundless on the noise-absorbing floor.

"Cat!" said Agent ter'Fendil, in disbelief.

The cat turned its head, blinked and continued on its way.

The Loop indicated that a cat in headquarters was an anomaly.

Agent ter'Fendil went after it.

❊ ❊ ❊

MIRI HIT the chair in the control center a little too hard, swore, and opened the board with a sweep of her good hand.

"Get me some painkillers," she said over her shoulder to the war 'bot. "And some stim."

"I regret," Jeeves said, his high-class voice sounding apologetic. "Stim is known to cause fetal damage."

The screens were up, she fumbled, then found the general shipping band.

"What's that got to do with me?" she asked, her mind more than half occupied with locating the other, more tricksy band. This one, even Val Con was hazy on . . .

"The 'doc reports that you are pregnant," Jeeves said.

In the midst of making an adjustment, Miri froze, before spinning the chair around to face the 'bot.

"That's the craziest—" she began, and then clamped her mouth shut.

Oh, Robertson, you prize fool.

Because it wasn't crazy, was it? Not with her fresh outta the 'doc, and him, too, both returned to normal baseline functioning— read 'fertile'—and neither one of them remembering to ask for the shot.

Miri, let us make love . . . He murmured in memory, and if she found out he'd known—that he'd *planned* . . .

She'd kill him.

Uh-huh. First he's gotta get home alive.

She spun back to the control board, adjusting the volume on the ship band, which had been plenty loud enough, and had another go at the local band.

This time, her fingers were smarter—or the three-times-damned Korval luck was in it. Whichever, her inquiry elicited an answer.

"Binjali's," said a woman's matter-of-fact voice.

Miri took a breath. "This is the Captain," she said, in the mode of Ultimate Authority. "Situation Red."

❊ ❊ ❊

"*DUTIFUL PASSAGE,* seal your weapons." Solcintra Tower said—which it had to say, as Shan knew well. Had he been portmaster, faced with a sudden battleship in orbit around his peaceful and orderly world, he would have said precisely the same thing, most likely with a good deal more heat.

Priscilla touched the reply stud. "This is Captain Mendoza. We are on business of Clan Korval. Our weapons are live and under our control."

"That is in violation of regulations, Captain Mendoza. The guild has been notified."

Priscilla's mouth tightened. "Copy," she said, voice steady, and closed the connection.

"Never fear, Priscilla, there remains one license between us. And the Code tells us that what one lifemate owns, the other owns as well."

She looked at him, black eyes betraying her amusement. "Tell it to the Pilots Guild."

Shan snapped his fingers with a grin. "*That* for the Pilots Guild! We'll get you a Terran license under an assumed name, and no one will be the wiser."

"Now, why don't I think that will work?"

"Because you are an innocent and pure of heart." He turned back to his screens. "The portmaster will satisfy herself with the complaint to the guild," he murmured, pulling in the traffic reports. "She can fire on us, of course, but we've done nothing to merit that."

"Yet," Priscilla said, with a glance to Ren Zel, quiet and efficient at third board.

"Any sign of our friends, pilot?"

"Not as yet, captain," he answered, "but we are ahead of schedule."

"By three entire minutes," Shan said. "Trust a scout to—"

"Jump-flare," Ren Zel said sharply. "Close in."

His fingers moved, and Shan's did, too, locating the flare and the coords—*close*, gods. Which meant it must be the expected scouts, though there was no reason—

The comm crackled as the flares died and the ships announced themselves, one, two, three, four: *Diamond Duty, Timonium Core, Crystalia, Survey Nine*. Tree-and-Dragon, Tree-and-Dragon. Tree-and-Dragon, Tree-and-Dragon.

"What the devil?" He isolated the four of them, Jumped as a unit, had they? Master pilots, then—or, yet, it could be scouts, though in such strange, unscout-like vessels . . .

"Jump-flare!" Ren Zel cried again—and so it was: a fifth ship Jumping into the hollow square formed by the first four, a maneuver so chancy that Shan half-averted his face from the expected collision.

But no. The comm crackled, and a fifth ID rang across the general band.

Fortune's Reward, Solcintra, Liad. Tree-and-Dragon.
Tree-and-Dragon.

THE TRANSFER was complete. The last light on the status board was lit.

Miri wiped a sleeve across her damp forehead, leaned forward in the chair, bum arm braced against the board; and pushed the button that connected to her to receivers located at the Council of Clans; Scout Headquarters; each of the major halls: accountants, pilots, trade, and Healer; the offices of Solcintra and Chonselta portmasters; the editorial offices of The Gazette; the general shipping band; and a number of strategically placed public speakers.

We cover the world, she thought, as the master light went to green. *You're on, Robertson. Don't forget your lines.*

NORMAL SPACE. The screens reformed. The comm came live.

On the private band: "Boss is here, let's party!" "Well flown." "Make a master outta you yet, son!" "Good work, Boss."

He'd done it.

Pat Rin sagged back into the pilot's chair, shivering with relief.

He'd done it.

Now, to do the rest.

THE VOICE that came out of the old, forgotten receiver was female. Her accent was Solcintran and her message, thought

Speaker for Council, raising her head and staring, entirely absurd.

" . . . Captain's Emergency. I say again: This is a Captain's Emergency. In accordance with the conditions put forward in paragraph 8, section 1 of the original contract of hire between the Houses of Solcintra and Captain Cantra yos'Phelium, which requires the captain, her heirs, or assigns to safeguard the welfare of the passengers, I, Miri Robertson Tiazan, Delm Korval, declare a Captain's Emergency. The Council of Clans will hold itself subservient to Captain's Law. Control of the planetary defense net rests with the Captain.

"Passengers are advised that the name of our enemy is the Department of the Interior. They have stolen and murdered members of every clan, High House and Low. They have subverted the cash flow of entire clans. They have pressed ships and pilots into service, to the detriment of Liad. They will be stopped. Now. Locations of known Departmental offices and safeplaces follows.

"Repeat, repeat: This is a Captain's Emergency."

IT WAS THE CUSTOM of Kilon pel'Meret to visit the old Waterway Park with her small son every day before Prime. This exercise gave double benefit, refreshing Kilon and allowing young Nev Art room to run off excess energy in a manner not likely to earn him a sharp rebuke from his grandmother.

The pattern of the walk was well known to both mother and child. Kilon would stroll along the old path from the park's entryway down to the silted-in pond, while Nev Art might run circles about her, or dart off in all directions at once, saving only that he did not disappear entirely from her sight. He would rejoin her at the pond and they would then both walk back along the path to the entrance, practicing seemliness; thence down the city sidewalks to home, and grandmother, and Prime.

Today, Nev Art darted up and grabbed her hand. "Thawla, look! Yxtrang!"

Kilon was a sensible woman. She was also familiar with her son's imaginative prowess. So, she did not scream, or gather him up in her arms and run. Rather, she allowed herself to be tugged 'round by the hand, fully expecting to see a tree wearing an uniform of shadow, or a stealthy weed peering over a crumbling section of ornamental stonework.

"Look!" Nev Art said again; and look Kilon did, breath caught in her throat.

For across the rumpled grass toward them came three tall persons—two much taller than the third—dressed in what was indisputably military style, packs on their backs and their belts hung about with all manner of objects.

"Yxtrang, Thawla," Nev Art insisted, pulling on her hand. "I want to see their guns!"

"No!" she said sharply, and tightened her hold on his hand. "They are only Terrans, my son." She hesitated. Terran soldiers, here, strolling through an abandoned and all-but-forgotten park in the Low House district of Solcintra? Abruptly, she turned, dragging Nev Art with her.

"Come along, child, it is time to go home."

"It's not!" he protested, but she was adamant.

Walking briskly, holding her son firmly by the hand, she went down the path. He stretched his short legs until he was all but running, and so they gained the entrance—and, a moment later, the street.

"GO AFTER THEM, Commander?" Diglon asked hopefully.

Liz shook her head. "No. It ain't like they're the only ones gonna see us." She pointed. "Let's go."

"BOSS?" Cheever McFarland's voice came low and easy across the tight band. "You ready to cook?"

Pat Rin took a deep breath, and another, deliberately calming.

"A moment, Mr. McFarland. I am afraid that I found the Jump in . . . exhilarating."

"Was close, wasn't it?" the Terran said, cheerfully. "Just think what we could do with practice."

Alone in his ship, Pat Rin smiled. "Next, you will have us touring as a precision flying unit."

"Something to that. We're out here if you need us, Boss. All lines open."

Pat Rin inclined his head. "Thank you, Mr. McFarland."

"Right." The line closed.

Another deep breath and Pat Rin leaned to the board, his finger on the switch . . .

The main screen flared, awash with Jump-flares—one! three! eight! one dozen! Two!—Pat Rin snapped back, eyes narrowed, the bands fizzing with static; and then the IDs hit, one after another, gathering intensity, until they blurred and became a single shout; a challenge:

Scout.

Tree-and-Dragon.

THE BEAST had vanished entirely.

Not a little disgruntled, Agent ter'Fendil returned to the accountant's bedside—and stared, heartbeat spiking, breath gasping— the Loop, barely submerged since his last check, kicked in, bringing both into normal range, but the bed—the bed remained empty; blankets rumpled, pillow showing an indentation.

dea'Gauss was gone.

THE OLD MAN was recovered.

REN ZEL SMILED AT HIS SCREEN, attention divided between the countdown in the lower corner and a wholly imaginary, but completely accurate, screen in his mind.

"Go home now, beloved," he sub-vocalized.

Soon, she answered. *We must wait for Merlin.*

THE SCOUT SHIPS had settled into their orbits, and if Tower had a sharp word or two to say to them, it was on a private band and not for the entertainment of common ships.

Steeling himself, Pat Rin extended a hand to the board. The bogus Ring flashed and flared in the cabin's light. He touched the comm switch.

"This is Pat Rin yos'Phelium, speaking for Korval and for the Captain. I call on the Council of Clans to witness formal Balancing with the Department of the Interior."

"SPEAKING FOR KORVAL?" Shan repeated blankly, but Priscilla had touched a key on the captain's board, releasing the recorded warn-away.

"*Dutiful Passage*, Solcintra, Liad, Captain Priscilla Mendoza. Stand clear. Stand clear! We are on business of Korval and we are armed." The touch of a second key sent the Tree-and-Dragon roaring across the general band.

Silence on all bands for a heartbeat . . . three.

"This is Scout Commander Clonak ter'Meulen. The Scouts call the Department of the Interior to answer for acts of murder and mayhem. We subordinate our claim to the Captain and Korval."

Silence on the bands . . .

"Have you all run mad?" Solcintra Tower demanded. "There is no Department of the Interior!"

"On the contrary," Pat Rin said. "I advise the Tower that I am transmitting a ship's recording of an incident of attempted piracy which took place in the sovereign space of the world Surebleak. You will note that the Department of the Interior claims to speak for Liad."

"Pirates, speaker-for-Korval," the Tower snapped. "Surely *you* know that pirates are not bound to speak the truth!"

Silence.

Aboard *Fortune's Reward*, Pat Rin laughed aloud, reached to the board—and froze.

Jump-flare distorted his screen. When the image was steady, there were six new ships in high orbit, their IDs stark and simple.

Juntavas.

Pat Rin bit his lip, remembering the courier who had departed at Natesa's word, leaving her partner to fly as part of this attack upon the homeworld.

In the screen, another flare, a sharp spike of static, and a ship's ID.

Implacable. High Judge. Juntavas.

The broad band crackled, fizzed, and produced a man's voice, speaking Liaden with a slight Terran accent.

"The Juntavas calls the Department of the Interior to answer for acts of murder and mayhem. We subordinate our claim to Tree-and-Dragon."

THE LINES WERE DRAWN, the orders given. Events were set in motion. There was the Plan and the end of the Plan—and the alternative plan, should, unthinkably, they fail.

Commander of Agents sat in his office, awaiting reports, and brooded upon Korval.

Perhaps it had been error, to allow them to continue so long. Perhaps they should have been weeded out quickly, at the very beginning of the Work.

For look at what Korval had cost . . .

First, the Scouts, backed by a ship piloted by a long-missing and presumed dead Korval elder, resist the Department's first open action on its way to fulfilling the Plan. Nor did the Scouts retreat to Liad, but withdrew entirely from the system . . . .

Next, on what should have been little more than a routine pick-up of the dismissible yos'Phelium ne'er-do-well, Departmental ships were lost in the discovery of a capable and disciplined fleet of war vessels flying the Tree-and-Dragon in Surebleak nearspace—a fleet led by none other than the supposed ne'er-do-well in a surprisingly well-armed pleasure yacht.

Then, as if unconnected, comes a ship full of mercenaries to Liad itself, claiming damage at the hands of the Department. Yet, in its many actions the Department had never dealt with the ship or its mercenaries.

In short order came a Korval battleship, several dozen openly Scout vessels—and who knew how many secret ones?—a Juntavas battleship and its escort—ah, and the Surebleak war fleet. All sitting in orbit, shouting Tree-and-Dragon to the universe, while here on the homeworld itself one Miri Robertson Tiazan publicly denounced the Department and described the location of several minor bases of operation, raising the citizenry to arms.

What more?

The Commander need not look at the charts that covered the desk. He need not look at the screens.

For, as difficult as they had been—as costly—Korval had in its actions against the Department revealed a weakness. There was a discernible pattern in their actions.

On Lytaxin, according to the intercepted mercenary reports, Val Con yos'Phelium had waited until action was in place and swept in with aircraft, sowing confusion and winning the battle and the war at once—all the while hiding behind the smoke-screen of his so-called Surebleak mercenary.

At Scout Headquarters, the same pattern—from nowhere came a ship to turn the tide of battle.

At Surebleak—a building of forces and then action by Pat Rin yos'Phelium. . . .

An emergency buzzer went off, startlingly loud. He touched the comm button.

"Commander—Agent ter'Fendil. I report that the accountant is gone. There is a cat inside the facility. My error is that I pursued, but lost it. Upon my return to my post, I found the accountant gone."

Commander of Agents stared. A cat, inside the facility? Impossible. dea'Gauss, in his weakened and doubtless disoriented state, gone? Preposterous.

And yet . . .

Commander of Agents stood, automatically checking the position of his weapons.

"I will lead the search myself. Meet me in the infirmary lobby. Be wary—we may be facing a rogue Agent of Change."

"Yes, Commander," Agent ter'Fendil said.

The Commander cut the connection, walked across his office and put his hand against the plate set into the wall.

The scan crackled across his palm. He reached into the safe and removed a short, squat rod, which he slipped into his sleeve.

KILON pel'MERET held tightly to Nev Art, her heart hammering with fear. Her son labored under no such affliction. *He* was enjoying one of the great days of his life. Not only had he spotted the soldiers walking in the park, but now came this parade of taxicabs, each stopping at the end of the placid dead-end street to allow even more soldiers to disembark. That these *were* soldiers was not in dispute; Kilon had no trouble identifying guns, missile launchers, backpacks.

Nev Art crowed as they dashed out of the cabs, forming into lines and units with bewildering speed as each cab roared away, to be replaced by another, and another, and . . .

"Excuse me, ma'am."

Kilon jumped back, staring up into the face of the sudden soldier. A Terran, dark-skinned and sober, carrying a rifle in her own streets, speaking to her in Trade. Why, she hardly ever—

"Ma'am?" he said again. "Please. We're holding a taxi for you and the boy."

"See, Thawla, I bet they're going after the Yxtrang I saw," Nev Art cried. And then, to the soldier, "Are you? Are you an admiral?"

"No." The man smiled as he answered, a slow smile. "I never do want to be an admiral, boy." He looked at Kilon, and pointed to the right, where indeed there was a taxicab, pulled slightly to one side of the street.

"I insist, ma'am. Please take the taxi. There's likely to be trouble and—"

"Ten'shun!" A large voice bellowed from lines of soldiers. "Group One, double time, move out!"

Kilon looked about wildly. "Trouble? Trouble? Soldiers in the street is trouble!"

The soldiers did something—one moment they had been still as rocks; the next, one group was spread out and hurrying toward the park, while another group broke away, trotting down the street toward the office complex.

Their own soldier waved at one of his comrades, and said to Kilon, "There's a good chance we'll be using weapons ma'am. I'm sorry. You've got to leave!"

"I saw the Yxtrang!" Nev Art announced, tugging so hard against her hand that she almost lost him. "I want to talk to them!"

The second soldier had waved the taxi close, and opened the door.

"You've got good eyes, youngster, if you saw the 'trang," the first soldier said. "Just remember what they looked like, and get into the cab."

Behind them someone yelled, "Group Three, weapons check!" followed by a loud series of clicks and slaps, and, "Arm your weapons!"

Kilon flung back, found her arm caught, not ungently, by the dark-faced soldier. "Calm down . . ." he began, and was interrupted by the arrival of yet another man, much lighter of face.

He bowed, recognizably the bow of a ranking public servant to person of unknown melant'i, and said in curiously accented Liaden, "I am Commander Higdon. This way, please, civilians must clear the area. I would not want to have to detain you."

He offered her a card, and automatically she took it, and was somehow gently pushed into the taxi, the while her son was proclaiming, "Yxtrang and soldiers, can't we stay?"

The dark soldier handed the driver a twelfth-cantra piece.

"Take them wherever they want to go that's more than five minutes from here. If there's any change from that give it to the kid."

"Look!" Nev Art shouted in her ear. "*Big* guns, Thawla!"

The cab accelerated into a turn, flinging Kilon sideways in the back seat, so she never did see what her son was pointing at. She righted herself, glancing down at the card she still held in her hand, as the cab slewed 'round a corner.

Higdon's Howlers, the Trade words stated. *Military missions. Security to mayhem. Guaranteed service.*

THE DEPARTMENT had long planned for this day. There was an undercurrent of expectation in the control room as the master switch was unshielded; the communications web checked; the technicians readied.

Before them the situation screen was clear; several orbiting stations would soon be under the direct control of the Department, and the destroyer *Heart of Solcintra*, long disguised as a freighter undergoing retrofitting, was already rising to orbit.

In the control room, they awaited the Commander's word. When it came, the flip of the master switch would shunt control of the planetary defense web from Solcintra port to the Department's control room, the power flowing from the selfsame uninterruptible source which supplied the portmaster's office.

The call came; the switch was activated. The screens came live; satellites and warning systems revealed their locations, weapon status, the locations of potential targets . . .

On the control board, an emergency light was blinking—not unexpected with so many ships coming in. An auxiliary monitor displayed the message *Captain's Emergency* in the lower left corner.

In the main screens, the stations, the destroyer, the satellites, the ships—

The master technician swore and leaned to her board.

Not a single Korval ship showed on the screens. *Dutiful Passage* was not there. Treacherous *Fortune's Reward* did not show. There was no range on Korval's four killer ships from Surebleak . . . .

But something *was* moving, near Station Three.

The master tech upped magnification, as the comm came alive with a shrill, "Danger! Danger! Hostile action on Station Three! Nine wounded, one dead . . ."

Ship ID came out: *Lifeboat A* off of *Jacksbucket Three*, Terraport. Somehow, it had escaped the Department's absorption of Station Three.

"Danger! Danger!" the Terran ship screamed, across all open bands, putting similar actions on the remainder of Liad's orbital stations at risk.

The merest touch of a dial and the proper blast-satellite was located. The master technician fed in the firing sequence.

Nothing happened.

The tech touched another switch, invoked a back up screen— Nothing.

"Check the lines," she snapped, to this aide. "Recycle the interface," to that one; and—"Rebooting . . ."

All for naught. The screen steadfastly refused to show any ship flying the Tree-and-Dragon. And the controls remained unresponsive.

Finally, an aide selected the flashing *Captain's Emergency* on the auxiliary monitor.

During a Captain's Emergency control of the planetary defense system is invested in the Captain or assigns. There will be a one minute warning when control is reassigned to the port office.

The master tech went to manual and ordered the nearest defensive device to use a pulse-beam against the fleeing escape pod.

Nothing happened.

"Alert *Heart of Solcintra*," she said to the comm-tech.

THE MOST POTENT dramliza on the planet stood at bay, cornered in a corridor leading to the sealed rooms. She held in her arms a rather large gray cat. Behind her, leaning against the stainless steel wall for support, was dea'Gauss, shivering.

Agent ter'Fendil had alerted what few fellow Agents remained at headquarters. They'd spread out from the infirmary, in a circular search-pattern, and had also triggered an automated rotating check of the internal sensors that had been turned off to conserve power—and which had ironically permitted the man responsible for the loss of power to escape. And quickly found him.

But not alone. It was obvious that the prisoner could not have risen from his bed without serious assistance from the woman holding the cat. It was equally obvious that, even with that assistance, his strength was fading, and would soon fail.

The woman was far more than the Commander had expected. Despite that she was dressed in the torn remnants of what had been formal Council attire, and that her face was dirty, she stood calm and alert before the not inconsiderable threat of three armed Agents.

She might well, the Commander thought, have a gun beneath the cat, or a bomb, or knife, or only her hands. The fact that she stood in this hallway at all meant that she was competent enough to make it past the outgoing attack teams without attracting notice. Worse, it meant that she had managed to avoid the carefully placed external sensors, and that she had slipped past guards on alert.

This was not someone to trifle with, despite her reported softness.

Without warning, the cat moved, flowing soundlessly out of the woman's arms—and fled away down the hall.

No one gave chase. They could take care of it later. The problem now was the woman, as she stood, catless, but holding a scout-issue pistol, pointed at the Commander's mid-section.

He inclined his head slightly in acknowledgment.

She said nothing; the gun remained steady.

"**DANGER! DANGER!** Hostile action on Station Three!"

Fortune's Reward located the source of the warning, and opened a window in the forward screen, showing Pat Rin an unarmed life pod, tumbling free of that same Station Three.

"Nine wounded, one dead! Hostile action on Station Three! Danger! Ho, the port!"

Tower came on-line, reciting coords for an emergency descent. Pat Rin watched the life pod move, clumsily, into compliance—and the glare of a beam weapon flashed across his screen.

"No!" he shouted, slapping up the magnification.

But, yes. The pod was gone, leaving a slight drift of debris along its descent path. Obligingly, *Fortune's Reward* redrew the detail window, tracing the path of the beam back to the originating vessel.

From the closed comm, Andy Mack's voice.

"I got a clear line to the bastid, Boss."

Pat Rin nodded. "Fire at will, Colonel."

VAL CON LED, now, Sheather and Nelirikk at his back. The lower service ways were empty, which was not surprising.

The Commander would surely have heard the *Passage* arrive in orbit, weapons hot and warn-away blaring. From it, he would have deduced Val Con's presence on-world. Being a bold man, he would have seen this circumstance as opportunity. If the Commander played well and audaciously now, the Department stood to win all: the extinction of Korval and the fruition of the Plan.

The goal was a man-high section of stainless steel access hatches built into the wall of a particular inner corridor. Behind those hatches were the cables, pipes, wires, and comm-fibers that connected and powered the facility and allowed the Commander to reach his hand out to the universe.

That the corridor in question was off one leading to the Commander's office was beside the point.

The hallway ahead was intersected by another. Val Con checked his inner map, and raised a hand. Behind him, Sheather and Nelirikk halted. Val Con proceeded at a crouch, hugging the wall, slipping his gun from its holster.

At the intersection of the hallways, he eased the safety off, and listened. He heard nothing but the hum of the air purification system, yet his hunch was that there was . . . something in the hall beyond.

Moving so slowly he scarcely seemed to be moving at all, he leaned forward, peering 'round the corner—

Directly into a pair of yellow eyes.

"Merlin?" Val Con breathed.

The yellow eyes blinked, happily, and Merlin burbled. Tail held high, he danced forward, stropped Val Con's leather-clad knee once, and strutted away importantly, pausing only once to look over his shoulder and be sure Val Con was paying attention. Since he was leading in the direction they needed to go, they followed, with Sheather drawing a long crystal blade as he hurried along.

THE LIFEBOAT was gone, vaporized.

Miri was bent over the schematic, swearing softly and continuously. She had an ID on the murderer—one *Heart of Solcintra*, claiming to be a freighter—but no clean shots. No shots at all, really, unless she wanted to go through a scout ship, a can carrier and a Juntavas courier to get her target, which did sorta seem a waste of allies and innocents.

A detail window blossomed in the corner of the situation screen—at least someone had a clear shot! The debris and gases of the lifepod lit in a lambent glow, and the destroyer itself was illuminated in a rush of scintillant brilliance. There was a flare then as the destroyer's shield went up and Miri could trace the beam to its source—one of the four monstrosities Jeeves assured her were nothing more exotic than asteroid miners.

There was sudden glare as the destroyer's shields were overwhelmed, and an odd coruscating flash as the mining beam oscillated the length and breadth of the target. The ship's hull expanded, peeled away, dissolved into a plasma of metal, evaporated before the beam, and then the seven decks could be seen clearly for a moment, as in some illustrator's cut-away of a slowly rotating warcraft. Multiple internal explosions speckled the obscuring mist and in one last flicker of the planet-killer ray—

Heart of Solcintra was gone.

"OF COURSE you realize," the Commander said, "that this cannot last long. We are several, you are one—and time sides with us. We merely need wait until your qe'andra collapses."

"Perhaps you overestimate your advantages," Anthora yos'Galan said, and her voice was soft and husky.

"Commander!" The aide's voice preceded her around the corner—she stopped, amazed at the tableau before her.

"Report!" the Commander ordered.

She bowed, hastily, one eye on the woman with the gun. "The planetary defense grid has been subverted by Korval."

Of course. Commander of Agents pointed at Agent of Change bin'Tabor.

"Give the command for the air units to attack Jelaza Kazone at low level. Detach a ground force to—"

"Give no command," said Anthora yos'Galan, her voice firm and gentle.

The Agent stood as if rooted.

"*I* command it," Commander of Agents snapped, and saw the man stir. "Bring in the air units and—"

"Be still," said Anthora yos'Galan; and the Agent froze.

"I see," said Commander of Agents, and raised his gun.

THERE WERE VOICES ahead, and a better lit corridor. Merlin strolled on, unconcerned. The rest of the invasion force shrank back into the plentiful shadows.

Came the hurried clatter of someone who was not an Agent in the halls. They remained in the shadows, despite a complaining burble from Merlin—and then moved, cautiously, on.

"Commander!" came the call from the hallway they approached; the answering voice sent a thrill down Val Con's spine.

"Report!"

The words grew indistinct and the invaders, weapons ready, ghosted quickly to the intersection. Val Con spied 'round the corner, and swallowed hard against a surge of sheer horror.

His sister Anthora, trapped by two Agents and the Commander himself, using her body to shield one who could only be Mr. dea'Gauss, but a dea'Gauss diminished and desperately ill. She held a gun, true enough, but so did her opponents. If all fired at once, even a dramliza—

The Commander raised his weapon. The Agents raised theirs. The aide gasped and bolted.

From the shadowed floor leapt a large gray cat, wrapping itself around the Commander's arm, pulling the gun down. A pellet whined by Val Con's ear as he jumped forward, his own gun out and up . . .

Training had prepared Agent ter'Fendil to face an opponent with a blade, a gun, or even a security dog. The apparition attacking the Commander bore no relationship to training—and he dared not fire again for fear of endangering the Commander. He reversed his gun, meaning to club the thing—

"Hold!" Anthora shouted, her voice a-glitter with power. "Do not move!"

Val Con kept moving, firing into the face of an Agent. Merlin snarled and dug his claws in the harder.

Everyone else in the hallway froze in place: ter'Fendil with his gun reversed, Sheather, his blade raised as if to behead him; Nelirikk, aim locked on the Commander.

The Commander struggled, as pain overrode the compulsion to stillness. But for Merlin's growls, there was silence in the hallway. The sound of dea'Gauss collapsing to the floor was loud—and so, too, was the sudden wail of alarms, and the sound of running feet.

Sheather shook himself; lowered his blade, and bowed in Anthora's direction.

"As you say."

THE MURDERER was gone; destroyed at his word. For the second time in his life, he had killed a ship. Pat Rin touched a switch, opening the comm line between himself and those sworn to serve him.

"Well done, Colonel," he said calmly.

"Thank you, sir," Andy Mack replied formally.

"First class shooting," Dostie chimed in, just ahead of Bhupendra's satisfied, "we teach the enemy to fear us."

"Which ain't exactly," Cheever McFarland added, "an unmixed blessing." He paused. "How many of them ships out there can we count on as back up, Boss? The battlewagon?"

Dutiful Passage, that would be, and a question near to his own heart and peace. That it was captained by Priscilla Mendoza, Shan's first mate and longtime lover, was . . . disturbing. And yet . . .

Pat Rin leaned to the comm. "I shall attempt to ascertain, Mr. McFarland. In the meanwhile, do me the kindness of speaking with the High Judge, as my deputy."

"Will do," Cheever said, as easily as if he spoke to such august persons daily, and signed off.

Pat Rin did the same, and sat for a moment, hands folded, as he gathered his courage—though what had he to fear? Priscilla Mendoza was well-known to him as a kind and generous lady. He had no need nor reason to fear her. Indeed, he could be certain that she would tell him, at long last, the truth.

The truth.

He reached to the board once more, fingering the keys with care, accessing the most secret Korval band . . .

"Well met, kinsman!" Shan's voice flowed cheerily into the cabin, as clear as if his cousin sat in the co-pilot's chair. Pat Rin closed his eyes, fingers gripping the edge of the board.

"Well met," he answered, shakily, knowing Shan would hear the tears in his reply, and caring not at all. "How fares the clan?"

"As it happens, we thrive—the more so now that the one who had fallen off-grid is returned to us. You must tell me all about your holiday—later. For the moment—rest assured that the *Passage* stands at your back as you speak for Korval. Oh, and check in with Jeeves, will you?"

"Jeeves?" Pat Rin cleared his throat. "Yes, I will. Shan—"

"Softly," his cousin interrupted, not ungently. "We cannot know that the line remains secure."

"Of course." He drew a careful breath. "Until soon, cousin."

"Until soon, Pat Rin. Stay the course."

The connection light went out.

"HOW FARE we, my brother?" Sheather inquired from his position as guard over the Commander, who lay unconscious, savaged hand hastily wrapped in a shirt.

Val Con was rapidly divesting Agent ter'Fendil of the tools of his trade: knives, smoke-gas pelletts, garrotte, capsules filled with poison, cunning button-sized explosives; the wallet, with its generous destructive possibilities; the boots, the interesting little blade under the sock, various guns in a diversity of calibers . . .

They had concealed themselves in the Commander's office—a questionable solution, at best. The advantages of the situation included a door that would not yield to the searchers, and access to the Commander's files, computers and comms. That there was no easy escape was . . . annoying.

Val Con removed a selection of pins and wires from the seams of Agent ter'Fendil's vest.

"We are in some disarray, I fear," he said to Sheather. "Behind enemy lines, burdened by prisoners and casualties . . ." He glanced over his shoulder to the place where Anthora kept watch over their two injured—an old man and an ancient gray cat—and returned to his task.

"On the whole, it would be best if we simply melted away into the night . . ."

As if to underscore the whimsy of that expressed desire, the loudspeaker in the ceiling gave tongue: "Intruder alert! Multiple intruders on Level Seven . . ."

"Enough." Val Con pushed the Agent against the wall, under Sheather's watchful blade, and edged past Nelirikk, who was happily removing the travel packing from their supply of explosives.

At the Commander's desk, he sat, and reached for the comm.

The access codes changed frequently, according to a pattern imbedded in the Loop of every Agent. Val Con frowned at the comm, trying to reconstruct the barely-glimpsed pattern—and, suddenly, gently, in the space behind his eyes that had previously been reserved for Loop display, there hung an access code.

SOMETHING HAD GONE terribly wrong.

Ren Zel felt himself a man of two separate but equal parts.

One part sat his board on the bridge of the *Dutiful Passage*, attending the minutia of piloting, monitoring the various bands that told of mayhem and dismay on the nearer stations, and minding his shields most closely.

The second part knelt next to Anthora on a cold metal floor, one hand on the chest of an old and fragile man, the other on the laboring side of a valiant gray cat.

"What's amiss?" he asked and felt her sigh.

"Mr. dea'Gauss must have a 'doc—and that soon. Merlin—he has been shot. I cannot—quite—understand how badly he is wounded. If I could but take both home . . . I have tried bespeaking the Tree, and there is no answer. We are trapped here."

"Are you?" He glanced around the cold metal room, seeing the golden lines running pure and true. "Perhaps not."

FINGERS POISED above the comm, Val Con considered the access code hanging just behind his eyes.

"Brother!" Anthora's voice was sharp with urgency.

He spun, heart clenched in fear of hearing the old man's

death—but no. His sister was standing tall, face animated—even eager.

"I require aid," she said quickly. "Do you put dea'Gauss on my back and I shall take him to Jelaza Kazone."

He blinked. Anthora was a wizard of some note, true enough, but . . .

"Will you walk through walls?" he asked.

She nodded. "I will. Assist me."

In the end, it required Nelirikk to gently lift dea'Gauss onto Anthora's back. Val Con lashed the man's wrists together on her breast, and used a length of fuse to tie them both 'round the waist.

"If I am able to return, I will do so," she said, breathless with bearing the unaccustomed burden. "Merlin . . ."

"If you make it to safety, you will remain there," Val Con said firmly. "We shall care for Merlin—and ourselves." He stepped back, waving at Nelirikk to do the same.

"If you are able, now is the time," he murmured.

"Yes." Slowly, awkward with the added weight, she walked directly toward the wall.

There was a flash of golden light, and an instant when the metal went to fog—then Anthora, and Mr. dea'Gauss, were gone.

"Jela's blood produces many wonders," Nelirikk commented, and returned to the unpacking of explosives.

After a moment, Val Con went back to the comm, and tapped in the code he had been given.

The unit light went from red to green. Scarcely daring to breathe, Val Con punched in the code for Jeeves' private line.

"Jelaza Kazone."

Val Con sat down in the Commander's chair.

"This is Korval," he said, keeping his voice steady, despite his foolishly pounding heart. "Pray confirm my ID. Also, please put a tracer on this call. Let Miri know that we are well, at liberty, but . . . contained. How stands the action?"

"ID confirmed. Miri will be informed. Working. How wide a theater?"

"Entire."

A small pause.

"The planetary defense net is ours," Jeeves said. "We control near space. A warship of the Department of the Interior has been destroyed by one of Lord Pat Rin's vessels. *Dutiful Passage* has been pressed into service for back up and link duty. Scout and Juntavas forces are prepared to allow Tree-and-Dragon central command if action is necessary."

"Jeeves, forgive me—Lord Pat Rin's forces?"

"Yes, quite an elegant group of ships flying Tree-and-Dragon, perfect for a low key planetary embargo, insurrection control, or as siege ships. They are precisely disciplined and well-crewed."

Ah, are they? And how came Pat Rin by such ships? Val Con moved his shoulders, putting aside such questions in favor of those more pressing.

"Planetary?" he asked Jeeves.

"Much of the planet is calm; Solcintra Portmaster has issued a flight hiatus, incidentally warning Captain Mendoza that her license is in danger. Solcintra City is not calm. There are riots in strategic locations, and we have signs of enemy action in Low Port. Higdon's Howlers are active at your location and at the spaceport. Here, we have withstood several attempts at penetration and anticipate— pardon, working . . ."

Across the room, Sheather moved, knife flashing. There was a scream—of metal, as the blade sheared through the floor. "Brother, he has initiated a device!"

The Commander's hand was still wrapped in his shirt; Nelirikk sprang forward and jerked the covering off, forcing the clenched hand open . . .

"Scout." He threw the object; Val Con snatched it out of the air and stared down at it—a short and stubby wand, its surface studded with tiny buttons and switches . . .

Agent ter'Fendil shrank against the wall, staring at the Commander in horror.

"You've given them orders. But—"

" . . . working!" Jeeves voice came out of the comm. "Alert! There has been a sixty thousand fold increase in neutrino emissions from Liad. Triangulation places the source at your location. Suggest immediate evacuation of all personnel."

Nelirikk had dragged the Commander up by the back of his collar. He shook him, as a dog shakes a rat. "Inform me!"

The Commander said nothing.

"The level of neutrino flux is consistent with old-style timonium powered armored units," Jeeves said. "Suggest immediate evacuation."

"Brother," Sheather said. "Something of much power is in motion. It moves strangely . . ." He turned and placed his three fingered hand flat against the wall.

"It comes . . ."

THERE WAS FIGHTING on the stations, there was fighting in the streets. Status reports poured in steadily, until Miri felt like she was drowning in details.

The Department's base in the commercial district of Solcintra city had been taken by an angry mob, led, she strongly suspected, by scouts—a victory for the angels, except for the civilians dead, of course.

Closer to the port, the news wasn't so good—the mob there had been repelled, expensively. Word was that there was a regroup in process.

Low Port was the worry—there'd been a couple unanticipated explosions. There were scouts there, too, trying to organize an evacuation.

The wall of books to her left shimmered and went foggy, for all the world like Clutch drive affect.

Miri blinked and came half out of her chair, too tired to even swear at the pain in her arm.

The books solidified and suddenly she wasn't alone. A dark-haired woman with an old man tied across her back was swaying in front of the bookcase.

"Help," she said.

THERE WAS A CRASHING sound behind the wall, and another.

" . . . Autonomous Semi-sentient Policing Systems," Jeeves said;

"or ASPS. They were deployed a number of times on outworlds, for the most part disastrously, which resulted in public backlash against applications of such technology to civilian situations. I was once assigned as back up, and then lead control in a military operation designed to rid a world of the devices . . . approximately seventeen million dead as a result of erroneous deployment . . ."

"You must define the enemy or they will destroy everything," Agent ter'Fendil said. He lurched to his feet, ignoring Sheather, his blade—and the Commander, who was all at once on his feet, a plain metal blade in his good hand, slashing at the unprotected back—

ter'Fendil spun, Agent-quick, slapped the knife away, closing and twisting, taking advantage of his adversary's momentum—

The Commander's neck broke with a *snap*. Agent ter'Fendil dropped the body and shrank back, staring.

" . . . do not draw attention to yourself in any circumstances . . ." Jeeves was saying, over the clanking in the hallway.

Val Con slapped up the screen, accessed the hallway camera, and sucked in his breath.

The hall was blocked with objects—four objects, in fact. Each as large as Edger, all of deep green metal, all bearing large Terran numerals—Val Con saw numbers 1, 3, 15 . . .

" . . . energy spike entirely consistent with an intact ASPS unit . . ." the voice continued from the comm.

"Jeeves, I confirm such a unit. Options?"

"Evacuate immediately. General use explosives slow them down; the most effective resistance, aside from vaporization, is placing obstructions in their way or dropping things on them. . . . When first mobilized they are methodical unless one triggers a self-defense program . . ."

"The control." Agent ter'Fendil was beside him. "They will destroy the planet. Give me the control."

Val Con looked at him, seeing honest fear in the Agent's eyes. "Can they be turned off?"

"There is a resting state, yes."

From the hallway outside, screams and the sounds of rending.

Val Con handed Agent ter'Fendil the control wand.

❈   ❈   ❈

THE OLD GENT was settled in the autodoc. Miri leaned against the unit, feeling a kind of hum in her bones, which was probably the 'doc working, and which she shouldn't have noticed at all.

An arm's length away, Anthora yos'Galan slumped in a massively carved chair, eyes closed and voice low as she complied with Miri's request to be brought up to speed.

She was doing a good job, hitting the high points and not wasting any words, and Miri wasn't much liking what she heard.

"They're surrounded," she said, by way of a sum-up when the low, careful voice came to an end. "And trapped." She bit her lip. "We can bust them out, but we're gonna need coords for that room. Think you can work with Jeeves and figure it?"

Anthora shook her head. "Going in, the Tree provided the path. Ren Zel showed me the way out."

Right. The hum from the 'doc was making her twitchy. Miri straightened out of her lean and looked down at the kid in the chair, hating what she was about to ask.

"So, you can get the Tree to provide a path back in, right? And this time, we'll rig you up with a findme, and—"

Anthora opened her eyes. Silver-blue, like Shan's, wide-spaced and dreamy-looking—which Shan's weren't. "Val Con said, if I got to safety, to stay there."

Miri sighed. "Yeah, well. Val Con says a lot of stupid things, especially where it bears on somebody he cares about maybe getting hurt. Figures he's tough enough to take his licks and ours, too. Also figures he's fast enough to outrun most common trouble. Sometimes, he's right; sometimes, he's lucky. This time, he needs help. That's us."

"You don't understand," Anthora said. "Val Con *said*, if I got to safety, to stay there. I cannot return."

Miri closed her eyes, counted to ten, and tried it again. "Val Con's half of one good delm." She reached inside her shirt and brought the Ring up on its cord, so the kid could see it. "I'm the other half. I'll make it an order, if I have to."

Anthora shook her head. "You do not understand," she

repeated. "Val Con—I am *forbidden*. He has this ability. I *cannot* return."

"I just saw you walk through a *wall*," Miri started—and blinked, as various memories from a young adulthood that was absolutely not hers unfolded, neatly, before her mind's eye.

"You're talking dramliza talent," she said to Anthora's soft silver eyes. "He can tell you no and make it stick."

"He can do it to Priscilla, too," Anthora offered helpfully.

"Great," Miri said, thinking that if there were one person in the universe who had to be a dramliza-brake, of *course* it would be—

"Miri." Jeeves' voice flowed out of the room speakers. "You are needed in the control room. A situation is developing."

THE LAST CHARGE was laid; the last timer set.

Val Con dropped out of the repair hatch to the floor below, counting in his head.

Six minutes before the charges blew, burying the ASPS unit in rubble. Three minutes from his location to the rendezvous point. Two minutes to the surface.

Plenty of time.

"LORD PAT RIN, your timing is impeccable, sir," Jeeves said—and surely, Pat Rin thought, it was an artifact of the transmission that yos'Galan's butler sounded breathless? "We have a situation. Stand by, of your goodness, while I ascertain . . ."

There was silence, though the connect light remained steady. Pat Rin recruited himself to patience which was very shortly rewarded.

"Working," Jeeves announced. "You will understand that control of the planetary defense net resides under the Captain's hand during this present time of emergency."

Pat Rin all but smiled. "Ah, does it? That will certainly expedite matters, should it become necessary to fire upon the planet. However—"

"Precisely," the robot said, cutting him off ruthlessly. "It is exactly the subject of firing upon the planet that must now be addressed. The nature of the fleet you chose to field dictates your task. It will shortly be necessary to fire upon Solcintra City. Coordinates and ranging will be supplied."

Necessary to fire upon Solcintra? Pat Rin closed his eyes. He had, of course, known that it might come to firing upon the home-world—why else had he brought destroyers with him? Truth told, he had pinned his hope on the Council of Clans, that the all-too-public crying of Balance would flush the Department of the Interior onto the surface, where it might be dealt with as any other transgressor against the Code.

"Lord Pat Rin?"

"One moment," he managed, holding up a hand that the robot could not see. "Jeeves, how is it necessary that we fire upon Solcintra, now? There has been no time for the Council to speak, nor time for the Department of the Interior to make answer . . ."

"The Department has made answer," Jeeves said. "Certain intelligence reports, confirmed by direct observation of trusted parties, indicate that the Department of the Interior has deployed timonium powered weapons capable of overwhelming anything that Liad may bring against them on the ground. The planetary defense net is unable—by its nature—to effect an attack against a target situated upon the planet." There was a pause, then Jeeves continued, hurriedly.

"It is my estimate that a failure to destroy these weapons in short order will lead to planetary disaster. In fact, it is necessary to fire upon the planet, bringing destruction to a portion of the city, in order to preserve the greater part. Your vessels are uniquely fitted to this task. *Dutiful Passage*, for instance, may only deploy a broad beam—far more destructive than those precision cutting units borne by your fleet."

"There are *people* in that city!" Pat Rin snapped.

"There are. Evacuation has been sounded. I expect confirmation from teams shortly. In the meantime, steps are being taken to contain the targets." Another pause, then, with a gentleness a robot could certainly never feel—

"It is our intention to destroy as small an area as possible.

However, we dare not err by the application of too little force. People will die, despite the call for evacuation and the best efforts of the teams. But more people will die, if the enemy is not destroyed."

Pat Rin bowed his head.

"I understand. I will require data."

"Uploading," Jeeves said promptly.

DIGLON RIFLE waited patiently for his next target. So far he had taken seven shots with this light rifle borrowed from Commander Carmody's troop; he felt confident of five hits.

Nearby, Commander Call-Me-Liz-Lizardi was speaking quietly into a comm unit. His duty was to guard her and to watch for break-outs at the door which was, by now, well shattered, and partly filled with bodies.

Their position was excellent—they had a large stone monument for cover when they stood, and a stone wall, half buried on the other side with soil, for cover when they sniped . . .

Hazenthull Explorer had not shot as much as he, but perhaps with more accuracy. The commander had told them to conserve their ammunition, and to be prepared to act as rearguard if need be—and to be rearguard with such as she, whose exploits were writ on books and worlds forever, such was a fate a solider could embrace.

There came another one of those slight shakes of the ground, and a vibration that was longer. He was leaning against the monument, his face feeling the stone—and . . . there was a shake, a—

"Explorer!" he called. "Something happens here!"

Hazenthull gave an assent signal, indicated to the commander that she was moving his way . . . .

"Feel," he whispered to her, pushing fingers to the stone. "Equipment!"

She looked at him in startlement, felt the stone herself, then leaned her ear against it.

Abruptly there was grinding noise close to hand and she jerked back, dragging Diglon with her.

A seam in the granite shivered, clunked, shrugged—and slid

quietly into the rest of the monument, revealing a metal wall. Almost immediately that wall moved aside, and smoke billowed free, carrying the smell perhaps of burnt meat. From within the monument came the scout, Nelirikk Explorer, and another, with blood on his cheek—pushing the Honored One, guiding him into the light . . . .

The scout was cradling something precious against his chest; gun held ready in his free hand. He looked around, caught Diglon's eye, smiled, and thrust the gray fur ball into his hands, saying in Troop, "Protect this hero from harm. Move away, move away!"

That quickly he was gone, dashing back to the monument, bending, making some unseen adjustment. There was a repeat of the clanking and grinding; the door shut, and the monument was as it had been.

"Medic! Medic!" yelled Commander Liz, and waved to him in his new troop-sign: *fast march that way* . . . .

They all started running then, away from the monument and the fighting in the street, and when the ground rumbled and knocked them down, the monument swayed and great gouts of smoke and flame blew out of it, into the pale green sky.

The breeze was fairly stiff, blowing away from the city center and—by extrapolation—away from Jelaza Kazone and Korval's valley.

" . . . **NOT NEVER** meant for atmospheric work . . . damn, but look at that!" That was Andy Mack, muttering publicly under his breath.

Everyone else—including the usually irrepressible Cheever McFarland—remained silent as rug mites, watching their separate screens and the results of their labors. There was fire—not all of Solcintra could be spared, no matter how precise the aiming Jeeves had contrived—and a black spout of soot and ash leaning away from the city. Already there was a darkening that was not mere shadow as the heaviest debris fell in a kind of non-volcanic pumice.

Pat Rin switched views quickly. Not all of the smoke above the city had its birth in their attack. Portions of Low Port and Mid Port were aflame, and elsewhere there were reports of scattered violence. The portmaster's jury-rigged comm was demanding answers, demanding control of the planetary net, demanding that the mercenary units vacate the planet, demanding Korval's surrender. . . .

That last had brought a burst of laughter from several of his crew members; then Jeeves had once again brought their attention to the task at hand and they fired what Pat Rin hoped was the last blast at the city he'd called home.

Jeeves supplied them with several views of the target now. The beams, meant to slice and cut, had done just that, lancing through the atmosphere of Liad in unison from the four mining craft, each cutting its own edge of a box centered on a green park and then crisscrossing toward the center. The initial gout of reflective white smoke had given way quickly to a dense ash-filled swirl, and then when the interior of the buried domain was opened there had been explosions. . . .

The while, Jeeves had spoken in the background, calmly instructing and coaxing minute beam corrections until at last, for good or for ill, the thing was finished.

Now, from above, Pat Rin, saw the terminator on the planet clearly as his ship entered shadow. Soon, night would fall on Solcintra. He wondered if anyone there would be able to sleep.

DAY 56

❋❋❋❋❋❋❋❋❋❋❋❋❋❋❋❋❋❋❋❋❋❋❋

Standard Year 1393
Solcintra
Liad

"MR. MCFARLAND, I thank you for your care, but I scarcely need *security* in the very heart of Solcintra."

The big Terran sighed. "Boss, use your head. Ships under your command fired on the planet not all that long ago." He held up a hand. "Yeah, we did for a good reason and likely saved a buncha folks their hides, if not exactly their homes. And we can take it as given the evacuation missed somebody—probably more than a couple somebodies. *And* there's a big glassy hole in the planet where we beamed them 'bots into vapor.

"All of which says to me that there're some who ain't gonna be real pleased to see you."

Pat Rin closed his eyes. *True enough*, he thought. Nor would it do to deprive the delm of the honor of dealing appropriately with Korval's erring child Pat Rin by getting himself murdered beforehand.

"Besides," Cheever said. "Natesa'd chew me out good if I let somethin' happen to you."

Natesa.

"Your point is taken, Mr. McFarland."

He opened his eyes, checked the gun in its hidden pocket, pulled the jacket into seemliness—and paused, his fingers tightening on the leather. *Jacket,* he thought. *This jacket. Before Korval.*

Pat Rin yos'Phelium, you are a fool.

"Boss?"

He smoothed the sleeves, feigning a finicky lordling's care, buying time—a few moments, only; long enough for his heart to stop pounding so, and for his face to find the proper expression of cool neutrality. What, after all, was a pilot's jacket, when he already wore a ring?

"Something I oughta know?" Cheever McFarland asked.

Jacket settled, he looked up into the face of his oathsworn, seeing worry and . . . care in the strong lines. Gods, when had Cheever McFarland's face become as precious to him as kin?

He inclined his head.

"There is something you should know, yes," he said, deliberately cold. "When we are with my cousin Val Con, you will forget that you are armed. You will protest nothing that may happen while he and I . . . converse." He looked closely into the Terran's eyes. "I will not insult you by asking for your oath on this. I will merely remind you that—I am the boss. Is this understood?"

Cheever's face tightened, but—"Yessir," he said, mildly enough.

"Good," Pat Rin murmured.

SOMETHING WAS BAD wrong, Cheever decided as Pat Rin bowed to the young buck from Binjali's who'd won the brief bowli ball game for the right to play taxi, and turned to look at the building where Val Con yos'Phelium had set up a temporary headquarters.

The slim shoulders rose and fell inside the leather jacket, then Pat Rin was gone, walking steadily across the street, head up, back straight. Cussing softly, Cheever went after him.

The door was flanked by two soldiers, male and female, each massing about as much as Cheever did. The male dropped his rifle across the door, barring the way.

"Name is?" the female asked, her Trade carrying a heavy accent that Cheever didn't quite place. "Business is?"

"My name is Pat Rin yos'Phelium Clan Korval. I have come to speak with my kinsman, Val Con yos'Phelium, on business of the clan."

"Hah." She snapped her fingers, the rifle was lifted away, and Pat Rin walked on, Cheever at his back.

They went down a short hallway, following the sound of voices to a room cluttered with people and equipment. Pat Rin hesitated on the threshold, scanning the crowd, maybe. A woman in working leathers pushed by, and ran down the hall. Still, Pat Rin stood there, oblivious to the jostling.

Suddenly, he moved, striding purposefully across the room toward a knot of people in leathers, uniforms, and Low Port motley. A dark haired man in working leathers turned his head, said a quick word to the group and stepped forward, hands extended, smiling across a face so familiar that Cheever had to shake his head and look again—by which time Pat Rin was on his knees before the younger edition of himself, forehead on the floor, the back of his neck exposed and vulnerable.

SOMETHING MOVED across the busy room. Val Con glanced aside and saw two pilots approaching, the Liaden walking with purpose; the Terran—

"A moment," he said quickly to the cluster of scouts, and went forward, hands extended in welcome.

"Cousin, well-met!"

Pat Rin flung to his knees, face against the floor. Behind him, the Terran slammed to a halt, openly shocked.

Val Con looked down at the exposed neck, at the dark hair curling softly, several fingers longer than its accustomed length, and the smooth, unmarred leather of the Jump pilot's jacket.

"As ill as that?" he murmured and bent forward, checking when he sensed the big man start.

Looking up, he met the man's eyes. "I will not hurt him."

The Terran nodded, brusquely. "Right."

Carefully, Val Con bent and put a hand on a bowed shoulder. The muscles were rock hard. "Come, cousin," he said softly. "You'd best tell me."

Nothing. Then, slowly, Pat Rin straightened. Val Con dropped lightly to one knee, putting them at the same level. Pat Rin, he saw, had lost weight; his face was chapped, as if he had spent too much time out in the cold; and there were new lines around his mouth and eyes.

"My lifemate and my oathsworn are blameless," he said, in the mode of transgressor to delm. "I claim all."

"Ever more terrifying," Val Con returned, lightly, deliberately, in the Low Tongue. "Pray reveal at once the horrific crimes of which they are innocent."

Pat Rin raised his left hand, on which gleamed Korval's—no.

"Ah, I see. Very prettily done, too. Though they should have been more careful about the emeralds."

The edge of a smile glimmered. "Just so." The smile faded, and he moved his hand again; light ran liquid over dragon scale and leaf.

"Using this, I have subjugated a world to my necessity. I have allied with the Juntavas. I have made promises in Korval's name. I have put things . . . into motion . . ."

"As well we all know, having seen that motion work wonders. Very well. And your necessity was—what? Usurpation of Korval?"

Pat Rin shuddered and closed his eyes. "They came to me," he whispered, and his voice was haunted. "They came to me and they said, *all your kin are dead*. They said, *Korval*. They expected that I would be *grateful* for their care of my interests—and that I would represent them to the Council."

"They were very foolish," Val Con said softly. "That was at Teriste? Where did you go after?"

The brown eyes opened. "First, to a Juntavas base. Then to Bazaar, to purchase stock. Finally to Surebleak, where I set up as a boss, and—and began my Balance—" the smile again, slightly more visible this time. "Among other necessary tasks."

"Ah." Val Con tipped his head. "And these are the crimes of which you alone are guilty?"

Pat Rin sighed. "I don't doubt there are others—impersonating a pilot comes to mind."

"Commander?" A voice called from behind. "We have word from the Low Port."

Val Con glanced over his shoulder. "A moment." He reached out and gripped Pat Rin's hand.

"Duty," he said. "Quickly now—tell me the name of your lifemate."

"Inas Bhar," Pat Rin said softly. "Called Juntavas Sector Judge Natesa the Assassin."

Val Con smiled. "The clan increases." He rose, pulling his cousin up, and embraced him, cheek to cheek.

"Bide," he murmured. "We will go home together."

DAY 59

※※※※※※※※※※※※※※※※※※※※※※※※

Standard Year 1393
Solcintra
Liad

SPEAKER FOR COUNCIL was enjoying the show, Miri thought. Come to think of it, she'd be having a better time herself if she was sitting behind a high table, with a pretty silver bell to ring whenever she felt like hearing it, and a cup of her favorite brew to hand.

Unfortunately, Defenders Before Council had to stand on the low floor facing the paid seats stretching up to the ceiling, with the Speaker's high desk behind them. As far as Miri was concerned, the whole set-up was a melant'i trick designed to make the Defenders feel all humble and unworthy. What she mostly felt was annoyed—and she wasn't exactly getting humble-vibes from Val Con, either.

"Korval has been called before this Council to answer for the following crimes against the homeworld," Speaker said from behind them and considerably over their heads.

"Landing a hostile force comprised of Terran and Yxtrang soldiers at Solcintra Port.

"Leading a military action against Liad.

"Subverting the planetary defense net.

"Firing upon the homeworld."

She paused a nice, long while, to let the assembled delms get a good look at them. Miri ran a quick Rainbow and felt her shoulders relax under the ceremonial delm costume. From Val Con she caught a flutter of warmth, as if he had quickly kissed her cheek.

"Korval's answer, given before this Council, invokes the contract originally made between Captain Cantra yos'Phelium Clan Torvin and the Combined Houses of Planet Solcintra. The Council's attention was directed most particularly to the articles discussing the duty of the captain toward the passengers; the charge upon successor captains; and the term of contract.

"It is Korval's contention that this contract, made before the Exodus from Solcintra, remains in force, according to its conditions of termination. They provide evidence that a call for Captain's Justice was made in Standard Year 1061, which Justice was dealt by the delm of Korval in her melant'i as Captain Genetic in this very chamber."

There was a pause, and a small clink. Miri sighed inwardly. A cup of tea would taste good right now. Especially if she could have it in the back kitchen at Jelaza Kazone.

Another clink, as Speaker put her teacup down.

"Korval argues that their *contract of employment* burdens them with the duty of protecting the residents of the planet Liad, whom they are pleased to term 'the passengers.'

"Korval provides evidence of the existence and the crimes of an organization calling itself the *Department of the Interior*. The list of names of those allegedly impressed or murdered by this organization is particularly notable in that it includes many of those whom Korval has been charged with harming.

"Korval's conclusion and final answer to this Council is that the Captain Genetic, having ascertained the mortal danger presented to the passengers by the Department of the Interior, acted to remove this danger. For the best good of Liad."

She didn't, Miri thought, sound too impressed with all Nova's careful compilations and cross-checks.

"I must note, with some surprise, that various organizations and individuals have indicated a willingness—on the side of Korval—to file briefs and informational materials or have in fact filed briefs and such material sufficient to fill several warehouses. These organizations and individuals have, for the most part, a clear, well-known, and on-going relationship with Korval. I mention a few—the Scouts of Liad, the Accountants Guild, the Pilots Guild, the Solcintra Feline Appreciation Society, the Taxicab and Pedicab Association of Solcintra, Binjali's Repair Shop and Jalopy Garage," here there was a clear and distinctly disapproving pause, " . . . the Juntavas."

That brought a murmur from the chamber and Miri raised her eyebrows Val Con-fashion as she glanced at him. He raised his back at her.

Robertson, she thought, *you ain't takin' this serious enough . . .*

"Also," Speaker continued, "University, the Defenders of the Code, the Little Festival Association, Tey Dor's Sporting Clubs—and the list is quite long, and will be appended to our decision which will be hung on the chamber door and published as required, with copies to all major parties. Given the seriousness and time-sensitive nature of the charges, the Council has decided to forego introduction of such material into the hearing process. We thank each of those who have offered assistance."

Hanging judge! Miri thought. *She don't want to be confused by the facts.*

A pause, the sound of a tea cup being placed too close to the microphone.

"The Council will now render its judgment. Hedrede is called."

From the fifth row up came a stir and a rustle, and finally a man, decked out like they all were, in formal delm gear, arose and bowed toward the floor.

"As Korval will doubtless recall," he said, his voice about as warm as a Surebleak winter morning, "House Hedrede was among the signers of the contract with Captain Cantra yos'Phelium."

"Korval recalls," Val Con said from beside her.

"The Dragon's memory," someone said, loudly, from high near the ceiling, "is not in question."

Sharon Lee & Steve Miller

There was a titter and a murmur of agreement through the hall.

"Mizel is found to be out of order," Speaker snapped. "Honored Hedrede, pray continue."

He inclined his head.

"The Council of Clans finds Korval in error," he stated coldly. "The contract between Captain yos'Phelium and the Houses of Solcintra was never intended to continue so long, or to place so much of a burden upon one clan. In undertaking the described actions against the so-called Department of the Interior, Korval has overstepped, to the endangerment and distress of the homeworld."

He paused, maybe expecting an answer from the floor. Miri preserved a dignified silence. Beside her, Val Con inclined his head slightly—courteous permission to continue.

"The Council of Clans likewise finds," Hedrede continued portentously, "that it has erred, in that it has not caused the contract in question to be terminated according to its articles, thereby removing the burden of captaincy from Korval." He bowed, employer to employee.

"The Council of Clans, successor to the Combined Houses of Solcintra, hereby terminates, closes, and declares fulfilled the contract of employment originally made between Cantra yos'Phelium Clan Torvin, captain-owner of the starship *Quick Passage*, and the Combined Houses of Solcintra."

From Val Con, a flare of joy so pure and so vivid, her breath caught in her throat.

"Korval hears," he said, his voice perfectly composed.

"This also means," said Hedrede, perhaps a bit testily, "that the defense of Liad shall no longer be the concern of Korval or its assigns. We require a timely transfer of the defense net to the duly constituted authority of the portmaster." Hedrede glanced up from the document he read from. "Is this clear?"

"To avoid potential conflicts of interest Korval relinquished control of the defense net to the Commander of the Liaden Scouts upon entering this chamber," Val Con murmured. "I am certain that the portmaster will contrive an orderly transfer."

There was a collective sigh in the hall.

Hedrede inclined his head. "We now come to the matter of Balance."

"It is the decision of this Council that Clan Korval is an active threat to the safety and security of this world. Therefore, Korval shall be cast out. No longer shall Korval have a voice in this Council nor may Korval look to the assembled clans for justice, sustenance, or comfort.

"Korval is required to vacate Liad and Liaden space. All and any Korval properties or persons remaining within Liaden space on the one hundredth forty-fifth day following this judgment shall be forfeit to the Council of Clans."

Miri blinked.

The bright joy radiating from Val Con went incandescent.

In the fifth row, Hedrede bowed once more.

"Thus, the Council's judgment."

He sat. The room was real quiet; nobody shuffled papers; nobody coughed, or whispered, or dropped a stylus. Everybody was watching them, Miri realized; waiting to see what they'd do.

"Cha'trez?"

She turned, saw green eyes smiling at her, and a slim golden hand extended. Grinning, she wove her fingers with his. Together, they bowed to the assembled delms—*farewell*. Nothing else.

Hand-in-hand, not hurrying, but not wasting any time, either, they walked up the long ramp. The door swung open as they approached.

Neither one looked back.

"ONE HUNDRED FORTY-FOUR days to leave planet, lock, stock and piglet?" Shan repeated incredulously. "Have they lost their wits?"

"Certainly not," Val Con said drily. "They merely hope to hurry us sufficiently that we will leave a few things behind, to their benefit."

"Did the Council forbid sales?" inquired dea'Gauss—this the new dea'Gauss, a woman in her early middle years, with a serious face and unexpectedly merry eyes. Her father was yet with the Healers and he would be well, with time. Though his notes were before her, it was happily clear to Val Con that her course was her own.

Val Con shook his head. "The vote was close, as I counted. Close enough that those who most dearly wished us gone dared not risk their victory by burdening the issue with petty Balance."

The dea'Gauss inclined her head. "That is good, then. Allow me . . ." She bent to her keyboard.

"Even supposing we can pack everything of importance," Shan continued. "How the devil are we going to ship it? Worse, where will we go? Somehow, I don't believe Erob would be willing to have us."

Miri laughed, and Merlin, who was curled up on her lap, muttered a sleepy protest.

"Bad idea, anyway," she said. "Given the family tendency to force things into our own mold."

"There's that. We might try for New Dublin, I suppose . . ."

"Or Surebleak," Pat Rin said quietly from his place next to Shan.

"Surebleak's at the back end of nowhere—and it's cold," Miri said, and then shook her head, with a half-grin. "Why'm I telling you that, Boss?"

"In fact, Surebleak is not so ill-placed as it first appears," Pat Rin replied, earnestly. "Certainly, the presence of trade and an upgraded port would be more than enough to overcome any difficulty of location. As to the weather—" He moved his shoulders. "The portmaster has specs for climate satellites on file. It does not need to remain cold."

There was a brief pause, then—

"He's right," Shan said. "There aren't any major trade routes close, but there are three solid mid-level routes through that sector. If there was any reason for ships to stop at Surebleak—"

"They would stop," Val Con concluded. He glanced aside. "Cha'trez?"

She sighed. "Well, it'll give us a base. Hafta buy up a buncha real estate and do some heavy renovating . . ."

"There is land beyond the city, which is only lightly lived in," Pat Rin said, looking at Val Con. "We might be situated as we have been here, near enough to port and city, with easy access at need."

"And thus be invested in keeping the Port Road open." Val Con grinned. "Well-played, cousin."

"If we liquidate all holdings," the dea'Gauss said abruptly, "over a period of one hundred forty-two days, we may be able to prevent the Exchange from collapse, assuming we get and give value." She looked up.

"Unless your lordship wishes to incept a market collapse?"

"It is not necessary. We prefer to sell at fair value, however."

"Certainly," she said. "We have a list of off-world investors who have previously expressed interest in various acquisitions." She paused, touched a key.

"The accounts currently held at the Bank of Solcintra must be moved. Shall I query the Bank of Terra?"

"Why not transfer everything equally among our existing accounts," Shan suggested, "and sort that out once we're settled? I have a feeling that the Council of Clans may find themselves able to overlook Korval investments in Liad, after a suitable period of uncertainty."

"That's a point," said Miri. "Can't really do banking on Surebleak." She looked at Pat Rin. "Unless you fixed that, too?"

"Not yet," he said, and she shook her head.

"The dies, your lordship?"

Val Con frowned. "How much longer on the current term?"

"Less than a Standard."

"If we close the treasury, that *will* crash the market," Miri protested.

"Yet the dies are ours," Val Con said. "How if we—"

Across the room, the door opened, admitting Nelirikk.

"Captain, the elder scout is returned."

"That was quick," Miri commented. "Let him in, Beautiful. We need all the heads we can get."

"Captain." He stepped aside and Daav strolled in, pausing half-a-dozen steps inside the room to bow casually to the delm's honor.

"Good afternoon, Father," Val Con said mildly. "I confess that we had not looked for you so soon."

"I rather expected that you hadn't," Daav retorted. "However, the Clutch Elders have the ability to act rapidly, when they see the need—much like Clutch ships. Of which more anon. I hear on the port that we are unemployed, outlawed, and homeless, all in one canny throw."

"Indeed we are. The Council chose to see us as a danger to Liad."

"All hail the Council, wise at last," Daav murmured, and tipped his head. "Is that Pat Rin? I'm delighted to see you, child."

"Uncle Daav . . ." his voice failed him and he inclined his head, taking a hard breath. "I am all joy to see you."

"So what did the Elders say?" Miri asked. "No dice?"

"Entirely the opposite," Daav said, favoring her with one of his edged smiles. "They are eager to assist us in any way they can—and have detached one of their larger vessels for Korval's use. It is understood that this use will include transporting the Tree, but no limit of service was set."

"A ship large enough to move Jelaza Kazone?" Pat Rin asked.

"Oh, easily. In fact, if you would care to step outside, you may see for yourself."

IT RODE ON THE HORIZON like a moon, glass smooth and subtly glowing.

Miri took a hard breath against the sudden tightness in her chest and slid her hand into Val Con's. He squeezed her fingers gently, his attention focused on the moon-ship.

"Volume?" he murmured.

"Sufficient to contain those portions of Solcintra City still standing," Daav replied. "Or the Tree, and most of the valley."

Behind them, Shan sighed. "Brother, we have our transportation problems solved. But is Surebleak ready for that?"

"All the more reason to set down in the country," Pat Rin said unsteadily.

"Edger professes himself ready to commence immediately," Daav continued. "He is accompanied by several of his kin. If the delm wishes to remove all that is ours . . ."

"Yes," Miri and Val Con said—and abruptly laughed.

"Yes!" Miri said again.

DAY 201

❈❈❈❈❈❈❈❈❈❈❈❈❈❈❈❈❈❈❈❈❈❈❈❈

Standard Year 1393
Solcintra Liad

"TOMORROW IS THE DAY," Edger boomed, one three fingered hand splayed flat against the trunk of the Tree. "The ship of the Elders shall descend with sample bay open and the lift active; it will be but a matter of a few hundred moments to adjust for Jelaza Kazone's necessity. We have spoken somewhat—the elder tree and I—and the vessel is ready to respectfully receive all into its interior."

Edger paused a short pause, thinking or watching or perhaps merely staring into the distance for some Clutch-required moment—and then continued in apparent haste.

"We have the coordinates for the new nesting place. There is no need for apprehension as Aelli has done the calculations. My brothers and I have consulted together, the boss kinsman of my brother and my sister has returned to put all into readiness. Thus, the work goes forth; art incarnate. Ephemeral and multi-stranded, it wends through time, space, and song, altering the very fabric of the universe. As I see, each day brings a new thread."

Miri stirred and squeezed Val Con's fingers. "Altering the fabric of the universe?" she whispered.

"Hyperbole," Val Con whispered back.

"Right."

There was a sound, somewhere beneath Edger's oration. Miri looked over her shoulder, and then turned—Val Con with her—staring at the apparition walking, none-too-steady, across the grass toward them, wary eyes on Edger.

She wasn't much more than a kid: undergrown, sharp-faced, and pale; her hair an uncertain sort of yellow, unruly rather than curly; dark eyes smudged by lack of sleep.

She stopped a couple paces away and bowed—out of mode and out of time, but, hell, the kid was dead on her feet. Her jacket told the story of how she'd gotten passed by security: Jump pilot.

"It is necessary that I speak to the delm of Korval, on business of the clan," she said, and her High Liaden was even worse than her bow.

Miri nodded—and blinked, feeling a rush of recognition from Val Con.

"*Another* one?" she complained, looking up at him.

"Shall you like odds?" he answered, and then nodded easily at the kid.

"You are addressing the delm of Korval," he said in Terran. "May we know your name?"

The kid frowned, equal parts irritation, exhaustion, and relief at not having to do the rest of conversation in Liaden.

"Theo Waitley," she said.

Apparently realizing that the name alone was a little scant, she added, "I'm here because my father's missing and he told me—he *always* told me to go the delm of Korval, if ever there was really bad trouble."

She paused, running one hand through her thoroughly draggled hair.

"My father's name is Jen Sar Kiladi. He teaches—"

"He teaches cultural genetics," Val Con interrupted, gently.

"Right. I mean, you might not think it was a big problem, if your father wasn't where you left him—"

"No, acquit me—I would think it a very large problem, indeed."

Theo might not have heard him; she swept on, caught up in the tide of her explanation. "But, he's never done anything like this before—just up and left, in the middle of the term and—" Her mouth tightened.

"I got trouble," she finished, "and since I can't find him . . . ."

"Well," Val Con murmured, eyes pointed over Theo's head.

Miri looked where he was looking, saw the tall shadow moving toward them from the house, and sighed.

"Theo," Val Con said; "please look behind you."

She blinked at him, then did what she was told.

"Father!" she shouted and leapt forward, slamming Daav into a full body hug.

"Father, where the *hell* have you been?"

Daav tousled the Jump pilot's hair, looking suddenly old.

"I have been busy, child," he said, returning the hug. "Very busy."

He paused, and shook his head, Terran-style.

"I can't tell you how glad I am to see you, Theo. And sorry, as well."

"Sorry!" she looked startled—and afraid.

"Gently, child," Daav said, touching her cheek. "Sorry, because you would not be here if there wasn't really bad trouble."

She nodded. "It's kind of complicated," she started . . .

AUTHORS' AFTERWORD

We Remember Uncle Harry
or
The Return of the Afterword That Ate Unity

YOU REALLY NEED TO KNOW about Uncle Harry. The Liaden Universe® is his fault, you know.

You see, long ago and far away, when we first started to learn about the trials of Clan Korval, the words, "The man who was not Terrence O'Grady had come quietly," appeared—almost without warning—on an otherwise clean sheet of paper sitting in the carriage of a well-used, but dignified, typewriter named Uncle Harry.

Uncle Harry barely managed to get us through that first adventure—belching, smoking and shuddering, he finally burst into flames as Sharon was typing the last page of the final draft of *Agent of Change*—but the course of our lives was by then inextricably entwined with the history and people of Clan Korval. The more we wrote of them, the more they revealed to us, and the more they revealed the more we needed to know. Oddly, the same thing—the needing to know more—happened to some readers, and then more readers, and now we're here, all of us together in one swell swoop, at the end pages of *I Dare*, a book we've been planning on writing for more than a dozen years.

Along the way we had some delays and some joys and some fun —and more recently a lot of fun as we've gotten to travel and meet some few of the readers who've made each additional book possible. We've also gone through several typewriters and numerous computer systems and printers (ah—remember that Star nine pin dot matrix printer that worked so hard and so long that we gave it to a school after it printed out—in 24 hours or so, mostly non-stop, the final version of *Carpe Diem*?), and with each new computer or printer we'd ask (one of us to another, without fail), "Do you remember when we brought Uncle Harry home?"

The funny thing is that so many things have changed since Uncle Harry flamed his way through that last page—like the state we live in, our publisher, our cats—that we're sometimes amazed that we've gotten to this point, the point where we can say "OK, Korval's set for the moment, now all we have to do is catch up on those details . . ."

What we've learned, seven books and more than a dozen years down the road, is that Uncle Harry's legacy is lasting. We keep finding new stories in the Liaden Universe®, new heroics, new details, and new characters who come out of the virtual woodwork with a sudden, "Hey, you. You there at the keyboard! I have something to say! Hop to it!"

Uncle Harry, by the way, was heavy. Carrying him upstairs the day we brought him home from the used typewriter pound he'd fallen into after his daring escape from an insurance company office was no easy thing. He went thunk! very much, thank you! when he was put down and when he was turned on the table he sat on vibrated and so then did the floor of the front bedroom we'd converted into an office, and so then did the ceiling of the kitchen below vibrate, and so then did our neighbors assume we had one of those vibrating recliners they were selling on TV that year . . .

The neighbors put up with our recliner-Uncle-Harry-typer and our late night kitchen world-building conclaves and all those other things that make people look at us and say—"Oh, them? They're— *writers* . . ."

And while the neighbors were likely relieved when we carried

Uncle Harry off to the shop, where the repair guy reverently removed the scorched cover, shook his head sadly and murmured, "I'm sorry, there's nothing I can do. We can't even use it for parts . . ." we still remember Uncle Harry, fondly.

Arguably, without those particular vibrations and clunks and patterings that transformed that cramped upstairs office into a view screen into elsewhere, there'd be no Liaden Universe® for any of us to enjoy. So the ghost of Uncle Harry whirs over our shoulders, reminding us that there are always more stories waiting to find the page.

Thanks, Uncle Harry. We still miss you.

Steve Miller and Sharon Lee
July 2001

Liaden/Terran Dictionary

A'nadelm: Heir to the nadelm

A'thodelm: Head-of-Line-to-Be

A'trezla: Lifemates

Al'bresh venat'i: Formal phrase of sorrow for another Clan's loss, as when someone dies.

Al'kin Chernard'i: The Day Without Delight

Balent'i Kalandon: Our local galaxy

Balent'i tru'vad: The starweb of all creation

Cha'leket: Heartkin (heartbrother, heartsister)

Cha'trez: Heartsong

Chernubia: Confected delicacy

Chiat'a bei kruzon: Dream sweetly.

Ckrakec: (derived from the Yxtrang) Approximately "Master Hunter"

Coab minshak'a: "Necessity exists"

Conselem: An absurdity

Delm: Head of Clan (Delm Korval, Korval Himself/Herself)

Delmae: Lifemate to the Delm

Denubia: Darling

Dramliza: A wizard. PLURAL: dramliz (The dramliz . . .)

Dri'at: Left

Eklykt'i: Unreturned

Eldema: First Speaker (most times, the delm)

Eldema-pernard'i: First-Speaker-In-Trust

Entranzia volecta: Good greetings (High Liaden)

Fa'vya: an aphrodisiac-laced wine sold at Festival

Flaran Cha'menthi: "I(/We) Dare"

Galandaria: Confederate? Countryperson?

Ge'shada: Mazel tov; congratulations

Glavda Empri: yo'Lanna's house

I'ganin brath'a, vyan se'untor: Play with the body, rest the mind

I'lanta: Right

Ilania frrogudon palon dox: (approx) Young ladies should speak more gently

Illanga kilachi: (no translation available)

Indra: Uncle

Jelaza Kazone: The Tree, also Korval's Own House. Approx. "Jela's Fulfillment"

Lazenia spandok: Son of a bitch (REAL approximate)

Lisamia keshoc: Thank you (Low Liaden)

Megelaar: The Dragon on Korval's shield

Melant'i: Who one is in relation to current circumstances. Also who one is in sum, encompassing all possible persons one might be.

Menfri'at: Liaden karate

Mirada: Father

Misravot: Altanian wine; blue in color.

Nadelm: Delm-to-Be.

Nubiath'a: Gift given to end an affair of pleasure

Palesci modassa: Thank you (High Liaden)

Prena'ma: Storyteller

Prethliu: Rumorbroker

Qe'andra: Man of business

Qua'lechi: Exclamation of horror

Relumma: Division of a Liaden year, equaling 96 Standard days. Four relumma equal one year.

Thawla: Mother (Low Liaden; approximately Mommy)

Thawlana: Grandmother

Thodelm: Head of Line

Tra'sia volecta: Good morning (Low Liaden)

Trealla Fantrol: The yos'Galan house.

Valcon Berant'a: Dragon's Price or Dragon Hoard, the name of Korval's valley

Valcon Melad'a: Dragon's Way, the Delm's Own ship

van'chela: beloved friend

va'netra: charity case, lame puppy

zerlam'ka: kinslayer